Nelson DeMille was born in New York City in 1943. He grew up on Long Island and graduated from Hofstra University with a degree in Political Science and History. After serving as an infantry officer in Vietnam, where he was decorated three times, DeMille worked as a journalist and short-story writer. He wrote his first major novel, *By the Rivers of Babylon*, in 1978 and has gone on to write 10 international bestsellers, with sales of over 55 million copies in 24 languages. He lives on Long Island.

For more information on Nelson DeMille contact:
www.nelsondemille.co.uk
www.nelsondemille.net

NELSON DEMILLE

GOLD COAST

timewarner
paperbacks

A *Time Warner* Paperback

First published in Great Britain in 1991
by Grafton Books
Published in 1993 by HarperCollins
This edition published in 2001 by Warner Books
Reprinted by Time Warner Paperbacks in 2002
Reprinted 2003 (twice)

A CIP catalogue record for this book
is available from the British Library.

ISBN 0 7515 3121 9

Printed and bound in Great Britain by
Clays Ltd, St Ives plc

Time Warner Paperbacks
An imprint of
Time Warner Books UK
Brettenham House
Lancaster Place
London WC2E 7EN

www.TimeWarnerBooks.co.uk

To my three budding authors:
Ryan, Lauren, and Alex.

ACKNOWLEDGEMENTS

I wish to thank Daniel and Ellen Barbiero for sharing with me their invaluable insights into Gold Coast life, and also Audrey Randall Whiting for sharing with me her knowledge of Gold Coast history.

I would also like to acknowledge my gratitude to Harry Mariani for his generous hospitality and support.

I also want to thank Pam Carletta for her tireless and professional work on the manuscript of this book.

And once again, my deepest gratitude to Ginny DeMille, editor, publicist, and good friend.

A man lives not only his personal life as an individual, but also, consciously or unconsciously, the life of his epoch and his contemporaries.

Thomas Mann
The Magic Mountain

GOLD COAST

PART I

The United States themselves are
essentially the greatest poem.

Walt Whitman
Preface to *Leaves of Grass*

CHAPTER 1

I first met Frank Bellarosa on a sunny Saturday in April at Hicks' Nursery, an establishment that has catered to the local gentry for over a hundred years. We were both wheeling red wagons filled with plants, fertilizers, and such toward our cars across the gravel parking field. He called out to me, 'Mr Sutter? John Sutter, right?'

I regarded the man approaching, dressed in baggy work pants and a blue sweatshirt. At first, I thought it was a nurseryman, but then as he drew closer, I recognized his face from newspapers and television.

Frank Bellarosa is not the sort of celebrity you would like to meet by chance, or in any other way, for that matter. He is a uniquely American celebrity, a gangster actually. A man like Bellarosa would be on the run in some parts of the world, and in the presidential palace in others, but here in America he exists in that place that is aptly called the underworld. He is an unindicted and unconvicted felon as well as a citizen and a taxpayer. He is what federal prosecutors mean when they tell parolees not to 'consort with known criminals'.

So, as this notorious underworld character approached, I could not for the life of me guess how he knew me or what he wanted or why he was extending his hand toward me. Nevertheless, I did take his hand and said, 'Yes, I'm John Sutter.'

'My name's Frank Bellarosa. I'm your new neighbour.'

What? I think my face remained impassive, but I may have twitched. 'Oh,' I said, 'that's . . .' Pretty awful.

'Yeah. Good to meet you.'

So my new neighbour and I chatted a minute or two and noted each other's purchases. He had tomatoes, eggplants, peppers, and basil. I had impatiens and marigolds. Mr Bellarosa suggested that I should plant something I could eat. I told him I ate marigolds and my wife ate impatiens. He found that funny.

15

In parting, we shook hands without any definite plans to see each other again, and I got into my Ford Bronco.

It was the most mundane of circumstances, but as I started my engine, I experienced an uncustomary flash into the future, and I did not like what I saw.

CHAPTER 2

I left the nursery and headed home.

Perhaps it would be instructive to understand the neighbourhood into which Mr Frank Bellarosa had chosen to move himself and his family. It is quite simply the best neighbourhood in America, making Beverly Hills or Shaker Heights, for instance, seem like tract housing.

It is not a neighbourhood in the urban or suburban sense, but a collection of colonial-era villages and grand estates on New York's Long Island. The area is locally known as the North Shore and known nationally and internationally as the Gold Coast, though even realtors would not say that aloud.

It is an area of old money, old families, old social graces, and old ideas about who should be allowed to vote, not to mention who should be allowed to own land. The Gold Coast is not a pastoral Jeffersonian democracy.

The *nouveaux riches*, who need new housing and who comprehend what this place is all about, are understandably cowed when in the presence of a great mansion that has come on the market as a result of unfortunate financial difficulties. They may back off and buy something on the South Shore where they can feel better about themselves, or if they decide to buy a piece of the Gold Coast, they do so with great trepidation, knowing they are going to be miserable and that they had better not try to borrow a cup of Johnnie Walker Black from the people in the next mansion.

But a man like Frank Bellarosa, I thought, would be ignorant of the celestial beings and great social icebergs who would surround him, completely unknowing of the hallowed ground on which he was treading.

Or, if Frank Bellarosa was aware, perhaps he didn't care, which was far more interesting. He struck me, in the few minutes we spoke, as a man with a primitive sort of *élan*, somewhat like a conquering soldier from an inferior civilization who has quartered himself in the great villa of a vanquished nobleman.

Bellarosa had, as he indicated, purchased the estate next to mine. My place is called Stanhope Hall; his place is called Alhambra. The big houses around here have names, not numbers, but in a spirit of cooperation with the United States Post Office, my full address does include a street, Grace Lane, and an incorporated village, Lattingtown. I have a zip code that I, like many of my neighbours, rarely use, employing instead the old designation of Long Island, so my address goes like this: Stanhope Hall, Grace Lane, Lattingtown, Long Island, New York. I get my mail.

My wife, Susan, and I don't actually live *in* Stanhope Hall, which is a massive fifty-room beaux-arts heap of Vermont granite, for which the heating bills alone would wipe me out by February. We live in the guesthouse, a more modest fifteen-room structure built at the turn of the century in the style of an English manor house. This guesthouse along with ten acres of Stanhope's total two hundred acres were deeded to my wife as a wedding present from her parents. However, our mail actually goes to the gatehouse, a more modest six-room affair of stone, occupied by George and Ethel Allard.

The Allards are what are called family retainers, which means they used to work, but don't do much anymore. George was the former estate manager here, employed by my wife's father, William, and her grandfather, Augustus. My wife is a Stanhope. The great fifty-room hall is abandoned now, and George is sort of caretaker for the whole two-hundred-acre estate. He and Ethel live in the gatehouse for free, having displaced the gatekeeper and his wife, who were let go back in the fifties. George does what he can with limited family funds. His work ethic remains strong, though his old body does not. Susan and I find we are helping the Allards more than they help us, a situation that is not uncommon around here. George and Ethel concentrate mostly on the gate area, keeping the hedges trimmed, the wrought-iron gate painted, clipping the ivy on the estate walls and the gatehouse, and replanting the flower beds in the spring. The rest of the estate is in God's hands until further notice.

I turned off Grace Lane and pulled up the gravel drive to the gates, which are usually left open for our convenience, as this is our only access to Grace Lane and the wide world around us.

George ambled over, wiping his hands on his green work pants. He opened my door before I could and said, 'Good morning, sir.'

George is from the old school, a remnant of that small class of professional servants that flourished so briefly in our great democracy. I can be a snob on occasion, but George's obsequiousness sometimes makes me uneasy. My wife, who really was to the manner born, thinks nothing of it and makes nothing of it. I opened the back of the Bronco and said, 'Give me a hand?'

'Certainly, sir, certainly. Here, you let me do that.' He took the flats of marigolds and impatiens and laid them on the grass beside the gravel drive. He said, 'They look real good this year, Mr Sutter. You got some nice stuff. I'll get these planted 'round the gate pillars there, then I'll help you with your place.'

'I can do that. How is Mrs Allard this morning?'

'She's very well, Mr Sutter, and it's nice of you to ask.'

My conversations with George are always somewhat stilted, except when George has a few drinks in him.

George was born on the Stanhope estate some seventy years ago and has childhood memories of the Roaring Twenties, the Great Crash, and the waning of the Golden Era throughout the 1930s. There were still parties, debutante balls, regattas, and polo matches after the Crash of '29, but as George once said to me in a maudlin moment, 'The heart was gone from everybody. They lost confidence in themselves, and the war finished off the good times.'

I know all that from history books and through a sort of osmosis that one experiences by living here. But George has more detailed and personal information on the history of the Gold Coast, and when he's had a few, he'll tell you stories about the great families: who used to screw whom, who shot whom in a jealous rage, and who shot themselves in despair. There was, and to some extent still is, a servants' network here, where that sort of information is the price of admission to servants' get-togethers in the kitchens of the remaining great houses, in the gatehouses, and in the local working-man's pubs. It's sort of an American *Upstairs Downstairs* around here, and God only knows what they say about Susan and me.

But if discretion is not one of George's virtues, loyalty is, and in fact I once overheard him tell a tree pruner that the Sutters were good people to work for. In fact, he doesn't work for me, but for Susan's parents, William and Charlotte Stanhope, who are retired in Hilton Head and are trying to unload Stanhope Hall before it pulls them under. But that's another story.

Ethel Allard is also another story. Though always correct and pleasant, there is a seething class anger there, right below the surface. I have no doubt that if someone raised the red flag, Ethel Allard would arm herself with a cobblestone from the walkway and make her way toward my house. Ethel's father, from what I gather, was a successful shopkeeper of some sort in the village who was ruined by bad investment advice from his rich customers and further ruined by the failure of those customers to pay him what they owed him for goods delivered. They didn't pay him because they, too, had been financially ruined. This was in 1929, of course, and nothing has been the same around here since. It was as though, I suppose, the rich had broken faith with the lower classes by going broke and killing themselves with alcohol, bullets, and leaps from windows, or simply disappearing, leaving their houses, their debts, and their honour behind. It's hard to feel sorry for the rich, I know, and I can see Ethel's point of view.

But here it is, some sixty years after the Great Crash, and maybe it's time to examine some of the wreckage.

If this place doesn't sound quite like America, I assure you it is; only the externals and the landscape are a bit different.

George was talking. 'So, like I was saying the other day, Mr Sutter, some kids got into the Hall a few nights ago and had themselves a party – '

'Was there much damage?'

'Not too much. Lots of liquor bottles, and I found a bunch of those . . . things – '

'Condoms.'

He nodded. 'So, I cleaned it all up and replaced the plywood on the window they got in. But I'd like to get some sheet metal.'

'Order it. Charge it to my account at the lumberyard.'

'Yes, sir. Now that spring is here – '

'Yes, I know.' The hormones are bubbling and the local bunnies are in high heat. I used to get into abandoned mansions myself, to be truthful. A little wine, some candles, a transistor radio tuned to WABC, and maybe even a fire in the fireplace, though that was a giveaway. There's nothing quite like love among the ruins. I find it interesting that condoms are back in fashion. 'Any sign of drugs?'

'No, sir. Just liquor. You sure you don't want me to call the police?'

'No.' The local police seem very interested in the problems of the gentry, but I find it awkward standing around a deserted fifty-room mansion with cops who are trying to look sympathetic. Anyway, there was no damage done.

I got into my Bronco and drove through the gates, the tyres crunching over the thinning gravel. It will take five hundred cubic yards of crushed bluestone at sixty dollars a yard to get barely an inch of new topping on the winter-ravaged drive. I made a mental note to write my father-in-law with the good news.

My house, the guesthouse, is about two hundred yards up the main drive and fifty yards from it, via a single-lane spur also in need of gravel. The house itself is in good repair, its imported Cotswold stone, slate roof, and copper-sheathed sash and drainpipes virtually maintenance free and nearly as good as aluminium siding and vinyl plastic windows.

We have ivy on the walls, which will be in need of cutting as its new pale-green tendrils begin to creep, and there is a rose garden out back that completes the image that you are in England.

Susan's car, a racing-green Jaguar XJ-6, a gift from her parents, was sitting in the turnaround. Another merrie-olde-England prop. People around here tend to be Anglophiles; it comes with the territory.

I went inside the house and called, 'Lady Stanhope!' Susan answered from the rose garden, and I went out the back doors. I found her sitting in a cast-iron garden chair. Only women, I think, can sit in those things. 'Good morning, my lady. May I ravage you?'

She was drinking tea, the mug steaming in the cool April air. Yellow crocuses and lilies had sprouted in the beds among the bare rose bushes, and a bluebird sat on the sundial. A very cheering sight, except that I could tell that Susan was in one of her quiet moods.

I asked, 'Were you out riding?'

'Yes, that's why I'm wearing my riding clothes and I smell of horse, Sherlock.'

I sat on the iron table in front of her. 'You'll never guess who I met at Hicks' Nursery.'

'No, I never will.'

I regarded my wife a moment. She is a strikingly beautiful woman, if I may be uxorious for a moment. She has flaming-red hair, a sure sign of insanity according to my Aunt Cornelia, and catlike green eyes that are so arresting that people stare. Her skin is lightly freckled, and she has pouty lips that make men immediately think of a particular sex act. Her body is as lithe and taut as any man could ask for in a forty-year-old wife who has borne two children. The secret to her health and happiness, she will tell you, is horseback riding, summer, fall, winter, and spring, rain, snow, or shine. I am madly in love with this woman, though there are times, like now, when she is moody and distant. Aunt Cornelia warned me about that, too. I said, 'I met our new neighbour.'

'Oh? The HRH Trucking Company?'

'No, no.' Like many of the great estates, Alhambra had passed to a corporation, according to county records. The sale was made in February for cash, and the deed recorded for public view a week later. The realtor claimed he didn't know the principals involved, but through a combination of research and rumours by the old guard, the field was narrowed down to Iranians, Koreans, Japanese, South American pharmaceutical dealers, or Mafia. That about covered the range of possible nightmares. And in fact, all of the above had recently acquired houses and property on the Gold Coast. Who else has that kind of money these days? The defences were crumbling, the republic was on the auction block. I said, 'Do you know the name Frank Bellarosa?'

Susan thought a moment. 'I don't think so.'

'Mafia.'

'Really? That's our new neighbour?'

'That's what he said.'

'Did he *say* he was Mafia?'

'Of course not. I know him from the newspapers, TV. I can't believe you never heard of him. Frank "the Bishop" Bellarosa.'

'Is he a bishop?'

'No, Susan, that's his Mafia nickname. They all have nicknames.'

'Is that a fact?'

She sipped her tea and looked distantly into the garden. Susan, not unlike many of the residents in this Garden of Eden, excludes much of the outside world. She reads Trollope and Agatha Christie, never listens to radio, and uses the television only to play videotapes of old movies. She obtains her weather reports from a recorded phone message. Local events are learned through the good-news weekly newspaper and from a few upscale magazines that serve the affluent Gold Coast communities. Regarding hard news, she has adopted Thoreau's philosophy: If you read about one train wreck, you've read about them all.

I asked, 'Does this news upset you?'

She shrugged, then asked me, 'Are *you* upset?'

As an attorney, I don't like people turning questions back to me, so I gave a flippant reply. 'No. In fact, Grace Lane will now be well protected by the FBI, joined by county detectives on stakeouts.'

She seemed to be processing that information, then said, 'This man . . . what's his name . . .?'

'Bellarosa.'

'Yes, well, I'll talk to him about the horse trails and rights of way over his land.'

'Good idea. Set him straight.'

'I will.'

I recalled a silly, though appropriate, joke for the occasion and told it to Susan. 'Christopher Columbus steps ashore in the New World – this is a joke – and he calls out to a group of native Americans, "*Buenos dias!*" or maybe "*Buon giorno!*" and one of the Indians turns to his wife and says, "There goes the neighbourhood."'

Susan smiled politely.

I stood and walked out the rear garden gate, leaving Susan to her tea, her mood, and her potential problem with explaining equestrian rights of way to a Mafia don.

CHAPTER 3

One of the local traditions here says that if you're crossing an estate on foot, you're trespassing; if you're on horseback, you're gentry.

I didn't know if Mr Frank Bellarosa was aware of that as yet, or if he was, if he was going to honour the tradition. Nevertheless, later that Saturday afternoon, I crossed over onto his land through a line of white pine that separated our properties. I was mounted on Yankee, my wife's second horse, a six-year-old gelding of mixed breeding. Yankee has a good temperament, unlike Zanzibar, Susan's high-strung Arab stallion. Yankee can be ridden hard and put away wet without dying of pneumonia, whereas Zanzibar seems to be under perpetual veterinary care for mysterious and expensive ailments. Thus the reason for Yankee's existence, just as my Ford Bronco fills in when Susan's Jag is in the shop every other week. But I suppose there's a price to pay for high performance.

Coming out of the pines, an open field lay ahead, a former horse pasture now overgrown with brush and various species of saplings that aspire to be a forest again if left alone.

I was certain that Bellarosa, like most of his kind, was not as concerned with his privacy as with his personal safety, and I half expected to be confronted by swarthy, slick-haired gunmen in black suits and pointy shoes.

I continued across the field toward a grove of cherry trees. It was just turning dusk, the weather was balmy, and there was a scent of fresh earth around me. The only sounds were Yankee's hoofs on the soft turf and birds trilling their twilight songs from the distant trees. All in all, a perfect late afternoon in early spring.

I took Yankee into the cherry grove. The gnarled and uncared-for old trees were newly leafed and just budded with pink blossoms.

In a clearing in the grove was a sunken mosaic reflecting pool, filled with dead leaves. Around the pool were toppled classical fluted columns and broken lintels. At the far end of the pool was a moss-covered statue of Neptune, his upraised hand minus his trident, so that he seemed to be halfway through a roundhouse punch. At Neptune's feet were four stone fish, whose gaping mouths once spouted water. This

24

was one of the classical gardens of Alhambra, built as a mock Roman ruin, now ironically a real ruin.

The main house of Alhambra is not itself a classical structure, but a Spanish-style mansion of stucco walls, stone archways, wrought-iron balconies, and red-tiled roofs. The four pillars that hold up the arched portico were actually taken from the ruins of Carthage in the 1920s when it was fashionable and possible to loot ancient archaeological sites.

I don't know what I would do if I had that much money myself, but I like to think I would show some restraint. But then restraint is a condition of our era with its dwindling supply of nearly everything vital to life. Restraint was not what the Roaring Twenties was about. One can be a product only of one's own era, not anyone else's.

I rode across the garden ruins, then up a small rise. About a quarter-mile to the east, sitting in shadow, was Alhambra. A solitary light shone from a second-floor balcony window that I knew to be the location of the library.

Alhambra's library, like many rooms in the greatest of the estate houses, had originally existed in Europe. The original owners and builders of Alhambra, a Mr and Mrs Julius Dillworth, on a tour of Europe in the 1920s, took a fancy to the hand-carved oak library of their host, an old English peer whose name and title escape me. The Dillworths made an uninvited but spectacular offer for the entire library, and the tweedy old gentleman, probably short of cash as a result of the same world war that had enriched the Dillworths, accepted the offer.

I watched the library window for a minute or so, then reined Yankee around and rode down the slope, back toward the garden.

I saw now a white horse nibbling on new spring grass between two toppled columns. Astride the horse was the familiar figure of a woman dressed in tight jeans and a black turtleneck sweater. She turned to me as I approached, then faced away. It was my wife, Susan, but I could tell from her look that she was not herself. What I mean is, she

25

likes to playact. So, to be cooperative, I called out, 'Who are you?'

She turned back to me and responded in an icy voice, 'Who are *you*?'

Actually, I wasn't sure yet, but I improvised. 'I own this land,' I said. 'Are you lost or trespassing?'

'Neither. And I doubt anyone dressed as you are, with so wretched a horse, could own this land.'

'Don't be insolent. Are you alone?'

'I was until you came by,' she retorted.

I pulled in Yankee side by side with the white Arabian. 'What is your name?'

'Daphne. What is *your* name?'

I still couldn't think of a name for me, so I said, 'You should know whose land you are on. Get down from your horse.'

'Why should I?'

'Because I said so. And if you don't, I'll pull you down and take my switch to you. Dismount!'

She hesitated, then dismounted.

'Tether him.'

She tethered her horse to a cherry limb and stood facing me.

'Take off your clothes.'

She shook her head. 'I won't.'

'You will,' I snapped. 'Quickly.'

She stood motionless a moment, then pulled off her turtleneck, exposing two firm breasts. She stood with the sweater in her hand and looked up at me. 'Do I have to do this?'

'Yes.'

She dropped the sweater, then pulled off her boots and socks. Finally, she slid her jeans and panties off and threw them in the grass.

I sidled my horse closer and looked down at her standing naked in the fading sunlight. 'Not so arrogant now, are you, Daphne?'

'No, sir.'

This is Susan's idea of keeping marital sex interesting,

though to be honest, I'm not complaining about acting out Susan's sexual fantasies. Sometimes these dramas are scripted and directed (by Susan); sometimes, as with this encounter, they are improv. The locales change with the seasons; in the winter we do it in the stable or, to relive our youth, in front of a fireplace in a deserted mansion.

This was our first alfresco encounter of the new spring season, and there is something about a woman standing naked in a field or forest that appeals to the most primal instincts of both sexes, while at the same time flouting modern conventions regarding where love should be made. Trust me on this; you get used to the occasional ant or bumblebee.

Susan asked, 'What are you going to do to me?'

'Whatever I wish.' I looked at Susan standing motionless, her long red hair blowing in strands across her face, waiting patiently for a command. She has no acting background, but if she had, she would be a method actress; there was not a hint in her face or bearing that she was my wife, and that this was a game. For all purposes, she was a naked, defenceless woman who was about to be raped by a strange man on horseback. In fact, her knees were shaking, and she seemed honestly frightened.

'Please, sir, do what you will with me, but do it quickly.'

I'm not good at the impromptu games, and I'd rather she scripted it so I know who I'm supposed to be or at least what historical epoch we're in. Sometimes I'm a Roman or a barbarian, a knight or an aristocrat, and she's a slave, a peasant, or a haughty noblewoman who gets her comeuppance.

I brought Yankee right up to Susan and reached out and held her upraised chin in my hand. 'Are you embarrassed?'

'Yes, sir.'

I should mention that Susan often takes the dominant role, and I'm the one who plays the part of a naked slave at auction or a prisoner who is stripped and given a few lashes, or whatever. Lest you think we are utterly depraved, I want you to know we are both registered Republicans and members of the Episcopal Church, and attend regularly except during the boating season.

Anyway, on this occasion, I had the feeling we were in the seventeenth century or thereabouts, thus the 'Don't be insolent' line and all the rest of the silly dialogue. I tried to think of another great line and finally said, 'Are you Daphne, wife of the traitor Sir John Worthington?'

'I am, sir. And if you are indeed Lord Hardwick, I've come to ask you to intercede on my husband's behalf with His Majesty, the King.'

I was indeed hardwick at that moment and wished I'd worn looser trousers. 'I am every inch Hardwick,' I replied, and saw a real smile flit across her face.

Susan dropped to her knees and wrapped her arms around my boot. 'Oh, please, my lord, you must present my petition to King Charles.'

History is not my strong point, but I can usually wing it. History wasn't the point anyway. I said, 'And what favour will you do me in return if I do this for you?'

'I will do *anything* you wish.'

That was the point. And in truth, the playacting usually got me jump-started before Susan, and I wanted to get on with the last scene. 'Stand,' I commanded.

She stood and I grabbed her wrist as I took my foot from the stirrup. 'Put your right foot in the stirrup.'

She put her bare foot in the stirrup, and I pulled her up facing me, both of us tight in the English saddle, with her arms around me and her bare breasts tight against my chest. I gave Yankee a tap, and he began to walk. I said, 'Take it out.'

She unzipped my fly and took it out, holding it in her warm hands. I said, 'Put it in.'

She sobbed and said, 'I do this only to save my husband's life. He is the only man I have ever known.'

A few clever replies ran through my mind, but the hormones were in complete control of my intellect now, and I snapped, 'Put it *in*!'

She rose up and came down on it, letting out an exclamation of surprise.

'Hold on.' I kicked Yankee, and he began to trot. Susan held me tighter and locked her strong legs over mine. She buried her face in my neck, and as the horse bounced along, she moaned. This was not acting.

I was now completely caught up in the heat of the moment. I'm only a fair horseman, and what little skill I have was not equal to this. Yankee trotted at a nice pace through the cherry grove, then out into the pasture. The air was heavy with the smell of horse, the trodden earth, our bodies, and Susan's musky odour rising between us.

God, what a ride, Susan breathing hard on my neck, crying out, me panting, and the wetness oozing between us.

Susan climaxed first and cried out so loudly she flushed a pheasant from a bush. I climaxed a second later and involuntarily jerked on the reins, causing Yankee to nearly tumble.

The horse settled down and began to graze, as if nothing had happened. Susan and I clung to each other, trying to catch our breath. I finally managed to say, 'Whew . . . what a ride . . .'

Susan smiled. 'I'm sorry I trespassed on your land, sir.'

'I lied. It's not my land.'

'That's all right. I don't have a husband in trouble with the King, either.'

We both laughed. She asked, 'What were you doing here?'

'Same as you. Just riding.'

'Did you visit our new neighbour?'

'No,' I replied. 'But I saw a light in his window.'

'I'm going to speak to him.'

'Perhaps you'd better put your clothes on first.'

'I may have better luck as I am. Was he good-looking?'

'Not bad, in a Mediterranean sort of way.'

'Good.'

I reined Yankee around. 'I'll take you back to Zanzibar and your clothes.'

She sat upright. 'No, I'll get off here and walk.'

'I'd rather you didn't.'

'It's all right. Hold my hand.'

She dismounted and walked off. I called after her, 'You have no time to talk with Bellarosa. We'll be late for the Eltons again.'

She waved her arm to show she'd heard me. I watched my wife walking naked through the pasture until she entered the shadows of the cherry grove, then I turned Yankee and headed for home.

After a minute or so, I was able to get Lord Hardwick back in his pants.

I *do* make love to my wife, Susan Stanhope Sutter, in our bed, and we enjoy it. Yet, I believe that marriages entirely grounded in reality are bound to fail, just as individuals who cannot escape into flights of fancy are bound to crack up. I'm aware that a couple who acts out sexual fantasies must be careful not to step over into the dark side of the psyche. Susan and I have come to the brink a few times but always drew back.

I crossed from Bellarosa's land through the white pines to Stanhope. I didn't much like leaving Susan with darkness coming and with a few hundred yards' walk in the nude back to her horse, but when she says she's all right, she means go away.

Well, I thought, the flowers were bought and planted, the main house resecured, we had chicken Dijon and asparagus delivered from Culinary Delights for lunch, I was able to get into the village to do some errands, and I had my afternoon ride, and got laid at the same time. All in all, an interesting, productive, and fulfilling Saturday. I like Saturdays.

CHAPTER 4

The Lord rested on the seventh day, which has been interpreted to mean that His sixth-day creations should do the same.

George and Ethel Allard take the Sabbath seriously, as do most working-class people from that generation who remember six-day workweeks of ten-hour days. I, on the other hand, have to take care of the Lord's English ivy creeping over my windowpanes.

I don't actually do any business on Sunday, but I do think about what has to be done on Monday morning as I do my Sunday chores.

Susan and I had cut ivy until about ten in the morning, then got cleaned up and dressed for church.

Susan drove the Jag, and we stopped at the gatehouse to pick up George and Ethel, who were waiting at their front door, George in his good brown suit, Ethel in a shapeless flower-print dress that unfortunately seems to be making a comeback with women who want to look like 1940s wallpaper.

The Allards have a car, William Stanhope's old Lincoln that he left here when he and Charlotte Stanhope moved to Hilton Head, South Carolina, in '79. George sometimes doubled as the Stanhopes' chauffeur and is still a good driver despite his advancing years. But as there is now only one service at St Mark's, it would seem snooty for us not to offer to drive, and perhaps awkward for us to ask him to drive us. Maybe I'm being too sensitive, but I have to walk a thin line between playing lord of the manor and being George and Ethel's assistant grounds keeper. We all have so many hang-ups from the old days. Anyway, George isn't the problem; Ethel the Red is.

The Allards climbed in, and we all agreed it was another beautiful day. Susan swung south onto Grace Lane and floored it. Many of the roads around here were originally horse-and-buggy paths, and they are still narrow, twist and turn a bit, are lined with beautiful trees, and are dangerous. A speeding car is never more than a second away from disaster.

Grace Lane, which is about a mile long, has remained a private road. This means there is no legal speed limit, but there is a practical speed limit. Susan thinks it is seventy, I think it's about forty. The residents along Grace Lane, mostly estate owners, are responsible for the upkeep of the road. Most of the other private roads of the Gold Coast have sensibly been deeded to the county, the local village, the State of New York, or to any other political entity that promises to keep them drained and paved at about a hundred thousand dollars a mile. But a few of the residents along Grace Lane, specifically those who are rich, proud, and stubborn (they go together), have blocked attempts to unload this Via Dolorosa on the unsuspecting taxpayers.

Susan got up to her speed limit, and I could almost feel the blacktop fragmenting like peanut brittle.

High speeds seem to keep older people quiet, and the Allards didn't say much from the back, which was all right with me. George won't discuss work on Sundays, and we had exhausted other subjects years ago. On the way back, we sometimes talk about the sermon. Ethel likes the Reverend James Hunnings because, like so many of my Episcopal brethren, the man is far to the left of Karl Marx.

Each Sunday we are made to feel guilty about our relative wealth and asked to share some of the filthy stuff with about two billion less fortunate people.

Ethel especially enjoys the sermons on social justice, equality, and so forth. And we all sit there, the old-line blue bloods, along with a few new black and Spanish Episcopalians, and the remaining working-class Anglos, listening to the Reverend Mr Hunnings give us his view of America and the world, and there is no question-and-answer period afterward.

In my father's and grandfather's day, of course, this same church was slightly to the right of the Republican Party, and the priests would direct their sermons more toward the servants and the working men and women in the pews, talking about obedience, hard work, and responsibilities, instead of about revolution, the unemployed, and civil rights. My parents, Joseph and Harriet, who were liberal for their day and social class, would gripe about the message from the pulpit. I don't think God meant for church services to be so aggravating.

The problem with a church, any church, I think, is that unlike a country club, anyone can join. The result of this open-door policy is that for one hour a week, all the social classes must humble themselves before God and do it under the same roof in full view of one another. I'm not suggesting private churches or first-class pews up front like they used to have, and I don't think dimming the lights would help much. But I know that, years ago, it was understood that one sort of people went to the early service, and the other sort of people to the later one.

Having said this, I feel I should say something in extenuation of what could be construed as elitist and antidemocratic thoughts: First, I don't feel superior to anyone, and second, I believe fervently that we are all created free and equal. But what I also feel is socially dislocated, unsure of my place in the vast changing democracy outside these immediate environs, and uncertain how to live a useful and fulfilling life among the crumbling ruins around me. The Reverend Mr Hunnings thinks he has the answers. The only thing I know for certain is that he doesn't.

Susan slowed down as she approached the village of Locust Valley. The village is a rather nice place, neat and prosperous, with a small Long Island Railroad station in the middle of town, from which I take my train into New York. Locust Valley was gentrified and boutiquefied long before anyone even knew the words, though there is a new wave of trendy, useless shops coming in.

St Mark's is on the northern edge of the village. It is a small Gothic structure of brownstone with good stained-glass windows imported from England. It was built in 1896 with the winnings of a poker game playfully confiscated by six millionaires' wives. They all went to heaven.

Susan found a parking space by hemming in a Rolls-Royce, and we all hurried toward the church as the bells tolled.

*

33

On the way back, Ethel said, 'I think Reverend Hunnings was right and we should all take in at least one homeless person for Easter week.'

Susan hit the gas and took a banked curve at sixty miles per hour, causing the Allards to sway left and quieting Ethel.

George, ever the loyal servant, said, 'I think Father Hunnings should practise what he preaches. He's got nobody but him and his wife in that big rectory of theirs.'

George knows a hypocrite when he hears one.

I said, 'Mrs Allard, you have my permission to take a homeless person into your house for Easter week.'

I waited for the garrote to encircle my neck and the sound of cackling as it drew tight, but instead she replied, 'Perhaps I'll write to Mr Stanhope and ask his permission.'

Touché. In one short sentence she reminded me that I didn't own the place, and since Susan's father has the social conscience of a Nazi stormtrooper, Ethel got herself off the hook. Score one for Ethel.

Susan crested a hill at seventy and nearly ran up the rear end of a neat little TR-3 – 1964, I think. She swerved into the opposing lane, then swung back in front of the Triumph in time to avoid an oncoming Porsche.

Susan, I believe, has hit upon a Pavlovian experiment in which she introduces the possibility of sudden death whenever anyone in the car says anything that doesn't relate to the weather or horses.

I said, 'Not too much spring rain this year.'

George added, 'But the ground's still wet from that March snow.'

Susan slowed down.

I drive to church about half the time, then there's the three-month boating season when we skip it altogether, so going to church is dangerous only about twenty times a year.

Actually, I notice that when Susan drives to and from church I feel closer to God than I do inside the church.

You might well ask why we go at all or why we don't change churches. I'll tell you, we go to St Mark's because

34

we've always gone to St Mark's; we were both baptized there and married there. We go because our parents went and our children, Carolyn and Edward, go there when they are home on school holidays.

I go to St Mark's for the same reasons I still go to Francis Pond to fish twenty years after the last fish was caught there. I go to carry out a tradition, I go from habit, and from nostalgia. I go to the pond and to the church because I believe there is still something there, though I haven't seen a fish or felt the presence of the Holy Spirit in twenty years.

Susan pulled into the drive, went through the open gates, and stopped to let the Allards out at the gatehouse. They bid us good day and went inside to their Sunday roast and newspapers.

Susan continued on up the drive. She said to me, 'I don't understand why he didn't come to the door.'

'Who?'

'Frank Bellarosa. I told you, I rode right up to the house and called up toward the lighted window. Then I pulled the bell chain at the servant's entrance.'

'Were you naked?'

'Of course not.'

'Well, then he had no interest in making small talk with a fully dressed, snooty woman on a horse. He's Italian.'

Susan smiled. 'The house is so huge,' she said, 'he probably couldn't hear me.'

'Didn't you go around to the front?'

'No, there was construction stuff all over the place, holes in the ground, and nothing was lit.'

'What sort of construction stuff?'

'Cement mixers, scaffolding, that sort of thing. Looks like he's having a lot of work done.'

'Good.'

Susan pulled up to our house. 'I want to get this thing straight with him about the horse trails. Do you want to come along?'

'Not particularly. And I don't think it's good manners to

approach a new neighbour with a problem until you've first paid a social call.'

'That's true. We should follow custom and convention, then he will, too.'

I wasn't sure about that, but one never knows. Sometimes a neighbourhood, like a culture or civilization, is strong enough to absorb and acculturate any number of newcomers. But I don't know if that's true around here any longer. The outward forms and appearances look the same – like the Iranians and Koreans I see in the village wearing blue blazers, tan slacks, and Top-Siders – but the substance has been altered. Sometimes I have this grotesque mental image of five hundred Orientals, Arabs, and Asian Indians dressed in tweeds and plaids applauding politely at the autumn polo matches. I don't mean to sound racist, but I am curious as to why wealthy foreigners want to buy our houses, wear our clothes, and emulate our manners. I suppose I should be flattered, and I suppose I am. I mean, I never had a desire to sit in a tent and eat camel meat with my fingers.

'John? Are you listening?'

'No.'

'Do you want to go with me and pay a social call on Frank Bellarosa?'

'No.'

'Why not?'

'Let him come to us.'

'But you just said –'

'I don't care what I just said. I'm not going over there, and neither are you.'

'Says who?'

'Says Lord Hardwick.' I got out of the car and walked toward the house. Susan shut off the car engine and followed. We entered the house, and there was that pregnant silence in the air, the silence between a husband and wife who have just had words, and it is unlike any other silence except perhaps the awful stillness you hear between the flash of an atomic bomb and the blast. Five, four, three, two, one. Susan said, 'All right. We'll wait. Would you like a drink?'

'Yes, I would.'

Susan walked into the dining room and got a bottle of brandy from the sideboard. She moved into the butler's pantry, and I followed. Susan took two glasses from the cupboard and poured brandy into each. 'Neat?'

'A little water.'

She turned on the faucet, splashed too much water in the brandy, and handed me the glass. We touched glasses and drank there in the pantry, then moved into the kitchen. She asked, 'Is there a Mrs Bellarosa?'

'I don't know.'

'Well, was Mr Bellarosa wearing a wedding ring?'

'I don't notice things like that.'

'You do when it's an attractive woman.'

'Nonsense.' But true. If a woman is attractive and I'm in one of my frisky moods, I don't care if she's single, engaged, married, pregnant, divorced, or on her honeymoon. Maybe that's because I never go past the flirting stage. Physically, I'm very loyal. Susan, on the other hand, is not a flirt, and you have to keep an eye on women like that.

She sat at the big round table in our English country-style kitchen.

I opened the refrigerator.

She said, 'We're having dinner with the Remsens at the club.'

'What time?'

'Three.'

'I'll have an apple.'

'I fed them to the horses.'

'I'll have some oats.' I found a bowl of New Zealand cherries and closed the refrigerator door. I ate the cherries standing, spitting the pits into the sink, and drank the brandy. Fresh cherries with brandy are good.

Neither of us spoke for a while, and the regulator clock on the wall was tick-tocking. Finally, I said, 'Look, Susan, if

37

this guy was an Iranian rug merchant or a Korean importer or whatever, I would be a good neighbour. And if anyone around here didn't like that, the hell with them. But Mr Frank Bellarosa is a gangster and, according to the papers, the top Mafia boss in New York. I am an attorney, not to mention a respected member of this community. Bellarosa's phones are tapped, and his house is watched. I must be very careful of any relationship with that man.'

Susan replied, 'I understand your position, Mr Sutter. Some people even consider the Stanhopes as respected members of the community.'

'Don't be sarcastic, Susan. I'm speaking as an attorney, not as a snob. I make about half my living from the people around here, and I have a reputation for honesty and integrity. I want you to promise me you won't go over there to call on him or his wife, if he has one.'

'All right, but remember what Tolkien said.'

'What did Tolkien say?'

'Tolkien said, "It doesn't do to leave a live dragon out of your calculations if you live near him."'

Indeed it does not do at all, which was why I was trying to factor in Mr Frank Bellarosa.

CHAPTER 5

Dinner at The Creek club with the Remsens, Lester and Judy, began well enough. The conversation was mostly about important social issues (a new resident whose property bordered our club had brought suit over the skeet shooting, which he claimed was terrorizing his children and dog), about important world issues (the PGA was going to be held in Southampton again this May), and about pressing ecological issues, to wit: The remaining land of the old Guthrie estate, some one hundred acres, had gone to the developers, who wanted a variance to put up twenty houses in the two-million-dollar price range. 'Outrageous,' proclaimed

Lester Remsen, who like myself is no millionaire, but who does own a very nice converted carriage house and ten acres of the former Guthrie estate. 'Outrageous and ecologically unsound,' Lester added.

The Guthrie estate was once a three-hundred-acre tract of terraced splendour, and the main house was called Meudon, an eighty-room replica of the Meudon Palace outside Paris. The Guthrie family tore down the palace in the 1950s rather than pay taxes on it as developed property.

Some of the locals considered the tearing down of Meudon Palace a sacrilege, while others considered it poetic justice, because the original Guthrie, William D., an aide to the Rockefeller clan, had purchased and torn down the village of Lattingtown – sixty homes and shops – in 1905. Apparently the structures interfered with his building plans. Thus, Lattingtown has no village centre, which is why we go to neighbouring Locust Valley for shopping, church, and all that. But as I said earlier, that was a time when American money was buying pieces of Europe or trying to replicate it here, and the little village of Lattingtown, a tiny hamlet of a hundred or so souls, could no more resist an offer of triple market value than could the English aristocrat who sold his library to adorn Alhambra.

And perhaps what is happening now is further justice, or irony if you will, as land speculators, foreigners, and gangsters buy up the ruins and the near ruins from a partially bankrupt and heavily taxed American aristocracy. I never came from that kind of money, and so my feelings are somewhat ambivalent. I'm blue blood enough to be nostalgic about the past, without having the guilt that people like Susan have about coming from a family whose money was once used like a bulldozer, flattening everything and everybody who got in its way.

Lester Remsen continued, 'The builders are promising to save most of the specimen trees and dedicate ten acres of park if we'll offer our expertise for free. Maybe you could meet with these people and tag the trees.'

39

I nodded. I'm sort of the local tree guy around here. Actually, there are a group of us, who belong to the Long Island Horticultural Society. All of a sudden I'm in demand as local residents have discovered that raising the ecological banner can hold off the builders. Ironically, that's one of the reasons that Stanhope's two hundred acres can't be sold, which is good for me but not for my father-in-law. That's a messy situation, and I'm caught right in the middle of it. More about that later. I said to Lester, 'I'll get the volunteers out, and we'll tag the rare trees with their names and so forth. How long before they break ground?'

'About three weeks.'

'I'll do what I can.'

It never ceases to amaze me that no matter how many million-dollar houses are built, there is an inexhaustible supply of buyers. Who are these people? And where do they get their money?

Lester Remsen and I discussed the skeet-shooting problem. According to yesterday's *Long Island Newsday*, a judge issued a temporary restraining order stopping the shoot, notwithstanding the fact that the shooting has been going on for more than half a century before the plaintiff bought his house or was even born. But I can see the other point of view. There is population pressure on the land, and there are noise and safety considerations to be taken into account. No one hunts deer or pheasant around here anymore, and the Meadowbrook Hunt Club, in its last days, had to plan a trickier route each year, lest the horses and hounds wind up charging through new suburban backyards or a shopping mall. Talk about terrorizing new residents.

I know that we are fighting a rearguard action here to protect a way of life that should have ended twenty or thirty years ago. I understand this, and I'm not bitter. I'm just amazed that we've gotten away with it this long. In that respect I say God bless America, land of evolution and not revolution.

Susan said, 'Can't you put silencers on the shotguns?'

'Silencers are illegal,' I informed her.

'Why?'

'So gangsters can't get ahold of them,' I explained, 'and murder people quietly.'

'Oh, I bet I know where you could get hold of a silencer.' She smiled mischievously.

Lester Remsen looked at her.

'Anyway,' I continued, 'half the fun is the noise.'

Lester Remsen agreed and asked Susan where in the world she could get a silencer.

Susan glanced at me and saw this was not the time to bring up the subject. She said, 'Just joking.'

The club dining room was full for Sunday dinner. The clubs around here, you should understand, are the fortresses in the fight against the Visigoths and Huns who are sweeping over the land and camping out around the great estates in cedar and glass tents that go up in less time than it takes to polish the marble floors of Stanhope Hall. All right, that was a bit snooty, but one does get tired of seeing these stark, skylighted contemporaries reproducing themselves like viruses everywhere one looks.

As for the clubs, there are many types: country clubs, yachting clubs, riding clubs, and so forth. I have two clubs: The Creek, a country club, which is where we were having dinner with the Remsens, and The Seawanhaka Corinthian Yacht Club, whose first commodore was William K. Vanderbilt. I keep my boat, a thirty-six-foot Morgan, anchored at the yacht club.

The Creek is what the media like to call 'very exclusive', which sounds redundant, and a 'private preserve of the rich', which sounds judgemental. It isn't true anyway. Rich counts around here, no doubt about it. But it doesn't count for everything the way it does with the new rich. To fully understand what is sometimes called the Eastern Establishment is to understand that you can be poor and even be a Democrat and be accepted in a place like The Creek if you have the right family background, the right school, and know the right people.

Remsen and I, as I said, are not rich, but we breezed through the membership committee interview right out of college, which is usually the best time to apply, before you screw up your life or wind up working in the garment industry. In truth, one's accent helps, too. I have what I guess you'd call an East Coast preppie accent, being a product of St Thomas Aquinas on Fifth Avenue in Manhattan, St Paul's in New Hampshire, and Yale. That's a good accent to have. But there is a more predominant accent around here, which is known (nationally as I've discovered) as Locust Valley Lockjaw. This condition usually afflicts women, but men often display strong symptoms. With Locust Valley Lockjaw, one has the ability to speak in complete and mostly understandable sentences – including words with lots of broad vowels – and to do so without opening one's mouth, sort of like a ventriloquist. It's quite a trick, and Susan can do it really well when she's with her bitchy friends. I mean, you can be having a drink on the club patio, for instance, and watch four of them sitting around a nearby table, and it looks as if they're silently sneering at one another, but then you hear words, whole sentences. I never get over it.

The Creek itself, named after Frost Creek, which runs through the north end of the property on the Long Island Sound, was originally an estate. There are about a dozen other country and golf clubs around here, but only one other that counts, and that is Piping Rock. Piping Rock is considered more exclusive than The Creek, and I suppose it is, as its membership list more closely matches the Social Register than does The Creek's. But they don't have skeet shooting. Though maybe we don't either. Susan, incidentally, is listed in the Social Register as are her parents, who still officially maintain a residence at Stanhope Hall. In my opinion, the Register is a dangerous document to have floating around in case there *is* a revolution. I wouldn't want Ethel Allard to have a copy of it. I have a John Deere cap that I plan to wear if the mob ever breaks through the gates of Stanhope Hall. I'll stand in front of my house and call out, 'We got this here place already! Main house is up the drive!' But Ethel would give me away.

Susan looked up from her raspberries and asked Lester, 'Do you know anything about anyone moving into Alhambra?'

'No,' Lester replied, 'I was going to ask you. I hear there have been trucks and equipment going in and out of there for over a month.'

Judy Remsen interjected, 'No one has seen a moving van yet, but Edna DePauw says she sees furniture delivery trucks going in about once a week. Do you think anyone has moved in yet?'

Susan glanced at me, then said to the Remsens, 'John ran into the new owner yesterday at Hicks'.'

Lester looked at me expectantly.

I put down my coffee cup. 'A man named Frank Bellarosa.'

There was a moment of silence, then Judy said contemplatively, 'That name sounds familiar . . .' She turned to Lester, who was looking at me to see if I was joking. Lester finally asked, '*The* Frank Bellarosa?'

'Yes.'

Lester didn't respond for a while, probably waiting for his stomach to unknot, then cleared his throat and asked, 'Did you *speak* to him?'

'Yes. Nice chap, actually.'

'Well, he may have been with you, but – '

Judy finally connected the name. 'The gangster! The Mafia boss!'

A few heads at other tables turned towards us.

'Yes,' I replied.

'Here? I mean, next door to you?'

'Yes.'

Lester asked, 'How do you feel about that?'

I thought a moment and made a truthful reply. 'I'd rather have one gangster next door than fifty *nouveau-riche* stockbrokers with their screaming kids, lawn mowers, and smoking barbecues.' Which, when I said it aloud, made sense. Only I wish I hadn't said it aloud. No telling how

43

it would be misinterpreted or misquoted as it made the rounds.

Lester Remsen looked at me, then went back to his apple pie. Judy spoke to Susan without opening her mouth. 'Would you pass the cream?' Susan replied without so much as a throat flutter – I think the sound came out of her nose – 'Of course, dear.'

I caught Susan's eye, and she winked at me, which made me feel better. I didn't feel sorry for what I'd said, but I wished I had remembered that Lester is a stockbroker.

The problems were beginning.

PART II

The business of America is business.

— Calvin Coolidge

CHAPTER 6

The following week passed without incident. I went to my law office in Locust Valley on Monday, then commuted by train to my Manhattan office on Tuesday, Wednesday, and Thursday. Friday found me back in Locust Valley. I follow this schedule whenever I can as it gives me just enough of the city to make me a Wall Street lawyer, but not so much as to put me solidly into the commuting class.

I am a partner in my father's firm of Perkins, Perkins, Sutter and Reynolds. The firm is defined as small, old, Wasp, Wall Street, carriage trade, and so on. You get the idea. The Manhattan office is located in the prestigious J. P. Morgan Building at 23 Wall Street, and our clientele are mostly wealthy individuals, not firms. The office's decor, which has not changed much since the 1920s, is what I call Wasp squalor, reeking of rancid lemon polish, deteriorating leather, pipe tobacco, and respectability.

The Morgan Building, incidentally, was bombed by the anarchists in 1920, killing and injuring about four hundred people – I can still see the bomb scars on the stonework – and every year we get a bomb threat on the anniversary of the original bombing. It's a tradition. Also, after the Crash of '29, this building chalked up six jumpers, which I think is the record for an individual building. So perhaps along with prestigious, I should add historic and ill-omened.

The Locust Valley office is less interesting. It's a nice Victorian house on Birch Hill Road, one of the village's main streets, and we've been there since 1921 without any excitement. Most of the Locust Valley clientele are older people whose legal problems seem to consist mostly of disinheriting nieces and nephews, and endowing shelters for homeless cats.

The work in the city – stocks, bonds, and taxes – is interesting but meaningless. The country work – wills, house closings, and general advice on life – is more meaningful but not interesting. It's the best of both worlds.

Most of the older clientele are friends of my father and of Messrs Perkins and Reynolds. The first Mr Perkins on the letterhead, Frederic, was a friend of J. P. Morgan, and was one of the legendary Wall Street movers and shakers of the 1920s, until November 5, 1929, when he became a legendary Wall Street jumper. I suppose the margin calls got on his nerves. My father once said of this incident, 'Thank God he didn't hurt anyone on the sidewalk, or we'd still be in litigation.'

Anyway, the second Mr Perkins, Frederic's son, Eugene, is retired and has moved down to Nags Head, North Carolina. The Carolinas seem to have become a respectable retirement destination, as opposed to Florida, most of which is considered by people around here as unfit for human habitation.

And the last senior partner, Julian Reynolds, is also retired, in a manner of speaking. He sits in the large corner office down the hall and watches the harbour. I have no idea what he's looking at or for. Actually, he occupies the same office from which Mr Frederic Perkins suddenly exited this firm, though I don't think that has any relevance to Julian's fascination with the window. My secretary, Louise, interrupts Mr Reynolds's vigil every day at five, and a limousine takes him uptown to his Sutton Place apartment, which offers an excellent view of the East River. I think the poor gentleman has old-timers' disease.

My father, Joseph Sutter, had the good sense to retire before anyone wanted him to. That was three years ago, and I remember the day with some emotion. He called me into his office, told me to sit in his chair, and left. I thought he had stepped out for a moment, but he never came back.

My parents are still alive, but not so you'd notice. Southampton is on the eastern side of Long Island, only about sixty miles from Lattingtown and Locust Valley, but my parents have decided to make it further. There is no bad blood between us; their silence is just their way of showing me that they are sure I'm doing fine. I guess.

As you may have gathered or already known, many white Anglo-Saxon Protestants of the upper classes have the same sort of relationship with their one or two offspring as, say, a sockeye salmon has with its one or two million eggs. I probably have the same relationship with my parents as they had with theirs. My relationship with my own children, Carolyn, age nineteen, and Edward, seventeen, is somewhat warmer, as there seems to be a general warming trend in modern relationships of all sorts. But what we lack in warmth, we make up for in security, rules of behaviour, and tradition. There are times, however, when I miss my children and wouldn't even mind hearing from my parents. Actually, Susan and I have a summer house in East Hampton, a few miles from Southampton, and we see my parents each Friday night for dinner during July and August whether we're all hungry or not.

As for Susan's parents, I call Hilton Head once a month to deliver a situation report, but I've never been down there. Susan flies down once in a while, but rarely calls. The Stanhopes never come up unless they have to attend personally to some business. We do the best we can to keep contact at a minimum, and the fax machine has been a blessing in this regard.

Susan's brother, Peter, never married and is travelling around the world trying to find the meaning of life. From the postmarks on his infrequent letters – Sorrento, Monte Carlo, Cannes, Grenoble, and so forth – I think he's trying the right places.

I have a sister, Emily, who followed her IBM husband on a corporate odyssey through seven unpleasant American cities over ten years. Last year, Emily, who is a very attractive woman, found the meaning of life on a beach in Galveston, Texas, in the form of a young stud, named Gary, and has filed for divorce.

Anyway, on Friday afternoon, I left the Locust Valley office early and drove the few miles up to The Creek for a drink. This is a tradition, too, and a lot more pleasant one than some others.

I drove through the gates of the country club and followed the gravel lane, bordered by magnificent old American elms, toward the clubhouse. I didn't see Susan's Jag in the parking field. She sometimes comes up and has a drink on Fridays, then we have dinner at the club or go elsewhere. I pulled my Bronco into an empty slot and headed for the clubhouse.

One of the nice things about having old money, or having other people think you do, is that you can drive anything you want. In fact, the richest man I know, a Vanderbilt, drives a 1977 Chevy wagon. People around here take it as an eccentricity or a display of supreme confidence. This is not California, where your car accounts for fifty percent of your personality.

Besides, it's not what you drive that's important; it's what kind of parking stickers you have on your bumper that matters. I have a Locust Valley parking sticker, and a Creek, Seawanhaka Corinthian, and Southampton Tennis Club sticker, and that says it all, sort of like the civilian equivalents of military medals, except you don't wear them on your clothes.

So I entered The Creek clubhouse, a large Georgian-style building. Being a former residence, there is nothing commercial looking about the place. It has instead an intimate yet elegant atmosphere, with a number of large and small rooms used for dining, card playing, and just hiding out. In the rear is the cocktail lounge, which looks out over part of the golf course and the old polo field, and in the distance one can see the Long Island Sound, where The Creek has beach cabanas. There is indoor tennis, platform tennis, possibly skeet shooting, and other diversions for mind and body. It is an oasis of earthly pleasure for about three hundred well-connected families. Someday it will be a housing subdivision and they will call it The Creek Estates.

Anyway, I went into the lounge, which was filled mostly

with men who were in that Friday mood that reminds me of grinning idiots at a locker room victory party.

There were the usual hellos and hi, Johns, a few backslaps, and assorted hale-fellow-well-met rituals. More interestingly, I caught a wink from Beryl Carlisle, whom I would dearly love to pop if I weren't so faithful.

I looked around the room, assured once again that there were still so many of us left. An Englishman once said that he found it easier to be a member of a club than of the human race because the bylaws were shorter, and he knew all the members personally. That sounds about right.

I spotted Lester Remsen sitting at a table near the window with Randall Potter and Martin Vandermeer.

I thought the best thing to do regarding Lester, whom I hadn't heard from since Sunday, was to just go over and sit down, so I did. Lester greeted me a bit coolly, and I had the impression the other two had just gotten a negative evaluation report on me. The cocktail waitress came by, and I ordered a gin martini, straight up.

Regarding bylaws, the rules of this club, like those of many others, prohibit the talking of business, the original purpose being to provide an atmosphere of forced relaxation. These days we like to pretend that this bylaw precludes members from having an unfair business advantage over people who are not allowed in the club. Americans take their economic rights very seriously, and so do the courts. But the business of America is business, so Randall and Martin went back to their business discussion, and I took the opportunity to address a question to Lester Remsen. 'I have a client,' I said, 'a woman in her seventies, with fifty thousand shares of Chase National Bank stock. The stock was issued in 1928 and 1929 –'

Lester leaned toward me. 'You mean she has the actual certificates?'

'Yes. She lugged them into my Locust Valley office in a valise. They were left to her by her husband, who died last month.'

'My Lord,' Lester exclaimed. 'I've never seen Chase

National certificates. That's Chase Manhattan now, you know.'

'No, I didn't know. That's what I wanted to speak to you about.' Of course I did know, but I could see Lester's feathers getting smoother and shinier.

Lester asked, 'What did they look like?'

Some men get excited by *Hustler*; Lester apparently got excited by old stock certificates. Whatever turns you on, I say. I replied, 'They were a light-green tint with ornate black letters and an engraving of a bank building.' I described the certificates as best I could, and you would have thought by the way Lester's eyes brightened that I'd said they had big tits.

'Anyway,' I continued, 'here's the kicker. On the back of the certificates, there is the following legend: "Attached share for share is an equal number of shares of Amerex Corp."' I shrugged to show him I didn't know what that meant, and I really didn't.

Lester rose a few inches in his club chair. 'Amerex is now American Express, a nothing company then. It says that?'

'Yes.' Even I was a little excited by this news.

Lester said, 'American Express is thirty-three and a half at today's close. That means . . .'

I could see the mainframe computer between Lester's ears blinking, and he said, 'That's one million, six hundred and seventy-five thousand. For American Express. Chase Manhattan was thirty-four and a quarter at the close . . .' Lester closed his eyes, furrowed his brow, and his mouth opened with the news: 'That's one million, seven hundred and twelve thousand, five hundred.'

Lester never says 'dollars'. No one around here ever says 'dollars'. I suppose if you worship money, then like an ancient Hebrew who may not pronounce the name of God, no one in this temple will ever pronounce the word *dollars*. I asked, 'So these shares are good front and back?'

'I can't verify that without examining them, but it sounds as if they are. And, of course, the figures I gave you don't take into account all the stock splits since 1929. We could be talking about ten, maybe ten point five.'

This means ten or ten and a half million. That means dollars. This was indeed good news to my client who didn't need the money anyway. I said, 'That will make the widow happy.'

'Has she been collecting dividends on these stocks?'

'I don't know. But I'm handling her deceased husband's estate, so I'll know that as I wade through the paper-work.'

Lester nodded thoughtfully and said, 'If for some reason Chase or American Express lost touch with these people over the years, there could also be a small fortune in accrued dividends.'

I nodded. 'My client is vague. You know how some of these old dowagers are.'

'Indeed, I do,' said Lester. 'I'd be happy to send the information to my research department for verification. If you'll just send me photostats of the certificates, front and back, I'll let you know how many times each company's shares have split, what they're worth today, and let you know if Chase or American Express is looking for your client so they can pay her dividends.'

'Would you? That would be very helpful.'

'The shares ought to be examined and authenticated, and they should really be turned in for new certificates. Or better yet, let a brokerage house hold the new certificates in an account. No need to have that kind of money lying around. I'm surprised they've survived over sixty years already without mishap.'

'That sounds like good advice. I'd like to open an account with you on behalf of my client.'

'Of course. Why don't you bring me the actual certificates to my office on Monday? And bring your client along if you can. I'll need her to sign some papers, and I'll need the pertinent information from the estate establishing her ownership as beneficiary and all that.'

'Better yet, why don't you come to my office after the close? Monday, four-thirty.'

'Certainly. Where are the shares now?'

'In my vault,' I replied, 'and I don't want them there.'

Lester thought a moment, then smiled. 'You know, John, as the attorney handling the estate, you could conceivably turn those shares into cash.'

'Now why would I want to do that?'

Lester forced a laugh. 'Let me handle the transaction, and we'll split about ten million.' He laughed again to show he was joking. Ha, ha, ha. I replied, 'Even by today's Wall Street standards, that might be construed as unethical.' I smiled to show I was sharing Lester's little joke, and Lester smiled back, but I could see he was thinking about what *he'd* do with ten million in his vault over the weekend. Lester wouldn't give it to the cats.

After a few more minutes of this, Randall and Martin joined our conversation, and the subject turned to golf, tennis, shooting, and sailing. In most of America that Friday night, in every pub and saloon, the sports under discussion were football, baseball, and basketball, but to the best of my knowledge no one here has yet had the courage to say. 'Hey! How about those Mets?'

Other taboo subjects include the usual – religion, politics, and sex, though it doesn't say this in the bylaws. And while we're on the subject of sex, Beryl Carlisle, who was sitting with her pompous ass of a husband, caught my eye and smiled. Lester and Randall saw it but did not say something like, 'Hey, Johnny boy, that broad is hot for your tool,' as you might expect men to say in a bar. On the contrary, they let the incident pass without even a knowing glance. Lester was going on about the damned skeet shooting again, but my mind was on Beryl Carlisle and the pros and cons of adultery.

'John?'

I looked at Randall Potter. 'Huh?'

'I said, Lester tells me you actually met Frank Bellarosa.'

Apparently someone had changed the subject during my mental absence. I cleared my throat. 'Yes ... I did. Very briefly. At Hicks' Nursery.'

'Nice chap?'

I glanced at Lester, who refused to look me in the eye and acknowledge that he had a big mouth.

I replied to Randall Potter, '"Polite" might be a better word.'

Martin Vandermeer leaned toward me. Martin is a direct descendent of an original old Knickerbocker family and is the type of man who would like to remind us Anglo-Saxons that his ancestors greeted the first boatload of Englishmen in New Amsterdam Harbor with cannon fire. Martin asked, 'Polite in what way, John?'

'Well, perhaps "respectful" is a better word,' I replied, searching my mental thesaurus and stretching my credibility.

Martin Vandermeer nodded in his ponderous Dutch manner.

I don't want to give the impression that I'm cowed by these people; in fact, they're often cowed by me. It's just that when you make a faux pas, I mean really blow it, like saying a Mafia don is a nice chap and suggesting that you would rather have him as a neighbour than a hundred Lester Remsens, well then, you've got to clarify what you meant. Politicians do it all the time. Anyway, I didn't know what these three were so unhappy about; I was the one who had to live next door to Frank Bellarosa.

Randall asked me, with real interest, 'Did he have any bodyguards with him?'

'Actually, now that you mention it, he had a driver who put his purchases in the trunk. Black Cadillac,' I added with a little smirk to show what I thought of black Cadillacs.

Martin wondered aloud, 'Do these people go about armed?'

I think I had become the club expert on the Mafia, so I answered, 'Not the dons. Not usually. They don't want trouble with the police.'

Randall said, 'But didn't Bellarosa kill a Colombian drug dealer some months ago?'

On the other hand, I didn't want to sound like a Mafia groupie, so I shrugged. 'I don't know.' But in fact I recall the news stories back in January, I think, because it struck me at the time that a man as highly placed as Bellarosa would have to be insane to personally commit a murder.

Lester wanted to know, 'What do you suppose he was doing at Hicks'?'

'Maybe he works there on weekends,' I suggested. This got a little chuckle out of everyone, and we ordered another round. I wanted desperately to turn my head toward Beryl Carlisle again, but I knew I couldn't get away with it a second time.

Martin's wife, Pauline, showed up and stood at the door near the bar, trying to get his attention by flapping her arms like a windmill. Martin finally noticed and lifted his great roast beef of a body, then ambled over to his wife.

Randall then excused himself to talk to his son-in-law. Lester Remsen and I sat in silence a moment, then I said, 'Susan tells me I made an unfortunate remark last Sunday, and if I did, I want you to know it was unintentional.' This is the Wasp equivalent of an apology. If it's worded just right, it leaves some doubt that you think *any* apology is required.

Lester waved his hand in dismissal. 'Never mind that. Did you get a chance to look at Meudon?'

This is the Wasp equivalent of 'I fully accept your halfhearted apology.' I replied to Lester, 'Yes, I took the Bronco over the acreage just this morning. I haven't seen it in years, and it's quite overgrown, but the specimen trees are in remarkably good shape.'

We spoke about Meudon for a while. Lester, you should understand, is no nature nut in the true sense, and neither are most of his friends and my neighbours. But, as I said, they've discovered that nature nuts can be useful to achieve their own ends, which is to preserve their lifestyle. This has resulted in an odd coalition of gentry and students, rich estate owners, and middle-class people. I am both gentry and nature nut and am therefore invaluable.

Lester proclaimed, 'I don't want fifty two-million-dollar tractor sheds in my backyard.'

That's what Lester calls contemporary homes: tractor sheds. I nodded in sympathy.

He asked, 'Can't we get Meudon rezoned for twenty-acre plots?'

'Maybe. We have to wait until the developer files his environmental impact statement.'

'All right. We'll keep an eye on that. What's the story with your place?'

Stanhope Hall, as you know, is not my place, but Lester was being both polite and nosey. I replied, 'There are no takers for the whole two hundred acres with the house as a single estate, and no takers for the house with ten surrounding acres. I've advertised it both ways.'

Lester nodded in understanding. The future of Stanhope Hall, the main house, is uncertain. A house that size, you understand, may be someone's dream palace, but even an Arab sheik at today's crude oil prices would have a hard time maintaining and staffing a place that's as big as a medium-size hotel.

Lester said, 'It's such a beautiful house. Got an award, didn't it?'

'Several. *Town & Country* noted it best American house of the year when it was built in 1906. But times change.' The other option was to tear the place down, as Meudon Palace had been torn down. This would force the tax authorities to reassess the property as undeveloped land. The guesthouse is Susan's, and we pay separate tax rates on that, and the gatehouse where the Allards live is theoretically protected by Grandfather Stanhope's will.

Lester said, 'What sort of people seem interested in the house?'

'The sort who think five hundred thousand sounds good for a fifty-room house.' That's what I'm trying to get for it with ten acres attached. The irony is that it cost five million dollars in 1906 to construct. That's about twenty-five million of today's dollars. Aside from any aesthetic considerations about tearing down Stanhope Hall, my frugal father-in-law, William Stanhope, would have to consider the cost of knocking down a granite structure built to last a millennium and then trucking the debris someplace as per the new environmental laws. The granite and marble used to build Stanhope Hall came here to Long Island by railroad from Vermont. Maybe Vermont wants the rubble back.

Susan, incidentally, does not care about the main house or the other structures – except the stables and tennis courts – which I find interesting. Whatever memories are attached to the house, the gazebo, and the love temple are apparently not important or good. She *was* upset the night that vandals burned down her playhouse. It was a sort of Hansel and Gretel gingerbread house, as big as a small cottage, but made of wood and in bad repair. One can only imagine a lonely little rich girl with her dolls playing lonely games in a house all her own.

Lester inquired, 'Did you hear from the county park people yet?'

'Yes,' I replied. 'A fellow named Pinelli at the park commissioner's office. He said he thought the county owned enough Gold Coast mansions for the time being. But that might only be their opening gambit, because Pinelli asked me if the house had any architectural or historical significance.'

'Well,' said Lester, 'it certainly has architectural significance. Who was the architect?'

'McKim, Mead, White,' I replied. Neither history nor architecture is Lester's strong point, but in addition to becoming a nature nut, he's becoming an authority on the social and architectural history of the Gold Coast. I added, 'As for historical significance, I know that Teddy Roosevelt used to pop over from Oyster Bay now and then, and Lindbergh dined there while he was staying with the Guggenheims. There were other noteworthy guests, but I think the county is looking for something more significant than dinner. I'll have to research it.'

'How about making something up?' Lester suggested half jokingly. 'Like maybe Teddy Roosevelt drafted a treaty or a speech at Stanhope Hall.'

I ignored that and continued, 'One of the problems with selling the estate to the county as a museum and park is that Grace Lane is still private, as you know, and that doesn't sit well with the county bureaucrats. Nor would I be very popular on Grace Lane if a thousand cars full of people from Brooklyn and Queens showed up every weekend to gawk.'

'No, you wouldn't,' Lester assured me.

'Bottom line, Lester, if the county did make an offer, it would only offer a price equal to the back taxes. That's their game.'

Lester did not ask how much that was, because he had probably looked it up in the public record or saw it published in the *Locust Valley Sentinel* under the heading TAX DELINQUENCIES.

The back taxes on Stanhope Hall, including interest and penalties, is about four hundred thousand dollars, give or take. You can look it up. Well, you might be thinking, 'If I owed four *thousand* dollars, let alone four *hundred* thousand dollars, in back taxes, they'd grab my house and kids.' Probably. But the rich *are* different. They have better lawyers, like me.

However, I've nearly exhausted all the legal manoeuvres that I learned at Harvard Law, and I can't forestall a tax sale or foreclosure on this potentially valuable property for much longer. I don't normally do legal work for free, but William Stanhope hasn't offered to pay me for my services, so I guess I'm making an exception for my father-in-law. Not only is it true that the rich do not pay their bills promptly, but when they do finally pay, they like to decide for themselves how much they owe.

Lester seemed to be reading my dark thoughts because he said, 'I trust your father-in-law appreciates all you've done.'

'I'm sure he does. However, he has lost touch with the new realities here regarding land use and environmental concerns. If he can't sell the whole estate intact, he wants it subdivided and sold to developers. Even if I could get the two hundred acres divided, there's the house to deal with. William has the idea that a developer will either tear down the old house or offer it to the new residents as a clubhouse or some such thing. Unfortunately, it's expensive to tear down and much too expensive for twenty new households to maintain it.'

'It certainly is a white elephant,' Lester informed me. 'But you *are* trying to preserve that land if not the house.'

'Of course. But it's not my land. I'm in the same situation as you are, Lester, living in splendid isolation on a few acres of a dead estate. I'm master of only about five per cent of what I survey.'

Lester thought about that a moment, then said, 'Well, maybe a white knight will come along to save the white elephant.'

'Maybe.' A white knight in this context is a non-profit group such as a private school, religious institution, or sometimes a health care facility. Estate houses and their grounds seem to lend themselves to this sort of use, and most of the neighbours can live with this arrangement because it keeps the land open and the population density low. I wouldn't mind a few nuns strolling around Stanhope's acres, or even a few nervous-breakdown cases, or, least desirable, private-school students.

Lester asked, 'Did you ever contact that real estate firm in Glen Cove that puts corporations together with estate owners?'

'Yes, but there seems to be a glut of estates and a dearth of corporations that need them.' I should point out that corporations have bought entire estates for their own use. The old Astor estate in Sands Point, for instance, is now an IBM country club, and one of the many Pratt estates in Glen Cove is a conference centre. Also, one of the Vanderbilt estates, an Elizabethan manor house with a hundred acres in Old Brookville, is now the corporate headquarters to Banfi Vintners, who have restored the sixty-room house and grounds to its former glory. Any of these uses would be preferable to . . . well, to twenty tractor sheds inhabited by stockbrokers and their broods.

William Stanhope, incidentally, is far enough removed from here not to fully appreciate the fact that my environmental activities and his instructions to me are very nearly mutually exclusive. This is called a conflict of interest and is both unethical and illegal. But I really don't care. He's getting what he's paying for.

My father-in-law, you understand, can, if pushed, come up with the four hundred thousand dollars in back taxes but chooses not to, not until he's got a buyer or until the day before a tax seizure takes place. He fully intends to protect his huge asset unless and until he determines it is a liability and cannot be sold in his lifetime.

If you're wondering what this white elephant is worth to William Stanhope and his heirs and successors, here are the figures: two hundred acres, if they could be rezoned into ten-acre plots, would fetch over a million dollars a plot on the fabled Gold Coast, which amounts to a total of over twenty million dollars before taxes.

Susan, I assume, will eventually inherit enough money to get herself a full-time stable mucker and someone to help me and old George with the gardening.

If you're wondering what else is in it for me, you should know that these sorts of people rarely let money get out of the immediate family. In fact, I entered into a prenuptial agreement long before the middle class even knew such a thing existed. William Stanhope and his paid attorney drew up the 'marriage contract', as it was then called, and I acted as my own attorney, proving the adage that a lawyer who represents himself has a fool for a client. Anyway, William has been getting free legal advice from the fool ever since.

On the brighter side, Edward and Carolyn have a trust fund into which Stanhope monies are deposited. And in fairness to Susan, the 'marriage contract' was not her idea. I don't want the Stanhope money anyway, but neither do I want the Stanhope problems. I said to Lester, 'Neither Susan nor I am in favour of suburban sprawl, nor, specifically, the development of Stanhope Hall for monetary gain. But if this paradise is to be down-zoned to limbo, then we each have to decide if we wish to stay or leave. That is also an option.'

'Leave for where, John? Where do people like us go?'

'Hilton Head.'

'Hilton Head?'

'Any planned little Eden where nothing will ever change.'

'This is my home, John. The Remsens have been here for over two hundred years.'

'And so have the Whitmans and the Sutters. You know that.' In fact, I should tell you that Lester Remsen and I are related in some murky way that neither of us chooses to clarify.

Families that predate the millionaires can indulge themselves in some snobbery, even if their forebears were fishermen and farmers. I said to Lester, 'We're on borrowed time here. You know that.'

'Are you playing devil's advocate, or are you giving up? Are you and Susan moving? Is this Bellarosa thing the last straw?'

Sometimes I think Lester likes me, so I took the question as a show of concern and not an expression of desire. I replied, 'I've thought of it. Susan has never once mentioned it.'

'Where would you go?'

I didn't know five seconds before he asked, but then it occurred to me. 'I would go to sea.'

'*Where?*'

'Sea, sea. That wet stuff that makes waterfront property so expensive.'

'Oh . . .'

'I'm a good sailor. I'd get a sixty footer and just go.' I was excited now. 'First I'd go down the Intracoastal Waterway to Florida, then into the Caribbean – '

'But what about Susan?' he interrupted.

'What about her?'

'The horses, man. The horses.'

I thought a moment. In truth, a horse would be a problem on a boat. I ordered another drink.

We sat and drank in silence awhile. I was beginning to feel the effects of the fourth martini. I looked around for Beryl Carlisle, but her idiot of a husband caught my eye. I smiled stupidly at him, then turned to Lester. 'Nice chap.'

'Who?'

'Beryl Carlisle's husband.'

'He's a schmuck.'

Lester picks up words like that where he works. *Putz* is another one. They seem like excellent words, but I just can't seem to find the opportunity to try one of them.

We sat awhile longer, and the crowd was starting to thin. I wondered where Susan was and if I was supposed to meet her somewhere. Susan has this habit of thinking she's told me something when she hasn't, and then accusing me of forgetting. I understand from friends that this is quite common among wives. I ordered another drink to jog my memory.

Horses and boats went through my mind, and I tried to reconcile the two. I had this neat mental image of Zanzibar, stuffed and mounted on the bow of my new sixty-foot schooner.

I looked at Lester, who seemed deep in his own reveries, which probably ran along the lines of horse-mounted gentry burning down tractor sheds and trampling tricycles.

I heard Susan's voice beside me. 'Hello, Lester,' she said. 'Are you still insulted? You look all right.' Susan can be direct at times.

Lester asked, 'What do you mean?' feigning ignorance.

Susan ignored that and asked, 'Where's Judy?'

Lester said with real ignorance, 'I don't know.' He thought a moment and added, 'I should call her.'

'First you have to know where she is,' Susan pointed out. 'What were you and John talking about?'

'Stocks and golf,' I answered before Lester could dredge up the subject of Stanhope Hall again, which is not Susan's favourite topic. I said to Lester, 'While you're trying to remember where your wife is, would you like to join us for dinner?' I shouldn't have had the fourth or fifth martini. Actually, the fifth was okay. It was the fourth I shouldn't have had.

Lester rose unsteadily. 'I remember now. We're having people for dinner.'

Susan said, 'You must get me the recipe.'

Susan was obviously irked at something. Poor Lester seemed muddled. He said, 'Yes, of course I can. Would you like to come along? I'll call.'

Susan replied, 'Thanks, but we have dinner plans.'

I didn't know if this was true or not, because Susan never tells me these things.

Lester wished us a good evening, and Susan told him to drive carefully.

I stood and steadied myself against the wall. I smiled at Susan. 'Good to see you.'

'How many of me do you see?' she asked.

'I'm quite sober,' I assured her, then changed the subject. I said, 'I see the Carlisles here. I thought we'd ask if they could join us for dinner.'

'Why?'

'Isn't she a friend of yours?' I asked.

'No.'

'I thought she was. I rather like . . .' – I couldn't remember his name – 'her husband.'

'You think he's a pompous ass.' She added, 'We have dinner plans.'

'With whom?'

'I told you this morning.'

'No, you didn't. With whom? Where? I can't drive.'

'That's obvious.' She took my arm. 'We're having dinner here.'

We made our way through the house to the opposite wing and arrived at the largest of the dining rooms. Susan directed me toward a table at which sat the Vandermeers, of all people.

It was obvious to me that Martin's wife had also failed to inform him of the evening's plans.

Susan and I sat at the round table with the white tablecloth and exchanged small talk with the Vandermeers. Sometimes I think that Eli Whitney got his idea of interchangeable parts from upper middle-class society where all the people are interchangeable. Everyone in that room could have switched tables all night, and the conversations wouldn't have missed a beat.

I realized that my growing criticism of my peers was more a result of changes within me than any changes in them. What had once made me comfortable was now making me restless, and I was, quite frankly, concerned about the compromises and accommodations that had taken over my life in insidious ways. I was fed up with being the caretaker of Stanhope Hall, tired of everyone's obsession with the status quo, impatient with the small talk, annoyed at old ladies who walked into my office with ten million dollars in an old valise, and generally unhappy with what had once made me content.

Oddly enough, I didn't recall feeling that way the week before. I wasn't certain how this revelation came about, but revelations are like that; they just smack you across the face one day, and you know you've arrived at the truth without even knowing you were looking for it. What you do about it is another matter.

I didn't realize it then, but I was ready for a great adventure. What I also didn't know was that my new next-door neighbour had decided to provide one for me.

CHAPTER 7

Saturday morning passed uneventfully except that I had a slight headache brought on, no doubt, by the Vandermeers' hot air. Also, the Allards both had the flu, and I paid them a sick call. I made them tea in the gatehouse's little kitchen, which made me feel like a regular guy. I even stayed for half a cup, while George apologized six times for being sick. Ethel's usual surliness turns to a sort of maudlinism when she's ill. I like her better that way.

I should mention that during the Second World War, George Allard went off to serve his country, as did all the able-bodied male staff at Stanhope Hall and, of course, the other estates. George once told me during a social history lesson that this exodus of servants made life difficult for the families who had managed to hold on to their huge houses through the Depression, and who still needed male staff for heavy estate work. George also tells me that higher wartime wages lured many of the servant girls away for defence work and such. George somehow associates me with this class of gentry and thinks I should feel retroactively saddened by the great hardships that the Stanhopes and others endured during the war. Right, George. When I picture William Stanhope having to lay out his own clothes every morning while his valet is goofing off on Normandy Beach, a lump comes to my throat.

William, by the way, did serve his country during this national emergency. There are two versions of this story. I'll relate Ethel's version: William Stanhope, through family connections, received a commission in the Coast Guard. Grandpa Augustus Stanhope, unable to make use of his seventy-foot yacht, *The Sea Urchin*, sold it to the government for a dollar, as did many yacht owners during the war. *The Sea Urchin* was outfitted as a submarine patrol boat, and its skipper turned out to be none other than Lt (j.g.) William Stanhope. Ethel says this was not a coincidence. Anyway, *The Sea Urchin*, with a new coat of grey paint, sonar, depth charges, and a .50-calibre machine gun, was conveniently berthed at the Seawanhaka Corinthian. From there, Lieutenant Stanhope patrolled up and down the Long Island Sound, ready to take on the German U-boat fleet, protecting the American way of life, and occasionally putting in at Martha's Vineyard for a few beers. And not wanting to take up government housing, William lived at Stanhope Hall.

Ethel is probably justified in her opinion that William Stanhope's wartime service symbolized the worst aspects of American capitalism, privilege, and family connections. Yet most of the upper classes, from all I've read and heard, did their duty, and many went beyond the call of duty. But Ethel excludes any realities that upset her prejudices. In this respect she is exactly like William Stanhope, like me, and like every other human being I've ever met, sane and insane alike. Needless to say, William does not regale his friends or family with war stories.

Anyway, George returned from the Pacific in 1945 with malaria, and he still has episodes from time to time, but this day I was sure it was just the flu. I offered to call the doctor, but Ethel said cryptically, 'He can't help us.'

George and Ethel had been married right before George shipped out, and Augustus Stanhope, as was the custom at the time, provided the wedding reception in the great house.

A few years ago, during a chance conversation with an older client of mine, I discovered that Grandpa Augustus, who would have been in his fifties then, also provided Ethel with some degree of companionship while George was killing our future allies in the Pacific. Apparently this small investment of time and effort on Ethel's part paid dividends, the Allards being the only staff not let go over the years. Also, there was the generous gift of the gatehouse, rent-free for life. I often wondered if George knew that his master was dipping his pen in George's inkwell. But even if he did, George would still be convinced that it was his loyalty, rather than his wife's disloyalty, that was responsible for the old coot's generosity. Well, maybe. Good help is still harder to find than a good lay.

I don't normally listen to gossip, but this was too interesting to resist. Besides, it's more in the category of social history than hot news.

As I drank my tea, I looked at Ethel and smiled. She gave me a pained grimace in return. Above her head on the wall of the small sitting room was a formal photograph of her and

George, he in his navy whites, she in a white dress. She was a very pretty young woman.

What interested me about this story was not that a lonely young war bride had had an affair with her older employer; what interested me was that Ethel Allard, the good Christian socialist, had done it for the lord of the manor and had perhaps blackmailed him, subtly or not so subtly.

A place like this is rife with interlocking relationships that, if explored, would be far more damaging to the social structure than depression, war, and taxes.

The Allards, by the way, have a daughter, Elizabeth, who looks enough like George to put my mind at ease concerning any more Stanhope heirs. Elizabeth, incidentally, is a successful boutique owner – a shopkeeper, like her maternal grandfather – with stores in three surrounding villages, and Susan makes a point of sending her acquisitive friends to all of them, though she herself is not much of a shopper. I saw Elizabeth's name in the local newspaper once in connection with a Republican Party fund-raiser. God bless America, Ethel; where else can socialists give birth to Republicans and vice versa?

I took my leave of the Allards and reminded them to call me or Susan if they needed anything. Susan, for all her aloofness, does have that sense of *noblesse oblige*, which is one of the few things I admire about the old monied classes, and she takes care of the people who work for her. I hope Ethel remembers that when the Revolution comes.

I spent the early afternoon doing errands in Locust Valley, then stopped at McGlade's, the local pub, for a beer. The usual Saturday crowd was there, including the pub's softball team, back from trouncing the florist's ten pathetic sissies, who were there also and had a different version of the game. There were a few self-employed building-trade contractors who needed a drink after giving estimates to homeowners all morning, and there were the weekend joggers who all seemed to have a suspicious amount of tread left on their hundred-dollar running shoes hooked around the bar rails. And then there were the minor gentry in their Land's End and L. L. Bean uniforms, and the major gentry whose attire is difficult to describe, except to say you've never seen it in a store or catalogue. The old gentleman beside me, for instance, had on a pink tweed shooting jacket with a green leather gun patch, and his trousers were baggy green wool embroidered with dozens of little ducks. I was wearing the L. L. Bean uniform: Docksides, tan poplin trousers, button-down plaid shirt, and blue windbreaker. Many of us were perusing wife-authored 'to do' lists as we sipped our beer, and our wallets, when opened for cash, revealed pink dry-cleaning slips. On the restaurant side, well-dressed women with shopping bags were chatting over cottage cheese and lettuce. It was definitely Saturday.

Good pubs, like churches, are great equalizers of social distinctions; more so, perhaps, because when you approach the rail in a pub, you do so with the full knowledge that talking is not only permitted but often required.

In fact, as I was having my second beer, I saw in the bar mirror my plumber, leaning against the wall behind me. I went over to him and we talked about my plumbing problems. To wit: I have a cracked cast-iron waste pipe, and he wants to replace it with PVC pipe, at some expense. I think it can be soldered instead. He asked me about the procedure for adopting his second wife's son, and I gave him an estimate. I think we were too expensive for each other, and the conversation turned to the Mets. You can talk baseball here.

I chatted with a few other acquaintances, then with the bartender and with the old gentleman with the pink tweed jacket, who turned out not to be major gentry but a retired butler from the Phipps' estate who was wearing the boss's cast-offs. You used to get a lot of that around here, but I see less of it in recent years.

It was too nice a day to spend more than an hour in the pub, so I left, but before I did, I gave my plumber the name of an adoption attorney whose fees are moderate. He gave me the name of a handyman who could try a weld on the pipe. The wheels of American commerce spin, spin, spin.

I got into my Bronco and headed home. On the way back, I passed my office and assured myself it was still there. I thought about the ten million in stocks stashed in the vault. It would not be a problem to have Mrs Lauderbach − that's my client's name − sign the necessary papers for me to liquidate the stocks, and for me to hop on down to Rio for a very long vacation. And I didn't need Lester Remsen's help in this at all. But I've never violated a trust or stolen a nickel, and I never will. I felt very pious. What a day I was having.

My mood stayed bright until I approached the gates of Stanhope Hall, when my brow, as they say, darkened. I'd never really noticed it before, but this place was getting me down. The truth, once it grabs hold of you, makes you take notice of the little buzzings in your head. This was not your garden-variety midlife crisis. This was no crisis at all. This was Revelation, Epiphany, Truth. Unfortunately, like most middle-aged men, I had no idea what to do with the truth. But I was open to suggestions.

I stopped at the gatehouse and looked in on the Allards, who were listening to the radio and reading. Ethel was engrossed in a copy of *The New Republic*, which may have been the only copy in Lattingtown, and George was perusing the *Locust Valley Sentinel*, which he's been reading for sixty years to keep abreast of who died, got married, had children, owed taxes, wanted zoning variances, or had a gripe they wanted to see in print.

I picked up Susan's and my mail, which is delivered to the gatehouse, and riffled through it on my way out. Ethel called after me, 'There was a gentleman here to see you. He didn't leave his name.'

Sometimes, as when the phone rings, you just know who's calling. And Ethel's stress on the word *gentleman* told me that this was no gentleman. I asked, 'A dark-haired man driving a black Cadillac?'

'Yes.'

Ethel never says 'sir', so George chimed in, 'Yes, sir. I told him you were not receiving visitors today. I hope that was all right.' He added, 'I didn't know him, and I didn't think you did.'

Or wanted to, George. I smiled at the image of Frank Bellarosa being told that Mr Sutter was not receiving today. I wondered if he knew that meant 'get lost'.

George asked, 'What shall I say if he calls again, sir?'

I replied as if I'd already thought this out, and I guess I must have. 'If I'm at home, show him in.'

'Yes, sir,' George replied with that smooth combination of professional disinterest and personal disagreement with the master.

I left the gatehouse and climbed back into the Bronco.

I drove past the turnoff for my house and continued on toward the main house. Between my house and the main house, on Stanhope land, is the tennis court, whose upkeep Susan had taken on as her responsibility. Beyond the tennis court, the tree-lined lane rises, and I stopped the Bronco at the top of the rise and got out. Across a field of emerging wildflowers and mixed grasses, where the great lawn once stretched, stood Stanhope Hall.

The design of the mansion, according to Susan and as described in various architectural books that mention Stanhope Hall, was based on French and Italian Renaissance prototypes. However, the exterior is not European marble, but is built of good Yankee granite. Spaced along the front are attached columns or wall pilasters with Ionic capitals, and in the centre of the house is a high, open portico with freestanding classical columns. The roof is flat, with a balustraded parapet running around the perimeter of the mansion's three massive wings. The place looks a bit like the White House, actually, but better built.

There were once formal gardens, of course, and they were planted on the descending terraces that surround the great house. Each year at this time the gardens still burst into bloom, wild with roses and laurel, yellow forsythia and multicoloured

71

azaleas, the survival of the fittest, a celebration of nature's independence from man.

For all the European detail, there are distinctly American features to the house, including large picture windows in the rear, a greenhouse-style breakfast room to capture the rising sun, a solarium on the roof, and an American infrastructure of steel beams, heating ducts, good plumbing, and safe electricity.

But to answer Lester Remsen's question, there is nothing architecturally significant or unique about this misplaced European palace. Had McKim, Mead, or White designed a truly new American house, whatever that might have been in 1906, then the landmark people and all the rest of the preservationists would say, 'There is nothing like this in the whole country.'

But the architects and their American clients of this period were not looking into the future, or even trying to create the present; they were looking back over their shoulders into a European past that had flowered and died even before the first block of granite arrived on this site. What these people were trying to create or re-create here in this new world is beyond me. I can't put myself in their minds or their hearts, but I can sympathize with their struggle for an identity, with their puzzlement which has troubled Americans from the very beginning – Who are we, where do we fit, where are we going?

It occurred to me that these estates are not only architectural shams, but they are shams in a more profound way. Unlike their European models, these estates never produced a profitable stalk of wheat, a bucket of milk, or a bottle of wine. There was some hobby farming, to be sure, but the crops certainly didn't support the house and the servants and the Rolls-Royces. And no one who was hired to work the land here could have felt the sense of wonder and excitement that comes with the harvest and the assurance that the earth and the Lord, not the stock market, has provided.

Well, what do I know about that? Actually, my ancestors

were mostly farmers and fishermen, and fishing I do understand, but my ability to coax things from the ground is limited to inedibles, as Mr Bellarosa pointed out. I recalled his red wagon filled with vegetable seedlings, purchased at top dollar from an upscale nursery, and I decided he was a sham, too.

This whole silly Gold Coast was a sham, an American anomaly, in a country that was an anomaly to the rest of the world. Well, no one ever said the truth would make you happy – only free.

Of course, there were other as yet undiscovered truths, and there were other people's truths, but that was yet to come.

I looked out at Stanhope Hall and beyond. The large gazebo, another American accoutrement, was visible on the back lawn, surrounded by overhanging sycamores, and in the distance was the English hedge maze, a ridiculous amusement for young ladies and their fatuous beaux, all of whom should have spent more time in the love temple and less time running around hedge mazes.

The land fell away beyond the hedges, but I could see the tops of the plum orchard, half of whose trees were now dead. The orchard, according to Susan, had originally been called the sacred grove, in the pagan fashion of nature worship. And in the centre of the grove is the Roman love temple, a small but perfectly proportioned round structure of buff marble columns that hold up a curved frieze carved with some very erotic scenes. In the domed roof is an opening, and the shaft of sunlight and moonlight that comes through at certain hours illuminates two pink marble statues, one of a man or a god, and the other of a busty Venus, locked in a nude embrace.

The purpose of this place mystifies me, but there were a number of them built on the more lavish estates. I can only conjecture that classical nudity was acceptable; Greco-Roman tits and ass was not just art, it was one of the few ways to see T and A in 1906, and only millionaires could afford this expensive thrill.

I don't know if young women, or even mature ladies,

ventured into the plum grove to see this porn palace, but you can be sure that Susan and I make good use of it on summer evenings. Susan likes being a vestal virgin surprised by John the Barbarian while praying in the temple. She's been deflowered about sixty times, which may be a record.

The temple may be a sham, but it is a beautiful sham, and Susan is no virgin, and I'm an imperfect barbarian, but the heart-stopping orgasms are real, and real things happen to real people even in Disney World.

I knew right then that despite my recent disenchantment with my enchanted world, I was going to miss this place.

I got back into my Bronco and headed home.

CHAPTER 8

Lester Remsen showed up at my Locust Valley office on Monday afternoon to take care of Mrs Lauderbach's ten-million-dollar problem. The actual figure according to Lester's research department was, as of three P.M. that day, $10,132,564 and a few cents. This included about sixty years of unpaid dividends on which, unfortunately, no interest was given.

Mrs Lauderbach had a hairdresser's appointment and could not join us, but I had power of attorney and was prepared to sign most of the brokerage house's paperwork on her behalf. Lester and I went to the second-floor law library, which had been the study of the Victorian house on Birch Hill Road. We spread out our paperwork on the library table.

Lester commented, 'This is one for the books. Good Lord, you'd think she'd be interested in this.'

I shrugged. 'She had grey roots.'

Lester smiled and we began the tedious paperwork in which I had less interest than Mrs Lauderbach. I ordered coffee as we neared the end of the task. Lester handed me a document and I handed him one. Lester seemed not to be focusing on the task at hand, and he laid down the

74

paper, stayed silent for a moment, and said, 'She's how old? Seventy-eight?'

'She was when we started.'

Lester seemed to miss my drollness and asked, 'And you're also the attorney for her will?'

'That's correct.'

'Can I ask who her heirs are?'

'You can ask, but I can't say.' I added, however, 'She has three children.'

Lester nodded. 'I know one of them. Mary. She's married to Phil Crowley. They're in Old Westbury.'

'That's right.'

'I never knew the Lauderbachs had so much money.'

'Neither did the Lauderbachs.'

'Well, I mean, they always lived well. They used to own The Beeches, didn't they?' He looked at Mrs Lauderbach's address on a document. 'But they've moved to a house in Oyster Bay village.'

'Yes.'

'They sold The Beeches to an Iranian Jew, didn't they?'

'I didn't handle that. But yes, they did. They got a fair price, and the new owners are maintaining the property quite well.'

'Hey, I don't care if they're Iranian Jews,' Lester smiled. 'Better than a Mafia don.'

Better than twenty Lester Remsens. The Lauderbachs, incidentally, had used a large law firm with no connections to the gentry for the property closing on The Beeches. This is sometimes done when the old homestead is being sold to people with funny last names. I suppose I see the point, which is that local attorneys might not want to be involved in a property transaction that other clients and neighbours disapprove of. Well, that was true in the Lauderbachs' day, but recently the Gold Coast reminds me of a nation that is about to fall, and no one is pretending any longer that everything is all right; instead, everyone is grabbing whatever he can and fleeing for the airport. I don't know if I would have handled the closing if asked. It was probably worth ten thousand dollars for a day's work, and I personally have nothing against Iranian Jews or any other foreigners. But some of my clients and neighbours do.

Lester asked, 'You don't think Mr Lauderbach *knew* he had ten million in stocks?'

'I don't know if he did, Lester. *I* didn't know or I'd have advised him to open an account with you.' I added, 'There were plenty of other assets. It didn't matter. You can spend only so much in a lifetime. Ernest Lauderbach ran out of time before he ran out of money.'

'But the *dividends* should have been reinvested. They just *sat* there not collecting a dime. That's like giving Chase Manhattan and American Express interest-free loans.'

Money that lies fallow upsets Lester. His children never had piggy banks. They had money market accounts.

Lester perused Ernest Lauderbach's will. 'Neither Mary nor the other two children, Randolf and Herman, inherited under this will?'

'No, they didn't.' It was Lester's right to examine the will to establish Mrs Lauderbach's ownership to all the property. My father had drawn up the sixth and last edition of Ernest Lauderbach's last will and testament about ten years before, but the stock and bond assets were only identified as 'securities and other money instruments that I may hold at the time of my death.' Clearly, no one, including the Lauderbachs' three children, knew precisely what was in the vault in the basement of the Oyster Bay house. I was fairly certain they still didn't know, or I'd have heard from all three of them and/or their attorneys by now.

Lester inquired, 'Where are Herman and Randolf?'

'Herman is retired in Virginia, and Randolf is a businessman in Chicago. Why?'

'I'd like to handle their stock assets when they inherit. That's why.'

Lester and I both knew that this conversation actually had to do with the possibility of making sure that Randolf,

Herman, and Mary did *not* inherit these stock assets. But I said, 'I'll recommend you to them if I'm satisfied with how this account is handled.'

'Thanks. I suppose they know about this?' He patted a pile of stock certificates.

I ignored the question and its implications and said politely but firmly, 'Lester, regarding your handling of this account, do not play the market for Mrs Lauderbach. Those are two perfectly good stocks. Just leave them in place and see that she gets her past and future dividend cheques. If she needs money for estate taxes, I'll advise you, and we'll sell off some shares for Uncle Sam.'

'John, you know I wouldn't churn this account for the commissions.'

Lester, to be fair, is an ethical broker, or I wouldn't deal with him. But he's in an occupation whose temptations would give Jesus Christ anxiety attacks. Such was the case now, with ten million sitting on the mahogany table in front of him. I could almost see that little devil on his left shoulder, and the angel on his right, both chattering in his ears. I didn't want to interrupt, but I said, 'It doesn't matter, you know, who knows about this money, who needs it, who deserves it, or that Agnes Lauderbach doesn't give a rat's ass about it.'

He shrugged and sort of changed the subject. 'I wonder why the Lauderbachs didn't hold on to The Beeches if they knew they had this kind of money.'

I replied, 'Not everyone *wants* a fifty-room house and two hundred acres, Lester. It's a waste of money even if you've got money. How many bathrooms do you need?'

Lester chuckled, then asked, 'Would you buy Stanhope Hall if you had ten million dollars?'

'You mean five million, partner.'

Lester smiled sheepishly and glanced at me to see if I was baiting him, then lowered his eyes, which swept across the paper-strewn table and rested on the piles of stock certificates. He asked, 'Or would you buy that sixty footer and sail off into the sunset?'

I was sorry I had confided in Lester. I didn't reply.

'Or think about getting Susan out of the guesthouse and back into the great house.' There was a silence in the room, during which Lester was thinking of what he'd do with five million dollars, and I guess I was thinking of what I'd do with ten, since I had no intention of compounding a crime with the sin of sharing any of it with Lester Remsen.

It occurred to me that Lester is the type of person who is honest out of fright, but he likes to flirt with dishonesty to see how it feels to have balls, if you'll pardon the expression. And he likes to see how other people react to his enticements.

Lester spoke in a way that suggested he was speaking apropos of nothing. 'It's very easy, John, now that I see the paperwork and the actual certificates. And it's a big enough sum to make it worthwhile. And I don't think we even have to leave the country afterwards, if it's handled right. When the old lady dies, you'll have seen to it that nothing appears in her will regarding this.'

Lester went on in this vein, never using bad words such as *federal tax evasion, steal, forge,* or *fraud.* I listened, more out of curiosity than a need to be educated in crime by Lester.

I don't know why *I* am honest. I suppose it is partially a result of my parents, who were paragons of virtue if nothing else. And when I was growing up in the fifties, the message from the pulpit and in Sunday school and my private school had less to do with the world's ills and injustices, and more to do with how to behave correctly toward others. It was the Ten Commandments and the Golden Rule, and believe it or not, young men and women were supposed to have personal mottoes to live by. Mine was, 'I will strive each day to give more than I receive.' I don't know where I got that, but it's a good way to go broke. But I must have lived by it once, maybe until I was eighteen. Maybe longer.

Yet millions of men and women of my generation were raised the same way, and some of them are thieves, and some much worse. So why am I honest? What is keeping me from ten million dollars and from the nearly naked ladies on

Ipanema beach? That's what Lester wanted to know. That's what I wanted to know.

I looked at the pile of stock certificates, and Lester interrupted his dissertation on how to safely steal ten million to inform me, 'No one cares anymore, John. The rules are out the window. That's not my fault or yours. It just is. I'm tired of being a sucker, of fighting by Marquess of Queensberry rules while I'm getting kicked in the groin, and the referee is being paid to look the other way.'

I made no reply.

Until very recently, one of the reasons for my honesty was my contentment with my life, the whole social matrix into which I fit and functioned. But when you decide you won't miss home, what keeps you from stealing the family car to get away? I looked at Lester, who held eye contact for a change. I said, 'As you once observed, money doesn't tempt me,' which was the truth.

'*Why* doesn't money tempt you?'

I looked at Lester. 'I don't know.'

'Money is neutral, John. It has no inherent good *or* evil. Think of it as Indian wampum. Seashells. It's up to you what you do with it.'

'And how you get it.'

Lester shrugged.

I said, 'Maybe in this case, I think that taking money from a batty old lady is no challenge and beneath my dignity and my professional ability to steal from sharp people. Find something dangerous and we'll talk again.' I added, 'I'll have the stocks delivered to your Manhattan office tomorrow by bonded courier.'

Lester looked both disappointed and relieved. He gathered the paperwork into his briefcase and stood. 'Well . . . what would life be like if we couldn't dream?'

'Dream good dreams.'

'I did. *You* should dream a little.'

'Don't be a schmuck, Lester.'

He seemed a little put off, so I guess I used the word right.

79

Lester said coolly, 'Don't forget I need Mrs Lauderbach's signature cards.'

'I'll see her tomorrow, on her way to her lunch date.'

Lester extended his hand and we shook. He said, 'Thanks for giving me this account. I owe you dinner.'

'Dinner would be fine.'

Lester left with a parting glance at the ten million dollars lying on the table.

I carried the stock certificates downstairs and put them in my vault.

The remainder of the week, which was Holy Week before Easter, passed in predictable fashion. On Thursday evening, Maundy Thursday, we went to St Mark's with the Allards, who were well again. The Reverend Mr Hunnings washed the feet of a dozen men and women of the congregation. This ceremony, if you don't know, is in imitation of Christ's washing the feet of his disciples and is supposed to symbolize the humility of the great toward the small. I didn't need my feet washed, but apparently Ethel did, so up she went to the altar with a bunch of other people who I guess had volunteered for this ahead of time because none of the women had panty hose on and none of the men wore silly socks. Now, I don't mean to make fun of my own religion, but I find this ceremony bizarre in the extreme. In fact, it's rarely performed, but Hunnings seems to enjoy it, and I wonder about him. One Maundy Thursday, when I get enough nerve, I'm going to volunteer to have my feet washed by the Reverend Mr Hunnings, and when I take my socks off, on each toenail will be painted a happy face.

Anyway, after services, we had George, and Ethel of the clean feet, to our house for what Susan referred to as the Last Supper, being the last meal she intended to cook until Monday.

Friday was Good Friday, and in recent years I've noticed that around here at least, people have adopted the European custom of not working on this solemn day. Even the Stock

Exchange was closed, and so, of course, Perkins, Perkins, Sutter and Reynolds, whose Wall Street office is in lockstep with the Exchange, was shut down. Whether this new holiday is a result of the religious reawakening in our country or a desire for a three-day weekend, I don't know, and no one is saying. But in any event, I had earlier in the week declared the Locust Valley office closed for Good Friday and then surprised the staff and annoyed the Wall Street partners by announcing that the Locust Valley office would also observe Easter Monday as the Europeans do. I'm trying to start a trend.

Susan and I, along with Ethel and George, went to St Mark's for the three-o'clock service, which marks the traditional time when the sky darkened and the earth shook and Christ died on the cross. I remember a Good Friday when I was a small boy, walking up the steps of St Mark's on a bright, sunny day that *did* suddenly turn dark with thunderclouds. I recall staring up at the sky in awe, waiting, I guess, for the earth to shake. A few adults smiled at me, then my mother came out of the church and led me inside. But this day was sunny, with no dramatic meteorological or geological phenomena, and had anything of the sort occurred, it would have been explained on the six-o'clock weather report.

St Mark's was filled with well-dressed people, and the Reverend Mr Hunnings, looking resplendent in his Holy Week crimson robes, stuck to business, which was the death of Jesus Christ. There were no social messages in the sermon, for which I thanked God. Hunnings, incidentally, also gives us a guilt break on Easter Sunday and usually at Christmas, except then he goes on a bit about materialism and commercialism.

After the austere service, Susan and I dropped off the Allards, parked the Jag, and took a long walk around the estate, enjoying the weather and the new blooms. I can picture how this place must have looked in its heyday – gardeners and nurserymen bustling around, planting, trimming, cultivating, raking. But now it looks forlorn: too much deadwood and layers of leaves from twenty autumns past. It's not quite returned to nature, but the grounds and gardens, like much around here – including my life – are in that transitional stage between order and chaos.

Edward and Carolyn were not coming home for Easter this year, having made travel plans with friends, and I suppose Susan and I, like many couples who have discovered their children are gone, were reflecting on a time when the kids were kids and holidays were family affairs.

As we walked up the drive toward Stanhope Hall, Susan said, 'Do you remember when we opened up the big house and had that Easter egg hunt?'

I smiled. 'We hid a hundred eggs for twenty kids, and only eighty eggs were found. There are still twenty eggs rotting in there somewhere.'

Susan laughed. 'And we lost a kid, too. Jamie Lerner. He was screaming from the north wing for half an hour before we found him.'

'Did we find him? I thought he was still in there, living on Easter eggs.'

We walked past the great house, hand in hand, onto the back lawn, and sat in the old gazebo. Neither of us spoke for a while, then Susan said, 'Where do the years go?'

I shrugged.

'Is anything wrong?' she asked.

This question is fraught with all types of danger when a spouse asks it. I replied, 'No,' which in husband talk means yes.

'Another woman?'

'No,' which in the right tone of voice means no, no, no.

'Then *what*?'

'I don't know.'

She remarked, 'You've been very distant.'

Susan is sometimes so distant I have to dial an area code to get through to her. But people like that don't appreciate it when it's reversed. I replied with a stock husband phrase: 'It's nothing to do with you.'

Some wives would be relieved to hear that, even if it weren't true, but Susan didn't seem about to break into a grin and throw her arms around me. Instead, she said, 'Judy Remsen tells me that you told Lester you wanted to sail around the world.'

If Lester were there, I would have punched him in the nose. I said sarcastically, 'Is that what Judy Remsen told you that I told Lester?'

'Yes. Do you want to sail around the world?'

'It sounded like a good idea at the time. I was drunk.' Which sounded lame, so in the spirit of truth, I added, 'But I have considered it.'

'Am I included in those plans?'

Susan sometimes surprises me with little flashes of insecurity. If I were a more manipulative man, I would promote this insecurity as a means of keeping her attention, if not her affection. I know she does it to me. I asked, 'Would you consider living in our East Hampton House?'

'No.'

'Why not?'

'Because I like it here.'

'You like East Hampton,' I pointed out.

'It's a nice place to spend part of the summer.'

'Why don't we sail around the world?'

'Why don't *you* sail around the world?'

'Good question.' Bitchy, but good. Time to promote insecurity. 'I may do that.'

Susan stood. 'Better yet, John, why don't you ask yourself what you're running from?'

'Don't get analytical on me, Susan.'

'Then let me tell you what's bothering you. Your children aren't home for Easter, your wife is a bitch, your friends are idiots, your job is boring, you dislike my father, you hate Stanhope Hall, the Allards are getting on your nerves, you're not rich enough to control events and not poor enough to stop trying. Should I go on?'

'Sure.'

'You're alienated from your parents or vice versa, you've

had one too many dinners at the club, attractive young women don't take your flirting seriously anymore, life is without challenge, maybe without meaning, and possibly without hope. And nothing is certain but death and taxes. Well, welcome to American upper-middle-class middle age, John Sutter.'

'Thank you.'

'Oh, and lest I forget, a Mafia don has just moved in next door.'

'That might be the only bright spot in the picture.'

'It might well be.'

Susan and I looked at each other, but neither of us explained what we meant by that last exchange. I stood. 'I feel better now.'

'Good. You just needed a mental enema.'

I smiled. Actually, I did feel better, maybe because I was happy to discover that Susan and I were still in touch.

Susan threw her arm around my shoulders, which I find very tomboyish, yet somehow more intimate than an embrace. She said, 'I wish it *were* another woman. I could take care of that damned quickly.'

I smiled. '*Some* attractive young women take me seriously.'

'Oh, I'm sure of that.'

'Right.'

We left the gazebo and walked on a path that led into a treed hollow that lay south of the mansion. I said, 'You're not always a bitch. And I don't dislike your father. I hate his guts.'

'Good for you. He feels the same way about you.'

'Excellent.'

We continued our walk into the wooded hollow, Susan's arm still thrown over my shoulders. I'm not usually into self-pity or self-analysis, but sometimes you have to stop and think about things. Not only for yourself, but also so you don't hurt other people.

I said, 'By the way, the Bishop stopped by last Saturday. George told him I wasn't receiving.'

'George said that to Bishop Eberly?'

'No, to Bishop Frank.'

'Oh . . .' She laughed. '*That* Bishop.' She thought a moment. 'He'll be back.'

'You think so?' I added, 'I wonder what he wanted.'

Susan replied, 'You'll find out.'

'Don't sound so ominous, Susan. I think he just wants to be a friendly neighbour.'

'For your information, I've called the Eltons and the DePauws, and they haven't heard from him or seen him.'

The Eltons own Windham, the estate that borders Alhambra to the north, and the DePauws have a big colonial and ten acres, not actually an estate, directly across from Alhambra's gates. I said, 'Then it appears as if Mr Bellarosa has singled us out for neighbourly attention.'

'Well, you met him. Maybe you said something encouraging.'

'Hardly.' And I still wondered how he knew who I was and what I looked like. That was upsetting.

We came out of the trees at a place where there was a small footpath, paved with moss-covered stone. I steered Susan toward the path and felt her resist for a moment, then yield. We walked up the stone path, which was covered by an old rose trellis, and at the end of the path was the charred ruin of the gingerbread playhouse. The remaining beams and rafters supported climbing ivy that had crept up from the stone fireplace chimney. The fireplace itself was intact with a mantel and a large black kettle still hanging from a wrought-iron arm. In true fairy-tale fashion, there was, and had been as I recalled before the fire, something sinister about the cute little cottage.

Susan asked, 'Why did you want to walk here?'

'I thought since you were analysing *my* head, *I'd* like to know why you never come here.'

'How do you know I don't?'

'Because I've never seen you walk here, and I've never seen a hoofprint near this place.'

85

'It's sad to see it this way.'

'But we never came here *before* the fire, never played our games here.'

She didn't reply.

'I suppose I can understand not wanting to have sex in a playhouse with childhood memories.'

Susan said nothing.

I walked up to what had been the front door, but Susan didn't follow. I could make out a flower box that had fallen from a window ledge, pieces of stained glass and melted lead, and the burned skeleton of a bed and mattress that had fallen through from the second floor. I asked, 'Well, are the memories good or bad?'

'Both.'

'Tell me the good ones.'

She took a few steps toward the house, knelt, and picked up a shard of pottery. She said, 'I had sleepovers here in the summer. A dozen girls, up all night, giggling, laughing, singing, and deliciously terrified at every noise outside.'

I smiled.

She approached the house and surveyed the blackened timbers, which still emitted an odour ten years after the fire. 'Lots of good memories.'

'I'm glad. Let's go.' I took her arm.

'Do you want to know about the bad things?'

'Not really.'

'The servants used to come here sometimes and have parties. And sex.' She added, 'I realized it was sex when I was about thirteen. They used to lock the door. I wouldn't sleep in that bed again.'

I didn't respond.

'I mean, it was *my* house. A place that I thought belonged to me.'

'I understand.'

'And . . . one day . . . I was about fifteen, I came here and the door wasn't locked and I went inside and up the stairs to get something I'd left in the bedroom . . . and this couple was

86

lying there, naked, asleep . . .' She glanced at me. 'I guess I was traumatized.' She forced a smile. 'Today, I don't know if a fifteen-year-old girl would be traumatized by that. I mean, how could they be? You see naked people on TV doing it.'

'True.' But I couldn't believe that still bothered her. There was more to it, and I sensed she was going to tell me what it was.

She stayed silent awhile before saying, 'My mother used to come here with someone.'

'I see.' I wondered if it was her mother that she'd seen in bed, and with whom.

She walked across the littered floorboards and stopped beside the burned bed. 'And I lost my virginity here.'

I didn't respond.

She turned toward me and smiled sadly. 'Some play-house.'

'Let's go.'

She walked past me, onto the path between the rose bushes. I came up beside her. I said, 'Was it you who burned the place down?'

'Yes.'

I didn't know what to say, so I said, 'Sorry.'

'It's all right.'

I put my arm around her and said in a lighter tone, 'Did I ever tell you about that Good Friday when I was a kid and the sky suddenly darkened?'

'Several times. Tell me how you lost your virginity.'

'I told you.'

'You told me three different versions. I'll bet I was your first lay.'

'Maybe. But not my last.'

She punched me in the ribs. 'Wise guy.'

We walked in silence back through the hollow, and when I ran my fingers over her cheek, I discovered she was crying.

'Everything's going to be all right,' I assured her.

'I'm too old for fairy tales,' she informed me.

At Susan's suggestion we turned toward the plum orchard,

the so-called sacred grove, and made our way toward the Roman love temple. More than half the plum trees were dead or dying, and each spring there were fewer blossoms, but still, the air was perfumed with their scent.

We came into the clearing where the round marble temple stood, and without speaking we mounted the steps and I swung open the big brass door.

The sun was low on the horizon and shone in on a slant through the opening in the domed roof, illuminating a section of the erotic carvings on the lintels. Susan walked across the marble floor and stood before the naked statues of Venus and the big Roman male. The statues of pink marble were seated side by side on an uncarved slab of black stone, and though they were in a partial embrace, about to kiss, the view from the waist down was of full frontal nudity. The man had forgotten his fig leaf, and his penis was in an excited state. As I said, this was all pretty risqué for 1906, and even today an erect penis in art is considered by some to be pornographic.

Anyway, it is possible for a woman to sit in the lap of this virile male and achieve penetration. In fact, in Roman times during the Saturnalia festival, virgins actually deflowered themselves in this way, using, I believe, the statue of Priapus, whose member is always at the ready.

You must keep in mind that these statues and this love temple were commissioned by Susan's great-grandfather, Cyrus Stanhope, and I believe that randiness runs in some families. Certainly Susan has inherited an as yet unidentified gene for an overactive libido from both sides of her family, who, by most accounts, couldn't seem to keep their pants up or their skirts down.

I told you, too, that Susan and I engage in some interesting sexual practices in this love temple, though not the aforementioned Roman practice of statuary rape, if you'll pardon my pun. I should also tell you that the two statues are slightly larger than life, and consequently the Roman gentleman's equipment is perhaps slightly larger than mine, but not by so much as to make me jealous.

Well, anyway, there we were in this pagan temple on a Good Friday, recently returned from church, and from a moment of truth at the gazebo and an emotional episode at the playhouse. And to be honest, this confluence of events left me with the uncomfortable feeling that this might not be the time or place for romance.

Susan, on the other hand, seemed more sure of what she wanted. She said, 'Make love to me, John.'

That request in that form means we are not going to playact, but are going to make love as husband and wife. This also means that Susan is feeling insecure, or perhaps melancholy.

So I took her in my arms, and we kissed and, still kissing, sat on the wide ledge at the base of the statues in unconscious imitation of their pose. We kicked off our shoes and, still kissing, removed our clothes, helping each other undress until we were naked. I lay down on my back on the cool marble, and Susan straddled me with her knees, then rose up and came down on me. She worked her pelvis up and down and rocked back and forth, her eyes closed, her mouth open, moaning softly.

I reached up and pulled her down to me and kissed her. She straightened her legs, and stretched her body out over mine. We embraced and continued to kiss as her hips rose and fell.

Susan's body went tense, then relaxed, and she continued to move her hips until she went rigid again, then went limp again. She did this three or four times until her breathing began to sound laboured, but she continued on until she had yet another orgasm. She might have gone on until she passed out, which actually happened once, but I let myself come, and this brought on her final climax.

She lay with her head buried in my chest, her long red hair draped over my shoulders. I heard her whisper between deep breaths, 'Thank you, John.'

It was pleasant lying there, Susan on top of me, our groins

all warm and wet. I played with her hair, rubbed her back and buttocks, and we rubbed our feet together.

I could see from the open dome that the sunlight was fading outside, and in fact the temple was darker now. But directly above me I could see the marble statues still locked in their eternal embrace, and from this perspective, their expressions and their whole demeanour looked more lustful and heated, as if their nine decades of frustration were about to explode into an act of sexual frenzy.

We must have fallen asleep, because when I opened my eyes, it was dark in the temple and I was cold. Susan stirred, and I felt her warm lips on my neck.

I said, 'That's nice.'

'Feel better?'

'Yes.' I replied. 'You?'

'Yes.' She added, 'I love you, John.'

'I love you.'

She got to her feet and said, 'Stand up.'

I stood and Susan took my shirt, put it on me and buttoned it, then put my tie on and tied it. Next came my shorts and my socks, then my trousers. She buckled my belt and zipped my fly. Having a woman undress me is very erotic, but only Susan has ever dressed me after sex and I find it a very loving and tender act. She put my shoes on and tied them, then brushed off my jacket and helped me into it. 'There,' she said as she straightened my hair, 'you look like you just left church.'

'Except my groin is sticky.'

She smiled, and I looked at her standing in front of me stark naked. I said, 'Thank you.'

'My pleasure.'

I tried to dress her, but I got the panties on backward and was having trouble with the bra fasteners. Susan said, 'John, you used to undress me in the dark with one hand.'

'This is different.'

We finally got Susan into her clothes and walked hand in hand back to the house in the dark. I said to her, 'You're right, you know. I mean your perceptive analysis of how I feel. I don't want to feel bored or restless, but I do.'

'Maybe,' she replied, 'you need a challenge. Perhaps I can think of something to challenge you.'

'Good idea,' I said, which turned out to be the stupidest thing I ever said.

CHAPTER 9

I skipped church on Holy Saturday, having had enough of the Reverend Mr Hunnings and the Allards. Susan played hooky, too, and spent the morning cleaning her stables with two college boys home on vacation. I don't do stables, but I did stop by with a cooler of soft drinks. As I pulled the Bronco up to the stable, I was struck by the awful smell of horse manure and the sounds of laughter and groans.

Zanzibar and Yankee were tethered to a post outside, under the huge, spreading chestnut tree, nibbling grass and oblivious to the humans slaving on their behalf. I think horses should clean their own stables. I used to like horses. Now I hate them. I'm jealous.

On the same subject, Susan, who can be cold as Freon to men her own age who show an interest in her, is very friendly to young men. This I'm sure is partly maternal, as she is old enough to be the mother of college-age children and in fact is. It's the part that is not maternal that annoys me. Anyway, they all seemed to be having a grand time in there shovelling shit.

I pulled the cooler out of the rear of the Bronco and set it down on a stone bench.

A pile of manure had risen on the cobbled service court in front of the stable, and this would find its way to the rose garden behind our house. Maybe that's why I don't stop and smell the roses.

I opened a bottle of apple juice and drank, my foot propped on the bench, trying to strike a real-man pose in case anybody came out of the stable. If I had tobacco and paper I would have rolled one. I waited, but the only thing coming out of the stable was laughter.

I surveyed the long, two-storey stable complex. The stables are built of brick with slate roofs in an English country style, more matching the guesthouse than the main house. I suppose there's no such thing as beaux-arts stables with Roman columns. The stables had been built at the same time as the house, when horses were a more reliable and dignified means of transportation than automobiles. There were thirty stalls for the riding horses, the carriage horses, and the draught horses, and a large carriage house that probably held two dozen horse-drawn conveyances, including sleds and estate equipment. The second storey was part haymow and part living quarters for the forty or so men needed to maintain the animals, buildings, tack, and carriages. The carriage house had become the garage by the 1920s, and the coachmen, grooms, and such had become chauffeurs and mechanics.

Susan and I sometimes used the garage for the Jag, and George always parks his Lincoln there, as he is of the generation that believes in taking care of possessions. The gatehouse, guesthouse, and main house were built without garages, of course, because if one needed one's horse, carriage, or automobile, one just buzzed the carriage house. I have a buzzer marked CARRIAGE HOUSE in my kitchen, and I keep pushing it, but no one comes.

Anyway, the stables are on Stanhope land, which presents a problem if the land is sold. The obvious solution to this is to construct a smaller wooden stable on Susan's property. I mean, we don't live in the great house: why should the horses live in the great stable? But Susan fears emotional trauma to her animals if they are forced to step down in life, so she wants at least part of the original stable moved, brick by brick, slate by slate, and cobble by cobble to her land. She wants this done soon, before the tax people start identifying assets. Her father has graciously given his permission to move all or part of the structure to her ten acres, and Susan has picked a nice tree-shaded patch of land with a pond for her precious horsies. All that remains to be done is to engage the Herculean Task Stable Moving Company and a hundred slaves to complete the job. Susan says she'll split the cost with me. I have to look at that prenuptial agreement again.

I finished my apple juice and hooked my thumb in my belt, waiting for somebody to push a wheelbarrow full of faeces out the door. I found a piece of straw and stuck it between my teeth.

After a minute or so in this pose, I decided to stop being silly and just go in. But as I walked toward the main doors, a puff of hay flew out of the loft overhead and landed on me. It sounded as if they were having a hay fight. Good clean American fun. Pissed off beyond belief, I spun around, got into the Bronco, and slammed it into gear, making a tight U-turn in front of the main doors. I could hear Susan calling after me from the open loft as I drove right through the pile of manure in four-wheel drive.

That afternoon, after a rational discussion regarding my childishness, we put on our tennis whites and walked down to the courts to keep a tennis date. It was warm for April, and after a few volleys while we waited for the other couple, Susan took off her sweater and warm-up pants. I have to tell you, the woman looks exquisite in tennis clothes, and when she fishes around in her panties for the second ball, the men on the court lose their concentration for a minute or two.

Anyway, we volleyed for another ten minutes, and I was blasting balls all over the place, and Susan was telling me not to be hostile. Finally, she said, 'Look, John, don't blow this match. Calm down.'

'I'm calm.'

'If we win, I'll grant you any sexual favour you wish.'

'How about a roll in the hay?'

She laughed. 'You got it.'

We volleyed a bit longer, and I guess I did calm down a bit, because I was keeping the balls in the court. I was not, however, a happy man. It's often little things, like Susan's horsing around in the hay, that sets you off on a course that can be vengeful and destructive.

Anyway, our tennis partners, Jim and Sally Roosevelt, showed up. Jim is one of the Oyster Bay Roosevelts still living in the area. Roosevelts, Morgans, Vanderbilts, and such are sort of a local natural resource, self-renewable like pheasant and nearly as scarce. To have a Roosevelt or a pheasant on your property is an occasion of some pride; to have one or the other for dinner is, respectively, a social or culinary coup. Actually, Jim is just a regular guy with a famous name and a trust fund. More important, I can beat his pants off in tennis. Incidentally, we don't pronounce *Roosevelt* the way you've heard it pronounced all your life. Around here, we say *Roozvelt*, teeth clenched lockjaw style, two syllables, rhymes with 'Lou's belt'. Okay?

Sally Roosevelt was née Sally Grace, of the ocean liner Graces, and Grace Lane, coincidentally, was named after that family, not after a woman. However, I'm certain that nearly all of Grace Lane's residents think their road is named after the spiritual state of grace in which they believe they exist. Aside from being a Grace, Sally is not bad to look at, and to get even for the hayloft incident I flirted with her between sets. But neither she nor Susan, nor Jim for that matter, seemed to care. My shots started to get wilder. I was losing it.

At about six P.M., in the middle of a game, I noticed a black, shiny Cadillac Eldorado moving up the main drive. The car slowed opposite the tennis courts, which are partially hidden by evergreens. The car stopped, and Frank Bellarosa got out and walked toward the courts.

Jim said unnecessarily, 'I think someone is looking for you.'

I excused myself, put down my racket, and left the court. I intercepted Mr Bellarosa on the path about thirty yards from the court.

'Hello, Mr Sutter. Did I interrupt your tennis game?'

'You sure did, greaseball. What do you want?' No, I didn't actually say that. I said, 'That's all right.'

94

He extended his hand, which I took. We shook briefly without playing crush the cartilage. Frank Bellarosa informed me, 'I don't play tennis.'

'Neither do I,' I replied.

He laughed. I like a man who appreciates my humour, but in this case I was willing to make an exception.

Bellarosa was dressed in grey slacks and a blue blazer, which is good Saturday uniform around here, and I was quite honestly surprised. But he also had on horrible white, shiny shoes, and his belt was too narrow. He wore a black turtleneck sweater, which is okay, but not très chic anymore. There were no pinky rings or other garish jewellery, no chains or sparkly things, but he did have on a Rolex Oyster, which I, at least, find in questionable taste. I noticed this time that he had on a wedding ring.

'It's a nice day,' said Mr Bellarosa with genuine delight.

I could tell the man was having a better day than I was. I'll bet Mrs Bellarosa hadn't spent the morning thrashing around in the hayloft with two young studs. 'Unusually warm for this time of year,' I agreed.

'Some place you got here,' he said.

'Thank you,' I replied.

'You been here long?'

'Three hundred years.'

'What's that?'

'I mean my family. But my wife's family built this place in 1906.'

'No kidding?'

'You can look it up.'

'Yeah.' He looked around. 'Some place.'

I regarded Mr Frank Bellarosa a moment. He was not the short, squat froggy type you sometimes associate with a stereotypical Mafia don. Rather, he had a powerful build, as if he lifted dead bodies encased in concrete, and his face had sharp features, dark skin, deep-set eyes, and a hooked Roman nose. His hair was blue-black, wavy, well-styled, grey at the temples, and all there. He was a few inches shorter that I, but I'm six feet, so he was about average height. I'd say he was about fifty years old, though I could look it up somewhere – court records, for instance.

He had a soft smile that seemed incongruous with his hard eyes and with his violent history. Except for that smile, there was nothing in his looks or manner that suggested a bishop. I didn't think the guy was particularly good-looking, but my instincts told me that some women might find him attractive.

Frank Bellarosa turned his attention back to me. 'Your guy – what's his name . . ?'

'George.'

'Yeah. He said you were playing tennis, but I could go on in and see if you were done. But that I shouldn't interrupt your game.'

Mr Bellarosa's tone told me he wasn't happy with George.

I replied, 'That's all right.' George, of course, knew who this man was, though we never discussed our new neighbour. George is the keeper of the gate and the keeper of the long-dead etiquettes, and if you were a lady or a gentleman, you were welcome to pass through the main gates. If you were a tradesman on business or an invited killer, you should use the service entrance down the road. I thought I should tell George to lighten up on Mr Bellarosa. I asked, 'What can I do for you?'

'Nothing. Just wanted to say hello.'

'That's good of you. Actually it was I who should have paid a call on you.'

'Oh, yeah? Why?'

'Well . . . that's the way it's done.'

'Yeah? No one's stopped by yet.'

'Now that's odd. Perhaps no one is sure you're there.' This conversation was getting weird, so I said, 'Well, thanks for coming by. And welcome to Lattingtown.'

'Thanks. Hey, you got a minute? I got something for you. Come on.' He turned and motioned me to follow. I glanced back at the tennis court, then followed.

Bellarosa stopped at his Cadillac and opened the trunk. I expected to see George's body, but instead Bellarosa took out a flat of seedlings and handed them to me. 'Here. I bought too much. You really don't have a vegetable garden?'

'No.' I looked at the plastic tray. 'I guess I do now.'

He smiled. 'Yeah. I gave you a few of everything. I left these little signs on so you know what they are. Vegetables need good sun. I don't know about the soil around here. What kind of soil you got here?'

'Well . . . slightly acid, some clay, but good loamy topsoil, glacial outwash – '

'What?'

'Glacial . . . silty, pebbly in places – '

'All I see around here is trees, bushes, and flowers. Try these vegetables. You'll thank me in August.'

'I thank you in April.'

'Yeah. Put that down. Not on the car.'

I put the tray down on the ground.

Bellarosa pulled a clear plastic bag from the trunk, inside of which was a mass of purplish leaves.

'Here,' he said. 'This is radicchio. You know? Like lettuce.'

I took the bag and examined the ragged leaves with polite interest. 'Very nice.'

'I grew it.'

'You must have warmer weather over there.'

Bellarosa laughed. 'No, I grew it inside. You know, my place has this room – like a greenhouse . . . the real estate lady said it . . .'

'A conservatory.'

'Yeah. Like a greenhouse, except it's part of the house. So I got that fixed up first thing in January. Every pane was broken, and the gas heater was gone. Cost me twenty thousand bucks, but I'm getting onions and lettuce already.'

'Very expensive onions and lettuce,' I observed.

'Yeah. But what the hell.'

I should tell you that Bellarosa's accent was definitely not

Locust Valley, but neither was it pure Brooklyn. Accents being important around here, I've developed an ear for them, as have most people I know. I can usually tell which of the city's five boroughs a person is from, or which of the surrounding surburban counties. I can sometimes tell which prep school a person has gone to, or if he's gone to Yale as I have. Frank Bellarosa did not go to Yale, but occasionally there was something odd, almost prep school, in his accent if not his choice of words. But mostly I could hear the streets of Brooklyn in his voice. Against my better judgement, I asked, 'Where did you live before Lattingtown?'

'Where? Oh, Williamsburg.' He looked at me. 'That's in Brooklyn. You know Brooklyn?'

'Not very well.'

'Great place. Used to be a great place. Too many . . . for-eigners now. I grew up in Williamsburg. My whole family is from there. My grandfather lived on Havemeyer Street when he came over.'

I assumed Mr Bellarosa's grandfather came over from a foreign country, undoubtedly Italy, and I'm sure the old Germans and Irish of Williamsburg did not welcome him with hugs and schnitzels. When this continent was inhabited by Indians, the first Europeans had only to kill them to make room for themselves. The succeeding waves of immigrants had it a little rougher; they had to buy or rent. I didn't think Mr Bellarosa was interested in any of these ironies, so I said, 'Well, I do hope you find Long Island to your liking.'

'Yeah. I know Long Island. I went to boarding school out here.'

He didn't offer any more, so I didn't press it, though I wondered what boarding school Frank Bellarosa could possibly have attended. I thought that might be his way of saying reform school. I said, 'Thanks again for the lettuce.'

'Eat it quick. Just picked. A little oil and vinegar.'

I wondered if the horses would like it without oil and vinegar. 'Sure will. Well – '

'That your daughter?'

Bellarosa was looking over my shoulder, and I glanced back and saw Susan coming down the path. I turned back to Bellarosa. 'My wife.'

'Yeah?' He watched Susan approaching. 'I saw her riding a horse one day on my property.'

'She sometimes rides horses.'

He looked at me. 'Hey, if she wants to ride around my place, it's okay. She probably rode there before I bought the place. I don't want any hard feelings. I got a couple hundred acres, and the horse shit is good for the soil. Right?'

'It's excellent for roses.'

Susan walked directly up to Frank Bellarosa and extended her hand. 'I'm Susan Sutter. You must be our new neighbour.'

Bellarosa hesitated a moment before taking her hand, and I guessed that men in his world did not shake hands with women. He said, 'Frank Bellarosa.'

'I'm pleased to meet you, Mr Bellarosa. John told me he met you at the nursery a few weeks ago.'

'Yeah.'

Bellarosa maintained good eye contact, though I did see his eyes drop to Susan's legs for half a second. I wasn't altogether pleased that Susan hadn't put on her warm-up pants and that she was presenting herself to a total stranger in a tennis skirt that barely covered her crotch.

Susan said to Bellarosa, 'You must forgive us for not calling on you, but we weren't certain if you were settled in and receiving.'

Bellarosa seemed to ponder this a moment. This receiving business must have been giving him problems. Susan, I should point out, slips into her Lady Stanhope role when she wants to cause certain people to be uncomfortable. I don't know if this is defensive or offensive.

Bellarosa did not seem uncomfortable, though he seemed a little more tentative with Susan than he had been with me. Maybe Susan's legs were distracting him. He said to her, 'I was just telling your husband I saw you riding on my place once or twice. No problem.'

I thought he was about to mention the scatological side benefits to himself, but he just smiled at me. I did not return the smile. This was indeed a horse shit day, I thought.

Susan said to Mr Bellarosa, 'That's very good of you. I should point out, however, that it is local custom here to allow for equestrian right of way. You may mark specific bridle paths if you wish. However, if the hunt is ever reinstated, the horses will follow the dogs, who are, in turn, following the scent. You'll be notified.'

Frank Bellarosa looked at Susan for a long moment, and neither of them blinked. Bellarosa then surprised me by saying in a cool tone, 'I guess there's a lot I don't understand yet, Mrs Sutter.'

I thought I should change the subject to something he *did* understand, so I held up the plastic bag. 'Susan, Mr Bellarosa grew this lettuce – radicchio, it's called – in Alhambra's conservatory.'

Susan glanced at the bag and turned back to Bellarosa. She said, 'Oh, did you have that repaired? That's very nice.'

'Yeah. The place is coming along.'

'And these seedlings . . .' I added, indicating the tray on the ground, 'vegetables for our garden.'

'That's very thoughtful of you,' Susan said.

Bellarosa smiled at Susan. 'Your husband told me you eat flowers.'

'No, sir, I eat thorns. Thank you for stopping by.'

Bellarosa ignored the implied brush-off and turned to me. 'What's your place called? It's got a name, right?'

'Yes,' I replied. 'Stanhope Hall.'

'What's that mean?'

'Well . . . it's named after Susan's great-grandfather, Cyrus Stanhope. He built it.'

'Yeah. You said that. Am I supposed to name my place?'

'It has a name,' I said.

'Yeah, I know that. The real estate lady told me. Alhambra. That's how I get my mail. There's no house number. You believe that? But should I give the place a new name or what?'

Susan replied, 'You may, if you wish. Some people do. Others keep the original name. Do you have a name in mind?'

Frank Bellarosa thought a moment, then shook his head. 'Nah. Alhambra's okay for now. Sounds Spanish though. I'll think about it.'

'If we can be of any help with a name,' Susan said, 'do let us know.'

'Thanks. You think I should put up a sign with the name of the place? I see signs on some of the places. You guys don't have a sign.'

'It's entirely up to you,' I assured our new neighbour. 'But if you change the name, notify the post office.'

'Yeah. Sure.'

Susan added – baitingly, I thought, 'Some people just put their own names out front. But others, especially if they have well-known names, don't.'

Bellarosa looked at her and smiled. He said, 'I don't think it would be a good idea to put my name out front, do you, Mrs Sutter?'

'No, I don't, Mr Bellarosa.'

Now *I* was getting uncomfortable. 'Well,' I said, 'we'd better get back to our guests.'

Bellarosa hesitated a moment, then said, 'I'm having a little Easter thing tomorrow. Some friends, a little family. Nothing fancy. Traditional Italian Easter foods.' He smiled. 'I went to Brooklyn to get *capozella*. Lamb's head. But we got the rest of the lamb, too. About two o'clock. Okay?'

I wasn't sure I'd heard him right about the lamb's head. I replied, 'I'm afraid we've got another Easter thing to go to.'

'Yeah? Well, see if you can drop by for ten minutes and I'll show you the place. Have a drink. Okay?' He looked at Susan.

She replied, 'We will certainly try to join you. But if we can't, have a very joyous and blessed Easter.'

'Thanks.' Bellarosa shut the trunk and went to his car door. 'You mind if I drive around a little?'

Susan said, 'Not at all. That's a rather long car to try to turn on this lane, so go on up to the main house and turn in the circle.'

I knew if I wanted to annoy Susan I should tell Mr Bellarosa that the old homestead was up for sale, but I figured we had enough to talk about for one day.

Bellarosa looked at us over the top of his car, and we looked back. It was a contest, or maybe the first skirmish in the clash of cultures, I thought. Susan and I were both raised never to be rude to social inferiors unless they presented themselves to you as equals. Then you could massacre them. But Mr Frank Bellarosa was not trying to put on any airs or ask for honorary gentry status. He was what he was and he didn't care enough about us to pretend he was something else.

I was reminded of my first impression of him, of a conqueror, curious about the effete society he had just trampled, maybe a little amused by the inhabitants, and certainly monumentally unimpressed by a culture that couldn't defend itself against people like Frank Bellarosa. This, I would learn later, was an accurate first impression and was, as I discovered from the man himself, part of the Italian psyche. But at that moment, I was just glad he was leaving. I knew, of course, I would see him again, if not to eat lamb's head together on Easter, then some other time in the near future. But I did not know, nor could I have possibly guessed, to what extent we three would bring ruin and disaster on one another.

Bellarosa smiled at us, and I was struck again by that gentle mouth. He said bluntly, 'I'm going to be a good neighbour. Don't worry. We'll get along.' He ducked into his car and drove off up the sun-dappled lane.

I handed Susan the bag of lettuce. 'Oil and vinegar.' I added, 'You were a bit snooty.'

'Me? How about you?' She asked, 'Well, do you want to drop by for a quick lamb's ear or something?'

'I think not.'

She stayed silent a moment, then said, 'It just might be interesting.'

I said, 'Susan, you're strange.'

She replied in a husky voice, 'Yeah? Ya think so?' She laughed and turned back toward the tennis courts. I left the tray of seedlings on the ground and followed. 'Do you think I should plant vegetables this year?'

'You'd better.' She laughed again. 'This is bizarre.'

The word was *scary* not *bizarre*, and we both knew that. Not scary in the physical sense perhaps; we weren't going to get rubbed out for not showing up at Bellarosa's house or not planting his seedlings or even for being a little curt with him. But scary in the sense that the man had the *power* to have people who annoyed him rubbed out. And despite Susan's aloofness and what I hoped was my cool indifference toward the man, you did not deal with Frank the Bishop Bellarosa in the same way you dealt with the Remsens, the Eltons, or the DePauws. And the reason for that was not too subtle; Frank Bellarosa was a killer.

Susan said, 'Maybe "Casa Bellarosa".'

'What?'

'His place. Maybe I'll get a nice sign made as a house-warming gift. Something in mother-of-pearl. Casa Bellarosa.'

I didn't reply to what I thought was nearly an ethnic slur.

Susan pulled a leaf of radicchio from the plastic bag and munched on it. 'A little bitter. It does need some oil or something. But very fresh. Want some?'

'No, thank you.'

'Should we have introduced Mr Bellarosa to the Roosevelts? You know, like, "Jim and Sally, may I present our newest friend and neighbour, Frank the Bishop Bellarosa?" Or would one say "don Bellarosa", to impress the Roosevelts?'

'Don't be inane.' I asked Susan, 'What did you think of him?'

She replied without hesitation, 'He has a certain primitive charm and a self-assurance even in the face of my well-bred arrogance.' She paused, then said, 'He's rather better looking than I'd imagined.'

'I don't think he's good-looking.' I added, 'And he dresses funny.'

'So do half the tweedbags around here.'

We walked back onto the court, where Jim and Sally were volleying. I said 'Sorry.' You should know that interrupting a tennis game for anything short of a death on the court is in bad taste.

Jim responded, 'Susan said that might be your new neighbour.'

'It was.' I picked up my racket and took the court. 'Where were we?'

Sally asked, 'Frank Bellarosa?'

'I think it was my serve,' I said.

Susan said to Sally, 'We just call him Bishop.'

Three of us thought that was funny. I repeated, 'My serve, two-love.'

Susan showed the Roosevelts the bag of radicchio and they all examined it as though it were Martian plant life or something.

'It's getting dark,' I said.

'What did he want?' Jim asked Susan.

Susan answered, 'He wants us to eat this and plant a vegetable garden.'

Sally giggled.

Susan continued, 'And he wants to know if he's supposed to put a sign out front that says Alhambra. And,' Susan added, 'he invited us over for Easter dinner.'

'Oh, no!' Sally squealed.

'Lamb's head!' Susan exclaimed.

'Oh, for God's sake,' I said. I've never seen a game delayed for conversation on the court except once at the Southampton Tennis Club when a jealous husband tried to brain the pro with his Dunlop Blue Max, but everyone got back to business as soon as the husband and the pro disappeared around the clubhouse. I said, 'My muscles are tightening. That's the game.' I gathered my things and walked off the court. The other three followed, still talking, and I led the way back to the house.

It was still warm enough to sit in the garden, and Susan brought out a bottle of old port. For hors d'oeuvres there was cheese and crackers, garnished with radicchio, which even I found amusing.

I drank and watched the sun go down, smelled the fresh horse manure in the rose garden, and tried to listen to the birds, but Susan, Sally, and Jim were chattering on about Frank Bellarosa, and I heard Susan using the words 'deliciously sinister', 'interestingly primitive', and even 'intriguing'. The man is about as intriguing as a barrel of cement. But women see different things in men than men see in men. Sally was certainly intrigued by Susan's descriptions. Jim, too, seemed absorbed in the subject.

If you're interested in the pecking order on my terrace, the Stanhope and the Grace sitting across from me are considered old money by most American standards, because there wasn't much American capital around until only about a hundred years ago. But the Roosevelt sitting beside me would think of the Graces and Stanhopes as new money and too much of it. The Roosevelts were never filthy rich, but they go back to the beginning of the New World and they have a respected name and are associated with public service to their country in war and peace, unlike at least one Stanhope I could name.

I told you about the Sutters, but you should know that my mother is a Whitman, a direct descendant of Long Island's most illustrious poet, Walt Whitman. Thus, in the pecking order, Jim and I are peers, and our wives, while rich, pretty, and thin, are a step down the social ladder. Get it? It doesn't matter. What matters now is where Frank Bellarosa fits.

As I listened to Susan and the Roosevelts talk, I realized they had a different slant on Frank Bellarosa than I did. I was concerned about Mr Bellarosa's legal transgressions against society, such as murder, racketeering, extortion, and little things like that. But Susan, Sally, and even Jim discussed larger issues such as Mr Bellarosa's shiny black car, shiny white shoes, and his major crime, which was the purchase of Alhambra. Susan, I think, acts and speaks differently when she's around people like Sally Grace.

I was also struck by the fact that these three found some entertainment value in Mr Frank Bellarosa. They spoke of him as if he were a gorilla in a cage and they were spectators. I almost envied them their supreme overconfidence, their assurance that they were not part of life's circus, but were ticket holders with box seats opposite the centre ring. This aloofness, I knew, was bred into Sally's and Susan's bones from childhood, and with Jim, it just flowed naturally in his blue blood. I suppose I can be aloof, too. But everyone in my family worked, and you can only be so aloof when you have to earn a living.

Listening to Susan, I wanted to remind her that she and I were not ticket holders at this particular event; we were part of the entertainment, we were inside the cage with the gorilla, and the thrills and chills were going to be more than vicarious.

At my suggestion, the subject turned to the boating season. The Roosevelts stayed until eight, then left.

I remarked to Susan, 'I don't see anything amusing or interesting about Bellarosa.'

'You have to keep an open mind,' she said, and poured herself another port.

'He is a criminal,' I said tersely.

She replied just as tersely, 'If you have proof of that, Counsellor, you'd better call the DA.'

Which reminded me of the underlying problem: If society couldn't get rid of Frank Bellarosa, how was I supposed to do it? This breakdown of the law was sapping everyone's morale – even Susan was commenting on it now, and Lester Remsen was convinced the rules were out the window. I wasn't so sure yet. I said to Susan, 'You know what I'm talking about. Bellarosa is a reputed Mafia don.'

She finished her port, let out a deep breath, and said, 'Look, John, it's been a long day, and I'm tired.'

Indeed it had been a long day, and I, too, felt physically and emotionally drained. I remarked, unwisely, 'Hay fights take a lot out of a person.'

'Cut it out.' She stood and moved toward the house.

'Did we beat the Roosevelts or not?' I asked. 'Do I get my sexual favour?'

She hesitated. 'Sure. Would you like me to go fuck myself?'

Actually, yes.

She opened the French door that led into the study. 'I'm certain you recall that we are due at the DePauws at nine for late supper. What one might call an Easter thing. Please be ready on time.' Susan went into the house.

I poured myself another port. No, I did not recall. What was more, I didn't give a damn. It occurred to me that if certain people found Frank Bellarosa not bad looking, 'deliciously sinister', 'interestingly primitive', 'intriguing', and worth an hour's conversation, then maybe those same people found me nice and dull and predictable. That, coupled with the hay fight earlier in the afternoon, got me wondering if Susan was getting a bit restless herself.

I stood, took the bottle of port, and walked out of the garden and into the dark. I kept walking until I found myself some time later at the hedge maze. A bit under the influence by now, I stumbled into the maze, whose paths were choked with untrimmed branches. I wandered around until I was sure I was completely lost, then sprawled out on the ground, finished the port, and fell asleep under the stars. Screw the DePauws.

CHAPTER 10

I could hear birds singing close by, and I opened my eyes but could see nothing. I sat up quickly in disoriented panic. I saw now that I was engulfed in a mist, and I thought for a moment that I had died and gone to heaven. But then I burped up some port and I knew I was alive, though not well. By stages I recalled where I was and how I'd gotten there. I didn't like any of the recollections, so I pushed them out of my mind.

Overhead, the first streaks of dawn lit up a purple and crimson sky. My head felt awful, I was cold, and my muscles were stiff as cardboard. I rubbed my eyes and yawned. It was Easter Sunday, and John Sutter had indeed risen.

I stood slowly and noticed the bottle of port on the ground and recalled using it as a pillow. I picked it up and took the final swallow from it to freshen my mouth. 'Ugh . . .'

I brushed off my warm-up suit and zipped the jacket against the chill. Middle-aged men, even those in good shape, should not wallow around on the cold ground all night with a snoot full of booze. It's not healthy or dignified. 'Oh . . . my neck . . .'

I coughed, stretched, sneezed, and performed other morning functions. Everything seemed to be working except my mind, which couldn't grasp the enormity of what I'd done.

I took a few tentative steps, felt all right, and began pushing aside the branches of the hedge maze. I tried following the trail of footprints and broken twigs of the night before, but tracking is not one of my outdoor skills, and I was soon lost. Actually, I started out lost. Now I was missing in action.

The sky was getting lighter, and I could make out east from west. The exit from the maze was on the eastern edge of the hedges, and I moved generally that way whenever I could, but I found myself crossing my path again and again. Whoever laid out this labyrinth was some kind of sadistic genius.

A full half hour after I'd begun, I broke out onto the lawn and saw the sun rising above the distant gazebo.

I sat on a stone bench at the entrance to the maze and forced myself to think. Not only had I walked out on Susan and missed a social engagement, but I had also missed sunrise services at St Mark's, and Susan and the Allards were probably frantic with worry by now. Well, maybe Susan and Ethel were not frantic, but George would be worried and the women, concerned.

I wondered if Susan had bravely gone to the DePauws with regrets from her husband, or had she called the police and stayed by the phone all night? I guess what I was wondering was if anyone cared if I was dead or alive. As I was brooding over this, I heard the sound of hoofs on the damp earth. I looked up to see a horse and rider approaching out of the sun. I stood and squinted into the sunlight.

Susan reined up on Zanzibar about twenty feet from where I stood. Neither Susan nor I spoke, but the stupid horse snorted, and the snort sounded contemptuous, which set me off, illogical as that may seem.

I thought I would be filled with guilt and remorse when I saw Susan, but strangely enough, I still didn't care. I asked, 'Were you looking for me, or just out riding?'

It must have been my tone of voice that kept her from a smart-aleck reply. She said, 'I was looking for you.'

'Well, now that you've found me, you can leave. I want to be alone.'

'All right.' She began reining Zanzibar around and asked over her shoulder, 'Will you come to eleven-o'clock service with us?'

'If I do, I'll drive my own car to church.'

'All right. I'll see you later.' She rode off, and Zanzibar broke wind. If I'd had my shotgun, I would have filled his ass with buckshot.

Well, I thought, that was easy. I felt good. I began walking, loosening my muscles, then I jogged for a while, sucking in the cool morning air. What a beautiful dawn it was, and what a beautiful thing it was to be up with the sun and running through the ground mist, getting high on beta blockers and endorphins or something. I spent an hour cavorting, I guess you'd call it, gambolling about the acreage, with no goal or reason except that it felt good.

I climbed a big linden tree at the rear edge of the property that overlooks The Creek Country Club. What a magnificent view. I stayed in the tree awhile, reliving this exquisite pleasure of childhood. With great reluctance I got down from the tree, then began jogging again. At about what I guessed was nine A.M., I was physically exhausted but as mentally alert as I'd been in a long time. I didn't even have a hangover. I pushed myself toward the line of white pine that separated the Stanhope property from Alhambra, sweat pouring from my body and carrying the toxins out with it.

I ran through Alhambra's overgrown horse pasture, my heart pounding and my legs wanting to buckle and drop me to the earth. But I went on through the cherry grove and reached the classical garden where Susan and I had enacted our sexual drama.

I collapsed on a marble bench and looked around. The imposing statue of Neptune still stood at the end of the mosaic reflecting pool, but there was now a bronze trident in his clenched fist. 'Look at that . . .' I saw, too, that the four fish sculptures were spouting water from their mouths and the water was collecting in a giant marble seashell, then spilling over into the newly cleaned reflecting pool. 'I'll be damned . . .'

I stood and staggered over to the fountain, which had not worked in over twenty years. I dropped to my knees and washed my face in the seashell, then lapped up the cold water. 'Ah . . . nice going, Frank.'

I gargled a mouthful of water and spit it up in a plume, in imitation of the stone fish. 'Gurgle, gurgle, gurgle.'

I heard a noise and turned. Not thirty feet away, on the path that led from the house, stood a woman in a flowery dress and pink hat, with a white shawl over her shoulders. She saw me and stopped dead in her tracks. I could imagine the picture I presented, slobbering around the fountain with a filthy warm-up suit and tangled hair. I spat out a mouthful of water and said, 'Hello.'

She turned and began walking quickly away, then looked back to see what I was up to. She was a woman in her mid-forties, full-figured, with blond hair that, even at this distance, looked bleached. Her make-up was not subtle, and I thought the purple eye shadow and hot-pink lip gloss might have been leftover Easter-egg dyes. Even in her Easter frock and bonnet she looked a little cheap and brassy. But she was well put together. I'm not a tit man, and my preference is for lithe, well-scrubbed, all-American types, like Susan. But having spent the morning alternating between atavistic and adolescent behaviour, I was in the right mood to find something crudely sexual in this woman's primitive paint job, with her big breasts and buttocks. In some vague way she reminded me of the Venus statue in the love temple.

She was still glancing over her shoulder as she put distance between us. I thought I should identify myself so she wouldn't be frightened, but if she was part of the Bellarosa clan, it might be best if we didn't meet under these circumstances. I was about to stand and walk away, which is what an uninteresting attorney and gentleman would have done. But, recalling my recent success with Susan, I got on all fours and growled.

The woman broke into a run, losing her high heels.

I stood and wiped my mouth with my sleeve. This was fun. It did occur to me that my behaviour was not in the normal range, but who am I to make psychiatric evaluations? As I walked along the edge of the reflecting pool contemplating my next move, I noticed something else new. At the far end of the long, narrow pool was a white statue. As I drew closer, I saw that it was one of those cheap plaster saints with the sky-blue niches that you see on Italians' lawns, usually in conjunction with a pink flamingo or two.

I saw now that it was a statue of Mary, her arms cradling the infant Jesus. I found the juxtaposition of this Christian icon across the pool from the pagan god rather curious. Here was this loving woman enveloping her child, and in the same setting staring at her, as it were, was this half-naked, virile god with upraised trident, the antithesis of the Judaeo-Christian God of love.

I was reminded of the first time I was in Rome and being surprised at how the two dominant strands of Italian culture – pagan and Christian – coexisted in art with no apparent contradictions. The tour guides seemed to have no theological or aesthetic problems with mixed motifs: for instance, a frieze of nubile nymphs and randy cupids adorning the same room that held a statue of *La Vergine*.

The Italians, I decided then, were themselves pagan and Christian, like their art, both cruel and gentle, Roman and Catholic. It was as if the wrong religion had been grafted onto a country and a people who by temperament made good pagans and lousy Christians.

It occurred to me, too, that the same Frank Bellarosa who restored the trident to Neptune, who knew what that clenched fist needed, was also the Frank Bellarosa who felt a need to balance his world with this symbol of love and hope. This was a man who covered all his bases. Interesting.

I heard a dog barking from the direction of the mansion, and I decided to wonder about all of this while moving rapidly away from the don's hit men. I may have been crazy, but I wasn't stupid.

I headed in the direction of Stanhope Hall, moving as fast as I could, considering I hadn't had anything more substantial to eat than radicchio and cheese since Saturday's lunch. The barking dogs, two of them now, were closer.

I put on a burst of speed, crossing the tree line at full tilt. I didn't slow up, however, figuring the dogs and the hit men, while not mounted gentry, would still surely cross into Stanhope land in hot pursuit.

I saw the shallow pond near where Susan intended to move her stable and charged into it, half wading, half walking on water, until I reached the other side. What I lacked in stalking skills, I made up for in escape and evasion techniques.

I kept running and I could hear the dogs yapping around the pond where they'd lost the scent. I had only assumed that the dogs were accompanied by men, but I wasn't certain until now when I heard the discharge of a shotgun behind me. My legs responded instinctively and began moving faster than my heart and lungs could take. I ran out of glucose, adrenalin, endorphins, and all that and collapsed on the ground. I lay perfectly still and listened.

After a few minutes, I stood slowly and began walking softly through the brush. I intersected an old gravel road that led to the service gate on Grace Lane. I followed the road until I saw the guesthouse through newly budded cherry trees. I was pretty sure the shotgun boys wouldn't penetrate this far into the Stanhope estate, so I took my time getting to the house. As someone once said, there's nothing quite so satisfying as being shot at and missed. I felt terrific, on top of the world. My only regret was that I couldn't tell this story to anyone. What I needed, I realized, were friends who would appreciate this escapade. I would have told Susan, but she wasn't my friend anymore.

I came into the house through the rose garden and saw by the clock in the study that I had apparently misjudged the time. It was past eleven, and Susan was gone. Again, I discovered that I didn't care. Finding out that you didn't care about things you used to care about was all well and good, but the next step was trying to find out what you *did* care about.

I went into the kitchen and saw a note on the table. It read: *Please remember to be at your aunt's at three.* I crumpled up the note. Screw Aunt Cornelia. I opened the refrigerator and grazed awhile, stuffing my mouth with whatever struck my fancy, leaving a mess of opened containers, wrappings, and half-eaten fruit. I grabbed a handful of blueberries, slammed the door, and went upstairs.

Primitive is one thing, but a hot shower is something else. I stripped, showered, and ate blueberries, but I didn't shave. I dressed casually in jeans, sweatshirt, and loafers without socks and got out of the house before Susan returned.

I jumped into my Bronco and drove onto the old, overgrown path that once connected the guesthouse to the service road and, subsequently, the service gate. These old estates had not only service entrances to the main house, but servants' stairways so that ladies and gentlemen never met staff on the stairs, and in addition, there was a system of roads or narrow tracks for deliveries, work vehicles, and such. These places were sort of forerunners to Disneyland, where armies of workers ran around on hidden roads, through tunnels and back doors, attending to every need, making meals appear like magic, cleaning rooms, and making gardens grow, always out of sight, like little elves.

Anyway, I crossed the service road, drove along a footpath to the pond, and got out of the Bronco. I examined the footprints left in the ground, saw the paw marks at the muddy edge of the water, and found an eight-gauge shotgun cartridge that I put in my pocket. Satisfied that I hadn't been hallucinating on beta blockers, I got back into the Bronco and proceeded down the road toward the service gate in order to avoid Susan and the Allards if they were coming home from church. The service gate, which is never used anymore, was padlocked, but like a good maintenance man, I had a ring of keys in the Bronco for every keyhole on the Stanhope estate. I opened the padlock and gates and drove out onto Grace Lane a few hundred yards from the main gate.

I headed north to avoid the Jag, which would be coming up from Locust Valley, meanwhile trying to figure out where to go. Errant husbands should have a destination, but few of them do, and they usually wander around in their cars, not wanting to go someplace where people will ask them how the missus is.

I passed the gate of Alhambra on my left and noticed two gentlemen in black suits posted at the entranceway.

I guess I was still royally ticked off about the events of the previous day, though I knew if I were to verbalize my complaints to a friend, he or she would not fully comprehend how the hayloft incident or the Bellarosa incident could have put me in high dudgeon. People never do. Of course I would say, 'There's more to it.' And there was, but most of that was in my head, unconnected to the physical world, and no one but a shrink would sit still for my monologue on all the injustices of life and marriage.

Anyway, I drove around a while and wound up in Bayville, which is sort of a blue-collar town sitting on prime Long Island Sound real estate. This place is ripe for gentrification, but I think there's a village ordinance against BMWs and health-food stores.

The main industries of the small village of Bayville are fishing, boatyards, nautical stores, and the dispensing of alcohol. You wouldn't expect to find so many gin mills in so small a place, but it's a matter of supply and demand. Some of the places are rough, some rougher, and the roughest is a place called The Rusty Hawsehole. A hawsehole, if you care, is the hole in the bow of a ship through which the anchor cable passes. I think the bars and restaurants on Long Island are scraping the bottom of the bilge for unused nautical names, but this place *looked* like a rusty hawsehole, and it was open for Easter services. I parked the Bronco in the gravel lot between a pickup truck and four motorcycles and went inside.

A waterfront gin mill at night has a degree of local colour, exuberance, and *je ne sais quoi*. But on a Sunday afternoon, Easter Sunday at that, The Rusty Hawsehole was as depressing as the anteroom to a gas chamber.

I found a stool at the bar and ordered a draught beer. The place was done up in standard nautical motif, but I wouldn't outfit a garbage scow from the junk on the walls and ceilings. I noticed that my fellow celebrants included three men and a woman in interesting black leather motorcycle attire, a few old salts whose skin had that odd combination of sun weathering and alcohol pickling, and four young men in jeans and T-shirts playing video games and alternating between catatonia and St Vitus' dance. I don't think there was a full set of teeth in the house. I was aware that the dark corners and booths held more of the damned.

I bought some bar snacks, the kind of stuff that should have warning labels, and munched away. The Seawanhaka Corinthian Yacht Club is a mile or so down the road from here, and in the summer the nautical gentry will visit places like The Rusty Hawsehole after a day of sailing. When one is safely back at one's country club, one will casually mention the visit, thus suggesting that one is a real man. But here I was in off-season, sipping suds and eating prole food, watching the blue haze of cigarette smoke float past the bar lights.

I ordered another beer and six of those beef jerky sticks for dessert. Just when it seemed that no one was interested in me or offended by my presence, one of the leather gentlemen at the bend in the bar inquired, 'You live around here?'

You have to understand that even in jeans and sweatshirt, unshaven, and with a Bronco outside, John Whitman Sutter was not going to pass for one of the boys, especially after I opened my preppie mouth. You understand, too, that there was deeper meaning in that question. I replied, 'Lattingtown.'

'La-di-da,' he responded musically.

I'm honestly glad there is no class animosity in this country, for if there were, the leather gentleman would have been rude.

He asked, 'You lost or what?'

'I must be if I'm in this place.'

Everyone thought that was funny. Humour goes a long way in bridging the gap between men of culture and cretins.

Leather said, 'Your old lady kick you out or what?'

'No, actually she's in St Francis Hospital in a coma. Hit-and-run. Doesn't look good. The kids are with my aunt.'

'Oh, hey, sorry.' Leather ordered me a beer.

I smiled sadly at him and went back to my beef jerky sticks. They're actually not bad, and if you chew them with a mouthful of bar nuts, it forms this pasty mass that absorbs beer. You swallow the whole wad. I learned that in New Haven. That's the way we say Yale. New Haven. It doesn't sound so snooty.

I was due at Aunt Cornelia's for cocktails at three, as the note said. It was sort of a family reunion that we do every Easter at Aunt Cornelia's home, which is in Locust Valley, about a fifteen-minute drive from here. It was now a few minutes to two. Aunt Cornelia is my mother's sister, and she is the aunt, you may recall, who has some theories regarding red hair. Wait until she sees her favourite nephew, I thought, staggering in without tie or jacket, unshaved, and smelling of beer and bar nuts.

Susan, to be fair, is good with my family. Not close, just good. Her family are few in number, not close to one another, and scattered far and wide. Perfect in-laws.

Anyway, as I was contemplating another hour in this hole, a woman took the empty stool beside me. She must have come from the dark recesses, because the front door hadn't opened. I glanced at her and she gave me a big smile. I looked in the bar mirror, and our eyes met. She smiled again. Friendly sort.

She was about thirty but could have passed for forty. She was divorced and was currently living with a man who beat her. She worked as a waitress somewhere, and her mother took care of her kids. She had a few health problems, should have hated men, but didn't, played the Lotto, and refused to accept the fact that life was not going to get any better. She didn't say any of this, she didn't say anything, in fact. But the sort of people you find in The Rusty Hawsehole are like those fill-in-the-adjective games. You wonder sometimes how a fabulously wealthy nation can create a white underclass. Or maybe it's just that some people are born losers, and in the year 3000 in a colony on Mars, there will be a Rusty Hawsehole whose clientele will have bad teeth, tattoos, and leather space suits, and they will tell each other their life stories and complain about bad breaks and people screwing them. I heard two shoes hit the floor.

'My feet are killing me.'

'Why is that?' I asked.

'Oh, jeez, I worked all morning. Never even got to Mass.'

'Where do you work?'

'Stardust Diner in Glen Cove. You know the place?'

'Sure do.'

'I never saw you there.'

And you never will. 'Buy you a drink?'

'Sure. Mimosa. Hate to drink before six. But I need one.'

I motioned to the bartender. 'Mimosa.' I turned to my companion. 'You want a beef jerky?'

'No, thanks.'

'My name's John.'

'Sally.'

'Not Sally Grace?'

'No, Sally Ann.'

'Pleased to meet you,' I said.

Her mimosa came and we touched glasses. We chatted for a few minutes before she asked, 'What are you doing in a place like this?'

'I think that's *my* line.'

She laughed. 'No, really.'

I suppose I was flattered by the question, my ego stroked by the knowledge that no one in that bar thought I belonged there even before they caught the accent. Conversely, I suppose, if any of these people were in The Creek, even in tweeds, I'd ask the same question of them. I replied to Sally, 'I'm divorced, lonely, and looking for love in all the wrong places.'

She giggled. 'You're crazy.'

'And my clubs are closed today, my yacht is in dry dock, and my ex-wife took the kids to Acapulco. I have my choice of going to a Mafia don's party, my Aunt Cornelia's house, or here.'

'So you came here?'

'Wouldn't you?'

'No. I'd go to the Mafia don's party.'

'That's interesting.' I asked, 'Are you by any chance a Roosevelt?' *Roozvelt.*

She laughed again. 'Sure. Are you an Astor?'

'No. I'm a Whitman. You know Walt Whitman, the poet?'

'Sure. *Leaves of Grass.* I read it in school.'

'God bless America.'

'He wrote that, too?'

'Possibly.'

'You're related to Walt Whitman?'

'Sort of.'

'Are you a poet?'

'I try.'

'Are you rich?'

'I was. Lost it all on Lotto tickets.'

'God, how many did you buy?'

'All of them.'

She laughed yet again. I was on. I swung my stool toward Sally. You could tell she had been attractive once, but the years, as they say, had not been kind. Still, she had a nice smile and a good laugh, all her teeth, and I'm sure a big heart. I could see she liked me and with a little encouragement would have loved me. A lot of my schoolmates were into fucking the poor, but I never did. Actually, I take that back. Around here, the local custom is that Wednesday night is maid's night out, and all the young bars on the Gold Coast were, and still are, I guess, filled with delicious Irish and Scottish girls over here on work visas. But that's another story. The point is, it's been a long time since I've been tête-à-tête with a working girl in a bar, and I wasn't quite sure how to act with Sally Ann. But I believe I should always be myself. Some people like twits. And besides, I was doing better with Sally Ann than with Sally Grace. And now, as of sunrise, I had the power. We chatted awhile longer, and she was giggling into her third mimosa, and the leather crew were starting to get suspicious about the wife-in-the-coma story.

I caught a glimpse of the bar clock, which informed me that it was Miller time and three P.M. Given the choice between taking Sally Ann back to her place or going to Aunt Cornelia's, I'd rather do neither. 'Well, I should go.'

'Oh . . . you in a hurry?'

'I'm afraid I am. I have to pick up the Earl of Sussex at the train station and get over to Aunt Cornelia's.'

'Seriously . . .'

'Can I have your number?'

She demurred for half a second, then smiled coyly. 'I guess.'

'Do you have a card?'

'Uh . . . let me see . . .' She rummaged through her bag and found her short stub of a waitress pencil. 'You want it on a card?'

'A napkin will do.' I pushed a dry one toward her, and she wrote her name and number on it. She said, 'I live here in Bayville. I can see the water from my place.'

'I envy you.' I put the napkin in my pocket with the shotgun shell. I might start a scrapbook. I said, 'I'll call you.' I slid off the bar stool.

'I'm on nights for the rest of the month. Five to midnight. I sleep when I can. So try anytime. Don't worry about waking me. I have an answering machine anyway.'

'Got it. See you.' I left my change on the bar and exited The Rusty Hawsehole into the bright sunlight. There must be some place in this world for me, but I didn't think The Rusty Hawsehole was going to make the short list.

I climbed into my Bronco. I had my choice now of don Bellarosa's or Aunt Cornelia's. I headed south along Shore Road, hoping, I guess, for some sort of divine intervention, like brake failure.

Anyway, I found myself on Grace Lane and passed Stanhope Hall, whose gates were closed. The Allards, I suppose, were at their daughter's house, and Susan was already at my aunt's or, more interestingly, at Frank's house, eating sheep's nose and putting out a contract on me.

I continued on and reached the beginning of the distinctive brick-and-stucco wall of Alhambra. I slowed down, then pulled off onto the shoulder opposite Alhambra's open gates. The two men in black suits were still there and they stared at me. Behind them, at the gatehouse, which was built into and part of the estate wall, was the Easter bunny. He was a rather large bunny, about six feet tall, not counting ears, and he held a big Easter basket, which I suspected was filled with coloured hand grenades.

I turned my attention back to the bunny's two helpers, who were still eyeing me. I had no doubt that one or both of these men – don Bellarosa's soldiers – had been pursuing me that morning.

Alhambra's main entranceway, unlike Stanhope's, is a straight drive to the main house, which you can see perfectly framed by the wrought-iron gates and pillars. The drive itself is paved with cobbles instead of gravel, and it is lined with stately poplars. On the drive now, stretching all the way to the house, were automobiles mostly of the long, black variety, and it occurred to me that these people with their black cars and black clothes were ready for a funeral at a moment's notice.

Looking at the scene across the street, I suspected that Frank Bellarosa knew how to throw a party. And I had the feeling that he did so in a manner that was in unconscious imitation of a Gatsby party, with everything a guest could want except the host, who watched his party from a distance.

In some bizarre way, Bellarosa's ostentatious Easter was a case of history repeating itself, according to the stories that are told of millionaires in the 1920s trying to outdo one another in bad taste. Otto Kahn, for instance, one of the richest men in the country, if not the world, used to hold Easter egg hunts on the six hundred acres surrounding his 125-room mansion in Woodbury. Guests included socialites and millionaires as well as down-and-out actors, writers, musicians, and Ziegfeld girls. To make the hunt interesting, each colourfully painted egg contained a one-thousand-dollar bill. This was a popular event and an original way to celebrate the Resurrection of Jesus Christ.

I know in my heart that I would not have gone to Kahn's estate for the thousand-dollar bills – about a year's salary for some people in the 1920s – but I might have been tempted by the Ziegfeld girls.

Similarly, while sheep's head didn't make my mouth water, curiosity about Frank Bellarosa, his family, and extended 'family' was getting the better of me. While I was weighing the pros and cons of passing through those gates, I noticed that one of the cons, obviously tired of keeping an eye on me, was motioning me to move on. As I am a shareholder in Grace Lane and was not interfering with Mr Bellarosa's party in any way, I rolled down my window and gave the man what is sometimes known as the Italian salute.

The man, apparently overjoyed at my familiarity with Italian customs, returned my salute energetically with both hands.

About this time, a limousine with dark windows came up beside me, then turned left into the gates and stopped. The windows went down, and one of the guards checked the passengers while the big bunny handed out goodies from his basket.

I heard a sharp tap on my passenger-side window and turned quickly. A man's face peered through the window, and he was motioning me to roll it down. I hesitated, then reached over and cranked down the window. 'Yeah?' I said in my best tough guy voice. 'Whaddaya want?' I felt my heart speed up.

The man pushed his head through the window and held out one of those badge cases with an ID photo in front of my face, then pushed the face to match through the window. 'Special Agent Mancuso,' he said. 'Federal Bureau of Investigation.'

'Oh . . .' I took a deep breath. This was really too much, I thought. Unreal. Right here on Grace Lane. Mafia, six-foot Easter bunnies, errant husbands, and now this guy from the FBI. 'What can I do for you?'

'You are John Sutter, correct?'

'If you're the FBI, then I'm John Sutter.' I assumed they'd run my licence plate through Albany in the last few minutes, or perhaps months ago when Bellarosa had moved in.

'You probably know why we're here, sir.'

A few sarcastic replies passed through my mind, but I answered, 'I probably do.'

'Of course you have every right to park here, and we have no authority to ask you to move.'

'That's right,' I informed him. 'This street is private property. My property.'

'Yes, sir.' Mancuso had folded his arms on the windowsill of my Bronco, and his chin was resting on his forearm, his head tilted as though he were an old friend just chatting. He was a man of about fifty, with incredibly large white teeth, like a row of Chiclets. His skin was sallow, and his eyes and cheeks were sunken as if he weren't getting enough to eat. And he had gone bald in a bad way, with a bushy fringe and a tuft of curly hair left on his peak like a circus clown. I added, 'I'm not even sure you have a right to be here.'

Mr Mancuso winced as if I'd offended him, or maybe he smelled the beer nuts and beef jerky. 'Well,' he said, 'I'm a lawyer and you're a lawyer and we could debate that intelligently some other time.'

I didn't know why I was being aggressive with the guy. Maybe I was still a little shook up about how he'd rapped on my window, and aggression was my response. Or maybe I was still in my primitive mode. Anyway, I realized I sounded as if I were a mouthpiece for the don. I calmed down a bit and said, 'So?'

'Well, you see, we're taking pictures and your vehicle is in our line of sight.'

'Pictures of what?'

'You know.'

He didn't offer and I didn't ask from where he or they were taking pictures, but it could only have been from the DePauw house, which sits about a hundred yards off Grace Lane on a rise, directly, as I said, across from Alhambra's gates. I found it interesting, but certainly understandable, that the DePauws, who are 'Support your local police state' types, would join the forces of good against the forces of evil. Allen DePauw would, I'm sure, let the Feds set up a machine-gun nest and supply the ammunition. Grace Lane was going through some changes.

I looked up at the DePauws' big clapboard colonial, then turned toward Alhambra's gate. I supposed that as the cars swung into the drive, the FBI was photographing the licence plates with a telephoto lens and probably even getting nice shots of the guests as they got out of their cars. I realized that I was not actually blocking the line of sight between the DePauws' house and the gates, and I thought there was more to this. I said, 'I was about to leave anyway.'

'Thank you.' Mancuso made no move to disengage himself from my vehicle. He said, 'I guess you're stopped here because you're curious.'

'Actually, I was invited.'

'Were you?' He seemed surprised, then not so surprised. He nodded thoughtfully. 'Well, if you ever want to talk to us' – he produced a business card and handed it to me – 'give me a call.'

'About what?'

'Anything. You going in there?'

'No.' I put the card in my pocket with the shotgun shell and cocktail napkin. Maybe a display case would be better.

'It's okay if you want to go in.'

'Thanks, Mr Mancuso.'

He flashed his pearly whites. 'I mean, we understand your situation. Being neighbours and all.'

'You don't know the half of it.' I glanced back at Alhambra's gates and saw the two men and the Easter bunny talking amongst themselves and looking at us. On a day when even the rich people that I knew couldn't get help with dinner (unless they ate at the Stardust Diner), don Bellarosa could run out two goons, a bunny, and probably more hired guns and help inside. I turned back to Mancuso, who was also missing Easter with his family, and asked a bit sarcastically, 'When can I expect Mr Bellarosa to go away for a while?'

'I can't comment on that, Mr Sutter.'

I said, 'I am not pleased with this situation, Mr Mancuso.'

'Neither are we, sir.'

'Well, then, arrest the guy.'

'We're gathering evidence, sir.'

I felt my anger rising, and poor Mr Mancuso, who represented the forces of official impotence, was going to get a piece of my civic mind. I snapped, 'Frank Bellarosa has been a known criminal for nearly three decades, and he lives a better life than you or I, Mr Mancuso, and you are still gathering evidence.'

'Yes, sir.'

'Perhaps crime does pay in this country.'

'No, it doesn't, sir. Not in the long run.'

'Is thirty years a short run?'

'Well, Mr Sutter, if all honest citizens were as outraged as you seem to be, and assisted – '

'No, no, Mr Mancuso. Don't give me that crap. I'm not a peace officer, a judge, or a vigilante. Civilized people may pay taxes to the government as part of the social contract. The *government* is supposed to get rid of Frank Bellarosa. I'll sit on the jury.'

'Yes, sir.' He added, 'Lawyers can't sit on juries.'

'I would if I could.'

'Yes, sir.'

I've spoken to a few Federal types over the course of my career – IRS agents, FBI men, and such – and when they get into their 'Yes, sir, Mr Citizen Taxpayer' mode, it means that communication has ended. I said, 'Well, go back to your picture-taking.'

'Thank you, sir.'

I threw the Bronco into gear. 'At least the neighbourhood is safe now.'

'It usually is in these situations, Mr Sutter.'

'Very ironic,' I observed.

'Yes, sir.'

I looked Mr Mancuso in the eye and asked, 'Do you know what *capozella* is?'

He grinned. 'Sure. My grandmother used to try to make me eat it. It's a delicacy. Why?'

'Just checking. *Arrivederci.*'

'Happy Easter.' He straightened up and all I could see now was his paunch. I hit the gas and released the clutch, throwing up some gravel as I headed up Grace Lane.

The lane ends in a turnaround in front of an estate called

Fox Point, which backs onto the Sound. Fox Point may become a mosque, but more about that later.

I drove around the circle and headed south on Grace Lane, passing Alhambra and the spot where Mr Mancuso had stood. He was gone now, as I expected he would be, but I had such a strong sense that the whole day was hallucinatory that I pulled his card from my pocket and stared at it. I recalled retrieving the shotgun cartridge for the same reason, to establish physical evidence of something that had just happened. 'Get hold of yourself, John.'

I thought of Mr Mancuso for a minute or two. Clown that he seemed, he was no fool. There was something quietly self-assured about him, and I rather liked the idea of an Italian on the case of another Italian. God knows, the establishment in Washington couldn't handle Bellarosa or his kind. The days of the erstwhile Elliot Ness were over, and Italian-American prosecutors and federal agents were having better luck with their felonious compatriots. In a sort of ironically historical twist, I thought, it was like the Roman senate hiring barbarian mercenaries to fight the barbarians. Satisfied with my analysis and nearly comforted by the chance meeting with the odd-looking Mr Mancuso, I headed toward Aunt Cornelia's.

Within ten minutes I was in the village of Locust Valley. Aunt Cornelia's house is a big Victorian on a quiet side street a few blocks from my office. The house has a turret, a huge attic, and a wraparound porch, the sort of home an Aunt Cornelia should live in, and I have fond childhood memories of the place. My aunt's husband, Uncle Arthur, is a retired failure: that is, he spent vast amounts of inherited income on ventures that went nowhere. But he never forgot the most important Wasp dictum: *Never touch the principal.* And so now, in retirement, the principal, handled by professionals, myself included, has grown and so has his income. I hope he stays out of business. His three sons, my brainless cousins, who have their father's flair for losing money, are made to repeat every morning, 'Never touch the principal.' They'll be all right, and so will their witless children, as long as they never touch the principal.

Aunt Cornelia's street was lined with cars, because it was a street where everyone's aunt, grandmother, and mother lived; a place, to paraphrase Robert Frost, where when you had to go home for a holiday, any home on the block would do.

I found a parking space and walked up to Aunt Cornelia's house. I stood on the porch awhile, took a deep breath, opened the front door, and entered.

The house was filled with people, all of them in some way or the other related to me and to each other, I suppose. I'm not good at the extended-family game, and I never know whom I'm supposed to kiss, whose kids belong to whom, or any of that. I'm always putting my foot in my mouth, asking divorced people how their spouses are, inquiring of bankrupt relatives how business is, and on more than one occasion, asking about the health of a parent who has been dead a few years. Susan, who is not related to any of these people except through me, knows everybody's name, their relationship to me, who died, who was born, and who got divorced, as if it were her job to make entries in the family Bible. I almost wished she were at my side now, whispering in my ear, something like, 'That's your cousin Barbara, daughter of your aunt Annie and your deceased uncle Bart. Barbara's husband, Carl, left her for a man. Barbara is upset, but is taking it well, though she hates men now.' Thus forewarned, I would be forearmed when I greeted Barbara, though there wouldn't be much to talk about except maybe women's tennis or something like that.

Anyway, there they all were, holding glasses in their left hands, gums flapping, and my mind raced ahead to possible pitfalls. I said a few hellos, but managed to avoid any real conversation by moving quickly from room to room through large double doors in the big old house, as if I were on my way to the bathroom.

I saw Judy and Lester Remsen, who always put in appearances at my family affairs, but for the life of me I can't find a single relative who knows how Lester is related to us. It may

127

be just a terrible mistake on his part, and he may have realized it at some point, but is afraid to stop coming to these things, thereby admitting he's been at the wrong family functions for thirty years.

As I slipped from room to room and out of conversational traps, I caught glimpses of my mother and father and of Susan, but I avoided them. I was acutely aware that I was underdressed and undergroomed. Even the kids were wearing pressed clothes and leather shoes.

I found the bar, set up in the butler's pantry, and made myself a scotch and soda. Someone tapped me on the shoulder, and I was surprised when I turned to see my sister, Emily, who I had understood could not make it from Texas. We embraced and kissed. Emily and I are close despite the years and miles that have separated us, and if there is anyone in this world I care about aside from Susan and my children, it is my sister.

I noticed a man standing behind her and assumed it was her new beau. He smiled at me, and Emily introduced us. 'John, this is my friend, Gary.'

I shook hands with Gary, who was a handsome, suntanned, young man, about ten years younger than Emily. He spoke in a Texas drawl. 'It's a real pleasure to meet you, Mr Sutter.'

'John. I've heard a lot about you.' I glanced at Emily and saw she was radiant, younger looking than when I'd last seen her, aglow with a new sexual fire that made her eyes sparkle. I was truly overjoyed for her and she knew it. The three of us chatted for a minute, then Gary excused himself, and Emily and I slipped into the big storage room off the butler's pantry. Emily took my hand. 'John, I'm so happy.'

'You look it.'

She fixed her eyes on mine. 'Is everything all right with you?'

'Yes. I'm on the verge of cracking up. It's marvellous.'

She laughed. 'I'm a slut and you look like a bum. Mother and Dad are scandalized.'

I smiled in return. 'Good.' My parents, as I've mentioned,

are socially progressive, but when their own family is involved in some sort of iconoclastic behaviour, my parents become keepers of the traditional values. I hesitate to use the word *hypocrites*.

Emily asked, 'Are you and Susan okay?'

'I don't know.'

'She told me you were unhappy and she was concerned. I think she wanted me to speak to you.'

I stirred my scotch and soda, then sipped it. Susan knows that, aside from herself, only Emily can speak to me intimately. I responded, 'Most of Susan's problems are of Susan's own making, and most of my problems are of my making. That's the problem.' I added, 'I think we're bored. We need a challenge.'

'So, challenge each other.'

I smiled. 'To what? A sword fight? Anyway, it's not serious.'

'But of course it is.'

'There's nobody else involved,' I said. 'At least not on my part.' I finished my drink and set the glass on a shelf. 'We still have a good love life.'

'I'm sure you do. So take her upstairs and make love to her.'

'Really, Emily.' People who are in steamy relationships think they've found a new cure for all life's ills.

'John, she really is devoted to you.'

I can't get angry with Emily, but I said, with an edge in my voice, 'Susan is self-centred, self-indulgent, narcissistic, and aloof. She is not devoted to anyone but Susan and Zanzibar. Sometimes Yankee. But that's Susan, and it's all right.'

'But she is in *love* with you.'

'Yes, she probably is. But she has taken me for granted.'

'Ah,' said the perceptive Emily. 'Ah.'

'Don't "ah" me.' We both laughed, then I said seriously, 'But I'm not *acting* different to get her attention. I really *am* different.'

'How so?'

'Well, I got drunk last night and slept outside, and I growled at a woman.' Since Emily is my good friend, I was happy to tell her about my morning, and we were both laughing so hard, someone – I couldn't see who – opened the door a crack and peeked in, then shut it.

Emily took my arm. 'Do you know that joke – "What is a real man's idea of group therapy?" Answer, "World War Two".'

I smiled tentatively.

She continued, 'Beyond midlife crisis, John, and male menopause, whatever that is, is the desire to simply be a man. I mean in the most basic biological sense, in a way no one wants to speak about in polite company. To fight a war, or knock somebody over the head, or some surrogate activity like hunting or building a log cabin or climbing a mountain. That's what your morning was about. I wish my husband had let himself go once in a while. He started to believe that his paper shuffling was not only important, but terribly challenging. I'm glad you cracked up. Just try to make it a constructive crack-up.'

'You're a very bright woman.'

'I'm your sister, John. I love you.'

'I love you.'

We stood there awkwardly for a few seconds, then Emily asked, 'Does this new fellow next door, Bellarosa, have anything to do with your present state of mind?'

It did, though I didn't completely understand myself how the mere presence of Frank Bellarosa on the periphery of my property was causing me to reevaluate my life. 'Maybe . . . I mean, the guy has broken all the rules, and he lives on the edge, and he seems at peace with himself, for God's sake. He's completely in control and Susan thinks he's interesting.'

'I see, and that annoyed you. Typical male. But Susan also tells me he seems to like you.'

'I guess.'

'And you want to live up to his estimation of you?'

'No . . . but . . .'

130

'Be careful, John. Evil is very seductive.'

'I know.' I changed the subject. 'How long are you staying?'

'Gary and I fly out early tomorrow. Come out and see us. We have a perfectly horrible shack near the water. We eat shrimps and drink Corona beer, we run on the beach and swat mosquitoes.' She added, 'And make love. Bring Susan if you wish.'

'Maybe.'

She put her hand on my arm and looked me in the eye. 'John, you have got to get out of here. This is the old world. No one lives like this in America anymore. This place has a three-hundred-year history of secret protocols, ancient grievances, and a stifling class structure. The Gold Coast makes New England look informal and friendly.'

'I know all that.'

'Think about it.' She moved toward the door. 'Are you going to hide in here?'

I smiled. 'For a while.'

'I'll bring you a drink. Scotch and soda?'

'That's right.'

She left and returned in a minute with a tall glass filled with ice and soda water and a whole bottle of Dewar's. She said, 'Don't leave without saying good-bye.'

'I may have to.'

We kissed and she left. I sat on a stool and drank, surveying the room filled with table linens, silver pieces, crystal, and other objects from what we call a more genteel age. Maybe Emily was right. This world was half ruin and half museum, and we were all surrounded by the evidence of former glory, which is not a psychologically healthy thing, or good for our collective egos. But what lies out there in the American heartland? Dairy Queens and K Marts, pickup trucks and mosquitoes? Are there any Episcopalians west of the Alleghenies? Like many of my peers, I've been all around the world, but I've never been to America.

I stood, braced myself, and made another foray into the cauldron of boiling family blood.

I walked upstairs where I knew there would be fewer people and went into the turret room, which is still a playroom for kids as it was when I was a child. There were, in fact, ten children in there, not playing make-believe as I had done, but watching a videotape of a gruesome shock-horror movie that one of them must have smuggled in. 'Happy Easter,' I said. A few heads turned toward me, but these children had not yet learned intelligible speech and were picking up points on how to become axe murderers.

I shut off the television and removed the videotape. No one said anything, but a few of them were sizing me up for the chain saw.

I sat and chatted with them awhile, telling them stories of how I had played in this very room before it had a television. 'And once,' I said to Scott, age ten, 'your father and I made believe we were locked in here and it was the Tower of London and all we had was bread and water.'

'Why?'

'Well . . . it was pretend.'

'Why?'

'Anyway, we made paper airplanes with messages written on them, asking for help, and we sailed the planes out the window. And someone's maid found one and thought it was for real, and she called the police.'

'Pretty stupid,' said Justin, age twelve. 'She must have been Spanish.'

A little girl informed Justin, 'They can't even read English, you dope.'

'The maid,' I said with annoyance, 'was black. There were a lot of black maids then and she read English and she was a very concerned woman. Anyway, the police came, and Aunt Cornelia called us downstairs to talk to them. We got a good lecture, then when the police left, we got punished by being locked up for real, in the root cellar.'

'What's a root cellar?'

'She locked you up? For what?'

'Did you ever get even with the maid?'

'Yes,' I replied, 'we cut off her head.' I stood. 'But enough about last Easter.' No one caught the subtle humour. 'Play Monopoly,' I suggested.

'Can we have the tape back?'

'No.' I walked out into the hallway with the videotape, sadder but wiser.

I felt like sitting in the root cellar again, but as I made the turn in the hallway, I ran into Terri, a stunning blonde, married to my cousin Freddie, one of Arthur's brainless sons. 'Well, hello,' I said. 'Where are you heading?'

'Hello, John. I'm checking on the kids.'

'They're fine,' I informed her. 'They're playing doctor and nurse.'

She gave me a tight smile.

'Have *you* had your complete physical yet?' I inquired.

'Behave.'

I walked over to a door across from the stairs and opened it. 'I was on my way to the attic. Would you like to join me?'

'Why?'

'There are some beautiful old gowns up there. Would you like to try some on?'

'How's Susan?'

'Ask Susan.'

Terri seemed a little nervous, but I couldn't tell if she was annoyed or considering the possibilities. I closed the attic door and moved toward the staircase. 'I guess we're too old for make-believe.' I started down the stairs, slowly.

'What's that?' she asked, pointing to the videotape in my hand.

'Trash. It's going in the garbage.'

'Oh . . . those damned kids . . .' She added, 'I'm glad you took it away from them.'

'That's my job. Uncle Creep.'

She laughed. 'I wish Freddie would do that once in a while.'

'It may be a lost cause. But it's our duty to civilization to try.'

'Yes.' She looked at me and smiled. 'You're very casual today, John.'

'I'm having an identity crisis, and I don't know how to dress for it.'

'You're crazy.'

'So what?' I stared at her.

She didn't reply, and I could see the hook was in, and all I had to do was reel up. This, you have to understand, is a woman who is used to men sniffing and drooling around her and has about fifty polite and impolite ways of handling it. But now she was just standing there, looking defenceless and ready for my next move. I started feeling guilty or something, so I said, 'See you later.'

'John, could I talk to you about a will? I think I need a will.'

'You do if you don't have one.'

'Should I call you?'

'Yes, I'm in the city Tuesday, Wednesday, and Thursday, Locust Valley Monday and Friday. We'll have lunch.'

'All right. Thanks.'

I went down the wide winding staircase, my feet barely touching the steps. I was on. I was magnetic, charismatic, interesting. I believed it, and that made it so. And I didn't even need my thousand-dollar cashmere sport jacket or my ninety-dollar Hermès tie. I had power over men and women. Children next. I wanted to tell Susan, but maybe I should keep my mouth shut and see if she noticed.

I also knew I should quit while I was ahead, before I got cornered by old people who are very good at scoping out a room, sizing up their prey, and making telepathically coordinated moves until they've got you cornered.

I dashed for the front door, pretending not to notice two male cousins who were calling my name. A lot of people are named John.

I got outside, bounded down the porch steps, and hurried

down the street, stopping only long enough to throw the videotape down a storm drain. I jumped into the Bronco and drove off.

It was twilight, and I drove slowly with the windows down, breathing in the cool air.

I like to drive, because it is one of the few times I am unreachable. I have no car phone with answering machine, call-waiting, and call-forwarding, no CB, no car fax, ticker tape, telex, or beeper. Only a fuzz buster.

I do have an AM radio, but it's usually locked into the U.S. Weather Service marine forecast out of Block Island. I like weather reports because they are useful information, and you can check the accuracy for yourself. And the guys who deliver the marine forecast talk in monotone, and they don't make jokes, like the idiots on regular radio or TV. They report an approaching hurricane in the same tone of voice they tell you it will be sunny and mild.

I turned on the weather station, and the voice recapped the day's weather without telling me what a nice day it had been for the Easter Parade on Fifth Avenue. I learned that cumulonimbus clouds were on the way and that heavy rains were expected for Monday morning, with winds from the northeast at ten to fifteen knots, and there were small-craft advisories. We'll see.

I drove for another hour or so, but traffic was starting to get heavy, so I headed home. Sunday evenings have never been a good time for me, and under the best of circumstances I'm moody and turn in early.

Susan came home after I'd settled into bed with the lights out. She asked, 'Can I get you anything?'

'No.'

'Are you feeling well?'

'I'm very well.'

'Your mother and Aunt Cornelia were wondering if there was anything wrong with you.'

'Then they should have asked me, not you.'

'You avoided them. Your father was disappointed he didn't have a chance to speak to you.'

'He's had over forty years to speak to me.'

'Do you want to speak to me?'

'No, I want to snore. Good night.'

'Emily passes on her best wishes. Good night.' Susan went downstairs.

I lay very still and looked up at the dark ceiling, feeling about as good as I'd felt in a long time, and about as bad as I'd ever felt in my life. What had happened to me in the last few days, I thought, was both apostasy and apotheosis; I had abandoned my old faith, and in the process had acquired new godlike powers. Well, that might be overstating the case, but certainly I wasn't the same man I had been a few weeks ago.

After a few minutes of metaphysics, I closed the door on the day. The sound of thunder rumbled in the distance, and I imagined myself out on the ocean at night, alone with my boat, the waves breaking over the bow, and the sails filled with wind. It was a good feeling, but I knew that ultimately, when the storm broke, I could not handle the helm and the sails alone. Wondering what to do about that, I fell asleep.

CHAPTER 11

Monday, Easter Monday, it rained as predicted, and the winds were indeed from the northeast, blowing in over Cape Cod and across the Sound, a bit of leftover winter.

I had risen at dawn and discovered that Susan had slept elsewhere, probably in a guest room. I showered and threw on jeans and a sweater, then headed into Locust Valley where I had breakfast at a coffee shop.

I lingered over my coffee and read the *New York Post* for the first time in ten years. An interesting paper, sort of like beef jerky for the mind.

I ordered a coffee to go, left the coffee shop, and drove the few blocks in the rain to my office. I went upstairs to my private office, which had once been the second-floor sitting room, and I built a fire in the fireplace. I sat in my leather wingback chair, put my bare feet up on the fender, and read a copy of *Long Island Monthly* as I sipped coffee from the paper cup. There was an article in the magazine about getting your East End house ready for Memorial Day, the official start of summer fun and sun. This, of course, reminded me that I had a place to go if I went into self-imposed exile or was declared persona non grata in Stanhope land.

My summer house in East Hampton is a cedar-shingled true colonial, built in 1769, surrounded by wisteria and fruit trees. I own that house with Susan – it is mine, hers, and the bank's.

My ancestors on my father's side were original settlers on the eastern end of this island, arriving from England in the 1660s when this New World was indeed very new. I actually have in my possession an original land grant given to one Elias Sutter by Charles II in 1663. That land encompassed about a third of Southampton Township, now one of the most exclusive beach communities on the East Coast, and if the Sutters still owned it, we'd all be billionaires.

That far eastern strip of this island, jutting out into the Atlantic, is a strikingly beautiful landscape, geographically different from the Gold Coast, but in some ways bound to it by family connections, money, and social similarities. More importantly, it is far less populated out there, and the nature nuts are in control. You can hardly put up a mailbox without filing an environmental impact statement.

This ancient connection to the eastern tip of Long Island has always interested me as an abstract footnote to my own life, but until now it has had little impact on my thinking. Lately, however, I've been wondering if the time has come to live in Sutter land rather than Stanhope land.

I tried to picture myself a country lawyer, my stocking feet on the desk in some storefront office, pulling in maybe thirty thousand a year and joining the rush down to the docks when the bluefish were running.

I wonder if Susan would live out there year-round. She would have to board her horses, but the riding there is spectacular, the public trails running through the Shinnecock Hills, right down to the Atlantic Ocean and along the white sand beach. Maybe that's what we needed to get ourselves together.

I sometimes like to come to the office on a day off and catch up on things, but I've never before used the office as a refuge from domestic problems. I put the magazine down, closed my eyes, and listened to the crackling fire and the wind and rain. Absolutely delightful.

I heard the front door open. I had left it unlocked in case any of the more enthusiastic troops wanted to put in a few hours or, like myself, just get away from home. I heard the door shut, then heard footsteps in the foyer. We have a dozen people working here: six secretaries, two paralegals, two junior partners, and two new law clerks, both young women who will take the bar exam this year. One of the budding new attorneys is Karen Talmadge, who will go far because she is bright, articulate and energetic. She is also beautiful, but I mention that only in passing.

I hoped that the footsteps I'd heard were Karen's because there were a few interesting legal concepts I wanted to discuss with her. But in the next instant, I realized that it didn't matter if it was her, my wife, my homely secretary, sexy Terri, or my little nieces and nephews with axes and chain saws. I just wanted to be alone. No sex or violence.

I listened and realized that the footsteps were slow and heavy, unlike a woman's tread. Perhaps it was the mailman or a deliveryman or even a client who didn't know I had made Easter Monday a new holiday. Whoever was down there was walking around, going from room to room, looking for someone or something.

I thought I should go down and investigate, but then I heard the bottom step squeak, and a voice called out, 'Mr Sutter?'

I put the coffee down and stood.

'Mr Sutter?'

I hesitated, then replied, 'I'm up here.' The heavy footsteps ascended the stairs, and I said, 'Second door to your left.'

Frank Bellarosa, wearing a shapeless raincoat and a grey felt hat, came through the door into my office. 'Ah,' he said, 'there you are. I saw your Jeep outside.'

'Bronco.'

'Yeah. Do you have a few minutes? I got some things I want to talk to you about.'

'We're closed today,' I informed him. 'It's Easter Monday.'

'Yeah? Hey, you got a fire. Mind if I sit?'

I sure did, but I motioned to the wooden rocker facing my chair across the hearth, and Mr Bellarosa took off his wet hat and coat and hung them on the clothes tree near the door. He sat. 'You religious?' he asked.

'No. Episcopalian.'

'Yeah? You take this day off?'

'Sometimes. Business is slow.' I picked up the poker and happened to glance at Bellarosa, whose eyes, I saw, were not on me or the fire, but on the heavy, blunt object in my hand. The man had very primitive instincts, I thought. I poked the logs in the fire, then with no abrupt movements, put the poker back. I had the urge to ask Bellarosa if this was a stickup, but I didn't want to strain our new relationship with bad humour. I said instead, 'Do *you* have the day off?'

He smiled. 'Yeah.'

I sat in the chair opposite him. 'What sort of business are you in?'

'That's one of the things I wanted to talk to you about.' He crossed his legs and tried rocking a few times as if he'd never sat in a rocker before. He said, 'My grandmother had one of these. Used to rock, rock, rock, all day. She walked with two canes, you know, before they had those walker things, and sometimes if you were trying to get past her to get into the kitchen, she'd swat you with one of the canes.'

'Why?'

'I don't know. I never asked her.'

'I see.' I regarded Mr Bellarosa a moment. He was wearing basically the same outfit as on Saturday, but the colours were sort of reversed; the blazer was grey and the slacks were navy blue, the shoes were now black, and the turtleneck was white. More interestingly, I could see his shoulder holster.

He looked at me and asked, 'You ever have trouble with trespassers?'

I cleared my throat. 'Once in a while. Nothing serious. Why?'

'Well, there was a guy on my property yesterday morning. Scared the hell out of my wife. My . . .'

'People sometimes like to walk on the estates. You get the vandalism at night with the kids.'

'This was no kid. White guy, about fifty. Looked like a derelict.'

'Really? Did he actually do anything to frighten your wife?'

'Yeah. He growled at her.'

'My goodness. Did you call the police?'

'Nah. My gardeners chased him with the dogs. But he went on to your place. I woulda called you, but you're unlisted.'

'Thank you. I'll keep an eye out.'

'Good. Now my wife wants to move back to Brooklyn. Maybe you can tell her this is a safe place.'

'I'll call her.'

'Or stop by.'

'Perhaps.' I sat in the wing chair and stared at the crackling fire. *Fifty?* She must be half blind. I hope so.

The wind had picked up, and the rain was splashing against the windowpanes. We sat in silence awhile, while one of us contemplated the purpose of this visit. Finally, Mr Bellarosa asked, 'Hey, you ever get those vegetables in the ground?'

'Not yet. But I did eat the radicchio.'

'Yeah? You like it?'

'Very much. I hope you gave me some to plant.'

'Oh, sure. It's marked. You got radicchio, you got basil, you got green peppers, and you got eggplant.'

'Do I have olives?'

He laughed. 'No. Olives grow on a tree. The trees are hundreds of years old. You can't grow them here. You like olives?'

'For my martini.'

'Yeah? I'm growing figs, though. I bought five green and five purple. But you got to cover the trees in the winter here. You wrap them with tar paper and stuff leaves around them so they don't freeze.'

'Really? Is gardening your hobby?'

'Hobby? I don't have hobbies. Whatever I do, I do for real.'

I was sure of that. I finished my coffee and threw the paper cup in the fire. 'So.'

'Hey,' said Frank Bellarosa, 'you missed a good time yesterday. Lots of good people, plenty to eat and drink.'

'I'm sorry we couldn't be there. How was the lamb's head?'

He laughed again. 'The old people eat that. You got to have things like that for them or they think you're getting too American.' He thought for a moment, then added, 'You know, when I was a kid, I wouldn't eat squid or octopus or any of that real greaseball stuff. Now I eat most of it.'

'But not lamb's head.'

'No. I can't do that. Jeez, they pluck the eyes out and cut the tongue off and eat the nose and cheeks and brains.' He chuckled. 'I just ate the lamb chops. What do you people have for Easter?'

'Headless spring lamb, with mint jelly.'

'Yeah, but you know something? In this country, I see the kids getting more interested in the old ways. I see it with my nieces and nephews and my own kids. At first they don't want to be Italian, then they get more Italian when they get older. You see it with the Irish, the Polacks, the Jews. You notice that?'

I hadn't noticed that Edward or Carolyn were dancing round the maypole or eating kippered herrings, but I had noticed that some ethnic groups were doing the roots thing. I don't entirely disapprove as long as there are no human sacrifices involved.

'I mean,' Bellarosa continued, 'people are looking for something. Because maybe American culture doesn't have some things that people need.'

I looked at Frank Bellarosa with new interest. I never thought he would be a complete idiot, but neither did I think that I would hear words such as 'American culture' from him. I asked, 'You have children?'

'Sure. Three boys, God bless 'em, they're healthy and smart. The oldest guy, Frankie, is married and lives in Jersey. Tommy is in college. Cornell. He's studying hotel management. I got a place in Atlantic City for him to run. Tony is at boarding school. He goes to La Salle, where I went. All my kids went there. You know the place?'

'Yes, I do.' La Salle Military Academy is a Catholic boarding school for boys, out in Oakdale on the south shore of Long Island. I have Catholic friends who have or had sons there, and I attended a fund-raiser there once. Its campus is on the Great South Bay and was once an estate, one of the few on the Atlantic side of this island, and belonged, I believe, to an heir to the Singer sewing machine fortune. 'A very fine school,' I said.

Bellarosa smiled, proudly, I thought. 'Yeah. They made me learn there. No bullshit there. You ever read Machiavelli? *The Prince*?'

'Yes, I did.'

'I can quote whole pages of it.'

And, I thought, *you can probably write the sequel to it*. I had heard rumours, and now it was confirmed, that boys with certain types of family connections, such as Mr Bellarosa's, were alumni of this school. On a somewhat higher level, there were a number of leaders from certain Latin American countries who were La Salle graduates, including General Samoza,

142

formerly of Nicaragua. This same school had also produced men who had made their marks in politics, law, the military, and the Catholic clergy. An interesting school, I thought, sort of the Catholic version of the Eastern Establishment Wasp prep school. Sort of. I asked, 'Didn't White House Chief of Staff John Sununu go there?'

'Yeah. I knew the guy. Class of '57. I was '58. Knew Peter O'Malley, too. You know him?'

'Dodgers' president?'

'Yeah. What a place that was. They break your balls there, the good Christian brothers. But maybe not so much anymore. The whole fucking country got soft. But they broke my balls back then.'

'I'm sure it did you some good,' I said. 'Perhaps you'll be rich and famous someday.'

He went along with the joke and replied, 'Yeah. Maybe if I didn't go there, I would've wound up in jail.' He laughed.

I smiled. Certain things about Frank Bellarosa were making sense now, including his nearly intelligent accent, and, I guess, his nickname, the Bishop. A Catholic military school had always struck me as a contradiction in terms, but I suppose on one level there was no contradiction. 'So,' I asked, 'were you a soldier?'

Bellarosa replied, 'If you mean an army soldier, then no.'

'What other kind of soldier is there?' I asked innocently.

He looked at me, and his lips pursed in thought a moment before he replied, 'We are all soldiers, Mr Sutter, because life is war.'

'Life is conflict,' I agreed, 'but that's what makes it interesting. War is something else.'

'Not the way I handle conflicts.'

'Then maybe you should take up conflict as a hobby.'

He seemed to ponder that, then smiled. 'Yeah.' He returned to the subject of his alma mater. 'I had six years at La Salle, and I got to appreciate military organization, chain of command, and all that. That helped me in my business.'

'I suppose it would,' I agreed. 'I was an army officer and

143

I still find myself applying things I learned in the military to my business and my life.'

'Yeah. So you see what I mean.'

'I do.' So there I was, having an almost pleasant chat with the head of New York's most powerful crime family, talking about food, kids, and school days. It seemed a relaxed conversation, despite my innuendoes regarding his business, and I admit the man was an okay guy, not in the least slimy, stupid, or thuggish. And if the conversation were being taped and played back to a grand jury or at a cocktail party, there would be a few yawns. But what did I expect him to talk about? Murder and the drug trade?

There was a chance, I thought, that he didn't want anything more than to be a good neighbour. But as a lawyer, I was sceptical, and as a socially prominent member of the community, I was on my guard. No good could come of this, I knew, yet I was reluctant to end the conversation. Yes, Emily, evil *is* seductive. Looking back on all of this, I can't say I didn't know or wasn't warned. I asked him, 'And did the religious part of La Salle's curriculum leave as lasting an impression on you as the military aspect?'

He thought a moment, then replied, 'Yeah. I'm scared shitless of hell.'

I remembered the Virgin at the end of his reflecting pool. I said, 'Well, that's a start.'

He nodded, then looked around my office, taking in the wood, the hunting prints, the leather, and the brass, probably thinking to himself, 'Wasp junk', or words to that effect. He said, 'This is an old law firm.'

'Yes.' I supposed he thought if the furniture was old, the firm was old, but I had underestimated his interest in me, because he added, 'I asked around. My lawyer knew the name right away.'

'I see.' I had the outlandish thought that he was going to make me an offer for the place, and decided that two million would be fair.

'Anyway,' he said, 'here's the thing. I'm buying a piece of

commercial property on Glen Cove Road, and I need a lawyer to represent me at contract and closing.'

'Are we talking business now?'

'Yeah. Start the clock, Counsellor.'

I thought a moment, then said, 'You just indicated you have a lawyer.'

'Yeah. The guy who knew your firm.'

'Then why don't you use him for this deal?'

'He's in Brooklyn.'

'Send him the cab fare.'

Bellarosa smiled. 'Maybe you know *him*. Jack Weinstein.'

'Oh.' Mr Weinstein is what is known as a mob lawyer, a minor celebrity in late twentieth-century America. 'Can't he handle a real-estate transaction?'

'No. This is one smart Jew, you know? But real estate is not his thing.'

'What,' I asked sarcastically, 'is his thing?'

'A little of this, and a little of that. But not real estate. I want a Long Island guy, like you, for my Long Island business. Somebody who knows the ropes out here with these people.' He added, 'I think you know all the right people, Mr Sutter.'

And, I thought, *you, Mr Bellarosa, know all the wrong people.* I said, 'Surely you have a firm that represents your commercial interests.'

'Yeah. I got a regular law firm in the city. Bellamy, Schiff and Landers.'

'Didn't they handle your closing on Alhambra?'

'Yeah. You checked that out?'

'It's public record. So why don't you use them?'

'I told you. I want a local firm for local business.'

I recalled the conversation I had with Lester Remsen regarding the Lauderbach estate, and I said to Bellarosa, 'My practice is rather select, Mr Bellarosa, and to be blunt with you, my clients are the type of people who believe that an attorney is known by the company he keeps.'

'Meaning what?'

'Meaning I could lose clients if I took you on as a client.'

He didn't seem offended, merely doubtful that I knew what I was talking about. He said with pointed patience, 'Mr Sutter, Bellamy, Schiff and Landers is a very upright firm. You know them?'

'Yes.'

'They don't have a problem with my business.'

'This is not New York City. We do things differently here.'

'Yeah? That's not what I'm finding out.'

'Well, you just found out that we do.'

'Look, Mr Sutter, you have a Manhattan office. Run my business out of there.'

'I can't do that.'

'Why not?'

'I told you, my clients . . . no, actually, I personally do not wish to represent you, and you know why.'

We both sat in silence a moment, and several things ran through my mind, none of them pleasant. It's generally not a good policy to argue with people who are armed, and I hoped that was the end of it. But Frank Bellarosa was not used to taking no for an answer. And in that respect, he wasn't much different from most American businessmen. He knew what he wanted and he wanted to get to yes, while I wanted to stay at no.

He crossed his legs and pulled at his lower lip, deep in thought. Finally he said, 'Let me explain the deal, then if you decide no, we shake hands and stay friends.'

I didn't recall the exact moment when we became friends, and I was upset to learn that we had. Also, I did not want to hear about the deal, but I couldn't be any more blunt without being insulting. Normally, I'm a lot smoother in these situations, but in some curious way, it was Frank Bellarosa himself who had caused me to change my style. Specifically, I blamed him in part for my fight with Susan, though he didn't know that, of course. And the fight had led to one thing after another, culminating in the new John Sutter. Hooray. And while I could appreciate a man like Frank Bellarosa now, I wasn't going to work for him. In fact, I found it easier to tell him to buzz off. I said, 'I can recommend a firm in Glen Cove that would probably handle your business.'

'Okay. But let me ask your opinion about this deal first. Just neighbourly advice. No formal agreement, no paperwork, and don't bill me.' He smiled. 'I'm buying the old American Motors showroom on Glen Cove Road. You know it?'

'Yes.'

'Prime property. Good for something. Maybe a Subaru dealership. Maybe Toyota. Some Jap dealership or other. Do you think that would be good?'

Against my better judgement, I gave him my opinion. 'I personally don't buy Japanese and most of the people I know around here don't either.'

'Is that so? Glad I asked. You see what I mean? You know the territory, and you're honest. Anybody else woulda just seen dollar signs.'

'Maybe. I'll give you another piece of free advice, Mr Bellarosa — you don't just buy property and decide what kind of car dealership you want to put in there. These dealerships are tightly controlled, with territories and all sorts of other requirements that you may not be able to meet. You must know that.'

'You're asking me if I know about territories?' He laughed. 'Anyway, I can get whatever dealership I want.'

'Is that so?'

'That is so.'

I should introduce Mr Bellarosa to Lester, but they probably wouldn't like or trust each other. They did, however, have that one thing in common: they wanted you to believe that everyone was doing it, doing it, doing it. I honestly believe that there is not as much corruption in this country as there is the perception of corruption, and it is that perception that a man like Frank Bellarosa uses to demoralize and ultimately corrupt businessmen, lawyers, police, judges, and politicians. But I wasn't buying it.

'So,' he continued, 'I'm offering six million for the land and the building. You know the property. Is that about right?'

'I'm not sure what the market is at the moment,' I said, 'but I had the impression you had already struck a deal and just needed an attorney at the closing.'

'Well, yes and no. There's always room to negotiate, right? The owners have some better offers, but I made my best offer, and I have to show them that my best offer is *their* best offer.'

'That's a novel approach to business.'

'Nah. I do it all the time.'

I studied Bellarosa's face, and he smiled at me, then said, 'I don't want to screw the guy, but I don't want to get screwed either. So let's say six is fair. So what do you get? A point? That's sixty thousand, Mr Sutter, for a few days' work.'

This is what you call a moment of truth. But there had been a lot of them in the last few weeks. Stealing ten million from an old lady was illegal and immoral. Earning sixty thousand dollars legally from a crook was borderline. I said, 'I thought we agreed I was giving you free neighbourly advice.'

'We also agreed you would listen to the deal.'

'I listened. Tell me how you can get any car dealership you want.'

He waved his hand in dismissal of my petty concerns and said, 'There is no problem with the real estate end of this deal. It's straight. Trust me on that.'

'Okay, I trust you.' I leaned toward him. 'But maybe the source of the money for this deal is not so straight.'

He looked at me, and I could see I had pushed his patience a bit too far. He said coolly, 'Let the government worry about that.'

I couldn't argue with that, because I had made a similar point with Mr Mancuso only yesterday. I stood. 'I sincerely appreciate your confidence in me, Mr Bellarosa, but I suggest you use Cooper and Stiles in Glen Cove. They will have no problem with the deal or the fee.'

Bellarosa stood also and gathered his coat and hat. He said, apropos of nothing, 'I've been reading up on the soil here. It's that glacial outwash you said.'

'Good.'

'I put in a grape arbour. Concord table grapes from upstate. They do good here, according to the book.'

'The book is right.'

'But I want to do a wine grape. Anybody around here grow wine grapes?'

'Mostly out east. But the Banfi Vintners in Old Brookville have been successful with chardonnay. You should talk to them.'

'Yeah? You see what I mean?' He tapped his forehead. 'You're a smart man, Mr Sutter. I knew that. No Jap cars, chardonnay grapes.'

'No charge.'

'I'll give you a case of my first wine.'

'Thank you, Mr Bellarosa. Just don't sell any wine without tax stamps.'

'Sure. What do you think of Saabs?'

'Good choice.'

'How about Casa Bianca? White House. Instead of Alhambra.'

'Sort of common. Sounds like a pizza place. Work on that.'

He smiled. 'Give my regards to Mrs Sutter.'

'I certainly will. And my best regards to your wife, and I hope she has gotten over her upset.'

'Yeah, you know women. You talk to her, okay?'

I opened the door for Mr Bellarosa and we shook hands. He left with two parting words. 'See ya.'

I closed the door behind him. 'Yeah.'

I went to the window and watched him walk across Birch Hill Road through the rain.

The village of Locust Valley is not all upper middle class, and there is another side of the tracks. And when I was thirteen, before I went up to St Paul's, I had the opportunity to know some tough guys. The odd thing, as I recall, was that many of them thought I was an okay guy for a twit. One of them,

Jimmy Curcio, a killer-in-training if ever there was one, used to shake my hand every opportunity he got. The little monster was irrepressible in his friendliness, and one time, I now remember, he was standing in the schoolyard with a group of his *capos* and foot soldiers around him, and as I was passing by, he tapped his forehead and said to them, 'That's a smart guy.'

I watched Frank Bellarosa approach his Cadillac and was not surprised to see a chauffeur – maybe I should say a wheelman or bodyguard – jump out and open the rear door for him. Vanderbilts and Roosevelts may drive their own cars these days, but not don Bellarosa or his kind.

I turned from the window, went back to the fire, and poked at it. Actually, I *am* a smart guy. And Frank Bellarosa, I was learning, was smarter than I had thought. I suppose I should have known that stupid people don't get that far and live that long in his business.

The real estate deal, I thought, may have been for real, but it was also bait. I knew it, and he knew I knew it. We're both smart guys.

But why me?

Well, if you think about it, as he obviously had done, then it made good business sense. I mean, what a team we would make: my social graces, his charisma, my honesty, his dishonesty, my ability to manage money, his ability to steal it, my law degree, his gun.

It was something to think about, wasn't it?

CHAPTER 12

I rattled around the big old house on Birch Hill Road all day, ignoring the ringing phone, watching the rain, and even doing some work.

No one else, except the mailman, came by, and I was irrationally annoyed that my employees had actually taken the day off on my made-up holiday. I would have written a nasty memo to the staff, but I can't type.

At about five P.M., the fax machine dinged, and I walked over to it out of idle curiosity. A piece of that horrible paper slithered out, and I read the handwritten note on it:

> John,
>
> All is forgiven. Come home for cold dinner and hot sex.
>
> Susan

I looked at the note a moment, then scribbled a reply in disguised handwriting and sent it to my home fax:

> Susan,
>
> John is out of the office, but I'll give him your message as soon as he returns.
>
> Jeremy

Jeremy Wright is one of the junior partners here. I suppose I was pleased to hear from Susan, though it was not I who needed forgiving. I wasn't the one rolling around in the hay with two college kids, and I wasn't the one who thought Frank Bellarosa was good-looking. Also, I was annoyed that she would put that sort of thing over the fax. But I *was* happy to see that she had regained her sense of humour, which had been noticeably lacking recently, unless you count the laughing from the hayloft.

As I was about to walk away from the fax machine, it rang again and another message come through:

> Jerry,
>
> Join me for dinner, etc?
>
> Sue

I assumed, of course, that Susan had recognized my hand-writing. I replied:

> Sue,
>
> Ten minutes.
>
> Jerry

On the way home, I saw that the sky was clearing rapidly with wisps of black cirrus sailing across a sunny sky as the southerlies brought the warm weather back. Long Island is not a large land mass, but the weather on the Atlantic side can be vastly different from the Sound side, and the East End has its own weather patterns. All of this weather is subject to change very quickly, which makes life and boating interesting.

I turned the Bronco into Stanhope's gateway and waved to George, who was on a ladder cutting some low branches on a beech tree.

As I headed toward my house, I tried to put myself in the right postbellum, precoital mood.

Susan swung open the door, wearing nothing at all, and called out, 'Jerry!' then put one hand over her mouth and the other over her pubic region. 'Oh . . !'

'Very funny.'

Dinner was indeed cold – a salad, white wine, and half-frozen shrimp. Susan has never taken to cooking, but I don't fault her. It's a wonder she knows how to turn on the oven considering she never even saw Stanhope Hall's downstairs kitchen until she was twenty. But dinner was served in the nude, so what could I complain about?

Susan sat on my lap at the dinner table and fed me icy shrimp with her fingers, poured wine into my mouth, and dabbed my face with a napkin. She didn't say much and neither did I, but I had the feeling everything was all right. It's quite pleasant to eat with a naked woman on your lap, especially if the meal isn't so good. I said, 'Well, so much for the cold dinner. What's for dessert?'

'Me.'

'Correct.'

I stood with her in my arms.

She shook her head. 'Not here. I want to make love on the beach tonight.'

Some women change partners for variety; Susan likes to change the scenery and costumes.

'Sounds fine,' I said, though, in truth, I would have preferred a bed, and I would have preferred it in the next two minutes.

Anyway, Susan dressed and we took the Jag. I drove and put the sunroof back and let in the spring air. It was getting on to that moody time of the day, twilight, when the long shadows make a familiar world look different. 'Do you want to go to the beach now?' I asked.

'No. After dark.'

I drove generally south and west toward the sinking sun, through a lovely landscape of rolling hills, shaded lanes, meadows, ponds, and pockets of woodland.

I tried to sort the events of the last few weeks, which compelled me into the wider subject of my life and my world. There still exists here, less than an hour's drive from midtown Manhattan, this great stretch of land along the northern coast of Long Island, which is almost unknown to the surrounding suburbanites and nearby city dwellers. It is a land that at first glance seems frozen in time, as though the clocks had stopped at the sound of the closing bell on October 29, 1929.

This semi-mythical land, the Gold Coast, is bordered on the north by the coves, bays, and beaches of the Long Island Sound, and on the south by the postwar housing subdivisions of the Hempstead Plains: the Levittowns, the tract housing, the 'affordable homes', built in cookie-cutter fashion, ten and fifteen thousand at a clip where the famous Long Island potato fields once lay, a fulfilment of the postwar promise to provide 'homes fit for heroes'.

But here on the Gold Coast, development has come more

slowly. Great estates are not potato fields, and their passing takes a bit longer.

I said to Susan, 'The interesting Mr Bellarosa dropped by my office today.'

'Did he?'

She didn't pick up on the word *interesting*, or if she did, she let it slide. Women rarely rise to the bait when the subject is jealousy. They just ignore you or look at you as if you're crazy.

We drove in silence. The sky had completely cleared, and the sunlight sparkled off the wet trees and roads.

The Gold Coast, you should understand, encompasses not only the northern coastline of Long Island's Nassau County, but by local definition includes these low hills that run five to ten miles inland toward the plains. These hills were left by the retreat of the last Ice Age glacier, some twenty thousand years ago, and are in fact the terminal moraine of that glacier. I will explain that to Mr Bellarosa one of these days. Anyway, when the Stone Age Indians returned, they found a nice piece of real estate, abundant with new plant life, game, waterfowl, and fabulous shellfish. Nearly all the Native Americans are gone now, their population probably equalling that of the remaining estate owners.

Finally, curiosity got the best of Susan, and she asked, 'What did he bring you this time? Goat cheese?'

'No. Actually, he wanted me to represent him on a real estate deal.'

'Really?' She seemed somewhat amused. 'Did he make you an offer you couldn't refuse?'

I smiled, despite myself, and replied, 'Sort of. But I did refuse.'

'Was he annoyed?'

'I'm not sure.' I added, 'It sounded like a legitimate deal, but you never know with these people.'

'I don't think he would come to you with anything illegal, John.'

'There is white and there is black, and there are a hundred

154

shades of grey in between.' I explained the deal briefly, then added, 'Bellarosa said that he had made his best offer, and he had to show the owners that it was *their* best offer. That sounds a little like strong-arming to me.'

'Perhaps you're overly sensitive to the situation.'

'Well, the deal aside, then, I have to consider my reputation.'

'That's true.'

'My fee for the contract and closing would have been about sixty thousand dollars.' I glanced at Susan.

'The money is irrelevant.'

I suppose if your name happens to be Stanhope, that's true. And that perhaps is the one luxury of the rich that I envy: the luxury to say no to tainted money with no regrets. I, too, indulge myself in that luxury though I'm not rich. Maybe it helps to have a wife who is.

I considered telling Susan about my Easter morning at Alhambra, but in retrospect, the whole incident seemed a bit foolish. Especially growling at the woman. I did, however, want Susan to know about Mr Mancuso. I said, 'The FBI is watching Alhambra.'

'Really? How do you know that?'

I explained that while I was out driving, I happened to see an Easter bunny and two goons at the gates to Alhambra. Susan thought that was funny. 'So,' I said, 'I pulled over for a minute, and this man, Mancuso, approaches me and identifies himself as an FBI agent.' I didn't mention that I was considering going to Mr Bellarosa's Easter thing.

'What did this man say to you?'

I related my brief conversation with Mr Mancuso as we drove past the Piping Rock Country Club. The day had turned out fine weatherwise and otherwise, and there was that fresh smell in the air that comes after a spring rain.

Susan seemed intrigued with my story, but I resisted the temptation to embellish it for entertainment purposes and concluded, 'Mancuso knew what *capozella* was.'

She laughed.

I turned my attention back to the road and the scenery. Not far from here is a huge rock, cleaved in half, with the halves sitting on each side of a tall oak, in the Indian fashion of burial sites. On the rock are engraved these words:

HERE LIES THE LAST

OF THE MATINECOC

The rock is in the churchyard of the Zion Episcopal Church, and at the base of the oak is a metal plaque that says PERPETUAL CARE.

So after thousands of years in these woods and hills, that is all that is left of the Matinecocs, swept away in a few decades by an historical event that they could neither resist nor comprehend. The Colonists came, the Dutch and the English – my forebears – and left their marks on the maps and on the landscape, building and naming villages and roads, renaming ponds and streams and hills, though sometimes letting the ancient Indian names stand.

But today, ironically, these place-names evoke few memories of Indians or Colonists, but are inextricably associated with that brief fifty years called the Golden Age. So if you say Lattingtown or Matinecoc to a Long Islander, he will think of millionaires and mansions, and more specifically perhaps the Roaring Twenties and the final frenetic days of that Golden Age and the Gold Coast.

'What are you thinking about?' Susan asked.

'About the past, about what it must have been like, and I was wondering if I would have liked living in a great house. Did you like it?'

She shrugged.

Susan and her brother, Peter, as well as her mother and father, had lived in Stanhope Hall while her grandparents were alive. You can get a lot of generations comfortably in one house if it has fifty rooms and as many servants.

After Susan's grandparents died, both in the mid-1970s, the

inheritance taxes that existed then effectively closed down Stanhope Hall as a fully staffed estate, though Susan's father and mother continued on there until the price of heating oil quadrupled, and they headed off to a warmer climate. I asked again, 'Did you *like* it?'

'I don't know. It was all I knew. I thought everyone lived like that . . . as I got older, I realized that not everyone had horses, maids, gardeners, and a nanny.' She laughed. 'Sounds stupid.' She thought awhile. 'But without sounding all pyschobabbly, I would have liked to have seen more of my parents.'

I didn't respond. I had seen enough of her parents, William and Charlotte, during the years they played lord and lady of Stanhope Hall. Susan's grandparents, Augustus and Beatrice, were alive when we first married and moved into Susan's wedding gift – deeded solely in her name as I have indicated. Her grandparents were old then, but I had the impression they were decent people, concerned for the welfare of their dwindling staff, but never really coming to terms with the dwindling money.

I asked Susan once, in perhaps a tactless moment, where the Stanhope money had originally come from. She had replied, truthfully I think, 'I don't know. No one as far as I know ever actually *did* anything for it. It just existed on paper, in big ledger books that my father kept locked in the den.'

Susan can be somewhat vague about money like many of these people. I suppose the definition of old money is money whose origins, whereabouts, and amounts are only dimly understood. But from 1929 through the Depression, the war, and the ninety per cent tax rates of the forties and fifties, there was less and less of this paper, and it finally vanished as mysteriously as it had first appeared.

Susan, as I indicated, is not poor, though I don't know how much she is worth. But neither is she fabulously wealthy as her grandparents were. I asked her, 'How do you feel about a man like Bellarosa being an illegal millionaire, while most of the Stanhope money was lost through legal taxation?'

She shrugged. 'My grandfather used to say, "Why shouldn't I give half my money to the American people? I got all of it from them."'

I smiled. 'That's very progressive.' On the other hand, some of the rich managed their assets and tax planning with far more care than the Stanhopes, and they are still rich, albeit in a quieter way. Others of the rich around here, the Astors, Morgans, Graces, Woolworths, Vanderbilts, Guests, Whitneys, and so on, were so unbelievably buried in money that nothing short of a revolution would put a dent in their fortunes.

I said, 'Do you ever feel you were cheated? I mean, if you were born, let's say, eighty years ago, you would have lived your life like an empress.'

'What good does it do to think about it? None of the people I know who are in my circumstances think like that.'

It's true that Susan doesn't talk much about life at Stanhope Hall. It's considered bad form among those people to bring up the subject of estate life with outsiders, and even spouses can be outsiders if they don't have an estate in their past. Sometimes, however, the rich and former rich can be prompted to talk if they don't think you're being judgemental or taking notes for publication. I inquired, 'Did you have a groom and stableboy for the horses?'

'Yes.'

The 'yes' came out sounding like, 'Of course, you idiot. Do you think I mucked out the stables?' I then asked, 'Did your grandparents see many of the old crowd? Did they entertain?'

She nodded. 'There were a few parties.' She volunteered, 'Grandfather would invite a hundred or so people at Christmas, and they would all dance in the ballroom. In the summer, he would have one or two parties out on the terrace and under tents.' She added, 'The old crowd would sometimes gather in the library and go through photo albums.'

We drove in silence awhile. There wasn't much more I was going to get out of Susan.

George Allard is a better source of information whenever I get interested in the subject of the old Gold Coast. George's stories are mostly anecdotal, such as the one about Mrs Holloway, who kept chimpanzees in the sitting room of Foxland, her estate in Old Westbury. From George, you can piece together what life was like between the world wars, whereas Susan's stories are mostly childhood memories of a time when the party was long over. George will sometimes tell me a story about Susan as a child that he thinks is funny, but that I find is a clue to my wife's personality.

Susan, by all accounts, was a precocious, snotty little bitch who everyone thought was bright and beautiful. That hasn't changed much, but the extroverted young woman I first met has become increasingly moody and withdrawn over the years. She lives more in her own world as the world around her closes in. I would not describe her as unhappy, but rather as someone who is trying to decide if it's worth the effort to be unhappy. On the other hand, she is not unhappy with me, and I think we're good for each other.

Regarding our current lifestyle, like many other people around here, we enjoy the good life, though as I said, we live among the ruins of a world that was once far more opulent. Susan, I should point out, can afford to provide us with more hired help, gardeners, maids, even a stableboy (preferably an old gent), but by mutual and silent agreement we live mostly within my income, which, while extravagant by most American standards, does not allow for live-in servants in this overpriced part of the world. Susan is a good sport about doing some house and garden chores, and I don't feel insecure or inadequate regarding my inability to move into Stanhope Hall and hire fifty servants.

Susan asked me, 'What beach do you want to make love on?'

'One without razor clams. I had a serious accident once.'

'Did you, now? That must have been before my time. I don't remember that. What was her name?'

'Janie.'

'Not Janie Tillman?'

'No.'

'You'll have to tell me about it later.'

'All right.' In our pursuit of fidelity within a twenty-year-old marriage, Susan and I, in addition to the historical romances, sometimes talk about a premarital lover as part of our foreplay. I read in a book once that it was all right to do this, to get the juices going, but afterward, as you're both lying there, one partner is usually sullen and the other is sorry he or she was so graphic. Well, if you play with fire to get heat, you can also get burned.

I asked, 'What did you do today?'

'I planted those vegetables that what's-his-name gave us.' She laughed.

'In the rain?'

'Don't they like the rain? I planted them in one of the old flower terraces in front of Stanhope Hall.'

I thought old Cyrus Stanhope, as well as McKim, Mead, and White, must be spinning in their graves.

I turned into an unmarked road that I don't think I was ever on before. A good many of the roads on the North Shore are unmarked – some say on purpose – and they seem to go nowhere and often do.

A modern map of this area would not show you where the great estates are; there is no Gold Coast version of the Hollywood Star Map, but there did once exist privately circulated maps of this area that showed the location of the estates and their owners' names. These maps were for use by the gentry in the event your butler handed you an invitation reading something like, 'Mr and Mrs William Holloway request the pleasure of your company for dinner at Foxland, the seventeenth of May at eight o'clock.'

Anyway, I have one of these old estate maps in my possession. Mine is dated 1928, and I can see on it the location of all the estates, great and small, in that year along with the estate owners' names written in. I said to Susan, 'You never met the original owners of Alhambra, did you? The Dillworths?'

'No, but they were friends of my grandparents. Mr Dillworth was killed in World War Two. I think I remember Mrs Dillworth, but I'm not sure. I do remember when the Vanderbilts lived there in the fifties.'

It seemed to me that the large Vanderbilt clan had built or bought half the houses on the Gold Coast at one time or another, allowing realtors to say of any great house with fifty per cent accuracy, 'Vanderbilts lived here.' I asked, 'Then the Barretts bought it?'

'Yes. Katie Barrett was my best friend. But they lost the house to the bank or the tax people in 1966, the year I went to college. They were the last owners until you-know-who.'

I nodded, then said to Lady Stanhope, baitingly, 'My grandfather once told me that the coming of the millionaires to Long Island was not looked on very favourably by the people who had been here for centuries before. The old Long Island families, such as my own, thought these new people – including the Stanhopes – were crass, immoral, and ostentatious.' I smiled.

Susan laughed. 'Did the Sutters and Whitmans look down on the Stanhopes?'

'I'm certain they did.'

'I think you're a worse snob than I am.'

'Only with the rich. I'm very democratic with the masses.'

'Sure. So, how will we treat Mr Bellarosa? As a crass, unprincipled interloper, or as an American success story?'

'I'm still sorting it out.'

'Well, I'll help you, John. You're as relieved as I am that Alhambra will not become a hundred little haciendas, which is very selfish but understandable. On the other hand, you'd have rather had someone next door whose crimes were not so closely associated with his fortune.'

'There are people out there who earn their money honestly.'

'I know there are. They live in Levittown.'

'Very cynical.'

Susan changed the subject. 'I heard from Carolyn and Edward today.'

'How are they?' I asked.

'Fine. They missed us at Easter.'

'It seemed different without them,' I said.

'Easter certainly was different this year,' Susan pointed out.

I let that alone. As for my children, Carolyn is a freshman at Yale, my alma mater, and I still can't get used to the fact that Yale has women there now. Carolyn went to St Paul's, also my alma mater, and that's even harder to picture. But the world is changing, and for women, perhaps, it's a slightly better place. Edward is a senior at St Paul's, which appeals to my male ego, but he's been accepted at Susan's alma mater, Sarah Lawrence. I suppose I should be happy that my children have chosen their parents' schools, but how my daughter has wound up at Yale and my son at Sarah Lawrence is beyond me. In Carolyn's case, I think she is making a statement. Edward's motives, I'm afraid, are a bit more base; he wants to get laid. I think they'll both succeed. I said, 'I came home every holiday when I was at school.'

'So did I, except one Thanksgiving I'd rather not discuss.' She laughed, then added seriously, 'They grow up faster now, John. They really do. I was so sheltered, I honestly didn't know a thing about sex or money or travel until I was ready to go to college. That's not good either.'

'I suppose not.' Susan actually went to a local prep school, Friends Academy here in Locust Valley, an old and prestigious school run by Quakers. She lived at home and was driven to school in a chauffeured car. Many of the rich around here favour the austere atmosphere of Friends for their children, hoping, I suppose, that their heirs will learn to enjoy simple pleasures in the event the market crashes again. Indeed we all try to raise our children as if *our* past experiences are important for *their* future, but they rarely are. Anyway, I'm glad Susan learned austerity between nine A.M. and three P.M. on school days. It may come in handy.

Susan said, 'Your mother called. They're back in Southampton.'

My parents are not the type to call to announce their movements. They once took a trip to Europe, and I didn't know about it until months afterwards. Obviously, there was more to the phone call.

Susan added, 'She was curious about your Easter behaviour. I told her you were just having a few bad days.'

I grunted noncommittally. My mother, Harriet, is a rather cold but remarkable woman, very liberated for her day. She was a professor of sociology at nearby C.W. Post College, which was once the estate of the Post family of cereal fame. The college has always been somewhat conservative, drawing its student body from the surrounding area, and Harriet was usually in some sort of trouble for her radical views in the 1950s.

She didn't have to work, of course, as my father did well financially, and there were people at Post who wished she didn't work. But by the 1960s the world had caught up with Harriet, and she came into her own, becoming one of the campus heroes of the counterculture.

I can remember her when I was home from St Paul's and Yale, running all over the place in her VW Beetle, organizing this and that. My father was liberal enough to approve, but husband enough to be annoyed.

Time, however, marches on, and Harriet Whitman Sutter got old. She now disapproves of four-letter words, loose sex, drugs, and sons who don't shave or wear ties at Easter. And this is the same lady who approved of co-ed streaking. I said to Susan, 'I'll call her tomorrow.'

Susan and my mother get along, despite their social and economic differences. They have a lot more in common than they know.

We slipped back into a companionable silence, and I turned my attention back to the scenery. It seemed to me that a traveller who put down his road map and looked out his window as he drove along these country lanes would not mistake his surroundings for some west-of-the-Hudson backwater, but would in some socially instinctive way know that he had entered a vast private preserve of wealth.

And as this traveller's car navigated the bends and turns of these tree-lined roads, he might see examples of Spanish architecture, like Alhambra, half-timbered Tudor manors, French châteaux, and even a white granite beaux-arts palace like Stanhope Hall, sitting in the American countryside, out of time and out of place, as if the aristocracy from all over Western Europe for the last four hundred years had been granted a hundred acres each to create an earthly nirvana in the New World. By 1929, most of Long Island's Gold Coast was divided into about a thousand great and small estates, fiefdoms, the largest concentration of wealth and power in America, probably the world.

As we drove along a narrow lane, bordered by estate walls, I saw six riders coming from the opposite direction. Susan and I waved as we passed, and they returned the greeting.

She said, 'That reminds me, I want to move the stable now that the good weather is here.'

I didn't reply.

'We'll need a sideline variance.'

'How do you know?'

'I checked. The stable will be within a hundred yards of you-know-who's property.'

'Damn it.'

'I have the paperwork from Village Hall. We need plans drawn up, and we'll have to get you-know-who to sign off on it.'

'Damn it.'

'No big deal, John. Just send it to him with a note of explanation.'

It's hard to argue with a woman to whom you want to make love, but I was going to give it my best shot. 'Can't you find another place for the stable?'

'No.'

'All right.' The idea of asking Frank Bellarosa for a favour didn't appeal to me in the least, especially after I had just told him to take his business elsewhere. I said, 'Well, it's your property and your stable. I'll get the paperwork done, but you take care of you-know-who.'

'Thank you.' She put her arm around me. 'Are we friends?'

'Yes.' But I hate your stupid horses.

'John, you look so good when you're naked. Now that the weather is warm, can I paint you outdoors in the nude?'

'No.' Susan has four main passions in life: horses, landscape painting, gazebos, and sometimes me. You know about the horses and about me. The Gazebo Society is a group of women who are dedicated to the preservation of the Gold Coast's gazebos. Why gazebos? you ask. I don't know. But in the spring, summer, and fall, they have these elaborate picnic lunches in various gazebos, and they all dress in Victorian or Edwardian clothes, complete with parasols. Susan is not a joiner, and I can't fathom why she hangs around with these ditsy people, but the sceptic in me says the whole thing is a front for something. Maybe they tell dirty jokes, or exchange hot gossip, or aid and abet marital infidelities. But maybe they just have lunch. Beats me.

As for the landscape painting, this is for real. Susan has gained some local notoriety for her oils. Her main subject is Gold Coast ruins, in the style of the Renaissance artists who painted the classical Roman ruins, with the fluted columns entangled with vines, and the fallen arches, and broken walls overgrown with plant life: the theme being, I suppose, nature reclaiming man's greatest architectural achievements of a vanished Golden Age.

Her most famous painting is of her horse, stupid Zanzibar, who if nothing else is a magnificent-looking animal. In the painting, Zanzibar is standing in the moonlight of the crumbling glass palm court of Laurelton Hall, the former Louis C. Tiffany mansion. Susan wants to do a painting of me, in the same setting, standing naked in the moonlight. But though

165

Susan is my wife, I'm a little shy about standing around naked in front of her. Also, I have the bizarre thought that I will come out looking like a centaur.

Anyway, Susan's clients are mostly local *nouveaux riches* who live in those tract mansions that cover the old estate grounds. These clients buy everything that Susan can paint and pay three to five thousand dollars a canvas. Susan does two or three landscapes a year and supports her two horses with the money. Personally, I think she could do another two or three and buy me a new Bronco.

'Why won't you pose in the nude for me?'

'What are you going to *do* with the picture?'

'Hang it over the fireplace. I'll give you another three inches and we'll have a cocktail party, and you'll be surrounded by admiring women.' She laughed.

'Get hold of yourself.' I headed in the direction of Hempstead Bay, where there are a few secluded beaches, on most of which I've had at least one sexual experience. There's something about the salt air that gets me cranked up.

I thought about Susan's paintings of the old estates and wondered why she chose to record and preserve this crumbling world in oil, and how she makes it look so alluring on canvas. It struck me that a painting of an intact mansion would be dull and ordinary, but there *was* an awful beauty to these fallen palaces. On the lands of these estates one can still see marble fountains, statuary, imitation Roman ruins such as Alhambra's, a classical love temple such as we have at Stanhope, gazebos, children's fantasy playhouses such as Susan's, teahouses, miles of greenhouses, pool pavilions, water towers built to look like watchtowers, and balustraded terraces overlooking land and sea. All of those lonely structures lend a whimsical air to the landscape, and it seems as if someone had built and abandoned a storyland theme park many years ago. Susan's paintings make me see these familiar ruins in a different way, which, I suppose, is the mark of a good artist. I asked her, 'Have you ever painted a man in the nude?'

'I'm not telling.'

I noticed the gates to the old Foxland estate ahead, now part of the New York Technical University. A number of these larger estates have become schools, conference centres, and rest homes. A few intact estates are owned by the county, as Lester and I discussed, and some of these have been restored for visitors, instant museums of a period in American history not quite dead yet.

Among the most enduring and useful structures of this Golden Age are the gatehouses and the staff cottages for gardeners, chauffeurs, and other servants who did not traditionally live in the great house. These quaint quarters are now occupied by former servants whose masters were good enough to deed them away or give them rent free – as in the case of the Allards – as a reward for past service, or occupied by people who have bought or rented them. They are quite desirable as homes or artist studios, and a stone gatehouse such as Stanhope's can sell for several hundred thousand dollars. If the Allards ever move on to their final, final reward, William Stanhope will sell the gatehouse.

An estate's guesthouse is an even more desirable home for a modern upper-middle-class family – perhaps because there are no working-class associations. It is in Stanhope's guesthouse, of course, where Susan and I live, which might be appropriate for me, but is a long step down for her.

As we came to another new subdivision, Susan said, 'Sometimes I can't remember the names of the old estates or their locations or what they were called, unless the builder uses the same name for his development.' She nodded toward the new homes going up in an open horse meadow surrounded by wrought-iron fencing. 'What was that place called?' she asked.

'That was part of the hedges, but I can't remember the last owner's name.'

'Neither can I,' she said. 'Is the house still there?'

'I think it was torn down. It was behind those blue spruces.'

'That's right,' Susan agreed. 'It was an English manor house.

The Conroys owned it. I went to school with their son, Philip. He was cute.'

'I think I remember him. Sort of a twit with terminal acne.'

Susan punched my arm. 'You're the twit.'

'I have clear skin.' We headed due west now, and as the last rays of the sun came through the windshield, I put the visor down. Sometimes these rides are pleasant, sometimes they aren't. I asked, 'Have you thought about moving?'

'No.'

'Susan . . . I give this place another ten years and you won't recognize it. The Americans are coming. Do you understand what I mean?'

'No.'

'The hamburger chains, shopping malls, twenty-four-hour convenience stores, pizza parlours – they're here already. There will come a day when there won't be a secluded beach left for us to make love on. Wouldn't you rather remember everything as it was?'

She didn't reply and I knew it was no use trying to introduce reality into her world.

In some ways, this place reminds me of the post-Civil War South, except that the decline of the Gold Coast is not the result of military operations, but of a single economic catastrophe followed by a more subtle class war. And whereas the ruined plantations of the old South were spread over a dozen states, the ruins of this fabled world are contained within an area of about ninety square miles, comprising about a third of the total area of this county.

Most of this surburban county's massive population of a million and a half people are contained in the southern two-thirds, and very close by are New York's teeming eight million. These facts – the numbers, the history, the present realities of population, taxes, and land development – colour our world and explain, I hope, our collective psyches and our obsession with wanting to freeze a moment in time, any moment in time except tomorrow.

I glanced again at Susan, who had her eyes closed now. Her head was still tilted back, and those magnificent pouty lips seemed to be kissing the sky. I was about to reach out and touch her when she seemed to sense my look or perhaps my thoughts, and she laid her hand on my thigh. She said, 'I love you.'

'And I love you.'

Susan caressed my thigh, and I shifted in my seat. I said, 'I don't think I can make it to the beach.'

'To the beach, my man.'

'Yes, madame.'

The sun had set now, and here and there I could make out the lights of a big house through the newly budded trees. I got my bearings and headed north through the village of Sea Cliff, then west to Garvie's Point, the former estate of Thomas Garvie, and the site of an old Indian camping ground, now returned again to nature as a wildlife preserve and an Indian museum, which was sort of ironic, I guess.

The park was closed, but I knew a way in through the adjoining Hempstead Harbor Yacht Club, where we parked the car.

I took a blanket from the trunk, and Susan and I held hands as we made our way down to the beach, a narrow strip of sand and glacial rock that lay at the base of a low cliff. The beach was nearly deserted except for a group of people a hundred yards farther up who had built a fire.

There was no moon, but the sky was starry, and out on Hempstead Bay, powerboats and sailing craft headed into the yacht club or continued south toward Roslyn Harbor.

It had gotten noticeably cooler, and a land breeze rustled through the trees at the top of the cliff. We found a nice patch of sand that the outgoing tide had deposited between two large rocks at the cliff's base. It was a well-sheltered spot, and we spread out the blanket and sat looking at the water.

There is something about the beach after dark that is both calming and invigorating, and the majesty of the sea and the vast sky makes anything you say sound feeble, yet any movement of the body seems graceful and divinely inspired.

We undressed and made love under the stars, then lay wrapped in each other's arms in the lee of the cliff and listened to the sound of the wind through the trees above us.

After a while, we dressed and walked along the beach, hand in hand. Across the bay I could see Sands Point, once home to the Goulds, the entire Guggenheim clan, August Belmont, and one of the Astors.

When I walk this beach and look across to Sands Point, I think of F. Scott Fitzgerald's Jay Gatsby, the location of whose mythical house is the subject of some local theories and literary essays. My own theory, shared by some others, is that Gatsby's house was Falaise, Harry F. Guggenheim's home in Sands Point. The colossal house that Fitzgerald described sounds like Falaise, including the coastline and high bluffs of Sands Point. Falaise is a county museum now, dark at night, but if it were lit in all its glory, I would be able to see it from here.

And on this side of the bay, up the beach on the next point of land, there is a big white colonial house which still stands and which I am certain is that of Gatsby's lost love, Daisy Buchanan. The long pier behind Daisy's house is not there any longer, but locals confirm that it existed, and the haunting green light at the end of the pier that Gatsby would stare at from his mansion across the water – well, I've seen it from my boat on summer nights, and Susan has seen it, too – a spectral glow that seems to float above the water where the pier must have ended.

I'm not sure what that green light meant to Jay Gatsby nor what it symbolized beyond the orgiastic future. But for me, when I see it, my worries seep away into the sea mist, and I feel as I did as a child one summer night many years ago when from my father's boat I watched the harbour lights playing off the sparkling waters of Hempstead Bay. When I see the green light, I am able to recall that innocent hour, that perfect, tranquil night with its sea smells and soft breezes, and the sound of gentle swells lapping against the swaying boat, and my father taking my hand.

Susan, too, says the green light can bring on a transcendental moment for her, though she won't or can't describe it precisely.

But I want to tell my children about this; I want to tell them to find their green light, and I wish that for one magic hour on a summer's evening, a weary nation would pause and reflect, and each man and woman would remember how the world once looked and smelled and felt and how nice it was to draw such supreme comfort and security by the simple act of putting one's hand into the hand of a father or mother.

The green light that I see at the end of Daisy's vanished pier is not the future; it is the past, and it is the only comforting omen I have ever seen.

CHAPTER 13

By Wednesday, I had gotten the necessary paperwork together to apply to the Village of Lattingtown for a building permit to erect a stable on Susan's property. I did not specifically state that the stable to be built already existed on Stanhope property, as the Stanhopes, of course, owe the village, the township, and the county a lot of money, and I suppose that the part of the stables that we were going to chop off and spirit away could be considered an asset on which there are tax liens. But if it's legal to tear down structures to save taxes, I guess it's legal to move them to property on which the taxes are paid, and will, in fact, go up because of the stables. I honestly don't know how anyone functions in this society without a law degree. Even I, Harvard Law, class of '69, have trouble figuring out legal from illegal, as the laws pile up faster than garbage in the county dump.

Anyway, I also drew up the petition for the variance on which we needed Mr Frank Bellarosa's autograph. Over dinner that Wednesday night, I said to Susan, 'It is customary, as you know, to hand the petition to our neighbour and chat for a while about what we intend to do.'

Susan replied, 'I'll take it over.'

'Fine. I'd rather not.'

'It's my stable. I'll take care of it. Would you please pass me the meat loaf?'

'Meat loaf? I thought it was bread pudding.'

'Whatever.'

I passed whatever it was to Susan and said, 'I suggest you go to Alhambra tomorrow during the day, so perhaps you can meet and deal with Mrs Bellarosa, who I'm sure is not allowed to go to the bathroom without asking her husband's permission, but who can pass the petition on to Il Duce, who can ask his consiglieri what to do.'

Susan smiled. 'Is that what you suggest, Counsellor?'

'Yes, it is.'

'All right.' She thought a moment. 'I wonder what she's like.'

I thought she might be like a busty blonde, which is why I was sending Susan and not me. 'Could you pass me . . . that over there?'

'That's spinach. I think I cooked it too long.'

'I'll just have the wine.'

*

The next day, Susan called me at my New York office and informed me, 'There was no one home, but I left the papers at the gatehouse with a young man named Anthony, who seemed to comprehend that I wanted them delivered to don Bellarosa.'

'All right.' I asked, 'You didn't say don Bellarosa, did you?'

'No. Anthony did.'

'You're kidding.'

'No, I'm not. And I want George to call us don and donna from now on.'

'I think I'd rather be called Sir John. See you about six-thirty.'

That evening, over one of Susan's special dinners – steak *au poivre* with fresh spring asparagus and new potatoes, delivered hot from Culinary Delights – I remarked, 'I'd call Bellarosa, but he's unlisted.'

'So are we. But I wrote our phone number on my calling card.'

'Well . . . I suppose that's all right.' Susan has calling cards, by the way, that say simply: *Susan Stanhope Sutter, Stanhope Hall*. This may sound to you like a useless and perhaps even pretentious thing to carry around, but there are still people here who use these cards, leaving them on a silver tray in the foyer after a visit. If the master and mistress are not at home, or are not receiving, the calling card – or visiting card, as it is also called – is left with the gatekeeper, maid, or nowadays anyone who's around to take it. Mr Frank Bellarosa, for instance, should have left his calling card with George when he first learned I was not receiving. I have calling cards, too, but only because Susan got them printed for me about twenty years ago. I've used four of them socially and a lot of them under wobbly table legs in restaurants.

As I was contemplating the importance of calling cards in modern society, the telephone rang. 'I'll get it,' I said. I picked up the extension on the kitchen wall. 'Hello.'

'Hello, Mr Sutter. Frank Bellarosa.'

'Hello, Mr Bellarosa.' I glanced at Susan, who had taken the opportunity to transfer my asparagus to her plate.

Bellarosa said, 'I'm looking at this thing here that your wife dropped off.'

'Yes.'

'You gonna build a stable?'

'Yes, if you have no objections.'

'What do I care? Am I going to smell the horse shit?'

'I don't think so, Mr Bellarosa. It's quite a distance from your house but near your property line, so I need what is called a sideline variance.'

'Yeah?'

'Yeah.' Susan was finished with my asparagus and was eating my steak now. She doesn't have that much of an appetite for her own cooking. 'Stop that.'

'Stop what?' asked Bellarosa.

I turned my attention back to the phone. 'Nothing. So, if you have no objections, would you sign that petition and mail it in the envelope to the village? I would appreciate that.'

'Why do you need my okay to do that?'

'Well, as I said, the new structure would be within a hundred yards of your property line, and the law – '

'Law?' exclaimed Mr Bellarosa as if I'd used a dirty word. 'Fuck the law. We're neighbours, for Christ's sake. Go ahead. I'll sign the thing.'

'Thank you.'

'I'm looking at these plans you sent along, Mr Sutter. You need somebody to build this thing?'

'No, I sent you those plans because the . . . the rules require that I show you the plans – '

'Yeah? Why? Hey, this thing is brick and stone. I could help you out there.'

'Actually . . . we're moving an existing stable.'

'Yeah? That thing I saw the other week when I was there? That's where the horses are now?'

'Yes.'

'You moving that whole fucking thing?'

'No, only part of it. You'll see by the plans – '

'Why? You could build a nice new thing for less.'

'That's true. Hold on.' I covered the mouthpiece and said to Susan, 'Frank says we can build a nice new thing for less, and put down that fucking potato.'

'Language, John.' She popped the last potato into her mouth.

I turned back to the telephone. 'The stables that you saw, Mr Bellarosa, have some historical and architectural value,' I explained, wondering why I was bothering, and getting a bit annoyed that he'd drawn me into this conversation.

174

'So,' said Mr Bellarosa, 'you got somebody to move that thing or not?'

'Actually, not yet. But there are some good restoration firms in the area.'

'Yeah? Listen. I have about a hundred greaseballs working over here trying to get this place fixed up. I'm gonna send the boss around to you on Saturday morning.'

'That's very kind of you, but –'

'Hey, no problem. These guys are good. Old World craftsmen. You don't find guys like that in this country. Everybody here wants to wear a suit. You want to move a brick stable? No problem. These guys could move the Sistine Chapel down the block if the Pope gave them the go-ahead.'

'Well –'

'Hey, Mr Sutter, these wops *live* cement. That's how they learn to walk – with a wheelbarrow. Right? The boss's name is Dominic. He speaks English. I personally guarantee his work. These guys don't fuck up. And the price is going to be right. Saturday morning. How's nine?'

'Well . . . all right, but –'

'Glad to help out. Just sign this thing, right?'

'Yes.'

'Go have your dinner. Don't worry about it. It's done.'

'Thank you.'

'Sure thing.'

I put the phone in the cradle and went back to the table. 'No problem.'

'Good.'

'Is there anything left to eat?'

'No.' Susan poured me some wine. 'What was he saying at the end there?'

'He's sending Dominic here to look at the job.'

'Who's Dominic?'

'Anthony's uncle.' I sipped my wine and thought about this turn of events.

Susan asked, 'Do you feel awkward now that you wouldn't take his business?'

'No. I have a professional life and a private life. Professionally I won't deal with him; privately I'll deal with him only when I have to as a neighbour. Nothing more.'

'Is that true?'

I shrugged. 'I didn't ask him to send Dominic over. Mr Frank Bellarosa is making it difficult for us to snub him.'

'He must like you. When he was in your office, did you get the impression he liked you?'

'I suppose. He thinks I'm smart.'

'Well, you are.'

'Sure. If I were smart, I never would have let you talk me into moving that stable, paying for half of it, and getting involved with Bellarosa.'

'That's true. Maybe you're not so smart.'

'What's for dessert?'

'Me.'

'Again? I had that last night.'

'Tonight I have whipped cream on it.'

'And a cherry?'

'No cherry.'

On Saturday morning, Dominic arrived punctually at our back door at nine A.M. He had parked his truck on the main drive and walked the last hundred yards to our house in a light drizzle. He refused offers of coffee or a hat, so Susan and I showed him to the Bronco and we drove to the stables.

Dominic was a man in his late forties, built something like a gorilla that lifts weights. He wore green work clothes, and his skin was already very sun-darkened for April. I still wasn't sure he spoke English or if he just pretended to. Susan speaks a little Italian and tried it out on Dominic, who kept looking at me as if he wanted me to translate or tell her to shut up.

Anyway, we all stood in the drizzle while Dominic gave the stable a cursory inspection.

Susan tried to make sure he understood we only wanted the central part moved, not the long wings or the carriage house. 'And we want this cobblestone moved, too,' she said, 'those

176

stone troughs, the wrought-iron work, the slate roof. And it has to be put together the same way over there.' She pointed off in the distance. '*Intatto, tutto intatto. Capisce?* Can you do that?'

He looked at her as though she'd just questioned his manhood.

I said to Dominic, 'We will take pictures of the stable from all angles.'

'Yes,' Susan said. 'I don't want it to wind up looking like the Colosseum, Dominic.'

He smiled for the first time.

'How much?' I asked. That's my line.

Dominic pulled a scrap of a brown paper bag from his pocket, wrote a number on it, and handed it to me.

I looked at his written estimate. It wasn't exactly itemized, containing only one number as it were, but the number was about half what I thought it should be. There are, as I've discovered over the years, many forms of bribes, payoffs, and 'favours'. This was one of them. But what could I do? Susan was intent on this and so apparently was Frank Bellarosa. I said something to Dominic that I thought I'd never say to a contractor. I said, 'This is too low.'

He shrugged. 'I gotta no overhead, I gotta cheap labour.'

Susan didn't bother to look at the number. She asked him, 'When can you start?'

'Monday.'

'Monday of what year?' she inquired.

'Monday. Monday. Day after tomorra, missus. Three weeks, we finish.'

Of course this seemed like a homeowner's fantasy come true, which it was. I said to Dominic, 'We'll think about it.'

Dominic looked at me, then said something odd. He said, 'Please.' He cocked his head in the direction of Alhambra.

He didn't exactly make a cutting motion across his throat, but I had the distinct impression that if Dominic went back to great Caesar without my okay, he was in trouble. I glanced at Susan, who seemed to be missing the subtleties here.

Susan said to me, 'Oh, John, I'm not in the mood to shop around. If it's too low, give him a bonus.' She laughed. 'Monday, John. *Capisce?*'

Against all my better instincts, I said to Dominic, 'All right.'

'*Molto bene*,' Susan said.

Dominic looked happy to be working for us for peanuts. I said to him, 'You want a cheque now?'

He waved his hand. 'No, no. We worka for Mr Bellarosa. You talka ta him. Okay?'

I nodded.

Dominic said, 'You taka you horses to Mr Bellarosa stable whila we work.'

Susan shook her head. 'We have many other stables here.' She motioned with her hand.

'But, missus, Mr Bellarosa stables all cleana for you. We maka lotta noise here with the jacka hammas.' He demonstrated using a jackhammer and reproduced the noise quite well. *Dadadadada*. He added, 'No gooda for you horses.'

That clinched it for Susan and she said, 'I'll take them over Monday.'

We got into the Bronco, and I drove back to where Dominic's truck sat in the main drive. I left Susan in the car and walked Dominic to the truck. I asked him, 'Is Mr Bellarosa home?'

He nodded.

'When you get to his house, tell him to call me.'

'Okay.'

I took my wallet out and handed Dominic my calling card. He examined both sides, obviously looking for a phone number. I guess the man never saw a calling card. 'Mr Bellarosa has my number,' I explained. 'Just give him the card and tell him to call me now.'

'Okay.'

I took a hundred dollars from my wallet and gave it to Dominic, who shoved it into his pocket without examining either side. 'Thanka you too much.'

We shook hands. 'See you Monday.' I walked back to the Bronco and drove it up to the house. Susan and I went in through the back way to the kitchen. I showed her the scrap of paper and said, 'Bellarosa is subsidizing this job.'

She glanced at the piece of paper. 'How do you know that?'

'After fifteen years of getting quotes for work here and having your father tell me it's too much, I know prices.'

Susan, who was in a good mood, wasn't about to be baited. She smiled, and said, 'As St Jerome wrote, "Never look a gift horse in the mouth."'

There are certain advantages in a classical education, and spouting fourth-century Roman saints to make a point with your spouse may be one of them. I replied, 'As a wiser man said, "There ain't no such thing as a free lunch."'

I poured two cups of coffee, and the phone rang. I answered it. 'Hello.'

'Mr Sutter.'

'Mr Bellarosa.'

'You all squared away there?' he asked.

'Maybe,' I replied. 'But I don't think he can bring the job in for that price.'

'Sure he can.'

'How?'

'Cheap labour, low overhead, and your materials.'

I glanced at Susan, who was watching me closely, then said to Bellarosa, 'All right. Whom do I pay?'

'You pay me. I'll take care of the boys.'

The last thing I wanted was to have one of my cheques drawn to Frank the Bishop Bellarosa. 'I'll give you cash,' I said.

He replied, 'I take cash for a lot of things, Mr Sutter, but I thought people like you want a record of every-thing.'

Not everything, Frank. I responded, 'It's still legal to pay in cash in this country. I *will* need a paid bill, from Dominic, on contractor's letterhead.'

Bellarosa laughed. 'Now I got to get letterheads printed up for the guy. That's how you get into overhead.'

'Perhaps you can get a rubber stamp for his brown paper bags.'

Bellarosa was in a merry mood and laughed again. 'Okay. You need something to show capital improvement for the government if you sell or something, right? Okay. No problem. Hey, what are these cards your wife and you got with nothing on them?'

'They have our names on them,' I said. 'That's how you know they're ours.'

'Yeah. But then it just says Stanhope Hall. Where's the phone number, the zip, and all that?'

'They're calling cards,' I informed him.

'I don't understand.'

'Neither do I. It's an old custom.'

'Yeah?'

'Anyway,' I continued, back on the subject, 'I just wanted to let you know that Dominic seems very professional and was very pleasant to deal with.' So don't kill him.

'Good. He knows his bricks and cement. It's in the blood. You know? You seen the Baths of Caracalla? That stuff impresses me. They don't build like that anymore. Two thousand years, Mr Sutter. You think this shit around here is going to be around in two thousand years?'

'We'll see. Also about the horses, thank you for the offer, but we'll have them boarded while – '

'Nah. Why throw your money away? I got a stable here. It's all ready, and it's nice and close by for you. I boarded out my dog once and it died.'

'But we both went to boarding school,' I reminded him, 'and we're both still alive.'

He thought that was very funny. I don't know why I feel compelled to use my razor-sharp wit on him. Maybe because he laughs.

He was still laughing as he said, 'Hey, I got to tell my wife that one. Okay, look, Mr Sutter, I want you to know I got no hard feelings about the other thing. Business is business, and personal is personal.'

'That's true.' I looked at Susan, who was reading the local non-newspaper at the kitchen table. I said to Bellarosa, 'My wife and I would like to thank you for your help in this and for signing the variance petition.'

'Hey, no problem. I noticed that thing was in your wife's name.'

I hesitated, then replied, 'This is her property. My estate is in the shop for repairs.'

Ha, ha, ha. I hoped he was writing these down. Then, being about fifty per cent certain the phone was tapped, and Mr Mancuso or someone like him was listening in, I said distinctly, 'If the job goes over cost, I insist on paying the difference. I will not accept a low bid, even as a personal favour, Mr Bellarosa, because you owe me no favours, and I owe you no favours, and it would be good if we didn't get into owing favours.'

'Mr Sutter, you gave me some good advice the other day. I don't see no bill, so that was a favour. I'm repaying the favour.'

I knew that I should watch my words, not only because of Mr Mancuso, but because of Mr Frank Bellarosa, who, like myself, makes his living with the spoken word, and who would not hesitate to use anything I said against me later. I asked him, 'Are we all evened up on favours?'

'Sure. If you let me keep the horse shit for my garden. Hey, I got a calling card — NYNEX. But I don't understand your calling card. I'm looking at it. What's it do?'

'It's . . . it's hard to explain . . .' By now, of course, I was sorry I had played my silly joke with Dominic. But Susan actually started it. I said, 'It's like a . . . like a handshake.'

There was another silence as he processed this. He said, 'Okay. My best regards to your wife, and you have a good day, Mr Sutter.'

'And you, too, Mr Bellarosa.' I hung up.

Susan looked up from her newspaper. 'What is like a handshake?'

'A calling card.'

She made a face. 'That's not quite it, John.'

'Then *you* explain it to him.' I remained standing and picked up my coffee mug from the table. 'I don't like this.'

'You made the coffee.'

'This *situation*, Susan. Are you mentally attending?'

'Don't get snotty with me. You use too many pronouns and too few antecedents. I've told you that.'

I felt a headache coming on.

Susan said in a kinder tone, 'Look, I understand your misgivings. I really do. And I am in complete agreement that you should not do any legal work for that man. However, we can't help but have some social interaction with him. He's our next-door neighbour.'

'Next-door? We live on two-hundred-acre estates. People in Manhattan don't even know the people in the next apartment.'

'This is not Manhattan,' she informed me. 'We know all our neighbours here.'

'That's not true.'

'I know them.' Susan stood and poured herself more coffee. 'Also, I don't want to give him or anyone the impression we are . . . well, bigoted. What if he were black and we were snubbing him? How would that look?'

'He's not black. He's Italian. He's arrived. So now we can snub him because we don't like him, not because of his race or religion. That's what makes this country great, Susan.'

'But you do like him.'

There was a silence in the kitchen, and I could hear that damned regulator clock tick-tocking.

'I'm your wife, John. I can tell.'

I said finally, 'I don't dislike him.' I added, 'But he's a criminal, Susan.'

She shrugged. 'So people say. But if he weren't a criminal, would you like him?'

'Possibly.' I'm not a bigot or too much of a snob. Half my friends are Catholic. Some are Italian. The Creek is half Catholic. In fact, many of the racial, religious, and ethnic barriers around here have tumbled, which is good because in some odd way these new people have brought a new vitality to a dying world, like a blood transfusion. But as I said, you can assimilate only so much new blood, and the new blood, to continue the analogy, has to be compatible.

In my world, certain types of occupations are okay, and some are not. Also, golf, tennis, boating, and horses are taken seriously, whereas theatre, concerts, fine arts, and such are okay, but not taken seriously unless one happens to be Jewish. It is still mostly a Wasp world in form and substance, if not in actual numbers.

Catholics and Jews are okay, you understand, if they act okay. Harry F. Guggenheim, one of the wealthiest men in America in his day, a friend of Charles Lindbergh, a staunch Republican and a Jew, was okay. The Guggenheim family opened the door through which other Jews have passed.

Before the last war, Catholics with French names such as the Belmonts and Du Ponts were okay, Irish Catholics were okay if they said they were Scotch-Irish Protestants, and Italians were okay if they were counts or dukes or had names that sounded as if they could be.

These days, Italians, Slavs, Hispanics, and even blacks are accepted, though on an individual basis. The new people, the Iranians, Arabs, Koreans, and Japanese, are still hanging out there in limbo, and no one seems to know if they're going to be okay or not.

But what I do know is this: Frank the Bishop Bellarosa of Alhambra is not okay.

I said to Susan, 'It's not personal, it's business. His business.'

'I understand.' She added, 'I'm discovering that he's quite famous. Everyone knows who he is. We have a celebrity next door.'

'Lucky us.' I finished my coffee. 'By the way, if you should ever have occasion to speak to him on the phone, remember that his telephone conversations are probably being recorded by various law enforcement agencies.'

She looked at me with surprise. 'Is that true?'

'I'm not certain, but it's a strong possibility. However, since neither of you will be discussing drug buys or contract murders, I only mention that so you don't say anything that could embarrass you if it were played back someday.'

'Such as what?'

'How do I know? Such as explaining what a calling card is, or discussing a new name for Alhambra. Something like that.'

'I see. All right.' She thought a moment. 'I never even thought of his phone being tapped. I'm so naive.'

Susan uses that expression once in a while, and I suppose in the ways of the world, this sheltered little rich girl is naive. But when it comes to people, she is sharp, discerning, and confident. That's her upper-class breeding.

She asked me, 'Did you get his telephone number?'

'No.'

'Should I get it?'

'He'll give it to us when he wants us to have it.'

'When will that be?'

'When he wants us to have it.'

Susan stayed silent a moment, then asked me, 'What does he want, John?'

'I'm not sure. Respectability, maybe.'

'Maybe.'

'Maybe he still wants me for a lawyer.'

'Perhaps,' Susan responded loyally. 'You're a good attorney.'

'But there must be more to it,' I admitted.

'There certainly must be,' Susan replied. She smiled. 'Maybe he wants your soul.'

That turned out to be true, and he wasn't even satisfied with that.

CHAPTER 14

The next few weeks passed uneventfully, unless you consider the moving of a big brick stable an event. Susan had shot a roll of film that Monday morning, before the disassembly began, making sure to include Dominic and a dozen of his compatriots in many of the pictures. I still have those photos, and it is obvious that Susan, who is in some of the shots with those big labourers, was having as good a time as they were. There must be something about stables that sparks her libido.

Anyway, it was May, and everything was in bloom. Susan's vegetable garden had survived the early planting, the cold rains, and the wildflowers that still considered the terraced garden their turf, if you'll pardon the pun.

I fully expected Mr Bellarosa to stop by one day to check on his labourers, but Susan said he never came around as far as she or the Allards knew, and if he had, she added, he'd forgotten to leave his calling card. Also, Bellarosa never telephoned, day or evening, and I was beginning to think I had overestimated his interest in us.

Susan, of course, had to drive to Alhambra to get to her horses each day, but she said she never saw the don or his wife. Susan had become quite friendly, however, with Anthony, who was apparently the full-time gatekeeper, to use a nice word for a Mafia foot soldier. Susan also reported that the Alhambra stables were in bad repair but recently cleaned, and one of Bellarosa's grounds keepers helped her with watering, feeding, and such. I, myself, felt no need to ride or feed horses, and avoided Alhambra.

Another work crew from the don's estate had already dug and poured footings to accommodate the stable, which was now a growing pile of brick and slate near the pond. Bellarosa's men and vehicles used the service entrance and service roads, of course, and we saw little of them unless we took ourselves to the job sites. And the more I saw of this work – ten to twenty men, eight to ten hours a day, six days a week – the more I realized I had gotten too good a deal on the price. But in some husbandly way, I was happy to make my wife happy. Don't misunderstand me, I'm not shifting the blame for this whole episode to her. We are partners in life, and we are each aware of our responsibilities to each other, to ourselves, and for our actions. In fact, people like us are locked into cages of responsibilities and correct actions, which, while offering protection, also make us easy prey to people who understand that we can't get out of the cage.

George Allard, I should mention, was not happy about the stable business, nor did I think he would be. But he never said anything critical, of course, he just asked questions like, 'Do you think we can plant a shrubbery to fill in the empty space between the two stable wings, sir?'

Not a bad idea. With the main section of the structure gone – the most architecturally interesting part – the two long wings looked forlorn, almost institutional. I might send a picture to William Stanhope of the result of his half-assed gift to his daughter, and pass on George's suggestion of shrubs so that this place will still show well to prospective buyers. Not that I care, but George does, and it's my job.

George, incidentally, bugged the workers and hung around the job, picking up their paper trash and beer cans, and generally being a nuisance. Susan told me that she once saw one of the men playfully measuring George with a ruler as two other men were digging a 'grave'. These were, indeed, the don's men.

Anyway, I rarely went to the job site, though when I did, everyone was polite and respectful. The Italians, I find, are heavily into respect, and I guess any friend of the Padrone's is due respect. Susan visited the job at least once a day, and I had the feeling her visits were welcome. She has an easygoing manner with working men, the opposite of the Lady Stanhope routine she pulls on near peers. I watched from a distance once as she moved around the job site, and the men looked at her as if she were hot antipasto. Italian men are not terribly subtle. Many women would feel intimidated by a dozen bare-chested labourers. Susan, you know, enjoys it.

Anyway, one morning during the week, I walked to the stables to see what progress was being made. There were a half dozen men there already, though it wasn't yet eight A.M.

I watched as the men removed the last of the bricks, painstakingly chipped off the old mortar, and loaded them carefully onto a flatbed truck. What remained now of the middle section of the stables was the old wooden stalls, which would be broken up and carted away, and the cobblestone floor which would be laid in the reconstructed stable. Also, to the left was the exposed tack room, and to the right was the blacksmith shop, looking very odd with no walls or roof, and with its anvil, furnace, and bellows sitting now outdoors. I hadn't seen the blacksmith shop in fifteen years or more, and no one had used it for at least seventy years.

Overhanging the roofless shop was the old chestnut tree. I don't know if a chestnut tree near a blacksmith shop is simply tradition, or if its spreading branches had the practical purpose of providing shade for the smithy in the summer. In either case, blacksmiths built their shops under the spreading chestnut tree. But in this land of make-believe, I know that Stanhope's architects first placed the stable where they wanted it, then transplanted the giant chestnut tree in front of the blacksmith's door. Tradition, Gold Coast style.

But, anyway, I saw now that the tree was not leafed out as it should have been by this time of year. It was, in fact, dying, as if, I thought, it understood now that the last seventy years had not been simply a pause, but the end. Well, perhaps I was in a mystical mood that May morning, but the tree had looked fine last summer, and I'm good at spotting tree problems. I wish I were as good at spotting my own problems.

I walked over to one of the men and asked, 'Dominic?'

The man pointed in the general direction of Stanhope Hall, so I started off toward the mansion. As I came to the rise in the main drive, Stanhope Hall came into view, and I could see Dominic standing in front of the three-storey-high portico, looking up at the house, with his hands on his hips.

I hesitated to make the two-hundred-yard trek, especially in suit and tie, and with a ten A.M. appointment in the city, but something told me to see what Dominic was up to.

He heard me approaching on the gravel drive and came part way to meet me. 'Hello,' I said. 'You like this house?'

'*Madonna*,' he replied. 'It's magnificent.'

Coming from a native-born Italian and a master mason, I took that as a high compliment. I asked, 'Do you want to buy it?'

He laughed.

'Cheap,' I added.

'Cheapa, no cheapa I no gotta the money.'

'Me neither. Is it well built?' I inquired.

He nodded. 'It's beautiful. All carva granite. Fantastic.'

Of course, Dominic may have had only an artistic interest in the house, but I wondered how he even knew it was back here. I looked him in the eye. 'Perhaps Mr Bellarosa would like to buy it.'

He shrugged.

'Is Mr Bellarosa at home?'

Dominic nodded.

'Did he ask you to look it over?'

'No.'

'Well, you tell him it will last two thousand years.' I put my hand on Dominic's shoulder and turned him around as I pointed. 'Go through that grove of plum trees and you will see a Roman temple. You know Venus?'

'Sure.'

'She's in the temple.' I added, 'She has magnificent tits and a fantastic ass.'

He laughed a bit uncomfortably and glanced at me.

I patted his back. 'Go on. It is very beautiful, very Roman.'

He looked sceptical, but shrugged and started off toward the sacred grove. I called after him, 'And take a walk in the hedge maze.'

I headed back up the drive and paused at the terraced garden that Susan had chosen for her vegetables. The seedlings were six to eight inches high now, the rows free of weeds and wildflowers. At the base of the terrace's marble retaining wall, I saw a large empty fertilizer bag. Susan was tending her garden well.

I continued back toward my house. I wasn't completely surprised that Frank Bellarosa would be interested in Stanhope Hall. It was, after all, an Italianate house, something that would strike his fancy and fit his mental image of a palazzo more so, perhaps, than the stucco villa of Alhambra.

But Stanhope Hall is about three times the size of Alhambra, and I couldn't conceive of Bellarosa's having enough money to abandon his new house and start over again. No, I'm not naive, and I know how much money is in organized crime, but only a fraction of it can surface.

For the past few weeks, I've been sending my New York secretary to the public library to gather information on Mr Frank Bellarosa. From the newspaper and magazine articles that she has come back with, I've pieced together a few interesting facts about the reputed boss of New York's largest crime family. To wit: He recently moved into a Long Island estate. But I knew that. I also discovered that he owns a limousine service, and several florists that I suppose he keeps busy with funerals. He owns a trash-hauling business, a restaurant supply company, a construction company, with which I assumed I was doing business, and the HRH Trucking Company, who are the recorded owners of Alhambra.

Those enterprises, I suppose, are where the legitimate money comes from. But I strongly suspect, as does the DA, that Frank Bellarosa is a partner in, or owner of, several other enterprises that are not registered with the Better Business Bureau.

But could he buy Stanhope Hall? And if he did, would he live there? What was this guy up to?

I got back to my house and took my briefcase from the den.

As it was getting late, and parking at the station was tight, I asked Susan for a ride to the train.

On the way there, she asked, 'Anything wrong this morning?'

'Oh . . . no. Just deep in thought.'

We reached the train station in Locust Valley with a few minutes to spare.

Susan asked, 'When will you be home?'

'I'll catch the four-twenty.' This is commuter talk and means that, barring a major Long Island Railroad horror show, I'd be at the Locust Valley station at 5:23. 'I'll catch a cab home.' This is husband talk for, 'Will you pick me up?'

'I'll pick you up,' Susan said. 'Better yet, meet me at McGlade's and I'll buy you a drink. Maybe even dinner if you're in a better mood.'

'Sounds good.' Susan was all lovey-dovey the last few weeks, and I didn't know if that was a result of my Easter crack-up or because her dream of uniting her stables with her property was coming true. I used to understand the opposite sex when I was younger, about five or six years old, but they have become less understandable over the last forty years. I said, 'Your garden looks good.'

'Thank you. I don't know why we never planted vegetables before.'

'Maybe because it's easier to buy them in cans.'

'But it's exciting to watch them grow. I wonder what they are?'

'Didn't you mark them? They were marked on the flats.'

'Oh. What should I do?'

'Nothing. I guess they know what they are. But I can tell you, you got radicchio, you got basil, you got green peppers, and you got eggplant.'

'Really?'

'Trust me.' I heard the train whistle. 'See you.' We kissed, and I left the car and walked onto the platform as the train pulled in.

On the journey into Manhattan, I tried to sort things out

that were not making sense. Bellarosa's silence for one thing, while welcome, was slightly unnerving in some odd way.

But then I thought of those stories of Mussolini keeping the crowds waiting for hours and hours in the hot Italian sun until they were delirious with fatigue, and half insane with anticipation. And then, as the sun was setting, he would arrive, and the crowd would weep and throw flowers and shout themselves hoarse, their frenzy mounting into near hysteria.

But they were Italians. I am not. If Bellarosa was playing a psychological game, he was playing it with the wrong person.

As it turned out, I didn't have long to wait before Il Duce decided to show himself.

The train was on time, and at 5:23 I stepped onto the platform at Locust Valley, walked across Station Plaza, and entered McGlade's. This is a good Irish pub on weekends, a businessman's lunch place during the week, and on Monday to Friday, from about five to seven P.M., it is sort of a decompression chamber for strung-out commuters.

Susan was at the bar having a drink with a woman whom she introduced to me as Tappy or something, a member of the Gazebo Society who was waiting for her husband, who had apparently missed his train. By the look of the woman, her husband had been missing trains since about three P.M. There are always more than a few women in this place around this time who seem to be waiting for husbands who can't seem to catch trains. Some of these ladies do sometimes go home with some husband or other. Anyway, I made a mental note to do some research on the Gazebo Society.

Susan and I excused ourselves and moved to a high-backed booth that she had reserved. Susan had on a very nice clingy, red, knit dress that I thought was a little too dressy for early evening at McGlade's Pub, but I supposed that she didn't want to underdress with me in a three-piece pinstripe, and she did look good across the table.

As we were finishing our simple but tasteless dinner, I said, 'The chef must have your recipe for mashed potatoes.'

She smiled. 'Thank you. But I thought these were a little raw and lumpy.'

That's what I meant, but I said, 'Well, I'm going to have dessert tonight.'

'Good. How about cannoli and some espresso?'

'They don't have that in an Irish pub,' I pointed out.

'And maybe a little sambuca.'

'Oh, no, Susan. No, no, no.'

'Yes. Anna Bellarosa called me this afternoon. She would like us there for coffee. About eight. I said yes.'

'Why didn't you call me?'

'Because you would have said no, no, no.'

I realized what the dress was all about now. 'I am not going.'

'Oh, look, John, this is better than doing dinner or some beastly Easter thing with lamb parts and a house full of *paesanos*.'

'Full of what?'

'Let's go and get it over with. It's easier than being evasive for the next few years.'

'No, it isn't.'

'John, his men are moving our stable.'

'Your stable, to your land.'

'We are at a distinct disadvantage. Be civil.'

'I am not going to be bullied, bribed, or embarrassed into accepting a social invitation.' I added, ' I have a *briefcase* full of work tonight.' I patted the briefcase beside me.

'Do it for me.' She pursed those magnificent pouty lips. 'Please.'

'I'll think about it.' I grumbled and looked at my watch. It was seven-fifteen. I called the waitress over and ordered a double Scotch. We sat in the booth, me nursing my Scotch and my resentment, Susan chatting about something or other. I interrupted her in mid-sentence. 'Does Anna Bellarosa wear glasses?'

'Glasses? How would I know? I couldn't tell over the phone.'

'That's true.'

'Why?'

'Just wondering.' I added, 'I thought I saw her someplace and wondered if she would recognize me. I saw her in town. I think she's a blonde with big hooters.'

'Big what?'

'Sunglasses.'

'Oh . . . how could you know . . .? I'm confused.'

'Me, too.' I went back to my Scotch. I replayed the fountain incident in my mind a few times and decided that there was a fifty-fifty chance she would recognize me in my pinstripes. I made a mental note not to get down on all fours and spit water.

Finally, at seven-thirty, I said to Susan, 'I've been doing some background research on Mr Bellarosa. He did do time once, back in '76. Two years for tax fraud. And that is what you call the tip of the iceberg.'

Susan responded, 'He paid his debt to society.'

I nearly choked on my ice cube. 'Are you serious?'

'I heard that line in an old movie once. It sounded good.'

'Anyway, it is *alleged* that Mr Bellarosa is involved in drug distribution, extortion, prostitution, bid rigging, bribery, murder conspiracy, and so on, and so forth. Additionally, the U.S. Attorney for the Southern District of New York, Mr Alphonse Ferragamo, is investigating allegations that Mr Frank Bellarosa personally murdered a man. So, do you still want to go to his house for coffee?'

'John, I absolutely *must* see what they've done to Alhambra.'

'Will you be serious a moment?'

'Sorry.'

'Listen to me, or read my lips. Ready? I am a law-abiding citizen, and I will not abide criminals.'

'I hear you. Now listen to me, or read my lips. Ready? Tax fraud? Bill Turner, one year, suspended sentence. Bid rigging? Dick Conners, your former golfing partner, two years for highway bid rigging. Drugs? I'll name you eight users with whom we socialize. And who is that lawyer you used to sail with who embezzled clients' funds?'

Properly chastised, I bowed my head into my Scotch and finished it. 'All right, Susan, so moral corruption is rampant. It just doesn't seem so bad when it's done by the right sort of people.' I chuckled to show I was joking.

'What a pompous ass you are sometimes. But at least you know it.'

'Yes.' I stayed silent for a while and listened to the ambient sounds of the nearby bar. The shell-shocked commuters were straggling out, and the singles had not yet arrived for the mating game. It was the quiet hour. Tabby or Tappy, I noticed, was still waiting for her husband, who, if he existed at all, was probably on a business trip out of town. Like all married people, I have often considered what it would be like to be single again.

This thought, for some reason, made me recall my cousin-by-marriage, the delicious Terri, wife of the brainless Freddie, who had indeed called about her will, and we have arranged a lunch date in the city next week. Around here, when you have a suburban office and a suburban client, yet still meet in the city for lunch, then there's more going on than lunch. However, I had already resolved to stick to business with Terri. But someday, my idiotic flirtations are going to get me in trouble. Beryl Carlisle is another case in point. I've seen her at The Creek a few times since I cast lustful looks at her last month. When I see her now, she looks at me as if she wants me to look at her lustfully again. But I'm fickle. And loyal. No Terris for me, no Beryls, no Sally Anns, and no Sally Graces. My wife is the only woman that keeps my interest up. Also, I'm chicken.

Somebody had put money in the jukebox, and his or her preference was for fifties tunes. The sound of The Skyliners, singing 'Since I Don't Have You', filled the nearly empty bar. The song brought back memories of a time that I suppose was more innocent, certainly less frightening.

I reached across the table and took Susan's hand. I said, 'Our world is shrinking and changing around us, and here we are in the hills like some sort of vanquished race, performing the old rituals and observing the ancient customs, and sometimes, Susan, I think we're ludicrous.'

She squeezed my hand. 'Here's another St Jerome for you – "The Roman world is falling, but we will hold our heads erect."'

'Nice one.'

'Ready to go?'

'Yes. Do I kiss his ring?'

'A handshake will be sufficient.' She added, 'Think of the evening as a challenge, John. You need a challenge.'

This was true. Challenge and adventure. Why can't some men be content with a warm fire and a hot wife? Why do men go to war? Why did I go to Alhambra to visit the dragon? Because I needed a challenge. In retrospect, I should have stayed in McGlade's and challenged Susan to a videogame of Tank Attack.

PART III

Wide is the gate, and broad is the
way, that leadeth to destruction.

– Matthew 7:13

CHAPTER 15

Alhambra. We were late but not fashionably so. Just ten minutes. I was driving Susan's Jaguar and I pulled up to the wrought-iron gates, which were closed. There was one of those post-mounted speakers near my window, and I pushed the call button. No one spoke to me through the speaker, but the gates began slowly swinging open. Technology is eerie. But it has allowed us to live tolerably well without our maids, cooks, charwomen, and other helpful humans. And now it gives us some of the security and convenience once provided by gatekeepers and estate managers.

But Mr Frank Bellarosa had both technology and servants, for as I drove the Jag through the open gates, a large *Homo sapiens* appeared in my headbeams. I stopped, and the figure moved toward my window, his knuckles dragging along the ground. It was a human male of about thirty, dressed in a dark silk shirt open to his navel, which revealed so much hair that I could see why he couldn't button it. Over his shirt he wore a dark sports jacket, which did not cover his shoulder holster when he leaned into the car.

The man had an unpleasant face with matching expression. He said to me, 'Can I help ya?'

'Yeah. Da Suttas ta see da Bellarosas.'

He spotted Susan and smiled. 'Oh, hello, Mrs Sutta.'

'Hello, Anthony.'

'Shoulda recognized ya car.'

'That's all right.'

'Mr Bellarosa's waitin' for ya.'

This was all going on a few inches from my face, but as I didn't exist, it didn't matter. Before Susan and Anthony had quite finished with their conversation, I hit the gas and the Jag bounced over the cobblestones. I asked Susan, 'Come here often?'

'He's nicer than he looks.'

'But is he paper trained?' I proceeded slowly up the drive. I like the sound of Michelins bouncing over cobble. It sounds like you've arrived before you stop the car.

Alhambra's drive is about a quarter-mile long, straight, as I said, and flanked by tall, statuesque Lombardy poplars, all leafed out now and perfectly pruned. Between the poplars were new garden lights that cast a soft amber glow over thousands of newly planted flowers. Ahead, I could see Alhambra's white stucco walls and red tile roofs looming larger. Jaded as I am, I always get a thrill when I drive up to one of the great houses at night. Their entranceways were designed to impress kings and millionaires and to intimidate everyone else. Unfortunately, the Bellarosas did not know about the custom of turning on the lights in all the front rooms when guests were expected, so the house looked dark and foreboding as we approached, except that the front door and the forecourt were lit.

I was not in the best of moods as you may have gathered, so despite the fact that I was impressed so far, I said, 'I can see why Bellarosa would buy this place. It looks like Villa di Greaseball.'

'Don't use that word.'

'*He* uses it.'

'I don't care,' she said. 'Anyway, Spanish architecture is fine if it's done right. *Vanderbilts* lived here, John.'

'Vanderbilts lived *everywhere*, Susan.' I pulled into the circular forecourt in the middle of which was a new three-tiered marble fountain from which water spouted and cascaded, lit by multicoloured lights. 'Early Italian catering hall.'

'Cut it out, John.'

I parked the car near the fountain, and we got out and walked across the cobblestones toward the front door. I stopped and turned back toward the drive we had just come up. The view out to the road with the line of poplars running down toward the gate was also very imperial. Despite my reservations about the abundance of coloured lights, it was nice to see this great estate coming alive again. 'Not bad,' I proclaimed. Beyond the gates and across Grace Lane, I could see the DePauws' stately colonial on the hill. I waved.

'To whom are you waving?' asked Susan.

'To Mr Mancuso,' I replied.

'Who? Oh . . .' She stayed silent for some time, then asked, 'Are you ready?'

'I suppose.' I turned back toward the house. I could see that the stucco was being repaired and there was scaffolding on the south wing. Several skids of red roofing tile sat in the forecourt, and on the grass were cement pans and wheelbarrows. I asked Susan, 'Do you know how Italians learn to walk?'

'No, John. Tell me.'

'They push wheelbarrows.' It didn't sound as funny as when Bellarosa said it.

Susan asked, 'How can they push wheelbarrows if they can't walk?'

'No, you're not getting it. You see . . . never mind. Listen, I want you to get a headache at nine-forty-five.'

'You're giving me a headache now.' She added, 'And why do I always have to get a headache? People are beginning to think I have a terminal disease. Why don't you say your haemorrhoids are acting up at nine-forty-five?'

'Are we having a tiff?'

'No, you're going to behave.'

'Yes, madame.'

We walked up the white limestone steps to a massive arched oak door with wrought-iron strap hinges.

Susan indicated one of the stone columns that held up the portico. 'Did you know that these are genuine Carthaginian columns?'

'I've heard.'

'Incredible,' she said.

'Plunder,' I replied. 'You millionaires plundered the Old World to adorn your houses.'

'That is what money is for,' Lady Stanhope informed me.

'You may recall that every marble fireplace in Stanhope Hall is from a different Italian palace.'

'Yes, I remember that palace in Venice with the missing mantelpiece.' I pulled the bell chain. 'Well, time for dessert.'

Susan wasn't attending. She was intrigued with the Carthaginian columns and ran her hand over one of them. She said reflectively, 'So, two thousand years after Frank Bellarosa's ancestors plundered Carthage, Frank Bellarosa and the plunder reunite a half world away.'

'That's very philosophical, Susan. But let's stick to the subject of vegetables and cement tonight.'

Susan whispered to me, 'If you play your cards right tonight, Counsellor, you may be a *consigliere* before the evening's done.'

'I am not amused,' I informed her.

'Well, then, if he pinches my ass, I want you to slug him.'

'If he pinches *my* ass, I'll slug him. Your ass is your business, darling.' I pinched her behind, and she jumped and giggled as the heavy oak door swung open to reveal don Bellarosa himself. He was smiling. '*Benvenuto a nostra casa.*'

'*Grazie,*' Susan replied, smiling back.

'Come in, come in,' said Mr Bellarosa in plain English.

I shook hands with my host on my way in, and Susan got a kiss on both cheeks, Italian style. This was going to be a long night.

We entered a cavernous colonnaded vestibule, a sort of palm court or atrium as they say now. The floor of the court was red quarry tile, and all around the court were pink marble columns that held up stucco arches. Without gawking, I could see a second tier of columns and arches above the first, from which protruded wrought-iron balconies. All the lighting was indirect and dramatic, and covering the entire court was a dome of glass and iron filigree. More interesting, I thought, was that on both levels of the colonnade, hung amid the flowering plants and the potted palms, were dozens of cages in which were brightly plumed tropical birds, squawking and chirping away. The whole thing seemed to me a cross between a public aviary in Rio de Janeiro and an upscale florist shop in a Florida mall.

Mr Bellarosa, always the subtle and self-effacing gentleman, said, 'Hell of a front hall, right?'

'It's beautiful,' Susan said breathlessly.

Bellarosa looked at me expectantly.

I inquired, 'How do you get the bird shit out of the cages up there?'

Susan threw me a mean look, but Frank explained. It had to do with a thirty-foot ladder on wheels that he'd had specially built. Very interesting.

Bellarosa looked me over. 'You're all dressed up.'

I realized he had never seen me in my Brooks Brothers' armour, and lest he think I had dressed for him, I said, 'I came directly from work.'

'Ah.'

Bellarosa, I should mention, was dressed casually in grey slacks and a white polo shirt, which accented a new tan. I snuck a look at his shoes and saw he was wearing sandals with socks. As if this wasn't bad enough, the socks were yellow. I wanted to draw Susan's attention to Bellarosa's feet but didn't have the opportunity. Around here, incidentally, when we have people to our home, the men usually wear tie and jacket to make sure they're not comfortable. The women wear whatever women wear. In this case, I found that I was slightly annoyed about the clingy red dress. But, she looked good in red, and I was both proud and jealous.

Bellarosa had turned his attention to Susan and asked, 'How's the barn coming?'

'The . . . it's coming apart quite well,' Susan replied. 'But can they put it back together?'

Bellarosa laughed politely. Haw, haw. He said, 'Dominic knows his stuff. But he might sneak in a few Roman arches on you.'

They shared a laugh. Haw, haw. Ha, ha.

'Come on,' said Mr Bellarosa, motioning for us to follow. 'Why are we standing here?'

Because you made us stand here, Frank.

We followed our host to the left through one of the archways of the palm court and entered a long, empty room that smelled of fresh paint. Bellarosa stopped and asked me, 'What is this room?'

'Is this a test?'

'No, I mean, I can't figure it out. We got a living room, we got a dining room, we got rooms, rooms, rooms. What's this?'

I looked around. 'Not a bathroom.'

Susan interjected. 'It's . . . actually *this* is the dining room.'

Bellarosa looked at her. 'You sure?'

'Yes. I was in this house when the last family lived here.'

'That stupid decorator . . . then what's the room over there?' He pointed through an archway.

'That is the morning room,' Susan informed him.

'Morning room?'

I could have had fun with that one, but I left it alone.

'It doesn't matter,' Susan assured him. 'These old houses are used in different ways now. Whatever works best for you.'

'Except,' I said helpfully, 'you can't cook in the bathroom, or go to the bathroom in – '

'John,' Susan interrupted, 'we get the idea, darling.'

We followed Mr Bellarosa through the newly discovered dining room, then through the archway that led to the morning room. It was rather a large room, right off the butler's pantry, which in turn led to the kitchen. Bellarosa seemed not in the least embarrassed to be entertaining us in the morning room – sometimes called the breakfast room – since, until very recently, he thought it was the dining room. But to be fair, I could see how a peasant might get confused. He pulled out two chairs at one end of a long dining table. 'Sit,' he commanded.

We sat. Mr Bellarosa went to a sideboard from which he took a tray of cordials and crystal glasses that he set on the table in front of us. 'Here. Help yourselves. Don't be shy. I'll be back in five minutes.'

He went through a swinging door into the butler's pantry, and I watched his retreating back as he headed for the kitchen. The door swung closed. Five, four, three, two, one —

'John, you were a bore.'

'Thank you.' I examined one of the bottles. 'Sambuca, my dear?'

'Behave. I'm serious.'

'All right. I don't want to get us killed.' I poured us both a glass of sambuca. There was a plate of coffee beans on the tray, and I dropped a bean into each glass. I raised my glass to Susan. 'Cheers.'

'*Centanni.*'

We drank. I asked, 'What was that about the Cosa Nostra?'

'*Nostra casa*, John. Our house. Welcome to our house.'

'Oh. Why didn't he say so?' I looked around the room as I sipped my cordial. The room was oriented to the south and east like most morning rooms to catch the rising sun at breakfast. Nowadays, this room in a mansion is used for almost all family meals as it is usually located close to the kitchen, but I suspected the Bellarosas ate in the kitchen and did their formal entertaining in the breakfast room, or perhaps the basement.

The south and east walls of the room were all windows, and as I was looking out, coloured floodlights suddenly came on, illuminating the newly reclaimed gardens in hues of red, blue, and green. I said to Susan, 'The motion detectors must have picked up an approaching hit squad. If you hear gunshots, hit the floor.'

'John.'

'Sorry.'

'And keep your voice low, please.'

I grunted and poured two more. I like sambuca. It reminds me of penny liquorice sticks. I surveyed the rest of the room. The furnishings were a sort of dark, formal Mediterranean, I guess, and seemed to go with the rest of the house.

Susan, too, was evaluating the place and commented softly,

'Not bad. He said they had a decorator, but they're not using anyone around here, or I'd know about it.'

'That's why they're not using anyone around here, Susan, or you'd even know Mrs Bellarosa's bra size.'

She smiled. 'Well, whoever they're using doesn't know a dining room from a breakfast room.'

'But you straightened that out in your tactful way,' I said.

She laughed. 'What was I supposed to say?'

I shrugged and poured my second or third. I was mellowing out a bit and decided to stop baiting Susan, who was nearly blameless for our being there. I asked her, 'Did anyone buy this place after the Barretts left?'

'No. It just sat vacant.' She stayed silent a moment, then added, 'In my junior year when I was home for spring break, Katie Barrett called me from the city. I hadn't heard from her in years. I met her at Locust Valley station and drove her here. We walked around for a long while, talking about when we were kids. It was sort of sad.'

I didn't say anything.

Susan continued, 'Then a few years later, this place was infested with squatters. Some sort of hippie commune. They lived here without water or electricity, and in the winter they burned whatever wood they could find in the fireplaces. Everyone on Grace Lane complained, but the police took their time about getting them out.'

I nodded. The sixties were sort of a test to see how much anarchy the system could take, and as it turned out, the system backed off.

Susan added, 'I remember my father was angry with the police. He told them that the bank didn't take so long to get the Barretts out and they owned the place.'

Again I nodded. There was certainly a moral there, and it had something to do with authority versus power, with voluntary compliance versus come and get me, pigs. Frank understood that. I said, 'Well, maybe the police will run Mr Bellarosa off.'

'Not if he pays his taxes, John.'

'True.' I guess I came into the picture here after the hippies, and I recall that Alhambra was used a few times for designer showcases. Although I never availed myself of the opportunity to see what these strange people do to the great houses, I've been told by other men that interior decorators with cans of mauve paint and rolls of iridescent wallpaper could do more damage to a vacant mansion than a hundred vandals.

I recalled, also, that in the middle and late seventies there were a few charity functions held at Alhambra, either in the house or on the half-acre patio in the summer. If the plumbing still works in these old mansions, and if the Long Island Lighting Company is paid up front for turning on the juice, then these houses can be rented from the bank or the county on a short-term basis for charity events, tours, designer showcases, movie sets, and such. So homes that once held Vanderbilts, Astors, and the like are now available to anyone with a few bucks and a need for floor space.

Susan once went to one of these charity things without me – a Save the Beluga Caviar Sturgeon benefit or something – but this was the first time I'd ever actually been inside Alhambra, though I knew that in the first fifteen years or so it had really fallen apart – its plumbing gone, windows broken, roof leaking – becoming unfit for interior decorators and even the charity ball crowd, who will usually dance and eat anywhere for a good cause.

In most respects, Alhambra's history is not much different from a few dozen other great houses that I know of. I asked Susan, 'Didn't you tell me you were here right before Bellarosa bought this place?'

'Yes, last autumn with Jessica Reid, the realtor, and a few other ladies. We were just snooping around. Jessica had a key, though you didn't need one because half the padlocks were broken.'

'I guess none of you bought the place.'

'It was really in awful condition. There were squirrels in the house, and birds had built nests all over.'

'There are still birds in the house.'

'Well, anyway, it was sad, you know, John, because I remember it as a happy, loving home when the Barretts lived here. But now it's coming alive again. It's amazing what a few hundred thousand dollars can do.'

'Yes, it is, which is nothing. Try a few million. And he's not done yet. Maybe this place will be what brings down the don. Join the home improvement club, Frank. Bottomless pit.'

'See, you two have something in common already.'

'Yes. He told me that Mrs Bellarosa wants to move the reflecting pool six feet to the left.'

'John.'

'Sorry.' I had another drink. Maybe the sambuca wasn't mellowing me. Maybe it makes people mean. I glanced at my watch. More than five minutes had gone by, and I was beginning to wonder if Bellarosa was pulling his Mussolini routine. Then I noticed a telephone on a small stand across the room. It was an elaborate instrument with several lines, one of which was lit. The don was dialling and dealing.

I looked around the room again and saw now above the sideboard a cheaply framed print. It was Christ, his arms outstretched, with a bright-red heart – a stylized exoskeletal organ – shining from his breast. At the bottom of the print were the words *Sacred Heart of Jesus*. I drew Susan's attention to the picture.

She studied it a moment, then observed, 'It looks very Catholic.'

'Looks like a pistol target.'

'Don't be blasphemous.' Susan turned back to me. 'You see, they're religious people. A religious person wouldn't be mixed up with – ' she lowered her voice to a whisper – 'with drugs, prostitution, or any of that.'

'I never thought of that,' I said dryly.

I must admit that, despite my cavalier attitude, I was a bit concerned about meeting Mrs Bellarosa. Not that I'd done anything particularly offensive or threatening – I'd just growled at her on my hands and knees – but that might be hard to explain if she called me out on it. Or worse yet, she might be the hysterical type. I had a mental picture of her screaming and pointing at me. 'Frank! Frank! He's the one! He's the one! Kill him!'

That wouldn't get us off on the right foot at all. I realized I shouldn't have come here, but I knew I would probably bump into Mrs Bellarosa eventually. Though if enough time had been allowed to pass, she might forget what I looked like, or I could grow a moustache.

With that thought, an idea came to me. As nonchalantly as I could, I took my reading glasses out of my breast pocket and put them on. I pulled a few bottles toward me and began reading the labels.

Out of the corner of my eye, I saw Susan looking at me. She asked, 'Interesting?'

'Yes. Listen to this. "Capella is a unique liqueur, produced from the nicciole, which is a native Italian nut. Capella is produced and bottled in Torino – "'

'Are you drunk?'

'Not yet.' I poured another sambuca for both of us.

'That's enough.'

'He said not to be shy.'

We drank in silence a few more minutes. The light on the telephone was out now, but then the phone rang once and was picked up somewhere, and a line button stayed lit. I pictured the don in the kitchen, supervising coffee and dessert while he was doing business on the phone, writing names on the wall of people to be killed.

'Are you going to keep your glasses on?'

I turned back to Susan. 'Yes.'

'Why?'

'Why is it that you never painted this place?' I asked, sort of changing the subject.

She seemed momentarily confused by the sudden shift but replied, 'I suppose it was too sad. But I did take a roll of colour slides when I was here with Jessica. Mostly of the palm court. You should have seen what it looked like.'

'Tell me.'

'Well, I'll show you the slides. Why are you wearing – '

'Tell me what it looked like when you were here.'

She shrugged. 'Well . . . the glass dome was broken, and water had gotten in. There was *grass* growing on the floor, lichen, mushrooms, moss on the walls, and ferns growing out of cracks in the stucco. An incredibly good study of ruin and decay.' She added, 'I thought I might paint it from the slides.'

I looked at her. 'I do not want you selling them a painting.'

She replied, 'I thought I'd give it to them as our house-warming gift.'

I shook my head.

'They would appreciate it, John. Italians love art.'

'Sure.' I cocked my head toward the Sacred Heart of Jesus print on the wall. 'Listen, Susan, that is much too extravagant. It could take you months to complete a canvas. And you *never* gave one away before. Not even to family. You charged your father six thousand dollars for the painting of the love temple.'

'He commissioned it. This is a different situation. I *want* to paint Alhambra's palm court as a ruin. Also, we came here empty-handed, and finally, we owe him a big favour for the stable.'

'No, I'm all evened up with him on favours – I gave him free advice. And I'll give you some free advice – don't get involved.'

'*I* don't feel we have repaid the favour, and if I want to – '

'What happened to the Casa Bellarosa sign in mother-of-pearl? Better yet, why don't you bake them a cake? No – maybe that's not a good idea. How about a bushel of horse manure for his garden?'

'Are you finished?'

'No.'

But before we could have a fight, Mr Frank Bellarosa burst through the swinging door, rear end first, carrying a big electric coffee urn. 'Okay, here's the coffee.' He set the urn on the sideboard and plugged it in. 'We got espresso, too, if anybody wants.' He took the seat at the head of the table and poured himself a glass of capella. 'You try this yet?' he asked me.

'No,' I replied, 'but I know that it's made from the nicciole nut.'

'Yeah. Like a hazelnut. How'd you know that?'

I smiled at Susan and answered Bellarosa. 'I read the label.'

'Oh, yeah.' He took some roasted coffee beans out of the dish and dropped two into Susan's glass and two into mine. He said, 'You either put no beans in, or you put three. Never more and never less.'

Damned if I was going to ask him why, but Susan bit. 'Why?' she asked.

'Tradition,' Bellarosa replied. 'No – superstition,' he admitted with a soft chuckle. 'The Italians are very superstitious. The three beans are for good luck.'

'That's fascinating,' Susan said.

Actually, it was bullshit. I asked Bellarosa, 'Are you superstitious?'

He smiled. 'I believe in good luck and bad luck. Don't you?'

'No,' I replied, 'I'm a Christian.'

'What's that got to do with it?'

'Everything,' I informed him.

'Yeah?' He thought a moment, then said, 'Yeah, I know what you're saying. But with the Italians, you got evil omens, evil signs, good omens, three coins in the fountain, three beans in the sambuca, and all that stuff.'

'That's pagan,' I said.

He nodded. 'Yeah. But you got to respect it. You just don't know.' He looked at me. 'You just don't know.' He changed the subject. 'Anyway, I got no cappuccino. I bought a beautiful machine direct from a restaurant when I was in Naples a few months ago. I had it shipped, but I think it got swiped at Kennedy. The guy in Naples says he sent it, and I believe him, so I asked around Kennedy, and nobody knows nothing. Right? And the Feds complain about organized crime there. You think organized crime steals coffee machines? No. I'll tell you who steals there – the *melanzane*.' He looked at Susan. '*Capisce?*'

'The eggplants?'

Bellarosa smiled. 'Yeah. The eggplants. The blacks. And the Spanish, and the punk airport rent-a-cops. *They* steal. But whenever there's a problem anyplace, it's organized crime, organized crime. Wrong. It's *dis*organized crime that's screwing up this country. The hopheads and the crazies. *Capisce?*' He looked at both of us.

I was, finally, at a loss for words after this bizarre mono-logue, so what could I say but, 'Capish.'

Bellarosa laughed. 'Ca-peesh. Have another.' He filled my glass with sambuca, and I tried the word again, but this time in my mind. *Capisce*.

Susan, who as I said is a little naive in some ways, asked the head of New York's largest crime family, 'Did you report the theft to customs?'

'Sure.' Bellarosa chuckled. 'That's all I need. Right? The papers get hold of that story and they'd laugh me out of town.'

'What do you mean?' Susan asked.

Bellarosa shot me a glance, then said to Susan, 'They think I steal from the airport.'

'Oh, I see. That *would* be ironic.'

'Yeah. Ironic.' Bellarosa sipped his capella delicately. 'Ah. Very nice.' He looked at Susan. 'My wife's coming. She has to make sure everything is perfect. I said to her, "Relax. These are our neighbours. They're good people."' He looked at me. 'But you know how women are. Everything's a big deal. Right?'

'No comment,' I replied wisely. Just then the swinging door opened. I adjusted my eyeglasses and prepared to stand, but it was not Mrs Bellarosa. It was a homely young woman in a plain black dress and a maid's apron, carrying a tray. She placed the tray on the sideboard, then set the table with cups and saucers, silverware, napkins, and such. She turned and left wordlessly, with no bow, curtsy, or even an Italian salute.

Bellarosa said, 'That's Filomena. She's from the other side.'

'The other side of what?' I inquired.

'The other side. Italy. She doesn't speak much English, which is all right with me. But these *paesan'* pick it up fast. Not like your Spanish. You wanna get ahead in this country, you gotta speak the language.' He added, 'Poor Filomena, she's so ugly she could never marry an American boy. I told her if she stayed with me three years and didn't learn English, I'd give her a dowry and she could go back to Naples and get herself a man. But she wants to stay here and be an American. I'll have to find somebody blind for her.'

I looked at Bellarosa. This was indeed the don, the *padrone*, in his element, running people's lives for them, being both cruel and generous.

Susan asked him, 'Do you speak Italian?'

He made a little motion with his hand. '*Così, così.*' He added, 'I get by. The *Napoletan'* understand me. That's what I am. *Napoletano.* But the *Sicilian'* – the Sicilians – who can understand them? They're not Italian.' He asked Susan, 'Where did you learn Italian?'

'Why do you think I know Italian?'

'Dominic told me.' He smiled. 'He said to me – in Italian – "Padrone, this American lady with red hair speaks Italian!"' Bellarosa laughed. 'He was amazed.'

Susan smiled. 'Actually, I don't speak it well. It was my language in school. I took it because I majored in fine arts.'

'Yeah? Well, I'm going to test you later.'

And so we chatted for another ten minutes or so, and I'd be lying if I told you it wasn't entertaining. The man knew how to hold court and tell stories, and although nothing of any importance or even intelligence was said, Bellarosa was lively and animated, using more hand gestures and facial expressions in ten minutes than I use in a year. He filled everyone's glass with sambuca, then changed his mind and insisted we try amaretto, which he poured into fresh glasses while he continued to talk.

This was a man who obviously enjoyed life, which, I suppose, was understandable for a person who knew firsthand how suddenly it could be cut short. I asked him bluntly, 'Do you have bodyguards here in the house, or just Anthony out there?'

He looked at me and didn't reply for a long time, then answered, 'Mr Sutter, a man of wealth in this country, as in Italy, must protect himself and his family against kidnapping and terrorism.'

'Not in Lattingtown,' I assured him. 'We have very strict village ordinances here.'

Bellarosa smiled. 'We have a very strict rule, too, Mr Sutter, and maybe you know about it. The rule is this – you never touch a man in his own house or in front of his family. So nobody in this neighbourhood should worry about things like that. Okay?'

The conversation had turned interesting. I replied, 'Perhaps you can attend the next village meeting and assure everyone for the record.'

Bellarosa looked at me but said nothing.

Feeling reckless, I pushed on, 'So then, why do you have security here?'

He leaned toward me and spoke softly. 'You asked me what I learned at La Salle. I'll tell you one thing I learned. No matter what kind of peace treaties you got, you post a twenty-four-hour guard. That keeps everybody honest, and makes people sleep better. Don't worry about it.' He patted my shoulder. 'You're safe here.'

I smiled in return and pointed out helpfully, 'You've got double protection, Mr Bellarosa, compliments of the American taxpayer. *Capisce?*'

He laughed, then snorted. 'Yeah. They watch the front gate, but I watch my ass.' He inquired, 'So, you know about that, do you, Mr Sutter? How'd you know about that?'

I was about to reply, but I felt a kick in the ankle. A kick in the ankle, of course, does not mean, 'You're being so charming and witty, my dear, please go on.'

Susan asked our host, 'Can I help Mrs Bellarosa in the kitchen?'

'No, no. She's okay. She makes a big deal. I'll tell you what she's doing now, because I know. She's stuffing cannoli. You know, when you buy them already stuffed, they sometimes get soggy, even in the good bakeries. So my wife, she gets the shells separate, and she gets the cream or makes it herself, and she stuffs, stuffs, stuffs. With a spoon.'

Susan nodded, a bit uncertainly, I thought.

It sort of surprised me, I guess, that this man was so artless and ingenuous, and that his wife was in the kitchen of their mansion stuffing pastry with a spoon. He wasn't putting on any airs for the Sutters, that was for sure. I didn't know if I was touched or annoyed.

Anyway, the door opened again, and in came a full-bodied blonde, carrying a huge tray, heaped with enough pastries to feed a medium-size Chinese city. I could barely see the woman's face, but her arms were stretched way out so that the pastry could clear her breasts, and I knew in a flash it must be Mrs B. I stood, and so did Bellarosa, who took the tray from the woman and said, 'This is my wife, Anna.' He put the tray on the table. 'Anna, this is Mr and Mrs Sutter.'

Anna brushed her hands on her hips and smiled. 'Hello.' She and Susan shook hands, then she turned to me.

Our eyes met, our hands touched, our lips smiled, her brow wrinkled. I said, 'I'm very pleased to meet you.' She kept looking at me, and I could almost hear the old synapses making connections between her narrowed eyes. Click, click, click. She asked, 'Didn't we meet or something?'

It was the 'or something' that caused me some anxiety. 'I think I saw you in Loparo's,' I said, mentioning the name of the Italian market in Locust Valley in which I wouldn't be caught dead.

'Yeah,' she agreed without conviction. 'No,' she changed her mind. 'No . . . I'll think of it.'

If I were a real man, I would have ripped off my glasses, jumped on the floor, and revealed my true identity. But I didn't see what good would come of that.

'Why are we all standing?' asked Mr Bellarosa, who also couldn't understand why we had stood around in the palm court. 'Sit, sit,' he commanded. We sat and he poured his wife an amaretto. We all made small talk.

Mrs Bellarosa was sitting directly across the table from me, which I didn't like, but it gave me the advantage of watching for signs that she was beginning to recall her terrifying Easter morning. If you're interested, she was wearing what I think are called hostess pyjamas. They were sort of an iridescent orange, but the colour kept changing every time she moved. She wore huge triangular gold earrings, which, if connected to a shortwave radio, could have picked up Naples. Around her neck was a gold cross sort of nestled in her cleavage, and for some reason I was reminded of Christ of the Andes. Also, five out of her ten fingers held gold rings, and on each of her wrists were gold bangles. If she fell into the reflecting pool, I wondered, would the gold sink her right to the bottom, or would the buoyancy of those two big lungs keep her afloat.

I should say something about her looks. She was not unattractive. It depends on what you like. The make-up was overdone, but I could see she had fair skin for an Italian woman. Her eyes were hazel, her full lips were painted emergency-exit red, and her hair, as I said, was bleached blond. I could see the dark roots. She seemed pleasant enough, smiled easily, and had surprisingly graceful gestures. She also wore a nice perfume.

I don't know what a Mafia don's wife should look like, since you never see one in public or on the news, but I guessed that Anna Bellarosa was better looking than most. Sometimes, when I'm in my male-chauvinist-pig mode – which, thank God, is infrequent – I try to imagine if I would go to bed with a woman I have just met. So, I looked at Anna Bellarosa.

When I was in college, there were five classifications for a woman's looks, based on the maximum light you would want on in the bedroom. There were the 3-way-bulb women – 100-watt, 70-watt, and 30-watt. After that you had your night-light-only women, and finally all-lights-out.

Anna Bellarosa saw me looking at her and smiled. She had a nice smile. So, I figured, with the number of drinks I'd already had, I'd probably turn on the 70-watt bulb.

Frank Bellarosa proposed a toast: 'To our new neighbours and new friends.'

I drank to that, though I had my fingers crossed under the table. Sure I'm superstitious.

We chatted awhile, and Susan made a big deal over the pile of pastry, then complimented the Bellarosas on all the work they were doing on Alhambra. We tossed around a few names for the estate, and I suggested Casa Cannoli. Frank Bellarosa inquired about Susan's vegetable garden, and Anna asked me if I wanted to take off my coat and tie. I certainly did not. And so it went for ten or fifteen minutes, breaking the ice as they say, until finally Frank Bellarosa said, 'Hey, call me Frank. Okay? And my wife is Anna.'

Susan, of course, said, 'Please call me Susan.'

It was my turn. I said, 'John.'

'Good,' said Frank.

I've never been on a first-name basis with a Mafia don, and I was just thrilled. I couldn't wait to get to The Creek with the news.

Mrs Bellarosa stood and served the coffee from the urn. We all helped ourselves to the pastry. The coffee and pastry were superb. No complaints there.

The conversation turned to children, as it usually does with parents, whether they be kings and queens, or thieves and whores. Parenting is the great equalizer, or more optimistically, a common human bond. I loosened up a bit, partly because of Mrs Bellarosa's presence, but partly because I felt oddly at ease.

Anna Bellarosa told us all about her three sons in detail,

then added, 'I don't want them in the family business, but Tony — that's the one at La Salle — wants to be in business with his father. He idolizes his father.'

Frank Bellarosa said, 'I got into the family business through my uncle. My father said, "Stay out of that business, Frank. It's not good for you." But did I listen? No. Why? I thought my uncle was a hero. He always had money, cars, clothes, women. My father had nothing. Kids look for what you call role models. Right? I think back now, and my father was the hero. He broke his tail six days a week to put food on the table. There were five kids and things were tough. But all around us was money. In America you see too much money. The country is rich, even stupid people can be rich here. So people say, "Why can't I be rich?" In this country if you're poor, you're worse than a criminal.' He looked at me and repeated. 'In America if you're poor, you're *worse* than a criminal. You're nobody.'

'Well,' I said, 'some people would still rather be poor but honest.'

'I don't know nobody like that. But anyway, my oldest guy, Frankie, he's got no head for the family business, so I sent him to college, then set him up in a little thing of his own in Jersey. Tommy is the one in Cornell. He wants to run a big hotel in Atlantic City or Vegas. I'll set him up with Frankie in Atlantic City. Tony, the one at La Salle, is another case. He wants in.' Bellarosa smiled. 'The little punk wants my job. You know what? If he wants it bad enough, he'll have it.'

I cleared my throat and observed, 'It's not easy to bring up kids today with all the sex, violence, drugs, Nintendo.'

'Yeah. But sex is okay. How about your kids?'

Susan replied, 'Carolyn is at Yale, and Edward is graduating from St Paul's in June.'

'They gonna be lawyers?'

Susan replied, 'Carolyn is pre-law. Edward is somewhat vague. I think because he knows he will inherit a good deal of money from his grandparents, he has lost some of his motivation.'

I've never heard Susan say this to anyone, not even me; and I was a bit annoyed at her for revealing family secrets in front of these people. But I suppose the Bellarosas were so far beyond our social circle that it didn't matter. Still, I felt I had to say something in Edward's defence. I said, 'Edward is a typical seventeen-year-old boy. His main ambition at the moment is to get — is girls.'

Bellarosa laughed. 'Yeah.' He asked, 'He's graduating college at seventeen?'

'No,' I replied. 'St Paul's is a prep school.' Talking to these people was like reinventing the wheel. I asked Bellarosa, 'Did you go to La Salle on scholarship?'

'No. My uncle paid. The uncle who took me into the family business. One less mouth to feed for my old man.'

'I see.'

Anna had another wifely complaint. 'Frank spends too much time at work. He's not enjoying his new house. Even when he's home, he's on the phone, people come here to talk business. I'm always telling him, "Frank, take it easy. You're going to kill yourself."'

I glanced at Bellarosa to see if he appreciated the irony of that last remark, but he seemed impassive. For about half a second I thought I had made a terrible mistake and that Mr Frank Bellarosa was just an overworked entrepreneur.

Susan chimed in, 'John doesn't keep long office hours, but he brings home a *briefcase* full of work every night. Though he does take Saturdays off, and of course he won't work on the Sabbath.'

Bellarosa said to Susan, 'And he took Easter Monday off. Wouldn't talk business with me.' He looked at me. 'I know a couple of Protestants. They don't work Sundays neither. Catholics will work on a Sunday. What if you had a real big case in court on Monday?'

'Then,' I informed him, 'I work on Sunday. The Lord wouldn't want me to make a fool of myself in front of a Catholic or Jewish judge.'

Ha, ha, ha. Haw, haw, haw. Even I smiled at my own wit. The sambuca was finally working its magic.

Bellarosa, in fact, picked up the bottle and poured some into my coffee, then everyone's coffee. 'This is the way we drink it.'

The coffee had steamed my glasses a few times, and I wiped them with my handkerchief without taking them off, which caused Susan to look at me with puzzlement. Anna Bellarosa, too, gave me a few curious looks. So far, the conversation had not touched on the unfortunate occurrence at Alhambra on Easter morning, and I hoped that Frank Bellarosa had forgotten his request that I speak to his wife about how nice and safe this area was. But Susan asked Anna, 'Do you miss Brooklyn?' and I knew where that was going.

Anna glanced at her husband, then replied, 'I'm not allowed to say.' She laughed.

Bellarosa snorted. 'These Brooklyn Italian women – I tell you, you can move them to Villa Borghese, and they still bitch about being out of Brooklyn.'

'Oh, Frank, *you* don't have to sit home all day. You get to go back to the old neighbourhood.'

'Listen to her. Sit home. She's got a car and driver and goes to Brooklyn to see her mother and her crazy relatives whenever she wants.'

'It's not the same, Frank. It's lonely here.' A little light bulb popped on in her head. I saw it, but before I could change the subject, she said, 'How about Easter morning?' She looked at me. 'I was walking out back on Easter morning, out near the pool we got out there, and this man –' she shuddered – 'this maniac is there, on his hands and knees like an animal, growling at me.'

'Really?' I asked, adjusting my glasses.

'My goodness!' Susan exclaimed.

Anna turned to Susan. 'I ran and lost my shoes.'

Frank said, 'I told John about that. He said he never heard of anything like that before. Right, John?'

'Right, Frank.' I asked, 'So, your son Frankie lives in New Jersey?'

Susan asked Anna, 'Did you call the police?'

Anna glanced at her husband again and replied, 'Frank doesn't like to bother with the police.'

'I got my own security here,' Bellarosa reminded us. 'There's nothing to worry about.'

Anna complained, 'It's scary here at night when Frank's away. It's too quiet.'

'Perhaps,' I suggested, 'you can get a recording of Brooklyn street noises.'

Anna Bellarosa smiled uncertainly, as if this weren't a bad idea.

Bellarosa said to me, 'When you try to make them happy, or you try to compromise with them, they think you're a faggot.'

I glanced at Susan to see how she reacted to that statement and saw she was smiling. I should point out that Susan is not a feminist. The women's movement is considered by women of Susan's class to be a middle-class problem that needs middle-class solutions. Women of Susan's class have owned property, entered into contracts, and gone to college for so many generations that they don't fully comprehend what all the fuss is about. As for equal pay for equal work, they're very sympathetic to that, as they are to starving children in Africa, and have about as much first-hand knowledge of the one as they do of the other. Maybe they will have a charity ball for underpaid female executives. Anyway, I mention this because many women would be somewhat offended by Frank Bellarosa's offhanded sexist remarks. But Susan Stanhope, whose family was one of the Four Hundred, is no more offended by a man such as Frank Bellarosa making sexist remarks than I would be offended by Sally Ann of the Stardust Diner telling me that all men were alcoholics, women beaters, and liars. In other words, you had to consider the source.

Anyway, Bellarosa made another pronouncement, this one, I guess, to balance his misogynist remarks. He said, 'Italian men can't compromise. That's why their women are always mad at them. But Italian women respect their men for not compromising. But when Italian men don't agree with each other on something, and they won't compromise, then there's a problem.'

Followed, I thought, by a quick solution, like murder. I asked, 'So Frankie's in New Jersey?'

'Yeah. I helped him buy into a thing in Atlantic City. None of my sons is ever going to work for nobody. Nobody's going to be over them. They got to have men under them. Either you're your own boss in this world, or you're nobody. You're your own boss, right?'

'Sort of.'

'Nobody says nothing when you come in late, right?'

'Right.'

'So, there you are.'

And there I was, off the subject of Easter morning. It was easy to change subjects with Mr Bellarosa, who seemed to have no agenda for social conversation but switched subjects in mid sentence the moment something else popped into his head. Business, I knew, was another matter. I knew the type. And I also knew that Mrs Bellarosa was not going to bring up the subject of the Easter monster again.

And so we talked for the next hour. We finished the urn of coffee – about twenty cups – and the second bottle of sambuca. The pile of pastry had dropped about six inches. I had, early in the evening, discovered that refusing food or drink was futile. '*Mangia, mangia,*' said Mrs Bellarosa, laughing, stopping just short of shoving pastry in my mouth. 'Drink, drink,' commanded Mr Bellarosa, filling cups and glasses with any liquid within his reach.

I went to the bathroom three times and each time considered throwing up in the toilet bowl, to purge myself, Roman style. When in Rome, to paraphrase St Ambrose, use the vomitorium as the Romans do. But I couldn't bring myself to do that.

On one of my returns from the bathroom, I saw that Mrs

Bellarosa had disappeared, probably into the kitchen, and Susan and Frank were sitting at the table alone. Before she saw me, I heard Susan say the words 'palm court' and feared she was making her pitch to paint the palm court. But when I sat down, she seemed to change the topic and said to me, 'I was telling Frank about our trip to Italy a few years ago.'

'Were you?'

Mrs Bellarosa returned with Filomena, who was carrying a platter of chocolates. I sat down, trying not to get a whiff of the chocolates or of anything on the table. I asked Mrs Bellarosa for some club soda, and she said something to Filomena, who left and returned with a bottle of something called Pellegrino and a glass. I had a glass of the mineral water, belched discreetly, and felt better.

As the conversation continued without my participation, I regarded Anna Bellarosa. She was deferential toward her husband, which was, of course, what her prenuptial agreement called for. But now and then she showed some Italian fire, and the don backed off. From what I gathered during the conversation, and the dynamics I observed between them, Anna Bellarosa, as the wife of don Bellarosa, had the status of a queen and the rights of a slave. And as the mother of his children, she was the *madonna*, revered like Mary for the fruit of her womb. Anna Bellarosa had borne three sons, suckled them, saw to their religious education, then let go of them when the father was ready to take charge of their lives, and perhaps, in the case of Tony, of the boy's death. How very different this family was from my own.

I noticed, too, that Anna Bellarosa, despite her good humour and easy laugh, had sad, faraway eyes, as if, I thought, decades of worry had dimmed the sparkle that must once have accompanied the laugh.

Bellarosa stood abruptly, and I thought the evening was over, but he said, 'Anna, show Susan around the house. She wants to see the place. John, come with me.'

The four of us made our way into the dining room, and Bellarosa informed his wife, '*This* is the dining room. Where we were is the *morning* room. For breakfast. I want you to ask Susan what all these rooms are. She knows this place. You give each other a tour. Okay?'

We all went into the palm court, and Frank took my arm and led me to the staircase. He said to his wife, 'We'll meet you later in the living room. Leave the greenhouse for me to show.' He corrected himself, 'The conservatory. Right?'

I caught Susan's eye, and she smiled at me, as if to say, 'See, you're having a good time.' I know that look. What I couldn't understand was why Susan seemed to be having such a good time. The nine-forty-five headache had not materialized, and being a macho man, I didn't want to complain about my nonexistent haemorrhoids, or admit honestly that I was tired and my Anglo-Saxon stomach was churning with Irish pub food and Italian dessert. So I let my buddy, Frank, steer me up the stairs.

We both navigated the winding steps without difficulty, and I saw that Bellarosa held his alcohol as well as I did. We got to the second level and walked around the mezzanine that ran in a horseshoe shape above three sides of the palm court. Every twenty feet or so we passed a heavy oak door, and finally Bellarosa stopped at one of them and opened it. 'In here.'

'What's in here?'

'The library.'

'Are we going to read?'

'No, we're going to have a cigar.' He motioned me inside.

Against my better judgement, I stepped through the door into the dimly lit room.

CHAPTER 16

Frank Bellarosa pointed to a black leather armchair. 'Sit.' I sat. I removed my reading glasses and put them in my breast pocket. Bellarosa took the chair opposite me. I hadn't thought that he was carrying a gun, and in fact saw no reason why he should in his own house. Nor did I see any place he could be packing it under his close-fitting shirt and pants. But when he crossed his legs, I saw the bulge of an ankle holster under his right cuff. He noticed that I noticed and said, 'I'm licensed.'

'Me, too.'

'You licensed to carry?'

'No. To drive. But I don't drive in my house.'

He smiled.

It's very difficult to get a pistol licence in New York State, and I wondered how Frank the Bishop Bellarosa had managed it. I asked him, 'New York?'

'Yeah. I got a little hunting place in an upstate county. They don't ask a lot of questions up there. I can carry anyplace in the state, but not in the city. You need a special licence in the city, and they won't give me one. But that's where I need a gun. Right? The fucking crazies carry. They got a licence? No. But I can't take the chance of a gun rap. So I walk around the city clean, so any two-bit junkie can take down Frank Bellarosa.'

How unfair. I said, 'How about your bodyguards?'

'Oh, sure. But it's not the same as having your own piece. Sometimes the bodyguards take a dive on you. And sometimes they got a new boss the night before, and you don't know about it. *Capisce?*'

'Oh, yes. I didn't realize all the stress in your business.'

'Hey. You don't want to know.'

'That's right.'

Between us was a low table on which was a box of real Havana cigars. Bellarosa opened the box and held it out toward me.

'I don't smoke.'

'Come on. Have a cigar.'

I took a cigar. In truth, all Wasp lawyers know how to have a cigar, because it's part of certain rituals. I took the cigar out of its metal tube and punctured the end with a silver pick that Bellarosa handed me. Bellarosa lit me up with a gold table lighter, then lit himself up. We puffed billows of smoke into the room. I asked, 'Aren't these illegal?'

'Maybe. We'd trade with the devil in hell if we needed fire. But cigars we don't need, so fuck Cuba. Right? Horseshit.'

So much for world events. Now, the local news. 'This is your office?'

'Yeah. When I first saw it, it was all painted pink and white. Even the wood floor was painted. The real estate lady liked it. She said decorators did it for some kind of show.'

'A designer showcase,' I informed him.

'Yeah. Every fucking room looked like some fairies got loose with paintbrushes.'

I looked around. This was the library that Susan had once told me about, the one that had existed in an English manor house and had been purchased by the Dillworths in the 1920s. The shelves were all dark oak, filled with books, though I was certain they were not from the original library. There was a fireplace on one wall, and on the opposite wall were double doors that led out to the balcony from which I'd seen the light when I was riding here in April. In the centre of the large room was an oak desk with a green leather top. Behind the desk in a large alcove, sort of a secretary's station, I could make out a word processor, copy machine, telex, and fax. The Mafia had gone high tech.

Bellarosa said, 'It cost me five large to get the paint stripped off this room. Then another five for the books. Books go for ten bucks a foot.'

'Excuse me?'

'There's five hundred feet of bookshelf. Books are ten bucks a foot. So that's five large . . . five thousand.' He added, 'But I had a few books of my own.'

I guess you can talk money here. I observed, 'That saved you a few bucks.'

'Yeah. I had my school books.'

'Machiavelli.'

He smiled. 'Yeah. And Dante. St Augustine. You ever read that guy?'

'Yes. Have you read St Jerome?'

'Sure. His collected letters. I told you, those Christian Brothers made me learn.' He jumped out of his chair, went to a shelf, located a book, and opened it. 'Here's St Jerome. I like this. Listen.' He quoted, '"My country is prey to barbarism, and in it men's only God is their belly, and they live only for the present."' He shut the book. 'So what's new? Right? People don't change. If this guy wasn't a priest, he would've said, "Their belly and their cock." Men follow their cocks around and that's how they ruin their lives. You gotta think with your head, not your cock. You got to think of the future before you stick it someplace it don't belong.'

'Easier said than done.'

He laughed, 'Yeah.' He looked at his books. 'Sometimes I sit here at night with one of those old school books. Sometimes I think I should've been a priest. Except for . . . you know . . . my cock.' He added, 'Women. Jesus Christ, they drive me nuts.'

I nodded in sympathy. 'You aren't a real bishop then?'

He laughed again and put the book back. 'No. My uncle used to call me his bishop because my head was all full of this stuff from La Salle. He used to say to his friends, "This is my nephew, the bishop." Then he'd make me recite something in Latin.'

'You speak Latin?'

'Nah. Just some stuff I leaned by memory.' He went to a serving cart and took a decanter and two brandy snifters from it and put them on the coffee table. He sat again and poured a dark fluid into the glasses. 'Grappa. You ever have this?'

'No.'

'It's like brandy, but worse.' He raised his glass to me.

I picked up my glass, we clinked, and I poured it down. I should have listened to Bellarosa's veiled warning about grappa. I can drink anything, but this was something else. I felt my throat burn, then my stomach heaved, and I thought I was about to blow the coffee hour all over the cigars. Through watery eyes I saw Bellarosa watching me over the rim of his glass. I cleared my throat. 'Mamma mia . . .'

'Yeah. Sip it.' He finished his grappa and poured himself another, then held the bottle toward me.

'No, thanks.' I tried to breathe, but the cigar smoke was thick. I put my cigar out, stood, and went out onto the balcony.

Bellarosa followed, with his cigar and his glass. He said, 'Nice view.'

I nodded as I breathed the clear night air. My stomach settled down.

He pointed off in the distance with his cigar. 'What's that place? You can't see it at night. It's like a golf course.'

'Yes. Exactly like a golf course. That's The Creek.'

'Greek?'

'Creek. A country club.'

'Yeah? They play golf there?'

'Yes. On the golf course.'

'You play golf?'

'A bit.'

'I can't see that game. How's it fun?'

I thought a moment, then replied, 'Who said it was?' I added, 'They have skeet shooting, too. Do you shoot?'

He laughed.

I thought it was time to let Frank Bellarosa know I was a real man. I said, 'I'm not bad with a shotgun.'

'Yeah? I fired a shotgun once.'

'Skeet or birds?' I inquired.

He stayed silent a moment, then replied, 'Birds. Ducks.' He added, 'I don't like shotguns.'

'How about rifles?' I asked.

'Yeah. I belong to a club in the city. The Italian Rifle Club. It's a social club. You probably heard of it.'

Indeed I had. An interesting establishment in Little Italy, some of whose members had never fired a sporting rifle in their lives, but who found the rifle range in the basement convenient for pistol practice. I asked, 'What type of rifle do you own?'

'I don't remember.'

I tried to recall how the Colombian drug king was murdered. Pistol, I think. Yes, five bullets in the head from close range.

'You feel better?' he asked me.

'Yes.'

'Good.' Bellarosa sipped his grappa, smoked his contraband cigar, and surveyed his kingdom. He pointed again with the cigar. 'I found a fountain over there and a statue of Neptune. That's where that guy scared the hell out of Anna. You ever seen that?'

'Yes. I've ridden all over this land.'

'That's right. Anyway, I fixed that whole place up. The pool, the fountain, the statue. I put a statue of the Virgin there, too, and had the whole thing blessed by a priest friend of mine. You gotta see it.'

'The priest blessed the statue of Neptune?'

'Sure. Why not? Anyway, there was these Roman ruins there, too. Broken columns and all. The landscape guy said it was built like that. That right?'

'Yes.'

'Why did they build a ruin?'

'That was popular once.'

'Why?'

I shrugged. 'Maybe to remind themselves that nothing is for ever.'

'Like, *sic transit gloria mundi.*'

I looked at him. 'Yes. That's it.'

He nodded thoughtfully and drew on his cigar.

I gazed out over Alhambra's acres. A half moon was high in a brilliantly clear sky, and a soft breeze blew in from the Sound, bringing with it the smell of the sea, as well as the perfume of May flowers. What a night.

Bellarosa, too, seemed to appreciate the moment. 'Brooklyn. Fuck Brooklyn. I go to Italy when I want to get away. I got a place in Italy, outside of Sorrento.'

'I've been to Sorrento. Where is your place?'

'I can't say. You know? It's a place where I might have to go someday. Only five people know where it is. Me, my wife, and my kids.'

'That's smart.'

'Yeah. You got to think ahead. But for now, I like it here. Brooklyn's finished.'

So was the Gold Coast, but that wasn't so apparent to Frank Bellarosa, who didn't comprehend that he was part of the problem.

He added, 'We had a nice house in Brooklyn. An old brownstone. Five storeys. Beautiful. But it was attached, and the yard was too small to have a big garden. I always wanted land. My grandparents were peasants. It's their old farm that I bought from the people who owned it. But I let the people farm the land for free. I keep the farmhouse. It's white stucco like this, with a red roof. But smaller.'

We both stayed silent a moment, then he said, 'You got a whole temple over there. Dominic said you showed him the temple. You got Venus over there.'

'Yes.'

'You people pagans over there?' He laughed.

'Sometimes.'

'Yeah. I'd like to see that temple.'

'Sure.'

'I'd like to see the inside of the big mansion.'

'Do you want to buy it?'

'Maybe.'

'Half a million.'

'I know that.' He added, 'You could have said more.'

'No, I couldn't, because the price is half a million. With ten acres.'

'Yeah? How about the whole place?'

'About twenty million for the land.'

'*Madonn*'! You got oil on that place?'

'No, we got dirt. And there's not much of that left around here. Why would you want another estate?'

'I don't know . . . maybe build houses on the land. Can I make money if I build houses?'

'Probably. You should be able to make a profit of five or six million.'

'What's the catch?'

'Well, you have to get permission to subdivide the property.'

'Yeah? From who?'

'Zoning people. But the neighbours and the environmentalists will hold you up in court.'

He thought awhile, and I knew he was trying to figure out who had to be paid off, who had to be offered the best deal, and who had to be actually threatened. I said, 'My wife's parents own the estate. Do you know that?'

'Yeah.'

'That doesn't include my house, and there is a stipulation in any contract that my gatekeeper and his wife live in the gatehouse rent free until they die. But the estate does come with the statue of Venus and she has nice tits.'

He laughed. 'I heard.' He added, 'I'll think about it.'

'Fine.' I thought about William Stanhope sitting down with a Mafia don at the house closing, and I decided I wouldn't take a fee for the pleasure of handling that. Actually, I wouldn't handle it. I still have to live around here. William and Charlotte visit friends here now and then, attend weddings and funerals, and all that. They have kept their Creek membership and on occasion stay in one of The Creek's cottages that are used by retired gentry who return from time to time. But if Frank Bellarosa bought Stanhope Hall, William and Charlotte would never again set foot on the Gold Coast. I liked this possibility, despite my reservations about being surrounded by mafiosi and FBI agents with cameras. I asked Bellarosa, 'How did you happen to find Alhambra?'

'I got lost.' He laughed. 'I was on the expressway, going to a restaurant in Glen Cove. I had to meet a guy there. My stupid driver takes the wrong exit, and we're all over the place trying to find Glen Cove. I notice all these big houses, and we go up

231

the road here and I'm pissed. But then I see the gates of your place there, and I tell the jerk to slow down. Then I see this place, and the house reminds me of the big villas near the water in Sorrento. You know? I can see that the place don't look lived in, so after my lunch thing, I go to a real estate office. I don't know where this place is, but I explain what it looks like. You know? So it takes a week for this dumb real estate lady to get back to me, but she sends me a picture. "Is this it?" Yeah, so I call her. How much? She tells me. It's owned by the bank, and the tax people got to be taken care of, or something. The bank just wants to dump it. So I pay the bank, pay the taxes, and some people named Barrett get some money, and I'm out about ten mill. *Madonn' mia.* But I like the poplar trees. Then I show it to my wife, and she don't like it. Jesus Christ – '

'You mean you bought this place without your wife seeing – ?'

'Yeah. So I say to her, "I like it, so you better learn to like it." She starts in, "It's a wreck, Frank! It's filthy, Frank!" Fucking women can't picture what things are going to look like. Right? So I get the greaseballs on the place and they bust their asses all winter and I take Anna out and she's crying all the way out. But I figure, soon as she sees it, she'll stop crying. But no, she still hates it. It's too far from her crazy mother and her crazy sisters. "Where's the stores, Frank? Where's the people?" Blah, blah, blah. Fuck the stores, fuck the people. Right?' He looked at me. 'Right?'

'Right. Fuck 'em.'

'Right.' He finished his grappa and drew on his cigar, then flipped the ash over the balustrade. '*Madonn'*, they drive you nuts. She misses her church. She used to walk to church three, four times a week and talk to the priests. They were all Italian. Some of them were from the other side. The church here is very nice. I went a few times. St Mary's. You know the place? But the priests are all Micks and one Polack, and she won't talk to them. You believe that shit? A priest's a priest, for Christ's sake. Right?'

'Well . . .'

'So what I want is, I want Susan to show Anna the ropes around here. You know? Take her around, meet some people. Maybe you'll show me that place over there. The Creek. If I like it, I'll join up.'

My stomach heaved again. 'Well – '

'Yeah. It just takes time. You talk to Susan.'

I had a maliciously bright thought. 'Susan belongs to the Gazebo Society. She can take Anna to the next meeting.'

'What the hell is that?'

Good question, Frank. I explained about the Victorian clothes and the picnic hampers.

'I don't get it.'

'Me neither. Let Susan explain it to Anna.'

'Yeah. Hey, look down there.' He pointed with the stub of his cigar.

I looked down at the expansive Spanish patio, lit with amber post lights.

'You see that? Next to the barbecue? That's a pizza oven. I had that built. I can make pizza right out there. I can bake ziti, I can heat stuff up. Whaddaya think?'

'Very practical.'

'Yeah.'

I glanced at Bellarosa. He had put his glass on the ledge and had ground out his cigar. He had his arms folded across his chest now as he surveyed the huge patio, the size of a piazza, below him. He caught me looking at him and laughed. 'Yeah. Like this.' He thrust his chin out in a passable impersonation of Mussolini. He looked at me. 'Is that what you're thinking? Frank Bellarosa thinks he's Il Duce. Right?'

'No comment.'

He thrust his hands into his pockets. 'You know, all Italians want to be Il Duce, Caesar, the boss. Nobody wants to be under nobody else. That's why Italy is so fucked up, and that's why people like me have people like Anthony around. Because every wop with a gun, a grudge, and fifty cents' worth of ambition wants to knock off the emperor. *Capisce?*'

'Do you trust Anthony?'

'Nah. I don't trust nobody but family. I don't trust my *paesanos*. Maybe I can trust you.'

'And you sleep well at night?'

'Like a baby. I told you, nobody has an accident in their own house.'

'But you carry a gun in your own house.'

He nodded. 'Yeah.' He stayed silent awhile, then said, 'I got some problems lately. I take precautions. I've got to get the bugs worked out of the security here.'

'But you just said your house is sacrosanct.'

'Yeah. But you got your Spanish now, and you got your Jamaicans, your Asians. They got to learn the rúles here. They got to learn that when you're in Rome, you do as the Romans do. Who said that? Saint Augustine?'

'Saint Ambrose.'

He looked at me and our eyes met. Here was a man, I suddenly realized, who had a major problem.

He said, 'Let's go inside.' He went back into the library and sat in his chair. He poured himself another grappa as I sat across from him.

My eyes fell on the school books on the shelf behind him. I couldn't make out the titles, but I was reasonably certain that most of the great thinkers, philosophers, and theologians of Western culture were up there, and that Frank Bellarosa had absorbed their words into his impressionable young mind. But he had apparently missed the essential message of the words, the message of God, of civilization, and of humanity. Or worse, he understood the message and had consciously chosen a life of evil, just as his son was going to do. How utterly depressing. I said to him, 'Well, thanks for the drink.' I looked at my watch.

He seemed not to hear me and sat back in his chair, sipping his drink, then said, 'You probably read in the papers that I killed a guy. A Colombian drug dealer.'

This was not your normal Gold Coast brandy-and-cigars

talk and I didn't know quite how to respond, but then I said, 'Yes, I did. The papers made you a hero.'

He smiled. 'Shows how fucked up we are. I'm a fucking hero. Right? I'm smart enough to know better.'

Indeed he was. I was impressed.

He said, 'This country is running scared. They want a gunslinger to come in and clean up the fucking mess. Well, I'm not here to do the government's job for them.'

I nodded. That was what I had told Mr Mancuso.

Bellarosa added, 'Frank Bellarosa works for Frank Bellarosa. Frank Bellarosa takes care of his family and his friends. I don't want nobody thinking I'm part of the solution. I'm definitely part of the problem. Don't you ever think otherwise.'

'I never did.'

'Good. Then we're off on the right foot.'

'Where are we going?'

'Who knows?'

I picked up my glass and sipped at the grappa. It didn't taste any better. I said, 'Alphonse Ferragamo doesn't think you're a hero.'

'No. That son of a bitch has a hard-on for me.'

'Maybe you embarrass him. I mean as an Italian American.'

Bellarosa smiled. 'You think that's it? Wrong. You got a lot to learn about Italians, my friend. Alphonse Ferragamo has a *personal* vendetta against me.'

'Why?'

He thought a moment, then said, 'I'll tell ya. I made a fool out of him in court once. Not me personally. My attorney. But that don't make a difference. This was seven, eight years ago. Ferragamo was the U.S. prosecutor on my case. Some bullshit charge that wouldn't hold. My guy, Jack Weinstein, got the jury to laugh at him, and Alphonse's balls shrunk to little nicciole — hazelnuts. I told Weinstein he fucked up. You don't do that to an Italian in public. I knew I'd hear from Ferragamo again. Now the jackass is the U.S. Attorney for the Southern

District of New York, and I got to live with him or move.'

'I see.' And all this time I thought Alphonse Ferragamo was a dedicated public servant. In truth, I didn't completely believe Frank Bellarosa's analysis of Ferragamo's motives. Thinking that I'd heard enough, I said, 'I have an early day tomorrow.'

Bellarosa ignored this and said, 'Ferragamo can't get anything on me, so he tells the papers that I hit this Colombian guy, Juan Carranza.'

My eyes rolled a bit. I said, 'I really can't believe that a U.S. Attorney would frame you.'

He smiled at me as though I were simple minded. 'Not to frame me, Counsellor. You really got a lot to learn.'

'Do I?'

'Yeah. You see, Ferragamo wants to get the Colombians on my case. *Capisce?* He wants them to do his dirty work.'

I sat up in my chair. 'Kill you?'

'Yeah. Yeah.'

I found this even harder to believe. I said, 'Are you telling me that the U.S. Attorney is trying to get you murdered?'

'Yeah. You don't believe that? You a Boy Scout or what? You salute the flag every morning? You people got a lot to learn.'

I didn't reply.

Bellarosa leaned toward me. 'Alphonse Ferragamo wants my ass *dead*. He don't want my ass in court again. He is a very pissed off *paesan'*. *Capisce?* He stewed for eight fucking years waiting for his chance to get even. And if I get hit by the Colombians, Ferragamo will make sure everybody on the street knows he was behind it. Then he's happy and he has his balls back.' He looked me in the eye. 'Okay?'

I shook my head. 'Not everyone thinks like you do. Why don't you give the guy credit for just doing his job? He thinks you killed somebody.'

'Bullshit.' He leaned back and twirled his glass.

'I have to go.'

'No. Just sit there.'

'Excuse me?'

He looked at me and I looked back. I finally saw don Bellarosa for a second or two. But then Frank was sitting there again. It must have been the light. He said, 'Let me finish, Counsellor. Okay? You're a smart guy, but you don't have the facts. Hey, I don't care if you think I hit this Colombian guy. But there's two, three, four sides to everything. A smart guy like you sees two sides, maybe three. But I'll show you another side, so when you walk out of here, you'll be a better citizen.' He smiled. 'Okay?'

I nodded.

'Okay. So when those assholes in Washington made Ferragamo the U.S. Attorney here, they knew what they were doing, for a change. They got it all figured out, those smart guys in the Justice Department. They want the Colombians to hit me, then my friends start hitting the Colombians, and the undertakers are happy, and the Feds are happy. The *melanzane* are not happy because now they have to go back to cheap wine because the white stuff is cut off while the stiffs are piling up. Understand? This talk make you uncomfortable?'

'No – '

'So the next time you talk to Mancuso out there, you tell him what I just told you. Mancuso is okay for a cop. He's got nothing against me personally, and I got nothing against him. We treat each other with respect. He believes in the law. I respect him for that even if it's stupid. He don't want a shooting war out there on the streets. He's a very responsible man.'

'You want me to pass on this conversation to Mancuso?'

'Sure. Why not? Let him go to Ferragamo and tell him that Bellarosa is onto his game.'

'You've been reading too much Machiavelli.'

'You think so?'

'Are you suggesting that not only Ferragamo, but the U.S. Attorney General and the Justice Department in Washington are in on a conspiracy to have you murdered and provoke a gang war?'

'Sure. Why do you think Alphonse is still here? It's so fucking obvious what he's up to with this Carranza shit. If Justice don't yank the guy out of here or tell him to cool it, then Justice is in on it. Right?'

'Your logic – '

'Then with the two biggest players blasting away at each other, the Feds take care of the Jamaicans and the other *melanzane* down there in the islands. Then they go for the Asians. Divide and conquer. Right?'

I shrugged. 'I do house closings.'

'Yeah. Let's say you buy what I'm saying. How do you feel about it as a good citizen?'

What I felt was distressed to think that the forces of law and order in this country were so desperate that they had to stoop to Bellarosa's level to get rid of Bellarosa. But I said, 'As a good citizen, I would be . . . angry to think the government would provoke a dangerous gang war.'

'Sure. But you kinda like the idea. Right? The spics and the wops finally knocking each other off.'

'No.'

'Bullshit.'

'No comment.' I asked, 'Why don't you go to the newspapers if you believe what you're saying?'

He laughed. 'Sure.'

'They'd print it.'

'You bet your ass they would. They print it when I fart. But you don't go public with your problems in my business. You shoot your mouth off to the press, and you piss off *everybody*, including your friends who don't even admit there's such a thing as the Mafia. You start talking to the press about your enemies, and your friends will kill you.'

'Why are you telling me this?'

'Because you're a lawyer.'

'I'm not *your* lawyer.' I added, 'Anyway, it's not a lawyer you need. You need bodyguards.' Or a psychiatrist.

'Yeah. But I need some outside advice. I listened to my friends, my counsellors, to Jack Weinstein. Now I want to hear from somebody who sees things different from the people around me.'

'You want my advice? Retire. Go to Sorrento.'

'You don't retire in this business. Did any of the Caesars retire? You can't set everything straight with the people you pissed off, you can't raise the dead, you can't go to the government and say, "I'm sorry, and I'm paying the taxes I cheated on and giving back all the businesses I bought with the illegal money." You can't let go of the tiger, because he'll turn and eat you. You got to stay on the tiger and keep the power in your hands.'

'No. You can go to Sorrento.'

He shrugged. 'Maybe I like what I do. Keeps me busy.'

'You like the power.'

'Sure. Sorrento is for when I'm old. When I'm tired of power, business, women. I got a few years yet.'

'Maybe not.'

He looked at me. 'I don't run. The spics are not running Frank Bellarosa off. The Feds are not running Frank Bellarosa off. *Capisce?*'

'Now I do.'

We both sat there a few minutes. I had the impression he was waiting for me to say something, to come up with some advice. As an attorney, I'm in the advice business, but I'm not predisposed to giving free and friendly advice. I said, 'Are we finished?'

'Almost. Here's the thing. Ferragamo can't be shooting his mouth off to the press that I'm a suspect in the murder of Juan Carranza, and let it go like that. Right?'

'Right.'

'He's got to follow up with a grand jury investigation.'

'Correct.'

'So, what I'm thinking is I want you to handle this for me.'

'If I wouldn't handle a real estate deal for you, why would I represent you in a criminal matter?'

'Because one thing is money, the other is justice.'

He didn't choke on that last word, but I almost did. I shook my head. 'I don't handle criminal matters. I'm not qualified.'

'Sure you are. You're a lawyer.'

'What kind of evidence is Ferragamo going to present to a grand jury to get you indicted?'

'He don't have shit. But you ever hear that expression – "a New York grand jury will indict a ham sandwich"? You hear that?'

'Yes.' New York grand juries are sort of like Star Chambers; twenty-three upright citizens sit in secret sessions, and the person under investigation is not present and neither is his attorney. So, without any evidence except what is presented by the government, the grand jury usually votes to indict. It was a safe bet to say that Frank Bellarosa would be indicted. I said, 'You think Ferragamo is just harassing you with this indictment?'

'Yeah. A regular jury won't convict me, because Ferragamo's got no evidence for them. So Frank Bellarosa versus the United States is not getting to trial. But meanwhile, Ferragamo's calling press conferences. He loves fucking press conferences. He's telling everybody that the Mafia is pushing out the Colombians, the Jamaicans, blah, blah, blah. That's bullshit. We all got our own thing. Then he says, "Bellarosa personally hit Juan Carranza to show them spics a lesson!" Understand? So the Colombians get their balls in an uproar – they get all macho. Christ, they're worse than Italians. Now they want to settle this *mano a mano*. Carranza was a big man with them. Okay, so now I got to worry about my own people, too. Understand? Because they don't want a fucking bloodbath, because they're all fat and soft. The South Americans are hungry and hard. They're the new guys and they work harder. They don't have the fucking brains they were born with, but they manage to get things done. Okay, maybe they're too stupid to get at me. You know? So what do they do? They go to my friends and they say, "Hey, let's settle this before Frank goes to trial, before people start getting hurt. We all got enough problems and we don't need this shit with Bellarosa." So maybe my guys say, "We'll take care of Frank." You see? The sons-of-bitches would give me up to save their own asses. Even though they know I didn't hit Carranza. Ten, twenty years ago, an Italian would say to a spic, "Fuck you. Get out of here before I feed you your balls for lunch." But things are different now. There's a whole new world out there. Understand?'

That, I understood. Now I discover that even the Mafia are having trouble adapting to this new New World. I said, 'That's absolutely fascinating, Frank. And I don't really see any way out for you.'

He laughed. 'Maybe something will come into your head. I need a very upright lawyer to go talk to Ferragamo. He's the key. He's got to call one of his press conferences and say that he has new evidence about who hit Carranza, or say he's got no evidence at all. You talk to him about that.'

'But maybe I don't believe your side of this.'

'You will when you see Ferragamo's face after you tell him I know what he's up to.'

Bellarosa, I realized, was a man who believed in his instincts. He would not need hard evidence, for instance, before he ordered the murder of someone he suspected of disloyalty. Like a primitive tribunal, all that Bellarosa required was the look of guilt, perhaps a word or phrase that seemed somehow wrong. And in the case of Alphonse Ferragamo, Frank Bellarosa first figured out a motive, then presumed the man guilty of the crime. I don't deny the value of instinct – I hope I use my instincts in court, and police use instinct every day on the streets. But Frank Bellarosa, whose good instincts had kept him free and alive, perhaps put too much faith in his ability to spot danger, tell friends from enemies, and to read people's minds and hearts. That was why I was sitting there; because Bellarosa had sized me up in a few minutes and decided I was his man. I wondered if he was right.

Bellarosa continued, 'The New York State Attorney General, Lowenstein, don't even want a piece of this case. I hear from some people close to him that he thinks it's bullshit. What's that tell you, Counsellor?'

'I'm not sure, and I still don't do criminal work.'

'Hey, you might have fun. Think about it.'

'I'll do that.'

'Good.' He settled back in his chair. 'Hey, I'm doing that real estate deal next week. I got that firm in Glen Cove you said. They gave me this guy Torrance. You know him? He any good?'

'Yes.'

'Good. I don't want no screw-ups.'

'Real estate contracts and closings are fairly simple if you pay attention to detail.'

'Then you should've done it, Counsellor.'

I regarded Bellarosa a moment. I couldn't tell if he was annoyed or just considered me a fool. I said, 'We've been through that.'

'Yeah. But I want you to know you're the first guy who ever turned down that kind of money from me.'

'That's discouraging.'

'Yeah? Well, people have turned down outright bribes. But never a legitimate fee. It *was* legit.'

'We've been through that, too.'

'Yeah. About the grand jury thing, I know you don't drop for money, but I'll pay you a flat fifty for talking to Ferragamo and another fifty if a grand jury isn't convened.'

'If I did criminal work, I'd get three hundred an hour, double for courtroom time. I don't take cash rewards if you're not indicted or convicted, and I don't give the money back if you are.'

Bellarosa smiled at me, but it was not a nice smile. 'I gotta tell you, some of your wisecracks are funny, some are not.'

'I know.'

'You got balls.'

'I know that, too.'

He nodded. 'I got too many guys around me kissing my ass, and any one of them would stick a knife in my back.'

'I feel sorry for you.'

'Hey, it's part of life.'

'No, it isn't.'

'My life. But I also got guys around me who respect me. People who don't kiss my ass, but kiss my hand.'

'Does anybody *like* you?'

He smiled. 'I don't really give a shit.'

'Work on that, Frank.'

He looked at me and said, 'Something else I gotta tell ya. Your people been here three hundred years, you said. Right? So you figure everybody who got here after you is uninvited company or something. But my family in Italy goes back a thousand years in that town outside Sorrento. Maybe they go back two thousand years to Roman times. Maybe one of my ancestors was a Roman soldier who invaded England and found your people wearing animal skins and living in mud houses. *Capisce?*'

'I understand enough history to appreciate the glory of Italian civilization, and you may well take pride in that heritage. But what we're discussing at the moment, the Mafia, is not one of Italian civilization's greatest contributions to Western culture.'

'That's a matter of opinion.'

'Well, it's most people's opinion.'

Bellarosa seemed deep in thought for a full minute, then said, 'Okay. Now you got to make a big decision, because you're jerking me around and yourself around. So you stand up, you turn around, and you go out that door. You get your wife and you leave, and you'll never hear from me again. Or, you have a drink with me.'

So. All I had to do was stand up and leave. Then why was I still sitting? I regarded Frank Bellarosa a moment. What had I learned in the last few hours? Well, I'd learned that Bellarosa was not only smart, but also more complex than I would have imagined. Also, to give Susan credit for an accurate first impression, Bellarosa *was* interesting. So, maybe this was Susan's gift to me; this was my challenge. I picked up my glass. 'What's this made of?'

'Grape. It's like brandy. I told you.'

We touched glasses, we drank.

He stood. 'Let's go find the women.'

CHAPTER 17

We left the library, and as we walked along the mezzanine, I said, 'Why don't you go right to the Colombians and explain that you're being set up?'

'Caesar does not go to the fucking barbarians and explain things. Fuck them.'

I could see that my straightforward Anglo-Saxon logic was not what the situation called for, but I said, 'A Roman emperor *did* go to Attila the Hun to talk peace.'

'Yeah. I know that.' We started down the sweeping stairs, and Bellarosa said, 'But what good did it do him? Made him look bad, and Rome got attacked anyway. Look, when people go for your balls, they're saying you got balls. As soon as they think you got no balls, they treat you like a woman. You might as well be dead.'

'I see.' Obviously my first advice as *consigliere* wasn't cutting it. I said, 'But Ferragamo is banking on that. He knows you won't go to the Colombians.'

'This is true. Only another wop could have understood that.'

'So? If you won't meet with the Colombians yourself, send somebody.' *But not me.*

'Same thing. Forget it.'

We walked across the palm court. I found this interesting as an intellectual challenge and on that basis would have liked to come up with a solution. But I also realized there was more to my interest in his problems than a mental exercise. I said, 'Tell the Colombians to come to you. Demand a meeting on your terms.'

He turned to me and smiled. 'Yeah? Maybe they'll come. But any way you cut that, it's me going to them to ask them for a break. Fuck them. If they think they're big enough to take me on, let them try. Maybe they need a lesson in respect.'

Mamma mia, this guy was tough. I recalled what he had said in my office. Life is war. And what he had said in the morning room. Italian men don't compromise. That about covered it. But I had a last solution. 'Find out who killed Carranza and deliver the guy to the State Attorney General, Lowenstein.'

'I don't do cop work.'

'Then deliver him to the Colombians.' I can't believe I said that.

'I can't do that.'

'Why not?'

'Because I already know who killed Carranza. The cops killed him. The fucking DEA – the Drug Enforcement Agency. They put five slugs in his head – mob style, like they say.'

'How do you know that?'

'I know the guys who did it. And it was no vigilante thing, if you're thinking they're good guys. It was no vendetta for a DEA guy who got hit in Colombia. They iced Carranza because he screwed them on a deal.'

God, this *was* depressing. What a world this man lived in. Right here, in America. Of course I'd read about it. But it's not the same as hearing it live. I asked, 'Why don't the Colombians know this?'

'Because they're stupid. They got no contacts, they got no sources. They're fucking outlaws. I got all kinds of sources – press sources, police sources, political sources, court sources.' Bellarosa stopped walking and put his hand on my shoulder. 'You know, the thing that the government calls the Mafia – the Sicilians, the Neapolitans – we've been in America for a hundred years. Christ, we're part of the establishment. That's why we're fat ducks now for the assholes in the Justice Department. But let me tell you something. Compared to these new people, we're nice guys. We play the fucking game. We don't hit cops, we don't hit judges, we don't go into people's houses and massacre families. We make contributions to the right people, we give to the Church, we provide services. If you run this kind of thing right, it don't have to be messy. You take your South Americans and your *melanzane* from the islands, they go right for the guns. Half of these assholes are on the junk they sell. But does Ferragamo go after these dangerous people, these crazies? No. The shithead wastes everybody's time and money going after his *paesanos*, because he can get to them, because he understands them. And he's got ambitions, this man. He wants to make a name. *Capisce?* And he knows we won't take him out. Is Ferragamo good for the public, the taxpayers? No. Well, fuck him. Maybe some *melanzane* will slice his throat for his watch someday. Meanwhile, we do business like nothing's wrong. Let him or the Colombians make the first move. Right?'

'You're absolutely right.'

'Good. Let's go talk to the women.' He took my arm and led me between two columns, then through an archway into the living room.

The room was about eighty feet long and half as wide, with a beamed cathedral ceiling. The walls were white stucco and the windows were arched. Unfortunately, this was not the living room. It was just too big, even for a great house. This must once have been the ballroom. At the far end was a grouping of chairs where Susan and Anna sat, looking very tiny and alone.

Bellarosa and I walked the eighty feet to the furniture, and I remembered to put my glasses back on. I sat before Bellarosa could say, 'Sit.' Bellarosa remained standing.

Susan addressed Bellarosa. 'The house is beautiful.'

Bellarosa smiled. 'Yeah.'

Susan asked both of us, 'What were you talking about all that time?'

I replied, 'Machiavelli.'

She smiled at Bellarosa. 'John's not much of a talker. But he pays attention.'

'Your husband's a smart man.'

Susan beamed proudly. Well, no, actually, she crossed her legs and sat back.

Anna addressed her lord and master. 'Susan knew the people who lived here before. The Barretts. Susan used to sleep in the guest room.'

Bellarosa smiled at Susan. 'It's yours if you have a fight with your husband.'

Susan smiled in return. Why wasn't I smiling?

Anna said to Frank, 'Susan knows some of the history here, Frank. The real estate lady wasn't lying about the Vanderbilts.'

'She lied about the plumbing,' Bellarosa said.

Anna had more news. 'This isn't the living room, Frank.'

'Jesus Christ.'

'It's a ballroom.'

'What?'

'And the room where we got the TV is the drawing room.' She looked at Susan. 'Tell him what that is.'

Susan explained, 'That's the room to which guests withdraw after dinner. But it's fine as a TV room.'

And so Susan gave the Bellarosas a crash course in great-house floor plans. Interestingly, however, she did it with some humour and self-effacement as if it were all very silly, thus not making the Bellarosas feel that they were vulgar half-wits who had no business living in a house they couldn't understand. This was a new Susan.

Meanwhile, I tried to figure out how I started the evening in an Irish pub and ended it as part of the Bellarosa family. Obviously none of this was happening. I'd wake up at Locust Valley station, get off the train, and try it again.

Bellarosa said to Susan, 'Come on. I'll show you my pride and joy. The conservatory.'

This didn't seem to include me, so I remained seated as Susan stood. Lady Stanhope and Squire Bellarosa walked off. I turned to Anna, and we smiled at each other.

She shook her finger at me. 'I *know* you from someplace.'

'Have you ever been to Plato's Retreat?'

247

'No . . .'

'I have a familiar face. Or maybe you saw my picture in the post office or the newspapers.'

'You in the papers?'

'The local paper sometimes.' I added, 'I recognized your husband, for instance, the first time I saw him in person. I felt I knew him from seeing him so many times on TV and in the papers.'

She looked embarrassed, and I felt just a bit sorry I'd said that. Henceforth, I would assume that Anna Bellarosa was a civilian and I would treat her as such unless I found out otherwise.

She said, 'Maybe this move was good for us. Maybe Frank will meet nice people here, like you and Susan.' She lowered her voice. 'I don't like some of the people Frank has to do business with.'

Little did she know I might be one of them. I was not altogether surprised that Frank the Bishop Bellarosa's wife thought he was a good man who only needed a few good people to get him on the path to salvation. She did not have a clue about her husband's commitment to villainy and perhaps outright evil.

We made small talk for a few minutes, and as we spoke, I removed my glasses and looked her right in the eyes. She hesitated for a second or two, then I think it was starting to come to her. I expected her to jump up and run the eighty feet out of the room. But she must have rejected as absurd whatever had popped into her tiny brain, and she went back to her chatting.

Normally, if left alone with a woman in this sort of situation, I'd do a little mild flirting, just to be polite, or to show I was still alive down where my oxford shirt ended. Sometimes, too, I flirt because I am honestly filled with lust. But I'd sworn off flirting, at least until the start of next Lent. And even if I hadn't sworn off, I wasn't going to screw around the Caesar's wife. Poor Anna, she probably hadn't been propositioned since Frank got his first gun. Still, I did stare at her mountainous bumpers, and she smiled openly at me.

To be honest, after Frank, Anna was a bit of a snooze. She was sweet, even a little funny, but I'd had enough Brooklyn English for one night. I wanted to go.

Anna leaned toward me and lowered her voice again. 'John?'

'Anna?'

'I want to ask you something.'

The top part of the hostess pyjamas, in case I hadn't mentioned it, was kind of loose and open. So when she leaned toward me, like it or not, I could see where those tremendous hooters lived. *Mamma mia*, those tits weighed more than Susan.

'John . . . this is a silly question, but . . .'

'Yes?' I tried to maintain eye contact.

Her hand went to the cross dangling free over her cleavage, and she fingered it. 'I asked Susan, and she said no . . . but are there any stories about ghosts?'

'Ghosts?'

'Ghosts. You know? In this house. Like you hear with the big old houses. Like on TV.' She looked at me as she continued to play with the cross.

'Oh . . .' I thought a moment, then remembered a ghost story. I said, 'Well, there is a story that I've heard . . . but it's really not worth repeating.'

Her free hand reached out and touched mine. 'Tell me.'

'Well . . . all right. Some years ago, it seems there was a governess here who looked after the two Barrett children, Katie and . . . Miles. The governess, an attractive young woman, came to suspect that Katie was . . . well, possessed by the ghost of the former governess, a woman named Miss Jessel – '

'Oh!' She squeezed my hand. 'No!'

'Yes. And to make matters worse, Miles was possessed by the ghost of the former estate manager, an evil man named Peter.'

Anna's eyes grew wider. 'Oh, John! Do you think . . . I mean, that the man I saw . . . could that have been . . .?'

I never thought of that. Why not? Better him than me. I said, 'Well, Peter, I understand, was about my age, my build — '

'Oh, my God.'

'Maybe I shouldn't go on.'

'No. Go on. I have to know.'

'All right. Well, from what I've been told, the governess made a startling deduction. She was convinced that the dead estate manager, Peter, and the dead governess, Miss Jessel, were continuing their mortal sexual affair through the possessed bodies of the young sister and brother.'

'No!' She released my hand and made a quick sign of the cross, then fell back in her chair. 'In this house? Where? Which room?'

'Well . . . the guest room.' I didn't want a fainter on my hands, so I said, 'I think that's enough. And I don't believe any of it — '

'No, John. Tell me the rest. Tell me!'

So, ever the good guest, I continued, 'There were some people who thought that the new governess was actually having an affair with the boy, Miles, who was of course only the innocent vehicle for the evil Peter. Others said the governess was also having a lesbian affair with Katie, who was of course Miss Jessel — '

'You mean that the governess was . . . and the two children were . . .? Susan's friend, Katie Barrett, and her brother . . . and the governess . . .?'

'Who knows?' Indeed, having read *The Turn of the Screw* twice, I still couldn't figure out who was doing it with whom. But somewhere in all that constipated Victorian gibberish was a fine sex-horror story. I said to Anna, 'I don't know how much, if any, of what I heard is true, but I know that the Barretts left suddenly in 1966 and never returned. The house has not been lived in until' — organ crescendo, please — 'until now. But don't tell Susan I told you this, as it still upsets her.'

She nodded her head as she tried to catch her breath. My, she had actually grown pale. 'Yes . . . I won't . . . John, are they still here?'

'The Barretts?'

'No, the *ghosts*.'

'Oh . . . I don't know.' I was feeling a wee bit like a bad boy, so I added, 'I doubt it. They were only interested in sex.'

'My God . . .' She made the sign of the cross again and informed me, 'We had a priest here to bless the house before we moved in.'

'There you go. Nothing to worry about. Can I get you some sherry? Grappa?'

'No. I'm okay.' She continued to hold on to her cross, blocking my view of Joy Valley.

I glanced at my watch. About twenty minutes had passed since Susan and Frank had taken a walk, and I was beginning to get a little annoyed.

I sat back and crossed my legs. Anna and I exchanged a few words, but the woman was clearly upset about something. Finally, a bit impatient with her silliness, I said sternly, 'A Christian does not believe in ghosts.'

'How about the Holy Ghost?'

'The Holy Spirit. That's different.'

'We used to say the Holy Ghost.'

This was a little frustrating. I said, 'Well, get the priests back. Let them check it out.'

'I will.'

Finally, Susan and Frank returned. Susan said to me, 'You should see the conservatory. It's bursting with flowers and tropical plants, palms, and ferns. It's gorgeous.'

'No zucchini?'

Bellarosa explained, 'I got all the vegetables outside now. My gardener grows all the houseplants and stuff in there. He switches everything around. Rotates stuff. You know?'

Susan and Frank sat. It was time for plant chat, and I tuned out. I replayed the balcony scene in my mind, then the library scene. The entire episode was so far removed from my experience, even as an attorney, that it had not fully sunk in yet. But I did have the feeling that Bellarosa and I had made some sort of arrangement.

A large, ornate tall-case clock in the far corner struck the hour, and twelve loud chimes echoed through the ballroom, stopping the conversation. I took the opportunity to say, 'I'm afraid we've overstayed our visit.' This is Wasp talk for 'Can we get the hell out of here?'

Bellarosa said, 'Nah, if I wanted you to leave, I woulda said so. So what's your rush?'

I informed everyone, 'My haemorrhoids are bothering me.'

Mrs Bellarosa, who seemed to have gotten over her ghost jitters, said sympathetically, 'Oh, that can drive you nuts. I had that with all my pregnancies.'

'So did Susan.' I stood, avoiding Susan's icy glare.

Everyone else stood, and we followed the Bellarosas out of the ballroom. I did a little soft-shoe routine to try to make Susan smile. She finally cracked a smile, then punched me in the arm.

We crossed the palm court, and I did a bird call, a yellow finch, which I'm good at, and all the caged birds began chirping and squawking.

Bellarosa glanced back at me over his shoulder as he walked. 'That's pretty good.'

'Thank you.' I felt another punch in the arm.

We stood at the front door, all ready to do the good-night routine, but Susan said, 'I would like to give you both a housewarming gift.'

I hoped she had opted for the cake, but no, she said, 'I paint Gold Coast houses, and – '

'She gets nine hundred a room,' I interjected, 'but she'll do any room in the house for free.'

Susan continued, 'I do oil paintings of the ruins. I have photos of this palm court when it was in ruins.' She explained and ended by saying, 'I have the slides, but I need to do some work here for three-dimensional perspective, proportion, and different lighting.'

Poor Mrs Bellarosa seemed confused. 'You want to paint it like it was when I first saw it? It was a wreck.'

'A ruin,' Susan corrected. Susan is very professional when she's in her *artiste* mode.

Frank chimed in. 'Sure, I get it. Like those pictures we saw in the museum in Rome, Anna. All these Roman ruins with plants growing out of them, and sheeps and people with mandolins. Sure. You do that?'

'Yes.' Susan looked at Anna Bellarosa. 'It will be beautiful. Really.'

Anna Bellarosa looked at her husband. Frank said, 'Sounds great. But I got to pay you for it.'

'No, it's my gift to you both.'

'Okay. Start whenever you want. Door's open to you.'

It seemed to me that Frank had some prior knowledge of this, and I would not have put it past Susan to have done an end run around me and Anna Bellarosa. Susan gets what Susan wants.

I moved to the door. 'Well, it's been a very enjoyable and interesting evening,' I said, going into my standard good-bye.

'Yeah.' Frank agreed.

Susan did her line. 'Anna, you *must* give me your recipe for cannoli cream.'

I felt my stomach heave again.

Mrs Bellarosa replied, 'I got no recipe. I just make it.'

'How wonderful,' Susan said, then finished her speaking part. 'I don't know *when* I've had so much fun. We *must* do this again. Come to us next time.'

Actually, Susan sounded sincere.

Anna smiled. 'Okay. How about tomorrow?'

'I'll call you,' Susan said.

Frank opened the door. 'Take it easy going home. Watch out for the fuzz.' He laughed.

I shook hands with my host and kissed Anna on the cheek. Anna and Susan kissed, then Frank and Susan kissed. Everyone was taken care of, so I turned toward the door, then stopped, took a calling card from my wallet, and left it on a plant table.

Susan and I walked to her car. Susan wanted to drive, and she got behind the wheel. She swung the car around in the forecourt, and we waved to the Bellarosas, who were still at the door. Susan headed down the drive.

We usually don't say much to each other after a social evening, sometimes because we're tired, sometimes because one or the other of us is royally ticked off about something, like flirting, close dancing, sarcastic remarks, and so on and so forth.

As we approached the gates, they swung open, and Anthony stepped out of the gatehouse. He waved as we went by. Susan waved back. She turned right, onto Grace Lane. Finally, she spoke, 'I had a nice evening. Did you?'

'Yes.'

She looked at me. 'Was that a yes?'

'Yes.'

'Good. Then you're glad you went?'

'Yes.'

She turned into the open gates of Stanhope Hall and stopped the car. Unlike the Bellarosas, we don't have electric gates, so I got out, closed the gates, and locked them. The gatehouse was dark, of course, as the Allards turn in early. It is at this point that I sometimes announce my preference to walk the rest of the way home. This is usually followed by spinning wheels and flying gravel. George sweeps and rakes it out in the morning.

'Are you coming?' Susan called out from the car. 'Or not?'

Nations sometimes go to war. Married couples live in a state of perpetual war, broken occasionally by an armed truce. *Don't be cynical, Sutter.* 'Coming, dear.' I got back into the car, and Susan drove slowly up the unlit drive. She said, 'You didn't have to leave your calling card.'

'Why not?'

'Well . . . anyway, what were you and Frank talking about all that time?'

'Murder.'

'Anna is rather nice. A bit . . . basic, perhaps, but nice.'

'Yes.'

'Frank can be charming,' Susan said. 'He's not as rough as he looks or talks.'

Wanna bet?

'I think Anna liked you, John. She was staring at you most of the evening.'

'Really?'

'Do you think she's attractive?'

'She has Rubenesque tits. Why don't you paint her naked, dancing around the palm court?'

'I don't paint naked women.' She stopped the car in front of our house, we got out, I unlocked the door, and we went inside. We both headed into the kitchen, and I poured club soda for us. Susan asked, 'Did you discuss any business?'

'Murder.'

'Very funny.' She asked, 'Did you and Anna figure out where you'd seen each other before?'

'Yes. Locust Valley. The pharmacy. Haemorrhoid remedies.'

'You're quick, John.'

'Thank you.'

'Why were you wearing your reading glasses? Quick now.'

'So Frank wouldn't hit me.'

'Excellent. You're crazy, you know.'

'Look who's talking.'

Susan finished her club soda and headed for the door. 'I'm exhausted. Are you coming up?'

'In a minute.'

'Good night.' She hesitated, then turned to me. 'I love you.'

'Thank you.' I sat at the table, watched the bubbles in my club soda, and listened to the regulator clock. 'Murder,' I said to myself. But he didn't commit *that* murder. I believed him. He has committed a dozen felonies, probably including murder. But not *that* murder.

As I've said, I'd had a premonition that Frank Bellarosa and I would one day go beyond vegetable chatter. But that was as far as my prophecy went. From here on – from the moment I sat there and had that last drink with him instead of leaving – I was on my own.

Looking back on that evening, I recalled that if Susan had told me she had a terrible evening and wanted to avoid the Bellarosas, then I would have done just that. But, incredibly, Lady Stanhope was going to do a painting of Alhambra that would put her into almost daily contact with don and donna Bellarosa. I suppose I should have foreseen the dangers inherent in this situation, and perhaps I did, but instead of demanding of Susan that she withdraw her offer to do a painting, I said nothing. Obviously, we were both responding to Bellarosa's unwanted attention for our own reasons; me, because I saw a challenge and because I wanted to show Susan that her husband was not just a dull attorney and was perhaps a little sinister himself, and Susan because . . . well, I didn't know why then, but I found out later.

So, it was a juxtaposition of events – the hayloft incident, the tennis court incident, and the Sutters' post-winter ennui – that had combined with Frank Bellarosa's proximity and his own problems to draw us together. These things happen, as unlikely as it seems, and if ever there was a case to be made for sticking with your own kind, this was it.

But that's all hindsight. That evening, my mind was cloudy, and my good judgement was influenced by my need to prove something. It goes to show you, you shouldn't stay out too late during the week.

PART IV

We will now discuss in a little more
detail the Struggle for Existence.

Charles Darwin
The Origin of Species

CHAPTER 18

We did not have the Bellarosas to our house the next evening as Anna suggested. In fact, as far as I knew, we had no immediate plans to see them again. Susan is the social secretary in our house and keeps a leather-bound calendar as her mother did. The Stanhopes did, at one time, have an actual social or private secretary, and I suppose the art has been passed down. I'm not very good at social planning, so I suppose I've allowed Susan to take full charge. I don't even think I have veto power anymore, as you might have noticed. So, regarding the Bellarosas, I was waiting for word from my resident Emily Post.

Susan had begun her painting of Alhambra's palm court, and that fact, plus the fact that her horses were still there, took Susan to Alhambra nearly every day. Susan, by the way, had decided on oils instead of water, so I knew this was going to be about a six-week project.

Susan Stanhope Sutter and Mrs Anna Bellarosa seemed to be forming a tentative relationship, perhaps even a genuine friendship according to Susan. This relationship, I was certain, was encouraged by Frank Bellarosa, who not only wanted his wife to have friends in the area, but also wanted her to get off his back about the move from Brooklyn to this dangerous frontier.

Susan barely mentioned Frank, and I never inquired after him. If I pictured him at all in this threesome, it was as a busy man who watched Susan set up her easel for a few minutes, jollied the two women along, and kept to himself for the rest of the day – or more likely, got into his limo and disappeared into the great city for a day of lawbreaking.

It is very difficult, I imagine, to run a large crime empire, especially since the emperor cannot say much over the telephone or, similarly, cannot send detailed instructions by fax or telex. Personal contact, the spoken word, handshakes, facial expressions, and hand gestures are the only way to run an underground organization, whether it be political or criminal. I recalled that the Mafia supposedly had its origins as an underground resistance organization during some foreign occupation of Sicily. I could certainly believe that, and that would explain why they were such a long-running hit in America. But maybe their act was getting a little old as the second millennium drew to a close. Maybe.

Susan said to me one evening, 'I saw the strangest thing next door.'

'What?'

'I saw a man kiss Frank's hand.'

'Why is that strange? My junior partners kiss my hand every morning.'

'Be serious, please. I'll tell you something else. Everyone who enters that house is taken into the coatroom and searched. I can hear that sound that a metal detector makes when it goes off.'

'Are you searched?'

'Of course not.' She asked, 'Why is he so paranoid?'

'He's not. People really are out to get him. Why don't you understand that?'

'Well, I suppose I do. But it just seems so bizarre . . . I mean, right next door.'

'Has Mr Mancuso spoken to you yet?'

'No. Will he?'

'Perhaps.'

But other than that brief conversation, there wasn't much mention of Frank, as I said.

Regarding Anna, Susan was more current. She told me that Anna did not ride horses, play tennis, sail, or engage in any athletic activities. This did not surprise me. Susan tried to get Anna on Yankee, but Anna wouldn't even go near the snorting beast. Anna Bellarosa, however, was interested in painting, as it turned out. According to Susan, Anna watched and asked questions about what Susan was doing. Susan encouraged her to get an easel and paints and offered to give her lessons, but Anna Bellarosa seemed as reluctant to paint as she was to ride, or to try anything new, for that matter. As fond as Susan seemed of the woman, I had the impression she was a bit exasperated by Anna's timidness. I informed Susan, 'Her reason for existence is cooking, cleaning, sex, and child care. Don't cause her any anxiety.'

'But I have the feeling that her husband would like her to develop new skills.'

So would *your* husband, Susan. Like cooking and house-keeping. In truth, I'd rather have a Susan than an Anna as my lifelong companion, but if I could combine the best qualities of both women, I'd have the perfect wife. But then what would I have to complain about?

Susan also informed me that Anna had a lot of questions about 'how you do things around here'. But I think these were more Frank's questions than Anna's.

Regarding the haunting of Alhambra, Susan mentioned to me a few days after she began her canvas that Anna had gone to Brooklyn by limousine one morning and returned a few hours later with two priests. 'They all looked pretty grim,' Susan said. 'They went around splashing holy water all over the place, and Anna was crossing herself eight times a minute.' Susan added, 'I sort of pretended not to notice, but it was hard to ignore them. Anna said they were blessing the house, but I think there was more to it than that.'

'They're very superstitious people,' I said. 'You didn't upset her with any of your ghost stories, did you, Susan?'

'No, of course not. I told her there are no ghosts in Alhambra.'

'Well, I'm sure she feels better now that the house is all sprinkled.'

'I hope so. They gave me the shivers.'

Anyway, there is a silver lining in every dark cloud, and in this case the silver lining was Italian food. Not that Susan was learning how to cook – no, she can no more cook than I can levitate. But she was bringing home a portion of the Bellarosas' evening fare almost every night:

Tupperware containers heaped with ravioli, baked ziti, eggplant parmigiana, fried zucchini, and other things with unpronounceable names. I had really struck pay dirt here, and I actually looked forward to dinner at home for the first time in twenty years.

Susan also brought home tomato seedlings and zucchini plants to add to her garden of radicchio, basil, green peppers, and eggplant. She never mentioned this to me, but I saw the new plants one day while I was out walking. Also, all the vegetables were now marked, correctly, I think, so we knew what we were rooting for (pardon the pun). Apparently, too, Susan had picked up some pointers from someone on vegetable gardening, because everything looked healthy, and by the end of May it seemed as though we might have a bumper crop. Stanhope Hall would now be a self-sustaining fiefdom, at least in regard to certain vegetables, and all its inhabitants – all four of us if you count the Allards – would be delivered from the ravages of scurvy and night blindness.

So far, to be honest, the changes in my life that had come about as a result of the cultural contact with the neighbouring fiefdom, to continue the metaphor, were for the better. The clash of cultures had not materialized in any significant way, but there was time for that.

I had no doubt that I had established a personal relationship with Frank Bellarosa, but I was not certain of the nature of that relationship; or if I did know, I wasn't letting on to anyone, myself included, what it was. And whatever it was, it seemed to be on hold, because by the end of that month I had not heard a word from him, directly or indirectly.

As for any business relationship with him, I considered that whole episode in his library as a bit of madness. Surely he must have regretted taking me into his confidence, which was probably why I hadn't heard from him. I mean, he certainly didn't think that he had retained me as his attorney. Right?

On the last Wednesday in May, Susan went to a meeting of the Gazebo Society, held at the old Fox Point waterfront estate at the end of Grace Lane. She mentioned this to me after the fact, and when I asked her if she had invited Anna Bellarosa, she said she had not and offered no explanation.

I knew that this relationship with the Bellarosas was going to be a problem, and I had tried to tell that to Susan. But Susan is not the type who thinks ahead. Everyone, I suppose, has friends, neighbours, or family with whom they'd rather not be seen in public. Much of that feeling is subjective; your goofiest cousin, for instance, may be a hit at your cocktail party. But with the Bellarosas, it was not a matter of my perception or interpretation as to their social acceptability; it was just about everyone's judgement. Yes, we would get past the front door at The Creek or Seawanhaka, and we would be shown to a table and even waited on. Once.

So, if in fact the Sutters and the Bellarosas were going to get together for dinner or drinks in public, I would be well advised to pick a restaurant out of the area (but even that was fraught with danger, as I myself discovered about a year ago when I was having dinner on the South Shore with a client, female, young, beautiful, who liked to touch when making a point, and in walked the damned DePauws. But that's another story.)

Anyway, I suppose the four of us could go to Manhattan if we had to have dinner. The city is supposed to be anonymous, but it seems I'm always running into someone I know in Midtown.

Also, there seems to be some sort of odd connection between Mafia dons dining out and Mafia dons being murdered, splattering blood all over innocent people and that sort of thing. This may seem a bit paranoid, but it's happened often enough to be a real possibility, and for me to plan for; thus, if I were dining out with the don, I would seriously consider wearing an old suit.

I believe Bellarosa when he tells me that the Mafia still maintains high, professional standards of murder, and in fact innocent people usually suffer no more than a stomach upset at these traditional dinner-hour murders. And of course, the dinner or what's left of it is always on the house for spectators as well as participants in the rub out. The murder, naturally, has to be committed *in* the restaurant to qualify for a freebie: not outside the front door as happened a while ago in front of one of New York's best steak houses. Hearing shots fired outside does not get you off the hook for the bill, unless you faint. On a more serious note, civilians *have* gotten caught in the crossfire, and there was at least one tragic case of mistaken identity some years ago when two suburbanite gentlemen were gunned down by accident in a Little Italy restaurant in front of their wives.

So, to sup or not to sup? Considering what Frank himself said about the U.S. Attorney, Alphonse Ferragamo, trying to provoke a gang war, I would opt for Chinese takeout. But what if my crazy wife asks them out to dinner? All things considered, I don't know if it would be worse to dine with the Bellarosas at The Creek and face social ostracism, or to go to Manhattan for a jittery dinner at a nice little place that Frank insists on showing us, where the food is great, the owner is a *paesano*, and everyone sits at banquettes with their backs to the wall.

Well, of course there are other options, and I don't mean to suggest that two headstrong people such as Frank and Susan could get me to do something I don't want to do. If the situation arises, I will insist on having Frank and Anna to our house for a quick drink and coffee to go.

A few days before the Memorial Day weekend, Dominic and his crew put the finishing touches on the stable. All in all, it was a masterful job of demolition and reconstruction. It was actually a bit eerie to see a familiar landmark disappear, then reappear in the same shape and form, in a new location. Dominic and his husky elves could indeed move the Sistine Chapel down the block if they had the Pope's okay. And if they had the don's okay, they could move my house onto Alhambra's patio. I was almost afraid to go on vacation.

And so that glorious day arrived when Zanzibar and Yankee came home. I suggested tricoloured bunting and garlands of flowers, but Susan ignored my suggestions and kept the ceremony simple and dignified, with only Dominic in attendance. I figured he was there to collect his money, but when I asked for the bill, he just jerked his thumb toward Alhambra. I gave him a bonus of five hundred dollars in cash for his men, and he seemed very happy for his men and looked as if he couldn't wait to distribute it.

Anyway, I sent a note over to Frank via Susan, but another week passed and still no bill. Now I owed the guy drinks and a chunk of cash, not to mention the fact that I was eating well.

Susan says that Italian food makes her passionate, and I, too, had noticed that our sex life, always good, had gotten better. Maybe Mrs B. had found the right combination of Italian herbs and spices. One evening, over one of these Alhambra take-out dinners, I said to Susan, 'My God, your tits are growing. Get the recipe for this ravioli.'

'Don't be a wiseass, John.' She added, 'You've put on a needed inch yourself, and I don't mean your waist.'

Touché. But anyway, I think our increased sexual appetites were more psychological than culinary in origin, and perhaps a result of the perfect spring weather, which always makes my sap run hot, to use a tree metaphor. But who knows? When you're middle age, whatever works is right. Suffice it to say, Susan and I were getting it on in the bedroom and kitchen. We weren't doing as well in the other rooms, however, as Susan, always somewhat distant, seemed now distracted, as if she had something on her mind. So I asked her one day, 'Is something bothering you?'

'Yes.'

'What?'

'Things.'

'Things? Like the recent outbreak of violence in Kurdistan?'

'Things around here. Just things.'

'Well, the children will be home in June, and in July I'll be on half schedule, and in August we'll go to East Hampton.'

She shrugged.

Remembering the immortal words of Frank Bellarosa on the subject of accommodating women, I said, 'Why don't you go back to Brooklyn?'

Anyway, I thought that with the stable moved and the horsies home at last, Susan's visits to Alhambra would taper off, but I had the impression she was still there quite a bit. I mean, I'm not around that much during the day, but whenever I called home, she was not there, and my messages on the answering machine went unanswered.

Also, George, the ever-faithful servant, would sometimes intercept me on my way to my house and say things like, 'Mrs Sutter hasn't been in all day or I would have asked her . . .' followed by an inane question. George is not subtle, though he thinks he is. Obviously, he disapproved of any relationship with the Bellarosas. George is more royal than the king, holier than the bishop, and a bigger snob than any Astor or Vanderbilt I've ever met. A lot of the old servants are like that, trying to make their younger masters and mistresses act more like their fathers and mothers, who were, of course, paragons of virtue, gentlemen and ladies of refined manners, and so forth. Servants have very selective memories.

The point is, George was not happy with us, and I knew that eventually, when he'd had a couple of stiff ones, he would say something to his cronies on the other estates, and the gossip would work its way up the social ladder. Well, if anything got back to me, I'd let George know how he'd kept his job and house all these years. No, I wouldn't. I liked George. And he liked Susan and me. But he *was* a gossip.

As for Ethel, I couldn't get a fix on her opinion of the Bellarosas or our relationship with them. She seemed non-committal, almost non-judgemental for a change. I suspect that this was because she couldn't fit the Bellarosas into her theory of class struggle. Socialist doctrine, I think, is somewhat vague on the subject of criminals, and Ethel gets most of her opinions from nineteenth-century radicals who believed that the oppressive capitalist system created crime and criminals. So, perhaps Ethel was wrestling with the idea that Frank Bellarosa was a victim of free enterprise rather than one of its beneficiaries. If Ethel and I agree on anything, it is probably Mark Twain's observation that 'there is no distinctly native American criminal class except Congress.'

Anyway, there was one day when I was in the city and I had to reach Susan to ask her if she could come into Manhattan to join me for dinner with two out-of-town clients, Mr and Mrs Peterson, who had dropped in unexpectedly, and who are old friends of her parents. I called home and left two messages on Susan's machine, then as my rendezvous time with the Petersons approached, I called the gatehouse and spoke to Ethel. She informed me that Mrs Sutter had taken Zanzibar to Alhambra in the morning and had not returned, to the best of her knowledge. So, what would you do if your gatekeeper's wife informed you that your spouse had taken the stallion to the neighbouring estate? One should, of course, send a servant to fetch one's spouse, and this is what Ethel offered to do; that is, to send George next door. Or, she suggested, I might call Alhambra to see if Mrs Sutter was actually there. I said it wasn't important, though of course it must be if I were calling the gatehouse. I hung up with Ethel, called Susan's phone again, and left a final, rather curt message regarding my dinner date and the name of the restaurant.

The fact was, I still didn't have the Bellarosas' phone number, and Susan said she didn't either. I had noticed, when I was at Alhambra, and Susan confirmed, that none of the telephones there have the phone numbers written on the instruments. This was good security, of course, and I'd seen that in other great houses, as a precaution against the occasional servant, repairman, or the like jotting down the phone numbers of the rich and famous.

Late that evening, upon returning home after my dinner with the Petersons (Susan had not shown up at the restaurant), I said to Susan, 'I was trying to get in touch with you today.'

'Yes, I got the messages on my machine and from Ethel.'

I *never* ask 'Where were you?' because if I did, then she

267

would start asking, 'Where were *you*?' – which leads to 'Who were you with and what were you doing?' What could be more lower-middle-class than asking your spouse to account for his or her day or evening? That's probably how Sally Ann got her first black eye. But I did say, 'I would like to be able to reach you if you are at Alhambra. Would you prefer that I send George over, or should you ask the Bellarosas for their telephone number?'

She shrugged. 'I don't have any reason to call them. I suppose you could just send George.'

I think Susan was missing my point. I responded, 'George is not always available. Perhaps you can get the Bellarosas' phone number, Susan. I'm quite sure you will have *some* reason to call them someday.'

'I don't think so. I just come and go as I please. If I have to leave a message, I leave it with Anthony, Vinnie, or Lee.'

'Who, may I ask, are Anthony, Vinnie, and Lee?'

'You've met Anthony – the gatekeeper. Vinnie is the other gatekeeper. They both live in the gatehouse. Lee is Anthony's friend. She lives in the gatehouse also. It has three bedrooms.'

'Lee is a woman. I see. And what does poor Vinnie do for a friend?'

'Vinnie has another friend, Delia, who comes by.'

The idea of Grace Lane's location being known by people whose origins were in Brooklyn was somewhat disturbing. I was at the point where I could almost tolerate Mafia dons and their peers in black limousines, but hit men, gun molls, and other riffraff were another matter. I said, 'I don't like the idea of a bordello down the street.'

'Oh, John. Really. What do you expect Anthony and Vinnie to do? Guard duty gets lonely. Twelve hours on, twelve hours off, seven days a week. They split it up. Lee keeps house.'

'That's interesting.' What was even more interesting, I thought, was that Lady Stanhope seemed to find these Damon Runyon characters *simpatico*. But I, narrow-minded, upper-middle-class John Sutter, was not so tolerant. I suggested, 'Perhaps we should introduce Anthony, Vinnie, Lee and Delia to the Allards, and they can exchange professional tips on gatekeeping.'

Getting no response, I went back to my main point and said, 'But surely, Susan, on a dark and stormy night, it might be easier to call Alhambra than to go to the gatehouse and interrupt something.'

'Look, John, if you want the phone number, you ask for it. How were the Petersons?'

'They were very sorry they missed you.' The question of the telephone number was now in my court, where it would stay. Do you see what I mean about Susan's unreasonableness? *Stubbornness* might be a better word. It's the red hair. Really it is.

Anyway, regarding the Bellarosas' phone number, I didn't really want it, except for those rare occasions when I needed to reach Susan, who seemed to have become part of the royal court at Alhambra. But the fact that Bellarosa hadn't called, written, sent word, or divulged his phone number to me confirmed in my mind that we had no lawyer/client relationship, either implied or inferred. And the next time he called me, I resolved that I would tell him that in no uncertain terms. Unfortunately, Fate, which had always been kind to me in the past, was pissed off at me for some reason and intervened again to push me into Bellarosa's deadly embrace.

I was busy at work, especially in my Manhattan office. My practice has as much to do with money as it does with law. Or to be more precise, my clients want to know how to legally keep their money out of the hands of the government. This spirited contest between the taxpayer and the Internal Revenue Service has been going on since the very moment Congress passed the income tax amendment in 1913. In recent years, because of people like me, the taxpayer has actually won a few rounds.

The result of this prolonged conflict has been the creation

of a large and thriving tax industry, of which I and my firm are important players. My clients are mostly people or heirs to people who were hit hard in 1929, and those who recovered faced income tax rates that reached ninety per cent by the 1950s. Many of these people, sophisticated in other ways, were unprepared for the onslaught of income redistribution from Washington. Some, in an idiotic display of guilt and altruism, even saw it as just and fair, like Susan's grandfather, who was prepared to give half his money to the American people. But when it got to be more than half, some of these socially progressive millionaires began to feel the pinch. It also became obvious that the few dollars of tax money that did get down to the people were getting to the wrong people for the wrong reasons.

And so, in a less sophisticated age, even those of my firm's clients who knew how to make money in the worst of times didn't know how to keep it from the government in the best of times. But they've seen the light, and they don't intend for this to happen again, for this is the age of greed, and of looking out for Number One. And through a process of social Darwinism, we have all evolved into specialized species who can smell the danger of a new tax law hatched on Capitol Hill all the way to Wall Street.

These people, my clients, hire me to be certain that they are not going to go to jail if they or their financial planners come up with a clever way to beat a tax. It's all legal, of course, and I wouldn't be involved with it if it weren't. The motto around here is this: *To evade taxes is illegal; to avoid taxes is legal.* And, I might add, a civil right and moral obligation.

So, for instance, when the new tax law swept away the old Clifford Trust for children, some bright guy like me (I wish it had been me) came up with something called a pseudo-Clifford Trust, which accomplished the same objective of transferring tax-free money to the little heirs and is so clever and complicated that the Internal Revenue Service is still trying to figure out a way to plug up the loophole. It's a game — maybe even a war. I play it well, and I also play it

270

clean and straight. I can afford to; I'm smarter than the other side, and if anyone in the IRS were as bright as I am, they'd be working for me.

Anyway, though I play it straight, I sometimes wind up in tax court with a client to settle a difference of opinion. But no client of mine has ever faced criminal charges for tax fraud unless he's lied to me about something or held back something. I try to keep my clients as honest as I am. When you cheat at poker, life, or taxes, you've taken the honour and fun out of winning, and ultimately you've cheated yourself out of the finest pleasure in life: beating the other guy fair and square. That's what I was taught in school.

Granted, the other side doesn't always play fair, but in this country you always have the option of yelling 'foul', and going to court. Maybe if I lived in another country with no honest and independent judiciary, I wouldn't fight fair. I am, after all, talking about survival, not suicide. But here, in America, the system still works, and I believe in it. At least I did up until eleven A.M. that morning. By noon, I had entered another stage of my life as an endangered species, trying to quickly evolve a few more specialized survival skills and stay out of jail myself. But more about that in a moment.

So there I was, sitting in my Wall Street office on that pleasant May morning, buried in work. My summer schedule generally consists of four-day weekends at my summer house in East Hampton during July, then I spend the whole month of August there. I knock off early, and Susan and I sail out of the yacht club and stay out until dark, or when the mood strikes us, we stay on the water until dawn, which is beautiful.

Susan and I have six or seven really good sex scenarios for the boat. Sometimes I'm a shipwrecked sailor and Susan pulls me aboard, nearly naked, of course, and nurses me back to health. In the rough-trade department, I'm a pirate who slips aboard at night and finds her in the shower, or undressing for bed. Then there's the stowaway drama in two acts, where I discover her hiding in the hold and administer appropriate corporal punishment as maritime law allows. I personally like the one where I'm a lowly deckhand and Susan is the yacht owner. She orders me around, sunbathes in the nude, and makes me perform demeaning acts, which I won't go into here. The point is, I look forward to sex on the high seas, and so I run, run, run through the treadmill of spring, my arms outstretched toward the Glorious Fourth.

I know this sounds as if I take it pretty easy from the Fourth of July to Labor Day, but I earned it. Also, I use the time to do my own taxes, which I put on extended deadline every year.

I mention this because as I was sitting in my office thinking about my summer house and my taxes, my secretary, Louise, buzzed me. I picked up the phone. 'Yes?'

'There is a Mr Novac on the line from the Internal Revenue.'

'Tell him to call me in September.'

'He says it is most important that he speak to you.'

I replied with annoyance, 'Well, find out what case or client it refers to, pull the file, and tell him to hold.' I was about to hang up with Louise when she said, 'I *asked* him that, Mr Sutter. He won't say. He says he must speak to you *personally*.'

'Oh . . .' I thought I knew what this was about. But why would the IRS call *me* about Frank Bellarosa? Then I thought it might be Mr Mancuso of the FBI calling undercover. But that didn't seem right. Frank Bellarosa had introduced a new dimension into my life, so naturally a call such as this took on a Bellarosa colouring, and it was not a pretty rose tint. I said to Louise, 'Put him through.'

'Yes, sir.' I heard a click, then a mealy-mouthed male voice, which I immediately took a disliking to, said, 'Mr John Sutter?'

'Yes.'

'My name is Stephen Novac, a revenue agent with the IRS.'

'Yes?'

'I'd like to stop up and discuss some matters with you.'

'*What* matters?'

'Serious matters, Mr Sutter.'

'Concerning what and whom?'

'I'd rather not say over the phone.'

'Why not?' I asked lightly. 'Are your phones tapped by the Taxpayers' Revolt Committee?' I waited for a polite chuckle, but there was none. Not good. I also waited for the word 'Sir,' but didn't hear that either. I pulled my calendar toward me. 'All right, how about next Wednesday at – '

'I'll be there in half an hour, Mr Sutter. Please be there and allow an hour for my visit. Thank you.'

The phone went dead. 'What nerve – ' I buzzed Louise. 'Clear my calendar until noon. When Mr Novac shows up, keep him waiting fifteen minutes.'

'Yes, sir.'

I stood, walked to the window, and looked down on Wall Street. Money. Power. Prestige. Corporate grandeur and layers of insulation against the world. But, Mr Stephen Novac, of the IRS, had done in fifteen seconds what some people couldn't do in fifteen days or weeks; he had breached all the fortifications and would be sitting in my office on the very same morning he'd called. Incredible.

Of course I knew by the tone of the man's voice and by his arrogance that this must be a criminal matter. (If it turned out to be a civil case, I'd throw him out the window.) So the question remained, which criminal was Mr Novac coming to see me about? Bellarosa? One of my clients? But Novac would not be that arrogant if he were looking for my co-operation. Therefore, he was not looking for my co-operation. Therefore . . .

At eleven-fifteen, Mr Stephen Novac was shown into my office. He was one of those people whose telephone voice exactly matched his looks.

After the mandatory limp handshake, Mr Novac showed me his credentials which identified him as a special agent, not a revenue agent as he'd said. A special agent, in case you haven't had the opportunity to meet one of these people, is actually with the IRS Criminal Investigation Division. I said to him, 'You misrepresented yourself over the telephone.'

'How so?'

I told him how so and added, 'You're speaking to an attorney, Mr Novac, and you've gotten yourself off on the wrong foot.' Of course, the man was royally pissed off and would now take every opportunity to stick it to me. But I had the feeling he was going to do that anyway. 'Sit,' I commanded.

He sat. I remained standing and looked down at him. That's my little power play. Mr Novac was about forty, and anyone still in the IRS after all those years was definitely a career officer, a pro. Sometimes they send kids over, spanking new CPAs or attorneys with the ink still wet on their diplomas, and I chew them up and spit them out before they even open their briefcases. But Stephen Novac looked cool, slightly smug, the way any cop is when he knows he has the full weight of the law in his badge case. He seemed not at all impressed with his surroundings, not intimidated by all the accoutrements of rooted, generational jurisprudence. This was not going to be pleasant. 'What can I do for you, Mr Novac?'

He crossed his legs and took a small notebook out of his pocket. He perused it without replying.

I had the urge to throw him out the window, but they'd just send another one. I regarded Novac a moment. He had on an awful grey poplin cotton suit, the sort of thing that prisons issue when they set you free. He wore shoes that actually had gum soles, and the uppers were made of a miracle synthetic that could be safely cleaned with Brillo. His shirt, his tie, socks, watch, even his haircut, were all bargain basement, and I found myself irrationally offended by the man because of the air of sensible frugality about him. Actually, I hate a man who won't splurge on a good suit.

What I really didn't like about Novac, of course, was that he was in my office to ruin my life. At least he could have come better dressed.

'Mr Novac,' I said, 'can I help you find something in that book?'

He looked up at me. 'Mr Sutter, you bought a house in East Hampton in 1971 for $55,000. Correct?'

Innocuous as that question may seem to you, it was not the question I wanted to hear. I replied, 'I bought a house in East Hampton in the early 1970s for about that price.'

'All right. You sold it in 1979 for $365,000. Correct?'

'That sounds about right.' Best investment I ever made.

'There was, then, a net long-term capital gain on the transaction of $310,000. Correct?'

'No. There was a *gross* gain of $310,000. There's a difference between net and gross, Mr Novac. I'm sure they taught you that in school, even if the IRS doesn't know the difference.' *Easy, Sutter.*

He looked at me. 'What, then, was your net capital gain?'

'You subtract capital improvements and other costs from the gross, and that's what we call the net in the world of private enterprise.'

'And how much was that, Mr Sutter?'

'I have no idea at this moment.'

'Neither do we, Mr Sutter, since you never reported a dollar of it.'

Touché, Mr Novac. I replied aggressively, 'Why should I report it as income? I bought another house in East Hampton for over $400,000. Therefore, the capital gain, whatever it is, was deferred. Would you like me to show you the pertinent section of the tax code?'

'Mr Sutter, you had eighteen months according to the law at that time to roll over the gain – to purchase a house with the proceeds of the house you sold in order to defer the capital gain. You waited *twenty-three* months before you bought the house on Berry Lane in East Hampton, in January of 1981. Therefore, a tax event took place, and you should have computed and paid taxes on your capital gain.' He added, 'You failed to report a significant amount of income.'

The man was right, of course, which was why he was still

sitting there and not being tossed bodily out into the hall. But lest you think I am a crook, there is an explanation. I said to Mr Novac, 'My intention was to *build* a house. The law, you may have heard, allows twenty-four months to roll over the capital gain if you build instead of buy.'

Mr Novac replied, 'But the house you bought and still own on Berry Lane was not built by you. It was an existing house, according to my research.'

'Yes. I had a binder on a piece of land on which I was going to build my house, but the seller reneged at the last moment. I began an action against him, but we settled. There are court records to substantiate that. So, as you can see, Mr Novac, my intention to build a new house was aborted. The clock was ticking, and I knew I could not find land and begin construction to satisfy the government's inane tax rules, which I think are an intrusion into my rights as a free citizen to make economic decisions based on *my* needs and not the government's. Therefore, Mr Novac, being thwarted in my intention to build, I quickly bought an existing house – the one on Berry Lane, which is quite nice, and if you're ever in East Hampton, drive by.' I added, 'To avoid taxes is legal, to evade taxes is illegal. I avoided. Thank you for stopping by on government time. I like to see how my tax money is spent.' I walked to the door and opened it, adding, 'I'll send you the pertinent records and court papers regarding the land deal that fell through, so you don't have to dig them up out in East Hampton. Please leave your card with my secretary.'

But Mr Novac was not on his way out the open door. He remained seated and said, 'Mr Sutter, you did not fulfil the requirements to *buy* a house within eighteen months. Therefore, a *tax event* took place at that point in time. There is nothing you can do or say retroactively to change that tax event.' He added, 'You have broken the law.'

Now, you have to understand how these people think. Mr Novac was certain that I had committed not only a crime under the ever-changing tax code, but that I had sealed my fate for eternity when a *tax event* took place without my notifying the government of it. Truly the angels in heaven were weeping for me all these years. Confess, said Mr Novac, repent and you will be absolved of this sin before we burn you at the stake. No, thanks. I closed the door so as not to upset Louise and moved toward Mr Novac, who stood his ground, or more precisely remained on his ass. 'Mr Novac,' I began at low volume, 'in this great nation of ours, a citizen is innocent until proven guilty.' Turning up the volume now: 'This is the central principle of our system of justice, a pillar of our civil liberties. Yet the Internal Revenue Service demands of American citizens that they supply proof of their innocence. Wrong, Mr Novac. Wrong.' Full volume. 'If you have proof of my guilt, I demand to see it. Now!'

He kept his cool, refusing to be baited or drawn into a shouting match, which was what I wanted for the record. He was a pro. 'Mr Sutter,' he said, 'like it or not, in matters of civil tax delinquency, the burden of proof is on you.'

'All right,' I said coolly, 'then listen carefully. It was my *intention*, which I can demonstrate in tax court, to *build* a house. Interestingly, the new tax law allows twenty-four months to build *or* buy a house in order to avoid a capital gains tax. So you see, Mr Novac, nothing is carved in stone, least of all the tax code, which is rewritten by little elves every night. So there you have my position in this case, Mr Novac. I have nothing further to say, but if you want to fill the remainder of the hour I have allotted to you, you can sit there and read the United States Tax Code while I work.'

Mr Novac got the message and stood. 'Mr Sutter, by your own admission, and based on my research, you are liable for capital gains taxes, plus interest and penalties.' Mr Novac took a piece of paper from his pocket, scanned it, and said, 'By my calculations, if you cannot show receipts and cancelled cheques for capital improvement deductions, then the capital gain in the year you sold your house was $310,000. Taking into account the tax structure at that time, plus the interest and penalties – negligence penalties, failure-to-file penalties, and a civil fraud penalty – you owe the United States $314,513.'

Now I wished I was sitting. I took a deep but discreet breath. This was the moment Mr Novac had been waiting for – perhaps for months – and I was not going to give him anything to savour about it. I said, 'And I still come up with zero.'

He handed the paper to me, but I refused to take it, so he left it on my desk. Mr Novac said, 'Your *intention* to legally avoid the tax is irrelevant.'

'Wrong,' I replied. 'In a civil tax case, my intent is very relevant. Where did you go to school?' Mr Novac only smiled, which made me uneasy. I continued, 'And don't expect me to agree to a negotiated settlement. My position is that I owe no taxes.' I added, 'And if you try to seize any of my assets, I will block you and sue you.' This threat, unfortunately, was so hollow that Mr Novac openly smirked. The IRS has nearly total power to take things from you, and you have to go to court to get them back. I added, 'I'm calling my congressman as well.'

Mr Novac seemed not impressed. He informed me, 'Normally, Mr Sutter, I would accept your explanation for the error if you would accept my figures. But as you are an educated man, a tax attorney at that, then the IRS is taking the position that this was not an error or oversight, but a case of premeditated tax evasion. Fraud. I must advise you at this time that, in addition to the civil penalties, *criminal* charges are being contemplated.'

I could smell that coming, and when a cop says 'criminal charges', I don't care who you are, how much money you have, or how many law degrees are hanging on your wall, your heart does a thump. I actually know a few men with more power and money than I have who were sent away for a while, as they say. I know two who have come back and they are not the same men. I looked Mr Novac in the eye. 'Grown men do not wear cotton suits.'

For the first time, Mr Novac showed some emotion; he turned red, but not, I'm afraid, with embarrassment over his poor attire. No, he was really pissed off now. He got his colour under control and said, 'Please prepare for a full audit of all your tax returns from 1979 to the present, including this year's return, which you have not yet filed. Have all your documentation and records available for an auditor, who will contact you this afternoon. If you do not voluntarily turn over these records, we will subpoena them.'

My tax records were in Locust Valley, but I'd worry about that this afternoon. Now I know what it feels like to be mugged. I walked to my door and opened it. 'And no one in the Free World wears synthetic leather shoes, Mr Novac. You must be a spy.'

'I am a vegetarian,' he explained, 'and will not wear leather.'

'Then for God's sake, man, have the decency to wear canvas tennis shoes or rubber galoshes, but not *plastic*. Good day.'

He left without another word, and as I was closing the door behind him, a word popped into my mind and I called out, 'Schmuck!' Louise almost dropped her dentures. I slammed the door shut.

Despite my cool, patrician exterior, I was somewhat disturbed over the prospect of coughing up about a third of a million dollars plus spending time in a federal prison. I poured a glass of ice water from a carafe, went to the window, and opened it, letting in some of the last breathable air that still exists at this altitude in Manhattan.

So, there it was; the Great Upper-Middle-Class Nightmare – a tax slip-up in six figures.

Now listen to me feel sorry for myself. I work my butt off, I raised two children, I contribute to society and to the nation, I pay my taxes . . . well, apparently not all of them, but most of them . . . and I served my country in time of war when others found ways to avoid their national duty. This is not fair.

Now listen to me build up rage. The nation is overrun with drug dealers and Mafia dons who live like kings. Criminals own the streets, murderers walk free, billions are spent on welfare, but there's no money to build jails, congressmen and senators do things that would put me behind bars, and big corporations get away with tax scams of such magnitude that the government would rather compromise than fight. And they call *me* a criminal? What the hell is wrong here?

I got myself under control and looked down into the street: Wall Street, the financial hub of the nation from which radiated the spokes of power and money that held up the rim of the world. And yet there was this perception out in the hinterlands that Wall Street was un-American, and the movers and shakers who inhabited it were parasites. Thus, Mr Novac entered Wall Street with a generally bad attitude, and I suppose I didn't do much to change his mind. Maybe I shouldn't have remarked on his plastic shoes. But how could I have possibly resisted? I mean, I learned *something* at Yale. I smiled. I was feeling a little better.

Now listen to me think rationally. The criminal charge would be difficult to prove, but not impossible. A jury of my peers, drawn from my friends at The Creek, would surely find me not guilty. But a federal jury, constituted in New York City, might not be so sympathetic. But even if I could avoid or beat the criminal charges and fines, I was probably on the hook for . . . I looked at the paper on my desk . . . $314,513, which was actually more than the entire so-called profit on the sale of the house. That is a lot of money, even for a successful Wall Street lawyer. Especially an honest one.

Also, Susan theoretically was on the hook for half of that. Though we file separate tax returns because of her complicated trust fund income, and because that is what our marriage contract stipulates we do, half the East Hampton house is hers, and she should have picked up half the supposed capital gain. But of course, even in this age of women's equality, Novac was talking jail to me, not Susan. Typical.

Anyway, thinking rationally, I knew I should call the Stanhopes' law firm and advise them of this problem. They'd probably go to the IRS and offer to help screw me in exchange for immunity for their little heiress client. You think marrying into a super-rich family is all fun and profit? Try it. Anyway, the next thing I had to do was have one of the partners here handle my tax case — you can't be objective when it's your own money — and then I should think about actually retaining a criminal attorney for myself.

This last thought led me into a word association, like this: Criminal — Bellarosa.

I thought about my buddy, Frank, for a moment. Mr Bellarosa went to jail once in his larcenous life, and that was for tax evasion. But obviously Bellarosa is still committing tax fraud, since he's certainly not declaring his income from drugs, prostitution, gambling, hijacking, or whatever else he does on the side.

So I stood there looking down on Wall Street, feeling sorry for myself, feeling angry at the injustices of life, and really pissed off at the thought of all the criminals who were not hassled today by the government.

It was just then, I suppose, that a strange thing began to happen to me: I started to lose faith in the system. Me, a champion of the system, a cheerleader for law and order, a patriot and a Republican for God's sake — suddenly I felt alienated from my country. I suppose this is a common reaction for an honest man and a good citizen who is thrown into the same category as Al Capone and Frank Bellarosa. I suppose, too, to be honest, that this had been brewing for some time.

I recalled Frank Bellarosa's words: *You a Boy Scout or something? You salute the flag every morning?*

Well, I did. But then I realized that all my years of good citizenship would only count toward a favourable pre-sentencing report to the judge.

My logic — no, my survival instincts — told me I needed to stop being a good citizen if I wanted to be a free citizen. So, voluntary compliance or come and get me, pigs? *Come and get me, pigs.*

I knew, of course, the one man who could really help me, and I wished I had his telephone number right then.

CHAPTER 19

'Give unto Caesar that which is Caesar's,' quoteth Frank Bellarosa. 'But,' he added, 'never more than fifteen per cent of your net.'

I give my clients similar advice, but I recommend seventeen per cent of the adjusted gross, and I charge for my time. So, I suppose, does Frank Bellarosa, in a manner of speaking.

It was Friday evening, and I was at my usual table in the cocktail lounge of The Creek. It was crowded, and everything was as I described it on an earlier Friday evening, except that sitting across from me was the Bishop.

Without even looking around, I could feel eyeballs bouncing between me and my friend Frank. Lester Remsen was at the next table, and with him were Randall Potter and Allen DePauw, who you may recall was providing the government with a forward observation post across the road from Alhambra.

The Reverend Mr Hunnings was also there, sitting with three other men at the corner table near the big picture window, a sports jacket thrown over his golfing clothes and a glass of red wine in his hand. Episcopalian and Catholic clergy, I've noticed, drink mostly red wine in public, which I suppose is okay for the image, because red wine is served at the altar, unlike cold beer.

At another nearby table, which apparently was reserved for people with Dutch blood, were Jim Roosevelt, Martin Vandemeer, and Cyril Vanderbilt, the latter I guess having come over from Piping Rock for a night of slumming.

The place was getting more crowded, and in the words of an old rock-Zen lyric, everybody there was there. Plus some. I had the bizarre thought that the word had gotten out that Sutter had brought Bellarosa up to the club, and everyone had turned out to watch. No, no. It was just a typical Friday night.

Frank snapped his fingers at old Charlie, a former dining-room waiter, who after having served his one-millionth meal was put out to pasture in the cocktail lounge where he could drink, smoke, talk, and take it easy like the club members. Charlie, of course, ignored the snapped fingers, and Frank snapped again and called out, 'Hey!'

I winced and said, 'I'll get us drinks.' I stood and walked to the bar.

Gustav, the bartender, had my martini going before I reached the rail. I said to him, 'And a rye and ginger ale.' Gustav's smirk told me what he thought of that drink.

Lester came up beside me, and I supposed he had been delegated with a few pokes in the ribs to approach me. 'Hello, John,' said Lester.

'Hello, Lester,' said John.

'Who's that fellow you're with?'

'That's Antonio Pugliesi, the world-renowned opera singer.'

'It looks like Frank Bellarosa, John.'

'Remarkable resemblance.'

'John . . . this is not good.'

The rye and ginger came, and I signed for the drinks.

Lester went on, 'What's this all about, John?'

'He's my neighbour.' I added, 'He wanted to come up here.' Which was the truth. It certainly wasn't my idea. But I found that I was annoyed with Lester for questioning me on the subject.

Lester inquired, 'Are you staying for dinner?'

'Yes, we are. Susan and Mrs Bellarosa will be here shortly.'

'Look . . . John, as a member of the club board, and as your friend — '

'And my cousin.'

'Yes . . . that, too . . . I think I should tell you that some people here tonight are unhappy, uncomfortable.'

'Everyone looks happy and comfortable.'

'You know what I mean. I understand the position you're

in, and I suppose drinks are all right, every once in a great while.' He added *sotto voce*, 'Like we do with some minorities. And even lunch now and then is all right. But not dinner, John, and not with the women.'

'Lester,' I replied curtly, 'you tried to involve me in fraud, forgery, and embezzlement just a few months ago. So why don't you get off your high horse and go fuck yourself.' I took the drinks and returned to my table.

As I sipped my martini, I found that my hand was a bit unsteady.

Frank stirred his highball. 'You forgot the cherry.'

'I'm not a fucking waiter.'

Frank Bellarosa, as you might imagine, is not used to being spoken to like that. But that being the case, he didn't know what to say and just stirred his drink.

I was not in the best of moods, as you may have guessed. I think that having a fight with an IRS man is the mood-altering equivalent of having a fight with your wife. I inquired of Mr Bellarosa, 'So, what would *you* do? Pay the guy off? Threaten to blow his brains out?'

Bellarosa's eyes widened as though he were shocked by what I'd said, and I found that almost comical. Bellarosa replied, 'You never, *never* hit a federal agent.'

'If you met Mr Novac, you'd make an exception.'

He smiled but said nothing.

I asked, 'So, should I bribe him?'

'No. You're an honest man. Don't do nothing you don't usually do. It don't work.' He added, 'Anyway, the guy's probably wired and thinks you are, too.'

I nodded. In truth, I'd find it less repugnant to shoot Mr Novac than offer him a bribe.

I regarded Frank Bellarosa, dressed in his standard uniform of blazer and turtleneck. He must have seen that outfit in a clothing ad with a mansion in the background and decided to stick with it, changing only the colours. The blazer was green this time, and the turtleneck canary yellow. In itself, the outfit would not draw much attention because after the tweed season around here most of the Wasps break out their silly summer colours and look like tropical birds until Labor Day. At least Bellarosa hadn't walked in wearing a grey iridescent sharkskin suit. I said to him, 'Ditch the Rolex, Frank.'

'Yeah?'

'Yeah. Some people can get away with it, you can't. Get a sports watch, and get some penny loafers or Docksides. You know what they are?'

'Sure.'

I didn't think he did. I finished my martini, got Charlie's attention without snapping my fingers, and ordered another round. 'And a maraschino cherry for this gentleman.'

'Would the gentleman like a green or red cherry, sir?' Charlie asked me, as if I'd brought my bulldog in and ordered him a saucer of milk.

'Red!' Bellarosa barked.

Charlie shuffled off.

A number of women had shown up to sit with or collect their husbands, and I noticed Beryl Carlisle now, at a table with her spouse, what's-his-name. She was in profile, and I watched her awhile, sucking on a drink stirrer. She did it well. She looked toward me, as if she knew right where I was, and we exchanged tentative smiles, sort of like, 'Are we at it again?'

Bellarosa looked at Beryl, then at me. 'That's a nice piece of goods there. I think she's got wet pants for you.'

I was happy to get a second opinion of this, but I informed him, 'We don't talk sex here.'

He smiled. 'No? Whaddaya talk here? Money?'

'We talk business but never money.'

'How the hell do you do that?'

'It's not easy. Listen, I want the name of your tax lawyer, Frank. Not the one you used when you went up for two years, the one you use now who's keeping you out of jail.'

The drinks came and Bellarosa dangled the horrible dyed cherry by its stem and bit it off.

'Your tax lawyer,' I prompted.

He chewed on the cherry. 'You don't need no lawyer. Lawyers are for when you gotta go to court. You got to head this off.'

'Okay. How?'

'You got to understand *why* before you know how.'

'I understand *why*. I don't want to fork over three hundred thousand dollars and go to jail for a few years. That's why.'

'But you got to understand *why*. Why you don't want to do that.'

'Because it was an honest mistake.'

'No such thing, pal.'

I shrugged and went back to my martini. I glanced around the room, sort of taking attendance. I caught a few people looking away, but a few, such as Martin Vandermeer and the good Father Hunnings, held eye contact in an unpleasant way. Beryl, on the other hand, gave me a wider smile as if we were on the right track again. I had the feeling that if Beryl Carlisle was, as Bellarosa grossly suggested, secreting, then it had something to do with my proximity to Mr Bellarosa. Beryl is one of those women who was once wild, married safe, has safe affairs, but still loves the bad boys. I guess I was now the best of both worlds for her; kind of a preppie thug.

I looked back at Bellarosa. I guess we were at an impasse until I figured out the why thing. I tried to recall some of his philosophy of life as imparted to me at Alhambra. I said, 'Novac has it in for me personally, that's why. I screwed his wife once and left her in a motel up in the Catskills during a snowstorm.'

Bellarosa smiled. 'Now you're getting closer.' He scooped up some of those awful pretzel goldfish from a bowl on the table and popped them in his mouth. I had intended to write to the club manager about pretzel goldfish, but after tonight, I'd be well advised not to complain about anything.

Bellarosa swallowed the goldfish and said to me, 'Okay, let me tell you how I see it. In this country, this very nice democracy we got here, people don't understand that there's a class war going on all the time. You don't believe that about

286

your country? Believe it, pal. All history is a struggle between three classes – high, middle, and low. I learned that from a history teacher at La Salle. You understand what the guy was saying?'

I guess so, Frank. I went to Yale, for God's sake. I asked him, 'Where does the criminal class fit in?'

'Same shit. You don't think there's different classes of criminals? You think I'm the same as some *melanzane* crack pusher?'

Actually, I sort of did, but now that he put it in historical and economic terms, I guess I didn't. Maybe I had more in common with Frank Bellarosa than I did with the Reverend Mr Hunnings, for instance, who didn't like me or my money. I said, 'My gatekeeper's wife, Ethel, believes in class struggle. I'll get you together with her someday. Should be fun.'

'Yeah. I don't think you buy this. Okay, it's not like in Europe with all the crazy political parties and all the crazy talk, but we got it anyway. Class struggle.'

'So that's why Novac is out to get me? He's a commie?'

'Sort of. But he don't even know he is.'

'I should have known when he told me he was a vegetarian.'

'Yeah. Also, you got another war going on which is just as old as the class war – you got a war between the jackasses in the government and the smart people outside the government. The jackasses in the government want the poor and stupid people to think they care about them. *Capisce?* So you know where that leaves guys like you and me? Protecting our balls with one hand and our wallets with the other. Right?'

The man was right, of course. But when I tell my clients the same thing, I say it differently. Maybe that's why they don't always get it.

Bellarosa went on. 'And it's not true that the IRS don't care about you, that you're just a number to them. That would be fucking terrific if it was true, but it ain't. They care about you in a way that you don't want them to care.'

I replied, 'But some of what they do, Frank, is not

malicious or philosophically motivated. It's just random, stupid bureaucracy. I know. I deal with them every day. I don't think the IRS or Novac is out to get me personally.'

'It don't *start* that way. It starts when they go after your *kind* of people. And that ain't random or stupid, pal. That's *planned*. And if it's planned, it's *war*. Then, when a guy like Novac gets on your case, it always turns personal.' He asked, 'Did you piss him off?'

I smiled. 'A little.'

'Yeah. Mistake number one.'

'I know that.'

'Look, Counsellor, Novac is a five-number guy, good for maybe thirty, forty a year. You do maybe ten times that. It's like with me and Ferragamo. Same thing. Thing is, they got the badges, so you don't insult them to their face.'

'The man annoyed me.'

'Yeah. They do that. Look, Novac didn't go into the IRS to protect your money. He went in there with an attitude, and if you knew what that attitude was, you'd shit.'

'I know that.'

Bellarosa leaned across the table toward me. 'Novac has power, see? Power to make a guy like you, and yeah, even me, squirm. And he gets his rocks off doing that, because he's got no power no place else – not at the bank, not in his office, maybe not even at home with his wife and kids. What kind of power you got at home when you bring in thirty thousand a year?' Bellarosa looked me in the eye. 'Put yourself in Novac's shoes for a day.'

'God, no. He wears synthetic leather.'

'Yeah? See? So go live in his shit house or his shit apartment, worry about the price of clothes for once in your life, the price of groceries, and lay awake at night and think about college tuition for your kids, and if you're gonna get a bad report from your boss, or if the government is going to spring for a raise this year. Then go and pay a call on Mr John Sutter in his fancy fucking office and tell how you're going to act with him.'

My Lord, I almost felt sorry for Stephen Novac. 'I under-stand all that, but I want to know – '

'Yeah, you got to understand first who you're dealing with, and understand this – they like to pick on very visible people. People like me and yeah, people like you. Guys whose tax problems are gonna make the news. You know why?'

'Yes, Frank. I do taxes for a living. The IRS likes to make the news so they can scare the hell out of a few million other taxpayers who they can't call on in person. That makes people pay their taxes.'

'They don't give a *shit* about collecting taxes for the gov-ernment. You still don't get it. They care about scaring the hell out of people. That's power. And that's jealousy, too. A guy like Novac don't have the balls to get rich like you and me, but he's got the brains to be pissed at not being rich. That's a dangerous man.'

I nodded. Bellarosa really did sound like Machiavelli in modern translation.

'Take a guy like Ferragamo,' Bellarosa continued. 'He pretends like it's all justice, democracy, equality, and caring about the poor and the victims of crime and all that shit. Wrong. That ain't what it's about, pal. It's about fucking *power*. It's jealousy, it's personal, and it's all covered up with nice sounding *bullshit*. Hey, I could take you to streets in Brooklyn where there's more crime in one block than there is in this whole fucking county. Do you see Ferragamo down there? Do you see Mancuso down there? You see Novac there asking those pimps and drug dealers if they filled out their tax return? And I'll tell you this, Counsellor, it don't matter if you led your whole life like *I* did, or like *you* did. When they decide to stick it up your ass with a felony, we're both looking at the same five or ten years, and maybe more. You get time off for good behaviour *after* you're inside, not before. *Capisce?* And I'll tell you something else you don't want to hear. When *you* look at a jury, they look back and size you up, and you try to look innocent and friendly. When *I* look at a jury, half of them think I fixed the other half, and all of them think they're gonna get blown away if they vote guilty. *That* is power, pal. I got it; you don't. Nobody fucks with me. And here's another news flash for you: If you think the government ain't after your ass because of what you do, because you're a fancy tax guy beating them at their own game then you still don't get it. Think about it.'

I'd already thought about that one and patriotically dismissed it. I said, 'You've got this all figured out.'

'I got most of it figured out. I'm still working on some of it.' He leaned back in his chair and finished the goldfish. 'So now you know *why*. Now you got to talk to Mr Melzer. He'll tell you how.'

I let a few seconds pass, then realized I had to ask, 'Who is Mr Melzer?'

'He was on the other side once. A big shot with the IRS. Now he's in private consulting. You know? And now he's rich from selling the enemy's secrets. He knows the jackasses personally. Understand? I met him too late for me. But maybe he can do the right thing for you.'

I thought a moment. There were, indeed, a few renegades out there selling guns to the Indians. But I would never recommend one of them to my clients. From what I knew, they operated in a sort of grey area, trading on personal relationships in the IRS, maybe even paying bribes and blackmailing former co-workers, for all I knew. Their clients never knew, which was part of the deal. No, John Sutter, Mr Straight, would not recommend a renegade IRS man to his clients, even if it was legal. It wasn't *ethical*.

I must have looked undecided, sceptical, or perhaps disappointed, because Bellarosa said, 'Mr Melzer will guarantee you, right up front, that you won't be indicted. No criminal charges, no jail.'

'How can he guarantee that?'

'That's his business, my friend. You want to fight this your way, you go ahead. You want to fight it with Melzer, with an up-front guarantee that you'll never see the inside of a Federal pen, then let me know. But you got to act quick before the jackasses get too far along for Melzer to settle things his way.'

I looked at Bellarosa. He, in effect, was personally guaranteeing me that I wasn't going to jail. I might still be out a third of a million dollars, but I wasn't going to be writing cheques to the IRS in the warden's office. What did I feel? Relief? Gratitude? A closeness to my new pal? You bet I did. 'Okay. Melzer.'

'Good. He'll get ahold of you.' Bellarosa looked around the room again. 'Nice place.'

'Yes.'

'They take Catholics, right? Italians?'

'Yes, they do.'

'My sons can come here if I'm a member?'

'Yes.'

'How's the food?'

'Not as good as Anna's.'

He laughed, then looked at me for a few long seconds. 'So you help me join up. Okay?'

'Well . . . you need three seconding sponsors. Understand?'

'Yeah. I belong to clubs. You find them. I don't know anybody here.'

I saw this coming. 'I'll tell you, Frank, even if I could do that, you won't get past the membership committee.'

'Yeah? Why?'

Why seemed to be the question of the evening. 'You know why.'

'Tell me.'

'Okay, because this is one of the most exclusive and prestigious clubs in America, and they don't want a . . . how do you describe yourself? I mean for real, Frank?'

He didn't reply, so I helped him. 'A Mafia don? Head of an organized crime family? What are you going to put on the application? What did you put on your tax return last year? Gangster?'

Again he made no reply, so I said, 'Anyway, this is one institution you can't coerce with threats, money, or political

291

connections. I've got more chance of becoming a Mafia don than you've got of becoming a member of this club.'

Bellarosa thought about that a moment, and I could see he wasn't pleased with this information, so I gave him more good news. 'You're not even welcome here as a guest. And if I take you here again, I'll be playing golf on the public course, and I'll have to do my skeet shooting in the basement of the Italian Rifle Club.'

He finished his drink and sucked up some ice cubes, which he crushed with his teeth, sending a shiver down my spine. 'Okay,' he said finally. 'So you do me another favour sometime.'

I had no doubt about that. I replied, 'If it's legal and possible, I'll do you a favour.'

'Good. I just thought of a favour. You represent me with this murder rap. As a favour.'

Checkmate. I took a deep breath and nodded.

'Good. I don't pay for favours.'

'I don't charge for them.'

Bellarosa smiled. 'But I'll cover your expenses.'

I shrugged. For a terrible moment, I thought Bellarosa was going to extend his hand to me across the table. I had this bizarre vision of a photo in the club newsletter, captioned: *Mafia don and prominent attorney make deal at Creek.* But he didn't want to shake, thank the Lord, and I changed the subject, saying, 'I owe you money for the stable.'

'Yeah. What did Dominic tell you?'

I told him Dominic's estimate but added, 'It must have gone over that.'

'These greaseballs work cheap for the first few years. Then they learn a little English, and they see what's going on here, and they start screwing the customers like everybody else.' He added, 'That's the American dream.'

Not quite. I said, 'Those guys didn't even make a minimum wage.'

He shrugged. 'So what? They ain't gonna learn if you

feel sorry for them and give them more. People got to be responsible for their own fuck-ups. Right?'

'Yes, but I think you subsidized the job. I think you're trying to get me in your debt.'

He didn't reply to that but asked, 'You satisfied with the job and the price?'

'Yes.'

'End of story.'

'Whom do I pay?'

'You pay me. Stop by for coffee one day. Cash, cheque, it don't matter.'

'All right.'

Bellarosa leaned back, crossed his legs, and regarded me a moment. He said, 'Now that you know you're not going to jail, you look happier.'

I would have been even happier if I knew that Frank Bellarosa was going to jail. What a mess.

Bellarosa informed me, 'Hey, that picture your wife is doing looks great. She won't let me look over her shoulder, you know. She chases me away, but when she's gone, I lift up the cloth and take a peek. She's a helluva painter.'

'I'm glad you like the painting.'

'Yeah. I got to find a place of honour for it. Anna likes it, too. Now she can see what Susan is talking about. You know? The ruins. Anna and Susan are getting along pretty good.'

'I'm happy to hear that. Your wife is very thoughtful to send over her cooking.' I'd slipped back into my inane Wasp speech patterns now that the important business was done with, and I could see that Frank was miffed. He'd probably thought we were soul mates, talking about bribery, murder, and Beryl Carlisle's damp pants, but I wanted to show him that even if we wallowed in the same slops for a while, I could still soar like an eagle. I think he appreciated this on one level. That's what he was buying: an eagle. Pigs were cheaper.

I became aware that something had caused a drop in the noise level. I looked toward the door and saw Susan coming toward me, Anna Bellarosa in tow.

Anna was wearing another one of those loose, flowing pant suits, emerald green this time, and her feet were encased in white sandals, studded with sparkly rhinestones. She had on enough gold to cause a fluctuation in the precious metals markets.

Anna was stealing glances at her surroundings as she moved toward us, and she became aware that she was the centre of attention. Her face broke into a silly, self-conscious smile, and I was actually embarrassed for her. Poor Anna. I wondered if she knew why people were looking at her; that everyone there thought she was dressed funny, that she had the biggest hooters in the whole club, and that everyone had made the correct deduction that she was the Mafia don's wife.

Susan, of course, was as self-possessed as a queen, completely at ease regarding her companion, whom she escorted as though Anna were European nobility.

Frank and I rose as the women drew nigh, and we all exchanged greetings and kisses. The way I figured it, everybody in the lounge got their money's worth even at four bucks a drink. I also noticed no one was leaving.

You have to understand, too, that despite what I said to Frank, Susan and I were not in immediate danger of social ostracism. No, John Whitman Sutter and Susan Stanhope Sutter could get away with a lot. People figure that the older the family, the more wacky and eccentric the members. Thus, just as radical chic was in during the sixties and seventies, with Rockefellers, Roosevelts, and so forth dining with black radicals and people without shoes, so perhaps criminal chic was in now. Maybe the Sutters were starting a trend. Take a criminal to The Creek.

The *nouveaux riches* among The Creek membership, however, would be the most vociferously judgemental, they being the most insecure and the most likely to be made uncomfortable by the Bellarosas, who reminded them of themselves when they lived in Lefrak City or Levittown.

Anyway, Susan looked stunning in a simple white silk dress, a sort of Greco-Roman thing that barely covered her knees and accentuated her tan. We all sat, and Charlie came over unbidden, because Lady Stanhope does not need a waiter summoned for her. Waiters, even in new restaurants, sense this and materialize by her side. This, by itself, is reason enough to stay married to her.

Drink orders were given, and the four of us fell into small talk. I said to Anna, 'You look lovely tonight.'

She smiled and her eyes sparkled. Clearly she liked me. For some reason, my eyes drifted to her cleavage, and there was that gold cross again, nestled between those voluptuous boobs, and if ever there was a mixed signal, that was it.

Susan inquired of Frank and me, 'Did you get your business finished?'

I replied, 'Frank was very helpful.'

'Good,' Susan replied. She said to Frank, 'My attorneys advised me to strike a separate deal with the government. In effect to abandon John. Can you believe that? What sort of people have we become?'

Bellarosa, on learning that Susan had her own attorneys, must have wondered the same thing. But to his credit he seemed to understand the underlying meaning of that question and replied, 'Governments come and go. Laws come and go. You owe loyalty to family, to your own blood, and to your wife or your husband.' He looked at me, 'And if your wife has given you children and if she is a good wife, you owe loyalty to her family, too. *Capisce?*'

Frank, of course, hadn't met the Stanhopes. I mumbled a reply.

Bellarosa continued, 'If you betray family, you are damned to hell for eternity.' He added, 'If family betrays you, then no punishment is severe enough.'

That sounded like something you'd pull out of a fortune cannoli if there were such a thing. I didn't mind the gospel according to Frank when we were alone, but when Susan was present, I didn't want it to appear that I actually hung on every grammatically incorrect piece of tripe he spouted. So I said, 'What do you mean by betrayal? How about sexual betrayal?'

Forgetting that I'd said we didn't talk sex here, he replied, 'A man can go with another woman without betraying his wife. This is the nature of a man. A wife cannot have another man without betraying her husband.'

I knew, of course, he was going to say something like that, and I wanted Susan to hear it, though I'm not certain why. A statement like that would usually set off a rather spirited discussion among two normal and contemporary couples, but if Frank Bellarosa had a weakness, it was this: The man had a faint sense of anachronism about him, a sort of 1950s persona, shaped by his unique subculture, his ethnic background, and his profession. He certainly understood the wider world in which he lived, and he understood human nature, which was why he made that statement and why, like it or not, it was a somewhat accurate statement. But he did not understand that you did not *say* things like that in America. You didn't refer to blacks as eggplants, and you didn't demean women or call Hispanics spics or make gross generalizations about women, minorities, the poor, the handicapped, immigrants, or any other group that was in special favour at the moment. Frank Bellarosa was not a sensitive man. Actually, he didn't have to be, which was one reason I was a little envious of him.

I glanced at Susan, who, as I suspected, was not offended, only amused at this primitive sitting beside her.

Anna, of course, had no comment, nor would she ever.

Frank went on, 'But a man must be careful when he goes with a woman who is not his wife. Great men have been ruined because women made them forget loyalty, made them forget their friends, and opened the door to their enemies.'

I had the feeling Frank would have gone on but I wanted the subject changed, so I changed it. I said to Susan, 'Frank told me he liked your painting.'

Susan smiled, then gave Bellarosa a stern look. 'If he keeps peeking, I'm going to paint his face.'

My, hadn't we become familiar with a Mafia don?

And so we chit-chatted through a round of drinks, giving our audience something to talk about over the weekend.

At eight, we retired to one of the dining rooms where Susan and I greeted a few people we knew and introduced the Bellarosas without using any of Frank's titles. No one, of course, snubbed the Bellarosas the way they would have twenty or thirty years ago. On the contrary, politeness grips most of American society now as if we'd been bombed with laughing gas, and your average white turkey will shake hands with a suspected murderer, converse on the street with bums who accost him, and probably open the door to armed robbers so as not to appear rude. Thus I knew we weren't going to have any scenes *vis-à-vis* the Bellarosas, and I was right.

We all sat, ordered more drinks, discussed the menu, and listened to the specials from Christopher, the *maître d'*, who Frank decided was a faggot.

We placed our orders with Richard, an elderly gent who prided himself on remembering every order without writing it down. Alas, that is no longer the case, and hasn't been for some years, so with Richard as your waiter, you either eat what he brings, or you embarrass him by sending it back. I eat what he brings.

I asked for a certain Bordeaux that I knew would go well with everything we ordered. I did this without consulting the wine list. That's my little restaurant gimmick, and people are usually impressed. Frank and Anna didn't seem to give a shit.

Susan smilingly explained to the Bellarosas that they might not get precisely what they ordered, or in fact anything they ordered. They didn't find this as amusing as our peers usually do, who are used to the eccentricities of old clubs.

Susan ended her story by saying, 'If we're lucky, Richard will bring the wrong wine with the wrong food and it might go well together.'

The Bellarosas seemed confused and incredulous. Frank demanded, 'Why don't they fire the guy?'

I explained that the members would not permit the firing of an old employee.

Frank seemed to comprehend that, being an employer, a

padrone, the don, a man who rewards loyalty. I asked him, 'You wouldn't fire someone who got too old for the job, would you?'

He replied with a smile, 'I guess not, but I never knew nobody in my business who got too old.' He laughed, and even I smiled. Susan chuckled, but Anna pretended not to hear or to understand. I think she would have liked to cross herself. Frank continued on his roll. 'Sometimes I got to fire people, but sometimes I got to fire *at* people.'

Three of us laughed. Anna studied a painting on the wall.

The appetizers came, two right, two wrong.

And so we dined, the Sutters and the Bellarosas. I was relaxed knowing that no one was going to be shot at our table. Susan was relaxed as well, unafraid, as I indicated, of social ostracism, but more than that, she was having a good time. In truth, the Bellarosas were more interesting than the Vandermeers, for instance, and certainly funnier once they got warmed up. Frank had a whole repertoire of jokes that were racist, sexist, dirty, and just plain offensive to anyone, Italians included. But the way he told them, with no apologies or self-consciousness, made them actually sound all right, and we all laughed until our faces hurt.

People around us seemed jealous that we were actually having a good time. The entrées came, one right, three wrong, but by this time no one cared. Susan had taken to calling me *consigliere*, which Frank found funny, but which I, even though drunk, didn't find terribly amusing.

Richard tried a few times to take away Frank's green salad, which had been untouched. But Frank told him to leave it, and the next time Richard reached for it, Frank grabbed his wrist. 'Look, pal,' said Bellarosa, 'I said leave the fucking salad alone.'

This sort of stopped the action for a few seconds. Richard backed off, almost bowing as he rubbed his wrist. I was glad for this little incident, for it assured me that Frank Bellarosa was who and what Alphonse Ferragamo said he was. And like most sociopaths, Mr Bellarosa had a short fuse and was liable to go from laughing to explosive violence in about one second. Even Susan, I saw, who found Bellarosa charming, interesting, and all that, was a bit taken aback.

Frank realized he should not have bared his fangs in human company and explained with a wave of the hand, 'Italians eat their salad after the main course. Cleans the palate. I guess that guy didn't know that.'

I guess he does now, Frank.

Frank ate his salad.

After about fifteen minutes, everybody forgot or made believe they forgot that Frank had forgotten his manners. In fact, Frank went out of his way to be nice to Richard, explaining about the salad, making a few dumb jokes about Italian waiters, and generally assuring Richard that he could move about the table freely without fear of losing a body part. Richard dropped a dish nevertheless.

We ordered coffee and dessert, and Frank ordered four glasses of marsala wine, explaining to Richard that Italians often had marsala with or before dessert, sometimes with cheese. Richard, who didn't give a shit, pretended to be fascinated.

The meal ended happily, without bloodshed or further incident, except that Frank insisted on paying even after I explained that no money could be used in the club. Finally, frustrated in his attempt to make amends with me, he shoved some bills in Richard's waistcoat pocket.

The truly inebriated never know when to quit, so we retired to a small study for liqueurs. A sleepy cocktail waitress glanced at her watch in preparation for telling us it was too late, then noticed Frank Bellarosa, who I knew had been pointed out to her at some time during the evening. She smiled and asked, 'What can I get for you?'

Frank took it upon himself to order for everyone. 'Sambuca, and you got to put three beans in each glass for good luck. Got it?'

'Yes, sir.' She hurried off.

Frank offered me a cigar and I took it. We lit up and

smoked. The cordials came with a whole plate of coffee beans so we could make our own luck.

Frank said, 'I got to take you two to a little place down on Mott Street. Little Italy, you know? A place called Giulio's. I'll teach you how to eat Italian.'

I asked, 'Do we need bulletproof vests?'

You never know with a guy like Bellarosa what he's going to find funny. Susan sort of chuckled. Anna seemed sad. But Frank laughed. 'Nah. They give you them when you sit. Like bibs.'

We finished our cordials and I stood unsteadily. 'They want to close up here.'

Frank sprung out of his chair. 'Come on back to my place.'

Susan accepted simultaneous to my declining. We're usually pretty much in sync when it comes to things like this, and we can communicate with a glance. But clearly we weren't on the same wavelength this evening. I said to Susan, 'I have a busy day tomorrow. You can go if you wish.'

'I guess I'll go home.'

Frank seemed neither disappointed nor relieved, though Anna looked at me in an odd way, almost as if she and I were *simpatico*, and the other two were nuts.

Susan and Anna had arrived in Frank's Cadillac, driven by the wheelman/bodyguard, and Susan and I accepted Frank's invitation to be driven home, as we were both somewhat impaired.

We staggered out into the balmy night, and Frank's car quickly pulled up to us as if the driver, out of force of habit, thought we'd just robbed the place.

We all squeezed into the backseat, which people who don't know each other well won't usually do if they're stone sober. Somehow, the order of seating turned out to be Susan, Frank, Anna, and me. The car pulled away and we all swayed and laughed. It was really tight, given Anna's ample hips, and so it seemed natural that Susan wound up half on Bellarosa's lap. Anna, for her part, seemed embarrassed if not actually panicky about the proximity of her right thigh and breast to my left thigh and arm, respectively. It didn't matter what was going on to her immediate left. Amazing.

Anyway, we laughed and joked, and it was all very silly, typical middle-aged suburbanites having alcoholic fun that in the morning would be embarrassing if you were stupid enough to think about it.

The driver, a man whom Frank called Lenny, actually checked us out in his rearview mirror and even glanced over his shoulder at me once. Lenny was a smirker, and I wanted to bash my fist in his idiotic young face, or tell Frank to put a bullet in the back of his head.

Anyway, Lenny seemed to know the way, pulling right through the open gates of Stanhope Hall, and without hesitation finding his way along the unlighted road to our house. Interesting. Lenny got out and opened Susan's door, helping her off Bellarosa's knee and onto the ground. I exited without help, unless you count Anna rearranging her hips, which inadvertently propelled me out the door.

Susan and I waved good-bye to the black windows of the Bellarosas' Cadillac, then went inside and climbed the stairs to our bedroom. We undressed and fell into bed. Susan and I both sleep au naturel all year round, which means the honeymoon is not over, and gives our young, Hispanic laundress something to talk about, i.e., 'I no wash no nightgowns or pyjamas at Stanhope Hall, but *mi Dios,* those sheets!'

Anyway, on the same subject, Susan reached over and grabbed me, finding, I'm afraid, not even four fingers' worth of John. I informed her, 'I've had too much to drink.'

Susan does not take that as a rejection, but as a challenge. In fact, once she gets going she could make my tie hard.

'Pretend,' she said, 'that I'm Anna Bellarosa, and we swapped spouses for the night.'

'Okay.' There was a distinct physical difference between Susan and Anna, so I had to pretend real hard. Susan switched off the lamp to facilitate this. She said, 'I'm with Frank now, in the back of his car, and we're getting out of our clothes as the chauffeur is driving us around.'

I didn't like that image, but a part of me must have because I felt that part getting harder in Susan's hand, and she giggled. 'See?' she said. 'There you go.' She added, 'And you're going to fuck Anna Bellarosa now. She's never been with any man except her husband, and she's shy, terrified, but excited. And you know she's going to love how you do it to her, and you're wondering how and when you're going to return her to her husband, and when he's going to give me back to you, and what we're all going to say to one another.'

My goodness, what an imagination this woman had. And she knows what turns me on, which can be a little uncomfortable for me. I mean, now that I thought about it, the idea of wife-swapping had briefly crossed my fuzzy mind on the way home in the car.

Anyway, there I was on my back, with Susan's hand cupped around my penis which was rising like an ICBM out of its silo. I heard her say, 'Oh, my God, John, you're bigger than Frank.'

'What?'

She said in a Brooklyn accent, 'I can't get alla this insida me. Please don't put it in me. My husband will kill me for this. He'll kill you.'

'He's fucking Susan right now,' I pointed out. 'Your husband is fucking my wife.'

She said, 'I am betraying my husband. God forgive me.'

I replied, 'I'm just having sex.' I rolled over on top of her and brought her legs over my shoulders.

'What are you doing?' she cried. 'What are you going to do?'

I thrust myself inside her and she let out a startled sound. As I made love to her, she moaned, sobbed, then settled down and began to enjoy herself. Between deep breaths, she gasped a few words in Italian which I didn't understand, but they sounded sexy and raunchy.

Well, look, I mean, we're a little kinky, okay? But we knew

where to draw the line and always had. But this time, for some reason, I had the feeling that we'd gone beyond the bounds of our game. Fantasy was one thing, but bringing people like the Bellarosas into our bedroom was dangerous. What was happening to us?

Afterwards, as we lay on the bed, uncustomarily separated by a few feet of sheets, Susan said, 'I think we should go away. On vacation.'

'Together?'

She let a few seconds go by, then replied, 'Of course. We have to get out of here, John. Now. Before it's too late.'

I didn't feel like asking what she meant by too late. I answered, 'I can't go now. There's too much happening.'

She didn't say anything for a long time, then replied, 'Don't forget I asked.'

And to be fair to her even in light of what happened, I'll never forget that she asked.

CHAPTER 20

July. The best-laid summer plans of hardworking men often go astray, and this promised to be as screwed up a summer as I'd had since my induction into the army.

Mr Melzer got in touch with me as Frank Bellarosa had said he would. We met, at Mr Melzer's insistence, at my house. He arrived at the appointed hour, six P.M. on a Wednesday, and I showed him into my study.

Mr Melzer was a white-haired gentleman, rather soft-spoken, which had surprised me on the telephone, and his voice fit his appearance as I now saw. He was dressed in a dove-grey suit that was expensive and surprisingly tasteful. His shoes were not only real, but they were lizard at about a thousand dollars a pair.

My, my, Mr Melzer, you struck it rich, didn't you? I wished Mr Novac could see his former co-worker.

We sat in my study, but I didn't offer Mr Melzer anything but a chair.

As he was a renegade, I had expected Mr Melzer to have somewhat of a furtive look about him. But he seemed instead completely at ease, and at times rather grave, as if what we were discussing was very weighty and thus very expensive.

I didn't dislike the man immediately as I'd disliked Novac, but there was something a bit oily about Mr Melzer, and I supposed he'd acquired that lubrication after he'd left the IRS, which is not known for greasing the shaft. The lizard shoes seemed appropriate footwear for Mr Melzer.

After fifteen minutes or so of conversation, he informed me, 'I require twenty thousand dollars as a retainer.'

That was actually reasonable considering the case. I would require more if it were my case. But then he added, 'I take half of what I save you in taxes.'

'*Half?* Attorneys are only allowed by law to charge a third of what they get a client in a civil suit.'

'I'm not an attorney, Mr Sutter. There is no law governing my fee. Also, you understand, I have rather heavy expenses.'

'You don't even have an office.'

'I've got other expenses. You don't want to know about them.'

'No, I don't.' I looked him in the eye. 'And there will be no criminal charges for tax fraud.'

'No criminal charges, Mr Sutter.'

'All right. You're hired.'

He added, 'However, according to what you've told me, you do owe the government most of that money. Perhaps all of it. But I can and will get it reduced. I have a good incentive to do that. You see?'

There is no harder worker than a former government employee who has discovered the word *incentive*.

He continued, 'And I will try to work out a payout schedule, but I must tell you, when they settle for less, they want it quickly.'

'Fine. But I don't want to see or hear from Novac again.'

'I'll deal with Steve.'

Steve? I asked him, 'How and when do you want to be paid your retainer?'

'A cheque is fine, and now would be convenient.'

'Not for me. I'll send you a cheque next week. But I want you to begin work as of now.' When clients say this to me, I raise my eyebrows like lawyers do.

But Mr Melzer just waved his hand. 'You are a friend of Mr Bellarosa. There is no problem with payment.'

That could be taken at least two ways. I stood and Mr Melzer stood also. He went to the window. I said to him, 'It's easier to get out through this door.'

He laughed softly and explained, 'I was admiring your place when I drove in.' He motioned out the window. 'It's very impressive.'

'It was.'

'Yes, was. It's incredible, isn't it, Mr Sutter, how the rich lived before income taxes?'

'Yes, it is.'

'It always pained me, when I was with the government, to see how much hard-earned personal wealth was taken through taxes.'

'It pains me, too, Mr Melzer. Truly it does. And I'm happy for your conversion.' I added, 'But we must all pay some taxes, and I don't mind paying my fair share.'

He turned from the window and smiled at me but said nothing.

I walked to the door. 'And you're certain you don't require my tax records?'

'I don't think so, Mr Sutter. I approach the problem differently.' He added, 'It's their records on you that interest me.'

'I see. And how can I reach you if the need arises?'

'I'll call you in a week.' Mr Melzer walked to the door, hesitated, and said, 'You're probably bitter about this, Mr Sutter, and you're probably thinking about some individuals who don't pay their fair share of taxes.'

'They have to live with that mortal sin, Mr Melzer. I simply want to settle up with my Uncle Sam. I'm a patriot, and a former Boy Scout.'

Again, Mr Melzer smiled. I could see that he thought I was a cut above the average tax cheat. He informed me, 'People who don't pay any taxes, the real tax evaders, appear to live like the old robber barons. But I assure you, eventually they go to jail. There is justice.'

That was similar to what Mr Mancuso had told me. That assurance must come with government work. They must know something I don't know. I replied, 'And I would be happy to sit on the jury.' I held the door open for him.

He took another step toward the door, then again turned to me. 'Perhaps I could use your services one day. I do very well, you understand, but I have no law degree.'

'Which is why you do very well, instead of just fairly well.'

He chuckled. 'You're well-known in the Manhattan IRS office. Did you know that?'

I suspected I was, but didn't know for certain. I asked, 'Do they throw darts at my picture?'

'Actually, when I worked there, we had a whole wall in the coffee room captioned "Rogues' Gallery".' He smiled, but I was not amused. He added, 'Not photos, of course, but names and Social Security numbers. Not of tax cheats, you understand, but of attorneys and CPAs who beat the IRS at their own game. They don't like that. So, you see, I knew you, or of you, before I heard from you.' He paused, then said, 'So, it is ironic, is it not, that you should find yourself in need of tax assistance from me?'

Irony to me often smells like a put-up job, and that's what he was hinting at. So I asked him, 'Do you believe this case is a personal vendetta against me?'

He let a meaningful second pass before answering, 'Who can say for sure? Bureaucrats can be so petty. The point is, even if they did single you out, they did find something, did they not? Even if it is a technicality.'

A rather expensive technicality. Well, if the only fitting death for a lion tamer is to get eaten by a lion, then the only fitting financial death for a tax man is to get eaten by the IRS.

Mr Melzer returned to his original subject and asked, 'I would like to call on you for advice.'

This was hardly the moment to tell him to fuck off, so I said, 'I'm available for my usual hourly rate.'

'Good. And would you be available for more extensive work? For instance, would you consider forming a limited partnership?'

Mamma mia, I was getting more offers than a Twelfth Avenue whore. I replied wryly, 'I hardly think that a man who is facing charges of tax fraud would be an asset to you, Mr Melzer.'

'You're too modest.'

'You're too kind.'

'Mr Sutter, I could double your present income in the first year.'

'So could I, Mr Melzer, if I chose to. Good evening.'

He took the heavy hint, put it around his neck, and left with a hanging head.

I felt I needed a shower, but made a drink instead. I loosened my tie and sat in my armchair, wiping my forehead with a handkerchief.

These old houses, all stone and with no duct work, are nearly impossible to air-condition properly, and my study was hot in the July heat. I could get a few window air conditioners, I suppose, but that looks tacky, and people around here are more concerned with appearances than comfort. That's why we wear ties and jackets in the heat. Sometimes I think we're crazy. Sometimes I know we are.

I sipped on a gin and tonic, my summer drink, made with real Schweppes quinine to ward off malaria, and real Boodles gin to ward off reality.

Double your present income. My God, I thought, this used to be a nation that produced useful goods, built railroads and

307

steamships, and subdued a continent. Now we perform silly services, make paper deals, and squander the vast accumulated capital of two hundred years of honest labour.

If Melzer could double my income to about $600,000, then Melzer must be good for over a million himself. And what did he do for that million? He fixed tax problems that were in large part created by people like himself. And the bozo probably went to a second-rate state university and squeaked out a degree in accounting. I made myself another drink.

Communism was dead, and American capitalism had a bad cough. So who and what would inherit the earth? Not the meek, as the Reverend Mr Hunnings preached. Not the parasites, such as Melzer, who could survive only while the organism was alive. Not Lester Remsen, who, though he specialized in mining and industrial stocks, wouldn't know a lump of coal from a cow pie. And certainly not me or my children, who had evolved along very narrow lines to be masters of a world that no longer existed.

People like the Stanhopes might survive because their ancestors had stashed away enough acorns to last for a long time. People like Bellarosa might survive if they could make deals with the new wolves in the woods. Evolution, not revolution. That was what America was all about. But you had to evolve fast.

I took my gin and tonic and went out on the back terrace. Susan, who had taken to drinking Campari and soda this summer (probably because it was served at Alhambra), joined me outside. She asked, 'Is everything all right?'

'Yes. But I need to borrow twenty thousand from you.'

'I'll have a cheque drawn to you tomorrow.'

'Thank you. I'll have it back to you as soon as I unload some stocks. What is your interest rate?'

'The vig is one per cent a week, compounded daily, and you got ninety days to pay up the principal or I break your legs.' She laughed.

I glanced at her. 'Where did you learn that? Next door?'

'No, no. I'm reading a book about the Mafia.'

'Why?'

'Why? You read books on local trees, I read books on local wildlife.' She added, 'Those wiseguys are not nice people.'

'No kidding.'

'But they make much better interest on their investments than my stupid trustees do.'

'So tell Bellarosa you want to capitalize his loan-sharking.'

She thought a moment, then said, 'Somehow, I think Frank is different. He's trying to go a hundred per cent legitimate.'

'He told you that?'

'Of course not. Anna did. But in a roundabout way. She doesn't even admit he's head of a Mafia family. I guess, like me, she never saw it in the papers.'

'Susan,' I replied, 'Frank Bellarosa is the number-one criminal in New York, perhaps in America. He could not legitimize his business or his life even if he wanted to, and I assure you he does not want to.'

She shrugged. 'Did you see that article in today's *Times*?'

'Yes. Are you reading the newspapers now?'

'Someone told me to read that.'

'I see.' The article in question concerned an announcement made by Mr Alphonse Ferragamo, the United States Attorney for New York's Southern District. Mr Ferragamo stated that he was presenting evidence to a federal grand jury that was looking into allegations that Mr Frank Bellarosa, an alleged underworld figure, was involved in the death of a Mr Juan Carranza, a Colombian citizen and a reputed drug dealer. The federal government was involved in the case, Mr Ferragamo stated, because both the victim and the suspect were reputed to be involved in ongoing interstate and international racketeering. Thus, the government was seeking a federal indictment for first-degree murder.

I always liked the *New York Times*' understated style, calling everyone 'Mr', and inserting lots of 'reputed's and 'alleged's. It all sounded so civilized. The *Times* should have heard what I heard in Bellarosa's study: fucking Ferragamo, fucking Carranza, fucking Feds, spics, shitheads, and *melanzane*. I made a mental note to pick up tomorrow's *New York Post* and *Daily News* and get the real scoop.

Susan said, 'Carolyn and Edward will be home tomorrow or the next day. But only for a few weeks, I'm afraid.'

'I see.' Neither of them had come home directly after school. Carolyn had gone to the summer home of her roommate's parents in Cape Cod, and Edward had remained at St Paul's for some vague reason, probably having to do with a girl. I asked Susan, 'Where are they going in a few weeks?'

'Carolyn is going to Cuba with a student exchange group to promote world peace and perfect her Spanish. Edward and some other graduating seniors are going to Cocoa Beach where there is a house available to them. I don't think they're going to promote world peace.'

'Well, but that's admirable on both counts. World peace begins with inner peace, with solving the problem of the groin area first.'

'That's very profound, John.'

I don't think she meant that. I should tell you that Susan finances these trips of Carolyn's and Edward's. The Stanhope money, in fact, has been a problem in the children's upbringing from the beginning. I don't say that Carolyn and Edward are spoiled; they are bright and they work hard in school. But their early nurturing was left to nannies hired by the Stanhopes. And their formative years were spent in boarding schools, which, while customary around here, is not mandatory. But I went along with it. So now, in a way, I barely know my children. I don't know what they think, what they feel, or who they are. Neither does Susan. I think we missed something, and I think they did, too.

July, so far, sucked.

Lester Remsen called me at my Locust Valley office one morning. The purpose of the call was social not business. Or more accurately, it was the business of being social. 'John,' he said, 'we had a meeting up at the club last night, and the subject was you.'

'Who was at the meeting?'

'Well . . . that's not important – '

'It most certainly is to me if I was the subject of the meeting.'

'It's more important what the meeting was about. It was about – '

'If it's important, Lester, we will present the topic at the next regularly scheduled meeting of the board. I will not be talked about behind my back in an unscheduled session of self-appointed busybodies who want to remain anonymous. This is a nation of law, and I am a lawyer. *Capisce?*'

'What?'

'Do you understand?'

'Yes, but – '

'While I have you on the phone, Lester, Mrs Lauderbach called and told me you suggested she sell half her American Express and buy United Bauxite. Why?'

'Why? I'll tell you why.' Whereupon he launched into a sales pitch.

I interrupted and asked, 'What is bauxite?'

'It's . . . it's like . . . an important . . . I guess you'd say mineral . . .'

'It's aluminium ore. Hardworking men dig it out of the ground so people can have beer cans.'

'Who cares? I told you, it's ten and a half today, a two-year low, and there's talk of a takeover bid by American Biscuit. They're a hot company. They make quality sporting goods.'

'Who makes biscuits? U.S. Steel?'

'USX. That's U.S. Steel now. They make . . . steel.'

'Leave the Lauderbach account alone, Lester, or I'll pull it from you.'

He mumbled something, then before I could hang up, he said, 'Listen, John, let me return to the other thing for a moment. I want to talk to you about that. Just between us.'

'Talk.'

'First of all, I think you owe me an apology.'

'For what?'

311

'For what you said to me at the club.'

'I think you owe me an apology for having the audacity to try to involve me in swindle.'

'I don't know what you're talking about. I want you to apologize for telling me to go fuck myself.'

'I apologize.'

'Oh . . . okay . . . next thing. The Bellarosa thing. I have to tell you, John, twenty years ago you'd have been asked to resign for that little stunt. We're all a little looser now, but by the same token, we're all a little more concerned about all these new people moving in. We don't want the club to get a reputation for being a place where these people can come, even as guests. We certainly do not want it known that a notorious Mafia boss is a regular at The Creek.'

'Lester, I have no desire to cause you or other club members any distress. I am as big a snob as you are. However, if John Sutter wishes to sup with the devil at the club, it is no business of yours or anyone's as long as no club rules are broken.'

'John, damn it, I'm talking about common sense and common courtesy, and yes, common decency –'

'And if you or anyone wishes to propose a house rule regarding alleged underworld figures, or the devil, I will probably vote for it. The days of gentlemen's agreements and secret protocols are over, my friend, because there are no gentlemen left, and secret protocols are illegal. If we are to survive, we had better adapt, or we had better get tough and get a plan of action. We cannot stand around any longer complaining because it's hard to dance on the deck of a sinking ship. Do you understand?'

'No.'

'Then let me put it this way. My prediction is that by the end of this century, Frank Bellarosa will be on the club board, or perhaps there won't be a Creek Country Club. And when it's a town park or a shopping mall, everyone can go there, and we can complain about tight parking and rowdy kids.'

'You may be right,' said Lester unexpectedly. 'But until

then, John, we would appreciate it if you didn't bring Mr Bellarosa in as a guest.'

'I will think about that.'

'Please do,' Lester said. 'My best regards to Susan.'

'And my regards to Judy. And Lester . . .?'

'Yes?'

'Go fuck yourself.'

I had decided to avoid The Creek for a while, partly because of my conversation with Lester, but mostly because I prefer to spend July at The Seawanhaka Corinthian Yacht Club.

So on a Friday evening, the day after Edward came home, and two days after Carolyn came home, Susan and I took the children to the yacht club for an early dinner, to be followed by a three-day sailing trip.

We took my Bronco, piled high with beer, food, and fishing gear. It was just like the old days, sort of, except that Carolyn was driving, and Edward wasn't bouncing all over the place with excitement. He looked instead like an adolescent who had things on his mind; probably the girl he left behind at school. And Carolyn, well, she was a woman now, and someone, not me, had taught her to drive a stick shift. Where do the years go?

Anyway, we entered the grounds of The Seawanhaka Corinthian Yacht Club. The club, founded by William K. Vanderbilt, is located on Center Island, which is actually more of a peninsula, surrounded by Oyster Bay, Cold Spring Harbor, the Long Island Sound, and an aura of old money. A no-trespassing sign would be redundant.

We approached the clubhouse by way of a gravel drive. The house is a three-storey building of grey cedar shingle and white trim, with a side veranda and gabled roofs. The building dates back to the 1880s and was built in a unique architectural style, which, on the East Coast, is called the American Shingle style. This is a sort of hybrid, combining native cedar shingles with classical ornamentation, though the classical touches are not of marble, but of white-painted wood. The clubhouse in fact had mock wooden pilasters all around, their capitals vaguely Corinthian, hence, I suppose, the club's second name. The Seawanhaka are an extinct tribe of Long Island Indians. Thus, the club's name, while as odd and hybrid as its architecture, has as its unifying theme the evocation of extinct civilizations, which may be fitting.

Anyway, it is a beautifully simple building, unpretentious, yet dignified, a combination of rough-hewn Americana with just a bit of frivolity, like an early settler in a homespun dress with imported ribbons in her hair.

Carolyn parked the Bronco and we climbed out, making our way to the clubhouse.

The dining room faces out onto Oyster Bay, and we took a table near the large, multi-paned window. I could see our boat, the thirty-six-foot Morgan, at the end of a distant pier. The boat is named *Paumanok*, after the old Indian name for Long Island.

I ordered a bottle of local wine, the Banfi chardonnay, produced on a former Vanderbilt estate that nearly became a housing tract. Perhaps, I thought, we could save the Stanhope estate by planting an expensive crop, maybe figs and olives, but I'd need a lot of sunlamps. Anyway, I poured wine for all of us and we toasted being together.

I believe that children should start drinking early. It gets them used to alcohol and removes the mystery and taboo. I mean, how cool can it be if your mother and father make you drink wine with dinner? It worked for me, and for Susan, too, because neither of us abused alcohol in our youth. Middle age is another matter.

We talked about school, about Carolyn's trip to Cape Cod and Edward's reluctance to leave St Paul's, which indeed had something to do with a girl, specifically an older girl who was a sophomore at nearby Dartmouth College. I fear that many of Edward's life decisions will be influenced by his libido. I suppose that's normal. I'm the same way, and I'm normal.

Anyway, we also talked about local happenings and about summer plans. Edward, on his third glass of wine, loosened up a bit more. Carolyn is always tightly wrapped, drunk or sober, and you don't get much out of her until she's ready to talk. Carolyn is also the perceptive one, like her mother, and she asked me, 'Is everything all right?'

Rather than pretend that it was, or be evasive, I replied, 'We've had some problems here. You both know about our new neighbours?'

Edward sat up and took notice. 'Yeah! Frank the Bishop Bellarosa. He threatening you? We'll go knock him off.' He laughed.

Susan replied, 'Actually, it's quite the opposite problem. He's very nice and his wife is a darling.'

I wasn't sure about any of that, but I added, 'He's taken a liking to us, and we aren't sure how to react to that. Nor do other people. So you may hear a few things about that while you're here.'

Edward didn't respond directly because when he has his own agenda, he doesn't want to be sidetracked. He said enthusiastically, 'What's he like? Can I meet him? I want to say I met him. Okay?'

Edward is an informal boy, despite all his private schooling and despite the fact that most of his family on both sides are pompous asses. He's sort of a scrawny kid with reddish hair that always needs combing. Also, his shirttails always need tucking in, his school tie and blazer are usually spotted with something, and his Docksides look as if they were chewed on. Some of this is affected, of course: the homeless preppie look, which was the fashion even when I was up at St Paul's. But basically, Edward is an undirected though good-hearted boy with a devil-may-care attitude. I said to him, 'If you want to meet your new neighbour, just knock on his door.'

'What if his goons come after me?'

Carolyn rolled her eyes. She always thought her younger brother was a bit of a jerkoff, without actually saying so. All in all though, they get along well in spite of, or perhaps because of, the fact they have been separated so much. I replied to the question about goons. 'You can handle them, Skipper.'

He smiled at his old nickname.

Carolyn said to me and to her mother, 'I wouldn't let other people tell me whom to associate with.'

Susan replied, 'We certainly don't. But some of our old friends are disappointed. Actually, there was an incident at The Creek a few weeks ago.' Susan related, in general terms, our evening with the Bellarosas. She concluded, 'Your father got a call from someone about it, and I got two calls.'

Carolyn mulled this over. She is, as I indicated, a serious young woman, self-assured, directed, and ambitious. She will do well in law school. She is attractive in a well-kempt sort of way, and I can picture her with glasses though she doesn't wear them, dressed in a dark suit, high heels, and carrying a briefcase. A lady lawyer, as we old legal beagles say. She gave us her considered opinion. 'You have a constitutional right to associate with whomever you please.'

I replied, 'We know that, Carolyn.' College kids sometimes think they are learning new things. For years I thought I was getting new information at Yale. I added, 'And our friends have that right, too, and some of them are exercising that right by choosing not to associate with us.'

'Yes,' Carolyn agreed, 'within the right to free association is the implied right not to associate.'

'And likewise, my club has the right to discriminate.'

She hesitated there, because Carolyn is what we call a liberal. She asked, 'Why don't you both just leave here? This place is anachronistic and discriminatory.'

'That's why we like it,' I said, and got a frown. Carolyn reminds me in many respects of my mother, whom she admires for her social activism. Carolyn is a member of several campus organizations that I find suspect, but I won't argue politics with anyone under forty. I asked her, 'Where do you think we should go?'

'Go to Galveston and live on the beach with Aunt Emily.'

'Not a bad idea.' Carolyn also likes Emily because Emily

broke the bonds of corporate wifedom and is now a beachcomber. Carolyn, though, would not do that. Her generation of iconoclasts are a bit less wild than mine, better dressed for sure, and won't leave home without their credit cards. Still, I think she is sincere. I said, 'Maybe we'll go to Cuba with you and see about world peace.'

'Why don't we order?' asked Susan, who always suspects me of baiting her daughter.

Carolyn said to me, 'I don't think Cuba is a good place, if that's what you're thinking. But I think by going there I can understand it better.'

Edward said, 'Who cares about Cuba, Cari? Come to Cocoa Beach and I'll introduce you to my friends.' He grinned at her.

She said icily, 'I wouldn't be caught *dead* with your twerpy friends.'

'Yeah? How come when I brought Geoffrey home for Christmas, you hung around us all week?'

'I did *not*.'

'You *did*.'

I looked at Susan, who looked at me and smiled. I said to Susan, 'And how come you can't remember to get your car serviced?'

'And why can't you learn to pick up your socks?'

Carolyn and Edward got the message, the way they always did, smiled, and shut up.

We chatted about George and Ethel Allard, about Yankee and Zanzibar and the relocation of the stables, and other changes in our lives since Christmas. We ordered dinner and another bottle of wine, though I won't drink more than two glasses before I sail.

As we ate, Carolyn brought up the subject of Frank Bellarosa again. She asked me, 'Does he know what you do for a living, Dad? Has he asked for tax advice?'

'On the contrary, I've asked him for tax advice. It's a long story. But now he wants me to represent him if he is indicted for murder.'

Again, it was Edward who failed to see any problem there. 'Murder? Wow! No kidding? Did he kill somebody? Are you going to get him off?'

'I don't actually think he did kill the person that he may be charged with killing.'

Carolyn asked me, 'Why does he want you to defend him, Dad? You don't do criminal work.'

'I think he trusts me. I think he believes that I would make a good appearance on his behalf. I don't think he would ask me to defend him if he were guilty. He thinks that if I believe in his innocence, then a jury would believe me.'

Carolyn nodded. 'He sounds like a smart man.'

'So am I.'

She smiled at me. 'We all know that, Dad.'

Edward grinned, too. 'Take the case. Beat the rap. You'll be famous. Are you going to do it?'

'I don't know.'

Susan said unexpectedly, 'I never get involved with your father's business, but if he does take this case, I'm behind him.'

Susan rarely makes public statements about standing by her man, so I had to wonder about this one.

Anyway, we had dinner, we all loosened up a bit more, and it did almost seem like old times, but this was the last time it would.

In truth, whatever relationship I have with Carolyn and Edward is based on a time when I could tease them, scold them, and hold them. They are older now, and so am I and so is Susan, and we all have other problems, other cares. I drifted away from my own father at about the age Carolyn and Edward are now, and we never came together again. But I do remember his holding my hand that evening on the boat.

I suppose this separation is a natural biological thing. And perhaps one day, Susan and I will have good adult relationships with our children. I always believed that animals in the wild who leave their nests someday find their parents again and recognize them, and perhaps even signal that recognition. Maybe they even say, 'Thank you.'

As Edward was shovelling pie into his mouth, he announced, 'I want to go out to East Hampton with you guys in August. Maybe for a couple weeks till school starts.'

I glanced at Susan, then informed Edward and Carolyn, 'We may be selling the East Hampton house, and it may be gone before August.'

Edward looked up from his pie as though he hadn't heard me correctly. 'Selling it? Selling the summer house? Why?'

'Tax problems,' I explained.

'Oh . . . I was sort of looking forward to going out there.'

'Well, you sort of have to make other plans, Skipper.'

'Oh.'

Edward seemed vaguely concerned, the way children are when adults announce money problems. Carolyn, I noticed, was eyeing Susan and me as if she were trying to find the real meaning in this. For all her interest in the disadvantaged, she could barely fathom money problems. Perhaps she thought her parents were getting divorced.

We finished dinner, and Carolyn and I walked down toward the pier where the *Paumanok* was berthed. Susan and Edward went to the parking field to bring the Bronco closer to the pier.

I put my arm around Carolyn as we walked and she put her arm around me. She said, 'We don't talk much anymore, Dad.'

'You're not around much.'

'We can talk on the phone.'

'We can. We will.'

After a few seconds she said, 'There's been a lot of things going on around here.'

'Yes, but nothing to be concerned about.'

After a few seconds, she asked, 'Are things all right between you and Mom?'

I saw that coming and replied without hesitation, 'The relationship between a husband and wife is no one's business,

Cari, not even their children's. Remember that when you marry.'

'I'm not sure that's true. I have a direct interest in your happiness and well-being. I love you both.'

Carolyn, being the good Stanhope and Sutter that she is, does not say things such as that easily. I replied, 'And we love you and Skipper. But our happiness and well-being are not necessarily tied to our marriage.'

'Then you *are* having problems?'

'Yes, but not with each other. We already told you about the other thing. Subject closed.'

We reached the pier and stood looking at each other. Carolyn said, 'Mom is not herself. I can tell.'

I didn't reply.

She added, 'And neither are you.'

'I'm myself tonight.' I kissed her on the cheek.

The Bronco came around, and we all unloaded our provisions onto the dock. Susan parked the Bronco again while Carolyn passed things to Edward, who handed them to me on the boat. We did all this without my having to say anything because this was my crew, and we'd done this hundreds of times over the years.

Susan hopped aboard and began putting things where they belonged in the galley, on the deck, and in the cabin. The kids jumped aboard and helped me as I went about the business of making ready to sail.

With about an hour of sunlight left, we cast off and I used the engine to get us away from the piers and the moored boats, then I shut off the engine and we set sail. Edward hoisted the mainsail, Carolyn the staysail, and Susan set the spinnaker.

There was a nice southerly blowing, and once we cleared Plum Point, it took us north toward the open waters of the Sound.

The Morgan is ideal for the Long Island Sound, perfect for trips up to Nantucket, Martha's Vineyard, Block Island, and out to Provincetown. The Morgan's major drawback in the bays and coves is its deep keel, but that's what makes it a safe family boat on the open seas. In fact, the original Morgan was developed by J. P. Morgan for his children, and he designed it with safety in mind. It's sort of an ideal club boat: good-looking and prestigious without being pretentious.

It would actually be possible for me to make a transatlantic crossing with this boat, but not advisable. And now that my children are older, the plodding Morgan may not be what I need. What I need, really need, is a sleek Allied fifty-five footer that will take me anywhere in the world. I would also need a crew, of course, as few as two people, preferably three or four.

I imagined myself at the helm of the Allied, heading east toward Europe, a rising sun on the horizon, the high bow cutting through the waves. I saw my crew at their tasks: Sally Grace mopping the deck, Beryl Carlisle holding my coffee mug, and the delicious Terri massaging my neck. Down in the galley is Sally Ann of the Stardust Diner making breakfast, and impaled on the bowsprit is the stuffed head of Zanzibar.

I took the Morgan west, past Bayville, where I could make out the lights of the infamous Rusty Hawsehole. I continued west into the setting sun, around Matinecoc Point and then south, tacking into the wind toward Hempstead Harbor.

I skirted the west shore of the harbour, sailing past Castle Gould and Falaise, then turned in toward the centre of the harbour where I ordered the sails lowered. Carolyn and Edward let out the anchor, and we grabbed fast, the boat drifting around its mooring with the wind and the incoming tide.

In the distance, on the eastern shore, the village of Sea Cliff clung to tall bluffs, its Victorian houses barely visible in the fading light. A few hundred yards north of Sea Cliff was Garvie's Point, where Susan and I had made love on the beach.

The sun had sunk below the high bluffs of Sands Point, and I could see stars beginning to appear in the eastern sky. I watched as they blinked on, east to west behind the spreading purple.

None of us spoke, we just broke out some beer and drank,

watching the greatest show on earth, a nautical sunset: the rose-hued clouds, the starry black fringe on the far horizon, the rising moon, and the gulls gliding over the darkening waters.

You have to pay close attention to a nautical sunset or you will miss the subtleties of what is happening. So we sat quietly for a long time, me, Susan, Carolyn, and Edward, until finally, by silent consensus, we agreed it was night.

Susan said, 'Cari, let's make some tea.' They went below.

I climbed onto the cabin deck and steadied myself against the mast. Edward followed. We both stared out into the black waters. I said to him, 'Are you looking forward to college?'

'No.'

'They will be the best years of your life.'

'That's what everyone keeps telling me.'

'Everyone is right.'

He shrugged. Presently, he asked, 'What kind of tax problems?'

'I just owe some taxes.'

'Oh . . . and you have to sell the house?'

'I think so.'

'Can you wait?'

I smiled. 'For what? Until you use it in August?'

'No . . . until I'm twenty-one. I can give you the money in my trust fund when I'm twenty-one.'

I didn't reply, because I couldn't speak.

He said, 'I don't need all of it.'

I cleared my throat. 'Well, Grandma and Grandpa Stanhope meant that money to be for you.' *And they'd have apoplexy if you gave it to me.*

'It's gonna be my money. I want to give it to you if you need it.'

'I'll let you know.'

'Okay.'

We listened to the waves breaking against the distant shore. I looked out to the east. Farther north of Garvie's Point, about five hundred yards from where we lay at anchor, I could see the lights of the big white colonial house on the small headland. I pointed to it. 'Do you see that big house there?'

'Yes.'

'There was a long pier there once, beginning between those two tall cedars. See them?'

'Yes.'

'Imagine where the pier ended. Do you see anything there?'

He looked in the black water, then said, 'No.'

'Look harder, Skipper. Squint. Concentrate.'

He stared, then said, 'Maybe . . . something . . .'

'What?'

'I don't know. When I stare, I think I can see . . . what do you call that stuff . . .? That algae stuff that grows in the water and glows kind of spooky green? Bioluminescence . . .? Yeah. I see it.'

'Do you? Good.'

'What about it?'

'That's your green light, Skipper. I think it means go.'

'Go where?'

I'm not good at the father-son talk, but I wanted to tell him, so somewhat self-consciously I replied, 'Go wherever you want. Be whatever you want to be. For me, that green light is the past, for you it is the future.' I took his hand in mine. 'Don't lose sight of it.'

CHAPTER 21

In retrospect, I should have tried the Atlantic crossing with my family and never returned to America; a sort of decolonization of the Sutters and the Stanhopes. We could have sailed into Plymouth, burned the *Paumanok*, set up a fish-and-chips stand on the beach, and lived happily ever after.

But Americans don't emigrate, at least not very many of us do, and the few who do don't do it well. We have created our own land and culture, and we simply don't fit anywhere else, not even in the lands of our ancestors, who can barely tolerate us on two-week holidays. In truth, while I admire Europe, I find the Europeans a bit tiresome, especially when they complain about Americans.

So we didn't cross the Atlantic, and we didn't emigrate, but we had a spectacular weekend of sailing with sunny weather and good winds.

We had stayed at anchor in Hempstead Harbor Friday evening, and at daybreak we set sail for Connecticut, putting in at Mystic for a few hours of sightseeing and shopping. Actually, after about an hour in town, Susan told Carolyn and Edward that she and I had to go back to the boat to get my wallet. Carolyn and Edward sort of grinned knowingly. I was a little embarrassed. Susan told them to meet us in front of the old Seaman's Inne in three hours.

'Three hours?' asked Edward, still smiling.

I mean, it's good for children to know that their parents have an active sex life, but you don't want to give them the impression that you can't go without it for a day or two. However, Susan was very cool about it and said to Edward, 'Yes, three hours. Don't be late.'

I took out my wallet and gave them each some money, realizing as I did so that I had created a slight inconsistency in the wallet story. But good kids that they are, they pretended not to see the wallet in my hands.

Anyway, on the way back to the dock, I said to Susan, 'That took me by surprise.'

'Oh, you handled it quite well, John, until you pulled out your wallet.' She laughed.

'Well, they knew anyway.' I said, 'Remember when we used to tuck them into their berths at night, then go out on top of the cabin and do it?'

'I remember you used to tell them that if they heard noises on the roof, it was only Mommy and Daddy doing their sit-ups.'

'Push-ups.'

We both laughed.

So, we took the *Paumanok* out again and sailed past the three-mile limit where sexual perversions are legal. We found a spot where no other craft were nearby, and I said to Susan, 'What did you have in mind?'

What she had in mind was going below, then reappearing on the aft deck stark naked. We were still under sail, and I was at the helm, and she stood in front of me and said, 'Captain, First Mate Cynthia reporting for punishment as ordered.'

My goodness. I looked at her standing at attention, those cat-like green eyes sparkling in the sunlight, the breeze blowing through her long red hair. I love this woman's body, the taut legs and arms, the fair skin, and the big red bush of pubic hair.

'Reporting for punishment as ordered,' she prompted.

'Right. Right.' I thought a moment. 'Scrub the deck.'

'Yes, sir.'

She went below and came back with a bucket and scrub brush, then leaned over the side and scooped up a bucket of salt water. She got down on her hands and knees and began scrubbing the deck around my feet.

'Don't get any of that on me,' I said, 'or you'll get a dozen lashes across your rump.'

'Yes, sir ... oops.' She tipped the bucket over, and the salt water soaked my Docksides. I think she did that on purpose.

She rose to her knees and threw her arms around my legs. 'Oh, Captain, please forgive me! Please don't whip me.' She buried her head in my groin.

You know, for a woman who's a bitch in real life, a real ball-buster if you'll pardon the expression, Susan has a rather strange alter ego. I mean, her favourite and most recurring roles are those of subservient and defenceless women. Someday, I'm going to ask a shrink friend of mine about this, though of course I'll change the names to protect the kinky.

Anyway, I made Susan lower the sails and drop anchor so we could stop for a little punishment. I tied her wrists to the mainmast and delivered a dozen lashes with my belt to her rump. Needless to say, these were light love-taps, though she squirmed and begged me to stop.

Well, we passed the next hour in this fashion, Susan performing all sorts of menial tasks in the nude, bringing me coffee, polishing the brass, cleaning the head. I can't get this woman to clean the crumbs out of the toaster at home, but she really enjoys being a naked slave on board the boat. It's good for her, I think, and very good for the boat.

Anyway, after about an hour she said to me, 'Please, sir, may I put my clothes on?'

I was sitting on the deck, my back against the cabin bulkhead, sipping a cup of coffee. I replied, 'No. You can get down on the deck on your hands and knees and spread your legs.'

She did what I ordered and waited patiently while I finished my coffee. I rose to my knees, lowered my pants, and entered her from behind. She was sopping wet as I discovered, and I wasn't in her for more than ten seconds when she came, and about five seconds later it was my turn.

On the way back into Mystic, Susan, who was fully dressed again, seemed somewhat distant. I had the impression that there was something very weighty on her mind. In fact, if I thought about it, Susan's behaviour over the past month or so had alternated between periods of clinging affection and bouts of sulkiness and withdrawal. I'm used to her moods, her sullenness, and her general nuttiness, but this was something different. As Carolyn observed, Susan was not herself. But then again, I was not myself either.

As we sailed back to Mystic, with me at the helm, I said to her, 'Maybe you were right. Maybe we should get away. We could take the boat down to the Caribbean and disappear for a few months. The hell with civilization.'

She didn't reply for a few seconds, then said, 'You have to settle your tax problem before it becomes a criminal matter.'

Which was true, and like most Americans, I resented any

326

government intrusion into my life that caused me an inconvenience. I said, 'Well, then, as soon as I take care of that, we should leave.'

She replied, 'Don't you think you owe Frank something?'

I glanced at her. 'Like what?'

'Well, you promised him you would handle that charge against him.' She added, 'When you told Carolyn and Edward about it, you made it sound as if you still hadn't decided.'

I stared out at the horizon for a while. I don't like people telling me how to run my business, or reminding me of what I said. Also, I didn't recall telling Susan that I promised Bellarosa I'd handle the murder charge.

She said, 'Didn't you exchange favours or something?'

I said, 'I suppose we did.' I asked. 'Why does it concern you?'

'Well, that's your challenge. I think it would do you some good to get involved in a criminal case.'

'Do you? Do you understand it would probably end my career with Perkins, Perkins, Sutter and Reynolds if I represented a Mafia don? Not to mention what it would do to us socially.'

She shrugged. 'I don't care, John, and neither do you. You've already chucked it all in your mind anyway.' She added, 'Go for it.'

'All right. I will.'

On Saturday afternoon, we sailed out of Mystic and headed south again to Long Island, spotting land at Montauk Point, which we rounded against a strong wind and tricky currents.

Out in the Atlantic, about ten miles southeast of Montauk, we saw whales breaching and lobtailing in the distance and we headed toward them but could not keep up. While still not a common sight, in recent years I've seen more whales, which is good news. But an hour later, we had a less happy sighting; not fifty yards off our port bow, the conning tower of a huge black submarine broke the water and rose up like some ancient obsidian monolith, dwarfing the thirty-six-foot Morgan. The tower had numbers on it but no other markings, and Edward gasped. 'My God . . . is it ours?'

I replied, 'No, it is theirs.'

'The Russians?'

'The government's. Russian or American. The Sutters don't own any nuclear submarines.'

And that, I think, completed the conversion of John Sutter from right-thinking, taxpaying patriot to citizen of the world, or more precisely, the sea.

With a few hours of usable light left, and a strong southwesterly wind, I headed back toward the south shore of Long Island and sailed west along the magnificent white beaches. We passed by East Hampton and Southampton, then turned into the Shinnecock Inlet and sailed past the Shinnecock Reservation, putting in at The Southampton Yacht Club where we anchored for the night.

The next morning, Sunday, we took on fresh water, then navigated around Montauk Point again and into the Great Peconic Bay. For small and medium-size craft, the sailing in Peconic Bay is some of the best on the East Coast, offering the appearance of open seas with the safety of protected water. Also, there is a lot to see in terms of other craft, seaplanes, islands, and spectacular shoreline, so we just explored for the entire day. Edward explored with a pair of binoculars, spotting four topless women. He kept offering the binoculars to me, but I assured him I wasn't interested in such things. Susan and Carolyn, on the other hand, told him to give them the binoculars if he spotted a naked man. What a crew.

On Sunday evening, we put in at the old whaling village of Sag Harbor for provisions. Susan, as I mentioned, is not much of a cook, even in her modern kitchen at home, so we don't expect much from the galley. Susan and Edward thought that provisions should consist of a decent meal at a restaurant on Main Street, but Carolyn and I voted for roughing it. Since I am the captain of the *Paumanok*, we had it my way. You see why I like sailing. So we took a walk through the village, which was quiet on a Sunday evening, and found an open deli where we bought cold beer and sandwiches. We took our provisions back to the ship, which was docked at the Long Wharf at the head of Main Street. As we sat on the aft deck drinking beer and eating baloney sandwiches, Susan said to me, 'If we get scurvy on this trip, it will be your fault.'

'I take full responsibility for the *Paumanok* and her crew, madam. I run a tight ship and I will not abide insubordination.'

Susan shook a bottle of beer, popped the cap, and sent a stream of suds into my face.

Normally, this sort of horseplay between Susan and me is actually foreplay, but there were children present, so I just joined in the laughter. Ha, ha. But I was horny. Boats make me horny.

We played cards that night, talked, read, and went to bed early. Sailing is exhausting, and I never sleep so well as when I'm on a gently swaying sailboat.

We rose at dawn on Monday morning and set sail for home. Out in Gardiners Bay, we sailed around Gardiners Island. The Gardiner family came to the New World about the same time as the Sutters, and the island that was granted to them by Charles I is still in their possession. The present occupant of the island, Robert David Lion Gardiner, has what amounts to the only hereditary title in America, being known as the Sixteenth Lord of the Manor. My father, who knows the gentleman, calls him Bob.

Anyway, the circumnavigation of the big island was a tricky piece of sailing, but the crew was up to it. As we sailed away from the north coast of the island, I couldn't help but reflect on the ancient idea that land is security and sustenance, that land should never be sold or divided. But even if that were true today, it was true only as an ideal, not a practicality. Still, I envied the Sixteenth Lord of the Manor.

We rounded Orient Point and lowered the sails, letting the *Paumanok* drift as we finally broke out the fishing gear. Susan, Carolyn, and I were going for bluefish, using as bait a tin of herring that we'd brought along for the occasion. Crazy Edward had brought a much bigger rod and reel with a hundred-pound line and was out for shark. He proclaimed, 'I'm going to get a great white.'

Carolyn smirked. 'See that he doesn't get *you*.'

Edward had kept a whole chicken in the refrigerator as bait, and he secured it to his big hook with copper wire. Bubbling with his old enthusiasm, he cast his line in the water.

We pulled in six blues, which we kept in a pail of seawater to be cleaned later by the captain. And indeed, Edward did tie into a shark, specifically a mako, which is prevalent in these waters in July, and I could tell when the mako broke water, and by the bend in the rod, that it weighed about two hundred pounds. Edward shouted with delight. 'Got 'im! Got 'im! He's hooked!'

The *Paumanok* has no fighting chair, which is a requisite if you're trying to land something that size, but Edward fought the fish from a kneeling position, his knees jammed against the bulwark. The shark was powerful enough to tow the boat and even to make it heel whenever Edward locked the reel. Eventually, Edward reached the end of his line, literally and figuratively, and he was so exhausted he could barely speak. The fish, however, had a lot of fight left in him. I recall a similar incident involving me, my father, and a blue shark. I had refused to let anyone relieve me on the rod and refused to let anyone cut the line and end the uneven battle. The result was that after an hour my arms and hands were paralysed from fatigue, and I lost not only the shark but the expensive rod and reel as well. What I was watching now was myself about thirty years ago.

A sailboat is not the ship you want to go shark hunting in, and there were a few times I thought that Edward was going to go over the side as the shark dived and the boat heeled. Finally, after nearly an hour, I suggested, 'Let him go.'

'No.'

'Then let me relieve you awhile.'

'No!'

Carolyn and Susan had stopped fishing for blues and were watching Edward silently. Edward, of course, was not going to blow it in front of the women, or in front of me for that matter. I tried to think of a graceful way out for him but couldn't. Actually, it was his problem, not mine.

Carolyn poured a bucket of fresh water over Edward, then wrapped a wet towel around his head and shoulders. Susan held cans of cola to his lips, and Edward drank three of them.

I could see that Edward was not in good shape. His skin was burning red, and his tongue was actually lolling around his mouth. His eyes had a faraway glazed look, and I suspected he was about to pass out from heat exhaustion. His arms and legs were wrapped around the pole in such a way that I didn't think the pole could get away from him but would take him with it if the fish gave a long, powerful lunge.

I wished in a way that he would pass out, or that the line would snap, or even that the shark would take him over the side; anything rather than his having to let go.

Carolyn said to him, 'Let it go, Edward. Let it go.'

He could not speak any longer, so he just shook his head.

I don't know what the natural outcome of this would have been, but Susan took matters into her own hands and cut the line with a knife.

Edward seemed not to understand what had happened for minute or so, then he sprawled out on the deck and cried.

We had to carry him below, and we put him in a bunk with wet towels. It was an hour before he could move his hands and arms.

We set sail for home. Edward was quiet and sullen for some time, then said to everyone, 'Thanks for helping out.'

Carolyn replied, 'We should have thrown you to the shark.'

'Shark?' I said. 'I thought he was fighting the dead chicken.'

Susan smiled and put her arm around her son. She said, 'You're as stubborn and pigheaded as your father.'

'Thank you,' said Edward.

We sailed into The Seawanhaka Corinthian late Monday afternoon, sunburned and exhausted. A boat is sort of a litmus test for relationships, the close quarters and solitude compelling people into either a warm bond or into mutiny and murder. As we tied the *Paumanok* up to its berth, the Sutters were smiling at one another; the sea had worked its magic.

But you can't stay at sea forever, and most desert islands lack the facilities for a quick appendectomy. So we tie up our boats, and we tie ourselves to our electronic lifelines, and we lead lives of noisy desperation.

I knew that the bond that the Sutters had renewed on the *Paumanok*, while solid in most respects, had a serious fissure, a fault line if you will, which ran between husband and wife. The children were not holding us together, of course, but they did draw us together, at least while they were around. But that evening, as I sat by myself in my study, I realized that I wanted this summer to end; I wanted Carolyn and Edward back at school so that Susan and I could talk, could connect or disconnect.

On Friday, the four of us drove out to the Hamptons, and I listed our house with the realtors for a quick summer sale. Alas, the summer was already a few weeks old, and most of the Manhattan turkeys had already been plucked. This, combined with a shaky stock market, high mortgage rates, and some nonsense about an income tax increase, was depressing the summer-house market. Nevertheless, I asked for a cool half million, which the realtor wrote down as $499,900. 'No,' I said, 'I told you half a million.'

'But –'

'I'm not looking for stupid buyers. List it my way.' And he did. Even if I got the half million, I wouldn't see much profit after I paid off the existing mortgage, the realtor's commission, Melzer, the IRS, and, of course, the new capital gains. God, how depressing. More depressing still was the fact that I liked the house, and it was the only solid piece of the earth that I owned.

So we spent Friday afternoon on our shingled bit of Americana, packing a few personal things that we didn't want around when the realtors brought customers through. Everyone was sort of quiet, and I suppose the reality of the situation was sinking in. Another reality, in case it crossed your mind, was that Susan could indeed come up with the money to pay off our tax debt. I don't know exactly how much the woman has (I'm only her husband and a tax lawyer), but I estimate about six hundred thousand dollars, which spins off perhaps fifty thousand a year for pin money. She doesn't spend that much, and probably it is ploughed back into the stocks, bonds, and whatever. But asking an old-money heiress to touch her principal is like asking a nun for sex.

Also, I don't think Susan is as fond of the Hamptons or our house there as I am. There are some practical reasons why this is so, but I think there is a psychological thing going on there that she is barely aware of, which has to do with whose home turf is whose. Anyway, we took care of the house, shopped for groceries, then had a drink on the porch. Edward said, 'If you don't sell it by the time I get back from Florida, can we come out for a few weeks?'

I replied, 'If I can spare the time.'

Carolyn said, 'Dad, you take every August off.'

'Yes, because taxes, though as inevitable as death, can be put off for a month. This year, however, I have a client with more serious problems than taxes, and I have to stay flexible. But we'll see.'

They both groaned, because 'we'll see' is father talk for 'no'. I said, 'No, really. We will see what happens.' I added, 'You can both come out on your own if we haven't sold the place. Perhaps your mother would like to join you.'

Susan said, 'We'll see.'

And that seemed to be the phrase of the moment, because the future was beginning to look tentative, subject to change without notice.

333

At seven P.M. the Sutter clan dutifully made the short trip to Southampton to visit Grandma and Grandpa Sutter, who were so overcome with joy at our arrival that they shook our hands. They own one of those glass and cedar contemporaries with every convenience known to late-twentieth-century American civilization. The house is actually on a computer/timer sort of thing, with all types of sensors that draw blinds open and shut depending on the sun, water lawns if they need watering, shut off lights if no one is in the room for more than five minutes, and so on. But as there are no uric acid sensors, you do actually have to flush your own toilet.

My mother announced that she would rather go directly to the restaurant instead of sitting and having a drink there, so we turned around and left in separate cars, meeting in the village of Southampton on Job's Lane. This is an interesting street, one of the oldest in America, going back to the 1640s, though none of the buildings actually go back that far. But speaking of Job, of all the miseries that God visited on that poor man, none – I repeat, none – could have been as bad as having to go to dinner with Joseph and Harriet Sutter.

Well, perhaps I exaggerate. But I do say this: There are times when I would rather eat worms in a root cellar than go to a restaurant with my parents.

Anyway, we had reservations at a trendy new place called Buddy's Hole. In the Hamptons, the more modest the name, like Sammy's Pizza or Billy's Burgers, and/or the more loathsome the name, like Buddy's Hole, the more pretentious the place will be. My parents, always avant-garde, seek out these dreadful places, filled with the dregs of the American literary world (which is barely distinguishable from the cream), and has-been actors, never-been artists, and a smattering of Euro-trash who probably swam here to sponge off the millionaires.

I myself, oddly enough, prefer the old-guard places of the Hamptons, dark, civilized sort of establishments with no hanging asparagus plants, and a menu that could be described as *ancienne cuisine*, heavy on the fatty Long Island duck and light on the kiwi fruit.

Be that as it may, we were shown to a nice table for two with six chairs around it and no tablecloth. On the floor under the table was a cat, which is supposed to be cutesy, but I know they rent them and rotate them like they do with the hanging plants. I've seen the same fat tiger cat in four different restaurants. I have little tolerance for these hip places, as you may have gathered, which may explain what happened later.

Well, to continue my complaining, the noise in the place sounded like the soundtrack in *The Poseidon Adventure* when the boat flips over, and the air-conditioning engineers hadn't taken into account that people might show up.

We ordered drinks from an irrepressibly friendly little college girl who didn't seem to realize we were not nice people.

My father, as patriarch, held up his glass as if to propose a toast, and we all did the same. But as it turned out, he was only checking for water spots, and having found some, he called the waitress over and reprimanded her. She was so bubbly and fascinated by the water spots that I began to think she was on a controlled substance.

New drink in hand, Dad examined the glass again, then set it down. So I proposed a toast. 'Here's to being together, and to a summer of love, peace, and good health.'

We touched glasses and drank. A vicious hanging fern kept trying to get its tendrils around my neck, so I ripped some of them off and threw them on the floor where the rent-a-cat was rubbing against my leg. Just as I was about to punt the fuzzy beast across the room, a college kid, probably on Quaaludes, dropped a full tray of food, and the cat, who like Pavlov's dogs, knew by now that this sound meant food, took off like a shot. I said to Susan, 'I'm going to recommend this place to Lester and Judy.'

Anyway, we chatted awhile, though my parents rarely make small talk. They don't care much about family news, don't

335

want to hear about Lattingtown, Locust Valley, or the law firm, and show about as much interest in their grandchildren as they do in their own children; i.e., zip.

Nevertheless, I tried. 'Have you heard from Emily recently?' I inquired. I hadn't seen my sister since Easter, but she had written to me in May.

My father replied, 'She wrote.'

'How recently?'

'Last month.'

'What did she write?'

My mother picked up the ball. 'Everything is fine.'

Susan said, 'Carolyn is going to Cuba next week.'

My mother seemed genuinely interested in this. 'Good for you, Carolyn. The government has no right to stop you.'

Carolyn replied, 'We actually have to fly to Mexico first. You can't get there from here.'

'How awful.'

Edward said, 'I'm going to Florida.'

My mother looked at him. 'How nice.'

My father added, 'Have a good time.'

We were really rolling now, so I tried this: 'Edward would like to spend some time out here in late August. If you're going away, he can house-sit for you.'

My father informed me, 'If we go away, we have the day maid house-sit.'

Neither of them asked why Edward couldn't stay at our house in East Hampton, so I volunteered, 'We're selling our house.'

'The market is soft,' said my father.

'We're selling it because I have a tax problem.'

He replied that he was sorry to hear that, but I knew he must be wondering how a tax expert could have been so stupid. So I briefly explained the cause of the problem, thinking perhaps the old fox might have an idea or two. He listened and said, 'I seem to recall telling you that would come back to haunt you.'

Good ol' Pop.

336

Carolyn said, 'Do you know who we have living next door to us?'

My father replied, 'Yes, we heard at Easter.'

I said, 'We have become somewhat friendly with them.'

My mother looked up from her menu. 'He makes the most fantastic pesto sauce.'

'How do you know?'

'I've had it, John.'

'You've eaten at the Bellarosas'?'

'No. Where is that?'

Obviously I was not paying attention.

Mother went on, 'He gets the basil from a little farm in North Sea. He picks it every day at seven P.M.'

'Who?'

'Buddy Bear. The owner. He's a Shinnecock, but he cooks marvellous Italian.'

'The owner is an Indian?'

'A *Native American*, John. A Shinnecock. And ten per cent of the bill goes directly to the reservation. He's a darling man. We'll try to meet him later.'

I ordered another double gin and tonic.

And so we passed the time, my parents not inquiring after Susan's parents or any of her family. They also did not ask about anyone in the Locust Valley or Manhattan office, or about the Allards, or in fact about anyone. And while they were at it, they made a special point of not asking Carolyn or Edward about school. There are certain types of persons, as I've discovered, who have a great love of humanity, like my parents, but don't particularly like people.

But my mother did like Buddy Bear. 'You absolutely must meet him,' she insisted.

'Okay. Where is he?' I replied graciously.

'He's usually here on Fridays.'

Edward said, 'Maybe he's at a powwow.'

My mother gave him a very cool look, then said to my father, 'We must get his mushrooms.' She explained to Susan and me, 'He picks his own mushrooms. He knows where to

337

go for them, but he absolutely refuses to let anyone in on his secret.'

I was fairly certain that Buddy Bear went to the wholesale produce market like any sane restaurateur, but Mr Bear was putting out a line of bullshit to the white turkeys who were gobbling it up. My God, I almost felt I would rather have been dining with Frank Bellarosa.

My mother seemed agitated that the owner had not put in an appearance, so she inquired of our waitress as to his whereabouts. The waitress replied, 'Oh, like he's *really* busy, you know? He's like, cooking? You know? Do you want to talk to him or something?'

'When he has a moment,' my mother replied.

I mean, who gives a shit? You know?

At my mother's suggestion, or insistence, I had ordered some angel-hair pasta concoction that combined three ingredients of Mr Bear's supposed foraging: the basil, the mushrooms, and some god-awful Indian sorrel that tasted like mouldy grass clippings.

There wasn't much said during dinner, but after the plates were cleared, my mother said to my father, 'We're going to have the Indian pudding.' She turned to us. 'Buddy makes an authentic Indian pudding. You must try it.'

So we had six authentic Indian – or should I say Native American – puddings, which I swear to God came out of a can. But I had mine with a tumbler of brandy, so who cares?

The check came and my father paid it, as was his custom. I was anxious to leave, but as luck would have it, the great Indian was now making the rounds of his tables, and we sat until our turn came.

To fill the silence, I said to my father, 'Edward tied into a mako last week. About two hundred pounds, I'd say.'

My father replied to me, not to Edward, 'Someone caught a fifteen-foot white out of Montauk two weeks ago.'

My mother added, 'I don't mind when they're eaten, but to hunt them just for sport is disgraceful.'

'I agree,' I said. 'You must eat what you catch, unless it's absolutely awful. A mako is very good. Edward fought him for an hour.'

'And,' my mother added, 'I don't like it when they're injured and get away. That is inhumane. You must make every effort to capture him and put him out of his misery.'

'Then eat him,' I reminded her.

'Yes, eat him. Buddy serves shark here when he gets it.'

I glanced at Edward, then Susan and Carolyn. I took a deep breath and said to my father, 'Do you remember that time, Dad, when I hooked that blue . . .?'

'Yes?'

'Never mind.'

Mr Bear finally got to us. He was rather fat and, in fact, didn't look like an Indian at all except for his long black hair. If anything, he was a white man with some Indian and perhaps black blood and, more importantly, a keen sense of self-promotion. My mother took his left hand as he stood beside our table, leaving his right hand free to shake all around. 'So,' said Buddy Bear, 'you like everything?'

Mother gushed forth a stream of praise for one of the most horrible meals I've ever eaten.

We made stupid restaurant chatter for a minute or two, mother still holding Mr Bear's paw, but alas, the last of the Shinnecocks had to move on, but not before my mother said to him playfully, 'I'm going to follow you one of these mornings and see where you pick your mushrooms.'

He smiled enigmatically.

I asked him, 'Do you have sorrel every day, or only after you mow your lawn?'

He smiled again, but not so enigmatically. The smile, in fact, looked like 'Fuck you.'

Edward tried to stifle a laugh, but failed miserably.

On that note, we left Buddy's Hole for the cool evening breezes of Southampton.

On the sidewalk of Job's Lane, my mother said, 'We would

339

invite you all back to the house, but we have a long day tomorrow.'

I addressed my parents. 'We have almost nothing in common and never did, so I would like to end these meaningless dinners if it's all the same to you.'

My mother snapped, 'What a hateful thing to say,' but my father actually looked saddened and mumbled, 'All right.'

In the Bronco on the way back to East Hampton, Susan asked me, 'Will you regret that?'

'No.'

Carolyn spoke up from the backseat, 'Did you mean it?'

'Yes.'

Edward said, 'I kinda feel sorry for them.'

Edward does not love all of humanity, but he likes people, and he feels sorry for everyone. Carolyn feels sorry for no one, Susan doesn't know what sorrow is, and I . . . well, sometimes I feel sorry for myself. But I'm working on that.

Actually, telling people what you think of them is not difficult, because they already know it and are probably surprised you haven't said it sooner.

I knew, too, that breaking off my relationship with my parents was good training for ending other relationships. I think Susan, who is no fool, knew this, too, because she said to me, 'Judy Remsen told me that you told Lester to go F himself. Is anyone else on your list?'

Quick wit that I am, I pulled a gasoline receipt from my pocket and pretended to study it as I drove. 'Let's see here . . . nine more. I'll call your parents tomorrow, so that will leave only seven . . .'

She didn't reply, because there were children present.

We drove back to Stanhope Hall on Monday, and for the next few days our house was lively as the children's friends came and went. I actually like a house full of teenagers on school break, and in short doses. At Christmas, Easter, and Thanksgiving especially, the presence of kids in the house lends something extra to the holiday mood and reminds me, I suppose, of my own homecomings from school.

The children of the old rich and privileged are, if nothing else, polite. They are acculturated early and know how to make conversations with adults. They'd rather not, of course, but they're learning early how to do things they don't want to do. They will be successful and unhappy adults.

Carolyn and Edward had booked flights on separate days, naturally, so that meant two trips to Kennedy Airport at inconvenient hours. It's times like those when I miss chauffeurs. We could have packed them off in hired limos, I suppose, but after telling my own parents to buzz off, I was feeling a wee bit . . . something.

After my children left, the house was quiet, and it rained for a few days straight. I went to the Locust Valley office to fill up the days, but didn't accomplish much except to find the file I needed on the East Hampton house. I spent a day figuring out my expenses on the house, so that when it was sold, I could calculate my profit accurately, and thus figure out my capital gains. Of course, as before, I could reinvest the so-called profit in another house and defer the tax, but I knew that I would not be buying another house in the near future; perhaps never. This realization, which was forced on me by the mundane act of having to crunch numbers, sort of hit me hard. It wasn't simply a matter of money that made me realize there would be no new house in my future; I might be doing very well in two years. It was more, I think, a decision on my part to stop making long-range plans. Modern life was geared toward a reasonably predictable future; thirty-year mortgages, seven-year certificates of deposit, hog belly futures, and retirement plans. But recent events convinced me that I can neither predict nor plan for the future, so screw the future. When I got there, I'd know what to do; I always know what to do in foreign countries. Why not the future?

The past was another story. You couldn't change it, but you could break away from it and leave it and the people in it behind. My objective, I suppose, was to float in a never-ending present, like the captain of the *Paumanok*, dealing with the moment's realities, aware but not concerned about where I've been and charting a general course forward, subject to quick changes depending on winds, tides, and whatever I could see on the immediate horizon.

As I was getting ready to leave the office, my phone rang and my secretary, Anne, came into my office instead of buzzing me. 'Mr Sutter, I know you said no calls, but it is your father.'

I sat there a moment, and for no particular reason, I saw us on that boat again, he and I, nearly forty years ago, in the harbour at night, and saw this sort of close-up of my hand in his, but then my hand slipped out of his hand, and I reached for him again, but he had moved away and was talking to someone, perhaps my mother.

'Mr Sutter?'

I said to her, 'Tell him I do not wish to speak to him.'

She seemed not at all surprised, but simply nodded and left. I watched the green light on my phone, and in a few minutes it was gone.

From the office, I went directly to my boat and sat in the cabin, listening to the rain. It was not a night you would choose to go out into, but if you had to go out, you could, and if you had been caught by surprise in the wind and rain, you could ride it through. There were other storms that presented more of a challenge, and some that were clear and imminent dangers. Some weather was just plain death.

There were obviously certain elemental lessons that you learned from the sea, most of them having to do with survival. But we tend to forget the most elemental lessons, or don't know when they apply. This is how we, as sailors, get ourselves into trouble.

We can be captains of our fate, I thought, but not masters of it. Or as an old sailing instructor told me when I was a boy, 'God sends you the weather, kid. What you do with it or what it does to you depends on how good a sailor you are.'

That about summed it up.

CHAPTER 22

Friday morning dawned bright and clear. Susan was up and out riding before I was even dressed.

She had finished the painting next door, and we were to have an unveiling at the Bellarosas' as soon as Anna found the right place for the painting, and Susan found an appropriate frame. I couldn't wait.

I was having my third cup of coffee, trying to decide what to do with the day, when the phone rang. I answered it in the kitchen, and it was Frank Bellarosa. 'Whaddaya up to?' he asked.

'Seven.'

'What?'

'I'm up to seven. What are you up to?'

'Hey, I gotta ask you something. Where's the beach around here?'

'There are a hundred miles of beaches around here. Which one did you want?'

'There's that place at the end of the road here. The sign says no trespassing. That mean me?'

'That's Fox Point. It's private property, but everyone on Grace Lane uses the beach. No one lives there anymore, but we have a covenant with the owners.'

'A what?'

'A deal. You can use the beach.'

'Good, 'cause I was down there the other day. I didn't want to be trespassing.'

'No, you don't want to do that.' Was this guy kidding or what? I added, 'It's a misdemeanour.'

'Yeah. We got a thing in the old neighbourhoods, you know? You don't shit where you live, you don't spit on the sidewalk. You go to Little Italy, for instance, you behave.'

'Except for the restaurant rubouts.'

'That's different. Hey, take a walk with me down there.'

'Little Italy?'

'No. Fox Place.'

'Fox Point.'

'Yeah. I'll meet you at my fence.'

'Gatehouse?'

'Yeah. Fifteen, twenty minutes. Show me this place.'

I assumed he wanted to discuss something and didn't want to do it on the telephone. In our few phone conversations, there was never anything said that would even suggest that I might be his attorney. I think he wanted to spring this on Ferragamo and the New York press as a little surprise at some point.

'Okay?' he asked.

'Okay.'

I hung up, finished my coffee, put on jeans and Docksides, and made sure twenty minutes passed before I began the ten-minute walk to Alhambra's gates. But was the son of a bitch pacing impatiently for me? No. I went to the gatehouse and banged on the door. Anthony Gorilla opened up. 'Yeah?'

I could see directly into the small living room, not unlike the Allards' little place, the main difference being that sitting around the room was another gorilla whom I supposed was Vinnie and two incredibly sluttish-looking women who might be Lee and Delia. The two sluts and the gorilla seemed to be smirking at me, or perhaps it was my imagination.

Anthony repeated his greeting. 'Yeah?'

I turned my attention back to Anthony and said, 'What the hell do you think I'm here for? If I'm expected, you say, "Good morning, Mr Sutter. Mr Bellarosa is expecting you." You do not say "yeah?" *Capisce?*'

Before Anthony could make his apologies or do something else, don Bellarosa himself appeared at the door and said something to Anthony in Italian, then stepped outside and led me away by the arm.

Bellarosa was wearing his standard uniform of blazer, turtleneck, and slacks. The colours this time were brown, white, and beige, respectively. I saw, too, as we walked, that

344

he had acquired a pair of good Docksides, and on his left wrist was a black Porsche watch, very sporty at about two thousand bucks. The man was almost getting it, but I didn't know how to bring up the subject of his nylon stretch socks.

As we walked up Grace Lane, toward Fox Point, Bellarosa said, 'That's not a man you want to piss off.'

'That's a man who had better not piss me off again.'

'Yeah?'

'Listen to me. If you invite me to your property, I want your flunkies to treat me with respect.'

He laughed. 'Yeah? You into the respect thing now? You Italian, or what?'

I stopped walking. 'Mr Bellarosa, you tell your goons, including your imbecile driver, Lenny, and the half-wits and sluts in that gatehouse, and anyone else you have working for you, that don Bellarosa respects Mr John Sutter.'

He looked at me for about half a minute, then nodded. 'Okay. But you don't keep me waiting again. Okay?'

'I'll do my best.'

We continued our walk up Grace Lane, and I wondered how many people saw us from their ivory towers. Bellarosa said, 'Hey, your kid came over the other day. He tell you?'

'Yes. He said you showed him around the estate. That was very good of you.'

'No problem. Nice kid. We had a nice talk. Smart like his old man. Right? Up-front like his old man, too. Asked me where I got all the money to build up the estate.'

'I certainly didn't teach him to ask questions like that. I hope you told him it was none of his business.'

'Nah. I told him I worked hard and did smart things.'

I made a mental note to talk to Edward about the wages of sin and about crime doesn't pay. Frank Bellarosa's advice to his children was probably less complex and summed up in three words: Don't get caught.

We reached the end of Grace Lane, which is a wide turn-around in the centre of which rises a jagged rock about eight feet high. There is a legend that says that Captain Kidd, who

345

is known to have buried his treasure on Long Island's North Shore, used this rock as the starting point for his treasure map. I mentioned this to Bellarosa and he asked, 'Is that why this place is called the Gold Coast?'

'No, Frank. That's because it's wealthy.'

'Oh, yeah. Anybody find the treasure?'

'No, but I'll sell you the map.'

'Yeah? I'll give you my deed to the Brooklyn Bridge for it.'

I think my wit was rubbing off on him.

We walked up to the entrance to Fox Point, whose gatehouse was a miniature castle. The entire front wall of the estate was obscured by overgrown trees and bushes, and none of the estate grounds were visible from Grace Lane. I produced a key and opened the padlock on the wrought-iron gates, asking Bellarosa, 'How did you get in here?'

'It was opened when I got here. Some people were on the beach. Do I get one of those keys?'

'I suppose you do. I'll have one made for you.' Normally, anyone who opens the padlock does not bother to lock it behind them, which was how Bellarosa had gotten in. But there was something about this man that made me rethink every simple and mundane action of my life. I had visions of his goons following us, or somebody else's goons following us, or even Mancuso showing up. In truth, you could scale the wall easily enough, but nevertheless, after we passed through the gates, I closed them again, reached through the bars and snapped the padlock shut. I said to Bellarosa, 'Are you armed?'

'Does the Pope wear a cross?'

'I imagine he does.' We began walking down the old drive, which had once been paved with tons of crushed seashells, but over the years, dirt, grass, and weeds have nearly obliterated them. The trees that lined the drive, mostly mimosa and tulip trees, were so overgrown that they formed a tunnel not six feet wide and barely high enough to walk through without ducking.

The drive curved and sloped down toward the shoreline, and I could see daylight at the end of the trees. We broke out into a delightful stretch of waterfront that ran about a mile along the Sound from Fox Point on the east to a small, nameless sand spit on the west. The thick vegetation ended where we were standing, and on the lower ground was a thin strip of windblown trees, then bulrushes and high grasses, and finally the rocky beach itself.

Bellarosa said, 'This is a very nice place.'

'Thank you,' I said, leaving him with the impression I had something to do with it.

We continued downhill along the drive, which was lined now with only an occasional salt-stunted pine or cedar. The drive led us to the ruin of the great house of Fox Point. The house, built in the early 1920s, was unusual for its day, a sort of contemporary structure of glass and mahogany with flat roofs, open decks, and pipe railings, resembling, perhaps, a luxury liner, and nearly as large. The house had been gutted by fire about twenty years ago, but no one had actually lived in it since the 1950s. Sand dunes had drifted in and around the long rambling ruin, and I was always struck by the thought that it looked like the collapsed skeleton of some fantastic sea creature that had washed ashore and died. But I do remember seeing the house before it burned, though only from a long distance when I was boating on the Sound. I had often thought I would like to live in it and watch the sea from its high decks.

Bellarosa studied the ruins for a while, then we walked on toward the beach. Fox Point had been, even by Gold Coast standards, a fabulous estate. But over the years the waterside terraces, the bathhouses, boathouses, and piers have been destroyed by storms and erosion. Only two intact structures now remained on the entire estate: the gazebo and the pleasure palace. The gazebo sat precariously on an eroded shelf of grassland, ready to float away in the next nor'easter.

Bellarosa pointed to the gazebo and said, 'I don't have one of those.'

'Take that one before the sea does.'

He studied the octagonal structure from a distance. 'I can take it?'

'No one cares. Except the Gazebo Society, and they're all nuts.'

'Oh, yeah. Your wife paints those things.'

'No, she has lunch in them.'

'Right. I'll have Dominic look at it.'

I gazed out over the Sound. It was a bright blue day, and the water sparkled, and coloured sails slid back and forth on the horizon, and in the distance the Connecticut coast was clear. It was a nice day to be alive, so far.

Bellarosa turned away from the gazebo and looked farther down the shore toward a building that sat well back from the beach on a piece of solid land protected by a stone bulkhead. He pointed. 'What's that? I saw that the other day.'

'That's the pleasure palace.'

'You mean like for fun?'

'Yes. For fun.' In fact, the wealthiest and most hedonistic of the Gold Coast residents constructed these huge pleasure palaces, away from their mansions, the sole purpose of which was fun. Fox Point's pleasure palace was constructed of steel and masonry, and during the Second World War the Coast Guard found the building convenient for storing ammunition. But as solid as it looks, or may have looked to German U-boats, from the air you can see that most of the roof is made of blue glass. Actually, on occasions that I've flown over the Gold Coast in a small plane, I could spot this and other surviving pleasure palaces because they all have these shimmering blue roofs.

Bellarosa asked, 'What kind of fun?'

'Sex, gambling, drinking, tennis. You name it.'

'Show me it.'

'All right.'

We walked the hundred yards to the huge structure, and I led him inside through a broken glass door.

The athletic wings of the pleasure palace resembled a

modern health club, but there were touches of art nouveau elegance in the mosaic tile floors and iron-filigreed windows. Considering that it hadn't been used since about 1929, it wasn't in bad shape.

In one wing of the building, there was a regulation-size clay tennis court covered by a thirty-foot-high blue-glass roof. The roof leaked, and the clay had crumbled long ago, and it sprouted some sort of odd plant life that apparently liked clay and blue light. There was no net on the court, so Bellarosa, who had shown some confusion in the past regarding interior design, asked me, 'What's this place?'

'The drawing room.'

'No shit?'

We walked through the larger adjoining wing, which was a full gymnasium, into the next section of the building, which held an Olympic-size swimming pool, also covered with blue glass. Adjacent to the gym and pool were steam rooms, showers, rubdown rooms, and a solarium. The west wing, more luxurious, contained overnight guest accommodations, including a kitchen and servants' quarters.

Bellarosa said very little as I gave him the tour, but at one point he remarked, 'These people lived like Roman emperors.'

'They gave it their best shot.'

We found the east wing, which was a cavernous ballroom where Susan and I had once gone to a Roaring Twenties party. '*Madonn'!*' said Frank. 'Yes,' I agreed. I remembered that there was a cocktail lounge near the ballroom, actually a speakeasy, as this place was built during Prohibition, but I couldn't find it. Walking through this building under the ghostly blue-glass roofs, even I, who have lived among Gold Coast ruins all my life, was awed by the size and opulence of this pleasure palace. We had retraced our steps and were back at the mosaic pool now. I said to Bellarosa, 'We have to hold a Roman orgy here. You bring the beer.'

He laughed. 'Yeah. Jesus, these people must've had lots of friends.'

'People with lots of money have lots of friends.'

349

'Hey, is this place for sale?'

I knew that was coming. This was the kind of guy who had to know the price of everything and wanted to buy everything he couldn't steal. I replied, 'Yes, it is. Are you going to buy all of Grace Lane?'

He laughed again. 'I like my privacy. I like land.'

'Go to Kansas. This is a million dollars an acre on the water.'

'Jesus. Who the hell can afford that?'

Well, Mafia dons. I said, 'The Iranians.'

'Who?'

'The Iranians are negotiating with the family who own this estate. People named Morrison who live in Paris now. They are filthy rich, but don't want to restore this place. Actually, they're not even American citizens anymore. They are expatriates.'

He mulled that over, figuring as many angles as he could, I'm sure, from that skimpy information. We found the broken door and walked out into the sunlight. Bellarosa asked, 'What the hell do Iranians want with this place?'

'Well, there are a lot of rich Iranian immigrants here on Long Island now, and they want to buy this estate and convert the pleasure palace into a mosque. Maybe the blue roof turned them on.'

'A mosque? Like an Arab church?'

'A Muslim mosque. The Iranians are Muslims, but not Arabs.'

'Ah, they're all sand niggers.'

Why do I bother to explain things to this man?

He jabbed his finger toward me. 'You people gonna allow that?'

'Whom do you mean by "you people"?'

'You know who I mean. You people. You gonna allow that?'

'I refer you to the First Amendment to the Constitution – written, incidentally, by my people – as it regards freedom of religion.'

'Yeah, but Jesus Christ, did you ever hear those people pray? We had a bunch of Arabs used to meet in a storefront near where I lived. This one clown used to get on the roof every night and wail like a hyena. Jesus, am I gonna have that down the street again?'

'It's a possibility.' We were walking, and I turned toward the gazebo.

I could see that my companion was unhappy. He grumbled, 'The real estate lady never told me about this.'

'She didn't tell me about you, either.'

He thought about that a moment, trying to determine, I suppose, if that was an ethnic slur, a personal insult, or a reference to the Mafia thing. He grumbled again, 'Fucking Iranians . . .'

It was really time for me to give this man a lesson in civics, to remind him what America stood for, and to let him know I didn't like racial epithets. But on further consideration, I realized that would be like trying to teach a pig to sing; it wastes your time and annoys the pig. So I said, 'You buy it.'

He nodded. 'How much? For the whole place?'

'Well, it's not nearly as much land as Stanhope or Alhambra, but it's waterfront, so I'd say about ten or twelve million for the acreage.'

'That's a big number.'

'It gets bigger. If you get into a bidding war with the Iranians, they'll run you up to fifteen or more.'

'I don't bid against other people. You just put me in touch with the people I got to talk to. The owners.'

'And you'll make them your best offer, and show them that it's their best offer.'

He glanced at me and smiled. 'You're learning, Counsellor.'

'What would you do with this place?'

'I don't know. Take a swim. I'd let everybody keep using the beach, too. The fucking Arabs wouldn't do that because they got this thing about seeing a little skin. You know? They swim with their fucking sheets on.'

'I never thought about that.' I wondered if this guy could actually buy Stanhope Hall *and* Fox Point, and still keep Alhambra. Or was he just blowing smoke? Also, it struck me that he had a lot of long-range plans for a man who was facing indictment for murder and who had an impressive list of enemies who wanted him dead. He had balls, I'll give him that.

We walked up the path to the gazebo and entered the big octagonal structure. It was made of wood, but all the paint on the sea side had been weathered off. It was fairly clean inside, probably tidied up by the weird ladies of the Gazebo Society before their luncheon. Someone should teach them how to paint.

Bellarosa examined the gazebo. 'You got one of these on your place. Yeah, I like it. Nice place to sit and talk. I'll get Dominic here next week.' He sat on the bench that ran around the inside of the gazebo. 'So, sit, and we'll talk.'

'I'll stand, you talk, I'll listen.'

He produced a cigar from his shirt pocket. 'Want one? Real Cuban.'

'No, thanks.'

He unwrapped his cigar and lit it with a gold lighter. He said, 'I asked your kid to ask your daughter to bring me back a box of Monte Cristos.'

'I would appreciate it if you didn't involve my family in smuggling.'

'Hey, if she gets caught, I'll take care of it.'

'I'm an attorney. I'll take care of it.'

'What's she doing in Cuba?'

'How did you know she was going to Cuba?'

'Your kid told me. He's going to Florida. I gave him some names in Cocoa Beach.'

'What sort of names?'

'Names. Friends. People who will take care of him and his friends if they use my name.'

'Frank – '

'Hey, what are friends for? But I got no friends in Cuba. Why'd your daughter go to Cuba?'

'To work for world peace.'

'Yeah? That's nice. How's it pay? Maybe I'll meet her next time she's in town.'

'Maybe. You can pick up your cigars.'

'Yeah. Hey, how's that income tax thing coming?'

'Melzer seems to have a handle on it. Thanks.'

'No problem. So, no criminal charges, right?'

'That's what he said.'

'Good, good. Wouldn't want my lawyer in jail. What's Melzer banging you for?'

'Twenty up front and half of what he saves me.'

'That's not bad. If you need some quick cash, you let me know.'

'What's the vig?'

He smiled as he drew on his cigar. 'For you, prime plus three, same as the fucking bank.'

'Thank you, but I've got the funds.'

'Your kid said you were selling your summer house to pay taxes.'

I didn't reply. It was inconceivable to me that Edward would say that.

Bellarosa added, 'You don't sell real estate in this market. You buy in this market.'

'Thank you.' I put my foot on the bench and looked out to sea. 'What did you want to speak to me about?'

'Oh, yeah. This grand jury thing. They convened last Monday.'

'I read that.'

'Yeah. Fucking Ferragamo likes to talk to the press. Anyway, they'll indict me for murder in two, three weeks.'

'Maybe they won't.'

He thought that was funny. 'Yeah. Maybe the Pope is Jewish.'

'But he wears a cross.'

'Anyway, I don't know if you know how these things work.

353

Okay, the U.S. Attorney gets his indictment from the grand jury. It comes down sealed, you know, and it's not going to be made public until the bust is made. So the U.S. Attorney takes his indictment to a federal judge, along with his arrest warrant, which he wants signed. Now this will usually go down on a Monday, you know, so they get the FBI guys out early on Tuesday morning, and they come for you, you know, they knock on your door about six, seven o'clock. Understand?'

'No. I do tax work.'

'Well, they come for you early so they usually find you home, you know, with your pants down, like in Russia. *Capisce?*'

'Why Tuesday?'

'Well, Tuesday is a good day for the news. You know? Monday is bad, Friday is bad, and forget the weekend. You think fucking Ferragamo is stupid?'

I almost laughed. 'Are you serious?'

'Yeah. This is serious stuff, Counsellor.'

'Arrests for murder aren't made to coincide with the news.'

Now it was his turn to laugh. Haw, haw, haw. He added, 'Grow up.'

That pissed me off a little, but I let it slide, because this was interesting. I said, 'But they *could* arrest you Wednesday or Thursday. Those are hot news days.'

'Oh, yeah. They could. But they like Tuesday for the big fish. This way they can make the Wednesday papers, too, and maybe a little Thursday action. What if they came for you on Thursday and you weren't home, and they got you Friday? They'd be fucked, news wise.'

'Okay. So they arrest you on a Tuesday. What's the point?'

'Okay. So they pick you up, they take you down to Federal Plaza, the FBI office, you know, and they jerk you around there awhile, give everybody a good look at you, then they get you over to Foley Square, the federal court, right? And the

FBI guys bring you in with cuffs about nine, ten o'clock, and by this time Ferragamo's got half the fucking newspeople in the world there, and everybody's shoving microphones in your face, and the cameras are rolling. Then you get printed and booked, blah, blah, blah, and at about that time is when they let you call your attorney.' He looked at me. 'Understand?'

'What if your attorney is in, say, Cuba?'

'He ain't gonna be. In fact, I don't have to call him. Because he's coming over to my place for coffee about five in the morning for the next few Tuesdays.'

'I see.'

'Yeah. So when the FBI comes, then my attorney is right there to see that everything is done right, that the FBI guys behave. And my attorney gets in my car with Lenny and follows me to Federal Plaza, then to Foley Square. My attorney is not in Cuba, or no place except with his client. *Capisce?*'

I nodded.

'Also, my attorney has a briefcase, and in that briefcase is cash and property deeds, and other shit that he needs to post bail for his client. My attorney will be given about four or five million dollars to post.'

'You're not going to get out on bail on a federal murder charge, Frank, not for any amount of money.'

'Wrong. Listen carefully. My attorney is going to convince the judge that Frank Bellarosa is a responsible man, a man who has strong ties to the community, a man who has sixteen legitimate businesses to look after, a man who has a house, a wife, and kids. My attorney will tell the judge that his client has never been convicted of a violent crime, and that he knew the FBI was coming for him and was waiting for them, and came along peacefully. My attorney was a witness to that. My attorney will tell the judge that he knows Mr Bellarosa personally, as a *friend*, and that he knows Mrs Bellarosa, and in fact my attorney lives next door to Mr and Mrs Bellarosa, and my attorney is making a personal guarantee that Mr Bellarosa will not flee the jurisdiction. Understand?'

Indeed I did.

'Okay. So now the judge, who does not like to grant any bail for murder, first degree, now he has to consider all this shit very seriously. By now, Ferragamo has been tipped by the FBI that Bellarosa knew he was going to get arrested that morning, and that Bellarosa has the cash on hand for bail, and that Bellarosa has a very high-quality attorney. So Ferragamo gets his ass into the courtroom personally and starts putting the pressure on the judge. Your Honour, this is a very serious charge, blah, blah, blah. Your Honour, this is a dangerous man; a murderer, blah, blah. But my attorney goes balls to balls with the U.S. Attorney and talks about bail not being unreasonably denied, blah, blah, and the charge is bullshit anyway, and we've got five million in the bag here, and I gave you my *personal* guarantee, Your Honour. John Sutter, of Wall Street, is putting his balls right on the table, Your Honour. Right? Now Ferragamo didn't expect this shit, and he's the one who's caught with his pants down. He's jumping through his ass to see that Frank Bellarosa doesn't walk. He's got a big hard-on about seeing me in jail with the *melanzane*. And that night he's gonna be home with his wife and friends having dinner, watching the fucking news while I'm in the slammer with a cork up my ass trying to keep the faggots out of my back door. You understand what I'm saying?'

Frank had a way with words. I replied, 'I do.'

'Yeah. And you understand that this is not going to happen, Counsellor. You are not going to let it happen.'

'I thought you told me that Ferragamo wants you on the street after your indictment. So that your friends or enemies could kill you before your trial.'

'Yeah. You remembered that? So here's the thing. Ferragamo knows if he gets me in jail, we are going to appeal the bail ruling. Right? But this takes a few weeks. And the next time we come up in front of the judge, Ferragamo has told the judge on the sly that bail is okay with him. He winks at the judge and whispers in his ear. The FBI wants to follow Bellarosa. Right? This is all bullshit. The FBI has been following me for twenty fucking years and they ain't seen

356

shit yet. So the judge winks back, and I'm sprung. But I've been in jail two, three weeks by that time. Follow? So Ferragamo puts the word out that I sang and sang in the slammer. That I'm ready to give up all kinds of people for a reduced charge. So now I'm dead meat. But listen, Counsellor, if I can walk out of that courthouse on the same day I walk in, then I got a chance to keep things under control. You understand?'

'Yes.' I understood perfectly well now why it was me and not Jack Weinstein who was going to represent Mr Frank Bellarosa. It was John Whitman Sutter, great-great-great-nephew of Walt, son of Joseph Sutter the Wall Street legend, husband of Susan (one of New York's Four Hundred) Stanhope, partner in Perkins, Perkins, Sutter and Reynolds, member of The Creek and Seawanhaka Corinthian, not to mention a High Episcopalian, a Yale graduate, Harvard Law, and a friend of Roosevelts, Astors, and Vanderbilts, and, incidentally, a friend and next-door neighbour to the accused – that very same John Sutter was going to guarantee personally in open court that his client, Mr Frank Bellarosa, was not going to skip bail. And that judge would listen, and so would every reporter in that court, and it would make every newspaper and every radio and TV news show in the tristate area, probably the country. The bastard was brilliant. He'd figured this out . . . when? The day I ran into him at Hicks' Nursery? That far back? *Mr Sutter? John Sutter, right?*

But of course, it had to be even before then. He had known who I was, that I was a lawyer, and that I was his next-door neighbour when he ran into me by accident or design. He had already seen in his mind this whole scenario that he had just laid out before me and had figured out how to survive before his enemies even made their first move. And what was even more impressive was that he had been reasonably sure that I was in his hip pocket even after I'd told him to buzz off a few times. It was no accident that this man was still alive and free after thirty years. His enemies – state and federal law enforcement agencies, rival Mafia bosses, Colombians, and other opportunists – were not lazy or incompetent. They simply were not up to the challenge of getting rid of Frank Bellarosa.

I mean, there was a time when I wanted to see him in jail . . . maybe even dead. But I had mixed feelings about that now, the way I do when a shark is hooked. You hate the shark, you fear the shark, but after about two hours, you respect the shark.

I heard his voice interrupting my thoughts. 'So you understand?'

I nodded.

He went on. 'We should be out of the courthouse before they break for lunch. I don't want lunch in the holding cell. Then you and me go have a nice lunch someplace. Maybe Caffè Roma. That's near the court. I gotta make you try fried squid. So around that time, Alphonse Ferragamo is holding one of his fucking press conferences. He's skipping lunch so he can make the late editions and the five-o'clock news. Right? He's announcing my indictment, my arrest, and all that shit. He wants to announce that I'm in jail, too, but that ain't gonna happen, so he has to eat a little shit from the press people and from his boss in Washington. But basically, he's a happy man, and he's going to fuck his girlfriend that afternoon, then go home and have a party. So we'll hang around town awhile, get a hotel room, watch the news, get some newspapers, have a few friends over. You can make a few statements to the press, too, but not too much. And remind me to call my wife. Oh, yeah, it would be nice if your wife could go over to my place about eight, nine in the morning and sit with my wife. You know how wives get about this shit. Well, maybe you don't. But I can tell you, they don't handle it too good. So your wife can kinda keep Anna's mind off things, maybe until her stupid relatives get out to my place and they can all hang around crying and cooking. Okay? But don't mention any of this to your wife yet. *Capisce?* And try to be around for the next two, three weeks. You going on vacation or anything?'

'I guess not.'

'Good. Stick around. Get lots of sleep on Monday nights. All right? Practise what you're gonna say in court. Get your brass balls on for the fucking Feds. We're gonna look good in court.' He looked at me. 'No jail, Counsellor. No jail. That's what I promised you, that's what you promise me. You understand?'

'I promise I will do my best.'

'Good.' He stood and slapped me on the shoulder. 'Hey, I got another problem. In Brooklyn, I got tomatoes the size of bull balls. Here it is the middle of July, and I got these small green things. But I see you got nice big ones, and those are the plants I gave you. Remember? So the soil must be different. I'm not embarrassed or anything, but this is hard to understand. So what I want is to trade you some of your tomatoes for something. I got lots of string beans. Okay? Deal?'

I don't like string beans, but we shook on it.

CHAPTER 23

Some days after the Fox Point powwow, I was up at the yacht club doing light maintenance on the Morgan. It was a weekday morning, and I was playing hooky from work, as usual. My partners had not commented directly on my extended absences, partly because they expect it in the summer, but also because they assume I am conscientious and would not let the firm down. In fact, they were wrong; my work was piling up, calls went unanswered, and the Locust Valley office had no one at the helm. People work better unsupervised anyway.

Though I enjoy tinkering around the boat, I enjoy sailing it more. But with a sailboat, you really should have at least two people aboard, and it's sometimes difficult to find a crew during the workday. Carolyn and Edward were gone, of course, and Susan is only moderately enthusiastic about sailing, as I am about riding, and she begged off.

There are friends who might be around during the week,

but I'd been avoiding people lately. One can always rustle up a few college kids to crew, but in some irrational way, because I missed my own children, I didn't feel like having other kids around. So, today, I contented myself with putting my boat in order.

I was aware of leather-soled footsteps coming toward me on the pier. It was low tide, so I had to look up from the deck and squint into the morning sun to see who it was. Whoever it was, he was wearing a suit. He stopped and said, 'Permission to come aboard.'

'Not in those shoes.'

So Mr Mancuso, of the Federal Bureau of Investigation, dutifully removed his shoes, then jumped down onto the teak deck in his stocking feet. 'Good morning,' he said.

'*Buon giorno*,' I replied.

He smiled with his big Chiclets. 'I'm here to bring some aggravation and worry into your life.'

'I'm already married.' That was a pretty good one, and he smiled wider. He wasn't a laugher, but he did appreciate my wit. He was on the right track.

He said, 'Do you have a few minutes?'

'For my country, Mr Mancuso, I have nothing but time. However, I'm out of money and short on patience.' I went about my business, which, at that moment, was coiling some half-inch line.

Mr Mancuso set his shoes down on the deck and watched me a moment, then looked around. 'Nice boat.'

'Thank you.'

'Nice place.' He waved his arm around, encompassing the whole club. 'First-class operation.'

'We try.' I finished with the line and regarded Mr Mancuso a moment. He was as sallow as when I'd last seen him in April. He wore a light-beige suit of summer wool, which was well cut, a good shirt and tie, and, as I was about to see clearly, very nice socks. However, the frizzy fringe of hair and the woolly tuft still amused me.

He said, 'You want to talk here, Mr Sutter? You feel

comfortable here? You want to go inside the boat? Someplace else?'

'How long is a few minutes?'

'Maybe half an hour. Hour.'

I considered a moment, then asked him, 'You sail?'

'No.'

'You do now. You probably won't need that tie and jacket.'

'Probably not.' He took off his jacket, revealing a shoulder holster that held a big automatic, perhaps a Browning.

I glanced around at the nearby boats, then said to him, 'Maybe you want to stow that below. You know, inside the boat.' I pointed. 'That's called below.'

'Sure.' He ducked down the companionway and reappeared a few minutes later, tieless and barefoot now, his cuffs and shirt sleeves rolled up. He looked even more ludicrous. I stood at the helm and started the engine. 'You know how to cast off?'

'Sure. I can do that.'

And he did. Within a few minutes we were under way. The Morgan's helm is a spoked mahogany wheel, and I stood there at it, feeling in control of something for a change. I would have preferred to be under sail, but with Mancuso as my crew I thought I'd better let the engine take us clear of the moored boats and shoals.

I took the *Paumanok* around Plum Point into Cold Spring Harbor, still under power, and pointed the bow north toward the Sound, then slowed the engine. Still at the helm I said to Mr Mancuso, 'See that winch? Crank that and it will raise the mainsail.'

He did as he was told and the mainsail went up. A light breeze caught it, and the *Paumanok* moved through the water. I cut the engine and told him how to trim the sail, then I got him to raise the jib, and we started to make some headway. Poor Mr Mancuso was scrambling all over the decks in his good wool trousers, which, I'm afraid, were ruined. All in all, though, he seemed to be enjoying himself, and I was

361

happy for this unexpected opportunity to sail. Mr Mancuso, of course, wanted to speak to me about something, but for the time being he seemed content to have been shanghaied aboard the *Paumanok*.

Mr Mancuso was a fast learner, at least as far as terminology, and within an hour, he knew a boom from a spreader, the headstay from the backstay, and presumably his ass from his elbow.

As I said, the wind was light, but it was from the south and got us well out into the Sound. About three miles off Lloyd's Neck, I showed him how to lower the sails. The wind was still southerly and the tide was ebbing, so we drifted safely away from the shore and shallow water. Still, I returned to the helm and played captain. I asked Mr Mancuso, 'Did you enjoy that?'

'Yes. I really did.'

'It's more fun at night with high winds and heavy seas. Especially if your engine conks.'

'Why is that, Mr Sutter?'

'Because you think you're going to die.'

'That does sound like fun.'

'But, of course, the objective is not to die. So you put out your trysails and see if you can run before the wind to safety. Or maybe you lower all your sails, put the engine on full power, and head into the wind. There are other times when you might want to ride to a sea anchor. You have to make intelligent decisions. Not like with desk work where it really doesn't matter.'

He nodded. 'About once a year I have to make a decision about pulling my gun. So I can appreciate what you're saying.'

'Good.' Having gotten the 'my balls are as big as your balls' stuff out of the way, I went below and poured two mugs of coffee from my thermos and brought them up. 'Here.'

'Thanks.'

I stood at the helm in my faded jeans and T-shirt, one hand resting on the wheel, the other holding my mug. I really looked good. I regarded Mr Mancuso with his silly outfit and his pale skin, sitting on a cushioned locker. I said to him, 'Did you say you wanted to speak to me about something?'

He seemed to be contemplating what it was he'd wanted to say, as if perhaps it was no longer relevant. Finally, he said, 'Mr Sutter, I have been an FBI agent for nearly twenty years.'

'It must be interesting.'

'Yes. Most of that time has been spent in various organized-crime task forces. The Mafia is my special area of concern.'

'Did you want sugar with that? I have no milk.'

'No, thanks. So, I've seen a lot of what life is like in the underworld, Mr Sutter, and there is nothing romantic about it.'

'Who ever said there was?'

'They hurt people, Mr Sutter. They sell drugs to children, force young girls into prostitution, extort money from honest businessmen. They engage in loan-sharking activities and beat people who can't make their payments. They corrupt unions and politicians – '

'I'm not sure who corrupts whom in that case.'

'They murder people – '

'They murder other types of scum. They do not murder cops, businessmen, judges, or people like you or me, Mr Mancuso. I hear what you're saying, but the average citizen is more concerned with, and outraged by, random street violence, rapists, muggers, car thieves, armed robbers, burglars, and drug-crazed maniacs running around. I personally know people whose lives have been touched by those sorts of criminals, and so do you. I don't know anyone personally who has been a victim of the Mafia. *Capisce?*'

He smiled at that word, then nodded in agreement. 'Yes, I understand that, Mr Sutter. But admit that organized crime and racketeering are hurting the entire nation in insidious ways that – '

'Okay. I admit it. And I told you I'd sit on a jury in a Mafia case. That's more than a lot of citizens would do. You know why? Because they are frightened, Mr Mancuso.'

'Well, there you are, Mr Sutter. People *are* frightened by mobsters. People – '

'Well, of course they would be frightened if they had to sit on a jury. But that's a remote possibility. What people are really frightened of is walking down the street at night.'

'The FBI doesn't patrol the streets, Mr Sutter. What you're talking about is another issue.'

'Well, then, let's talk about the Mafia. *Why* would the average citizen be frightened to sit on a jury or testify in an organized-crime case? I'll tell you why; because *you* are not doing your job.'

For the first time, Mr Mancuso seemed annoyed with me. In truth, he had shown a good deal of patience on this occasion and the last, but I could see I'd gotten to him. Actually, I was only blowing smoke at him, and I wanted him to tell me that everything was under control, that the republic was safe, and that I would be able to walk the streets of New York in a few more weeks, maybe a month. But that wasn't the case. He did, however, give me some hopeful news.

He put his mug on the deck and stood. He said, 'In fact, Mr Sutter, we are doing our job. In fact, sir, we are winning the war against organized crime.'

'Have you told the Mafia this?'

'They know it very well. Better than the American public, which is fed mostly bad news. But let me give a good-news headline: MAFIA ON THE RUN.'

I smiled but said nothing.

Mr Mancuso went on, 'Since 1984, Mr Sutter, the federal government has obtained hundreds of convictions under the Racketeer Influenced and Corrupt Organizations Act – the RICO Act. We have seized millions of dollars in property and cash, and we have destroyed or seriously damaged nearly all of the twenty-four organized-crime families in this country. There is only one remaining stronghold of the Mafia in America, and that is here in New York. And of New York's five traditional crime families, four have been crippled by prosecutions and by death and by early retirements. The old legendary dons are all gone now. The calibre of the remaining leadership is very low. Only one family remains strong, and only one leader commands respect.'

'Who could that be?'

Mr Mancuso, having delivered himself of this satisfying monologue, smiled. 'You know who.'

I asked him, 'What is your point?'

'Well, the point, obviously, is Frank Bellarosa and your relationship with him.'

'I see.' Mr Mancuso had intrigued me, and it occurred to me that he could answer some questions for me, rather than vice versa. I asked him, 'How rich is Mr Bellarosa?'

He thought a moment, then replied, 'We estimate that his illegal empire grosses about six hundred million dollars a year –'

'Six hundred *million*? *Mamma mia,* Mr Mancuso.'

Mr Mancuso smiled. 'Yes. But I don't know how much profit there is and how much of that he keeps personally. We do know that he is involved in fourteen legitimate businesses –'

'Sixteen.'

Mr Mancuso regarded me a moment, then continued, 'Fourteen or more legitimate businesses, from which he showed a taxable income last year of five and a half million dollars.'

'And he paid his taxes?'

'Oh, yes. Overpaid, actually. The IRS refunded him some two hundred thousand dollars. He had a serious tax problem some years back that sent him away for nineteen months. So he's very careful with his taxes on his legitimate income.' Mr Mancuso added, 'I would not be surprised if he asked you to do his tax work at some point.'

I didn't reply, but asked, 'Why do you suppose he's not satisfied with five million legitimate dollars a year?'

Mr Mancuso informed me, 'There are other factors at work, Mr Sutter. Bellarosa is a unique personality. He does not make decisions the way you or I would. This man fought his way to the top of New York's largest crime family, and he killed or caused to be killed at least nine men whom he perceived to be a danger to him, or who were, in fact, a danger to him, or men who were simply in his way during his pursuit of the emperor's crown. Personalities like this exist, of course, and history is full of them. Frank Bellarosa is a power freak. The money is incidental. Do you see?'

'I understand.'

'Understand, too, that he *likes* living on the edge. You may find this hard to believe, Mr Sutter, but in his primitive way he enjoys being the target of assassins. His enemies can pay him no higher compliment than trying to kill him. *Capisce?*'

I smiled involuntarily. '*Capisce.*'

'No, you say *capisco.* I understand. *Capisce?*'

'*Capisco.*'

'Very good. But work on your accent. I understand your wife speaks some Italian. Maybe she can help you.'

I didn't reply. In fact, neither of us spoke for a while. As the *Paumanok* drifted, I realized that I should, at some point, let Mr Mancuso know that I was representing the man who was the subject of our conversation. But as he hadn't asked, and since nothing of a confidential nature was being discussed yet, I let it slide. I wanted to know more about my client, and since my client wouldn't even admit that there was a Mafia, let alone that he was the emperor of it, I figured that Mr Mancuso was my best source. I asked, 'How big is his empire, actually? Not money, but people.'

Mr Mancuso studied me awhile, then replied, 'Well, again, these are estimates, but we think that Bellarosa controls the activities of three thousand men.'

'That's a big company.'

'Yes. And at the core of his organization are three hundred of what we call "made" men. Men who have made their bones. Do you understand what that means?'

'I'm afraid I do.'

'And all of these hard-core mafiosi are Italian, mostly Sicilian or Neapolitan.'

'And which are you, Mr Mancuso?'

'Neither, Mr Sutter. I am a true Roman on both sides of my family.'

'Interesting. And Mr Ferragamo?'

He smiled. 'I hear that his ancestors were from Florence. They are very cultured there. Why do you ask?'

'I'm just trying to read the subtexts, Mr Mancuso.'

'I assure you, Mr Sutter, there are no subtexts.'

'Perhaps not. But tell me about these Sicilians and Neapolitans.'

He hesitated a moment, then replied, 'I suppose it might matter where Bellarosa's crime family had its ancestral origins, in that there are historical and family ties that we must consider and comprehend in order to effectively prosecute these people.'

'I see. So there are about three hundred hard-core members, and about three thousand others.'

'Yes. Associates. At the top is Frank Bellarosa. He has an underboss, a man named Salvatore D'Alessio, aka Sally Da-da, who is Bellarosa's wife's sister's husband. Sort of his brother-in-law. Family relationships are very important to these people. When they can't determine if a bloodline exists, they try to determine if they are related by some marriage or another. Lacking anything there, they will form ties and bonds through christenings. You know, godparents and godchildren. These ties are important because they are used to claim and to reinforce loyalty. Loyalty and respect are number one and number two on the agenda. After that, everything else follows. That's why they have been so incredibly difficult to penetrate, and so successful for a century.'

I nodded. 'And why pale Wasps like me might tend to glamorize and romanticize them.'

'Perhaps.'

'But you see them more clearly, Mr Mancuso.'

'I believe I do.'

'Good. So, there is an underboss. Where does the *consigliere* fit in?'

'He is next in the chain. Their hierarchy is somewhat unique in that respect. This trusted adviser sometimes has more power than the underboss. He is the one who relays instructions to the *capos*, who are in charge of the gangs. Why do you want to know this?'

'I'm just trying to get a picture of my next-door neighbour. Where does a man like Jack Weinstein fit it?'

'Weinstein? Bellarosa's attorney?'

'Yes. Where does he fit in?'

'Well, if the attorney is not Italian, and I presume Jack Weinstein is not, then he occupies some sort of limbo. In Weinstein's case, he has beaten two serious criminal charges for Frank Bellarosa, before Bellarosa became the boss. Bellarosa, therefore, would be grateful, and he might respect Jack Weinstein, the way you or I would be grateful to and respectful of a surgeon who twice saved our lives. Understand?'

'Yes.'

'Why do you ask about Jack Weinstein, Mr Sutter?'

'Professional curiosity. Also, I'm a little tired of the tax business.'

Mancuso smiled, but it was a worried smile. He said, 'This is all abstract, Mr Sutter. Let me tell you a story about Mr Bellarosa. There are many, but I'll tell you one that I can swear to. When Bellarosa was a *capo*, he summoned a man named Vito Posilico to meet him in his social club on Mott Street. When Mr Posilico arrived, Frank Bellarosa ordered coffee and they sat and talked. Bellarosa then accused Posilico of withholding money from the proceeds of an extortion of a building contractor. The contractor, an honest business-man incidentally, paid Posilico fifty thousand dollars for a guarantee of labour peace during the time the builder was working on a big project. Bellarosa had taken his half share from Posilico – twenty-five thousand dollars – but now claimed that Posilico had shaken the contractor down for one hundred thousand dollars. Posilico denied this, of course, and offered to prove this to his *capo* in several ways. But Frank Bellarosa did not want to be proven wrong, especially in front of other people. What he wanted was for Posilico to show respect, to confess, to crawl and beg for mercy. Or, if he still insisted on his innocence, to do so in a way that showed he was frightened. But Vito Posilico had too big an ego, and though he *was* respectful, he was firm in his denial. He said, 'I'll get the contractor here in fifteen minutes, Frank. You can talk to him.' Then Posilico raised his cup to his lips to drink, and Frank Bellarosa drew a lead pipe from somewhere and smashed Posilico's fingers, the cup, and his teeth. Then he stood and proceeded to break nearly every bone in the man's body. To give you an example.'

Wow. I let go of the wheel and leaned back against the rail. Yes, I could easily picture Bellarosa, wielding a lead pipe, cigar in his mouth, cracking a man's bones because of some suspicion of thievery. In truth, Bellarosa would have broken old Richard's arm for taking his salad away if we had been in Bellarosa's club rather than mine. And this was the man whom Susan liked. I watched the wheel move to and fro as the rising wind and current carried the boat farther out. Evil and viciousness, I thought, are only fully understandable in anecdotal form. To hear that a man murdered nine nameless people to get to the top is distressful, but to hear in detail how he smashed Vito Posilico's face and teeth with a lead pipe is gut wrenching.

Mr Mancuso broke into my thoughts. 'Why would a man like you associate with a man like that?'

'Are you here on government business, Mr Mancuso, or are you here to save my soul?'

'Both, Mr Sutter, as they happen to coincide.' He regarded me a moment, then said, 'I don't know you, but I know a lot about you. I know that you are a church-going man, a law-abiding citizen, a family man, a successful and respected attorney, a respected member of your community, and an army veteran. Frank Bellarosa is a malignancy on society, a vicious criminal, and a man whose soul is going to burn in hell for eternity.'

The last thing caught me by surprise, and I must have shown it. I replied, 'I'm not arguing with you. Come to the point.'

'I would like your help.'

'How?'

'We have a court order to tap Bellarosa's phones. But he knows that, of course, and he doesn't say anything on the telephone, so – '

'And you overheard my conversations with him?'

'Yes. We know about the variance, the stables, and about his asking you to walk with him to Fox Point. Incidentally, you have a good sense of humour. And I'm happy to discover that you are not intimidated by him. He puts up with a lot of your sarcasm. I wonder why.'

'I think it goes over his thick head, Mr Mancuso.'

'Perhaps. Anyway, we know that you and your wife went there one night, of course, and I have photos of you waving at us, and photos of you walking with Bellarosa to Fox Point. We know, too, that you took him and his wife to your country club, and that this caused you some problems with your friends. Also, we've heard your wife talking to Mrs Bellarosa on the phone, and even with Mr Bellarosa a few times.' He watched me a moment, then added, 'Your wife spends a good deal of time at Alhambra. We understand that she is painting a picture of the house. Correct?'

'My wife is a professional painter. Artists, writers, and whores work for anyone with the cash.'

'But attorneys don't?'

'Depends on the cash.'

'Your wife did not charge the Bellarosas for the painting.'

'How do you know that?'

'There are things I know that I would be happy to share with you, Mr Sutter, if you would do me a few favours.'

I did not reply.

He said, 'What we need is for you to plant three or four bugs in Bellarosa's house. One in his den, one in the entranceway, maybe one in his greenhouse where we see him talking to his goombahs, and definitely one in the kitchen where he probably does most of his business because he's Italian.' Mr Mancuso flashed all his Chiclets.

'How about his bedroom?'

'We don't do that.' He added, 'Not too much goes on there anyway.' He walked toward me on the rolling boat and put his hand on my arm as though to steady himself. 'Can we count on you?'

'No.'

'Why not?'

'Well . . . I'm his attorney.'

He took a step back as if I'd said I had a communicable disease. 'Are you serious?'

'Yes. I am. Specifically, he wants me to represent him in the matter of the murder of Juan Carranza.' I studied Mr Mancuso's face and saw it was not a happy face.

He went to the portside rail and looked out to sea awhile.

I realized that I had made a tactical blunder in relating this to him if Bellarosa actually wanted it to remain a secret until his arrest, arraignment, and bail hearing. But that was a small mistake, and I was bound to make a few more since I do mostly taxes, wills, and house closings. Also, Bellarosa had, at one point, wanted me to speak to Mancuso about Ferragamo, so I was not actually violating a privileged conversation. I said to Mancuso, 'Do you want to know why I agreed to represent him?'

Without turning around, Mancuso replied, 'I could speculate, Mr Sutter, and if I did, I would say it had nothing to do with cash.'

'No, it doesn't. In fact, I'm repaying a favour. But the main reason is that I believe Bellarosa is innocent of that particular allegation.'

He turned toward me. 'Do you? Why do you believe that?'

'Among other reasons, because Bellarosa has convinced me

that the U.S. Attorney, Mr Alphonse Ferragamo, is framing him for that murder. Actually not just framing him, but setting him up to be murdered by the Colombians or by Bellarosa's own people to keep the peace with the Colombians.' I watched Mr Mancuso closely.

He has a very expressive face, which is not good for a cop, and I could see that he did not find this statement absurd. Bellarosa was right about watching faces when I made this accusation. I said to Mr Mancuso, 'I will relate to you what Bellarosa told me.' And for the next ten minutes, I did just that. I concluded by saying, 'Bellarosa said you are an honest man. So if you are, then tell me honestly, does this sound plausible to you?'

He stared down at the deck for a full minute, then without looking up at me replied, 'A United States Attorney is not going to jeopardize his career and his very freedom for personal revenge.'

'Well, I wouldn't have thought so three months ago, but – ' – I affected an Italian accent – 'but now I'ma learna abouta you *paesanos*, Mistah Mancuso, an' I'ma thinkin', maybe Mistah Bellarosa knowsa whas ina Mistah Ferragamo's head. *Capisce?*'

Mr Mancuso didn't seem amused.

I added, reverting to my normal accent, 'Save Mr Ferragamo's soul, Mr Mancuso. Remind him that revenge is a sin. If he backs off, that will let me off the hook as well. Tell him to find something better than a frame-up for Frank Bellarosa. Tell him to play fair.'

Mr Mancuso did not respond.

I glanced at my watch, then said to Mr Mancuso, 'I'll show you how to tack. Raise the mainsail first.'

And so we set sail for home, tacking through the wind, and fighting the tide, which was still running out. After about an hour with little headway, a weary Mr Mancuso inquired, 'Can't you just start the engine?'

'I could, but sailing into the wind is very instructive. It's a test of skill and patience. It is allegorical.'

'It's a useless exercise,' declared the crew.

We rounded Plum Point, and the wind shifted in a more favourable direction, so we made better headway. Mr Mancuso was kneeling on the foredeck, holding on to the rail. He seemed to enjoy the wind in the sails and the bow cutting through the water. I had advised him to put on a life jacket or tie on a lifeline, but he assured me he was an excellent swimmer. I called out to him, 'Did you people screw me up with the IRS?'

He turned and looked at me, then called back, 'No. But we know about that.'

'I'm sure you do.'

He added, 'I didn't do that. You have my word on that.'

I called over the sound of the wind and water, 'Maybe not you, but someone in your office.'

'No. We don't fool around with the IRS. It's not legal, and we don't trust them.'

'Then you couldn't get me off the hook with them?'

'We could put in a good word for you. But I can't promise you anything.'

But Frank Bellarosa and Mr Melzer could unconditionally promise me things. How utterly depressing and demoralizing.

He called to me, 'Would you like me to put in a good word for you?'

'Sure. Tell them I go to church and I'm a good sailor.'

'Will do. You want to plant some bugs for me?'

'I can't do that.'

'Sure you can. But you have to resign as his attorney. You have to be ethical.'

Mr Mancuso was into ethics. I called to him, 'Lower the jib.'

'The what?'

'The sail flapping over your head.'

He lowered the jib, then the staysail and the mainsail, and I started the engine. When you have an inexperienced crew, it's best to go into port under power and avoid a major embarrassment, like ploughing into a moored boat while people are having drinks on the clubhouse veranda.

We came alongside the pier, and I cut the engine as Mr Mancuso expertly lassoed a piling. We secured the *Paumanok*, and we both went below to collect our things.

As Mr Mancuso put on his tie and gun, he said to me, 'You're not defending Frank Bellarosa solely on the basis of your belief that he is innocent of this murder, Mr Sutter. Any attorney can do that. I think you are just playing with high explosives because you enjoy the danger. Like sailing in a storm at night. I know life can get boring, Mr Sutter, and people with time and money on their hands often need something to get their blood moving. Some men gamble, some race cars or boats, some climb mountains, some have affairs, some do it all.'

'At the same time?'

'But, Mr Sutter, there is a price to pay for the thrill. There are consequences. Danger is dangerous.'

'I know that, Mr Mancuso. Where did you get your law degree, if I may ask?'

'Georgetown.'

'Excellent. Can I double your salary, Mr Mancuso? We need a Catholic. You have your twenty years in with the FBI.'

He smiled. 'I'm not counting years, Mr Sutter. I want to finish this job. If it takes another twenty years to smash the Mafia in New York, then, God willing, I'll still be at it.'

'Please keep my offer in mind. It is a serious offer.'

'I appreciate the thought. It is seductive. But what I want to say to you, Mr Sutter, is that evil is seductive, and –'

'What did you say?'

'Evil is seductive. Do you understand?'

'Yes . . .'

'And virtue is boring. Evil seems to pay better than virtue, but virtue, Mr Sutter, is its own reward. You know that.'

'Of course I know that. I am an honest man. I am doing nothing dishonest with Frank Bellarosa.'

Mr Mancuso put his jacket on and gathered his shoes and socks. 'But being involved with Frank Bellarosa is unethical, immoral, and unwise. Very unwise.' He stepped closer to me in the small galley where we were standing. 'Listen to me, Mr Sutter. Forget that I asked you to bug Bellarosa's house, and that he may be innocent of this particular charge. The man is *evil*. I like you, Mr Sutter, and I want to give you good advice. Tell Frank Bellarosa to go away and stay away from you and your wife.' He actually grabbed me by the arm and put his face near mine. 'I am the voice of truth and reality. Listen to my voice. That man will destroy you and your family. And it will be *your* fault, Mr Sutter, not his fault. For the love of God, tell him to leave you alone.'

He was absolutely right, of course, so I said, 'Thank you. I like you, Mr Mancuso. You restore my faith in humanity, but not in much else. I'll think about what you've said.'

Mr Mancuso released my arm. 'Thank you for the ride, Mr Sutter. Have a pleasant day.' He went up the companionway and disappeared on deck.

After a minute, I followed and saw him on the pier slipping into his shoes. There were a few other people around now, and they were all watching this man in a suit who had come off my boat. At least a few people probably thought that Mr Mancuso was a friend of Mr Bellarosa's – as was John Sutter – and that Sutter and this Mafia fellow had just dumped a few bodies at sea.

I called out to Mr Mancuso, 'Ferragamo and Bellarosa belong in the same cell. You and I should go sailing again.'

He waved to me as he disappeared behind a big, berthed Allied fifty-five footer that I would buy if I had three hundred thousand dollars.

I got some polish from the locker and shined up a brass cleat until it gleamed in the sunlight.

CHAPTER 24

The week after Mr Mancuso and I went sailing, I was helping George Allard plant boxtrees where the central wing of the stables had once been. It was hard work, and I could have had it done professionally, but I like planting trees, and George has an obsession with saving old skinflint Stanhope a few dollars.

When men work together, despite class differences, they revert to a natural and instinctive sort of comradeship. Thus, I found I was enjoying my conversation with George, and George himself seemed a little looser, joking and even making an indiscreet remark about his employer. 'Mr Stanhope,' said George, 'offered the missus and me ten thousand dollars to leave the gatehouse. Who's he think is going to do all this work if I weren't here?'

'Mr Stanhope may have a buyer for the entire estate,' I said.

'He's got a buyer? Who?'

'I'm not sure he does, George, but Mr Stanhope wants to be able to offer an empty gatehouse if and when he does, or he wants to be able to sell the gatehouse separately.'

George nodded. 'Well, I don't want to be a problem, but . . .'

'Don't worry about it. I've looked at August Stanhope's will, and it's clear that you and Mrs Allard have lifetime rights of tenancy. Don't let William Stanhope pressure you, and don't take his offer.' I added, 'You couldn't rent comparable housing for less than twenty thousand a year around here.'

'Oh, I know that, Mr Sutter. It wasn't much of an offer, and even if he offers more, I wouldn't leave. This is my home.'

'Good. We need you at the gate.'

It was a hot day, and the work was heavy for a man his age. But men are competitive in this regard, and George was going to show me that he could keep up.

At noon, I said to him, 'That's enough for now. I'll meet you back here at about two.'

I walked home and had lunch alone as Susan was out, then wrote to my sister, Emily. When I returned to meet George, I found him lying on the ground between unplanted trees. I knelt beside him, but there were no signs of life.

George Allard was dead. The gates to Stanhope Hall were unguarded.

The wake, held in a funeral home in Locust Valley, was well attended by other elderly estate workers whom the Allards had known over the years. Interestingly, a few older gentry put in appearances as well, ladies and gentlemen of the old vanished world, looking like ghosts themselves, come to pay their respects to one of their own.

The Stanhopes, of course, felt obligated to come in from Hilton Head. They hadn't actually wished George dead, of course, but you knew that the subject had come up in their private conversations over the years, and that it had come up in a way that if you overheard them, you might think they were looking forward to it.

Susan's brother, Peter, still trying to find the meaning of life – this month in Acapulco – could not make it in to contemplate the meaning of death.

I was sorry that Carolyn could not be reached in time in Cuba, but Edward flew up from Cocoa Beach.

Many of my family in and around Locust Valley and Lattingtown stopped by the funeral home as they all knew and liked the Allards. My parents, according to Aunt Cornelia, had gone to Europe so I'll never know if they would have driven in for the funeral, and I really don't care, as all gestures on their part are meaningless, I've decided.

There was no reason for Emily to come in from Texas, as she didn't know the Allards that well, but she sent me a cheque to give to Ethel. It is customary when an old servant dies to take up a collection for the widow, this being a holdover, I suppose, from the days before servants had life insurance or Social Security. A good number of people passed cheques or cash to me to give to Ethel. William Stanhope knew this, of course, but didn't come up with any cash of his own. His reasoning, I'm sure, was that he was still obligated to pay Ethel her monthly stipend, as per Augustus's will, and that Ethel was still in the gatehouse, and now George was about to occupy a piece of the Stanhope family plot; though in point of fact, there is more Stanhope family plot left than there are Stanhopes left to occupy it. So he wasn't giving away anything valuable, as usual.

There was no reason for the Bellarosas to come to the funeral home, of course, but Italians, as I've discovered over the years, rarely pass up a funeral. So Frank and Anna stopped in for ten minutes one afternoon, and their presence caused a small stir of excitement, as if they were celebrities. The Bellarosas knelt at the coffin and crossed themselves, then checked out the flower arrangement they'd sent – which incidentally took two men to carry in – then left. They looked as if they did this often.

The Remsens stopped by the funeral home late Friday afternoon – after the closing bell and before happy hour at The Creek – but they pointedly avoided me, though they chatted with Susan for a minute.

One would think that, in the presence of death, people would be compelled into a larger appreciation of life and a sharper perspective of its meaning. One would think that. But to be honest, whatever petty grievances I, myself, had outside the funeral parlour were the same ones I carried inside. Why should Lester Remsen or William Stanhope or anyone be any different?

People like the DePauws, Potters, Vandermeers, and so forth, who might have stopped by for a moment as our friends and neighbours out of a sense of *noblesse oblige*, sent flowers instead. I didn't want to read anything into this, but I could have. I was sure they would make it to my funeral. Jim and Sally Roosevelt did come, and Jim was very good with Ethel, sitting for an hour with her and holding her hand. Sally looks good in black.

So we buried George Allard after church services at St Mark's on a pleasant Saturday morning. The cemetery is a few miles from Stanhope Hall, a private place with no name, filled with the departed rich, and in pharaonic style, with a few dozen loyal servants (though none of them had been killed for their masters' burials), and dozens of pets, and even two polo ponies, one of which was responsible for his rider's death. The old rich insist on being batty right to the end, and beyond.

As I said, George was interred in the Stanhope plot, which is a good-sized piece of land, and ironically the last piece of land the Stanhopes were destined to own on Long Island.

At graveside, there were about fifteen people in attendance, with the Reverend Mr Hunnings officiating; there was the widow, Ethel, the Allards' daughter, Elizabeth, her husband and their two children, William and Charlotte Stanhope, Susan, Edward, and I, plus a few other people whom I didn't know.

On the way to the cemetery, the funeral cortege, as is customary, passed by the house of the deceased, and I saw that someone had put a funeral wreath on the gates of Stanhope Hall, something I hadn't seen in years. Why that custom has died out is beyond me, for what could be more natural than to announce to the world, to unwary callers, that there has been a death in the house and that, no, we don't want any encyclopedias or Avon products today.

'Ashes to ashes, dust to dust,' said the Reverend Mr Hunnings, throwing a handful of soil atop the coffin. This is when clergy earn their pay. But Hunnings always struck me as a method actor who was playing the part of a priest in a long-running off-Broadway show. Why do I dislike this man? Maybe because he's conned everyone else. But George had seen through him.

Hunnings actually delivered a nice eulogy, though I noticed that he never once mentioned the possibility of heaven as a real place. No use talking about a place you've never been to and have no chance of ever going to.

Anyway, I was glad, in some perverse way, that I was the last one to see George alive and that we had spoken, and that he died doing what he liked best and where he liked doing it. I had spoken to Ethel and to his daughter, Elizabeth, about our last conversation, and of course, I embellished it a bit in an effort to bring them some comfort. But basically George had been a happy man on the day he died, and that was more than most of us can hope for.

I, myself, would not mind dropping dead on my own property, if I owned any property. But better yet, perhaps, I'd like to die on my boat, at sea, and be buried at sea. The thought of dying at my desk upsets me greatly. But if I could choose how and when I wanted to die, I would want to be an eighty-year-old man shot by a jealous young husband who had caught me in bed with his teenage wife.

The graveside service was ended, and we all threw a flower on the casket as we filed past on our way to our cars.

As I was about to climb into the Jaguar with Susan, I looked back at the grave and saw that Ethel was still there. The limousine that we had gotten for her and her family had drawn abreast of the Jag and I motioned for the driver to stop. The rear window of the limousine went down, and Elizabeth said to me, 'Mom wants to be alone awhile. The driver will come back for her.'

'I understand,' I replied, then added, 'No, I'll go back for her.' It's so easy to let professionals handle all the unpleasant aspects of dying and death, and it takes some thought and will to take charge.

Elizabeth replied, 'That would be nice. Thank you. We'll see you back at the church.' Her car drove off and I slid behind the wheel of the Jaguar. 'Where is Edward?' I inquired of Susan.

'He is riding with his grandparents.'

'All right.' I fell in behind someone's car and exited the cemetery.

Burial customs differ greatly in this country, despite the homogenization of other sorts of rites and rituals such as weddings, for instance. Around here, if you're a member of St Mark's, you usually gather after the funeral at the church's fellowship room, where a committee of good Christian ladies have laid on some food and soft drinks (though alcohol is what is needed). It's not quite a party, of course, but it can be an occasion to speak well of the deceased, and to prop up the bereaved for a few more hours.

As I drove toward the church, I was impressed by Ethel's decision not to go along with the planned programme, but to spend a little time at the grave of her husband; just she and George.

Susan said to me, 'That was very thoughtful of you.'

I replied, 'I am an uncommonly thoughtful man.'

Susan didn't second that, but asked me, 'Would you weep over my grave?'

I knew I was supposed to reply quickly in the affirmative, but I had to think about it. I finally replied, 'It would really depend on the circumstances.'

'Meaning what?'

'Well, what if we were divorced?'

There was a second of silence, then she said, 'You could still weep for me. I would cry at your funeral even if we had been divorced for years.'

'Easy to say. How many ex-spouses do you see at funerals?' I added, 'Marriages may or may not be until death do us part. But blood relatives are for ever.'

'You Italian, or what?' She laughed.

'What did you say?'

'Nothing . . . anyway, you recently told two of your blood relatives – Mater and Pater to be specific – to take a hike.'

'Nevertheless, they would attend my funeral, and I theirs. My children will attend my funeral and yours. We may not attend each other's funeral.'

'I will be at yours. You have my word on that.'

I didn't like this subject, so I changed it. 'Do you think Ethel will be all right alone in the gatehouse?'

'I'll check on her more often. Perhaps we'll have her to dinner a few times a week.'

'Good idea.' Actually, it wasn't, as I don't care for Ethel's company, though I care for her as a person, even if she is a socialist. She might be better off living with her Republican daughter, but I didn't think that was a possibility.

I noticed, too, that William Stanhope had been eyeing her as though he were sizing her up for a casket. I had no doubt that he would pull me off to the side sometime in the next few days and ask me to suggest to Ethel that she leave the gatehouse. William, of course, was desirous of selling the quaint house to yuppies, or successful artists, or anyone with a romantic bent and about a quarter million dollars. Or of course, if anything came of Bellarosa's interest in the entire estate, then, as I'd said to George, William would like all the serfs gone (unless he could sell them as well).

Naturally, I would assure my father-in-law that I would do my best to get old Ethel out, but actually I'd do the opposite as I'd done with George just a few days ago. William Stanhope is a monumental prick, and so outrageously insensitive and self-centred that he actually believes he can ask me for my help in enriching him, and I'm supposed to do his bidding (for free) because I'm married to his daughter. What a swine.

'Mother and Father looked good,' Susan said. 'Very tan and fit.'

'It's good to see them again.'

'They're staying for three or four more days.'

'Can't they stay longer?'

She gave me a sidelong glance, and I realized I was pushing my credibility. I hadn't told William or his wife to go to hell yet, as I'd promised myself I would, and I'm glad I hadn't because that could only confuse the issue between Susan and me.

I pulled up to the church, and Susan opened her door. 'That was very touching. I mean what Ethel did, staying behind to be with her husband. They were together a half century, John. They don't make marriages like that anymore.'

'No. Do you know why men die before their wives?'

'No, why?'

'Because they want to.'

'I'll see you later.' Susan got out of the car and headed toward the fellowship room, and I headed back to the cemetery.

Funerals are, of course, a time to reflect on your life. I mean, if you need any evidence that you're not immortal, that hole in the ground is it. So you naturally start to wonder if you're getting it right, then you wonder why it matters if you do. I mean, if Hunnings and his cohorts have removed the fear of a fiery hell and the promise of a four-star heaven, who gives a damn what you do on earth? Well, I do, because I still believe in right and wrong, and without embarrassment I'll tell you I believe in a comfortable heaven. I know that George is there even if Hunnings forgot to mention it.

But afterlife considerations aside, one does wonder if one could be getting a little more fun out of life. I mean, I still enjoy life, but I recall very well a time when things were better at home. So, I must answer the age-old question: Do I move or make home improvements?

I pulled into the gate of the cemetery and drove along the tree-shaded lane to the Stanhope section. It was interesting that the Stanhopes, who needed so much land in life, were all comfortably situated on an acre now, with room for more.

I stopped a short distance from the new grave and noticed that the gravediggers were nearly finished covering it. I noticed, too, that Ethel was nowhere to be seen.

I got out of the car and started for the grave to inquire of the gravediggers where she might be. But then I turned toward the south end of the Stanhope section, the older section where weathered marble headstones rose amid thick plantings.

Ethel Allard stood with her back to me at a grave whose headstone bore the name AUGUSTUS STANHOPE.

I watched for a second or two, but felt as if I'd intruded on a private moment. Though in truth, I hadn't stumbled upon this scene by accident; I somehow knew that Ethel would be there. I suppose I could have backed off behind the hedges and called out for her, like the old John Sutter would have done, but instead I said, 'Ethel, it's time to go.'

She glanced over her shoulder at me without surprise or embarrassment and nodded. But she remained at the grave for some time longer, then took a white rose that

383

she had been holding and tossed it on Augustus Stan-hope's grave.

Ethel turned and came toward me, and I could see there were tears in her eyes. We walked side by side toward my car and she said to me, 'I loved him very much.'

Who? 'Of course you did.'

'And he loved me dearly.'

'I'm sure he did.' *Who?*

She began sobbing and I put my arm around her. She actually leaned her head on my shoulder as I led her to the car. She said, 'But it could never be. Not in those days.'

Ah. My God, what funny people we are. I said, 'But it's good that you had *something.* That's better than nothing.'

'I still miss him.'

'That's very nice. Very lovely.' And it was, odd as the circumstances were, considering why we were there. And the moral was this: Go for it; it's later than you think.

I put her in the car and we drove back to the church without exchanging another word.

The morning after the funeral, Edward and I finished planting the boxtrees. As we dug in the hot sun, he sort of looked at me as if I might keel over myself and die on the spot. He said, 'Take a break, Dad.'

'I'm in top shape. *You* need the break.'

We sat under the chestnut tree and we drank spring water. Children don't think much about death, which is as it should be. But when they are confronted with it, it is not always processed properly or understood in its context. Some children shrug it off, others become maudlin. We spoke about death and dying for a while, coming up with no great revelations, but at least talking it out.

Edward is fortunate in that he has all four grand-parents – well, *fortunate* might not be the right word in the case of those four – but this is more common today as people live longer. And in fact, George Allard's funeral was the first one Edward had attended. Carolyn, at nineteen, has not gone to a funeral. And, I think, we've all, to some extent, come to believe that death is unnatural in modern American society, that somehow the deceased and the family of the deceased have been cheated. I said to him, 'Death is the natural order of things. I would not want to live in a world without death, Edward. In the old days, they used to call death the final reward. It still is.'

'I guess. But how about when a kid dies?'

'That's harder to comprehend or deal with. I have no answers for that.'

And so we kicked death around awhile. American parents are obsessed with the First Sex Talk; when it should occur, what should be said. Parents, I think, should give as much time and thought to preparing their children for their first experience with the death of a loved one.

We finished the plantings, and Edward said to me, 'Would you mind if I went back to Florida tomorrow?'

'Were you having a good time?'

'Yes.'

'Then get back there. How are the girls?'

'Well . . . okay.'

'You were taught about safe and responsible sex in health class?'

'Yes.'

'Anything else you want to know about safe sex?'

'No. I've had it up to here with that subject.'

I smiled. 'Anything you want to know about good sex?'

He grinned. 'Sure. If you know anything about it.'

'Hey, watch yourself, wise guy.' I think I know where this kid gets his sense of humour.

We went back to the house, cleaned up, then went riding, Edward on Zanzibar, me on Yankee. As we crossed Bellarosa's land, I asked Edward, 'Did you ever say anything to Mr Bellarosa about my having to sell the summer house for tax money?'

He looked at me as we rode. 'No. Why would I tell him that?'

'He seemed to know about that.'

'Not from me.'

After a minute, he made an unconscious mental connection and said, 'I saw the picture Mom painted. It's really terrific. You seen it?'

'Not yet.'

We rode until dusk, then we met Susan at a seafood restaurant on the Sound and had dinner together. We talked about the shark that got away, about the submarine sighting, and about dinner at Buddy's Hole, which was funny and sad at the same time. We spoke about the things that would become family history in this summer of change, growth, and death.

The next morning, I drove Edward to the airport. We don't see people off at the gate anymore, but I shook his hand before he passed through the metal detector and watched him disappear into the crowd.

William and Charlotte Stanhope were staying at one of the cottages at The Creek, and not with us, thank you, God. William took the opportunity of George's funeral to do some business while he was in New York.

At Susan's suggestion, Squire Stanhope made an appointment with the Bishop of Alhambra. They met at Alhambra first, without me present, then came back to Stanhope Hall, walked around, kicked the bricks, and struck a deal. I didn't actually see them strike the deal, but I could picture them, standing in the sacred grove, pitchforks in hand, cloven hooves bared, touching horns and wiggling their tails.

Anyway, we had dinner that night in Locust Valley; Susan and John, William and Charlotte. William fittingly picked an Italian restaurant, a very good restaurant, and very expensive. William does have good taste in restaurants, as opposed to my parents. But as William is my client, and as we were going to do a few minutes' worth of business, I was supposed to bill the dinner to Perkins, Perkins, Sutter and Reynolds. William pulls this every time he's in town, but my firm has never done a dime's worth of business with him, and he doesn't even pay me personally. Therefore, I always pay the bill with my own credit card.

So William gave me the business. 'John,' said he, 'your neighbour bought not only the house, but all the acreage. We'll draw up a contract tomorrow morning. Two million down, eighteen million at closing. I'll meet you at ten in the Locust Valley office, and we'll go over the details. He uses Cooper and Stiles in Glen Cove for real estate deals. You know them, so we won't have any problems with this deal. Now, let's close in a few weeks. He's got the money. No use waiting. You notify the tax people tomorrow that they can take the property off the auction block. They'll have their money in about thirty days. Do that first thing. And call Cooper and Stiles first thing and tell them to expect to receive and to read the contract by tomorrow afternoon. And I want them to get to their client with the contract the following day. None of this lawyerly foot-dragging. The whole Japanese Empire was surrendered with a one-page document that took five minutes to sign.'

How would you know? You were fishing off Martha's Vineyard. 'Yes, sir.'

'And John, you'll keep this strictly confidential.'

'Yes, sir.'

William went on, 'I think the idiot believes he can subdivide the acreage and make a killing. I want to nail this down before he learns otherwise. You speak to Cooper and Stiles about that without making it obvious what you *don't* want them to say to their client. They won't say anything anyway, because they want the fee.'

'Yes, sir.' Frank Bellarosa was many things, but an idiot wasn't one of them.

'He probably thinks he can bribe or threaten government officials to have the land rezoned. He's got a lot to learn about how we conduct public affairs here.'

I said, 'I think he wants the land to bury bodies.'

William gave me a look of annoyance. He doesn't appreciate my humour at all, which is probably why I hate him.

He said, 'Bellarosa's deed will include the gatehouse, too, of course. He wasn't happy about the Allards' lifetime tenancy. But I told him that if he made the widow a reasonable offer, she'd leave. If *he* can't get her out, no one can.' William nearly smiled, and I nearly put my fist in his mouth. He added, 'Meantime, the son of a bitch wants to hold a half million in escrow until the gatehouse is vacated and unencumbered. So put that in the contract, but let's see if we can get a promise from Ethel to move, and pass that on to Bellarosa.'

'Yes, sir.'

He looked at me and said, 'I discovered why you didn't want to dine at The Creek tonight, John. You're the subject of some heated debate over there. That's very awkward for me.'

And it will get a lot more awkward for you when your friends find out you sold Stanhope Hall to Frank Bellarosa. I said, 'Yes, sir. I'm sorry about that.'

He looked at me closely, then said, 'I'd like to give you some advice. Don't get involved with that man.'

'You just sold him Stanhope Hall,' I pointed out.

He stopped eating and his yellow eyes narrowed. 'That was business.'

'So is my involvement with him, sir. Your daughter handles our social involvements.'

So, there was what you call dead silence for a while, during which time I thought Susan might say something on my behalf. But Susan pays me the compliment of not defending me or speaking for me. I do the same for her.

Charlotte Stanhope finally broke the silence and said, 'Poor Ethel. She looked frightful.' She turned to me. 'Do you think she can manage alone?'

Charlotte has a trilly sort of voice that you think is going to trail off into a series of chirps. She's well bred, of course, and seems on the surface to be a nice lady, but in her own quiet way, she's as vicious as her husband.

'John? Do you think poor Ethel can manage alone?'

I replied, 'I'll inquire as soon as a respectable period of time has passed.'

'Of course. The poor dear, she would be so much better situated with her daughter.'

We chatted about this and that while we ate, or at least they did. I was simmering.

William returned to the subject of the sale. He said to my wife, 'I'm sorry, Susan, if this sale causes you any inconvenience. But it had to happen. And I don't think you need worry about houses going up so soon. Now that Bellarosa owns the land, you and I will contribute five or ten thousand to the Preservation Fund, anonymously, of course, so he doesn't get wind of it. They'll hold him up in court for years. But meanwhile, Bellarosa assured me that you may continue to use the land in any way you see fit, for riding, gardening, walks, just as if I still owned it. In fact, he's willing to sign a covenant to that effect.'

'That's very good of you to think to ask him about that,' said Susan to Mr Thoughtful.

William smiled at his daughter. 'It could have been worse, you know. At least you know this fellow. And he speaks well of you.' He paused. 'He's quite a character. But not the thug I expected.'

I didn't think William would find much fault with a man who was about to hand him twenty million dollars. William, of course, was ecstatic in his own shitty little way. What annoyed me, I think, was not his attitude toward me, or the fact that he had just made a fortune, but the fact that he shed not one tear for the passing of Stanhope Hall. Even I, who had come to hate the place, felt some nostalgia for it, and it hadn't been in *my* family for generations.

William was still talking to his daughter. 'Susan, I'm glad you got the stable moved – '

'I paid for half of the moving of the stable.'

William glanced at me, then turned back to his daughter and continued, 'Bellarosa told me he wants to move the love temple to his property. He says this fellow of his, Dominic, who did your stable – '

'You are a schmuck.'

He looked at me in a funny sort of way. 'Excuse me?'

'You are an unprincipled asshole, an utterly cynical bastard, a monumental prick, and a conniving fuck.'

Charlotte made a little choking sound. Susan continued eating her raspberries, with no apparent problem. William tried to say something, but only succeeded in going like this: 'You . . . you . . . you . . . you . . .'

I stood and poked William in the chest. '*You*, tightwad, pay for dinner.' I touched Susan's arm. '*You* come with me.'

She stood without a word and followed me out of the restaurant.

In the car on the way home, she said, 'Can the love temple actually be moved?'

'Yes, it's post and lintel construction. Sort of like building blocks. It has to be done carefully, but it's possible, and actually easier than the stable.'

'Interesting. I think I'd like to take some courses in building and architecture at Post. That would help me understand more fully what I paint, how it was built, the very soul of the structure, you know, the way Renaissance painters studied skeletons and muscle to paint those fantastic nudes. Perhaps that's all I'm lacking by way of becoming a great painter. What do you think?'

'You may be right.'

We pulled into the gates at Stanhope Hall. The gatehouse was dark, as Ethel was staying with her daughter awhile. Susan said, 'I'm going to miss George very much.'

'Me, too.' I didn't bother to get out of the car and close the gates, since I intended to pass through them again in about five minutes. Susan, of course, noticed this and remained silent all the way to our house. I brought the Jag to the front door, and Susan looked at me.

A few seconds passed, then I said, 'I'm not coming inside. I'll be back for my things tomorrow.'

'Where are you going?'

'That is really not your concern.'

She began to get out of the car, then turned back and said,

'Please don't leave me tonight.' She added, 'But if you do, take your own car.' She put out her hand and smiled. 'Keys, please.'

I shut off the Jag and gave her the keys. Susan unlocked the front door and we both went inside – I to the kitchen to get my own keys, she upstairs to go to bed. As I headed for the front door again, the phone rang and she answered it upstairs. I heard her say, 'Yes, Dad, I'm fine.'

I opened the door to leave, then heard her saying, 'Well, but that must be what he thinks of you or he wouldn't have said it. John is very precise in his choice of words.'

Though I don't like eavesdropping, I paused at the front door and heard her go on, 'No, he will not apologize, and I won't apologize for him.' Silence, then, 'I'm sorry Mother is upset. Actually, I think John would have said more if she *weren't* there.' Silence again, then, 'All right, Dad, I'll speak to you tomorrow. Yes, Dad . . .'

I called up the stairs, 'Tell the son of a bitch to find another free lawyer.'

I heard Susan say, 'Hold on, Dad. John just said, and I quote, "Tell the son of a bitch to find another free lawyer." Yes . . .' She called down to me, 'Father says you're an ambulance chaser, an embarrassment to your father, and an incompetent.'

'Tell him he's not half the man *his* father was, and the best part of him ran down Augustus's leg.'

Susan said, 'Dad, John says he disagrees with that. Good night.' I heard her hang up. She called down to me, 'Good night, John.'

I headed up the stairs. 'I need my overnight bag.'

I went into our bedroom to get my bag out of the closet, and Susan, who must have been undressing as she spoke on the phone, was lying on top of the sheets, her legs crossed and reading a magazine, stark naked.

Well, I mean, there's something about a naked woman, you know, and I was really feeling my oats and all, having just told William Stanhope what I thought of him, and there was his

391

bitchy daughter, lying there stark naked. In some instinctive sort of way, I knew I had to ravish her to complete my victory. So I did. She seemed to enjoy it.

Now, a real primitive would have left afterward, to show his contempt for her and her whole clan. But I was pretty tired, and it was late, so I watched some TV and fell asleep.

PART V

The public be damned.

William Henry Vanderbilt
Reply to a newspaper reporter, 1882

CHAPTER 25

Despite my announcement that I was leaving home, or perhaps because of it, Susan and I were getting along better. We both agreed that I had been under some financial and professional strain, and that George's death had caused us both some emotional trauma, and even the sale of Stanhope Hall had probably contributed to my outburst in the restaurant and my announcement when we got home. I assured Susan, however, that I still thought her father was a monumental prick. She seemed willing to let it go at that.

Anyway, toward the end of July, Mr Melzer called me at home to inform me that he had worked out a deal with the Internal Revenue Service. To wit: I would pay them $215,000 within sixty days and they would consider the obligation fulfilled. Mr Melzer seemed pleased with his work. He said, 'That is a savings to you of $99,513.'

'But then I would owe you about fifty thousand dollars, Mr Melzer, and I've already paid you twenty thousand. So really, Mr Melzer, if you do a little arithmetic, you have saved me only about thirty thousand dollars. I could have done as well myself.'

'But I did the work for you, Mr Sutter.' He cleared his throat over the phone. 'And there was the matter of the criminal charges. That alone is worth – '

'Get them down another ten or shave your commission.'

'But – '

I hung up. After a decent interval of an hour or so, Mr Melzer called back. 'They will take two hundred and ten thousand dollars, Mr Sutter. That is the best I can do. I will make up the other five to you. Considering they could *still* bring criminal charges against you, I suggest you settle.'

'I never understood, Mr Melzer, why the IRS and the Mafia haven't merged.'

Mr Melzer chuckled and replied, 'Professional jealousy.'

He added, 'Can you have the cheque ready within sixty days?'

'Yes.'

'Fine. I'll hand-deliver the cheque to the IRS and see that it is properly credited. That is part of my service.'

There was a not-too-subtle subtext there. I said, 'And I suppose you'd like to pick up your cheque at the same time.'

'That would be very convenient.'

'All right. Call me in thirty days.'

'Fine. And thank you, Mr Sutter. It has been a delight working with a man of such refinement.'

I couldn't say the same, so I said, 'It's been educational.'

'That only adds to my delight.'

'By the way, Mr Melzer, did you happen to hear anything regarding how the IRS discovered this oversight on my part?'

'I did make some inquiries regarding that very question. I did not receive any direct answers, but we can assume this was not a random examination of your past tax returns.'

'Can we then assume that someone was out to make difficulties for me?'

'Mr Sutter, I told you, you are not popular with the IRS.'

'But I have not been popular with the IRS since I began beating them at their game twenty years ago. Why would they examine my return *now*?'

'Oh, I think they knew about this oversight of yours for years, Mr Sutter. They like to see the interest and penalties accumulate.'

'I see.' But I found that hard to believe, even of the Internal Revenue Service. They were tough but generally honest, even going so far as to return money that you didn't know you overpaid them.

'However,' Mr Melzer continued, 'I would not pursue that if I were you.' He added, 'Or you will be needing me again.'

'Mr Melzer, I will never need you again. And I am not intimidated by any agency of the government. If I believe

I've been singled out for persecution, I will certainly pursue the matter.'

Mr Melzer let a moment pass, then said, 'Mr Sutter, if I may be blunt, your type of man is nearly extinct. Accept your loss, swallow your pride, and go live your life, my friend. No good will come of your trying to take on forces more powerful than yourself.'

'I enjoy fighting the good fight.'

'As you wish.' He added, 'By the way, I would still like to call on you for your professional advice if I may. Your work for me would be strictly confidential, of course.'

'Better yet, it will be nonexistent. Good day.'

Well, things always seem to work out, don't they? The very next day, on one of my rare appearances in my Wall Street office, there was a phone call for me. It was a Mr Weber, a realtor in East Hampton, informing me that he had good news. He had, in fact, a bid of $390,000 for my little summer cottage. 'That is not good news at all,' I informed him.

'Mr Sutter, the market has fallen to pieces. This is the only serious offer we've had, and this guy's looking around at other houses right now.'

'I'll call you back.' I then phoned every other realtor who had the house listed and listened to an earful of bad news and excuses. I called Susan, since she is joint owner of the house, but as usual, she wasn't in. That woman needs a pager, a car phone, a CB radio for her horse, and a cowbell. I called Weber back. 'I'll split the difference between asking and bid. Get him up to four hundred and forty-five.'

'I'll try.'

Mr Weber called me back in a half hour, making me wonder if his customer wasn't actually sitting in his office. Weber said, 'The prospective buyer will split the difference with you again, making his final offer $417,500. I suggest you take that, Mr Sutter, because – '

'The housing market is soft, the summer is waning, and

the stock market is down sixteen and a quarter today. Thank you, Mr Weber.'

'Well, I just want you to know the facts.'

Mr Weber, by now, could smell his commission, which I figured at six per cent to be about twenty-five thousand dollars. I said, 'I want four and a quarter for me, so you'll give me the difference from your commission.'

There was silence on the phone as Mr Weber, who had been smelling prime ribs, realized he was being offered T-bone or nothing. He cleared his throat as Mr Melzer had done and said, 'That's do-able.'

'Then do it.' Normally, I would be more aggressive in real estate deals and also with the IRS. But I didn't have much strength from which to bargain. In fact, unbeknownst to Mr Weber, I had none, and time was running out.

Mr Weber said, 'It's done. Did I tell you that the buyer wants to rent the house starting immediately? No? Well, he does. He wants to use it for all of August. He's offering a hundred a day until closing. I know you could get more now in high season, but it's part of the deal, so I suggest – '

'His name isn't Melzer, is it?'

'No. Name's Carleton. Dr Carleton. He's a psychiatrist in the city. Park Avenue. They don't see patients in August, you know, and he has a wife and two kids, so he wants – '

'My family wants to use the house in August, Mr Weber.'

'It's a deal breaker, Mr Sutter. He insists.'

'Well, in that case, I had better make new summer plans, hadn't I? Perhaps I'll go down to the town dump and slug rats with a rake.'

'Actually, I could find you another rental out here – '

'Never mind. Do it your way and Dr Carleton's way.'

'Yes, sir. Dr Carleton really likes the house. The furniture, too.'

'How much?'

'Another ten. Cash.'

'Fine. Did he see the picture of my wife and kids in the den?'

Mr Weber chuckled. Making deals was fun. I said, 'If this bonzo is trying to pull off a cheap summer rental, I'll hang his balls over my mantel.'

'Sir?'

'Get a one per cent binder, now. Today. And I want to go to contract in a week with twenty per cent down.'

'A week? But – '

'I'll fax you a contract this afternoon. You get this guy in high gear, Mr Weber. If there are any problems, get back to me pronto.'

'Yes, sir.' He asked, 'Are you looking to buy any other property out east?'

'What do you have east of Montauk Point?'

'Ocean.'

'How much?'

'It's free, Mr Sutter.'

'I'll take it.' I hung up. *Madonn'*, when the shit happens, it happens. Well, I thought, I broke even today. Not bad for a man who's only in his mid-forties.

I took the train home that evening and met Susan at McGlade's for dinner, as we'd planned that morning. I explained the deal to her and said, 'I tried to call you to get your approval.' Which was more than Frank Bellarosa did when he bought Alhambra without mentioning it to his wife.

Susan didn't seem to care about the sale. But you never know with women. To paraphrase what Churchill said about the Germans, 'Women are either at your feet or at your throat.'

Anyway, I had my calculator out and I was doing some number-crunching over my third gin and tonic. 'So, we pay the IRS, we pay Melzer, we pay the real estate commission, we satisfy the existing mortgage, we damned sure put money aside for the capital gains tax since we're not buying another house, and we add in the ten thousand for the furniture and about three thousand for rent, and deduct the taxes on that as though it were income to play it safe . . . then, let's see, we factor in some out-of-pocket expenses . . .'

Susan was yawning. The rich are bored by money talk.

I scratched some figures on my place mat. 'Well, I think we cleared ninety-three bucks.' I thought a moment, then said, 'A potential half-million-dollar asset wiped out.' I looked at Susan. 'What does the government do with all my money?'

'Can we order dinner?'

'I can't afford it. I'll drink.' I played around with the numbers again, but I still couldn't afford solid food, so I ordered another gin and tonic.

Susan said, 'Oh, by the way, are you figuring in the twenty thousand dollars you owe me?'

I looked up at her. 'Excuse me, Mrs Sutter, this is a joint liability.'

'Well, I know that, John. But it wasn't my fault.'

Understand, please, this woman needs twenty thousand dollars like I need to move another stable across the property. I cleared my throat, the way Messrs Melzer and Weber had done. 'Why are you bringing that up?'

'My attorneys want to know – '

'Your *father*.'

'Well . . . I don't really care about the money. But it's not a good habit to get into. I mean, mingling assets.'

'We mingle *my* assets. Look, Susan, rest assured I have no claim on your property, even if we do occasionally mingle assets. You have a very tight marriage contract. I'm a lawyer. Trust me.'

'I do, John, but . . . I don't actually need to have the money, but I do need a sort of promissory note. That's what my . . . lawyers said.'

'All right.' I scribbled an IOU for $20,000 on the place mat, signed and dated it, and pushed it across the table. 'It's legal. Just ignore the part about lunch, and dinner, and cocktails, steaks and chops.'

'You needn't be so touchy. You're a lawyer. You understand – '

'I understand that I've given your father free legal services for nearly two decades. I understand that I paid half the cost for the moving of your stable – '

'Your horse is in there, too.'

'I don't want the stupid horse. I'm going to have him turned into glue.'

'That's an awful thing to say. And by the way, you bought the boat in your name only.'

'The cheque had my name on it, lady.'

'All right, then . . . I don't like to bring this up, but you've never had to make a mortgage or rent payment since we've been married.'

'And what did *you* do to get that house except to get born with a silver spoon up your ass?'

'Please don't be so crude, John. Look, I don't like to talk about money. Let's drop it. Please?'

'No, no, no. Let us not drop it. Let us have our very first and very overdue fight about money.'

'Please lower your voice.'

I may or may not have lowered my voice, but the jukebox came on, and so everyone who was listening to us had to listen to Frank Sinatra singing 'My Way'. Great song. I think the guy at the end of the bar played it for me. I gave him a thumbs-up.

Susan said, 'This is very ugly. I'm not used to this.'

I addressed Lady Stanhope. 'I'm sorry I lost my temper. You're quite right, of course. Please put that IOU in your bag and I will repay the loan as soon as I can. I'll need a few days.'

She seemed embarrassed now. 'Forget it. Really.' She ripped up the IOU. 'I don't understand any of this.'

'Then, in the future, keep my business and our business to yourself, and do not discuss any of it with your father. I strongly suggest you get a personal attorney who has nothing to do with your father or your trustees. I will deal with that

401

attorney in any future matters.' *Including matrimonial*. 'And please keep in mind that, for better or worse, I am your husband.'

She was really quite red now, and I could see she was vacillating between my feet and my throat. She finally said, 'All right, John.' She picked up the menu and I couldn't see her face.

I told you about the red hair, and I knew she was still wavering between her good breeding and her bad genes. I suppose, as a purely precautionary move, I should have put the steak knives out of her reach, but that might be overreacting. I was still pretty hot myself, of course, and I had to get one last zinger in. I said, 'I didn't appreciate your father calling you the other night to see if you were all right. Does he think I beat you?'

She glanced up from the menu. 'Of course not. That was silly of him.' She added, 'He's really quite angry with you.'

'Why? Because I stuck him with the dinner bill?'

'John . . . what you said was a bit strong. But . . . he asked me to tell you that he would accept an apology from you.'

I clapped my hands. 'What a magnificent man! What a beautiful human being!' I wiped a tear from my eye.

The song had ended, and we had our audience back.

Susan leaned across the table and said to me, 'You've changed. Do you know that?'

'And how about you, Susan?'

She shrugged and went back to the menu, then looked up again. 'John, if you apologized, it would make things so much less tense. For all of us. Even if you don't mean it. Do it for me. Please.'

There was a time, of course, not so long ago, when I would have. But that time had passed, and it was not likely to come again. I replied, 'I will not say something I don't mean. I will not crawl for you, or for anyone. My only regret in that episode is that I should have grabbed his tie and yanked his face into his cheesecake.'

'You're really angry, aren't you?'

'No, anger is transient. I hate the bastard.'

'John! He's my father.'

'Don't bet on that.'

So, I had dinner alone. But I figured I should get used to it. Someday my quick wit is going to get me into trouble. Actually, I guess it did.

CHAPTER 26

This elderly couple walked into my office and announced that they had not gotten along for about fifty years and they wanted a divorce. They looked as if they were around ninety – stop me if you've heard this – so I said to them, 'Excuse me for asking, but why have you waited so long to seek a divorce?' And the old gentleman replied, 'We were waiting for the children to die.'

Well, there are times when I feel the same way. Susan and I were reconciled yet again, and I had apologized for suggesting that her paternal origin was in question and that her mother was a whore. And even if Charlotte had once had hot pants, what difference did it make? But there was still the open question of whether or not her father was a monumental prick and so forth. I honestly believe he is, plus some. In fact, I even jotted down a few more descriptions of him in the event I ever saw him again. Susan, of course, knew what he was, which was why she wasn't terribly upset with me; but William *was* her father. Maybe.

Anyway, I was still living rent-free in Susan's house, and we were speaking again but not in complete or compound sentences.

I had been getting to bed early on Monday evenings, as per Mr Bellarosa's suggestion, rising early on Tuesdays and joining him for coffee at dawn. Susan hadn't questioned me about my two early-Tuesday departures on foot to Alhambra, and as per my client's instructions, I hadn't told her about his imminent arrest.

403

The FBI knew now, of course, that I was Frank Bellarosa's attorney, but my client did not want them to know that we had anticipated an early-Tuesday-morning visit. So, for that reason, I had to walk across our back acreage and approach Alhambra from the rear so as not to be seen from the DePauw outpost.

Incidentally, I had run into Allen DePauw a few times in the village, and with that profound lack of moral courage that is peculiar to rat finks, stool pigeons, and police snitches the world over, he did not snub me, but greeted me as though we were still buddies. On the last occasion that I ran into him, at the hardware store, I inquired, 'Do you trust your wife alone with all those men at your house around the clock? Don't you go to Chicago a lot for business?'

Instead of taking a swing at me, he replied coolly, 'They have a mobile home behind my house.'

'Come on, Allen, I'll bet they're always coming inside to borrow milk while you're away.'

'That's not very funny, John. I'm doing what I think is right.' He paid for his machine-gun oil or whatever it was and left.

Well, probably he was doing what he thought was right. Maybe it *was* right. But I knew that he was one of the people at the club who were making anonymous demands for my expulsion.

Anyway, in regard to Tuesday early A.M., even if the FBI came for Frank Bellarosa on another day, I was ready every morning to jump out of bed and be at Alhambra quickly. This was really exciting.

It was early August now, a time when I should have been in East Hampton. But Dr Carleton, whoever the hell he was, was in my house with his feet on my furniture, enjoying East End summer fun and the instant respectability of an eighteenth-century shingled house. I'd spoken to the psychiatric gentleman on the phone once to get him squared away with the house, and he'd said to me, 'What is your rush in going to closing, if I may ask?'

'My mother used to take money from my piggy bank and never replaced it. It's sort of complicated, Doc. Next week, okay?'

So, I had that date out east and I needed the bucks for the Feds, but the other Feds across the street here wanted to bust my client and I had to stay on top of that, too. It was hard to believe that it was as recently as March when I'd had a safe, predictable life, punctuated only now and then by a friend's divorce or a revealed marital infidelity and occasionally a death. My biggest problem had been boredom.

I had called Lester Remsen the day after the battle of McGlade's and said to him, 'Sell twenty thousand dollars' worth of some crap or another and drop the cheque with my secretary in Locust Valley.'

He replied, 'This is not the time to sell anything that you're holding. Your stuff got hit harder than most. Hold on to your positions if you can.'

'Lester, I read the Wall Street Journal, too. Do as I say, please.'

'Actually, I was going to phone you. You have margin calls –'

'How much?'

'About five. Do you want me to give you an exact figure so you can send me a cheque? Or, if money is a little tight, John, I can just liquidate more stocks to cover the margin calls.'

'Sell whatever you have to.'

'All right. Your portfolio is a little shaky.'

This is Wall Street talk for, 'You've made some very stupid investments.' Lester and I go back a long way, and even when we're not speaking, we talk. At least we talk about stocks. I realized I didn't like stocks or Lester. 'Sell everything. Now.'

'*Everything?* Why? The market is weak. It will rally in September –'

'We've been talking stocks for twenty years. Aren't you tired of it?'

'No.'

'I am. You know, Lester, if I had spent the last twenty years looking for Captain Kidd's treasure, I would have lost less money.'

'That's nonsense.'

'Close my account,' I said, and hung up.

Well, anyway, it was six A.M. on the first Tuesday in August, and I was brooding about this and that. In reality, even if Dr Carleton wasn't in my summer house, I wouldn't be there this August, owing to the fact that my client next door wanted me to stick close. I suppose I could have moved into Alhambra, to be very close, but I don't think the don wanted me around while he conducted business and consorted with known criminals. And I certainly didn't want to be a witness to any of that.

So on that overcast Tuesday morning, I walked out of Susan's house and began my cross-country trek in a good suit, carrying a big briefcase into which I would place five million dollars in cash and assignable assets with which to make bail.

I had examined all these assets one night at Bellarosa's house in order to list and verify them. Thus, I saw a small piece of the don's empire. Most of what I saw was recorded property deeds, which the court would accept. There were some bearer bonds and a few other odds and ends, together totalling about four million, which would meet even the most excessive bail. But to be certain, Bellarosa had dumped a shopping bag onto his kitchen table that contained a million dollars in cash.

As I was making my third trip to Alhambra in as many weeks, the birds were singing and the air was still cool. A ground mist sat about chest high on the fields between our property, and it was sort of eerie, as if I were going to Wasp heaven in my Brooks Brothers suit and briefcase.

I reached the reflecting pool with the statue of Mary and Neptune still glaring at each other, and a figure moved toward me out of the mist. It was Anthony, who was being taken for a walk by a pit bull. He barked at me. The dog, I mean. Anthony said, 'Guh mornin', Mistah Sutta.'

He must have sinus condition. 'Good morning, Anthony. How is the don this morning?'

'He's 'spectin' ya. I'll walk ya.'

'I'll walk myself, thank you.' I proceeded up the path to the house. Anthony was quite nice when you got to know him.

I approached the rear of the big house, noticing that the security lights were still on. I crossed the big patio and pulled the bell chain. I saw Vinnie through the glass doors politely holstering his gun as he recognized me. 'Come on in, Counsellor. The boss is in the kitchen.'

I entered the house at the rear of the palm court, and as I made my way across the large space, I noticed Lenny, the driver, sitting in a wicker chair near one of the pillars, drinking coffee. He, like Vinnie, was wearing a good suit in expectation of visitors and for the possible trip into Manhattan. Lenny stood as I approached and mumbled a greeting, which I made him repeat more distinctly. This was fun.

I made my way alone through the dark house, through the dining room, morning room, butler's pantry, and finally into the cavernous kitchen, which smelled of fresh coffee.

The kitchen had been completely redone, of course, and the don had told me exactly how much it cost to import the half mile or so of Italian cabinetry, the half acre of Italian floor tile, and the marble countertops. The appliances, sensibly, were American.

The don was sitting at the head of an oblong kitchen table, reading a newspaper. He was dressed in a blue silk pinstripe suit, a light blue shirt, which is better than white for television, and a burgundy tie with matching pocket handkerchief. The newspapers had dubbed him the Dandy Don and I could see why.

Bellarosa glanced up at me. 'Sit, sit.' He motioned to a chair and I sat to his right near the head of the table. He poured me coffee while still reading his paper.

I sipped on the black coffee. I suspected that one would never find a round table in the house of a traditional Italian, because a round table is where equals sat. An oblong table has a head where the patriarch sat. So, there I was, sitting at his right hand, and I wondered if that was significant or if I was getting into this thing too much.

He glanced up from the newspaper. 'So, Counsellor, is this the morning?'

'I hope so. I don't like getting up this early.'

He laughed. 'Yeah? *You* don't like it. You're not the one going to jail.'

I'm not the one who's broken the law for thirty years.

He put down the newspaper. 'I say this is it. The grand jury sat for three weeks. That's long enough for murder. The RICO shit can take a year, nosing around your business, trying to find what you own and where it came from. Money is complicated. Murder is simple.'

'That's true.'

'Hey, fifty bucks says that this is the morning.'

'You're on.'

'Yeah, I know what you're thinking. You think they're not going to indict me. You think you squared it with Mancuso.'

'I never said that. I said I told him what you asked me to tell him – about Ferragamo. I know Mancuso is the type of man who would pass that on to Ferragamo and maybe even to his own superiors. I don't know what will come of that.'

'I'll tell you what's going to come of it. Nothing. Because that scumbag Ferragamo is not going to back off after making his pitch to a grand jury. That would make him look like a real *gavone*. But I'm glad you talked to Mancuso. Now Ferragamo knows that Bellarosa knows.' Bellarosa went on, 'But maybe you shouldn't've told him you were my attorney.'

'How could I speak to him on your behalf without telling him I was representing you?'

He shrugged. 'I don't know. But maybe if you didn't say anything, he might've opened up to you.'

'That's unethical and illegal, Frank. Do you want a crooked lawyer or a Boy Scout?'

He smiled. 'Okay. We'll play you straight.'

'I'll play myself straight.'

'Whatever.'

We drank coffee awhile and the don shared his newspaper with me. It was the *Daily News*, that morning's city edition, which someone must have delivered to him hot off the printing press in Brooklyn. I flipped through the lead stories, but there was no early warning, no statement from Ferragamo about an imminent arrest. 'Nothing about you in here,' I said.

'Yeah. The scumbag's not that stupid. I got people in the newspapers and he knows it. He's got to wait for the bulldog edition, about midnight. We'll get that tonight. This prick loves the newspapers, but he loves TV more. You want something to eat?'

'No, thanks.'

'You sure? I'll call Filomena. Come on. Get something to eat. It's gonna be a long morning. Eat.'

'I am really not hungry. Really.' You know how these people are about eating, and they actually get annoyed when you refuse food, and they're happy when you eat. Why it matters to them is beyond me.

Bellarosa motioned to a thick folder on the table. 'That's the stuff.'

'Right.' I put the folder containing the deeds and such in my briefcase.

Bellarosa produced a large shopping bag from under the table. In the bag was one hundred stacks of one-hundred-dollar bills, a hundred bills in each stack, for a total of one million dollars. It looked good like that.

He said to me, 'Don't get tempted on the way to court, Counsellor.'

'Money doesn't tempt me.'

'Yeah? That's what you say. Watch, I'll get to court and find out you cold-cocked Lenny and stole the money. And I'll be in jail and I get this postcard from you in Rio, and it says, "Fuck you, Frank."' He laughed.

'You can trust me. I'm a lawyer.'

That made him laugh even harder for some reason. Anyway,

I have this large briefcase, almost a suitcase, that lawyers use when they have to drag forty pounds of paper into court, plus lunch. So I transferred the paper money into the briefcase along with the four million in paper assets. Paper, paper, paper.

Bellarosa said, 'You looked at those deeds and everything the other day, right?'

'Yes.'

'So you see, I'm a legitimate businessman.'

'Please, Frank. It's a little early in the morning for bullshit.'

'Yeah?' He laughed. 'Yeah, you see, I got Stanhope Hall in that briefcase now. I got a motel in Florida, I got one in Vegas, and I got land in Atlantic City. Land. That's the only thing that counts in this world. They don't make no more land, Counsellor.'

'No, they don't except in Holland where –'

'There was a time when they couldn't take land away from you unless they fought you for it. Now, they just do some paperwork.'

'That's true.'

'They're gonna take my fucking land.'

'No, it's just going to be used as collateral. You'll get it back.'

'No, Counsellor, when they see that shit in your briefcase, they're gonna come after it. Ferragamo is going to start a RICO thing next. They're gonna freeze everything I got, and one day they're gonna own it all. And that stuff you got in there makes their job easier. The murder bullshit smoked out a lot of my assets.'

'You're probably right.'

'But fuck them. Fuck all governments. All they want is to grab your property. Fuck them. There's more where that came from.'

I guess so, if Mancuso was correct. A lot more.

'Hey, did I tell you I made an offer for Fox Point? Nine mill. I talked to that lawyer who you told me handles things here for the people who own the place.' He asked me, 'You want to handle that for me?'

I shrugged. 'Why not?'

'Good. I'll give you a point. That's ninety large.'

'Let's see if they accept nine. Don't forget the Iranians.'

'Fuck them. They're not owners. They're buyers. I only deal with owners. I showed this lawyer that my best offer was his client's best offer. So he's going to make his clients understand that. His clients are not going to know about any more Iranian offers. *Capisce?*'

'I surely do.'

'And now we got a place to swim. I'm gonna let everyone on Grace Lane keep using the beach. And nobody has to worry about a bunch of sand niggers running around wrapped in sheets. *Capisce?*'

'Do you think you could avoid using that word?'

'*Capisce?*'

'No, the other word.'

'What the fuck are you talking about?'

'Forget it.'

He shrugged. 'Anyway, you can count on ninety large in a few months. Glad you came?'

'So far.' I said to him, 'You're obviously not too concerned about facing murder charges, racketeering charges down the line, or possible assassination.'

'Ah, it's all bullshit.'

'It's not, Frank.'

'Whaddaya gonna do? You gonna curl up and die? You see a deal, you make a deal. One thing's got nothing to do with the other.'

'Well, but it does.'

'Bullshit.'

'Just thought I'd mention it.' I poured myself more coffee and watched the sun burning through the mist outside the kitchen window. *You see a deal. You make a deal.* I recalled a story I'd had to read once in history class, up at St Paul's. In the story, two noble Romans were standing on the ramparts

411

of their city, negotiating the price of a piece of land in the distance. The seller extolled the virtues of his land, its fertility, its orchards, and its proximity to the city. The potential buyer did his best to find some faults with the land to get the price down. Finally, they struck a deal. What neither man mentioned during or after the negotiations was that an invading army was camped on the land in question, preparing for an assault on Rome. The moral of this apocryphal story, for Roman schoolboys, and I suppose for modern preppies at St Paul's who were supposed to be sons of the American ruling class, was this: Noble Romans (or noble preppie twits) must show supreme confidence and courage even in the face of death and destruction; one went about one's business without fear and with an abiding belief in the future. Or, as *my* ancestors would say, 'Stiff upper lip.' I said to Bellarosa, 'I didn't know you'd closed on Stanhope Hall.'

'Yeah. Last week. Where were you? You don't do legal work for your father-in-law? What kind of son-in-law are you?'

'I thought it would be a conflict of interest if I represented him for that transaction, and you for this matter.'

'Yeah? You're always thinkin' about that kind of stuff.' He leaned toward me. 'Hey, can I tell you something?'

'Sure.'

'Your father-in-law is a little hard to take.'

I had this utterly irrational mental flash: I could get Bellarosa to have William rubbed out. *A contract. A closing. This is from your son-in-law, you son of a bitch. BANG! BANG! BANG!*

'Hey, you listening? I said how do you get along with that guy?'

'He lives in South Carolina.'

'Yeah. Good thing. Hey, you want to see the painting?'

'I'll wait until it's hung.'

'Yeah. We're gonna get some people here. Susan's gonna be the guest of honour.'

'Good.'

'How's she doin'? Don't see her much anymore.'

'Is that so?'

'Yeah. She around today? To keep Anna company?'

'I think so. We don't exchange daybooks.'

'Yeah? You got a modern wife there. You like that?'

'How's Anna?'

'She's getting used to living here. She has all her crazy relatives drive out, and she shows off now. Donna Anna.' He added nonchalantly, 'She got over that ghost thing.' He smiled at me unpleasantly. 'You shouldn't have told her that crazy story.'

I cleared my throat. 'I'm sorry if it upset her.'

'Yeah? That was a hell of a story. The kids fucking. *Madonn'*. I told a lot of people that story. But I don't know if I got it right. Then I told it to my guy, Jack Weinstein. He's a smart guy like you. He says it was a book. That you got the story out of a book. It's not a story about Alhambra. Why'd you do that?'

'To amuse your wife.'

'She wasn't amused.'

'Well, then to amuse myself.'

'Yeah?' He didn't look too pleased with me. 'Somethin' else,' he said. 'Anna thinks you were the guy who growled at her. Was that you?'

'Yes.'

'Why'd you do that?'

I pictured myself at the bottom of the reflecting pool wearing concrete slippers unless I had a better answer than 'To amuse myself.' I said, 'Look, Frank, that was months ago. Forget it.'

'I don't forget nothin'.'

True. 'Well, then accept my apology.'

'Okay. That I'll do.' He added, 'And that's more than I usually do.' He stared at me, then tapped his forehead. '*Tu sei matto. Capisce?*'

It helps when they use their hands. I replied, '*Capisco.*'

'You people are all crazy.'

We both went back to our newspaper, but after a few minutes of silence, he asked me, 'How much am I paying you?'

'Nothing. I'm returning a favour.'

'Nah. You already did that by talking to Mancuso. Get me sprung today, and you get fifty large.'

'No, I –'

'Take it now, Counsellor, because I might need you later for something, and if they grab all my money under RICO, you ain't gonna get shit.'

I shrugged. 'All right.'

'Good. See? You got ninety and fifty already and you ain't even had your breakfast yet.' He wagged his finger at me. 'And don't forget to report it on your income tax.' He laughed.

I managed a smile. Fuck you, Frank.

We spoke about family for a while, and Frank asked me, 'Your daughter still in Cuba?'

'Yes.'

'If you talk to her, tell her it's number fours.'

'Excuse me?'

'Monte Cristo number four. I forgot to tell your son to tell her that. That's the big torpedoes. Number four.'

I wasn't going to argue with him about smuggling, so I nodded. He asked me, 'Do you think the old lady is going to stay in the gatehouse?'

'I advised her to do that.'

'Yeah? What would she take to get out?'

'Nothing, Frank. That's her home. Forget that.'

He shrugged.

I played with the idea of telling him that William Stanhope had probably contributed money to the Gold Coast Preservation Fund, earmarked for the Stanhope Hall zoning battle. But I couldn't bring myself to reveal a confidence like that. However unethical William's action was, it wasn't illegal, and he'd confided his thoughts in front of me about four minutes before I told him to fuck himself. But I did ask Bellarosa, 'What are you going to do with Stanhope Hall?'

'I dunno. We'll see.'

'You could use it to bury bodies.'

He smiled.

I asked him, 'Where's your son, Tony?' I'd met the little La Salle student the previous week, and he seemed like a sharp kid. He also reminded me of his father in his appearance and mannerisms. Bellarosa seemed very proud of him. I'd taken to calling the kid Little Don, but only in my mind, of course.

Bellarosa answered me, 'I sent him to his older brother for the rest of the summer.'

'Which older brother?'

He looked at me. 'It don't matter, and forget you heard that. Understand?'

'Absolutely.' My Lord, you really had to think before you asked any questions of this man. The rich and famous were like that, of course, and I had wealthy friends who didn't advertise the whereabouts of their children either. But they would tell *me* if I asked.

He asked me, 'Hey, your son still in Florida?'

'Maybe. Maybe not.'

He smiled again and went back to his paper. He was doing the crossword puzzle. 'American writer, first name Norman, six letters . . . ends in *r*.'

'Mailer.'

'Never heard of him.' He filled in the boxes. 'Yeah . . . that's it. You're a smart guy.'

Filomena came into the kitchen, and she really was ugly, kind of hard to take in the morning. She and Frank chatted away in Italian for a few minutes, and I could tell his Italian wasn't good because she was impatient with him. She dragged out all sorts of biscuit tins with Italian writing on them and dumped them on the table. She was giving Bellarosa a hard time about something, then started giving me a hard time.

Frank explained to me, 'She wants you to eat.'

So, I ate. There were different kinds of breakfast biscuits, and they weren't bad with butter. Bellarosa had to eat, too. Filomena watched us for a while, motioning to me to keep shovelling it in. Bellarosa said something sharp to her, and she gave it right back to him. This was sort of like a power breakfast, and Filomena had the power.

Finally, Filomena found something else to do, and Frank pushed his plate away. 'Pain in my ass.'

'Well, that hit the spot.'

He leaned toward me. 'You know any men around here for her?'

'Not offhand.'

'She's twenty-four, probably a virgin, cooks like a chef, cleans, sews, and works hard.'

'I'll take her.'

He laughed and slapped me on the shoulder. 'Yeah? You want an Italian woman? I'm gonna tell your wife.'

'We've already discussed it.'

We had another cup of coffee. It was approaching eight A.M., and by this time I was beginning to think it was a little late for an arrest, but then Vinnie came into the kitchen as though he were walking on eggs. 'Boss, they're here. Anthony called from the gate. They're coming.'

Bellarosa made a motion of dismissal, and Vinnie dematerialized. Bellarosa turned to me. 'You owe me fifty bucks.'

I had the feeling he wanted it right then, so I gave it to him and he shoved it in his pocket. 'See?' he said. 'Ferragamo is a dishonest man. He lied to the grand jury and they gave him his indictment. So I'm getting arrested for something I didn't do, and he *knows* I didn't kill Juan Carranza. Now there's going to be blood in the streets, and innocent people are going to get hurt.'

People who get into trouble with the law start sounding like saints and martyrs. I've noticed that with my clients who get caught doing creative accounting.

Bellarosa stood and said to me, 'On January fourteenth of this year, on the day Juan Carranza was killed in Jersey by the DEA guys, I got a very good alibi.'

'Good.' I stood, too, and grabbed my briefcase.

'You never asked me about my alibi for that day because you're not a criminal lawyer.'

'That's true. I should have asked.'

'Well, as it so happens, I was here. That's one of the days I drove out here to look at this place. I was here almost the whole day, walking around, eighty miles from where Carranza got hit. They blew his head off in his car on the Garden State Parkway. But I wasn't anywhere near there. I was here.'

'Was anyone with you?'

'Sure. Someone's always with me. Lenny was driving. Another guy was keeping me company.'

I shook my head. 'No one wants to hear that crap, Frank. That's not an alibi. Did anyone around *here* see you?'

He looked me in the eye. I don't know why I hadn't seen that coming. I said, 'Forget it.'

He pointed his finger at me. 'Counsellor, if you tell that judge at the bail hearing that you saw me that day, you blow Ferragamo out of the water, and I walk in two minutes, maybe without even posting bail.'

'No.' I moved toward the door.

'Hey, maybe you did see me. What were you doing that day? You out riding?'

'No.'

He moved toward me. 'Maybe your wife was out riding. Maybe she saw me. Maybe I should talk to her.'

I dropped the briefcase and came toward him. 'You son of a bitch!'

We stood there, about a foot apart, and I kept thinking about the lead pipe. I said, 'I'm not going to commit perjury for you, and neither is my wife.'

We stared at each other and finally he said softly, 'Okay. If you don't think you got to say that to get me sprung, then you don't have to say it. Just get me sprung.'

I poked my finger at him. 'Don't try that shit on me again, Frank. Don't you *ever* ask me to do anything illegal. I want an apology or I walk out of here.'

I couldn't read anything in his normally expressive face, except that his eyes were somewhere else, then he focused on me. 'Okay. I apologize. Okay? Let's go.' He took my arm, I took the briefcase, and we went out to the palm court.

Lenny and Vinnie stood at the small peep windows that flanked the front door. Vinnie turned to his boss. 'Somethin' screwy here.'

Bellarosa brushed him aside and looked out the window. 'I'll be goddamned. . . .' He turned to me. 'Hey, look at this.'

I moved to the window, not knowing what I expected to see – tanks, SWAT teams, helicopters, or what. I did expect to see vehicles, and in the vehicles at least a dozen men: federal types in suits and maybe a few uniformed county police and detectives so that everyone felt they had a piece of the action. But what was coming up the long cobblestone drive now was a solitary man on foot, taking his time, looking at the flower beds and poplars, as though he were out for a stroll.

As the man got closer – actually long before that – I recognized him. I turned to Bellarosa. 'Mancuso.'

'Yeah?'

Lenny, at the other window, exclaimed, 'He's alone! The son of a bitch is *alone.*' He turned to Bellarosa. 'Let's off the motherfucker.'

I didn't think that was a good idea.

Bellarosa said, 'The man has balls. What balls he has.'

Vinnie was scandalized. 'They can't do that! They can't send one guy!'

Mr Mancuso wasn't alone, of course, but had the full weight and power of the law with him. That was the lesson to be learned this morning, not only by Frank Bellarosa and his men, but by me.

Lenny said, 'Here he comes!' He put his right hand inside his jacket, reaching, I hoped, for his appointment book. But no, he drew his revolver and said, 'Should we take him, boss?' Actually, he didn't sound too sincere.

Bellarosa replied, 'Shut up. Put that away. Both of you get back. Over there. Counsellor, you stand there.'

418

Lenny and Vinnie moved far back near a column, and I stood to the side.

There were three raps on the door.

Frank Bellarosa strode to the door and opened it. 'Hey, look who's here.'

Mr Mancuso held up his badge case, though we all knew who he was, and got right to the point. 'I have a warrant for your arrest, Frank. Let's go.'

But Bellarosa did not make a move to leave and both men stared at each other, as if they had both anticipated this moment for years and wanted to let it hang there awhile to be fully appreciated. Finally Bellarosa said, 'You got some balls, Mancuso.'

Mancuso replied, 'And you are under arrest.' Mancuso pulled a pair of handcuffs from his pocket. 'Hands to your front.'

'Hey, goombah, let me take care of a few things first. Okay?'

'Cut the goombah stuff, Frank. Are you resisting arrest?'

'No, no. I just want to talk to my wife. No funny stuff. I was waiting for you. Look, we got a civilian here.' He stepped aside and motioned toward me. 'See? You know him. He'll vouch for me.'

Mr Mancuso and I made eye contact, and I could tell that he already knew I was there. I said to him, 'Mr Mancuso, you can see that my client was expecting this arrest, and he has made no attempt to resist or to flee. He wants some time to speak to his wife. That is reasonable and customary.' I didn't know if that was true or not, but it sounded as if it could be. I think that's the way they do it in the movies.

Mr Mancuso said to Bellarosa, 'All right, Frank. Ten minutes. Just a hug and a smooch. No boomba, boomba.'

Bellarosa laughed, though I was certain he wanted to smash Mancuso's face with a lead pipe.

Bellarosa moved out of the doorway, and Mancuso walked a few paces into the palm court, looked at me, then saw

Vinnie, then Lenny. He glanced around to make sure he hadn't missed anyone.

Bellarosa said, '*Benvenuto a nostra casa.*'

Mr Mancuso replied in Italian, and though I couldn't understand what he'd said, it didn't sound like 'Thank you.' In fact, if I didn't know firsthand that Mr Mancuso didn't use profanity, I'd swear he said, 'Fuck you.' Maybe he only swears in Italian. Anyway, whatever he said caused Frank, Vinnie, and Lenny to be unhappy with their *paesano*.

Frank kept his smile in place, excused himself, and climbed the stairs to the second floor.

Mr Mancuso turned his attention to Lenny and Vinnie. He said to them, 'Carrying?'

They both nodded.

'Licensed?'

Again they nodded.

Mr Mancuso put out his hand. 'Wallets.'

They both put their wallets in his hand, and he rummaged through them, letting money and credit cards fall to the floor as he retrieved their pistol licences. He compared their faces to the photos and said, 'Vincent Adamo and Leonard Patrelli. What do you do for a living, boys?'

'Nothin'.'

He threw their wallets to them and said, 'Get out.'

They hesitated, then scooped up their money and cards from the floor and left.

Mr Mancuso turned his attention now to his surroundings, looking up at the birds, the hanging plants, and the mezzanine and balconies.

I asked him, 'Would you like some coffee?'

He shook his head and began ambling around the palm court, checking on the health of the potted palms, making sure the birds in the lower cages had food and water, then contemplating a pink marble column.

This was indeed a different Mr Mancuso than the one I'd gone sailing with. He turned and looked at me, then motioned me to a big wicker chair.

I sat, and he pulled another chair over and sat across from me. We listened to the birds awhile, then he looked at me and asked, 'What's the problem, Mr Sutter?'

'Problem? What problem?'

'That's what I asked you. You have to have problems or you wouldn't be here. Family problems? Money problems? Wife problems, life problems? You're not going to solve any problems here. Are you trying to prove something? What's making you unhappy?'

'You, at the moment.'

'Hey, I'm not in the happiness business.'

'Are you in the priest business?'

'Sometimes. Look, I'll let Bellarosa call his attorney, Jack Weinstein. Weinstein will meet him at Federal Court. I'll give you five minutes with Bellarosa to explain to him any way you want that you don't want to represent him or, in fact, ever see him again. Believe me, Mr Sutter, he will understand.'

'You're not supposed to try to come between a lawyer and his client.'

'Don't tell me the law, Mr Sutter. You know, it doesn't matter to me, as a federal agent making this arrest, who Bellarosa's attorney is. But it matters to me as a citizen and as a man that his attorney is you.'

I thought about that for a moment, then replied, 'I truly appreciate that. But I cannot walk away from this, Mr Mancuso. Only I know how I got here, and why. I have to see it through, or I'll never break out on the other side. Do you understand?'

'I have always understood. But you should have explored your alternatives.'

'Probably I should have.'

We sat in silence for a few more minutes, then I heard Bellarosa's heavy tread on the staircase.

Mancuso stood and met him at the bottom step, cuffs in hand. 'Ready, Frank?'

'Sure.' Bellarosa extended his hands, and Mancuso cuffed him. Mancuso said, 'Against the post.'

Bellarosa leaned against the marble stair post, and Mancuso frisked him. 'Okay.'

Bellarosa straightened up, and Mancuso said to me, 'As long as you're here, *you* tell him his rights.'

I didn't really remember the wording of the so-called Miranda warning, which was a little embarrassing. (I do mostly taxes, wills, and house closings.) Anyway, Mancuso and Bellarosa helped me out, though Mancuso had a little cheat card with him. He said to me, 'Okay? Your client understands his rights?'

I nodded.

Mancuso took my client's arm and began leading him away, but I said, 'I'd like to see the arrest warrant.'

Mr Mancuso seemed annoyed, but fished it out of his pocket and handed it to me. I studied it carefully. I'd never really seen one, and I found it rather interesting. I figured I was earning a little of the fifty large already, and making up for the Miranda thing, but I could sense that Mancuso and even Bellarosa were a little impatient. I handed the warrant back to Mancuso, but I wondered if I was supposed to ask for a copy for my files.

Mancuso led Bellarosa to the door and I followed. I said to Mancuso, 'Are you going directly to the FBI office at Federal Plaza?'

'That's right.'

'How long will you be there?'

'As long as it takes to book my prisoner.'

'And after the booking, will you be taking my client directly to the Federal Court at Foley Square?'

'That is correct.'

'At about what time, Mr Mancuso?'

'Whenever I get there, Mr Sutter.'

'Will there be newspeople there?'

'That's no concern of mine, Mr Sutter.'

'It's a concern of Alphonse Ferragamo, who is going to stage a media circus.'

'It's still no concern of mine.'

I said, 'I plan to be with my client every step of the way, Mr Mancuso. I expect everyone to behave properly and professionally.'

'You can count on that, Mr Sutter. May I remove my prisoner? I'd like to get on the road.'

'Certainly.' I said to Frank Bellarosa, 'I'll see you at Federal Plaza.'

Bellarosa, trying to look very nonchalant despite the cuffs and Mancuso's hand on his arm, said to me jokingly, 'Don't forget the briefcase, and don't stop for coffee, and don't get lost. *Capisce?*'

I noticed that Frank Bellarosa was not as eloquent with his hands cuffed, but I understood him. '*Capisco.*'

He laughed and said to Mancuso, 'See? Another few months and I'll have him cursing in Italian.'

'Let's go, Frank.' Mancuso led Bellarosa out the door.

I stood at the open door, and Lenny and Vinnie joined me. I watched Mancuso take Frank Bellarosa down the long drive toward the gate where Anthony stood watching. There is something about that scene that I won't ever forget. But I don't think that Anthony, Vinnie, or Lenny were as profoundly impressed with the scene, nor would they make the logical deduction that crime doesn't pay.

Lenny said to me, 'Ready to go, Counsellor?'

I nodded and retrieved my briefcase as Lenny went out to bring the Cadillac around front.

I found myself standing with Vinnie, who still seemed annoyed that the house hadn't been surrounded by SWAT teams and paratroopers. 'We shoulda offed the motherfucker. You know? Who the fuck does he think he is?'

'The law.'

'Yeah? Fuck him.' Vinnie stomped out the door.

I started to follow, but heard a noise behind me and turned. Coming down the winding staircase, wailing at the top of her big lungs, was Anna, wearing a robe and slippers. I started to back out the door, but she saw me. 'John! John! Oh, my God! John!'

Madonn'. Do I need this?

'John!' She came rushing toward me like a '54 Buick with oversized bumper guards. 'John! They took Frank! They took him away!' She collided with me — Boom! – and wrapped her arms around me, which was all that kept me from sprawling across the floor. She buried her face in my chest and gushed tears over my Hermès tie. 'Oh, John! They arrested him!'

'Yes, I was actually here.'

She kept sobbing and squeezing me. *Madonna mia*. Those tits and arms were crushing the air out of my lungs. 'There, there,' I wheezed. 'Don't cry. Let's sit down.'

I steered her over to a wicker chair, which was like trying to manhandle a side of beef. She wasn't wearing much under her robe, and despite the circumstances and the early hour, I found I was a wee bit cranked up by her proximity. An incredibly insane thought passed through my mind, but I got it right out of there before it got me killed.

She was sitting now, clutching my hands in hers. 'Why did they take my Frank?'

Gee, Anna, I can't imagine why. I said, 'I'm sure it's a mistake. Don't worry about it. I'll have him home by tonight.'

She yanked me down to my knees and our faces were close. I noticed that, as upset as she was, she'd dallied upstairs long enough to comb her hair, put on a little make-up, and that nice scent she used. She looked me straight in the eye and said, 'Swear to me. Swear to me, John, that you will bring Frank home.'

Mamma mia, what a morning this was going to be. I never had these problems at a house closing. I cleared my throat and said, 'I swear it.'

'On the grave of your mother. Swear it on the grave of your mother.'

As best I knew, Harriet was still alive and well in Europe. But a lot of people think my parents are dead, including me sometimes, so I said, 'I swear on the grave of my mother that I'll bring Frank home.'

'Oh . . . dear Lord . . .' She kissed my hands and blubbered awhile. I managed to get a look at my watch. 'Anna, I have to go meet Frank.' I stood, her hands still grasping mine. 'I really have to go – '

'Hey, Counsellor! Got to move!' It was Vinnie, who, seeing Anna clutching me, said, 'Oh, hi, Mrs Bellarosa. Sorry about this. I gotta take Mr Sutter to court.'

I disengaged my hands and said to Anna, 'Call Susan and she'll come over to keep you company. Maybe you can go shopping, play a little tennis.' I hurried toward the door, snatched up my briefcase, and left quickly.

On the expressway into Manhattan, Lenny, behind the wheel, said, 'Did you see how cool the don was?'

Vinnie, also in the front seat, replied, 'Yeah. He ain't afraid of nuthin'.' He looked back at me. 'Right, Counsellor?'

I was a little annoyed with these two, who had been singing Bellarosa's praises for the last ten miles, as though he'd been arrested by the KGB for pro-democracy activities and was on his way to the Lubyanka for torture. I said, 'There was nothing to be afraid of except bad drivers on the expressway.'

'Yeah?' snapped Vinnie. 'I've been arrested twice. You got to show balls or they fuck you around. How'd you like to be looking at ten or twenty years?'

'Hey, Vinnie,' I replied, 'if you can't do the time, don't do the crime. *Capisce?*'

Lenny laughed. 'Listen to this guy. He sounds like fucking Weinstein now. Hey, Counsellor, how'd you act if you was thrown in a cell full of *melanzane* and spics?'

'I might prefer it to being in a car with two greaseballs.'

They thought that was very funny and they laughed, slapped their knees, pounded the dashboard, and Lenny hit the horn a few times while Vinnie whooped. The Italians, I'd discovered, were pretty thick-skinned when it came to ethnic humour at their expense. But there were other kinds of jokes they didn't find so amusing. You had to be careful.

Vinnie said to me, 'The don is lookin' forward to lunch

at Caffè Roma today, Counsellor. He's gonna be there, right?'

'I hope so. If not, we'll get Caffè Roma to deliver to his cell.'

Now there's an example of the kind of joke they don't find funny. In fact, Vinnie said, 'That's not too fuckin' funny.'

Lenny said, 'If you don't walk out of that court with the don, maybe you should find another way home.'

That wasn't quite a threat, but it had possibilities. I replied, 'Let me worry about that. You worry about driving.'

No one spoke for a while, which was fine with me. So there I was, in a black Cadillac with two Mafia goons, heading into the maws of the federal criminal justice system.

It was just nine A.M. now and the worst of the rush hour was over, but traffic was still heavy, so I didn't think there was any chance that we'd overtake Mancuso, and in fact, I didn't even know what sort of vehicle he was driving. But as it turned out, though we never saw the car that Mancuso and Bellarosa were in, I began to realize that the same four nondescript grey Fords had been keeping pace with us for some time.

Lenny said, 'Look at those cocksuckers.'

So I did. Each car held two men, and they were staring at us as they played a game of changing positions around us. The car to our front suddenly slowed down, and Lenny hit his brakes. 'Cocksuckers!'

The grey Fords to our sides and rear boxed us in, and they slowed us down to ten miles an hour, causing the other Long Island Expressway motorists behind us, who are not known for road courtesy in the best of times, to go nearly hysterical. Horns were blaring, insults hurled, drivers pounded their foreheads against their steering wheels. They were really upset back there.

So we caused what they call on the radio 'major delays' approaching the Midtown Tunnel.

This wasn't just harassment, of course, but a rather unethical attempt to separate me from my client. I saw Ferragamo's hand in this and began to suspect that it wasn't the FBI in those cars, but Ferragamo's men from the Justice Department. I said to Lenny, 'Go right to Federal Court in Foley Square.'

'But the don said to meet him at the FBI headquarters.'

'Do what I say.'

'He'll kill us!'

'Do what I say!'

Vinnie, who had about half a functional brain, said, 'He's right. We gotta get straight to the court.'

Lenny seemed to understand. 'Okay. But I ain't takin' this fuckin' rap, Vinnie.'

I settled back in the seat and listened to the horns blaring around us. I didn't think Mancuso was in on this, and as best I could figure it, Mancuso would get a call over his car radio instructing him to go straight to Federal Court. Bellarosa could and would be booked there instead of at FBI headquarters. Then Bellarosa would be whisked in front of a judge for arraignment, and the head of New York's largest crime family would be standing there in his nice suit without an attorney. The judge would read the charge and ask Bellarosa to enter a plea. Bellarosa would say, 'Not guilty,' and the judge would order him held without bail. Frank would put up a big stink, but to no avail. Murder is a tough charge, and it would take me about two weeks to get a bail hearing. Actually, I would be well-advised to just head on down to Rio and send a postcard.

I looked at my briefcase beside me. Some of the paper assets were negotiable, and there was a cool million in cash. The Brazilians didn't ask many questions when you deposited a million U.S. in the bank, except maybe what colour cheques you wanted.

I looked at my watch. They were probably at Foley Square by now, but the booking process, even if it was speeded up, still had to be done according to law; there would be a body search, fingerprinting, photographs, a personal history taken, and forms to fill out. Only then would they haul Bellarosa in front of a waiting judge. So it was possible for me to charge into the courthouse, find out where Bellarosa was to be arraigned, and get into the courtroom on time. It was possible.

I remember I had a house closing in Oyster Bay once, and my car broke down . . . but maybe that's not a good comparison.

Well, but what could I do? I took down the licence plate numbers of our escorts, stared back at them, then picked up a newspaper lying on the seat. The Mets had beaten Montreal and were two games out of first place now. I said to my friends up front, 'Hey, how 'bout them Mets?'

Vinnie said, 'Yeah, you see that last night?'

We did baseball chatter awhile. I knew we had to have something in common besides the same boss and the fear of our lives.

There was a car phone in the rear, and I could have called Susan, but I had no desire to. The next time she heard anything of me would be on the afternoon news. But then I remembered she didn't read, hear, or watch the news. But maybe she'd make an exception in this case. Thanks for the challenge, Susan.

We approached the tunnel tolls, and I looked at my watch. This was going to be very close.

CHAPTER 27

We lost our escort at the Midtown Tunnel and got on the FDR Drive. Lenny turned out to be a better driver than a conversationalist, which is saying very little, and he got us quickly into and through the narrow, crowded streets of lower Manhattan. But the closer we got to Foley Square, the slower the traffic was moving. I looked at my watch. It was nine-forty, and I estimated that Mancuso and Bellarosa could have been at Foley Square for as long as thirty minutes. The wheels of criminal justice move slowly, but they're capable of a quick grind if someone such as Alphonse Ferragamo is standing there squirting oil on them.

But the wheels of the Cadillac were not moving fast at all. In fact, we were stalled in traffic near City Hall Park, and the first arraignments would begin at ten A.M. *Damn it*. I grabbed my briefcase and opened the door.

'Where you goin'?' asked Vinnie.

'Rio.' I exited the car before he could process that.

It was hot and humid outside the air-conditioned Cadillac, and it's not easy to run in wing-tip shoes despite their name, but all lawyers have done this at one time or another, and I headed up Center Street toward Foley Square at a good clip. On the way, I practised my lines. 'Your Honour! Don't bang that gavel! I got money!'

The streets and sidewalks were crowded, and many of the people in this section of town were civil servants of the city, state, or federal government who, by nature, were in no particular hurry. However, there were a few other Brooks Brothers runners whom I took to be attorneys on missions similar to mine. I fell in behind a good broken-field runner, and within ten minutes I was at Foley Square, covered with sweat, my arms aching from the weight of the briefcase. I'm in pretty good shape, but running through Manhattan heat and carbon monoxide in a suit is equivalent to about three sets of tough tennis at the club.

I paused at the bottom of the forty or fifty courthouse steps and contemplated the summit a moment, then took a deep breath and charged toward the colossal columned portico. I had a mental image of my passing out and of good samaritans crowding around me, loosening my Hermès tie, and relieving me of my five-million-dollar burden. Then I'd have to hitchhike to Rio.

But the next thing I knew, I was inside the cooler lobby of the Federal Courthouse, walking purposefully across the elegant ivory-coloured marble floor, then through a metal detector, which didn't go off. But a U.S. Marshal, obviously intrigued by my dishevelled appearance and huge briefcase, asked me to put the briefcase on a long table and open it. So, there I was, in this massive lobby amid the hustle and bustle of a courthouse at ten A.M., opening a briefcase stuffed with wads of money. If you've ever emptied a bag of dirty underwear at Customs, you know the feeling.

The marshal, an older man who probably thought all marshals should look and act like Wyatt Earp, stood there with his thumbs hooked in his belt, chewing a wad of something. Despite his cowboy pose, he was not wearing boots or spurs or anything like that. Instead, he was dressed in the standard marshal's courthouse uniform, which consisted of grey slacks, white shirt, red tie, and a blue blazer with the U.S. Marshal's service patch on the breast pocket. His shoes were penny loafers, and his six-gun was not strapped around his waist, but was somewhere else, probably in a shoulder holster. I was very disappointed in this outfit, but chose not to remark on it. Wyatt Earp inquired, 'What's that?'

It's money, you stupid ass. 'It's bail money, Marshal.'

'Oh, yeah?'

'Yup. I have a client being arraigned this morning.'

'Is that so?'

'It is. And in fact, I don't want to miss it, so – '

'Why're you all sweaty?'

'I was actually running so as not to be late for the arraignment.'

'You nervous about something?'

'No. I was running.'

'Yeah? You got some kind of identification?'

'I believe I do.' I pulled my wallet out and showed him my driver's licence with my photo, and my bar association card. A few other marshals were standing around now, watching me and the money. Wyatt Earp passed my driver's licence around and everyone took a look. Needless to say, a crowd was gathering, enchanted by the green stuff, so I closed the briefcase.

After my licence made the rounds, including, I think, a passing janitor, I got my ID back. Earp asked me, 'Who's your client, Counsellor?'

I hesitated, then replied, 'Bellarosa, Frank.'

The marshal's eyebrows arched. 'Yeah? They got that sucker? When?'

'He was arrested this morning. I really want to get to the courtroom before he comes before the judge.'

'Take it easy. He'll be lucky if he sees a judge by lunchtime. You new around here?'

'Sort of.' I added, 'I need to speak with my client before the arraignment. So I'll just be on my way.' And I was.

'Wait!'

I stopped. The marshal moseyed over to me, sort of bowlegged as if he'd been on a horse all morning, or maybe he had haemorrhoids. He said, 'You know where the lockup is?'

'Actually, no.'

'Well, I'll tell ya. You go to the third floor – '

'Thanks.'

'Hold on. The lockup is between the marshal's area where your guy is going to be fingerprinted and photographed, and . . .' He stopped talking and moved closer to me. 'You gotta go to the bathroom or something?'

I guess I seemed a little fidgety, and Wyatt could see it. He looked suspicious again, so I took the bull by the horns. 'Look, Marshal, my client is going to be processed very quickly because of who he is. In fact, he's already processed. I do not want to miss the arraignment because if I do, he will not be happy with me.' I almost added, *'Capisce?'* but the guy looked Irish.

He grinned. 'Yeah, you don't want to miss *that* arraignment, Counsellor. You know where to go?'

'Third floor?'

'Right you are. Your guy been indicted and arrested, or just arrested and waiting indictment?'

'Indicted and arrested.'

'Okay, then you don't want the Magistrate, you want the District Judge, Part One.'

Mamma mia, this guy was going to give me a course in the

Federal court system. In truth, I didn't know any of this, but neither did I care. I just wanted to get to the third floor before it was too late. However, I didn't want to look panicky, which would only cause him to be more helpful or more suspicious. I smiled. 'Part One. Right.'

'Yeah. Part One. Third floor.' He looked at this watch. 'Hey, it's after ten. You better get a move on.'

'Yes, I'd better.' I walked, not ran, toward the elevators. I heard him call after me, 'I hope you got enough money there.'

I hope I have enough time, Wyatt. I took the elevators up to the third floor.

As bad luck would have it, the elevator stopped outside the Magistrate's Court, not Part One, so I was already lost. I picked a direction and walked. There were dozens of handcuffed prisoners in the corridors of justice with their arresting officers, U.S. Marshals, FBI men, attorneys for the government, attorneys for the accused, witnesses, and all sorts of people, none of whom looked happy to be there. There is something uniquely depressing about the hallways in any criminal court; the prisoners, the guards, the visible evidence of human frailty, misery, and evil.

I picked a corridor and went down it. The Federal courts are distinctly different from state or municipal courts in many respects. For one thing, you usually get a higher-quality criminal, such as Wall Street types and other white-collar rip-off artists who were stupid enough to use the U.S. mails for their schemes or to branch out across state lines. Occasionally, you get a spy or traitor, and now and then (but not often enough) you get a congressman or member of the Cabinet. But I'd heard, and now I saw with my own eyes, that with the increase in federal drug cases, the quality of federal defendants was somewhat lower than in years past. In fact, I saw men who looked as if they were definitely part of the international pharmaceutical trade, and I could see why Frank Bellarosa, tough guy that he was, would just as soon avoid trouble with these new guys.

In fact, I didn't even want to be in the same hallway as these dangerous felons, even if they *were* cuffed. For one thing, they smelled, and the stink was overpowering. I had smelled that odour in state criminal court once and knew it; it was the smell of the junkie, a sort of sugary-sweet smell at first whiff, but underlying it was a stench like a rotting animal. I almost gagged as I walked down the corridor. John Sutter, what are you doing here? Get back to Wall Street where you belong. No, damn it, see it through. Where're your balls, you finicky twit? Push on.

I pushed on, through the stinking corridor of Magistrate Court, and found Part One, where the defendants were uncuffed and smelled better.

I asked a deputy marshal, 'Has Frank Bellarosa come before a judge yet?'

'Bellarosa? The Mafia guy? I didn't even know he was here.'

'He's supposed to be here. I'm his attorney. Could he have been arraigned already?'

He shrugged. 'Maybe. Judge Rosen's been doing arraignments for a while.'

'Where is his courtroom?'

'Her. Judge Rosen's a woman.'

'How many judges are arraigning this morning?'

'One, same as every morning. You new here?'

'I guess so. Where is Judge Rosen's courtroom?'

He told me and added, 'She's a bitch on bail, especially for wiseguy types.'

So, with that encouraging news, I walked quickly but with no outward signs of the anxiety that was growing inside me to the door of the courtroom marked JUDGE SARAH ROSEN and opened it.

Indeed, the court was in session, and two marshals eyed me as I entered. Sitting in the benches where spectators normally sit at a trial were about thirty people, mostly men, and almost all, I suspected, were defence attorneys, though there might be some arresting officers as well, and perhaps a few defendants who were deemed not dangerous and thus were uncuffed. I looked for my client's blue suit and for Mancuso's distinctive pate among the heads and shoulders but did not see either.

There was an arraignment in progress. A defendant and his attorney stood in front of Judge Sarah Rosen. To the right of the defendant was a young assistant U.S. Attorney, a woman of about twenty-five. She was in profile, and for some reason, she reminded me of my daughter, Carolyn. The courtroom was quiet, yet everyone up front was speaking so softly that I could catch only a word or two. The only thing I heard clearly was the defendant, a middle-aged, well-dressed man, say, 'Not guilty,' as if he meant it and believed it.

The criminal justice system in America is basically an eighteenth-century morality play that the actors try to adapt to twentieth-century society. The whole concept of arraignments, for instance, the public reading of the charges, the haggling over bail in open court, is somewhat archaic, I think. But I suppose it's better than other systems where justice is done in dark, private places.

One of the marshals was motioning me to sit down, so I sat.

The arraignment in progress was finished, and the defendant was led away in cuffs, bail denied. Not good.

The court officer called out the next case. 'Johnson, Nigel!'

Presently, a tall, thin black man wearing a white suit and dreadlocks was escorted into the courtroom through the side door, rubbing his wrists where the cuffs had been. An attorney rose and made his way toward the judge's bench. If I had to guess, I'd say the gentleman standing before Judge Rosen was a Jamaican and the charge probably had something to do with drug trafficking or illegal immigration or both. The arraignment could take as long as fifteen minutes if there was an argument over bail. Meanwhile, Ferragamo could have pulled a really neat trick, and my client could be standing in front of another judge in Brooklyn Federal Court, offering his Rolex watch for bail. The courtroom was cool, but I was still sweating. Think, Sutter.

As I thought, I was aware that the door behind me had opened a few times, and I noticed that men and women were making their way to the front of the court and finding seats. I also noticed two men and one woman in the otherwise empty jury box. They were sketch artists, which I thought was unusual at an arraignment.

Sitting a few feet to my left was an attorney doing some paperwork on his briefcase. I leaned toward him and asked, 'Have you been here long?'

He looked over at me. 'Since nine.'

'Have you heard Frank Bellarosa's case called?'

He shook his head. 'No. Is he going to be arraigned here?'

'I don't know. I'm representing him, but I'm not familiar with the Federal Courts. How would I find – '

'Quiet in the court!' bellowed the fat marshal, who probably saw me rather than heard me. These guys are power freaks, all full of themselves with their guns and badges and potbellies. I recalled that Mark Twain once observed, 'If you want to see the dregs of humanity, go down to the jail and watch the changing of the guard.' I wish Uncle Walt had said that. Anyway, I settled back and considered my options.

The arraignment of the tall fellow had begun, and indeed it was a drug charge. The U.S. Attorney, the defence attorney, and Judge Rosen were conferring. Apparently, the defence attorney wasn't getting his point across, because the judge was shaking her head and the U.S. Attorney, still in profile, seemed smug, and the defendant was staring at his feet. Presently, a guard came, and the defendant became the prisoner again. *She's a bitch on bail.* Yes, indeed. If, in fact, Frank Bellarosa came before her, I could think of no reason in the world why she would set bail for him on a murder charge.

The longer I sat there, the more convinced I became that this whole thing had been stacked against me from the beginning. I was sure that my client was in Federal Court in Brooklyn right now. I could ask for a bail hearing, take an appeal, get a writ of habeas corpus, and try to get him sprung sometime in the near future. But that's not what I was getting paid for, nor what he wanted. I got up, took my briefcase, and left.

I went to the holding cells located in a far corner of the third floor and checked with the U.S. Marshal who was in charge of the cells. But my client had disappeared as surely as if he had been swallowed into the Gulag.

I went to the public phone booths and called both my offices, but there was no message from my client. So, I sat there, contemplating my next move. Just then, the deputy marshal that I'd spoken to regarding the arraignments came up to me. He said, 'Oh, I'm glad I found you, Counsellor. Your guy, Bellarosa, is going to be arraigned at Brooklyn Federal Court.'

I stood up. 'Are you sure?'

'That's what I hear from my boss. Too bad. I wanted to see him.'

'I'll get you his autograph,' I said as I raced toward the elevators. I rode down to the lobby, rushed out the doors, down the steps, and hailed a cab in Foley Square. I could be across the Brooklyn Bridge and in Federal Court in about twenty minutes. A taxi stopped and I opened the door, but as I was getting in, I happened to notice an NBC news van. Then it hit me. That group of people who had walked into the courtroom, and the three sketch artists in the jury box. 'Damn it!' I left the taxi door open and raced back toward the courthouse. 'That bastard! That bastard Ferragamo! What a conniving son of a bitch!' I took a deep breath and charged back up the steps – there were forty-six of them, and the five million dollars was getting heavier.

I passed through the metal detector again, smiled at Wyatt Earp, who gave me a surprised look as I walked in long strides toward the elevators. I watched Earp out of the corner of my eye until an elevator came. I got in and rode up to the third floor.

I went directly to Part One and pulled open the door to

Judge Rosen's courtroom in time to hear the court officer bellow, 'Bellarosa, Frank!'

A murmur went up from the crowd, as they say, and people actually began to stand, then a few people moved into the aisle to get a better view, and I found myself pushing to get through.

The courtroom deputy was shouting, 'Order in the court! Sit down! Sit down!'

Through the crowd, I caught a glimpse of Bellarosa as he was escorted in through the side door.

As I made my way to the front, the courtroom deputy called out, 'Is the attorney for Frank Bellarosa present?'

I reached the spectator rail and said, 'Here!'

Bellarosa turned to me but did not smile, though he nodded to show he appreciated my resourcefulness in figuring out what had happened that morning. I actually felt very proud of myself despite the fact that what I was doing was not serving humanity or Western civilization in the least.

I passed through the gate in the spectator rail and put the briefcase on the defence table. I glanced at Judge Rosen, who registered no surprise that I was there, and I deduced that she was not part of the set-up. But the Assistant U.S. Attorney seemed rather surprised, and she couldn't hide it. She looked around the courtroom as if she expected someone to come to her assistance.

Judge Rosen said to me, 'Counsellor, have you entered your appearance in court?'

'No, Your Honour. I just now arrived.'

She looked at me, and I could tell she had seen me earlier. She shrugged. 'Your name?'

'John Sutter.'

'Let the record show that the defendant is represented by counsel.' Judge Rosen then advised Frank Bellarosa of his right to remain silent and so forth. 'Do you understand?' she asked him in a tone of voice that suggested she was unimpressed by his notoriety.

'Yes, Your Honour,' replied Bellarosa in a pleasant voice.

She looked down at the charge sheet that had been handed to her and scanned it for a minute, then read the charge of murder to Bellarosa and asked him, 'Do you understand the charge against you?'

'Yes, Your Honour.'

'And have you seen a copy of the indictment?'

'No, Your Honour.'

Judge Rosen turned to me. 'Have you been given a copy of the indictment, Mr Sutter?'

'No, Your Honour.'

Judge Rosen looked at the Assistant U.S. Attorney and addressed her by name. 'Miss Larkin, why hasn't the accused or defence counsel seen a copy of the indictment?'

'I'm not sure why the accused hasn't, Judge. But defence counsel was not present during the processing of the accused this morning.'

Judge Rosen said, 'He's here now. Give him a copy of the indictment.'

'Yes, Your Honour.'

I went to the prosecution table, and Miss Larkin handed me a thick sheaf of papers. I made eye contact with her, and she said, 'Perhaps you'd like a few hours to read that. I have no objection to a second call on this arraignment.'

'I do.'

Judge Rosen said, 'Mr Sutter, will you waive your client's right to a public reading of the indictment?'

I didn't have to, of course, and I could have had the indictment read line by line for the next few hours. In the eighteenth century, when people had more time and indictments were handwritten and a lot shorter, part of the drama was the reading of the grand jury's findings. But the fastest way to piss off Judge Rosen was to exercise any right that took more than two minutes of the court's time. I said, therefore, 'Though we have not had an opportunity to read the indictment, we waive a public reading of it.'

She inquired of me, 'Have you seen the arrest warrant, Mr Sutter?'

'I have.'

'And you have heard the charge read by me in open court?'

'We have.'

She nodded and looked at Frank Bellarosa. 'How do you plead to the charge?'

'Not guilty!' he replied in a tone of voice that sounded almost aggrieved, as if a monumental injustice was being done.

Judge Rosen nodded, somewhat inattentively, I thought. Someday, someone would shout out to her, 'Guilty as charged!' But she wouldn't hear it, nor would it register. She then said to Bellarosa, 'You also have the right to be released on a reasonable bail.'

That was true, but it wasn't likely.

Judge Rosen looked at me and said, 'However, in a case of murder, Mr Sutter, I do not grant bail. Furthermore, under federal law in a case involving narcotics, which in a manner of speaking this case does, there is a presumption against the defendant. But I assume you want to say something to me which would overcome that presumption.'

'Yes, Your Honour. May I confer with my client for a moment?'

'If you wish.'

I leaned toward Bellarosa and said, 'We were delayed.' I explained briefly.

He nodded and said, 'They don't play fair. See?' He added, 'Hey, I heard of this judge. She's a tough bitch. They made sure she was doing arraignments this morning. Understand?'

I regarded Judge Rosen a moment. She was a woman of about forty-five, young for a federal judge, and somewhat attractive, if you're into stern-looking women. I didn't think my boyish-charm routine would do me any good, unless she happened to get off on scolding boyish men. You have to play every angle. Judge Rosen looked at the Assistant U.S. Attorney and asked her, 'Miss Larkin? Do you wish to say something?'

Miss Larkin replied, 'Your Honour, in view of the presumption under the statute, the government requests that Frank Bellarosa be detained. However, if the court is inclined to hear arguments for bail, the government is entitled to and requests a three-day continuance for a bail hearing.'

'Why?'

'So that the government can gather evidence for the court to show why the accused should be detained.'

Judge Rosen said to me, 'Is that all right with you, Mr Sutter?'

'No, Your Honour. It isn't.'

'Why not, Mr Sutter?'

'I don't see any reason for my client to sit in jail for three days. The government has been investigating this case since January. They know everything they're going to know about my client already, and it's not likely they are going to learn anything new in the next seventy-two hours.'

Judge Rosen nodded and said to Miss Larkin, 'Request denied.'

Miss Larkin did not look happy. She said to Judge Rosen, 'Well, then, Your Honour, the U.S. Attorney would most probably wish to be present for any discussion of bail.'

'Why?'

Miss Larkin replied, 'Because of the . . . the seriousness of the charge and the notoriety of the accused.'

Judge Rosen looked at me. 'Mr Sutter? Would you like some time to confer with your client? We can schedule a bail hearing for this afternoon.'

I replied, 'No, Your Honour. We have entered a plea of not guilty, and we request bail in the amount of one hundred thousand dollars, which we are prepared to post right now.'

Judge Rosen's eyebrows rose at that statement. She turned her attention back to Miss Larkin and said, 'If Mr Ferragamo wished to be here for this arraignment, he should be here now. The attorney for the accused has indicated that he wants to discuss bail at this time.' Judge Rosen added, 'I assume you have read the indictment and are familiar with this case, Miss

440

Larkin. I'm sure you can present the government's arguments for detention.'

The subtext here was that it wasn't necessary to bother the U.S. Attorney since no bail was going to be granted anyway, and let's get on with it. But Miss Larkin, at a young age, had developed a nose for trouble, and she knew her limitations, which marked her as a potentially great attorney. She replied, 'Your Honour, will you instruct the deputy to call Mr Ferragamo's office and pass on my request for his presence? In the meantime, we can proceed.'

Judge Rosen motioned to her courtroom deputy, who disappeared into the judge's robing room to make the call. I wondered how fast Ferragamo could run in wing tips.

I looked into the courtroom and saw that the word had gotten out and the room was packed. In the jury box were the three sketch artists, scratching away at their pads now. I brushed my hair with my fingers.

Judge Rosen said to me, 'Mr Sutter, go ahead and present your argument for bail.'

'Yes, Your Honour.' You could literally hear ballpoint pens clicking in the courtroom behind me. Courtrooms don't terrify me the way they do some lawyers. But in this case, I had some real anxieties, and the cause of those anxieties was not the audience or Miss Larkin or the judge, but my client, who wanted to be on his way in ten minutes.

I spoke in a normal conversational tone, but I sensed that I could be heard clear to the back of the silent court. I said, 'Your Honour, first I want to bring to your attention the fact that my client had previous knowledge, through the newspapers, that the U.S. Attorney was presenting evidence of murder to a grand jury. He made no attempt to flee during that time. And furthermore, anticipating that an indictment might be handed down and an arrest warrant issued, he instructed me to remain available in that event. He, too, remained available for arrest, and in fact, when the arrest came at approximately eight A.M. this morning, I was with him and can attest to the fact that he made no attempt to flee or resist.' I added, 'If the arresting officer, Mr Mancuso, is here, he, too, can attest to that.'

Judge Rosen looked toward the side door, then out into the court. 'Is Mr Mancuso present?'

A voice called out from the side of the court. 'Here, Your Honour.'

As Mr Mancuso made his way through the standing-room-only crowd, I said to Bellarosa, 'They tried to send me to Brooklyn. Your buddy Alphonse is a snake.'

He smiled. 'Yeah, we shoulda known they'd pull some stunt. I never got to FBI headquarters neither. Mancuso gets this call on the radio, and next thing I know, we're pulling up to the back of the courthouse. You see what I mean? Fucking Alphonse.'

Mancuso came through the rail and stood a few feet from us. Bellarosa said to me, loud enough for him to hear, 'They wanted to get you over to FBI headquarters where they were going to jerk you around until this was over in court. But I dragged my ass through the booking. Fucked up six sets of prints.' He laughed and poked me in the ribs. 'I knew you'd figure it out. You're a smart guy. Hey, we leaving here together?'

'Maybe.'

Judge Rosen said, 'Mr Sutter? Do you need a moment?'

I turned back to the bench. 'No, Your Honour.'

She said to Mr Mancuso, 'Please relate the circumstances of the defendant's arrest.'

Mr Mancuso did so, very precisely, professionally, and unemotionally, leaving out only the conversation that he and I had had regarding my midlife crisis.

Judge Rosen said to him, 'What you're saying, Mr Mancuso, is that Mr Bellarosa appeared to be expecting you, and he made no attempt to flee or resist arrest.'

'That is correct.'

'Thank you, Mr Mancuso. Please remain in the court.'

'Yes, Your Honour.' Mancuso turned and looked at me,

then at Bellarosa, but I could read nothing in his face but weariness.

He took a seat at the prosecution table.

Judge Rosen said to me, 'It appears that the accused made no attempt to resist or flee. However, I am not going to grant bail based solely on that fact. Unless you can convince me otherwise, Mr Sutter, and do so very quickly, I am going to order that the accused be taken to the Metropolitan Correction Center right now to await trial.'

We did not want that, did we? So I looked at Judge Rosen and said, 'Your Honour, I also want to bring to your attention the fact that my client has never been convicted of a violent crime in any jurisdiction. He has, in fact, no history of violence.' Someone in the courtroom laughed. 'Further, Your Honour, my client is a legitimate businessman whose' – I could actually hear some tittering behind me. People are so cynical these days – 'whose absence from his companies would impose an undue hardship on him, would interfere with his livelihood, and with the livelihoods of people who depend on my client for employment –'

The laughing was becoming a little more overt now, and Judge Rosen, too, smiled, but then caught herself and banged her gavel. 'Order!'

Miss Larkin, I noticed, was smiling also, and so was the court reporter, the two marshals, and the courtroom deputy. Only Frank and John were not smiling.

Judge Rosen motioned me to approach the bench, and I did. She leaned over and our faces were only inches apart. We could have kissed. She whispered to me. 'Mr Sutter, at your request, I let you say your piece, but this is really very silly, and you're wasting my time and making a fool of yourself. Now, I understand the pressure you must be under to keep your client out of jail, but you can forget it. He can go to jail and await a more formal bail hearing where you may present more substantial evidence than your own characterization of him as a gentle man and a good citizen. I have a lot of arraignments before me today, Mr Sutter, and I'd like to

443

get moving on them.' She added, 'A few days or weeks in jail won't kill him.'

I looked her in the eye. 'But it will. Your Honour, at least let me say what I have to say. Can we retire to your chambers?'

'No. Your client is not any different from anyone else who will come before me today.'

'But he *is* different, Judge. You know that and so do I. This courtroom is packed with newspeople, and they're not here to report on the general state of the criminal justice system. They have, in fact, been tipped off by the U.S. Attorney's office to be here at your court to see Frank Bellarosa led away in cuffs.' I added, 'The press knew before even you or I knew that Frank Bellarosa would be in this courtroom.'

Judge Rosen nodded. 'That may be true, Mr Sutter. But it doesn't change the charge or the general policy of refusing bail in cases of homicide.'

Still *tête-à-tête*, I whispered, 'Your Honour, my client may or may not be involved in so-called organized crime. But if he is who the press alleges he is, you must be aware that no major figure such as Mr Bellarosa has fled U.S. jurisdiction for many decades.'

'So what?' She looked at me a moment, then said, 'Mr Sutter, I sense that you are not a criminal lawyer and that you are not familiar with Federal Court. Correct?'

I nodded.

'Well, Mr Sutter, this is another world, different, I'm sure, from the one you come from.'

You can say that again, lady. But good Lord, do I really look and sound like some sort of Wall Street Wasp, or worse yet, a la-di-da society lawyer from Long Island? I said to Judge Rosen, 'I'm here to see that justice is done. I may not know how things are usually done here, but I know that my client has a right under Constitutional law to have a fair bail hearing.'

'He does. Next week.'

'No, Judge. Now.'

444

Her eyebrows rose, and she was about to throw me out and put Bellarosa in the slammer, but as luck would have it, Miss Larkin interrupted. Obviously Miss Larkin didn't like all this talk that she couldn't hear, so she said, 'Your Honour, may I speak?'

Judge Rosen looked at her. 'All right.'

Miss Larkin came closer to the bench but spoke in a normal volume. 'Judge, whether or not the accused came into custody peacefully is not relevant in determining bail when the charge is murder. Nor is this the time or place to consider other circumstances that defence counsel might wish to put before the court. The government has reason to believe that the accused committed murder, and is a danger to the community, and has the resources and ample reason to flee the country if released on bail.'

Judge Rosen, who had had enough of me a minute before, now felt obligated, I think, to give the defence the last word before she kicked me out. She looked at me. 'Mr Sutter?'

I glanced at Miss Larkin, who still reminded me of Carolyn. I had an urge to scold her but said instead to her, 'Miss Larkin, the suggestion that my client is a danger to the community is ludicrous.' I turned to Judge Rosen and continued, loud enough now for everyone to hear, 'Your Honour, this is a middle-aged man who has a home, a wife, three children, and no history of violence.' I couldn't help but glance back at Mr Mancuso, who made a funny face, sort of a wince as if I'd stepped on his foot. I continued, 'Judge, I have here in this briefcase the names and addresses of all the companies that my client is associated with.' Well, maybe not *all*, but most. 'I have here, also, my client's passport, which I am prepared to surrender to the court. I have here also –'

Just then, the side door swung open, and in strode Alphonse Ferragamo, looking none too happy. Ferragamo was a tall, slender man with a hooked nose set between eyes that looked like tired oysters. He had thin, sandy hair and pale, thin lips that needed blood or lip rouge.

His presence caused a stir in the court because nearly

everyone recognized him; such was his ability to keep his face before the public. Ferragamo had been called an Italian Tom Dewey, and it was no secret that he had his eye on either the governor's mansion or, *à la* Tom Dewey, the bigger house in Washington. His major problem in running for elective office, I thought, was that he had a face that no one liked. But I guess no one wanted to tell him that.

Judge Rosen, of course, knew him and nodded to him but said to me, 'Continue.'

So I continued. 'I have here, too, the ability to post a substantial bail, enough to – '

'Your Honour,' interrupted Alphonse Ferragamo, ignoring all court etiquette. 'Your Honour, I can't *believe* that the court would even *entertain* a discussion of bail in a case of wilful and wanton *murder*, in a case of execution-style *murder*, a case of drug-related, underworld assassination.'

The jerk went on, describing the murder of Juan Carranza with more adjectives and adverbs than I thought anyone could muster for a single act. Also, he was into word stressing, which I find annoying in court, almost whiny.

Judge Rosen did not look real pleased with Alphonse Ferragamo charging into her court like – pardon the expression – gangbusters, and running off at the mouth. In fact, she said to Alphonse, 'Mr Ferragamo, a man's liberty is at stake, and defence counsel has indicated that he wishes to present certain facts to the court which may influence the question of bail. Mr Sutter was speaking as you entered.'

But Alphonse did not take the hint and put his mouth into gear again. Clearly, the man was agitated, and for whatever reason – justice or personal vendetta – Alphonse Ferragamo desperately wanted Frank Bellarosa in prison. Meanwhile, Miss Larkin, who in her own way had handled this open-and-shut case better by keeping her mouth mostly shut, sort of slipped off and sat beside Mr Mancuso at the prosecutor's table.

'Your Honour,' Ferragamo continued, 'the accused is a notorious *gangster*, a man who the Justice Department

446

believes is the head of the nation's largest organized *crime* family, a man who we believe, through investigation and through the testimony of witnesses, has committed a drug-related *murder*.' In a monumental Freudian slip, Ferragamo added, 'This is *not* a personal vendetta, this is *fact*,' leaving everyone wondering about personal vendettas.

Obviously, this guy hadn't been in a courtroom for some time. I mean, I don't do much court work either, but even I could do better than this clown. I listened as Mr Ferragamo did everything in his power to snatch defeat from the jaws of victory. I was tempted to interrupt a few times, but as that old Machiavellian Napoleon Bonaparte once said, 'Never interrupt an enemy while he's making a mistake.'

I glanced at Judge Rosen and saw that she was clearly and openly annoyed. But even a judge has to think twice before she tells a U.S. Attorney to shut up, and the more Ferragamo talked, the more time I felt I would be given to present my arguments.

The interesting thing about what Ferragamo was saying now was that it didn't relate directly to the question of bail. Instead, Ferragamo was going on about Bellarosa's alleged problems in the drug trade, especially in regard to Colombians and rival Mafia gangs. The man sounded as if he were holding a press conference. Actually, he was. Ferragamo informed everyone, 'The heroin trade, which has been traditionally controlled by the *Cosa Nostra*, the *Mafia*, is now only a small part of the lucrative trade in illegal drugs. The Bellarosa *crime family* is seeking to muscle in on the cocaine and crack trade, and to do so, they must *eliminate* their rivals. Thus, the *murder* of Juan Carranza.'

Good Lord, Alphonse, why don't you just paint a target on Bellarosa's forehead and turn him loose in a Colombian neighbourhood? I glanced at Frank and saw he was smiling enigmatically.

Judge Rosen coughed, then said, 'Mr Ferragamo, I think we understand that you believe the defendant has committed murder. That's why he's here. But pre-trial incarceration is not

447

a punishment, it is a precaution, and Mr Bellarosa is innocent until proven guilty. I want you to tell me why you believe he will forfeit his bail and flee.'

Mr Ferragamo thought about that a moment. Meanwhile, Frank Bellarosa just stood there, the object of all this attention but with no speaking part. I'll give him credit for his demeanour though. He wasn't sneering at Ferragamo, he wasn't cocky or arrogant, nor did he seem deferential or crestfallen. He just stood there as if he had a Sony Walkman stuck in his ear, listening to *La Traviata* while waiting for a bus.

Rather than answer Judge Rosen's direct question, Alphonse Ferragamo had some advice for her, and she clearly did not like his tone, but she understood the words. What he was saying in effect was this: 'Listen, lady, if you let this guy go free on bail, public opinion (the press) will crucify you. If he flees the country, you might as well go with him.' And the final point, though not in these exact words, was this: 'Judge, you have no reason whatsoever to stick your neck out. Just bang the goddamned gavel and have the prisoner taken to jail.'

Judge Rosen did not seem happy with the lecture, but she did seem to grasp the import of it. Still, to irk Ferragamo, I think, she turned to me. 'Mr Sutter?'

I began my counterattack, and that son of a bitch kept interrupting. I was scoring points, but clearly the home team started with lots of points. Bail proceedings, you understand, are not stacked in favour of the defendant as a trial by jury is, and it was all I could do just to keep Judge Rosen from banging the gavel and ending the whole thing. I mean, what was in it for her to listen to me tell her to make an insane decision that would jeopardize her career and lead to speculation that she was on the mob's payroll or was sleeping with Italian gangsters? There was nothing in it for her except that she was ticked off at Ferragamo's grandstanding, and in some deeper sense, she was not now fully convinced that Bellarosa was a bail risk. In short, she was interested in justice.

I went on with my description of Bellarosa as if I were introducing him for a Knights of Columbus award. 'He has deep roots in his former Brooklyn neighbourhood, having lived within a mile of his birthplace all his life. Recently, he has become my neighbour, and I know this man personally.' This brought a few murmurs from the crowd, but having started on this tack, to use a nautical term, I had to sail with it. 'My wife and his wife are friends. We have entertained at one another's house' – sort of – 'and I've met some of his family –' *Oh, shit. Wrong word.* Everyone laughed again, and the gavel crashed down again. 'Order!'

I recovered nicely and went on, 'Your Honour, I will personally guarantee that my client will not leave the Southern District of New York and that he will appear in court to face this charge on the date assigned to this case. I repeat, Your Honour, my client, despite all innuendos and allegations and public smears to the contrary, is a substantial, taxpaying citizen, a man with friends and fami – and relatives all over the metropolitan area, a man who counts among his friends many prominent businessmen, clergy, politicians –' More chuckles from the peanut gallery, though I could see I had made a few more points, but was anyone keeping score? I said, 'And further, Your Honour –'

Ferragamo couldn't stand not hearing himself talk for this long, so he cut me off again. 'Judge, this is *ridiculous*. This man is a known *gangster* –'

It was Judge Rosen's turn to interrupt. 'The charge before the court is murder, Mr Ferragamo, not racketeering. If the charge were racketeering and he had these roots in the community, I would have already set bail. I'm not interested in allegations of racketeering. I'm interested in the question of whether or not this man will flee a drug-related murder charge.'

Ferragamo was annoyed. He looked at Bellarosa, and their eyes met for the first time. Then he looked at me, as if to say, 'Who the hell are you to get in the middle of this thing between Ferragamo and Bellarosa?' Ferragamo said to the judge, 'Then let's concentrate on that aspect; this is a man who has vast *resources,* not only in *this* country, but in *foreign* countries, and it is not inconceivable that – '

'Your Honour,' I interrupted, since this seemed the way to get the floor with Mr Ferragamo, 'Your Honour, I stated earlier that I have here my client's passport – '

Ferragamo interrupted by yelling at me directly, 'Your client, Mr Sutter, can buy *fifty* passports!'

I found myself, for the first time in my life, shouting in court. 'Mr Ferragamo, I gave the court my word! I am personally guaranteeing that – '

'Who are *you* to personally guarantee – ?'

'Who are *you* to doubt – ?'

And so it went, degenerating very quickly into courtroom histrionics. Everyone loved it. Except Judge Rosen, who banged her gavel. 'Enough!' She looked at me. 'Mr Sutter, the court appreciates your personal guarantee and is impressed with your foresight in dragging a suitcase full of money into court' – laughter – 'and acknowledges your offer to turn over the defendant's passport. However, your request for bail is deni – '

'Your Honour! One more thing, if I may.'

She rolled her eyes, then motioned wearily for me to go on.

'Your Honour . . . Your Honour . . .'

'Yes, Mr Sutter? Speak. Please.'

I took a deep breath, caught Bellarosa's eye, and spoke. 'Your Honour, regarding the charge itself . . . the charge as read . . . the charge states that the alleged murder of this Juan Carranza individual took place on January fourteenth of this year in New Jersey. Well, Your Honour, my client has an alibi for that day, and I didn't think it appropriate or advisable to introduce that alibi at this time, but it's obvious that I must address myself to that alibi. So, if I may approach the bench. . . .'

There was a silence in the courtroom, broken by Ferragamo's voice. 'What *kind* of alibi, Mr Sutter? I want to hear what alibi *you* have.' He looked at the judge. 'Your Honour,

I have *five* witnesses who have testified under *oath* in front of a *grand jury*, who have implicated Frank Bellarosa in the *murder* of Juan Carranza. The grand jury voted to indict the defendant based on this testimony. What *possible* alibi could the defence counsel present here . . .?' He threw up his hands in a dramatic gesture. 'Oh, this is inane. Really, Mr Sutter. *Really*. You have wasted my time and everyone's time.'

He really looked pissed off. *Really*. But I was more pissed off. In fact, the more this jerk spoke, the more I realized he was a ruthless, egocentric media hound. I said to him, loud enough for everyone to hear, 'Mr Ferragamo, I have the licence plate numbers of four cars that attempted to delay my appearance here in court. I believe that when I run those numbers through the DMV, I will find those cars are registered to the U.S. Attorney's office. I believe that you engaged in an unlawful act to keep – '

'How dare you? How *dare* you?'

'How dare *you*?' I shot back, doing a little word stressing of my own. 'How dare *you* obstruct – '

'Are you insane?'

I mean, I was really hot now. Needless to say, it's not a good idea to make an enemy of a man like this, but what the hell, I had enemies in high places now: the IRS, the FBI, The Creek, the Stanhope dynasty and their attorneys, and so forth. What was one more? I said, 'I'm not the one displaying aberrant behaviour in open court.'

'*What*?'

The crowd loved it. I mean, *really* loved it. There they sat, only ten minutes before, bored out of their minds with pro forma early-morning arraignments, and suddenly, in walks Frank Bellarosa, then his button-down attorney, who turns out to be a little bit nuts, and the ambitious Alphonse Ferragamo, who has completely lost control of himself. I glanced into the courtroom and saw reporters scribbling furiously, artists looking up and down between their pads and the bench as though they were following a vertical Ping-Pong game, and the rest of the crowd, smiling attentively, like people who had been sitting through a dull opera only to discover there was a nude scene in the second act.

Bellarosa and I made eye contact again, and he smiled at me.

Meanwhile, Alphonse and I were getting in good jabs at each other, not really addressing any issue except the issue of egos. Judge Rosen let us spar for about a minute, not wanting to be thought of as a killjoy, but finally she rapped her gavel. 'That's enough, gentlemen.' And she used the term loosely. 'Mr Sutter,' she said, 'that is a serious accusation, but even if it were true, it has no bearing on this discussion. And regarding any alibi you say your client has for the day of the alleged crime, Mr Sutter, such alibi evidence may be considered by the court in determining whether to set bail or not. However, I don't see how I can give your argument any credence unless you happen to have witnesses in this court. And even if you did, Mr Sutter, I am not prepared to delay this morning's arraignments by swearing in witnesses at this time.' She added, 'I'm sorry, Mr Sutter, but the question of bail must be decided at a future session – ' The gavel went up again.

'Judge,' I said quickly, 'Judge, on the day in question, January fourteenth of this year – '

'Mr Sutter – '

'My client, Your Honour, was, in fact, inspecting property adjacent to my property on Long Island. And though he was unknown to me personally at that time, I recognized him from newspapers and television, and I realized that I had, in fact, seen Mr Frank Bellarosa.'

Judge Rosen leaned toward me and waited for the gasps and all that to subside. 'Mr Sutter, are you telling me that *you* are Mr Bellarosa's alibi?'

'Yes, Your Honour.'

'You saw him on January fourteenth?'

'Yes, Your Honour. I was home that day. I checked my daybook.' Actually I hadn't, but I should have before I committed perjury. I continued, 'I was riding my horse and

452

saw Mr Bellarosa with two other gentlemen walking around the property that he subsequently purchased. I saw them and they waved to me and I returned the wave, though we did not speak. I was not more than thirty feet from Frank Bellarosa and recognized him immediately. This was at nine A.M., then I saw them get into a black Cadillac at about noon and leave. Mr Carranza was murdered at about noon as his car left an exit of the Garden State Parkway in New Jersey, about eighty miles from where I saw Mr Bellarosa at the same time.'

What could Alphonse Ferragamo say? Only one word and he said it. 'Liar.'

I gave him my best withering Wasp look, and he actually turned his oyster eyes away.

Judge Rosen sat quietly for a full minute, probably wondering why she had wanted so badly to be a judge. Finally, she asked me, 'How much money do you actually have there, Counsellor?'

'Five million, Judge. Four in assignable assets, one million in cash.'

'Good. I'll take it. See the clerk downstairs.' She banged her gavel as Ferragamo bellowed. Judge Rosen ignored him and said, 'Next case!'

On the way to see the district clerk down in the basement, Bellarosa said to me, 'See, I knew you could do it.'

My stomach was churning, my head ached, and yes, my heart ached. Never in a billion years would I have imagined that I would perjure myself in court for *any* reason, let alone to spring a Mafia don.

But neither did I ever think I would be charged with criminal tax fraud for a stupid misjudgement. Nor would I have imagined that a U.S. Attorney would frame a man because of a personal grudge, or try to obstruct justice by delaying me on my way to court, then trying to send me on a wild-goose chase to Brooklyn. Yes, I know that two wrongs don't make a right – that's one of the first ethical lessons I learned as a small boy – but part of life and part of growing up is the ability to do what has to be done to survive. When the stakes go from baseball cards and pennies to life and death, then sometimes you make adjustments. Concessions, I guess you'd say. Sometimes you lie.

The history of the world is filled with dead martyrs who would not compromise. I used to admire them. Now I think that most of them were probably very foolish.

Bellarosa said to me, 'See what a prick that guy is?'

I didn't reply.

He went on, 'You pissed him off. I didn't want you to do that. It's personal for him, but it's not personal for me. *Capisce?*'

'Frank. Shut up.'

*

I was still sort of in a daze as I moved through the corridors of the courthouse, reporters with pads and pencils swarming around us. They can't bring cameras or tape recorders into the courthouse, but why they let these crazy people inside at all is beyond me. Freedom of the press is one thing, but blocking the hallway is inconvenient and probably a misdemeanour.

Finally, out on the courthouse steps, minus my heavy briefcase and my virginity, we ran into the press again, who had fallen back to regroup and join up with their cameramen and photographers.

Reporters were asking all sorts of pertinent and dangerous questions, but all they were getting from the don in return were wisecracks, such as: 'Hey, what're you all doing here? No autographs. You want me to smile? Get my good side.' And so forth.

Also, he knew some of the reporters by name. 'Hey, Lorraine, long time. Where'd you get that tan?' Lorraine smiled at the charming man.

'Tim, you still working for the paper? They don't know about your drinking?' Ha, ha, ha.

A TV reporter got his microphone under Bellarosa's nose and asked, 'Is there a power struggle going on between the Mafia and the Medellin cartel over the control of the cocaine trade?'

'The who and the what over the which? Talk English.'

A more sensible reporter asked, 'Do you think Alphonse Ferragamo is pursuing a personal vendetta against you?'

Frank lit up a big cigar, Monte Cristo number four. 'Nah. People lie to him about me, and he's got to follow up. He's my good goombah.'

Everyone laughed.

'You happy to be free this morning, Frank?'

He puffed on his stogie. 'I gotta tell ya, I had the worst breakfast of my life in there. That's what I call cruel and unusual punishment.'

That got a good laugh, and as it became obvious that Mr Bellarosa was not going to make any newsworthy statements, the emphasis shifted to the entertainment value of the story. Frank was good entertainment. Someone asked him, 'How much did that suit cost you, Frank?'

'Peanuts. I go to a little guy on Mott Street. I don't pay uptown prices. You could use a good tailor yourself, Ralph.'

So the don held court for a few minutes as we made our way down the forty-six steps toward the street, surrounded by about fifty members of the press, including cameramen and photographers. Worse, a crowd of several hundred onlookers had materialized. It doesn't take much to draw a crowd in New York.

I was not being completely ignored, of course, and reporters who couldn't get the don's attention were settling for me, but I was just reciting my mantra, which was, 'No comment, no comment, no comment.'

We were near the bottom of the steps, but the crowd around us was so thick now, I couldn't see any way to get to the street where Lenny was supposed to meet us with the car.

A reporter asked me, 'How much does five million dollars weigh?'

It seemed silly to say 'No comment' to a silly question, so

I replied, 'It was heavy enough for me to think that it was excessive bail.'

Well, you should never encourage these people, and by answering one question I opened myself up for a lot of attention. I was really getting grilled now, and I glanced at Bellarosa, who gave me a look of caution through his cigar smoke.

'Mr Sutter,' asked a newspaper reporter, 'you said in court that you were delayed by four cars on your way here. How did they delay you?'

'No comment.'

'Did they cut you off?'

'No comment.'

'Do you really think those cars were driven by people from Alphonse Ferragamo's office?'

'No comment.'

And so it went. I seemed to have a permanent microphone under my nose now, recording my 'no comment' for posterity. I spotted the Cadillac parked illegally in the square about fifty yards away, with Lenny behind the wheel. Then I noticed Vinnie approaching the courthouse with two patrolmen in tow.

Meanwhile, the press were really getting on my nerves. I glanced again at my client and saw that he was still smiling, still puffing away, and still at ease despite being surrounded by aggressive A-type personalities. But though he was at ease, Bellarosa did not have the reputation of being a publicity hound. He could handle it, but he did not seek it out as did some of his predecessors, certain of whom were – partly as a result of their fondness for talking too much to the press – dead.

A particularly persistent and pesky female reporter, whom I recognized from one of the TV networks, was bugging me about the alibi. She asked me, 'Are you *certain* it was Frank Bellarosa you saw?'

'No comment.'

'You mean you're not *sure* it was Frank Bellarosa.'

456

'No comment.'

'But you *said* it was Frank Bellarosa.'

And on and on she went, as if we were married or something. 'Mr Sutter,' she said very snottily, 'Mr Ferragamo has five witnesses who put Frank Bellarosa at the scene of the murder. Are you saying they're all liars? Or are *you* the liar?'

It must have been the heat, and I guess my own state of mind, or maybe that woman's tone of voice finally got to me. Anyway, I snapped back, 'Ferragamo's witnesses are liars, and he *knows* they are liars. This whole thing is a frame-up, a personal vendetta against my client, and an attempt to start trouble between –' I got my mouth under control, then glanced at Bellarosa, who touched his index finger to his lips.

'Trouble between who? Rival mobs?'

Someone else, a Mafia groupie or something, asked, 'Trouble with his own mob? Trouble with his underboss? With Sally Da-da?'

Mafia politics were not my strong point, but obviously the initiated knew all sorts of underworld gossip and they thought I did, too.

'Trouble with who?' asked someone else. 'With the Colombian drug kings? With Juan Carranza's friends?'

'Is it true that the Mafia is trying to push out the Colombians?'

'Mr Sutter, did you say in court that Alphonse Ferragamo ordered people to run you off the road?'

I thought someone already asked that question.

'Mr Sutter, are you saying that the U.S. Attorney is framing your client?'

Mr Sutter, blah, blah, blah. I had this image of the television set over the bar at The Creek. I wonder if people really do look heavier on TV. I hope not. I could hear my pals now. 'Look at him.' 'He's getting fat.' 'He's sweating like a pig.' 'His tie is crooked.' 'How much is he getting paid for that?' 'His father must be rolling over in his grave.' My father is actually alive and well in Europe.

Finally, the two cops, with Vinnie encouraging them on, got through to us. Frank bid the press fond adieu, waved, smiled, and followed Vinnie and the two cops through the throng with me bringing up the rear. We got out to the street, and Lenny inched the car closer through the onlookers. I was annoyed that the government could set the stage for a media circus, then not provide crowd control. Actually, I never realized how many annoying things the government did.

Vinnie got to the Cadillac and opened the rear door. Bellarosa ducked inside, and one of the cops said, 'Take it easy, Frank.'

Bellarosa said to the two cops, 'Thanks, boys. I owe you one.'

Meanwhile, I can't even get a cop to interpret complex and contradictory parking signs for me. But that was yesterday. Today, the cop near the open car door touched his cap as I slid in beside the don. What a screwy country.

Vinnie had jumped into the passenger's seat up front, and Lenny pulled away, moving slowly until he was clear of the crowd, then he gassed it.

We headed downtown, then Lenny swung west toward the World Trade Center, then downtown again to Wall Street. Obviously, he was trying to lose anyone who might be following.

We passed my office building, the J. P. Morgan Building at 23 Wall Street, and though I was still supposed to work there, I felt a sudden nostalgia for the old place.

We drove around for a while, no one saying much, except that Vinnie and Lenny were congratulating the don *ad nauseam* about his great escape, as though he had something to do with it. I really detest flunkies.

Bellarosa said very little in return, but at one point he leaned over to me. 'You did real good, Counsellor. Right up until the end there.'

I didn't reply.

He continued, 'You got to be careful what you say to the press. They twist things around.'

I nodded.

He went on, 'The press ain't lookin' for facts. They think they are, but they want a good story. Sometimes a good story has no facts. Sometimes it's funny. They think this stuff is all funny. This stuff with the Mafia and all. The big Cadillacs, the cigars, the fancy suits. Somehow they think this is all funny. *Capisce?* That's okay. That's better than them thinking it's not funny. So you keep it funny. You give them funny stuff. You're a funny guy. So lighten up. Make it all sound funny, like it's a big joke. Understand?'

'*Capisco.*'

'Yeah. You did fine with that lady judge. Alphonse fucked himself up. He talks too much. Every time he opens his mouth, somebody wants to put their fist in it. He's pissed off now, but he's gonna be a lot more pissed off when the press starts asking him about the car bullshit this morning and the frame-up thing. You didn't have to say all that shit. You know?'

'Frank, if you don't like the way – '

He patted my knee. 'Hey, you did okay. Just a few points I gotta make so you know. Okay? Hey, I walked. Right?'

'Right.'

We kept driving around lower Manhattan. Frank ordered Lenny to pull over at a newsstand, and Vinnie got out and bought the *Post* for Frank, the *Wall Street Journal* for me, and some medical journals for himself, mostly gynaecology and proctology. Lenny shared the journals with Vinnie at stoplights. I like to see people try to improve their minds.

I had some paperwork with me relating to the bail: the receipt for five million dollars, the bail forfeiture warning, and other printed matter that I looked over. I also had the arrest warrant now, and the charge sheet, which I now read. Most important, I had a copy of the indictment, which ran to about eighty pages. I wanted to read it at my leisure, but for now, I perused it, discovering that, indeed, all the evidence against Frank Bellarosa was in the form of five witness statements. There was no physical evidence putting him at the scene of the crime, and all the witnesses had Hispanic names.

I had never asked Bellarosa about the actual murder, and I only vaguely remembered the press accounts of it. But from what I could glean from the witness statements, Juan Carranza, driving his own car, a Corvette, left the Garden State Parkway at about noon on January fourteenth, at the Red Bank exit. With him was his girlfriend, Ramona Velarde. A car in front of the Corvette came to a stop on the single-lane exit ramp, and Carranza was forced to stop also. Two men then exited the car behind Carranza, walked right up to his car, and one of them fired a single bullet through his side window, striking Carranza in the face. The assassin then tried the driver's door, and finding it unlocked, he opened it and fired the remaining four bullets from the revolver into Carranza's head. The girlfriend was untouched. The assassin then threw the revolver on the girlfriend's lap, and he and his companion got into the front car that had blocked the exit ramp, abandoning their car behind Carranza's.

The witnesses to this assassination were Ramona Velarde and four men who were in a car behind the car from which the assassins exited. Each of the four male witnesses stated frankly that they were Juan Carranza's bodyguards. I noted that none of them said they fired at the men who had bumped off their boss. In fact, they stated that they put Ramona Velarde in their car and jumped the kerb onto the grass, driving around the assassins' abandoned car and the Corvette, but they made no attempt to pursue the assassins. The subtext here was that they recognized that their boss had been hit by the Italian mob, and they didn't want to be dead heroes. The New Jersey State Police determined that this rubout had federal drug and racketeering implications and contacted the FBI. Through an anonymous tip, Ramona Velarde was picked up, and she subsequently identified the four bodyguards, who were all picked up or surrendered within a few weeks. All of them agreed to become federal witnesses.

The issue of identification seemed to me a little vague. Ramona Velarde was only a few feet from the assassin, but I don't see how she could have seen his face if he was standing beside a low-slung Corvette. All she could have seen was the hand and the gun. Similarly, the assassin and his partner would have exited their car with their backs to the four bodyguards, who had let that car come between them and their boss. However, all four men stated that the assassin and his partner glanced back at them a few times as the two men stepped up to Carranza's Corvette. All four of the men said they recognized the face of Frank Bellarosa. Ramona Velarde picked Bellarosa's photo out of mug shots.

Well, as I read this interesting account of gangland murder, it did certainly sound like a mob hit, Italian style. I mean, it was classical Mafia: the boxed-in automobile, the girlfriend left untouched, even the bodyguards left alone so that the hit didn't become a massacre, which would draw all sorts of unwanted negative press. And the abandoned car was stolen, of course, and also Italian style, the murder weapon was left behind and was clean as a whistle. The amateurs liked to use the same gun over and over again until somebody got caught with it, and ballistics showed it had about a dozen murders on it. The Italians bought clean guns, used them once, and dumped them immediately at the scene before strolling off.

I thought about this testimony I was reading in Bellarosa's Cadillac. It was quite possible that the murder had taken place exactly this way, and the witnesses were telling the truth, except for the identification of Frank Bellarosa. I'm no detective, but it doesn't take many brains to realize that a man such as Bellarosa, even if he wanted to commit a murder personally, wouldn't do it in broad daylight where half the population of the New York metropolitan area could identify his face.

But apparently someone in the FBI office or the U.S. Attorney's office saw this murder as an opportunity to cause problems in the underworld. Therefore why not assign it to the number-one Mafia boss? And I thought, if Bellarosa was right that the murder was done by the Drug Enforcement Agency, then the DEA would most probably choose a modus operandi of the underworld, e.g. an Uzi sub-machine-gun attack to imitate Colombians, a knife or machete attack to imitate the Jamaicans, a bomb assassination as the Koreans had used a few times, or the cleanest, safest, and most easily imitated attack – a Mafia rubout.

I realized that what I was doing was formulating a defence in my mind, but beyond that I was trying to convince myself that I was defending an innocent man. Trying to be objective, trying to be that universal juror, I evaluated what I knew of the case so far and found that there was a reasonable doubt as to Frank Bellarosa's guilt.

I glanced at Bellarosa as I flipped through the indictment. He noticed and said to me, 'They named the guys who testified against me. Right?'

'Yes. Four men and one woman.'

'Oh, yeah. Carranza's girlfriend. I remember that from the papers.' He asked, 'She said she saw me?'

'Yes.'

He nodded but said nothing.

I said to him, 'They're all under the federal witness protection programme.'

'That's good. Nobody can hurt them.' He smiled.

I said to him, 'They won't made good witnesses for a jury. They're not upright citizens.'

He shrugged and went back to his newspaper.

Lenny stopped in front of a coffee shop on Broadway. Vinnie took coffee orders, then went inside to fetch four containers.

We drove through the Holland Tunnel into New Jersey, then came back into Manhattan via the Lincoln Tunnel.

The car phone in the rear rang, and Bellarosa motioned for me to answer it, so I did. 'Hello?'

A familiar voice, a man, asked, 'Is Mr Bellarosa there?'

John Sutter is a fast learner, so I replied, 'No, he's at Mass. Who is this?'

Bellarosa chuckled.

The man answered my question with one of his own, 'Is this John Sutter?'

462

'This is Mr Sutter's valet.'

'I don't like your sense of humour, Mr Sutter.'

'Most people don't, Mr Ferragamo. What can I do for you?'
I looked at Bellarosa.

'I would like your permission to speak to your client.'

Bellarosa already had his hand out for the phone, so I gave
it to him. 'Hello, Al . . . Yeah . . . Yeah, well, he's kind of new
to this. You know?' He listened for a while, then said, 'You
ain't playing the game, either, goombah. You got no right to
complain about this.' He listened again, a bored expression
on his face. 'Yeah, yeah, yeah. So what? Look, you gotta do
what you gotta do. Am I complaining? You hear me shooting
my mouth off?'

I couldn't hear the other end of the conversation, of course,
but I couldn't believe the end I *was* hearing. These guys were
talking as if they'd just had a disagreement over a game of
boccie ball or something.

Bellarosa said, 'You think I'm gonna use dirty money for
bail? Check it out, Al. You find it's dirty, it's yours, and I'll
come back to jail . . . Yeah. Save yourself some time. Don't
get technical.' He glanced at me, then said into the phone,
'He's an okay guy. Get off his case. He's a real citizen. An
important citizen. You don't fuck with him, Al. You fuck
with him, you got serious problems. *Capisce?*'

Me? Was he talking about *me*?

Bellarosa said to the U.S. Attorney, 'I'm sorry you're pissed
off, but you should just think about it. Okay? . . . Yeah. I'll
do that. Catch you on TV tonight, right?' Bellarosa laughed.
'Yeah. Okay. See ya.' He hung up and went back to his
newspaper.

Madonna mia. These people were crazy. I mean, it was
as if they were playing at being Americans in public, but
between themselves some sort of ancient ritual was taking place.

No one spoke for a while, then Bellarosa looked up from
his paper and asked his boys, 'Okay?'

Lenny replied, 'I never spotted nobody, boss.'

Bellarosa glanced at his watch, then asked me, 'You hungry?'

'No.'

'You need a drink?'

'Yes.'

'Good. I got just the place.' He said to Lenny, 'Drive over to Mott Street. We'll get a little lunch.'

Caffè Roma is a fairly famous spot in the heart of Little Italy. I'd been there a few times for dinner with out-of-towners. But it wasn't on Mott Street. I said to Bellarosa, 'Mulberry Street.'

'What?'

'Caffè Roma is on Mulberry Street.'

'Oh, yeah. We're not going there. We're going to Giulio's on Mott Street.'

I shrugged.

He saw that I didn't appreciate the significance of what he was saying, so he gave me a lesson. 'Something else you got to remember, Counsellor – what you say you're doing and what you're doing don't have to be the same thing. Where you say you're going and where you're going are never the same place. You don't give information to people who don't need it or to people who could give it to other people who shouldn't have it. You're a lawyer. You know that.'

Indeed I did, but a lunch destination was not the kind of information I kept secret or lied about.

But then again, nobody wanted to shoot me at lunch.

CHAPTER 28

Little Italy is not far from Foley Square and is also close to Police Plaza, the FBI headquarters at Federal Plaza, and the state and city criminal courts. These geographical proximities are a convenience to attorneys, law enforcement people, and occasionally to certain persons residing in Little Italy who might have official business with one of these government agencies. So it was that we could actually have pulled up in front of Giulio's Restaurant on Mott Street in Little Italy within five minutes of leaving Foley Square. But instead, because of other considerations, it took us close to an hour. On the other hand, it was only now noon, time for lunch.

Giulio's, I saw, was an old-fashioned restaurant located on the ground floor of one of those turn-of-the-century, six-storey tenement buildings bristling with fire escapes. There was a glass-panelled door to the left, and to the right, a storefront window that was half-covered by a red café curtain. Faded gold letters on the window spelled out the word GIULIO'S.

There was nothing else in the window, no menus, no press clippings, and no credit-card stickers. The establishment did not look enticing or inviting. As I mentioned, I come to Little Italy now and then, usually with clients, as Wall Street is not far away. But I've never noticed this place, and if I had, I wouldn't have stepped inside. In truth, my clients (and I) prefer the slick Mulberry Street restaurants, filled with tourists and suburbanites who stare at one another, trying to guess who's Mafia.

Lenny drove off to park the car, and Vinnie entered the restaurant first. I guess he was the point man. I stood on the sidewalk with Bellarosa, who had his back to the brick wall and was looking up and down the street. I asked him, 'Why are we standing outside?'

Bellarosa replied, 'It's good to let them know you're coming.'

'I see. And you really can't call ahead, can you?'

'No. You don't want to do that.'

'Right.' He never looked at me, but kept an eye on the block. There are many fine restaurants in Little Italy, all trying to keep a competitive edge. A shortcut to fame and fortune sometimes occurs when a man like don Bellarosa comes in and gets shot at his table. A terrible headline flashed in front of my eyes: DANDY DON AND MOUTHPIECE HIT.

I asked my lunch companion, 'Has anyone been knocked off here?'

He glanced at me. 'What? Oh . . . no. Yeah. Once. Yeah, back in the Prohibition days. Long time ago. You like fried squid? *Calamaretti fritti?*'

'Probably not.'

Vinnie opened the door and stuck his head out. 'Okay.'

We entered. The restaurant was long and narrow, and the rows of tables had traditional red-checkered cloths. The floor was ancient white ceramic tile, and the ceiling was that pressed tin with glossy white paint on it. Three ceiling fans spun lazily, keeping the smell of garlic circulating. On the plain white plaster walls were cheap prints, all showing scenes of sunny Italy. The place wasn't much to look at, but it was authentic.

There weren't many diners, and I could see waiters standing around in red jackets, all stealing glances at don Bellarosa. A man in a black suit rushed toward us, his hand prematurely extended, and he and Bellarosa greeted each other in Italian. Bellarosa called him Patsy, but did not actually introduce him to me, though he was obviously the *maître d'*.

Patsy showed us to a corner table in the rear. It was a nice comfortable table with good fields of fire.

Lenny had arrived, and he and Vinnie took a table near the front window with a good view of the door. Now we had interlocking fields of fire, which was the first requirement for a pleasant lunch at Giulio's.

Patsy was obsequious, the waiters bowed and bowed and bowed as we walked by, and a man and a woman, apparently the owner and his wife, ran out of the kitchen and stopped just short of prostrating themselves on the floor. Everyone was grinning except Frank, who had this sort of Mafia poker face on that I'd never seen before. I said to him, 'Come here often?'

'Yeah.' He said something to the owner in Italian, and the man ran off, perhaps to kill himself, I thought, but he returned shortly with a bottle of Chianti and two glasses. Patsy uncorked the wine but Frank poured. Finally, after a lot of fussing around our table, everyone left us alone. Frank banged his glass against mine and said, *'Salute!'*

'Cheers,' I replied, and drank the wine, which tasted like grappa diluted with tannic acid. *Yuk!*

Frank smacked his lips. 'Aahh . . . that's good. Special stuff. Direct from the other side.'

They should have left it there.

A few more people had entered, and I looked around. The clientele at lunch hour seemed to be mostly locals, mostly men, and mostly old, wearing baggy suits without ties. I could overhear a mixture of English and Italian around me.

There were a few younger men in good suits, and like a vampire who can tell its own kind at a glance, I recognized them as Wall Street types, trendy twerps who had 'discovered' Giulio's the way Columbus discovered America, i.e., it ain't there until I find it.

Here and there I noticed tables at which were men who I thought might be in Frank's business. And in fact, Frank nodded to a few of these people, who nodded back. Despite the informality of the place and the fact that it was warm, only the Wall Street twerps and a few of the old men had removed their jackets. The rest of the clientele, I was sure, were either wearing shoulder holsters or wanted everyone to think they were. Frank, I knew, could not be armed, as he had just been through a booking and search. Lenny and Vinnie, I knew, *were* armed. I was basically unarmed, except for my three-hundred-dollar Montblanc pen and my American Express Gold Card.

I said to my client, 'Are you satisfied with the way it went this morning?'

He shrugged. 'It went like it went. I got no complaints with you.'

'Fine. Do you want to discuss the charge against you? The defence?'

'I told you, it's bullshit. It's not getting to trial.'

'It could. Ferragamo had five witnesses for the grand jury.

Those witnesses said enough to implicate you in the murder of Juan Carranza.'

'Ferragamo's probably got something on them. They maybe saw the hit, but they didn't see my face there.'

I nodded. 'Okay. I believe you.'

'Good. Then you did the right thing today.'

'No. I committed perjury.'

'Don't worry about it.'

The owner, whose name was Lucio, came by with a bowl of fried onion rings, and a waiter put down two small plates.

'*Mangia*,' Frank said as he took a clawful of the onion rings.

'No, thanks.'

'Come on. Eat.'

They weren't onion rings, of course, but I was trying to pretend they were. I put a few of the things on my plate, then put one in my mouth and washed it down with the Chianti. Ugh, ugh, ugh.

There was a big loaf of Italian bread sitting right on the tablecloth, unsliced, and Frank ripped it apart with his big mitts and flipped a few pieces my way. I didn't see a bread plate and probably never would. I ate some of the bread, which was the best I've ever had.

Between chews, Bellarosa said, 'You see what I mean about how law-abiding I am? Mancuso came in by himself, and I'm waiting for the fucking cuffs. Now how do you think they take a spic out of one of those social clubs? They go in there with a fucking battalion, armed to the fucking teeth, and they got to beat off spics and drag the guy out screaming. Half the time somebody gets a split head or gets shot. You see the difference? You think Mancuso is a fucking hero? No. He knew I wasn't going to put him away.'

'Still, Frank, that took balls.'

He smiled. 'Yeah. That little, skinny wop bangs on my door and says, "You're under arrest." Yeah.' He added, 'But you think Mancuso is going to be a star? No fucking way.

Ferragamo runs his show his way, and he's the star. You'll see on the news.'

Unbidden, the waiter brought over a bowl of what looked like scallops covered with red sauce. Bellarosa shovelled some on my plate beside the fried squid. He said, 'This is *scungilli*. Like . . . conch. Like a shellfish. *Sono buone.*'

'Can I order something from the menu?'

'Try that. Try it.' He dug into his whatever it was. 'Eat. Come on.'

I positioned my wine and a piece of bread, swallowed a piece of the conch, drank the Chianti, and bit on the bread.

'You like it?'

'*Sono buone.*'

He laughed.

We ate, drank, and talked awhile. No one offered us a menu, and I noticed that most of the customers were not using menus but were talking food with the waiters in a mixture of Italian and English. The waiters seemed friendly, happy, enthusiastic, knowledgeable, patient, and helpful. Obviously they weren't French.

It struck me as I sat there that this restaurant could have been a hundred years old, older than The Creek, older than The Seawanhaka Corinthian. And very little in the restaurant had changed, not the decor, the cuisine, or the clientele. In fact, Little Italy was a sort of time warp, a bastion of Italian immigrant culture that seemed to be resisting change and assimilation against all odds. If I had to bet on what would last into the next century – the Gold Coast or Little Italy – I'd bet on Little Italy. Similarly, I'd put my money on Giulio's over The Creek.

I regarded Frank Bellarosa as he ate. He looked more comfortable here, obviously, than he had in The Creek. But beyond that, he belonged here, was part of this place, part of the local colour, the fabric and decor of Giulio's, and Mott Street. I watched him, his tie loosened, a napkin stuffed in his collar, and his hands darting around the table, relaxed in the knowledge that no one was going to take anything away from him; not his food, nor his pride.

We were working on our second bottle of Chianti, and I said to him, 'You're from Brooklyn. Not Little Italy.'

'Yeah. But most of Brooklyn's gone. My old neighbourhood is gone. This is still the place. You know?'

'How so?'

'I mean, like every Italian in New York comes here at least once in his life. Most come once or twice a year. It makes them feel good, you know, because they live in the suburbs now, and maybe their old neighbourhood is full of blacks or Spanish, or something, so they can't go back there, so they come here. This is everybody's old neighbourhood. *Capisce?* Well, maybe not your old neighbourhood.' He laughed. 'Where you from?'

'Locust Valley.'

'Yeah. You don't have far to go home.'

'It gets farther every year.'

'Well, I like to come down here, you know, to walk on the streets, smell the bakeries, smell the cheese, smell the restaurants. Lots of people come for San Gennaro – you know, the Feast of San Gennaro, the patron saint of Napoli . . . Naples. They come for St Anthony's feast, too. They come here to eat Italian, see Italians, feel Italian. You understand?'

'Is that why you come here?'

'Yeah. Sometimes. I have some business here, too. I see people here. I got my club here.'

'The Italian Rifle Club?'

'Yeah.'

'Can you take me there?'

'Sure. You took me to The Creek.' He smiled. 'I take Jack Weinstein there. He loves it. I get him drunk and take him down to the basement and let him blast the targets. I got a silhouette target down there that says "Alphonse Ferragamo."' He laughed.

I smiled. 'I think they throw darts at my picture in the IRS office.'

'Yeah? Darts? Fuck darts.' He stuck his finger at me and

cocked his thumb. 'Ba-boom, ba-boom. That's how you make holes in targets.'

He finished another glass of wine and repoured for both of us. The Chianti was getting better. By the third bottle it would taste like Brunello di Montalcino, 1974.

I looked around the restaurant again. During my mental absence it had gotten full and was noisy now, lively and hopping. I said to Bellarosa, 'I like this place.'

'Good.'

Actually, I was feeling better. Sort of like the high you get after a close call. I couldn't come to terms with the perjury, you understand, but I was working on it. In fact, I took my daybook out of my pocket and, for the first time, turned to January fourteenth. I write in ink, partly because, as an attorney, I know that my daybook is a quasi-legal document and, therefore, should be done in ink in the event it ever had to be shown as evidence. On the other hand, I always use the same pen, the Montblanc with the same nib and the same black Montblanc ink, so if I had to add something after the fact, I could. But I don't like to do that.

Anyway, with some real trepidation, knowing a lot rode on this, I looked at the space for January fourteenth and read: *Light snow. Home in* A.M., *lunch with Susan at Creek, Locust Valley office* P.M., *meet with staff, 4* P.M.

I stared at the entry awhile. *Home in* A.M. Did I really ride that day? Maybe I did. Did I ride over to Alhambra? Perhaps. Did I see three mafiosi walking around? I said I did.

I began to close the book, but then I noticed the entry for January fifteenth: *7:40* A.M., *Eastern flight #119, West Palm Beach.* If I had gone to Florida on the morning of the fourteenth, Ferragamo and the FBI would eventually have discovered that by subpoenaing my daybook, or by other means. And John Sutter would be sharing a cell with Frank Bellarosa. But I was in the clear; *Home in* A.M. The Sutter luck was holding. If I were a Catholic, I would have crossed myself and said the Rosary. I put the book in my pocket.

Bellarosa said, 'You got someplace else to go?'

'No. Just checking something.'

'Yeah? Does it check out?'

'Yes, it does.'

'Good.' He looked me in the eye. *'Grazie,'* he said, and that was all the thanks or acknowledgement I would ever get, and more than I wanted.

Bellarosa said, 'I want to take the women here with us at night. You'll like it at night. This old ginzo plays the little squeeze box' — he pantomimed someone playing an accordion — 'whaddaya call that? The concertina. And they got this old fat donna who sings like an angel. Your wife will love it.'

I asked, 'Are you safe to be with?'

'Hey, what's this thing you got about that?' He tapped his chest. 'If I'm the target, I'm the target. You think anybody gives a shit about you? Just don't get in the way and don't be looking at people's faces. *Capisce?*' He laughed and slapped my shoulder. 'You're funny.'

'So are you.' I knocked back another glass of that nectar of the gods and asked him, 'But how about the other people? The Spanish? The Jamaicans? Do they play by the rules?'

He was chewing on olive pits now and spoke as he chewed. 'I'll tell you one rule they play by. They come into Little Italy to make a hit, there won't be a fucking black or Spanish left in New York. They understand that rule. Don't worry about them around here.'

I've always like New York because of its ethnic diversity, this great American melting pot. *Give me your tired, your poor, your huddled masses . . .* I've forgotten the rest of it. Maybe we've all forgotten it.

Bellarosa leaned toward me and said, 'As long as this stuff bothers you, you ever think about getting a gun permit?'

'It's not on my "must do" list, no.'

'Well, if you're going to be around, you know, you should think about it.'

'Why?'

472

He quoted. '"Among other evils which being unarmed brings you, it causes you to be despised." Who said that?'

'Mother Teresa?'

He laughed. 'Come on. Machiavelli. Right?'

'Right. Do I get combat pay?'

'Sure. Hey, I owe you fifty large. Right?'

'No. I don't want it.'

'That don't matter. You got it.'

A waiter set down a platter of antipasto. There seemed to be no sequence to this meal, at least none that I could determine.

Bellarosa pointed to the items on the plate. 'That's prosciutto – you know that stuff, right? This is *stracchino,* and this is *taleggio.* This cheese here has worms in it, so I won't make you eat it.'

'Excuse me?'

'Worms. Little worms. You know? They give the cheese a flavour. You don't eat the worms. You crumble the cheese like this and get the worms out. See? See that one?'

I stood. 'Where is the men's room?'

He jerked his thumb over his shoulder. 'Back there.'

I walked to the men's room, a horrible little place, and washed my face and hands. *Worms?*

The door opened and Lenny came in. He stood at the sink beside me and combed his greasy hair. He asked me, 'You enjoyin' your lunch, Counsellor?'

'Shouldn't you be out there keeping an eye on the door?'

'Vinnie got two eyes.' He washed his hands. 'Fucking city. Everything's got dirt on it.' He dried his hands on a towel roll that had dirt on it. 'You're the don's lawyer, so you're not wired. Correct?'

'Wired? Are you out of your mind?'

'No. Sometimes people got wires. Sometimes they come in the shitter to drop a wire, sometimes to pick up a wire. If I see people go to the shitter when they're talking to the don, I think wire, I think gun.'

'I think you've been watching too much TV.'

473

He chuckled. 'So? You mind?' He held out his clean hands toward me.

I stood there a moment, then nodded. The son of a bitch gave me a thorough frisking, then said, 'Okay. Just checking. Everybody got a job.'

I put a quarter on the sink. 'That's for you, Lenny. Good job.' I left. Boy, I was really getting the hang of it now. I returned to the table and saw that the worm cheese had been removed from the antipasto.

Frank said, 'Yeah. I got rid of that for you. You find the back'ouse okay?'

'The what?'

He laughed. 'The back house. Back'ouse, they say in Little Italy. From when it was out back. You know?'

'Yes, I found it.' I saw Lenny return to his table, glaring at me as he sat. I asked Bellarosa, 'Did you send him in to frisk me?'

'Nah. He just does it. Look, I know Mancuso tried to get to you, and I trust you more than I trust a lot of my own people. But when I *know* I'm talking to a guy who's clean, I feel better.'

'Mr Bellarosa, a lawyer cannot, may not, will not, act as an agent for the government against his own client.'

'Yeah. But maybe you're writing a book.' He laughed. 'Fuck it. Let's eat. Here. This is called *manteche*. No worms.' He put a piece of the cheese on a biscuit he called *frisalle* and held it near my mouth. 'Come on. Try that.'

I tried it. It wasn't bad. I sipped some Chianti and popped a black olive in my mouth. These people dined out differently from what I was used to. For instance, none of the previous plates had been cleared, and Bellarosa returned to his fried squid.

I said to him, 'Mancuso told me you once beat one of your men with a pipe and broke every bone in his body.'

He looked up from his squid. 'Yeah? Why'd he tell you that? What's he trying to do? He trying to make me sound like a bad guy?'

'Well, that certainly didn't show you in the best light.'

'Mancuso should learn how to keep his fucking mouth shut.'

'The issue is not Mancuso, Frank. The issue is you beating a man with a pipe.'

'That's not an issue.' He pulled apart some bread and dipped it in the red sauce as he spoke. 'When you're young, you sometimes do things you don't want to do, but got to do. I wasn't the boss when that thing happened. The boss was a guy who you'd know. He's dead now. But when he said to me, "Frank, you got to do this or you got to do that," I did it. *Capisce?*'

I didn't reply.

'Just like in the army or in the Church. You follow orders. I give the orders now, and I don't like the rough stuff. Times are changing. Not everybody wants to get into this business anymore. You got to treat your people better.'

'At least offer them Blue Cross and Blue Shield.'

He thought that was funny. 'Yeah. If you break their legs, they're covered. Yeah. Blue Cross.'

There was no reason to pursue the bone smashing incident; it was only important that he knew I knew about his peculiar managerial style. In truth, there were times when I would have liked to beat my partners with a lead pipe, but that would only give them an excuse to do the same to me. And that made me think of Signor Niccolò Machiavelli. I said to Frank, 'An enemy must either be caressed or annihilated.'

He looked up from his food. 'Yeah. That's the problem with pissing somebody off, Counsellor. I'm happy you understand that. In my business, you treat people with respect or you put them away. Now that thing with the pipe, for instance, that was not a good idea. That was one pissed-off *paesano*, so when he was feeling better again, I knew I had to settle that. You know? He had to be caressed or annihilated. You don't leave people around like that with vendettas against you.'

'So you bought him dinner and gave him a raise.'

'Yeah.' He thought a moment, then added, 'I'll tell you the

main thing that's wrong with what the priests teach you – the main thing wrong with religion. It's the bullshit about turning the other cheek. You do that and everybody's gonna take a pop at your face. But sometimes you got to take a hit. Like with Ferragamo. There's not a fucking thing I can do to him. All I can do is make sure there's not a fucking thing he can do to me. Understand? And if you can't get rid of a guy, you don't piss him off, even if he's on your case.'

'But you piss Ferragamo off just by being alive.'

He smiled. 'Yeah. That's *his* problem. But *you* piss him off by smart-assing him.'

'So what? There's not a thing he can do to me.'

'Maybe yes, maybe no. So maybe he comes after your friends. Maybe you want to give him a call and discuss the case. He would like you to do that. He would like you to show a little respect.

'The man is an asshole, Frank, and everybody in New York knows it.'

'That's why he needs all the respect he can get.'

We both laughed at that one. Bellarosa said, 'Hey, maybe the son of a bitch will be the Governor someday, or even the President. Be nice to him. He'll make you the Attorney General.'

In fact, by taking Mr Frank Bellarosa as a client, I would never be considered for any public office. Not that I want to be a judge or to run for the State Assembly or anything like that, but in the back of every lawyer's mind is that possibility. I was once elected to the Lattingtown Village Board, but after this fiasco, I would be well-advised to stay out of public life for a decade or so.

Frank said, 'So maybe you'll call him. I'll give you his private number.'

I looked at him. 'Frank, he's not going to drop any charges against you after today.'

'Yeah, I know that. I'm not talking about that. I thought you understood.'

'You mean, you want me to apologize to him?'

'You don't have to say, "Mr Ferragamo, I'm sorry I made you look like an asshole and a fool." In fact, you don't mention that. You just talk to him about the case with respect. He'll forgive you, because he's an asshole. *Capisce?*'

Here was a client who wanted me to call the prosecution – not to try to make a deal or plea bargain, but to apologize for beating his pants off in court. *Mamma mia,* I don't remember any of this from Harvard Law. I replied, 'I'll call him. And I'll be respectful toward his office.'

'There you go. Sometimes assholes hold important positions. You think every Caesar was a bright guy? Whaddaya gonna do? You got to deal with it.' He poured more wine. 'Ready for your pasta?'

We'd been there an hour already, and I had consumed a lot of food, mostly bread, cheese, and olives, which were the only edible things served so far. Also the Chianti was working its way through my duodenum. I said, 'I'll pass on pasta.'

'No. You have pasta. They have *lingue de passero* here – the sparrow's tongue.'

'Can I get meatballs instead?'

'It's not real sparrow tongue. It's the name of the pasta. You think we eat sparrow's tongue?'

'You eat worms, Frank, and sheep's brains.'

'You don't eat the worms. You'll have sparrow's tongue. It comes from a little town called Faro San Martino in Abruzzo – the province of Brutus. That's where my wife's family is from. They're very thickheaded there. But they have magnificent pasta.' He put his thumb and forefinger to his lips and kissed. '*Magnifico.* And we're gonna have it with the *puttanesca* sauce. The whore's sauce.'

'Say again?'

'Whore. Whore. I don't know why they call it that. Maybe because it's got anchovies in it.' He laughed. 'You understand?'

'I believe I do.'

He raised a finger and a waiter appeared. Bellarosa made

a sweeping motion with his hand, and the waiter snapped his fingers, and two busboys hurried over and cleared away round one.

I settled back in my chair and had some water. I noticed that the Wall Street types had left, and so had some of the local tradesmen. But the old men stayed on, sipping wine or coffee. Also still present were the men who looked like Frank. Obviously, there were two kinds of lunches served here: American Italian and Italian Italian.

Frank stood and excused himself but did not head for the back'ouse. Instead, he walked to a table where four men in dark suits sat. They greeted him cordially but with obvious reserve. I watched as a waiter ran over with a wineglass and one of the men poured Bellarosa some Chianti. They all touched glasses and I heard them mumble, 'Salute.' They drank, then they all hunched forward over the table and said grace. Well, maybe not.

Good Lord, I thought, these people really exist. I mean, right there, not twenty feet away, were five mafiosi drinking wine in a restaurant in Little Italy. I was sorry I hadn't brought my video camera. Look, kids, here's Daddy having lunch with a Mafia don. Now the don is walking over to talk to his mobster friends. See? Okay, the camera's swinging around to those two men near the door. See them? They're bodyguards. See the door? Close-up of the door. Okay, back to the table with the Mafia men.

I watched them, sans video camera. They all talked with their hands. One of them made a motion as if he was pushing something down into the table, another one touched his forefinger to his right eye, Bellarosa tapped the tips of his fingers on the table, and another guy flicked his thumb under his chin. One thing they didn't do with their hands, however, was to point at or touch one another.

I noticed, too, that their expressions were for the most part stoic, sort of that Mafia poker face that Frank put on when he walked in here. But now and then their eyes or their mouths would convey something without revealing anything.

I had no idea what was being discussed, of course, but I assumed that Bellarosa was telling them about his morning. Maybe they knew about the arrest by now, if it was on the radio or if they had another source of information. In any event, they would be interested in the outcome of his court appearance. The fact that he was in Giulio's was a point in his favour regarding any rumours floating around town that he was making deals with Alphonse Ferragamo.

The other order of business would be the Juan Carranza problem. By now, I could actually imagine a conversation among these people. Frank was saying something like, 'We gotta stick together on this Carranza thing. Okay? We don't want a bunch of spics making us do things we don't wanna do. Right? And we don't want the fucking Feds to start something between us. You know? I don't wanna see no Italian blood spilled over a bunch of spics. Agreed? We don't want to hurt business, so if we gotta go to the mattresses with these spics, we hit them hard and fast. Understand? We don't make no separate deals with spics, chinks, *melanzane,* Feds, DAs, or nobody. *Capisce?*'

How's that? The scary thing is that four months ago, if I'd heard that conversation, I wouldn't have understood half of it. Now I could make it up. *Madonn'.* What was happening to me? I didn't know, but it was interesting.

I regarded Lenny and Vinnie at their nice table for two in the corner. They hadn't had any alcohol as far as I could see, but they were puffing up a smoke screen and drinking cup after cup of coffee. The Italians seem to have the capacity to sit for hours at a table, talking and consuming things. Lenny and Vinnie seemed content doing nothing except sitting and watching the door. But I guess watching the door was about as important a job as there was in Giulio's at the moment. Both of them, I noticed, were also watching the remaining clientele, especially the four men with Frank. But the lingerers in the restaurant all seemed to be known by the waiters and *maître d'*, and I thought it was unlikely that one of them would suddenly stand up and start blasting away. No, it was the door that had to be watched. So, to help Vinnie and Lenny, I watched the door, too.

After about fifteen minutes, Frank returned to our table. 'I'm sorry, Counsellor. I had some business there.'

'No problem.'

The pasta came and Frank dug right in. 'Whaddaya think? Smell like a whore's pussy? Yes? No?'

'No comment.'

I picked at the pasta, which I guess did resemble little sparrow tongues. Actually, it was quite good, including the fishy sauce, but I was stuffed.

Bellarosa tore off a piece of bread and actually stuck it in my dish. 'Here, dunk. Don't be shy.'

I don't even like it when Susan takes food off my plate. But I took the bread from him and ate it.

I glanced at my watch. 'Do you want to call your wife?'

'Yeah. Later.'

'Maybe we should let her know you're out on bail.'

'She's okay.'

'She was upset after you left.'

'Yeah? I told her to stay upstairs. You see? They don't fucking listen anymore.'

'Nevertheless, a call —'

'What made you think of my wife? The *puttanesca* sauce?' He laughed. 'Is that what made you think of calling my wife?'

I wasn't going to touch that one. I played around with the pasta and sipped the wine.

Bellarosa finished his pasta and spilled some of mine onto his plate, commenting, 'You're not eating. You don't like it?'

'I'm stuffed.' I glanced at my watch. It was two-thirty. I informed Bellarosa, 'I told your wife I'd have you home this afternoon.'

'Yeah? Why? I told you, we got to stay around here. I got more people to talk to. I want you to say something to the newspeople later. We got a nice big suite at the Plaza. We'll hang around town for a few days.'

'A few days?'

'Yeah.'

'Frank, I have a business, appointments – '

'What can I tell ya? The shit hit the fan, Counsellor. I'll make it up to you.'

Actually, I had no appointments and nearly no business left to worry about. And for fifty large, I could stick around for a few days.

Frank took the rest of my pasta. 'Yeah, we'll send home for some clothes. Your wife will pack some things for you.'

'Will she?'

'Sure. That's what wives are for.'

Not my wife, goombah.

He waved his hands over the plates as if he wanted them to go away by themselves, but a waiter popped up out of the floor and whisked them away.

Another waiter brought two plain salads. Frank said, 'Cleans your palate.' He sprinkled oil and vinegar over his greens and tomatoes, then did the same for me. 'Eat,' he said.

I poked at the salad.

'Eat it. The vinegar helps you digest.'

'What does the oil do?'

'Helps you shit. *Mangia.*'

The salad I could handle, but I said, 'Don't order any more food for me.'

'You have to have the main course. What did you come here for?' Bellarosa called over the waiter. They discussed the main course in Italian, then Bellarosa turned to me. 'Whaddaya like? Veal? Chicken? Pork? Fish?'

'Sheep's head.'

'Yeah?' He said something to the waiter and I heard the word *capozella.* They both laughed. He turned to me. 'They got a special chicken dish here. Nice and light. Okay? We'll share it.'

'Fine.'

Bellarosa ordered, then turned back to me. 'This dumb wop

481

walks into a pizzeria, you know, and says to the guy, "I want a whole pizza." And the guy says, "You want it cut in eight pieces or twelve?" And the dumb wop says, "Twelve, I'm really hungry."' Bellarosa laughed. 'Twelve slices. I'm really hungry. Get it?'

'I think so.'

'Tell me one.'

'Okay. This Wasp walks into Brooks Brothers, you know, and he says to the guy, "How much is that three-piece pinstripe suit?" And the guy says, "Six hundred dollars." And the Wasp says, "Fine, I'll take it."' I went back to my salad.

Bellarosa let a few seconds pass, then said, 'That's it? That's the joke? That's not funny.'

'That's the point.'

'What's the point?'

'Wasps aren't funny.'

He processed that a moment, then said. 'You're funny.'

'No one else thinks so.'

He shrugged.

We drank awhile, and the nice little chicken dish came, and it was enough to feed half the dining room in The Creek. Bellarosa spooned the stuff onto two plates. 'This is called *pollo scarpariello*. Say it.'

'Pollo . . . scarp . . .'

'*Scarpariello*. Chicken, shoemaker style. Maybe a shoemaker invented it. Maybe they make it with old shoes.'

I turned over a piece of meat with my fork. 'What part of the chicken is that?'

'That's sausage. You make it with sausage, too. It's sautéed in oil and garlic, with mushrooms.'

'That does sound light.'

'Eat it. Here, try this. This is escarole with more oil and garlic. The garlic gets that pussy smell outa your mouth. Here. You got to try everything.'

I called the waiter over. 'Bring me a bottle of that water with the bubbles in it and a glass of ice.'

'Yes, sir.'

He brought a green bottle of Pellegrino, and I made a mental note of it for the future. I poured and drank three glasses of the sparkling water while Frank ate the chicken and sausage.

It was nearly three-thirty but the place was not completely empty. Frank's four friends had left, but a few old men sat around with coffee and newspapers. Two old guys were actually snoozing. Vinnie and Lenny were still drinking coffee and smoking.

The door opened, and I instinctively tensed. A man entered, about fifty years old, wearing a dark grey suit and sunglasses. Behind him was a younger man whose eyes darted around the tables. I poked Bellarosa's arm and he followed my gaze to the door. I glanced at Vinnie and Lenny and saw they were on the case. The two men who had come in were aware of Bellarosa's bodyguards and didn't make any abrupt movements, but just stood there near the front door looking at Bellarosa and me. The waiters stood still, staring at their shoes. The few old men in the place gave the two intruders a glance, then went back to their coffee and newspapers.

Frank stood and stepped away from the table, and the man with the sunglasses took them off and came toward Bellarosa. They met in the middle of the restaurant and embraced, but I could see it was more a demonstration of respect than affection.

Frank and his buddy sat at an empty table. The man's partner, or bodyguard or whatever, took a seat with Vinnie and Lenny at their suggestion. I turned my attention back to Bellarosa and his *paesano*. If you watched these people long enough, you could figure out the pecking order. Whereas Frank the Bishop Bellarosa seemed to have no peers this side of Augustus Caesar, this man who had just come in was close. The man had lit Bellarosa's cigarette, but he did it in such a way as to suggest that he didn't like doing it and might not do it again. Bellarosa, for his part, purposely blew smoke at the man. They were both smiling, but I wouldn't want anyone to smile at me like that.

The conversation lasted five minutes, then the man patted

Bellarosa's shoulder as if he were congratulating him on getting out of the slammer. They both stood, embraced again, and the man left with his friend.

The waiters reappeared. I relaxed a bit, but I noticed that Lenny and Vinnie had their eyes glued to the door.

Frank sat down across from me. 'That was a guy who used to work for me.'

'The guy whose bones you broke?'

'No. Another guy.'

'He looked familiar. Is his picture in the papers sometimes?'

'Sometimes.'

I could see that Frank Bellarosa was a bit distracted. Obviously, that man had said something that upset my client. But whatever it was, I would probably never know about it.

It was apparent to me, however, that don Bellarosa was doing some politicking, some public relations on his own behalf, and that he had more personal appearances to make. I had the sense, too, that this was galling to him, but he was going to do it just the same. He might not compromise or make deals with the law or with blacks or Hispanics or with women. But he had to deal with his own kind, and he had to do it with just the right balance of force and respect.

Bellarosa seemed to have come out of his pensive mood and he said to me, 'Hey, you drink cappuccino, espresso, or American?'

'American.'

He signalled a waiter and gave an order. The coffee came and behind it was a man carrying a tray of pastry. *Mamma mia*, I couldn't even swallow my own saliva anymore. But good old Frank, playing both host and waiter, insisted on describing each of the pastries before asking me to pick two for myself. There was no use declining, so I picked two, and he told me I didn't want those two and picked two others for me.

I nibbled at the pastry, which was good enough to find room for, and I also got my coffee down. We chatted with

484

Patsy, with Lucio and his wife, and with a few of the waiters. Everyone seemed happy that the meal was coming to a blood-less conclusion. Patsy smiled at me. 'You like everything?'

'Very good.'

'You come back for dinner. Okay?'

'Sure will.'

Lucio and his wife were not smooth like Patsy, but I tried to draw them out. 'How long have you owned this place?'

Lucio replied, 'It was my father's restaurant, and his father's restaurant.'

'Your grandfather was Giulio?'

'Yes. He came from the other side and opened his restaurant, right here.' He pointed to the floor.

'In what year?'

He shrugged. 'I don't know. Maybe 1900.'

I nodded. A real slick entrepreneur would have made the most of that: *Giulio's; family-owned on Mott Street since 1899.* (The last century always sounds better.) But I had the impression that Lucio was concerned only with the day's fare and his customers' satisfaction a meal at a time. Maybe that's why he was successful, like his father and his father's father.

The chef came out, complete with apron and chef's hat, which he removed prior to bowing to the don. Good Lord, you would have thought Bellarosa was a movie star or nobility. Actually, he was even more important than that; he was mafioso, and these people, mostly from Sicily and Naples, I suspected, had good ancestral memories.

We chatted a minute longer. They all could not have been friendlier, but nevertheless I felt a bit out of place, though not uncomfortable. Lucio and company could tell, of course, that I was an important person, but not an important Italian person. I felt actually like an American tourist in Italy.

Frank stood and I stood, and the chairs were pulled away for us. Everyone was grinning wider as they held their breaths. A minute more and they could all collapse on the floor.

I realized that the only thing missing from this meal was

the bill. But then Frank took a wad of cash from his pants pocket and began throwing fifties around the table. He hit the chef with a fifty, Patsy with a fifty, and three waiters with a fifty each. He even called over two young busboys and slipped them each a tenner. The man knew how to take care of people. We all bid each other *buon giorno* and *ciao*.

Lenny was already gone, and Vinnie was outside checking the street. I saw Lenny pull the Cadillac up in front of the restaurant, and Vinnie opened the rear car door while we were still inside the restaurant. Vinnie motioned through the glass door, and it was only then that Bellarosa exited the restaurant. I was right behind him but not too close. He slid into the backseat and I got in beside him. Vinnie jumped into the front and Lenny pulled quickly away. And this guy wanted to take the wives here? Get serious, Frank.

But maybe he was just taking normal precautions. I mean, maybe even when peace reigned in the regions of the underworld, Frank Bellarosa was just a careful man. Maybe I *would* take Susan here with the Bellarosas. Couldn't hurt. Right?

We travelled south on Mott Street, which is one-way like all of the narrow streets in the old part of Manhattan.

Frank said to Lenny, 'Plaza Hotel.'

Lenny cut west on Canal and swung north on Mulberry, driving through the heart of Little Italy. Bellarosa stared out the window awhile, recharging his Italian psyche. I wasn't sure, but I suspected that he did not walk these streets freely; that, like a celebrity, he saw most of the world through tinted car-windows. Somehow I felt sorry for him.

He turned to me and said, 'I've been thinking. Maybe you had enough of this shit.'

Maybe I did. Maybe I didn't. I didn't reply.

He went on, 'You did what I needed you to do. You got me sprung. You know? Jack Weinstein can take over from here. He knows how to deal with those scumbags in the U.S. Attorney's office.'

'It's up to you, Frank.'

'Yeah. This could get messy. You got a nice law practice,

you got a nice family. You got friends. People are gonna bust your balls. You and your wife go take a nice vacation someplace.'

What a nice man. I wondered what he was up to. I said, 'It's your decision, Frank.'

'No, it's your decision now. I don't want you to feel pressured. No problem either way. You want, I'll drop you off at the train station. You go home.'

I guess it was time for me to bail out or take an oath of loyalty. The man was a manipulator. But I already knew that. I said, 'Maybe you're right. You don't need me anymore.'

He patted my shoulder. 'Right. I don't need you. I *like* you.'

Just when I think I've got this guy figured out, I don't. So we went to the Plaza Hotel.

What I didn't know was that half the Mafia in New York were going to show up that night.

CHAPTER 29

The Plaza is my favourite hotel in New York, and I was glad that Frank and I shared the same taste in something, since I was apparently going to be there awhile.

We checked into a large three-bedroom suite overlooking Central Park. The staff seemed to appreciate who we were – or who Bellarosa was – but they were not as obvious about it as the *paesanos* at Giulio's, and no one seemed particularly nervous.

Frank Bellarosa, Vinnie Adamo, Lenny Patrelli, and John Whitman Sutter sat in the spacious living room of the suite. Room service delivered coffee and sambuca, and Pellegrino water for me (which I discovered is an antidote for Italian overindulgence). By now it was twenty minutes to five, and I assumed we all wanted to catch the five-o'clock news on television. I said to Frank, 'Do you want to call your wife before five?'

'Oh, yeah.' He picked up the telephone on the end table and dialled. 'Anna? Oh . . .' He chuckled. 'How you doin' there? Didn't recognize your voice. Yeah. I'm okay. I'm in the Plaza.'

He listened for a few seconds, then said, 'Yeah. Out on bail. No big deal. Your husband did a terrific job.' He winked at me, then listened a bit more and said, 'Yeah, well, we went for a little lunch, saw some people. First chance I had to call . . . No, don't wake her. Let her sleep. I'll call later.' He listened again, then said, 'Yeah. He's here with me.' He nodded his head while my wife spoke to him, then said to her, 'You want to talk to him?' Bellarosa glanced at me, then said into the phone, 'Okay. Maybe he'll talk to you later. Listen, we got to stay here a few days . . . Yeah. Pack some stuff for him, and tell Anna I want my blue suit and grey suit, the ones I had made in Rome . . . Yeah. And shirts, ties, underwear, and stuff. Give everything to Anthony and let him send somebody here with it. Tonight. Okay? . . . Turn the news on. See what they got to say, but don't believe a word of it . . . Yeah.' He laughed, then listened. 'Yeah . . . Okay . . . Okay . . . See you later.' He hung up, then almost as an afterthought, he said to me, 'Your wife sends her love.'

To whom?

There was a knock on the door, and Vinnie jumped up and disappeared into the foyer. Lenny drew his pistol and held it in his lap. Presently, a room service waiter appeared wheeling a table on which was a bottle of champagne, a cheese board, and a bowl of fruit. The waiter said, 'Compliments of the manager, sir.'

Bellarosa motioned to Vinnie, who tipped the waiter, who bowed and backed out. Bellarosa said to me, 'You want some champagne?'

'No.'

'You wanna call your wife back and tell her what you need?'

'No.'

488

'I'll dial it for you. Here . . .' He picked up the telephone. 'You go in your room for privacy. Here, I'll get her.'

'Later, Frank. Hang up.'

He shrugged and hung up the phone.

Vinnie turned on the television to the five-o'clock news. I hadn't expected a lead story, but there was the anchorman, Jeff Jones, saying, 'Our top story, Frank Bellarosa, reputed head of the largest of New York's five crime families, was arrested at his palatial Long Island mansion early this morning by the FBI. Bellarosa was charged in a sealed sixteen-count federal indictment in the murder of Juan Carranza, an alleged Colombian drug lord who was killed in a mob-style rubout on the Garden State Parkway on January fourteenth of this year.'

Jeff Jones went on, reading the news off the teleprompter as if it were all news to him. Where do they get these guys? Jones said, 'And in a startling development, Judge Sarah Rosen released Bellarosa on five million dollars' bail after the reputed gang leader's attorney, John Sutter, offered himself as an alibi witness for his client.'

Jones babbled on a bit about this. I wondered if Susan recalled the morning of January fourteenth. It didn't matter if she did or not, since I knew she would cover me so I could cover Frank Bellarosa. Oh, what tangled webs we weave, and so forth. Mr Salem taught me that in sixth grade.

Jeff Jones was saying now, 'We have Barry Freeman live at Frank Bellarosa's Long Island estate. Barry?'

The scene flashed to Alhambra's gates, and Barry Freeman said, 'This is the home of Frank Bellarosa. Many of the estates here on Long Island's Gold Coast have names, and this house, sitting on two hundred acres of trees, meadows, and gardens, is called Alhambra. And here at the main gates of the estate is the guard booth – there behind me – which is actually a gatehouse in which live two, maybe more of Bellarosa's bodyguards.'

The camera panned in on the gatehouse and Freeman said, 'We've pushed the buzzer outside there and we've hollered and shaken the gates, but no one wants to talk to us.'

The camera's telescopic lens moved in, up the long driveway, and the screen was filled with a fuzzy picture of the main house. Freeman said, 'In this mansion lives Frank the Bishop Bellarosa and his wife, Anna.'

I heard Frank's voice say, 'What the fuck's this got to do with anything?'

Freeman went on for a while, describing the lifestyle of the rich and infamous resident of Alhambra. Freeman said, 'Bellarosa is known to his friends and to the media as Dandy Don.'

Bellarosa said, 'Nobody better call me that to my face.'

Vinnie and Lenny chuckled. Clearly they were excited about their boss's television fame.

The scene now flashed back to Freeman, who said, 'We've asked a few residents on this private road about the man who is their neighbour, but no one has any comment.' He continued, 'We don't think the don has returned home from Manhattan yet, so we're waiting here at his gate to see if we can speak to him when he does.'

Bellarosa commented, 'You got a long wait, asshole.'

Barry Freeman said, 'Back to you, Jeff.'

The anchor, Jeff Jones, said, 'Thanks, Barry, and we'll get right back to you if Frank Bellarosa shows up. Meanwhile, this was the scene this morning at the Federal Courthouse in lower Manhattan. Jenny Alvarez reports.'

The screen showed the video tape of that morning: Frank Bellarosa and John Sutter making their way down the steps of the courthouse as savage reporters yelled questions at us. My blue Hermès tie looked sort of aqua on camera, and my hair was a bit messy, but my expression was a lawyerly one of quiet optimism. I noticed now that the snippy female reporter who had given me a hard time on the lower steps was on my case even then as we first left the courthouse, but she hadn't really registered in my mind at the time. I saw, too, by her microphone, that the station I was watching was her station.

I guess that was Jenny Alvarez. She was yelling at me, 'Mr Sutter? Mr Sutter? Mr Sutter?'

Obviously, she had been fascinated by me the moment she laid eyes on me. Actually, she wasn't bad-looking herself.

But neither Frank nor I had said much as we descended the steps, and the scene shifted to the lower steps where we got stuck for a while. And there was Great Caesar, with the majestic classical columns of the courthouse behind him, puffing on his stogie, wisecracking and hamming it up for the cameras. I hadn't noticed when I was there, but from the camera's perspective I could see a line of federal marshals on the top steps of the courthouse, including my buddy, Wyatt Earp.

Frank commented to the three of us, 'I gotta lose some weight. Look how that jacket's pulling.'

Vinnie said, 'You look great, boss.'

Lenny agreed, 'Terrific. Fuckin'-ay-terrific.'

It was my turn. 'You could drop ten pounds.'

'Yeah? Maybe it's just the suit.'

I turned my attention back to the television. You could hear a few questions and a few answers, but mostly it was just entertainment, a street happening, impromptu theatre. Then, however, Ms Snippy's cameraman got a close-up of her bugging me again. 'Mr Sutter, Mr Ferragamo has five witnesses who put Frank Bellarosa at the scene of the murder. Are you saying they're all liars. Or are *you* the liar?'

And stupid John replied, 'Ferragamo's witnesses are liars, and he *knows* they are liars. This whole thing is a frame-up, a personal vendetta against my client, and an attempt to start trouble between – '

'Trouble between who?' asked Ms Snippy. 'Rival mobs?'

And so it went.

Frank didn't say anything, but I had the feeling he wished this wasn't going out over the air to Little Italy, Little Colombia, Little Jamaica, Chinatown, and other quaint little neighbourhoods where exotic people with big grudges, big

491

guns, and extreme paranoia might decide to engage in what was called a drug-related murder.

I turned my attention back to the television. The classical columns and crowded steps of the courthouse were gone, and the background was now grey stone. And there was Ms Alvarez live, apparently recently returned from her engagement in lower Manhattan. In fact, she had changed from the morning's neat suit and was now wearing a clingy, red fuck-me dress and holding a bulbous phallic symbol to her lips. But did she put it in her mouth? No. She spoke into it. 'And this is Stanhope Hall. Or at least its walls and towering gates. And over there, right behind the gates, is the gatehouse where an old woman tried to shoo us away a little while ago.'

Funny, but I hadn't recognized the place at first. It was odd that you could sometimes believe in the imagist world of television, but when the person or place was someone or something you knew personally, it didn't look real; the perspective was wrong, the colours were off. The very diminution of size made the person or place nearly unrecognizable. But there it was: the gateway to Stanhope Hall on television.

Ms Alvarez did ten seconds of travelogue, then said, 'You can't see the fifty-room mansion from here, but in that mansion lives John Whitman Sutter and Susan Stanhope Sutter.'

This was not at all accurate, of course. Susan *had* lived in the mansion once, but had stepped down in the world. I'll write to Ms Alvarez.

Anyway, Jenny Alvarez went on about blue bloods, high society, Susan's parentage, and all that nonsense, then she came to the point, which was, 'Why would John Sutter, a respected and successful attorney with the old Wall Street firm of Perkins, Perkins, Sutter and Reynolds, with rich and powerful friends and clients, defend Frank the Bishop Bellarosa on a charge of murder? What is the connection between these two men, between these two families? Did John Sutter, in fact, see Frank Bellarosa on the morning of January fourteenth when Alphonse Ferragamo charges that

Bellarosa murdered Juan Carranza in New Jersey? Is that why Sutter chose to take on this case? Or is there more to it?'

There's more to it, Ms Snippy.

Bellarosa asked, 'Where'd they get all that shit on you, Counsellor?'

'I handed out press kits on myself.'

'Yeah?'

'Just kidding, Frank.'

Ms Alvarez was still at it. Where she got all that shit was from Mr Mancuso and/or Mr Ferragamo. This was called payback time, aka 'Fuck you, Sutter.' Thanks, boys.

Frank Bellarosa said, half jokingly, 'Hey, who's the fucking star of this show? Me or you? I didn't know you were a big shot.'

I stood and walked toward my bedroom.

'Where you goin'?'

'The back'ouse.'

'Can't you hold it? You're gonna miss this.'

'I won't miss it at all.' I went into my bedroom and into the bathroom. I peeled off my jacket and washed my hands and face. 'Good Lord . . .' Well, aside from my personal reasons for being here, the fact remained that Frank Bellarosa was not guilty of the murder of Juan Carranza. 'Not guilty,' I said aloud. 'Not guilty.'

I looked in the mirror and held eye contact with myself. 'You fucked up, Sutter. Oh, you really fucked up this time, Golden Boy. Come on, admit it.'

'No,' I replied, 'I did what I had to do. What I wanted to do. This is a growing experience, John. A learning experience. I feel fine.'

'Tell me that in a week or two.'

I am the only man I know who can get the best of me in an argument, so I turned away before I said something I'd regret.

I dropped my clothes on the bathroom floor and stepped into the shower. Oh, that felt good. The three best things in life are steak, showers, and sex. I let the water cascade over my tired body.

By tomorrow morning, this story would be spread all over the newspapers. The *Daily News,* New York's premier chronicle of the Mafia, would headline it, and so would the *Post. USA Today* would give it some play, and the *Wall Street Journal,* while not seeing any real news value to the story per se, would report it. My fear there was that they would decide that the story was not Frank Bellarosa, but John Sutter of Perkins, Perkins, Sutter and Reynolds. In fact, they might massacre me. Woe is me.

And by tomorrow morning, anyone in Lattingtown, Locust Valley, or the other Gold Coast communities who had missed the story in the above-mentioned newspapers, or missed it on the radio, or somehow missed it on New York's dozen or so TV news shows, could read it in the local Long Island newspaper, *Newsday,* with special emphasis on the local boy, John Sutter. I saw the headline: GOLD COAST TWIT IN DEEP SHIT. Well, maybe not in those words. But *Newsday* was a left-of-centre sort of publication in a heavily Republican county, and they delighted in being antagonistic toward the nearly extinct gentry. They would have fun with this one.

I tried to imagine how this would sit with my partners, my staff, and my two secretaries when they discovered that Mr Sutter had expanded the scope of Perkins, Perkins, Sutter and Reynolds into criminal law. As the water flowed over my head, I had this mental image of my mother and father flipping through the *International Herald Tribune,* somewhere in darkest Europe, looking for depressing stories of famine and political repression, and stumbling upon an odd little article about Mr Frank Bellarosa, Mafia gang leader in New York. Mother would say, 'Isn't that the fellow who lives next to our son, what's-his-name?' And Father would reply, 'Yes, I believe . . . well, look, here is a mention of John Sutter. That must be our John.' And Mother would say, 'It must be. Did I tell you about that darling little café I saw yesterday in Montmartre?'

Of course my friends at The Creek would be some-what more interested. I pictured Lester, Martin Vandermeer,

Randall Potter, Allen DePauw, and a few others sitting around the lounge, nodding knowingly, or perhaps shaking their heads in stunned disbelief, or doing whatever they thought everyone else thought was appropriate, and Lester would say, 'If only John had had more strength of character. I feel sorry for Susan and the kids.'

Jim and Sally Roosevelt, though, were real friends, and nonjudgemental people. I could count on them to tell me straight out what they thought and felt about me. Therefore, I would avoid them for about a month.

Then there were my relatives, my aunts and uncles such as Cornelia and Arthur, and my too many cousins, and their spouses, and the whole crew of silly people I had to associate with because of things like Easter, Thanksgiving, Christmas, weddings, and funerals. Well, Thanksgiving was three months away, I didn't know about any upcoming weddings, and no one seemed about to croak (though after today I wouldn't be surprised if Aunt Cornelia did). And if they all snubbed me, I wouldn't care one whit, but they were more likely to pester me for details of my secret life as a Mafia mouthpiece.

And of course, there were Carolyn and Edward. I was glad I'd tipped them off about this, so when they heard it from other sources, they could say, 'Yes, we know all about that. We support our father in whatever he does.' What great kids. Anyway, I guessed that Carolyn would be outwardly cool, but inwardly worried. That girl keeps everything in. Edward would start a scrapbook. But I'm not concerned about the judgement of children, my own included.

As for my sister, Emily, she had passed through her own midlife rejection of upper-middle-class values and had already reached the other side. I knew she would be there waiting for me when I arrived at my destination, and bless her, she wouldn't want to know anything about my journey, only that I'd made it.

Ethel Allard. Now there was a tough call. If I had to put major money on that, I would say she was secretly pleased that another blue blood had been exposed as morally corrupt. Especially me, since she could never find a chink in my shining armour. I mean, I never beat my wife (except at her own suggestion), I didn't owe money to tradesmen, didn't use the gatehouse to screw women, I went to church, hardly ever got drunk, and I treated her reasonably well. 'But,' she would ask, 'what good have you done lately, Mr John Sutter?' Not much, Ethel. Oh, well.

I'm only glad that George isn't alive to see this, for surely it would have killed him. And if it didn't, he would have annoyed me with his superior and disapproving attitude, and I would have killed him myself.

But, you know, there's a bright spot even in a pile of horse manure. For instance, the Reverend Mr Hunnings would be secretly and sneeringly happy that I was shown up for what I was: a gangster groupie who probably dealt drugs to support his alcohol habit. And I liked the idea that he was probably happy. I was happy that he was happy. I couldn't wait to get to church next Sunday to put my envelope in the collection plate with a thousand dollars in it.

Then there were the women; Sally Grace Roosevelt, for one, who had found Susan's description of don Bellarosa so interesting. And there was Beryl Carlisle, who I was sure now would peel off her damp pants the moment I walked into the room. And there were women like the delicious Terri, who would take me a little more seriously after this.

Ah, we're getting a little closer to the crux of this matter, you say. Perhaps. Let's discuss Charlotte and William Stanhope for one half-second: Fuck them.

Now on to Susan. No, I can't *blame* her for what happened, for my being at that moment in the Plaza Hotel with a mobster, an accused murderer, and a man who had about two hundred people looking to kill him. I couldn't blame her for my decision to be Bellarosa's attorney. And I couldn't blame her for the unwanted press attention she and I were both now getting and would continue to get until perfect strangers knew all about us. No, I couldn't *blame* her. But you do see that it was mostly her fault.

I mean, no, not her *fault,* but sort of her responsibility. In a very small nutshell, it was like this: Susan thought Frank Bellarosa was interesting and, perhaps by inference, more of a man than her own husband. Her husband, who truly cares what his wife thinks of him, did not like that. Her husband is a jealous man. And her husband thinks he is every inch the man that Frank Bellarosa is. More of a man in many ways. But it doesn't do a bit of good to say such a thing. You have to show it.

And so, when the opportunity to do so presented itself, ironically through the person of Frank Bellarosa himself, the husband, showing more ego than judgement, proceeded to ruin his life so he could show everyone a thing or two.

Did I have any regrets as of that moment? Not a one, really. In fact, I felt better than I'd felt in a long time. I knew I would.

I stepped out of the shower and dried myself off. In the misty mirror I drew a nice big smiling face. 'Smile, stupid, you got what you wanted.'

It was a wild night. The phone rang non-stop, and people came and went. Obviously, the don was not in hiding, but had simply moved his court from Alhambra to the Plaza.

There were phone calls from the news media, too, and I suppose the word had gotten out via the hotel staff, or perhaps some of the invited guests. But Bellarosa was taking no calls from the press and told me not to make any statements until the morning. A few enterprising, not to mention gutsy, reporters had actually shown up at the door of the suite and were greeted by Vinnie, official gatekeeper for don Bellarosa, who had a funny line. 'I'll let ya in but ya ain't gettin' out.' No one accepted the invitation. But I could have sworn I heard Jenny Alvarez's voice arguing with Vinnie.

Waiters set up a bar and brought food all night. The television was on constantly, tuned to an all-news channel that re-ran the Bellarosa story every half hour or so with a few variations. I could barely hear the television above the chatter, but I could see Bellarosa and Sutter walking down those courthouse steps every half hour.

Most of the men who arrived at the suite seemed to be vassals of the great *padrone*, captains and lieutenants in his own organization. They hugged and kissed him, and the lesser of them satisfied themselves with a handshake. A few older men actually bowed as they took his hand. Obviously, they were there to swear fealty to this man who was their don. Bizarre, I thought; this so-called empire of Bellarosa's sort of reminded me of a medieval principality where none of the affairs of state or the rules of behaviour were written down, but simply understood, and where oaths were binding on pain of death, and court intrigue was rampant, and succession to power was accomplished through a mixture of family blood, consensus, and assassination.

The men present were dressed in standard Mafia suits of blue, grey, and black, some with pinstripes. The suits could almost pass for Wall Street, but there was something subtly different about them, and the dress shirts ran mostly to shiny satin or silk, and the ties were drab monotones. There were lots of gold cuff links, expensive watches, even jewelled tiepins, and every left pinky in that room had a diamond ring, except mine.

The men around me spoke mostly in English, but every once in a while, someone would say something in Italian; just a line or two that I couldn't understand, of course. I regretted that I'd wasted eight years in French class. I mean, what can you do with French? Insult waiters? I did get lucky in Montreal once, but that's another story.

Anyway, not everyone who came to the Plaza suite was there to pay homage and swear loyalty. A few men showed up with their own retinues, men with unpleasant faces whose embraces and kisses were strictly for show. These were men who were there for information. Among them were the four whom Bellarosa had sat with at Giulio's, and also the steely-eyed man who had come in later with the bodyguard. Bellarosa would disappear with these men into his bedroom, and they would emerge ten or fifteen minutes later, their arms around one another, but I couldn't tell who screwed whom in there.

At any given time, there were about a hundred men in the big sitting room, though, as I said, they were coming and going, but I estimated that as of about ten o'clock, two or three hundred people must have shown up. I wonder what the office Christmas party looks like.

Anyway, Bellarosa paid very little attention to me, but he wanted me to stay in the room, I suppose to show me off, or to immerse me in Mafiana, maybe even to impress me with his world. However, he barely introduced me to anyone, and when he did think to introduce me, I didn't get any kisses or hugs, only a few surprisingly limp handshakes. But I wasn't put out by this. In fact, I noticed that these people were not big on introductions in general and barely bothered with them or acknowledged them, even among themselves. I thought that odd, but perhaps it was only my cultural bias; I mean, in my crowd, and with Americans in general, introductions are a big deal, and I even get introduced to people's maids and dogs. But with Bellarosa and his goombahs, I think there was this ingrained sense of secrecy, silence, and conspiracy that precluded a lot of idle chatter, including people's names.

It was sort of an Italians-only party, I guess, but then Jack Weinstein showed up and I was never so happy to see a Jewish lawyer in my life. Weinstein came right up to me and introduced himself. He didn't seem at all professionally jealous, and in fact, he said, 'You did a nice job. I never could have sprung him.'

I replied, 'Look, Mr Weinstein – '

'Jack. I'm Jack. They call you Jack or John?'

Actually they call me Mr Sutter, but I replied, 'John is fine. Look, Jack, I don't think I should have any further involvement in this case. I don't do criminal work, and I simply don't know the ropes at Foley Square.'

He patted my shoulder. 'Not to worry, my friend. I'll be in the wings the whole time. You just schmooze the judge and jury. They'll love you.'

I smiled politely and regarded him a moment. He was a tall, thin man of about fifty with a deep tan, dark eyes, and a nose that could be described as Semitic or Roman; in fact, Weinstein could have passed for a *paesano*. Giovanni Weinstein.

He informed me, 'You shouldn't have said that about Ferragamo. About the aberrant behaviour in court. Crazy people are very sensitive about being called crazy.'

'Screw him.'

Weinstein smiled at me.

I said, 'Anyway, you know, of course, that Frank doesn't think he will make it to trial. He thinks he'll either be . . . you know . . . before then, or that Ferragamo will drop it for lack of evidence.'

Weinstein looked over both his shoulders and said softly, 'That's what this is all about. This gathering. This is public relations. He has to show that he's not afraid, that he has the support of his business associates and that he's still an effective manager. He smiled. '*Capisce?*'

'*Capisco.*'

Weinstein chuckled. Boy, what a good time we were having. He said, 'And I'm not going to bug you about that statement you made to the reporter out on the steps, John, because I put my foot in it a few times myself when I first came to work for this outfit. But you've got to be careful. These people speak their own brand of English. For instance, take the words "pal" and "talk". If someone here says to you, "Hey, pal, let's go outside for a talk," don't go. Same with, "Let's take a walk." *Capisce?*'

'Sure. But – '

'I'm just making you aware of this stuff – expressions, nuances, double meanings, and all that. Just be aware. And don't worry about facial expressions or hand gestures. You'll never understand any of that anyway. Just listen closely, watch closely, keep your hands still, your face frozen, and say very little. You're a Wasp. You can do that.'

'Right. I think I figured that out already.'

'Good. Anyway, I'm glad you were ready to go this morning. You know, usually the State Attorney General and sometimes even the U.S. Attorney will make an arrangement so that they don't have to come and arrest a man like Bellarosa at his home, or on the street or in a public place. You understand, when you have a middle-aged man with money and ties, the prosecutor can work something out with the guy's attorney. A voluntary surrender. But sometimes these bastards get nasty, like when they arrested those Wall Street characters in their own offices and marched them out in cuffs. That was bullshit.'

I shrugged. There were two ways of looking at that, depending on if you were watching it on TV or if you had the cuffs on.

Weinstein said, 'We were pretty sure they'd come for Frank on a Tuesday, so when our snitch rang me last night and let me know it was on for seven this morning, I wasn't too surprised.'

'What snitch?'

'In Ferragamo's office . . . oh . . . forget where you heard that.'

'Sure.' I thought a moment. That son of a bitch cheated me out of fifty bucks. I couldn't believe it. Here was a guy who threw fifty-dollar bills around, who offered me exorbitant fees for doing very little, and he screws me out of fifty bucks. Obviously, it wasn't the money, it was his obsessive need to win, and to impress people. And this was also the guy who gave me his alibi two minutes before he was arrested, then told me to forget it while making it clear to me he didn't intend to spend one day in jail. This guy was slick.

Weinstein said, 'See what I mean? I figured you knew about that. You can't figure these people, John. And they say Jews are tricky. Hell, this guy . . . well, enough of that.'

I inquired, 'Is he in any real danger? I ask that because I

don't want to get caught in the crossfire, and I don't mean that figuratively.'

Again Weinstein glanced around, then said, 'The Hispanic gentlemen will never get to him, and really don't want to get to him themselves, because that will cause them many problems. This is fine, because they tend to be indiscriminate with their sub-machine-guns. However' – his eyes travelled around the crowded room as he spoke – 'someone here can and will get to him if they smell weakness, if they think he is more of a liability than an asset.' He added, 'Think of a school of hungry sharks, and think of the biggest shark with a wound that leaves a trail of blood in the water. How long does that big shark have? Understand?'

I nodded.

'It's not that they don't like him,' Weinstein said, 'or that he hasn't done his job. But that's history. They want to know about today and tomorrow. The bottom line with these people, Counsellor, is keeping out of jail and making money.'

'No,' I informed him, 'keeping out of jail and making money are the subtotals. The bottom line with these people is respect. Appearances. Balls. *Capisce?*'

He smiled and patted my cheek affectionately. 'I stand corrected. You learn fast.' He said, 'Give me a call when you get some time. We have a few things to discuss. We'll have lunch.'

'Any place but Little Italy.'

He laughed, turned, and greeted someone in Italian. They hugged but didn't kiss. That would be me in a year or so if I wasn't careful.

A very short and very fat man came up to me, and his stomach hit me before I could back away. He said, 'Hey, I know you. You work for Jimmy, right? Jimmy Lip. Right?'

'Right?'

He stuck out his fat, sweaty hand. 'Paulie.'

We shook and I said, 'Johnny. Johnny Sutta.'

'Yeah. You're Aniello's godson, right?'

'That's right.'

'How's he doin'?'

'Very good.'

'The cancer ain't killed him yet?'

'Uh . . . no . . .'

'He's a tough son of a bitch. You see him at Eddie Loulou's funeral last month? You there?'

'Of course.'

'Yeah. Aniello walks in, half his face gone, and the fucking widow almost drops dead in the coffin with Eddie.' He laughed and so did I. Ha, ha, ha. He asked me, 'You see that?'

'I heard about it when I got there.'

'Yeah. Jesus, why don't he wear a scarf or something?'

'I'll mention it to him when we have lunch.'

We talked for a few more minutes. I'm usually good at cocktail party chatter, but it was hard to find things in common with Paulie, especially since he thought I was someone else. I asked him, 'Do you play golf?'

'Golf? No. Why?'

'It's a very relaxing game.'

'Yeah? You wanna relax? What for? You relax when you get old. When you're dead. What's Jimmy doin' with himself?'

'Same old shit.'

'Yeah? He better watch his ass. None of my business, but if I was him, I'd lay off the chinks for a while. You know?'

'I told him that.'

'Yeah? Good. You can push the chinks so far, you know, but if you keep leanin' on them, they're gonna get their little yellow balls in an uproar. Jimmy should know that.'

'He should.'

'Yeah. Hey, tell Jimmy that Paulie said hello.'

'Sure will.'

'Remind him about the place on Canal Street we got to look at.'

'I will.'

Paulie waddled off and bumped into someone else. I took a few steps toward the bar and someone tapped me on the shoulder. I turned to see a large gentleman whose features looked Cro-Magnon. He asked me, 'What's Fat Paulie talkin' to you about?'

'Usual shit.'

'What's the usual shit?'

'Who wants to know?'

'Hey, pal, if you don't know who I am, you better fucking ask around.'

'Okay.' I moved to the bar and poured myself a sambuca. How, I wondered indignantly, could anyone here mistake me, John Whitman Sutter, for one of them? I caught a glimpse of myself in a wall mirror. I still looked the same. But maybe my breath still smelled of *puttanesca* sauce and garlic.

Anyway, I asked a young man at the bar, 'Who is that?' I cocked my head toward the Cro-Magnon gentleman.

He looked at the man, then at me. 'You don't know who that is? Whaddaya from Chicago or Mars?'

'I forgot my glasses.'

'Yeah? If you don't know who that is, you don't gotta know.'

This sounded like Italian haiku, so I dropped the subject. 'Play golf?'

'Nah.' The young man leaned toward me and whispered, 'That's Sally Da-da.'

'Right.' Now I had three Sallys in my life: Sally Grace; Sally of the Stardust Diner; and a gentleman who, if I recalled Mancuso correctly, was born Salvatore with a whole last name, but who had apparently not mastered much speech beyond the high-chair stage. How's little Sally? Da-da-da. Sally want ba-ba? I said, 'That's the Bishop's brother-in-law.'

'Yeah. Sally is the husband of the Bishop's wife's sister. What's her name?'

'Anna.'

'No, the fucking sister.'

'Maria, right?'

'Yeah . . . no . . . whatever. Why you asking about Sally Da-da?'

'He told me to ask around about him.'

'Yeah? Why?'

'He wants to know what I was talking to Fat Paulie about.'

'You shouldn't be talkin' to Fat Paulie about nothing.'

'Why not?'

'If you don't know, you better find out.'

'Fat Paulie talks too much,' I ventured.

'You got that right. Fat Paulie better watch his ass.'

'And Jimmy Lip better watch his ass, too,' I said.

'Why?'

'He's leaning too hard on the chinks.'

'Again? What's wrong with that asshole?'

'He listens to his godson too much.'

'Which godson?'

'Aniello. No, Johnny. No . . .' I had to think how that went. The young man laughed. 'I thought you was gonna say his godson Joey. I'm Joey. Who are you?'

'John Whitman Sutter.'

'*Who?*'

'The Bishop's attorney.'

'Oh . . . yeah . . . I saw you on the news. Jack is out?'

'No, Jack is still in. I'm doing the front stuff.'

'Yeah. I heard that. Whaddaya want with Sally Da-da?'

'Just talk.'

'Yeah. You wanna stay away from that guy. You let the Bishop talk to him.'

'*Capisco. Grazie.*' I made my way to the window and looked out over Central Park. Basically all cocktail parties are the same. Right? You just have to get a few drinks in you, get warmed up a little, and work the room. The only thing missing at this little gathering was women. Actually, I realized I didn't miss them. *Capisce?*

*

At about ten P.M., a short, squat gentleman with hairy hands arrived, wheeling four suitcases on a luggage cart, one of which looked like my Lark two-suiter. Lenny directed the man, whom he knew, into the appropriate bedrooms. I wondered if Lady Stanhope enjoyed packing my suitcase. I'm glad Frank asked her, not me.

At eleven P.M., someone switched to a network news channel and turned up the volume. People began to quiet down and drift over to the TV set.

The lead story was still the arrest of Frank Bellarosa, but the slant this time was Alphonse Ferragamo's noontime news conference, which had been given short shrift earlier. I had no doubt that the U.S. Attorney's office had complained vigorously about media sensationalism and too much human-interest fluff regarding don Bellarosa and his attorney. Time for hard news.

After the anchor's lead-in, the screen showed yet another cameraman's perspective of the steps of the courthouse, with Bellarosa waving to everyone, and with me looking tan, fit, tall, and well dressed. No wonder the women love me.

Anyway, this lasted only five seconds or so, then the scene shifted to a crowded press-conference room, probably in the bowels of the Foley Square complex. A close-up of the podium showed Alphonse Ferragamo looking more composed than when I'd last seen him in court. A few people around me made interesting observations about the U.S. Attorney, such as 'motherfucker', 'cocksucker', 'asshole', 'shithead', and 'faggot'. I'm glad Alphonse's mother wasn't in the room.

Mr Ferragamo shuffled some papers and read a prepared statement. 'At seven forty-five this morning,' he began, 'agents of the Federal Bureau of Investigation, working within a Federal Organized Crime Task Force, which includes New York City and State police and agents of the Drug Enforcement Agency, acting in coordination with the Nassau County police, effected the arrest of Frank Bellarosa at his Long Island mansion.'

506

I could have sworn I saw only Mancuso there. But I guess everybody else was out on Grace Lane, and they wanted to be mentioned.

Ferragamo went on, 'This arrest is the culmination of a seven-month investigation by New Jersey state police acting in concert with the U.S. Attorney's office and the FBI. The evidence presented to the grand jury, which led to the indictment and arrest of Frank Bellarosa, implicates Bellarosa as the triggerman in the slaying of the reputed Colombian drug king, Juan Carranza.'

So Ferragamo went on, fashioning a hangman's noose for my client, and I wondered who in that hotel room would put it around his neck. From where I was standing, I could see Bellarosa's face, and he betrayed no emotion, no uneasiness or discomfort. He was listening to *La Traviata* in his head again. But I could see several other men in the room who looked uneasy. Others looked deep in thought, and a few glanced quickly at Bellarosa.

Ferragamo tied the last knot in the rope by announcing, 'Federal witnesses have testified in closed session that there is an ongoing power struggle within the Bellarosa organization and that the murder of Juan Carranza was not sanctioned by the organization or by the other four crime families in New York. The murder was carried out by Bellarosa and a faction of his organization that wants to regain dominance of the drug trade and push out the Colombians, the Caribbean connections, and the East Asian connections.'

Ferragamo continued, 'This murder indictment is only the first of many more indictments to come in the war against organized crime. The scope of this investigation has been widened to include other charges against Frank Bellarosa including charges of racketeering under the RICO Act. Other figures in Bellarosa's organization are also under investigation.'

That didn't get a round of applause. On one level, everyone knew that Ferragamo was beating the bush to see who would panic and run to him. But on another level, everyone in that room had a friend or relative in jail. Mancuso had been right about the mob's being crippled by a slew of recent convictions. But there were others in the five families who saw this as an opportunity, a period of cleansing. Out with the old blood, in with the new. Gang wars used to accomplish the same thing.

And speaking of gang wars, Ferragamo was right on top of it. He said, 'The U.S. Attorney's office and other federal, state, and city law enforcement agencies are concerned that this struggle for control of the drug distribution may lead to a new type of gang war on the streets of New York: a war between and among different ethnic groups who live in uneasy peace among themselves, but who may now resort to violence.' Ferragamo looked up from his prepared statement.

For a half second you could hear the breathing in the room around me, then a reporter at the press conference asked Ferragamo, 'Did you expect Bellarosa to show up with a Wall Street lawyer and five million dollars?'

A few people in the press room laughed, and in the hotel room many heads turned toward me.

Ferragamo smiled sardonically. 'We had some indication of that.'

Then, there she was, Ms Snippy, aka Jenny Alvarez, standing up and asking, 'You have five witnesses, Mr Ferragamo, who say they saw Frank Bellarosa shoot Juan Carranza. Yet Bellarosa's lawyer, John Sutter, says he saw Bellarosa on Long Island that morning. Who's lying?'

Alphonse Ferragamo gave a nice Italian shrug. 'We'll let a jury decide that.' He added, 'Whoever is lying will be charged with perjury.'

Including you, Alphonse. I'm not taking this rap alone.

And so it went for another minute, but then it was time to get on to the standard story of the fire in the South Bronx, which was only newsworthy because nobody could believe there was anything left in South Bronx to burn. Actually, I think they run the same footage of the last fire on slow news days.

Lenny flipped through the other two networks, but we only caught the last few seconds of the Ferragamo news conference, which had apparently been everyone's lead story.

Lenny turned back to the all-news channel, which at that particular moment was doing sports. The Mets did it again, trouncing Montreal six to one. What a day.

Why did I feel eyes on me? Well, time to fade to black as they say, so I opened the door to my bedroom, but saw it was being used for a meeting. Sitting around on my chairs and bed were six unhappy-looking men, including Mr Sally Da-da, who stared at me and inquired, 'Yeah?'

'This is my room.'

They all looked from one to another, then back at me. 'Yeah?'

I said, 'I'll give you ten minutes.' I closed the door and went right to the bar. Actually, they could have longer if they needed it.

The crowd had thinned to about thirty men now, and I noticed that Jack Weinstein was gone. I took my drink and went to one of the windows again and opened it, breathing in some fresh air.

Frank Bellarosa came up beside me with a drink in his hand, and a cigar in his mouth. We both stared out at the park and the lights of the great city. Finally he said, 'You have a good time tonight?'

'Interesting.'

'You talked to Jack.'

'Yes. Smart guy.'

'Yeah. Who else you talk to?'

'Fat Paulie. Some other people. I didn't catch many names.'

'Yeah? You meet my brother-in-law?'

'Sort of.' I added, 'He's in my bedroom now with five other men.'

Bellarosa said nothing.

We continued looking out into the summer night, and I was reminded of the night on his balcony. He offered me a cigar and I took it. He lit it with a gold lighter, and I blew smoke out the window. He said to me, 'You understand what's happening here?'

'I think I do.'

'Yeah. We got a long, hard fight ahead of us, Counsellor. But we won round one today.'

'Yes. By the way, I'd like my fifty dollars back.'

'What?'

'I heard about your snitch in Ferragamo's office.'

'Yeah? From who?'

'Doesn't matter who.'

He fished around in his pocket and pulled out a fifty, which I took. He said, 'Wanna make another bet?'

'What's the bet?'

'I bet that's the last time you catch me cheating.' He laughed and slapped me on the back.

So we puffed away on the Monte Cristos, then he said to me, 'A lot of these goombahs think you're magic or something. *Capisce?* They respect your world. They think you people still hold the power in your hands. Maybe you do. Maybe it's slipping away. Maybe if the Italians and the Anglos could somehow get together, we could get New York back. Maybe get this country back.'

I didn't reply, because I couldn't tell if he was serious, joking, or crazy.

He said, 'Anyway, you have this . . . what do you call it . . .? This like aura, you know, around you, like you are connected to powerful sources. That's what they said on television. That's what a lot of these goombahs believe.'

'You sure got your fifty thousand worth.'

He laughed. 'Yeah.'

'You understand, I hope, that I have no such power. I'm socially and financially connected, but not politically connected at all.'

He shrugged. 'So what? That's between us.'

'All right. I'm going to bed. Can I kick your brother-in-law out of my room?'

'Later. We'll wait up for the bulldog editions. I can get the

Post and the *Daily News* hot off the press in about half an hour. I got people waiting for them now.' He asked me, 'Hey, you call your wife?'

'No. Did you call yours?'

'Yeah, she called before. She's okay. She said to tell you hello. She likes you.'

'She's a nice woman. A good wife.'

'Yeah, but she drives me nuts with her worrying. Women. *Madonn'*.' He let a second or two pass, then said, 'Maybe it's good that we get away from them for a few days. You know? They appreciate you more when you're gone awhile.'

I wondered if Anna appreciated her husband more after he returned from two years in a federal penitentiary. Maybe she did. Maybe if I got nailed on a perjury rap and went away for five years, Susan would really appreciate me. Maybe not.

At about midnight, with about a dozen people left in the suite, two men arrived within a few minutes of each other, each carrying a stack of newspapers. One had the *Post,* the ink still wet on it, and the other, the *Daily News.* They threw the papers on the coffee table.

I read the *Post* headline: GOTCHA, FRANK. The *Post* is not subtle. Beneath the headline was a full-page photo of Frank Bellarosa being led down a corridor of the Federal Court in cuffs, with Mancuso holding his arm. I learned from the caption that Mr Mancuso's first name was Felix, which explained a lot.

It was obvious that despite the prohibition against cameras in the courthouse, Ferragamo had arranged for the daily newspapers to have photo opportunities during the time that Bellarosa was in cuffs. A picture is worth a thousand words, and maybe as many votes when November rolled around.

Bellarosa picked up one of the copies of the *Post* and studied the photo. 'I'm taller than Mancuso. You see? Ferragamo likes to have big FBI guys around the guy in cuffs. He don't like Mancuso for a lot of reasons. Plus the guy's short.' He laughed.

The remaining men in the room, including me, Frank, Lenny, Vinnie, Sally Da-da and two of his goons, and a few other soldier types each took or shared the newspapers. I picked up a copy of the *Daily News,* whose headline read: BELLAROSA ON MURDER CHARGE.

Again, there was a full-page photo, this one of Bellarosa holding his cuffed hands up, clenched together like a victorious prizefighter. The caption read: *Frank Bellarosa, reputed boss of New York's largest crime family, taken into custody in Federal Court yesterday morning.* I held the newspaper up for Bellarosa. 'You'll like this shot.'

He took the paper. 'Yeah. Good picture. I remember that one.'

Vinnie said, 'You look good, boss.'

Lenny nodded. 'Yeah. Nice shots, boss.'

Everyone else added their congratulations on a fine photo, cuffs notwithstanding. I wondered if Frank Bellarosa got tired of full-time sycophants.

I did notice that Sally Da-da was not adding his congratulations, but was reading the *News.* I did not like this man, and he knew it. And he did not like me, and I knew it, so it sort of balanced out. But aside from not liking him, I didn't trust him.

I opened the *Daily News* to a byline story and saw a small photo of Frank and a man who looked vaguely familiar. The caption read: *Bellarosa leaving courtroom with Attorney John Sutter.* Ah. I thought he looked familiar.

Bellarosa was reading the *Post.* He said, 'Hey, listen to this.' He read, '"In a move that surprised and even shocked veteran court observers, Bellarosa showed up at the arraignment with blue-blood lawyer John Sutter of Lattingtown, Long Island."' Bellarosa looked at me. 'You really got blue blood?'

'Of course I have.'

He laughed and went back to the story and read, '"Sutter is the husband of Susan Stanhope Sutter, heiress daughter of a socially prominent Gold Coast family."' He looked up at me again. 'Does that mean your wife's got blue blood, too?'

'Absolutely.'

Bellarosa scanned the article and said, 'They got a lot of shit here on you, Counsellor. Your law firm, your clubs, all that stuff.'

'That's nice.'

'Yeah? Where do you think they got all that shit so fast? Your pal Mancuso and scumbag Alphonse. Right? They're really trying to stick it up your ass.'

And doing a rather nice job of it, I should say. Oh, well, what did I expect? When people like me step out of bounds, the government is right there to pounce, and the press eats it up. There are unwritten rules in this society, too, just like in Bellarosa's society, and if you break the unwritten rules, you won't get your bones broken, but you'll get your life broken.

I looked again at the *Daily News* article and found my name. Here's what the article did not say: 'John Sutter is a good man, an okay husband, and a fairly good father. He served honourably in the U.S. Army, and is active in conservation efforts. He contributes thousands of dollars to charity, is a generous employer, and plays a good game of golf.'

Here is what the article did say: 'Sutter himself has been under investigation by the IRS for criminal tax fraud.'

I thought I'd solved that problem. I guess it was a matter of verb tenses. Has been. Had been. Journalese was interesting. It was an art form. I wondered if I should write a letter to the editor or begin a lawsuit. Probably neither.

I poured myself a Scotch and soda, and without wishing my fellow revellers good-night, I went into my bedroom and closed the door.

I saw my suitcase on the luggage rack and opened it. Susan had risen to the occasion and had done a nice job. She had packed my toilet kit, a grey suit, and a blue suit of summer-weight wool. There were matching ties and pocket handkerchiefs and dress shirts. There was also enough underwear for about two weeks, which might have been a subtle hint.

As I unpacked, I saw an envelope with my name on it and opened it. It was a 'Dear John' letter from Susan, which didn't surprise me since my name is John. But I'm being flip. As I brushed my teeth in the bathroom, I read the letter, and here's what it said:

> Dear John,
>
> You looked marvellous on television, though I'm not certain about the green tie with the blue suit. Or was the TV colour off? You handled that bitchy female reporter quite well, I thought. I spent the day with Anna, who was very impressed with you and thanks you. I had to go home through the back way as there were reporters at the gates of both houses. How long will that nonsense last? Lots of messages on our answering machines, though I haven't played any of mine yet. But there was a Fax from your New York office asking you to call. Urgent. I wonder what that's all about? What a break for Frank that you happened to see him on that day. Was I out riding with you? Call me tonight if you have a moment.
>
> Love,
> Susan

Well, that was vintage Susan Stanhope. Anna Bellarosa probably spent the whole day blubbering and wailing, and Susan spent the day arranging flowers. Well, look, this is the way people like us are. We *can* be passionate, affectionate, angry, sad, or whatever, but we don't show much of it. I mean, what good does it do? It's self-indulgent, and, contrary to popular opinion, it doesn't make you feel any better.

Still, Susan's note was a bit *sang-froid*, to use a French expression. On the other hand, I hadn't expected any note at all. I wonder if she wrote to Bellarosa.

I undressed, and as she hadn't packed any pyjamas, I went to bed in my underwear. No, I wasn't going to call her.

I drank my Scotch and listened to the muted murmur of Manhattan street sounds eight floors below. I still smelled that horrible fishy sauce and that garlic on my breath. No wonder Italy was the only country in Europe without vampire legends; they turned back at the Alps.

I may have drifted off for a while, but I woke up remembering that I had to tell Jimmy Lip that Fat Paulie wanted him to look at that place on Canal Street. More important, I had to tell Jimmy to lighten up on the chinks.

The phone rang and it was Susan, and I spoke to her, but in truth, I think it was a dream.

The phone rang again and it was Jenny Alvarez with an interesting proposition. I said to her, 'Come on up. Tell Lenny or Vinnie it's okay. I'm in the first bedroom to the left.'

Later I heard a knock on my bedroom door and she entered. I said to her, 'If you like me, why were you so bitchy to me?'

'That's my way.'

She took off her shoes, but not her red fuck-me dress, and crawled into bed beside me. What a tease. I wanted to kiss her but I was concerned about the anchovies and garlic on my breath.

I'm not sure what happened next, but when I woke up again before dawn, she was gone. Actually, I doubt she was ever there.

CHAPTER 30

The next morning while having coffee in the suite, I called a few select newspaper people whose names Bellarosa had given me. The story I put out was this: Frank Bellarosa wants a speedy trial within the next month, and any delay on the part of the U.S. Attorney's office would be construed as justice denied. Mr Bellarosa is innocent of the charge and wants to prove so in open court.

This, of course, would put Alphonse Ferragamo on the spot to develop a case quickly, and since there apparently was no case, Ferragamo had to either drop the charges or go into court with little chance of winning. Ferragamo wanted to do neither; what he wanted was for someone to knock off Bellarosa soon.

Anyway, after coffee that morning in the littered living room of the suite, I went into my bedroom and dialled Susan. 'Hello,' I said.

'Hello,' she replied.

'I'll be in the city for a few days and I wanted you to know.'

'All right.'

'Thank you for packing my bag.'

'Think nothing of it,' she said.

'Thank you just the same.' When husbands and wives get on this frigid roll, you'd think they were total strangers, and they are.

Susan asked, 'Did you see my note?'

'Note . . .? Oh, yes, I did.'

'John . . .?'

'Yes?'

'We really have to talk about it.'

'The note?'

'About us.'

'Not *us*, Susan. About *you*.'

She didn't reply for a few seconds, then asked, 'What *about* me? What is really bothering you about me?'

I took a deep breath and said, 'Did you call me last night? Did we speak?'

'No.'

'Well, then, it was a dream. But it was a very realistic dream, Susan. Actually it was my subconscious mind trying to tell me something. Something I've known for some time, but couldn't come to grips with. Has that ever happened to you in a dream?'

'Maybe.'

'Well, in my dream I realized that you were having an affair with Frank Bellarosa.'

There, I said it. Well, sort of. She didn't reply for a few seconds, then asked, 'Is that why you're in a bad mood? You dreamed that I was having an affair with Frank?'

'I think it was more than a dream. It was a nocturnal revelation. That's what's been bothering me for months, Susan, and it's what has come between us.'

Again there was a long silence, then she said, 'If you suspected something, you should have come to grips with it, John. Instead, you've become withdrawn. You've indulged yourself in playing Mafia mouthpiece and telling off all your friends and family. Maybe what's happened to us is as much your fault as mine.'

'No doubt about it.'

Again, silence, because neither of us wanted to return to the issue of adultery. But having come this far, I said, 'So? Yes or no? Tell me.'

She replied, 'You had a silly dream.'

'All right, Susan. If that's what you say, I will accept that because you've never lied to me.'

'John . . . we have to talk about this . . . in person. There's probably a lot we've been keeping from each other. You know I would never do anything to hurt you . . . I'm sorry if you've been upset these last few months . . . you're a very unique man, a very special man. I realize that now. And I don't want to lose you. I love you.'

Well, that was about as mushy as Susan ever got, and while it wasn't a full confession of marital infidelity, it was something very like it, sort of like plea bargaining. I was pretty shaky, to be honest with you, and I found myself sitting on the bed in my room, my heart pounding and my mouth dry. If you've ever confronted your spouse with charges of sexual misconduct, you know the feeling. I finally said, 'All right. We'll talk when I get back.' I hung up and stared at the telephone, waiting, I guess, for it to ring, but it didn't.

You have to understand that prior to that day in court and the subsequent media exposure, I wasn't ready to confront this other issue of Susan and Frank. But now, having put my old life behind me for ever, and now that I felt good about myself, I was prepared to hear my wife tell me she had been sexually involved with Frank Bellarosa. What's more, I still loved her, and I was prepared to forgive her and start over again, because in a manner of speaking, we'd both had an affair with Frank Bellarosa, and Susan was right that this was as much my fault as hers. But Susan was not yet at the point where she could tell me it had happened or tell him it was over.

So, lacking a confession from Susan, I had to remain in that limbo state of the husband who knows but doesn't know, who can't ask for a divorce or offer to forgive, and who has to deal with the parties as if nothing were going on, lest he make a complete fool of himself.

Or maybe I could just ask Frank, 'Hey, goombah, you fucking my wife, or what?'

Later that morning, Bellarosa and I met Lenny and Vinnie with the Cadillac outside the plaza. We drove back down to Little Italy where we stopped at Bellarosa's club for espresso. The Italian Rifle Club had few similarities to The Creek, as you might guess, except that it was private and that men discussed things there that had to do with manipulating the republic for the benefit of the club members. Maybe there were more similarities than I realized.

That morning Bellarosa had a series of meetings scheduled in his club, which was actually a large storefront with a black-painted picture window, dark inside, and divided into various dim coffee rooms and private rooms.

I was pretty much ignored most of the time, and sometimes they spoke in Italian, and sometimes when someone present didn't speak any Italian, I was asked to leave the room with the words, 'You don't want to hear this, Counsellor.' I was sure they were right.

So I drank a lot of coffee and read all the morning papers and watched some old geezers playing a card game that I couldn't follow.

After an hour or so in the club, we left and got back into the car. Though there was a layer of clouds blocking the sun, the morning was getting hot, an urban heat produced by cars and people and yesterday's sun still trapped in the concrete. Country squires can tolerate only about a week in Manhattan in the summer, and I hoped we wouldn't be much longer in the city, but with this guy you didn't ask questions about times and places.

We made a stop at Ferrara's, where Bellarosa picked out a dozen pastries for Anna, which were put into a nice white box with green and red string and which Bellarosa carried to the car. I can't describe to you why the sight of this big man carrying that little box daintily by the string struck me as so civilized, but it did. It wasn't exactly Aristotle contemplating the bust of Homer, but it was a profoundly human act that made me see the man, the husband, and the father. And yes, the lover. Whereas I'd always seen Bellarosa as a man's man, I saw now that my original impression of him as a man whom women would find attractive was accurate. Well, not all women, but some women. I could see Susan, Lady Stanhope, wanting to be debased and sexually used by this insensitive barbarian. Maybe it had something to do with her seeing her mother in bed with a gardener or stableboy or whoever it was. Maybe this is something that all highborn ladies fantasize about: taking off their clothes for a man who is not their social or intellectual equal, but is simply a sexual turn-on. And why should this be such a shock to men? Half the wealthy and successful men I know have screwed their secretaries, cocktail waitresses, and even their maids. Women have libidos, too. But maybe Susan Stanhope and Frank Bellarosa had a more complex relationship.

Anyway, we spent the rest of the morning in Little Italy, Greenwich Village, and environs, making a few quick stops, sometimes for talk, sometimes for taking provisions aboard the Cadillac. The car soon smelled of cheese and baked goods, and some horrible salted codfish called *baccalà*, which I suppose couldn't be put in the trunk because of the heat. Bellarosa explained to me, 'I'm going to send all this stuff home later. This is all stuff Anna likes. You want to send something to your wife?'

It annoyed me that he always referred to Susan as my wife, instead of by her name. What did he call her when they were alone?

'You want to stop for something? Flowers or something?'

'No.'

'I'll send these pastries from Ferrara's like it was from you.'

'No.'

He shrugged.

As we headed up toward Midtown, he said to me, 'You called this morning? Everything's okay at home?'

I replied, 'Yes. How's *your* wife? You call this morning? Everything okay at home?'

'Yeah. I'm just asking you because if you got problems at home, you don't have your mind on business. And because we're friends. Right?'

'How was I yesterday in court?'

'You were fine.'

'Subject closed.'

He shrugged again and looked out the window.

We stopped at the Italian Sailor's Club on West Thirty-fourth Street, and Bellarosa went inside by himself. He came out fifteen minutes later with a brown bag and got into the car. Now what do you suppose was in that brown bag? Drugs? Money? Secret messages? No. The bag was filled with small crooked cigars. 'These are from Naples,' he said. 'You can't get them here.' He lit one up and I could see why you couldn't. I opened the window.

'You want one?'

'No.'

He passed the bag up to Vinnie and Lenny, who took a

cigar apiece and lit up. Everyone seemed happy with their little duty-free cigars. Of course, today it was cigars, tomorrow it could be something else that came out of the Sailor's Club. Interesting.

Instead of stopping for a three-hour lunch at an Italian restaurant, we stopped at an Italian sausage cart near Times Square. Bellarosa got out and greeted the vendor, an old man who hugged and kissed Bellarosa and nearly cried. Without asking us what we wanted, Bellarosa got us all hot sausage heros with peppers and onions. I said, 'Hold the mayo.' We ate outside the double-parked car as we chatted with the old vendor, and Bellarosa gave the man a hunk of goat cheese from Little Italy and three crooked cigars. I think we got the best of that deal.

If a man is known by the company he keeps, then Frank Bellarosa was sort of a populist, mixing with the masses the way the early Caesars had done, letting the common people hug and kiss him, venerate him, and lay hands on him. At the same time, he mixed with the highborn, but if the Plaza was any indication, he seemed to treat the powerful with cool contempt.

The sausage man was not tending his cart and, in fact, shooed away a few people so he could better tend to his luncheon guests, dining al fresco in expensive suits in the heat of Times Square with the Cadillac blocking traffic. What a bizarre little scene, I thought.

We wiped our fingers on paper napkins, bid our host *buon giorno*, and got back into the car. Still chewing on a mouthful of sausage, Bellarosa said to Vinnie, 'You tell Freddie to hit these guys up for another fifty cents a pound on the sausage and let them pass it on to their customers.' He said to me, 'It's a good product and everybody eats it – your Spanish, your *melanzane*, they love this shit. Where they gonna go for lunch around here? Sardi's? The coffee shops serve shit. So they eat on the street and watch the pussy go by. Right? That's worth another quarter. Right? You like the sandwich? You pay another two bits for it? Sure. So we hit the vendors for another fifty cents a pound and they pass it along. No problem.'

'Now that we've all discussed it,' I said, 'should we take a vote?'

He laughed. 'Vote? Yeah, we'll vote. Frank votes yes. End of vote.'

'Good meeting,' I said.

'Yeah.'

Actually, I was impressed with Bellarosa's attention to the smaller outposts of his empire. I suppose he believed that if he watched the price of sausage, the bigger problems would take care of themselves. He was very much a hands-on man, both in his professional life and his personal life, if you know what I mean.

We crossed the East River into the Williamsburg section of Brooklyn by way of the Williamsburg Bridge. After that, I was lost. Brooklyn is a mystery to me, and I hope it remains so. Unfortunately, I had a guide who pointed out everything to me, the way people do who think you care about their squalid little part of the world. Bellarosa said, 'There on the roof of that building is where I got my finger wet for the first time.'

I had the impression he wasn't talking about sucking his thumb. I said, 'How interesting.'

Anyway, we stopped at a beautiful old baroque church covered with black grime. 'This is my church,' Bellarosa explained. 'Santa Lucia.'

We got out of the car, went to the rectory, and knocked on the door, which was opened by an old priest, who went through the hugging and kissing routine.

Bellarosa and I were shown into a large second-floor commons room where two more elderly priests joined us and we had coffee. These people drink a lot of coffee, in case you hadn't noticed, though it's not so much the caffeine they're after, but the shared experience, sort of a wet version of breaking bread together. And wherever Frank Bellarosa went, of course, coffee was made and served, usually with something sweet.

Anyway, we had coffee, and we chatted about this and that, but not about yesterday's difficulties with the law. The three priests were old-school Italians, naturally, and didn't use their first names, so there was none of that Father Chuck and Father Buzzy nonsense. On the other hand, they all seemed to have difficult first and last names, and with their accents, it sounded as if they were all named Father Chicken Cacciatore. I called them all Father.

So the head guy was talking about how the bishop (the real bishop of the diocese) wanted to close up Santa Lucia unless it could become self-sufficient, which seemed unlikely since there were hardly enough Italian Catholics left in the parish to support it. The priest explained delicately that the Hispanic Catholics in the parish, mostly from Central America, thought that ten cents in the collection basket covered the overhead. The priest turned to me and said, 'The old people of this parish can't go to another church. They want to be close to their church, they wish to have their funeral Mass here. And of course, we have those former parishioners, such as Mrs Bellarosa, who return to Santa Lucia and who would be heartbroken if we had to close.'

Okay, Father, bottom line.

He cleared his throat. 'It costs about fifty thousand dollars a year to maintain and to heat the church and rectory, and to put food on the table here.'

I didn't reach for my wallet or anything, but while the priest was telling me this for the don's benefit, the don had scribbled out a cheque and put it on the coffee table face down.

So, after a few more minutes, we made our farewells and embraces and got our God-bless-yous, and we left.

Out on the street, Bellarosa said to me, 'Nobody can shake you down like a Catholic priest. *Madonn'*, they hit me for fifty large. But whaddaya gonna do? Ya know?'

'Just say no.'

'*No?* How ya gonna say no?'

'You shake your head and say, "No."'

'Ah, you can't do that. They know you got the money and they do a guilt thing on you.' He chuckled, then added, 'You know, I was christened at Santa Lucia, my father and mother was christened here, I was married here, Anna had the kids christened here, Frankie got married here, my old man was buried here, my mother – '

'I get the picture. I've got a church like that, too. I give five bucks a week, ten at Easter and Christmas.'

'It's different here.'

Instead of getting back into the car, Bellarosa turned and looked back at the sad old church and surveyed the mean streets around us. He said, 'I used to play stoopball on those rectory steps there. You ever play stoopball?'

'I've heard of it.'

'Yeah. The slum kids played it. What did you play? Golf?' He smiled.

'I played the stock market.'

'Yeah?' He laughed. 'Well, we played stoopball right there. Me and my friends . . .' He stayed quiet for a few seconds, then said, 'Father Chiaro – that was the old pastor you just talked to – he used to charge out of the rectory and run us off. But if he got hold of you, he'd drag you by the ears into the rectory and put you to work on some shit job. You see those doorknobs in there? They're brass, but they don't look it now. I used to have to polish those fucking knobs until they looked like gold.'

'He's still got you by the ears, Frank.'

He laughed. 'Yeah. What a sovanabeech.'

'A what?'

He smiled. 'That's the way my grandfather used to say it. *Sovanabeech.* Son of a bitch.'

'I see.' Well, I tried to picture fat little Frank Bellarosa on these streets, playing ball, making zip guns, kneeling in the confessional, getting his finger wet, kneeling in the confessional, and so on. And I could picture it, and I'm a nostalgic guy myself, so I'm partial to people who are

524

sentimental about their childhood. I guess that's a sign of middle age, right? But with Bellarosa, there was more to it, I think. I believe he knew then that he was going home for the last time, and that he had to take care of Santa Lucia so that the priests there would take care of him when the time came. There had been a few stories in the newspapers over the last ten years or so about problems with certain priests and churches providing burial services for people in Frank's line of work. I guess this frightened Frank Bellarosa, who had assumed all along that he was dealing with a church that was under direct orders from God to forgive everyone. But now people were trying to change the rules, and Bellarosa, not one to take unnecessary chances and knowing he couldn't take it with him, prepaid for his burial service at Santa Lucia. That's what I think.

Bellarosa put his hands in his pockets and looked down the intersecting street. 'In those days you could walk down this street here late at night and nobody bothered you, but a lot of the old ladies would yell at me from the windows, "Frankie, get home before your mother kills you." You think anybody says that on this street anymore?'

'I doubt it.'

'Yeah, me too. You wanna see where I lived when I was a kid?'

'Yes, I would.'

Instead of getting into the car, we walked from Santa Lucia in the heat, the way Frank Bellarosa must have done many years before. Lenny and Vinnie tailed behind us in the Cadillac. The area around the church was mostly black, and people glanced at us, but they'd probably witnessed similar scenes, and they knew this was a prodigal son with a gun, so they went about their business while Frank went about his.

We stopped in front of a burned-out five-storey brick tenement, and Bellarosa said, 'I lived on the top floor there. It was a hundred degrees in the summer, but nice and warm in the winter with those big steam radiators that banged. I shared a room with two brothers.'

I didn't respond.

He went on, 'Then my uncle took me out of here and sent me to La Salle, and the dorms looked like a Park Avenue penthouse to me. I started to understand that there was a world outside of Williamsburg. You know?' He was quiet again, then said, 'But I got to tell you, looking back on this place in the 1950s, I was happy here.'

'We all were.'

'Yeah.' We got back into the car and drove some blocks to a better street, and he showed me the five-storey brownstone where he and Anna had spent much of their married life. He said, 'I still own the building. I made apartments on each floor and I got a bunch of old people in there. I got an old aunt in there. They pay what they can to the church. You know? The church takes care of the whole thing. It's a good building.'

I asked, 'Are you trying to get into heaven?'

'Yeah, but not this week.' He laughed, then added, 'Everything's got an angle, Counsellor.'

We drove around the old Italian section of Williamsburg, which had never been very large, and what was left of Italian Williamsburg seemed rather forlorn, but there were stops to be made, and the trip was not all nostalgia, but partly business. As I said, it must be difficult to run a crime empire when you can't use the telephone, or even the mail for that matter. And this fact obviously necessitated a lot of driving and quick stops to call on people. Frank was the three-minute Mafia manager.

After Williamsburg, we drove into more lively Italian neighbourhoods in Bensonhurst, Bay Ridge, and Coney Island, where we made more stops and saw more people, mostly in restaurants and in the back of retail stores and in social clubs. I was quite honestly amazed at the number of branch offices and affiliates of Bellarosa, Inc. – or would one say franchises and chain outlets? More amazing, there didn't seem to be any written lists of these stops. Bellarosa would just say a few words to Lenny and Vinnie, such as, 'Let's see Pasquale at the fish place,' and they'd drive somewhere.

I could hardly believe that their pea-size brains could retain so many locations, but I guess they had good incentives to do their job.

We left Brooklyn and went into Ozone Park, Queens, which is also an Italian neighbourhood. Frank had some relatives there, and we stopped at their row house and played boccie ball in an alleyway with a bunch of his old goombahs who wore baggy pants and three-day whiskers. Then we all drank homemade red wine on a back porch, and it was awful, awful stuff, tannic and sour. But one of the old men put ice in my wine and mixed it with cream soda, of all things. Then he sliced peaches into my glass. Frank had his wine the same way. It was sort of like Italian sangria, I guess, or wine coolers, and I had an idea to market the concoction and sell it to trendy places like Buddy's Hole where the clientele could drink it with their grass clippings. Ozone Park Goombah Spritzers. No? Yes?

Anyway, we moved on into the late afternoon, making a few more stops at modest-looking frame houses in other Queens neighbourhoods.

Frank Bellarosa had entertained the movers and shakers of his world, the chiefs and the 'made men', at the Plaza Hotel. Now he was going out into the streets to talk to his constituents, like a politician running for office. But unlike a candidate, I never heard him make any promises, and unlike a Mafia don, I never heard him make a threat. He was just 'showing his face around', which seemed to be an expression with these people that I kept hearing. Showing your face around must have a lot of subtle connotations, and must be important if Bellarosa was doing it.

The man had a natural instinct for power, I'll say that for him. He comprehended on some level that real power is not based on terror, or even on loyalty to an abstract idea or organization. Real power was based on personal loyalty, especially the loyalty of the masses to the person of don Bellarosa, as I witnessed with the sausage vendor and with everyone else we'd stopped to see. Truly the man was an intuitive and charismatic leader – the last of the great dons.

And as evil as he was, I nearly felt sorry for him, surrounded now by enemies within and without. But I had also felt sorry for proud Lucifer in *Paradise Lost* when he was brought down by God and heaven's host of goody-goody androgynous angels. There must be a serious flaw in my character.

We headed back to Manhattan after dark. New York is truly a city of ethnic diversity, but I don't have much occasion or desire to hang around with the ethnics. However, I have to admit that I was intrigued by the Italian subculture that I had caught a glimpse of that day. It was a world that seemed both alive and dying at the same time, and I remarked to Bellarosa in the car back to Manhattan, 'I thought all that Italian stuff was a thing of the past.'

He seemed to understand what I meant and replied, 'It is in the past. It was past when my old man took me around on Saturdays to sit with the goombahs and sip wine and talk. It's always in the past.'

The old immigrant cultures, I reflected, still exerted a powerful influence on their people and on American society. But truly they were losing their identity as they became homogenized, and ironically they were losing their power as they filled the vacuum created by the so-called decline of the Wasp. But more important, back there in the shadows, somewhere in the outer boroughs, were the new immigrants, the future that neither Frank Bellarosa nor I understood or wished to contemplate.

As the car approached the skyline of Manhattan, Bellarosa said to me, 'You have a good time today?'

'It was interesting.'

'Yeah. Sometimes I have to just get out and see these people. You know? To see that everybody's still out there. I've been losing touch, kind of holed up at Alhambra. You can't do that. You go out there and if somebody wants to take a pop at you, then at least you went down out on the street, and not holed up someplace waiting for them to corner you. You know?'

'Yes, I do. But do you need a lawyer along while you're tempting fate?'

'No. I need a friend.'

I had several sarcastic replies right on the tip of my tongue, but I said nothing, which said it all.

He added, 'I'm gonna make you into an honorary Italian like Jack Weinstein. You like that?'

'Sure, as long as that doesn't make me an honorary target.'

He sort of laughed, but I think he was finding less humour in the subject of his assassination. He did say, however, 'I talked to some people. You got nothing to worry about. You're still a civilian.'

Great news. And I trusted these people, right? Well at least they probably all belonged to the rifle club and were good marksmen. I surely hoped so.

CHAPTER 31

We went back to the Plaza Hotel. Bellarosa gave Vinnie and Lenny the night off, and Frank and I ordered dinner in the suite.

As we ate at the table in the dining area, we made small talk, mostly about vegetables and real estate. I sliced my steak, and as I did so, I wondered what new and exciting course my life would take if I plunged my steak knife into Bellarosa's heart.

I think he was reading my thoughts because he said, 'You know, Counsellor, you're probably thinking that your life is getting fucked up and you think I fucked it up for you. Wrong. You fucked yourself up and you did it before you ever laid eyes on me.'

'Maybe. But you're not part of the solution.'

'Sure I am. I helped you get rid of all the bullshit in your life. So now you got to go on.'

'Thank you.'

'Yeah. You think I'm some kind of dumb greaseball. Wrong again.'

I was getting a little annoyed with this guy now. I said, 'Stupid people think you're stupid. I know better.'

He smiled. 'Yeah. It's an old Italian trick. Claudius did it to save his life before he became emperor. There's a guy in my business up in the Bronx – you know the guy – he's been acting simple-minded for ten years because the feds are on his case. You know? But Ferragamo *is* stupid and he thinks I'm stupid, so I surprise him every time, but he's too stupid to get it.' He laughed.

We went back to our steaks and didn't speak until coffee, then he asked me, 'You ever play dumb?'

'Sometimes.'

'Like, I mean, you *know* something, but you don't let on you know. You hold on to it until the right time. You don't go off hot and get yourself hurt. You wait.'

I replied, 'Sometimes I *never* let on. Sometimes I just let the other guy go crazy wondering if I know.'

He nodded appreciatively. 'Yeah. Like what, for instance? Give me a for instance.'

We looked at each other across the table, and I replied, 'Like the bullshit with the IRS, Frank. You told Melzer to go to his friends in the IRS and see if they could find something on me, and they did. Then you turn me on to Melzer, who fixes things for me, and I owe you a favour. You're a real pal.'

He played around with his dessert and didn't reply.

I asked, 'But what if I hadn't come to you with the problem?'

He shrugged.

'Then,' I said, 'you'd find another problem for me. Or maybe I'd need another kind of favour from you, like the variance for the stables. I'm not sure that was a coincidence or a set-up, but apparently you have my wife's ear, so you can get to me through her.'

The man obviously knew there was trouble between Susan and me, and if he had a conscience at all, it was a guilty one.

In fact, he actually looked uncomfortable. I mean, beyond class differences and political differences, and ethnic and racial tensions, and all the other problems that people have with one another in society, the most primitive and elemental cause of violence, murder, and mayhem is sexual possessiveness. To put it more simply, people get angry when other people are fucking or trying to fuck their mate. Anyway, Bellarosa must have been feeling a little uneasy or he wouldn't have prodded me into the subject to see my reaction. He looked at me, waiting to see, I think, if I was actually going to broach the subject of him and Susan. But since it was he who was feeling a little uneasy, not me, I decided to leave him hanging awhile longer.

Without a word, I stood and went to the sideboard on which were a few dozen telephone messages, one of which was from Susan advising me that she'd changed her telephone number. I suppose the media were getting to her, not to mention our friends and relatives. I threw the message with the new phone number in the wastebasket and left the suite.

Down in the lobby, I was accosted by none other than Jenny Alvarez, the lady in red, except that she was not wearing red that evening. 'Hello, Mr Sutter,' she said.

She was, in fact, wearing a black silk dress, sort of an evening dress, I guess, as if she'd just come from dinner. She really looked good, and I wanted to ask her if we'd spent the night together, but it seemed like a silly question, so I just replied, 'Hello.'

'Can I buy you a drink?' she asked.

'I don't drink.'

'Coffee?'

'I'm in a bit of a hurry.'

She seemed hurt, and I began to believe we really had spent the night together. I'm a lot of things, but a cad isn't one of them, so I accepted the offer of a drink, and we went into the Oak Bar and got a table. She ordered a Scotch and soda, and I made it two. She said, 'I saw the statements you made to the newspapers this morning.'

'I didn't know TV journalists read the papers. Or read at all.'

'Don't be a snot.'

'Okay.'

'Anyway, I'd like to do an interview with you.'

'I don't think so.'

'It won't take long. We can do it right here in the Plaza, live for the eleven-o'clock news.'

'I'd be dead for the morning news.'

She laughed as though this were a joke. This was not a joke. She said, 'Could you get Mr Bellarosa to join you?'

'I think not.'

'Maybe we could tape an in-depth interview and run it on our nightly news show at eleven thirty. That's a national show. That would give you both an opportunity to present your side of the case.'

'We're actually going to present our side in court.'

So we went on in this vein for a while, Ms Alvarez thinking I was playing hard to get, and I, to be honest, not blowing her off because I was enjoying the company. She had nice full lips.

We ordered a second round. She could not comprehend, of course, that not everyone in America wanted to be on television. Finally, growing a little weary with her obsessive badgering, I said, 'I had a dream last night that I slept with you.'

She seemed like a tough sort of lady who'd heard it all before, but this took her by surprise, and she actually got flustered. I was smitten. I said, 'Look, Ms Alvarez – can I call you Jenny?'

'Yes.'

'Look, Jenny, you must know that these people don't appear TV shows. You have a better chance of getting the Premier of the Soviet Union on your show than getting Frank Bellarosa.'

She nodded, but only, I think, to get her brain working better. She said, 'But *you* are not in the Mafia –'

'There is no Mafia.'

'*You* can talk to us. Mr Ferragamo has agreed to come on the show – '

'He'd do a sitcom if the ratings were high enough.'

She giggled. 'Come on, Mr Sutter . . . John. Don't you see how this can help your client?'

So we began round three with another round of drinks. She went on for a while, making a good case for television exposure, but I'm afraid I wasn't paying much attention. I said, 'It was a very realistic dream.'

She replied, 'Look, if it means getting you on the air . . .'

I paid more attention. 'Yes?'

'Well . . . we can scramble you.'

'Excuse me?'

'You know. Scramble your face and voice. No one will know it's you.'

'Unless you introduce me by name.'

'Don't be silly. What would be the point of – ?'

'You had on that red dress.'

'The scrambled interview would have a different slant, of course. Not John Sutter as attorney, but as an unidentified source. We've done that before with organized crime reports. You'd talk about – '

'Do you have an apartment in town?'

Round three ended in a draw, and we went to round four, both optimistic. At seven bucks a pop in the Oak Bar, one of us was down fifty-six dollars already, plus tax and tip. There was a bowl of really good smoked almonds on the next table, but our table had a bowl of those disgusting goldfish pretzels. They're all over the place.

She went on again, glancing at her watch a few times. I asked, 'Are you doing the news tonight?'

'I don't think I have a story tonight since you're not co-operating.'

'Do you get paid anyway?'

'Maybe. Look, at least consider the news show at eleven thirty. We have a show put together, but we need a focus.'

'Does that mean you won't scramble my face?'

'I mean an *angle*. I want someone to speak intelligently about different aspects of this case. I don't want any more so-called experts. I want someone who can give the American public the other side of this issue.'

'What other side?'

'The constitutionality of RICO, the government's harassment of certain ethnic groups under the guise of justice, Ferragamo's statements about a possible gang war between Hispanics and Italians. That sort of thing. I really want to get a different view on this thing.'

'Sounds like a good show. I'll watch it.'

'Let's go talk to Mr Bellarosa. See if he wants to be interviewed. See if he wants his attorney to go on.'

'Stay here.' I stood. 'See if you can get a bowl of smoked almonds.' I went out to a house phone and called the suite, but Bellarosa's line was busy. I had no intention of presenting Ms Alvarez's offer to him, but I wanted to see if he was still in. I went back to the Oak Bar, sat, and informed Ms Alvarez, 'He says no. And no means no.' She had gotten the smoked almonds and I took a handful.

'Then how about you?' she asked. 'Will you go on the air?'

'What's in it for me?'

'I take off the red dress.'

'Before or after I go on the air?'

She looked at her watch. 'Before.' She added, 'Fuck me, but don't screw me.'

We both smiled. Well, dreams do come true if you let them. But this one looked like trouble. I stood. 'Sorry. I can't live up to my end of the deal. But it's been fun.' I left her with the tab.

In the lobby, I checked for messages, and there were a few from TV, press, and radio people. Most criminal attorneys would parlay this opportunity into fame and fortune. But mob attorneys such as Jack Weinstein and John Sutter had to satisfy themselves with 'No comment' and tainted money

534

that could be seized under the RICO Act. Hey, who said this was going to be good for my career?

Anyway, I turned toward the lobby doors, intending to take the walk I had intended to take before, but once again I was waylaid by Jenny Alvarez. She said, 'Let me ask you a question. A personal question, off the record.'

'I like the regular missionary position, but I'm open to anything.'

'What I want to know is, why did you get involved with Frank Bellarosa?'

'It's a long story. Truly it is.'

'I mean, I saw your estate out there on Long Island. My God, I didn't think people still lived like that.'

'I live in the guesthouse on the estate. You got that wrong on TV. And what difference does it make where I live?'

'It makes all the difference. We're talking TV, John. Entertainment. You're a star. You look like a star. You act like a star. You're well dressed, you carry yourself well, and you speak extremely well. You're a class act.'

'Thank you.'

'Even if you did stick me with the tab.'

'That's the classiest thing I've done all week. Look . . . Jenny, you're very attractive, and I'd like to take you upstairs, but I think you're giving me a line of bull because you want something from me, and it's not sex. And I can't deliver, not sex or information. I'm a faithful husband, plus I'm impotent and simpleminded. So – '

'What's the matter?'

Coming from the direction of the Oak Bar, staring at me, were Lenny and Vinnie. I guess they had seen me in the bar and wondered why I was having a drink with a TV reporter. Jenny Alvarez's face is well-known in New York, and even cretins like Lenny and Vinnie watch the news. Anyway, Cretin One and Cretin Two were making stupid movements with their heads, indicating they wanted me to join them.

Ms Alvarez inquired, 'Who are those men?'

'Those are my law clerks.' Well, the best way to cover

myself, of course, was to make it clear to Lenny and Vinnie that my intentions in speaking to Ms Alvarez were sexual and not traitorous. How's that for a rationalization? So, I put my arm around her and led her to the elevators. I said, 'Let's have a drink in my room.'

'All right.'

Lenny and Vinnie got on the elevator with us. As we rode up, I said to my pals, 'This is Jenny Alvarez. She's a famous TV reporter.'

They glanced at each other. Vinnie asked, 'The don want to see her?'

'No, I want to see her. Alone, and I don't want to be bothered.'

They both smirked, leered, and drooled. Class acts.

We got out on the eighth floor. Lenny unlocked the door to the suite, and we all entered. Bellarosa was lying on the couch, watching TV with his shoes off.

Jenny Alvarez went right up to him and introduced herself as he stood. Bellarosa said, 'Oh, yeah. You're the lady who gave this guy here a hard time. You friends now?'

She smiled. 'Yes, we are.'

Well, the next thing, of course, was that she was going to start hammering poor Frank for an interview. Right? Wrong. She turned out to be the class act of the evening. She said, 'John invited me for a drink. I hope I'm not intruding on business.'

Bellarosa replied, 'Nah. We're on vacation.'

I said to Ms Alvarez, 'Let's go to my room.' I snagged a bottle of Scotch and a bucket of ice from the bar, and she took two glasses and a bottle of soda.

I showed her to my room, but as I began to follow her in, Bellarosa tapped me on the shoulder. He closed the door to my room and said to me, 'You couldn't get yourself a house whore? You have to bring this TV broad up here?'

I replied tersely, 'It's my business who I spend my free time with. But to set the record straight, my relationship with that woman is and will remain platonic.'

Bellarosa glanced at the Scotch and ice bucket in my hands and smiled. I guess that did seem like a pretty idiotic statement from one man of the world to another. However, I added, 'And it's not a business relationship either.'

'Yeah? So no pillow talk. Okay? Watch what you say to her. Understand?'

I stepped toward the door, but he didn't move aside. Instead, he said, 'What's on your mind, Counsellor? What's bugging you?'

'If you spoke to my wife tonight, and I assume you did, then you know.'

He stayed silent a moment, then added. 'Yeah. Okay. I spoke to her. But you got that all wrong. That's a bad thing to be thinking about. That's a very dangerous thing, when a guy gets something like that in his head. I've seen that kind of thing get people hurt and killed. So you just put that out of your head.' He grabbed my shoulders and gave me a shake. 'Okay?'

So I guess I was outvoted, two to one, on the question of a sexual triangle. I said, 'All right, Frank. Subject closed. Open the door for me.'

He opened my bedroom door, and carrying the ice bucket and Scotch, I went inside and kicked the door shut, then put the Scotch and bucket on a cocktail table.

Jenny Alvarez said, 'Are you sure I'm not interrupting business?'

'I'm sure. Make yourself comfortable. Have a seat.'

We sat in the two facing club chairs in the corner with the drinks on the cocktail table between us.

As I put ice in our glasses, I noticed that my hand was a little unsteady. Confronting one's wife with an accusation of adultery was a little tense, but confronting the other man, especially when the guy was a killer, was not one of life's better moments. But I felt strangely at peace, as if I'd gotten rid of a great burden and put it on the people who'd stuck me with it in the first place. I mean, if you analysed it with cold logic, it really wasn't my problem, unless I chose to make it so. Still, I knew that the cold logic would eventually give way to more basic feelings such as heartache, pain, betrayal, jealousy, and other standard marital miseries. But tonight, I felt on top of things, and I had a drinking companion.

Jenny Alvarez said, 'Nice suite. Crime pays.'

I replied, 'Thanks for laying off Bellarosa.'

'I came up here to have a drink with you.'

'Right.' Cynic though I am, I believed her, and it felt good to believe what someone said for a change. I mixed us Scotch and sodas, and we touched glasses and drank. I have to be honest with you; I was nervous. I said, 'Don't you have to be on the air or something?'

'You're my only assignment tonight. But since you're not going on the air, neither am I. But I'll call in later.' She added, 'Late enough so they can't get me on something else before airtime. So I'm free tonight. Feels good.'

Well, I mean, she rearranged her whole schedule, you know, so she could have a drink with me. So what was I supposed to do? Kick her out after one drink? Get room service to deliver a Monopoly game? I cleared my throat. 'I'm very flattered.'

She smiled. Oh, those lips. I have to tell you, I'm not usually into Latin beauties, but this woman was absolutely gorgeous. She had a soft brown complexion, dark eyes that sparkled, and thick black hair that cascaded over her shoulders. When she smiled, she had dimpled cheeks that I wanted to pinch.

She said, 'You're separated, I understand.'

'I hadn't heard that.'

'Well, I did.'

'From whom?'

'People out where you live.'

'Is that a fact? I didn't even know that.'

She smiled. 'Most men would just say yes to that question under these circumstances.'

'I'm not most men. I'm into truth. Are *you* married?'

'I was. I had a baby on TV. Remember? Two years ago.'

I seemed to recall some mawkish and tasteless coverage of the progress of her pregnancy and final delivery. But I don't watch much TV news, and until now I didn't even realize that this was the same woman. I replied, 'I do remember that. TV cameras in the delivery room. Sort of vulgar.'

She shrugged. 'Not for television.'

'I also seem to recall a proud father.'

'I'm divorced now.'

'So no more babies on television.'

She smiled. 'Not for a while.'

We chatted a bit, but I watched my consumption of Scotch, in the event I had to rise to the occasion. I can't do it when I'm loaded, which is frustrating because that's usually when I want to do it the most. Alcohol is a cruel drug.

I said, 'Look, I asked you up here to cover myself with those two goons. Understand?'

'I think so. Do you want me to fake orgasmic noises, then leave?'

'Well . . . no. I enjoy your company. But . . . I just wanted you to know why I invited you here.'

'So now I know. Do you know why I accepted the invitation?'

'You find me interesting.'

'That's right. Very interesting. Intriguing. You intrigue me.'

'Well, that's good news. You may not believe this, but I used to be dull.'

'That's not possible.' She smiled. 'When was that?'

'Oh, back in March, April. I was really dull. That's why my wife left me.'

'You said you didn't know anything about that.'

'Well, I haven't been home in a few days. Maybe I should call my answering service.'

But I didn't. We talked about this and that, bantered and teased, but we never talked about Frank Bellarosa. However, it occurred to me that there was more than one way to put a knife into his heart. I mean, I could use this woman as a conduit to the news media. I could remain anonymous, and she would vouch for the reliability of her source. I could feed

539

the media all sorts of things that could put Frank Bellarosa into jail or into the grave. And that would take me off the hook for the perjured alibi, and Bellarosa would be out of my life. I mention this because it did cross my mind. I guess I had been hanging around Bellarosa too long. But I was determined not to let my life become obsessed with vendetta the way his was. Whatever he had done to me, he had to live with it, and perhaps one day, he would answer for it. *Vengeance is mine, saith the Lord.* So I dismissed my thoughts of revenge (for the moment) and got back to the business at hand. I said to Jenny Alvarez, 'There's no payoff, you know. I mean, even if you spend the night, I'm not telling you anything.'

'I told you I'm here because I want to be with you. I don't really give sex for stories and you don't really proposition women who need something from you. That was a game downstairs.'

'And it's another game up here. And I'm out of practice.'

'You're doing fine. I'm still interested. By the way, did you see yourself on TV?'

'Sure did.'

'Your hair was messy.'

'I know. And my tie looked the wrong colour, but it wasn't. I can show you the tie.'

'Oh, I believe you. That happens on TV sometimes.'

The phone rang, but I didn't answer it. Jenny made a call to her studio and told them she was through for the night. I had a club soda, and she had another Scotch. We both kicked our shoes off at some point. There was a TV in the bedroom and we watched her news show at eleven. The Bellarosa story got a minute, mostly reports about the published stories in the newspapers, including my press statements. Ferragamo, who was good at the ten-second sound bite, said, 'We are investigating Mr Bellarosa's alibi for the day in question, and if we find evidence that contradicts that alibi, we will ask that bail be rescinded, and we will take Mr Bellarosa into custody again, and we will consider action against the individual who supplied the alibi.'

Ten seconds on the head. The man was a pro.

Ms Alvarez inquired, 'He means you, doesn't he?'

I replied, 'I think so.'

'What sort of action? What can they do to you?'

'Nothing. I was telling the truth.'

'So the five other witnesses were lying? No, don't answer. No business. It's a habit. Sorry.' She seemed lost in thought, then blurted out, 'But it just doesn't make *sense*, John.'

'Does it make sense that Frank Bellarosa would commit murder in broad daylight?'

'No, but . . . you're sure you saw him?'

'Is this on the record?'

'No, off the record.'

'Okay . . . I'm positive it was him.'

She smiled. 'If you're going to keep talking business, I'm leaving.'

'My apologies.'

The sports came on, and I was delighted to discover that the Mets trounced Montreal again, nine to three. 'They're going all the way,' I said.

'Maybe. But the Yankees will take the first four of the Series.'

'The Yankees? They're lucky if they finish the season.'

'Baloney,' she said. 'Have you *seen* the Yankees this year?'

'There's nothing to see.'

We discussed this for a few minutes, and though I could tell she was knowledgeable, it was obvious that she was very biased. I explained, 'They don't have one long-ball hitter on the team.'

'Pitching is the name of the game today, buddy, and the Yankees have real depth in the bullpen.'

This was very frustrating. I tried to explain the facts of baseball life to her, but she said, 'Look, I can get us into the press box at Yankee Stadium. You come and see the Yankees play, then we can discuss this intelligently.'

541

'I wouldn't go to the Bronx if you paid me. But I'll watch a Yankee game with you on TV.'

'Good. I want you to watch them against Detroit next week.'

Well, anyway, it was a good night, and we had fun, and the next morning I felt a little better than I had the morning before. *Capisce?*

CHAPTER 32

We spent a few more days at the Plaza, but neither Frank nor I ever mentioned or alluded to the subject of my wife's being his mistress. But I could tell he was still burdened by the subject, and he could tell I was not. I don't mean to suggest I was playing with him; he was not a man to be played with. But apparently he had some human feelings like the rest of us mortals, and I sensed he felt he'd gone beyond the bounds of even Machiavellian behaviour and crossed into actual sin. Well, Father what's-his-name could issue him a quick absolution over the phone. 'Say two Hail Marys, Frank, when you get a chance. See you at Communion.'

Anyway, on one of those days at the Plaza, I had lunch with Jack Weinstein, whom I took a liking to. On another day, I called Alphonse Ferragamo, whom I had taken a disliking to. But I was nice to Alphonse, as per my client's orders, and Mr Ferragamo and I agreed to fight fair and clean, but we were both lying.

Alphonse – not me – brought up the subject of my client's co-operating in other matters of interest to the Justice Department in exchange for Justice dropping the charge of murder. I replied, 'He's not guilty of murder.'

Mr Ferragamo informed me, 'Well, we think he is. But I'll tell you what. I'll talk to Washington about a blanket immunity for Bellarosa if he wants to talk.'

'How about absolution?'

Ferragamo chuckled. 'That's between him and his priest.

I'm talking immunity from prosecution for good information.'

Good information? What kind of information did the stupid son of a bitch think the don of dons had – the location of a bookie joint in Staten Island? Bellarosa had plenty of good information; he just wasn't going to give it to the Justice Department.

'Immunity on anything he testifies about under oath,' said Alphonse, which is not quite the same as blanket immunity in exchange for unsworn information. This guy played it slick. I thought a moment. If, in fact, Frank Bellarosa squealed, the Mafia in New York would be crippled for years, maybe for ever. And perhaps for that reason alone, his *paesanos* wanted him dead. He simply had too much information and he had a good memory.

I said to Alphonse, 'Mr Ferragamo, my client knows nothing about organized crime. But if he did, I think he'd rather speak to the State Attorney General than to you.'

This got Alphonse a little worked up. The nice thing about a federal form of government is that you can play off one level of government against another. They taught me that in civics class. Well, they didn't, but they should have. Alphonse said, 'That's not a good idea, Mr Sutter. That won't get your client off the hook with the United States Government.'

'And co-operating with you won't get my client off the hook with the New York State government.'

'Well . . . let me work on a joint immunity sort of thing. Would that be what you're looking for?'

'Maybe. And we have six parking violations in the city. We want those fixed, too.'

When I heard him force a laugh, I knew I had him by the short hairs. He said, 'So you present this possibility to your client, Mr Sutter. You seem a bright and reasonable man. Maybe a man like you could convince your client to make a really smart move.'

'I'll tell him what we discussed.' You have to understand that every prosecutor in America would like to get just one break like that in a lifetime; a top-level bad guy who was willing to sing for a year into a tape recorder and rat out a thousand other bad guys. To tell you the truth, it *was* a good deal for Frank. Ferragamo, in effect, was offering Frank Bellarosa his life. But very few of these *paesanos* made deals, and Frank Bellarosa was the last man in America you would approach with a government offer. But Alphonse was asking, and I had to make sure he was offering the real thing, and it was my duty to pass it on. I said to the U.S. Attorney, 'Meanwhile, we really want a quick trial date, Mr Ferragamo, or I have to start complaining to the press.'

'My case is ready, Mr Sutter. My office is working on a date.'

Bullshit. 'Fine. When can I speak to the government witnesses?'

'Soon.'

Horseshit. 'Thank you.'

Understand that U.S. Attorneys don't often speak directly to defence lawyers, and when they do, they're a bit arrogant and bullying. But Mr Ferragamo had probably been reading about John Whitman Sutter in the newspapers, and he must have gotten the impression that I was someone with power, and he was being nice to me at least until he had me checked out. Also, of course, he wanted me to get Frank to sell out. But there was the matter of my perjury, which must have perplexed him. I said to Alphonse, 'I saw you on TV the other night, Mr Ferragamo, and I didn't appreciate the inference you made that I was lying about my client's whereabouts.'

'I didn't actually say you were lying, nor did I use your name. I said we are investigating the alibi.'

'Meaning you're sending Justice Department investigators around to my community and my offices to see if anyone can tell you where *I* was on January fourteenth of this year. I don't like that.'

'Be that as it may, Mr Sutter, that is how I must proceed.' He added, 'It may have simply been a case of mistaken identity on your part. Correct?'

'I know whom I saw.'

'Well, if you're willing to say that, and ten years in jail for perjury doesn't frighten you, then I suppose you know where you were on January fourteenth. That was the day before you flew to Florida for vacation, wasn't it?'

Mamma mia, first the IRS, then this guy. Why was everyone so intent on getting me into a federal prison? It must be my attitude. I replied, 'You're wasting your time and the taxpayers' money, Mr Ferragamo. But I respect your thoroughness and diligence.'

'Thank you. Please think about what I've said. Whatever we can work out for your client, we can also work out for you.'

I bit my lip, my tongue, and a pencil, and replied, 'Thank you for your time.'

Anyway, I spoke to Jack Weinstein in his Midtown office the next day, as you don't talk about these things on the telephone. I outlined what Alphonse Ferragamo had said and added, 'I know what Frank's answer is going to be, Jack, but this is perhaps his one last chance to save his life, and to start a new life.'

Weinstein stayed silent a few minutes, then said to me, 'Okay, John, I'm Ferragamo and I have you for perjury and you're looking at maybe ten in a federal prison. Okay, what I want from you is all the information you have on your friends and relatives and business partners that can put them away for cheating on their taxes, for playing fast and loose with SEC rules, for doing a little coke and marijuana, maybe for price-fixing, and for all those other little white-collar things that you winked at over the years. Okay, so your partners will go to jail, your wife's family goes to jail, *your* family goes to jail, your old school buddies go to jail, and you go free. What do you say, John?'

'I say fuck you, Alphonse.'

'Precisely. And it goes deeper than that with those people,

my friend. It's some kind of ancient distrust of government, some primitive code of honour and of silence. *Capisce?*'

'Yes, but the world has changed, Jack. Really it has.'

'I know. But nobody's told these people yet. You go tell Frank the world has changed and tell him to give up every last *paesano* he knows. Go tell him.'

I stood to leave. 'I suppose if Frank Bellarosa plays by the old rules, then he holds the old world together.'

'I think that's it.' He added, 'But you do have to tell him what Ferragamo said. Schedule about two minutes for that conversation.'

'Right.'

'Hey, how does "Weinstein and Sutter" sound?'

Not real terrific, Jack. But I smiled and replied, 'How about "Sutter, Weinstein and Melzer"?'

He laughed. '*Melzer?* I wouldn't share a match with that guy.'

I left Weinstein's office knowing that despite my ambivalent feelings about Frank Bellarosa's being alive, well, and free, I had done my job.

But to be certain, I did present Ferragamo's offer to Bellarosa. However, I didn't need a whole two minutes because after about thirty seconds, Bellarosa said to me, 'Fuck him.'

'That's your final decision?'

'Fuck him and fuck his dog. Who the hell does he think he's dealing with?'

'Well, he just took a shot at it. Don't take it personally. He has a job to do.'

'Fuck him and fuck his job.'

Pride goeth before the fall. Right?

Anyway, Frank and I and Lenny and Vinnie drove to the rifle club one night. We went down to the basement with a bunch of other sportsmen, all armed with revolvers and automatics, and we blasted away at paper targets and drank wine all night. Jolly fun, almost like bird shooting out in the Hamptons, lacking only a beautiful autumn landscape, tweedy old gentlemen, vintage sherry, and birds. But not bad for Manhattan.

Lenny and Vinnie, as it turned out, were really good shots, which I suppose I should have known. But I discovered it the hard way after losing about two hundred dollars to them on points.

So there I was at a Mafia shooting range, blasting away at paper targets with my wife's boyfriend and his Mafia pals, wondering if perhaps I should have taken in a movie instead. Anyway, we were all a little pie-eyed from the wine, and the shots were getting wilder, and one of the club members presented Bellarosa with a silhouette target on which someone had sketched in the features of Alphonse Ferragamo. The drawing was not Michelangelo quality, but it wasn't bad, and you could identify Alphonse with the owl eyes, aquiline nose, thin lips, and all that. Frank hung the target and put four out of six rounds through its heart at thirty feet, much to everyone's delight. It was not bad shooting considering he'd had enough wine to make him unsteady on his feet. But the whole incident made me a little uncomfortable.

The next few days passed with phone calls and meetings, mostly in the suite. I had expected a man like Bellarosa to have a girlfriend, or many girlfriends, or at least to get someone for a night. But I saw no signs of impropriety during the time we were at the Plaza. Maybe he was being faithful to his wife and his mistress.

As for my impropriety, Bellarosa said to me, 'Hey, I don't mind you bring women up here, but no more lady reporters. She's just trying to get something out of you.'

'No, she just likes my company.'

'Hey, I know that type. They use their twats to get ahead. You don't find that type in my business.'

Indeed, no one in Frank's business had female genitalia. If the government couldn't get him on murder or racketeering, maybe they could nail him on discriminatory hiring.

He went on, 'I'm telling ya, Counsellor, I'd rather see you talking to the devil than some *puttan'* who's trying to make a name for herself.'

Well, what was I going to say? That I was infatuated with Jenny Alvarez and it was strictly personal? I mean, it was hard for me to hold the moral high ground after dragging Ms Alvarez and a bottle of Scotch into my room. You know? But did I have to listen to a sermon from Frank Bellarosa? Maybe I did.

The Bishop went on, 'Men's business is men's business. Women don't play by the same rules.'

'Neither do men,' I informed him.

'Yeah. But some do. I try to keep my business in the family. You know? My own kind. That's why I had to make you an honorary Italian.' He laughed.

'Am I Sicilian or a Neapolitan?'

He laughed again. 'I'll make you a Roman because you're a pain in the ass.'

'I'm honoured.'

'Good.'

Indeed, everyone in Frank's world was male, and nearly all of them were Italian, and most of them were of Sicilian ancestry or from the city or region of Naples, as Bellarosa's family was. This did make the rules of behaviour and business easier, but there weren't many outside ideas that penetrated this closed world.

Jack Weinstein's roots, though, were obviously not southern Italian, and he was perhaps Bellarosa's link to the outside. I had learned, incidentally, that Weinstein's family and Bellarosa's family had known one another in Williamsburg. That section of Brooklyn, you should understand, was not predominantly Italian, but was mostly German, Jewish, and a little Irish. A real melting pot, to use an inaccurate term, since no one mixed much, let alone melted. However, because of the proximities of other cultures, the Williamsburg immigrants were not quite as insular as the immigrants in other areas of New York, who created tight little worlds. Thus, the

Williamsburg Italians, such as those around Santa Lucia, went to school with and even made friends with non-Italians. This information came from Mr Bellarosa, who didn't use the words *proximity* and *insular,* but I understood what he was saying. Anyway, he and Weinstein went back a lot of years, which I found interesting, and, like me, Jack Weinstein did not want to be, nor could he ever be, under Mafia constitutional law, the don. Thus, Weinstein was Bellarosa's Henry Kissinger, if you'll accept that analogy. So how did I fit into the Bellarosa crime family? Well, I was the noblest Roman of them all.

We checked out of the Plaza on Sunday and returned to Long Island in a three-car convoy, each car packed with Italian men and Italian food. I was in the middle car with Bellarosa, and the interior smelled of ripening cheese and cigars. I didn't know if I would have to boil my clothes or burn them.

Regarding Susan, she hadn't called again; at least she hadn't called *me* again. And I never did return her call and couldn't if I wanted to since I'd thrown away her new unlisted number. So, to be honest, I was a little tense about walking through the front door.

Bellarosa said to me, 'The girls will be happy to see us.'

I didn't reply.

'They probably thought we were having a good time in the city. Whenever you go away on business, they think you're having a ball. Meantime, you're busting your ass to make a buck. Right?'

'Right.'

'Anyway, Anna's cooking all my favourite things tonight.' Whereupon he rattled off all his favourite things in this sort of singsong voice that Italians use when talking about food. I actually recognized a few of the things. I'm an honorary Italian. Anyway, this food talk must have made him hungry because he ripped open a bag of *biscotti* and unwrapped a hunk of cheese that smelled like gym socks. He borrowed a stiletto from Vinnie and went to work on the cheese. Executive lunch. He asked, 'Want some?'

'No, thanks.'

'You know what a garbage truck is called in an Italian neighbourhood?'

'No, I don't.'

'Meals on wheels.' He laughed. 'Tell me one.'

'Did you hear about the dumb Mafia guy who tried to blow up a police car?'

'No.'

'He burnt his mouth on the tail pipe.'

He liked that one and slid the Plexiglas divider open and told it to Lenny and Vinnie, who laughed, though I could tell they didn't get it.

We rode in silence for a while, and I reflected on the present state of affairs. Despite the unspoken and unresolved issues between Frank Bellarosa and me, I was still his lawyer, and if I took him at his word, his friend. I could believe that if it weren't for the fact that I was also his alibi, and he was protecting his interest in me, which sort of coloured things.

Actually I didn't want to be his lawyer anymore, or his friend or his alibi. I could have told him that a few days ago, but since his arraignment it had become vastly more complicated for me to cut ties to him. As a lawyer, and therefore an officer of the court, what I had said in court was perjury even though I hadn't been under oath. And as a lawyer, if I recanted what I'd said, I'd probably be facing disbarment, not to mention a bullet in the head. There was, of course, this other side to being made an honorary Italian. It wasn't all wine and rigatoni, it was also *omertà* – silence – and it was us against them, and it was some sort of unspoken oath of loyalty that I must have taken, accepting Frank Bellarosa as my don. *Mamma mia*, this shouldn't happen to a High Episcopalian.

Bellarosa impaled a hunk of cheese on the point of the knife and held it under my nose. 'Here. You make me nervous when you watch me eat. *Mangia*.'

I took the cheese and bit into it. It wasn't bad, but it stunk.

Bellarosa watched me with satisfaction. 'Good?'

'*Molto bene.*' Not only were we partners in crime, but we were beginning to talk and smell the same.

After a few minutes of silence, he said to me, 'Hey, I know you're pissed about some things, you know, things that you think I did to you, like the Melzer thing. But like I told you once, sometimes you can't get even. Sometimes you got to take the hit and be happy you're still on your feet. Then the next time you're a little tougher and a little smarter.'

'Thank you, Frank. I didn't realize all you've done for me.'

'Yeah, you did.'

'Don't do me any more favours. Okay?'

'Okay. But here's some more free advice. Don't do me those kinds of favours, either. You don't talk to people like that reporter broad, and you don't even think about ways to even up the score. I'm telling you that for your own good. Because I like you, and I don't want to see nothing happen to you.'

'Look, Frank, I'm not into vendetta like you are. I took the hit and I learned my lesson as you said. But if I was into revenge for the Melzer thing and for those other things, I guarantee you, you wouldn't even see it coming. So we let bygones be bygones, and we finish out our business, and we part friends. *Capisce?*'

He looked at me a long time, then said, 'Yeah, you're smart enough to take a shot at me, but you ain't tough enough.'

'Fuck me again and we'll find out.'

'Yeah?'

'Yeah.'

I could tell he wasn't real happy with me, but he thought about it and said, 'Well, I'm not going to fuck you again, so we'll never find out. Okay?'

'Sure.'

He put out his hand and I took it. We shook, but I wasn't

sure what we were shaking on, and I don't think he knew either. Neither did he believe me that I wasn't looking for revenge, and I didn't believe that he wouldn't screw me again the first time it was in his interest to do so.

Anyway, as we approached the expressway exit to Lattingtown, Bellarosa said in a tone of conciliation, 'Hey, come on over for dinner tonight. We got lots of food. Anna invited a bunch of people over. All relatives. No businesspeople.'

'Are we related?'

'No, but it's an honour to be invited to a family thing.'

'Thank you,' I said noncommittally.

'Good. Susan, too. I think Anna talked to her already.' He added, 'Hey, I got an idea. Let's make this the picture party. Everybody's going to be there who I want to see the picture. Let's do that.'

I had the distinct impression everybody knew about this already. In polite suburban society, this would be a sort of friendly ruse to get a couple back together again. But Frank Bellarosa had all sorts of other angles as usual.

He said, 'Your wife will be the guest of honour. That okay with you?'

Well, the prospect of spending an evening at an Italian family homecoming party for a Mafia don with my estranged wife as the guest of honour was not that appealing, as you may conclude.

'Okay? See you about six.'

Vinnie suddenly burst out laughing and slid back the Plexiglas. He looked at me. 'Burned his mouth on the tail pipe. I get it.'

I should have taken the train home.

CHAPTER 33

The convoy turned into Stanhope Hall and proceeded up the gravel drive of Bellarosa's newly acquired fiefdom until we reached the little enclave of Susan Stanhope, where I bid my felonious friends good-day and carried my suitcase up to the front door.

Susan's Jaguar was out front, but with horse people that doesn't necessarily mean anyone is at home, and as I entered the house, it had that empty feeling about it. So the joyful reunion was postponed.

I went to my den and erased twenty-six messages on my answering machine, then took a stack of faxes and burned them in the fireplace unread. I did go through my mail because I respect handwritten letters. There was only one of those, however, a letter from Emily, which I put aside. Everything else turned out to be business mail, bills, ads, and assorted junk, which I also burned.

I sat down and read Emily's letter:

> *Dear John,*
>
> *Where in the name of God did you get that horrid tie? I kept adjusting the colour on my TV, but the tie didn't go with the suit unless your face was green. And I see you still don't carry a pocket comb. I saw that Spanish woman — Alvarez, I think — on the affiliate station here, and she hates you or loves you. Find out which. Gary and I are fine. Come on down. Soon!*
>
> *Love,*
> *Sis*

I put the letter in my desk drawer and went into the kitchen. We have a family message centre, formerly known as a bulletin board, but the only message on it said, *Zanzibar, vet, Tuesday* A.M. Fuck Zanzibar. He can't even read, and he's not allowed in the kitchen anyway.

I carried my suitcase upstairs and entered the former master bedroom, now called the mistress bedroom, and threw my suitcase in the corner. I changed into jeans, Docksides, and

T-shirt and went into the bathroom. My mouth still smelled of that cheese, so I gargled with mint mouthwash, but it didn't do any good. The stuff was in my blood.

I left the house and got into my Bronco, which I had trouble starting after it had sat idle for a while. George Allard was indeed dead. The engine finally turned over, and I headed down the driveway. I was on my way to go see my boat, but as I approached the gatehouse, Ethel stepped out of the door and stood in the drive, wearing her Sunday flower dress. I stopped the Bronco and got out. 'Hello, Ethel.'

'Hello, Mr Sutter.'

'How are you?'

'I'm fine,' she replied.

'You look well.' Actually she didn't, but I'm pretty easy on recent widows, orphans, and the severely handicapped.

She said to me, 'It's not my place to say this, Mr Sutter, but I think the press is treating you unfairly.'

Was this Ethel Allard? Did she use that George-ism 'it's not my place to say this'? Obviously this woman was possessed by the ghost of her husband. I replied, 'That's very good of you to think so, Mrs Allard.'

'This must be very trying for you, sir.'

I think my eyes moved heavenward to see if George was up there smiling. I said to Ethel, 'I'm sorry for any inconvenience this may have caused you regarding unwanted visitors.'

'That's all right, sir. That's my job.'

Really? 'Nevertheless, I do appreciate your patience. I'm afraid this might go on for some time.'

She nodded, actually sort of bowed her head the way George used to do to show he'd heard and understood. This was a little spooky, so I said, 'Well, you take care of yourself.' I moved back toward the Bronco.

She informed me, 'Mrs Sutter and I went to church this morning.'

'How nice.'

554

'She said you might be coming home today.'

'Yes.'

'She asked me to tell you if I saw you that she will be on the property this afternoon. She may be tending her garden or riding or at the stables. She asked that you look for her.' Ethel added hesitantly, 'She hasn't seemed herself the last few days.'

Neither have you, Ethel. Neither has anyone else around here. Just then, I would have given anything to go back to April when the world was safe and dull. Anyway, I really didn't want to see Susan; I wanted to see my boat, but I couldn't very well ignore Ethel's message, so I said, 'Thank you. I'll take a look around.' I got back into the Bronco, turned around, and headed back up the long drive.

I drove to the stable and looked inside, but Susan wasn't there, though both horses were. I put the Bronco into four-wheel drive and drove across the property to Stanhope Hall, but I didn't see her tending her vegetables in the terrace gardens. I drove past the gazebo and the hedge maze, but there was no sign of her.

I was aware, as I drove over the acreage, that this was no longer Stanhope property, but Bellarosa property, and in fact even my access to Grace Lane was by way of the long driveway that was now Bellarosa's, though I assumed that whoever had handled the sale for William was bright enough to put an easement clause into the contract. Actually, since I didn't own the guesthouse, what did I care? Susan and Frank could work out an easement arrangement. How's that for whiny self-pity? But put yourself in my position: landless, moneyless, powerless, jobless, and cuckolded. But I was also free. And I could stay that way unless I was foolish enough to get myself land, money, power, a job, and my wife back. As I skirted around the plum orchard, however, I noticed a straw sun hat on a stone bench at the edge of the grove, and I stopped the Bronco. I got out and saw that beside the hat was a bouquet of wildflowers, their stems tied together with a ribbon from the hat.

I hesitated, then went into the grove. The plum trees were planted far apart, and despite the fact that they had grown wild over the years, there was still an openness inside the grove.

I saw her walking some distance away wearing a white cotton dress and carrying a wicker basket. She was gathering plums, which were few and far between in this dying orchard. I watched her awhile, and though I couldn't see her face clearly at that distance in the dappled sunlight, she seemed to me downcast. If this whole scene seems to you a bit too set, I assure you the same thought occurred to me. I mean, she told Ethel to have me look for her. On the other hand, Susan is not manipulative, not prone to using feminine wiles, or any of that. So if she had gone through the trouble of setting this up, that in itself said something. I mean, if I'd found her tending the vegetables that Bellarosa had given us, then that, too, would have said something. Right? Well, enough horticultural psychology. She seemed to sense she wasn't alone, and she looked up at me and smiled tentatively.

Now picture us running toward each other through the sacred grove, in slow motion, the boughs parting, the wicker basket thrown aside, shafts of sunlight beaming on our smiling faces, our arms outstretched, picture that.

Cut to John Sutter, his hands in the pockets of his jeans regarding his wife with cool detachment. Close-up of Susan's tentative smile getting more tentative.

Anyway, she moved toward me and called out, 'Hello, John.'

'Hello.'

She kept coming, the basket swinging slightly by her side. She looked more tan than when I'd seen her five days before, and her freckles were all out. I noticed that she was barefoot and her sandals were in her basket. She looked about nineteen years old at that moment, and I

556

felt my heart thumping as she got to within a few feet of me. She took a plum out of the basket and held it toward me. 'Want one?'

I had an ancestor who once accepted a piece of fruit from a woman in a garden, and it got him into deep trouble, so I said, 'No, thanks.'

So we stood a few feet apart, and finally I said, 'Ethel told me you wanted to speak to me.'

'Yes, I wanted to say welcome home.'

'Thank you, but I'm not home.'

'You are, John.'

'Look, Susan, one of the first things those of us who were not born in a manor learn is that you can't have your cake and eat it, too. There is a price to pay for indulging yourself. You made your choices, Susan, and you have to accept responsibility for your actions.'

'Thank you for that Protestant, middle-class sermon. You're right that I was brought up differently, but I've made my adjustments to the new realities far better than you have. I've been a good wife to you, John, and I deserve better treatment than this.'

'Do you? Does that mean you deny any sexual involvement with Bellarosa?'

'Yes, I deny it.'

'Well, I don't believe you.'

Her face flushed red. 'Then why don't you ask him?'

'I don't have to, Susan, since you told him what I said to you. Am I supposed to believe you or him when it's obvious that you're both in cahoots? Do you think I'm an idiot?'

'No, you're a sharp lawyer. But you've become overly suspicious and cynical.' She paused and looked at me. 'I'll tell you something, though. Frank and I have become good friends, and yes, we talk, and we talk about you and about things, and I suppose that has the appearance of impropriety. I apologize for that.'

I looked into her eyes and I wanted to believe her, but I

557

had too much circumstantial evidence to the contrary. I said to her, 'Susan, tell me you are having an affair with him and I will forgive you. I mean that unconditionally, and we'll never speak of it again. You have my word on that. But you must tell me now, this minute, with no more lies.' I added, 'This is a onetime offer.'

She replied, 'I told you the extent of our relationship. It was close, but not sexual. Perhaps it was too close, and I will deal with that. Again, I apologize for confiding in him, and if you're angry, I understand. You are all the man I need.' She added, 'I missed you.'

'And I missed you.' Which was true. What was not true was her confession to a lesser crime. It's an old trick. I could see this was going nowhere. Susan is a cool customer, and if she were on a witness stand for eight straight hours and I were a savage lawyer, I could still not shake her. She'd made her decision to lie, or more accurately, Bellarosa had made it for her, for his own reasons. I felt that if it were anyone else but him, she'd stand up and tell me the truth. But this man had such a hold over her that she could look me in the eye and lie, though it was against everything in her nature and breeding to do so.

I felt worse at that moment than if she had just said, 'Yes, I've been screwing him for three months.' Actually, I was frightened for her because she was less able to handle Mr Bellarosa and his corruption than I was. I knew instinctively that this was not the time to push her and continue the confrontation. I said, 'All right, Susan. I understand that you were seduced by him in another way. And yes, I am angry and jealous of your relationship with him, even if it's not sexual. I wish it were simply physical and not metaphysical.' This was not true, of course, because I'm a man first, and a sensitive, intellectual, modern husband second, or third, or maybe even fourth or lower. But it sounded like the right response to her confession of emotional infidelity.

She said to me, 'You were seduced by him, too, John.'

'Yes, that's right.'

'Well, can we be friends?'

'We can work on it. But I'm still angry about a lot of things. Maybe you are, too.'

'Yes, I'm angry that you've accused me of adultery and that you've been emotionally withdrawn for months.'

'Well,' I said, 'maybe we should separate for a while.'

She seemed to mull that over, then replied, 'I'd prefer it if we could work out our problems while living together. We don't have to sleep together, but I'd like you to live at home.'

'Your home.'

'I've instructed my attorneys to amend the deed in both our names.'

Life is one surprise after another, isn't it? I said to her, 'Instruct them not to.'

'Why?'

'I don't want assets if I have tax problems. And I don't want your assets under any circumstances. But thank you for the gesture.'

'All right.' She asked, 'Well, will you be staying?'

'Let me think about it. I'm going to spend a few days out on the boat. I'm afraid I won't be able to come to your unveiling this evening.'

She replied, 'If you'd like, I'll tell . . . Anna to call it off.'

'No, Anna would be disappointed. Please pass on my regrets to Anna.'

'I will.'

'I'll see you in a few days.' I turned to leave.

'John?'

'Yes?'

'I just remembered. Mr Melzer came around the other day. Thursday or Friday, I think.'

'Yes?'

'He said you were supposed to make some sort of initial payment on your taxes.'

'Did you tell him we haven't gone to closing on the East Hampton house yet?'

'Yes, I did. He said he'd see what he could do, but he sounded concerned.'

'I'll get in touch with him.' I hesitated, then said, 'Susan, we have a long way to go.'

She nodded. 'Maybe we can go away together as soon as things settle down, John. Just you and I. We can take the boat to the Caribbean if you'd like.'

She was certainly trying, and I was certainly not. But the hurt was too deep, and the lies were not making it any better. I had the sudden compulsion to tell her I'd slept with a famous TV news reporter, and I might have if I thought it would do either of us any good. But I felt no guilt at all and didn't need to confess, and Susan didn't need to hear a confession that was given out of vengefulness.

'Think about a boat trip, John.'

'I will.'

'Oh, Edward and Carolyn both called. They send their love to you. They're drafting letters, but that might take a while.' She smiled.

'I'll call them when I get back. See you in a few days.'

'Be careful, John. You really shouldn't go out alone.'

'I'll stay in the Sound. Nothing tricky. I'll be fine.' I added, 'Good luck tonight.' I turned and walked away and heard her call out, 'Don't go to the Caribbean without me.'

I pulled into the yacht club an hour later, having stopped at a deli in Bayville to pick up beer, baloney, and bread. You can live on beer, baloney, and bread for three days before scurvy and night blindness set in.

I carried the case of beer and the bag of groceries to the boat in one trip and set everything down on the dock. As I was about to jump aboard, I noticed a cardboard sign encased in a sheet of clear plastic, hanging from the bow rail. I bent down and read the sign:

I stared at the sign awhile, trying to comprehend how this thing got on my boat. After a full minute, I stood and loaded my provisions on board.

As I went about casting off, I noticed that people in nearby boats were looking at me. I mean, if I needed a final humiliation, this was it. Well, but it could have been worse. Let's not forget that right here on Long Island in colonial times, people were put in wooden cages and dunked in ponds, they were tarred and feathered, locked in pillories, and whipped in public. So one little cardboard sign was no big deal. At least I didn't have to wear it around my neck.

I started the engine and took the *Paumanok* out into the bay. I noticed that on the door that led below was the same sign as the one on the bow rail. I saw yet another one tied to the main mast. Well, I couldn't say I didn't see the sign, could I?

I cut the engine and let the boat drift with the tide and wind. It was late afternoon, a nice summer Sunday in August, a bit cooler than normal, but comfortable.

I really missed this while I was in Manhattan: the smell of the sea, the horizons, the isolation, and the quiet. I opened a can of beer, sat on the deck, and drank. I made a baloney sandwich and ate it, then had another beer. After five days of menus, room service, and restaurants, it was nice to make myself a baloney sandwich and drink beer from a can.

Well, I went through about half the case, drifting around the bay, contemplating the meaning of life and more specifically wondering if I'd done and said the right things with Susan. I thought I had, and I justified my not telling her I didn't buy her story by reminding myself that she was borderline nuts even under the best of circumstances. I wasn't looking to destroy her or the marriage. I really wanted things to work out. I mean, on one level, we were still in love, but there's nothing more awkward than a husband and wife living together when one of them is having an affair, and the other one knows about it. (What I had done is called a fling. Susan was having an affair. Bellarosa had explained that when we were all having dinner at The Creek that night. Right?) Well, you don't sleep together, of course, but you don't necessarily have to separate and file for divorce, either. Especially if you're both still emotionally involved. There are other less civilized responses, I know, like having the big scene, or one or the other spouses going completely psychotic and getting violent.

But in this case, the entire mess had evolved in such a bizarre way that I felt I shared in the responsibility.

Actually Susan had not verbally acknowledged that she *was* having an affair with our next-door neighbour, and that sort of complicated the situation. To make a legal analogy, I had made an accusation but had never presented evidence, and the accused exercised her right to remain silent, sulky, and withdrawn. And in truth, though Bellarosa had tacitly acknowledged the affair, my evidence was purely circumstantial as far as Susan was concerned. So, I think we both figured that if we just avoided the issue and avoided each other, we might eventually both come to believe none of this had happened. It was sort of the reverse, I suppose, of our sexual fantasies; it was using our well-developed powers of make-believe to pretend that what was happening was just another sexual melodrama, this one titled, 'John Suspects Susan of Adultery.'

Anyway, somewhere around the tenth or eleventh beer, I realized that it was Frank Bellarosa who stood in the way of a real and lasting reconciliation.

Well, the sky was turning purple, and the gulls were swooping, and it was time to go back. I rose unsteadily, went below, and retrieved a fire axe that was clipped to a bulkhead. I went into the forward head and swung the axe, cutting a five-inch gash in the fibreglass hull below the waterline. I pulled the axe out and watched the sea water cascade down the hull between the sink and shower. I swung the axe a few more times, cutting a good-size hole in the hull. The sea gushed in, swamping the floor and spilling out into the forward stateroom.

I went topside and opened the flag locker, pulling out seven pennants and clipping them to the halyard. I ran the pennants up the main mast.

Proud of my idiocy, and with the *Paumanok* listing to starboard and me listing to port, I lowered myself onto the aft deck and pulled a small inflatable life raft from under the cockpit seat. I put the remainder of the beer aboard the raft along with two small oars, and I sat in the raft. I popped a beer and drank while my boat settled deeper into the water around me.

The sea came over the starboard side first, sloshed around the tilting deck and raised the life raft a few inches.

The *Paumanok* took a long while to sink, but eventually the stern settled into the water and the lifeboat drifted away over the swamped stern. I watched my boat as it settled slowly into the sea, listing at about 45 degrees to starboard, its bow rising up out of the water and its mast flying the seven signal pennants that proclaimed to the world *Fuck you*.

It was nearly dark now, and as I drifted away, it became more difficult to see my boat, but I could still make out the mast and the pennants lying almost perpendicular to the water. It appeared as though the keel had touched bottom and that she was as far down as she was going to go.

I drifted with the tide for a while, working on a fresh beer and thinking about this and that. Obviously, what I had done was a very spiteful thing, not to mention a class A felony. But so what? I mean, someone was being very spiteful toward me. Right? I saw Alphonse Ferragamo's hand in this, and Mr Novac's hand, too. And perhaps even Mr Mancuso's hand and possibly Mr Melzer's influence. *No good will come of your trying to take on forces more powerful than yourself.* True, but I was enjoying the fight.

What I didn't enjoy was the loss of my boat, which in some semi-mystical way had become a part of me over the years. The *Paumanok* had always been my ace in the hole, my rocket ship to other galaxies, my time machine. That's why they'd taken her from me. Well, as the signal flags said, Fuck you.

Of course, if I hadn't been so spiteful and impulsive, I'd have gotten the boat back after I'd come up with the taxes, but that wasn't the point. The point was that the *Paumanok* was not going to be used as a pawn or a knife in my ribs. It was a good boat, and it should not suffer the indignity of a government tax-seizure sign on it. So I hoisted the beer to her and lay down in the life raft and drifted around the bay.

Around midnight, after counting a billion stars and wishing on a dozen shooting stars, I stirred myself and sat up.

I finished the last half of a beer, oriented myself, and began rowing for shore. As I pulled on the oars, I asked myself, 'What else can go wrong?' But you should never ask that question.

PART VI

At two hours after midnight appeared
the land at a distance of two leagues.

Christopher Columbus
Journal of the First Voyage,
October 12, 1492

CHAPTER 34

'You gotta try the *sfogliatelli*,' said Frank Bellarosa.

Susan took the pastry and put it on her plate beside two other 'gotta try' pastries. Oddly, this woman, who looks like a poster girl for famine relief, packed down an entire 'gotta try' meal without even turning green.

Anna Bellarosa was watching her weight, as she announced about six times, and was 'just picking'. She picked her way through enough food to feed the slums of Calcutta for a week. She also picked out two pastries, then put artificial sweetener in her coffee.

Where this was taking place was Giulio's, and it was now mid-September. Actually, it was Friday, September seventeenth, to be exact, and you'll see shortly why the day sticks out in my mind.

As for the great unveiling, I understand everyone loved the painting, and everyone had a good time that night. Terrific. I had a good excuse for missing the art event of the year, of course, if I had wanted an excuse: 'Sorry, but I was busy sinking my boat to piss off the Feds.' Regarding that, I hadn't heard from the IRS yet, and I doubt they even knew the *Paumanok* was gone. It didn't mean as much to them as it did to me. Maybe in the end, it was a futile gesture, but I wasn't sorry I'd done it. And if they asked me about it, I'd say, 'Yes, I sunk her, just as my ancestors dumped tea into Boston Harbor. Give me liberty or give me death.' I'd probably get about a year and a six-figure fine.

But I did have a closing date on the East Hampton house, and I'd probably be able to settle my tax delinquency within a few weeks. Then I could get out my scuba gear and remove the tax-seizure signs from the *Paumanok*.

Regarding my marital status, I'd accepted Susan's suggestion and remained in residence. However, we were married in name only, as they used to say when describing a couple

569

who shared the same house and attended social and family functions together, but who no longer engaged in conjugal sex. This may have been all right for our ancestors, but to most modern couples, it's the worst of both worlds.

Anyway, back at Giulio's, the fat lady was still singing, belting them out in Italian, a mixture of sweet melodic songs and sad songs that made the old goombahs weepy, plus a few numbers that must have been pretty raunchy judging by the way she sang them and the reaction of the crowd.

The crowd, incidentally, was slightly different from the lunch group. There were, to be sure, a few suspected mafioso types, but there were also some uptown Manhattanites as well, people who spent their entire urban lives trying to discover new restaurants that nobody knows about yet, except the two hundred people in the place. Well, the uptown crowd was going to have something interesting to report after this meal. Anyway, there were also a lot of greasy young Guidos in the place with their girlfriends, who looked like slim Annas, just dying to get married so they could blow up like stuffed cannelloni.

And there was this old geezer with a four-day beard squeezing the whaddayacallit – the concertina – while the fat lady sang. Frank gave the old guy a twenty to play 'Santa Lucia', and this must have been on the goombah hit parade because everybody joined in, including Susan, who somehow knew all the words in Italian. Actually, it's a pretty song and I found myself humming it. Well, the place was packed and smelled like garlic and perfume, and everybody was in a very jolly mood.

Susan seemed really fascinated by Giulio's and its denizens. Her infrequent excursions into Manhattan are confined to Midtown, Broadway, and the East Side, and she probably hasn't been down in the old ethnic neighbourhoods since my company gave a party in Chinatown five years ago. But if I had thought she would enjoy something like this, I would have taken her to Little Italy, or Chinatown or Spanish Harlem or any place other than The Creek. But I didn't know. Then again, neither did she.

Well, a few events of note had transpired since the night I'd sunk the *Paumanok* that may be worth mentioning. Edward and Carolyn had come home from the southern climes. Edward with a deep tan, and Carolyn with a deeper understanding of the Cuban people, and also with a box of Monto Cristo number fours. So the Sutter clan was reunited for about a week before Labor Day, and we had a good time despite the fact that the *Paumanok* was at the bottom of the bay and the East Hampton house was sold. Incidentally, I hadn't told Susan that I'd sunk the boat and would not have mentioned it, except that when Edward and Carolyn came home, they wanted to go sailing. So I sat everyone down and said, 'The government slapped a tax-seizure sign on the boat, and it looked so obscene, I took her into the middle of the bay and sunk her.' I added, 'I think her mast is still above water, and if it is, you can see seven signal flags that say "Fuck you". Well, I hope she's not a hazard to navigation, but if she is, the Coast Guard will take care of it.'

There was a minute of stunned silence, then Edward said, 'Good for you.' Carolyn seconded that. Susan said nothing.

Anyway, we took some day trips, saw a matinee in Manhattan, swam at Fox Point, and even played golf one day at The Creek, though I had the distinct feeling some people were snubbing us. I resigned from the club the next day – not because, as Groucho Marx, a onetime Gold Coast resident, once said, 'I wouldn't belong to any club that would have me as a member' – but because if I belonged there, then I *belonged* there. And I didn't, so I don't. *Capisce?*

Anyway, the day after Labor Day, Susan decided to visit her parental units in Hilton Head, leaving Carolyn, Edward, and me to finish out the last days of school vacation by ourselves. It was a nice few days, and we spent them mostly at Stanhope Hall, riding and walking the property. Carolyn got the idea to do a photographic essay of the estate, and that took two days with me supplying the history and the captions for the pictures as best I could. Carolyn is not the sentimental type, but I think she knew that might be one of the last times that such a thing would be possible. One night, Edward, Carolyn, and I camped out in the mansion with sleeping bags, and we had a picnic on the marble floor of the dining room by candlelight.

Sitting around the candles, deep into a bottle of wine, Carolyn said to me, 'You've changed, Dad.'

'Have I? How?'

She thought a moment, then replied, 'You're more . . . grown-up.' She smiled.

I smiled in return. 'And my voice is changing.' I knew what she meant, of course. The last few months had been a time of challenge and change, and so I suppose it had been good for my character. Most American men of the upper middle classes never really grow up unless they are fortunate enough to go to war or go through a bankruptcy or divorce or other major adversity. So this was the summer I got hair on my balls, and it felt good and bad at the same time. I asked Edward, 'Do you think your old man has changed?'

Edward, who is not usually tuned in to the subtleties of human behaviour, replied, 'Yeah, I guess.' He added, 'Can you change back?'

'No. There's no going back.'

A few days after that, I rented a van and drove the kids to school. We went first to Sarah Lawrence, and Edward was nervous about starting college, but I assured him that the liberal arts curriculum he was taking was similar to the one I took at Yale, and that I slept for four years. Thus assured, he strode confidently into the formerly all-girls school, his hair combed for the first time since his baptism, and his body smelling of some awful lotion.

Carolyn and I drove alone to Yale, and I always enjoy going back to my alma mater, as my college memories are good despite the turmoil of those years in the mid-sixties. Carolyn said to me on the way to New Haven, 'Are you legally separated?'

'No. Your mother just went to visit her parents.'

'It's sort of a trial separation?'

'No.'

'Why are you sleeping in separate rooms?'

'Because we don't want to sleep in separate cities. End of conversation.'

So I drove her up to Yale. As a sophomore this year, Carolyn enters what we call a 'college', actually a dorm where she will spend the next three years. She is, in fact, in my old college, Jonathan Edwards. J E, as we call it, is a beautiful, old Gothic building with arches, climbing ivy, and turrets, situated around a large quadrangle. It is, in fact, the greatest place on the face of this earth, and I wished I was staying and not leaving.

Anyway, I helped her unload half a vanful of clothes and electronics, which barely fit in her room. It was a nice suite like my old place down the hall, with oak panelling and a fireplace in the living room. I met her roommate, a tall, blonde young woman from Texas named Halsey, and I wondered if I shouldn't go back to Jonathan Edwards to do a little more undergraduate work. You're never too old to learn.

But I digress. Carolyn and I walked down to Liggett's Drugstore, which is sort of a tradition, and with a few hundred other Yalies and parents, we stocked up on notions and sundries. We stowed the Liggett's bags in the van, then walked the few blocks to York Street, 'to the tables down at Mory's, to the place where Louie dwells.' Don't ask me what that means.

Mory's is a private club, and I've kept my membership for this past quarter of a century, though I doubt if I get there once a year. But though I may have resigned from The Creek, and may eventually resign from my job and my marriage and from life in general, I will never resign from Mory's, for to do that is to sever the ties to myself, to the John Sutter whom I used to know and like. I may indeed be a poor little lamb who has lost his way, but that night I was home again.

So Carolyn and I had dinner at Mory's along with a hundred other families, many of whom I noticed were missing one or

573

the other spouse. Carolyn is not a member of Mory's, and may never be, as she discriminates against private clubs. Nevertheless, I regaled her with Mory stories, and she sat there and smiled at me, sometimes amused, sometimes bored, and once or twice disapproving. Well, yesterday's high jinks are today's insensitive behaviour, I suppose, and maybe the reverse is also true. But it was a nice dinner, an exquisite few hours between father and daughter.

The oak tabletops at Mory's have been carved with thousands of names and initials, and though we couldn't find mine without clearing off someone else's dinner, I did produce a sharp pocketknife for Carolyn, who carved away while I went around the dining room and said hello to a few old school chums.

I walked Carolyn back to Jonathan Edwards, we kissed good-bye, and I got in the van, opting for the two-hour drive back to Long Island rather than prolonging the nostalgia trip, which could easily have turned from pleasant to maudlin.

Regarding my legal career, my association with Perkins, Perkins, Sutter and Reynolds seemed to be rather vague, perhaps even tentative. I put myself on half salary, which is, I think, fair since I spend half the week in the Locust Valley office, albeit with my door closed and the phone turned off. But I feel a sense of responsibility to my old clients, and I'm trying to put their affairs in some semblance of order and to parcel them out to other attorneys in the firm. As for my Wall Street business, that's completely gone. My Wall Street clients would fire an attorney after two missed phone calls, so my sense of loyalty and responsibility toward the yellow-tie guys is not deep and not reciprocal. But I have to settle the question of my status with the firm and I suppose if I ever show up at the Wall Street office, I could discuss this with the senior partners.

As for the *United States* v. *Frank Bellarosa*, that seemed to be moving rather more slowly than Mr Ferragamo promised. Not only did we not have a trial date, but I hadn't had an opportunity to examine any of the five witnesses against my client. Alphonse informed me one day by phone, 'We have them all in hiding under the witness protection programme. They're very frightened about testifying in open court against a Mafia chief.'

'There is no Mafia.'

Ha, ha, said Alphonse, and he added, 'They didn't mind the grand jury, but now they're getting cold feet.'

'Four Colombian drug goons and a gun moll have cold feet?'

'Why not? So for that reason, Mr Sutter, I've asked for a delay in the trial date. I'll keep you informed.' He added, 'What's your rush? This should make you happy. Maybe the witnesses will refuse to testify.'

'Maybe they were lying from the beginning,' I pointed out.

'Why would they do that?'

He and I both knew why, but I wasn't allowed to bug him. 'Maybe,' I said, 'it was a case of mistaken identity. All Italians look alike, don't they?'

'Actually, they don't, Mr Sutter. I don't look anything like Frank Bellarosa, for instance. By the way, regarding mistaken identity, I discovered that you were at your country club at about one P.M. on January fourteenth, for lunch with your wife.'

'So what? I said I saw Bellarosa at about nine A.M., then again at about noon.'

'And you went home, took care of your horse, presumably showered, changed into a suit, and were at your club at one P.M.'

'They don't call me superman for nothing.'

'Hmmm,' said Alphonse. I mean, this guy thought he was Inspector Porfiry Petrovich, hounding poor Raskolnikov into a confession, but I found him a bore.

Anyway, I was more convinced than ever that Alphonse was stalling and would continue to stall until somebody out on the street solved his problem. He didn't have long to wait.

Regarding my relationships with friends and family, that

was also on hold. Part of the reason for this was that I was keeping out of touch, which is no easy thing to do these days. Try it. But I disconnected my home fax, changed my phone number to an unlisted one, and had all my mail forwarded to a P.O. box in the Locust Valley Post Office, which I never visited. Also, Ethel as gatekeeper proved to be a lot more nasty than George ever was, and nobody gets past the gate while Ethel is in the gatehouse. When she's not around, the gate is locked.

Jenny Alvarez. Well, that relationship, too, is on hold, which is best for all concerned, as men and women say to each other when they get involved, panic, run, brood, call, run, and so on. But really, there was no use complicating the situation any more than it was. Actually, I didn't even know if Jenny Alvarez cared anymore, and I would have been relieved to hear that she didn't, and pretty annoyed and hurt, too. But I did watch her nearly every night on the news at eleven, and Susan asked me once if I had suddenly become a news junkie. Spouses who are carrying on often display a change in behaviour, as we know, but watching the news is not usually a tip-off. Goes to show you.

But watch I did, and I hoped that one night Jenny Alvarez would just break down on the air and cry out, 'John! John! I miss you!' or at least, I thought, perhaps when she was out in the field reporting, and she was turning it back to the anchorman, Jeff what's-his-name, she would say, 'Back to you, John.' But that never happened, at least not on the nights I was watching.

Anyway, I had moved into one of the guesthouse's guest rooms, the smallest one, badly and barely furnished, where we always put people whom we don't want around for more than twenty-four hours. Susan had said to me, 'I understand your reasons for not wanting us to sleep in the same bed, of course. But I'm glad you decided not to move out. I very much want you to stay.'

'Then I will. How much is it a night?'

576

'Twenty dollars would be fair for that room, but I can let you have a better room for only five dollars more.'

'I'll stay in the smaller room.'

Well, we're still making jokes, and that's a hopeful sign. Right? It's when it becomes really grim that it becomes insufferable. So we lived in that sort of cool limbo that husbands and wives have invented and perfected for the purpose of coexisting until the moving van arrives or until they fall into each other's arms and swear undying love for ever, which in connubial terms means about thirty days.

In truth, I was angry, hurt, and vindictive every morning, but by noon I was philosophical, resigned, and willing to let fate take its course. By late evening, however, I was lonely and ready to forgive and forget, unconditionally. But then the next day, the cycle would start over again. Unfortunately, Susan called from Hilton Head about eight A.M., one morning when I was in cycle one, and I said a few things that I regretted by evening. Things like, 'How's William Peckerhead of Hilton Head?'

'Settle down, John.'

Or, 'Did you want to speak to Zanzibar?'

'Go have your coffee and call me back.'

Well, I did that night, but she wasn't in. Anyway, in the week or so since she's been back, I've been civilized.

So, there we were in Giulio's, having dinner, which was a little bizarre considering the circumstances. But my client had really insisted on this little get-together, though for what reason I couldn't guess except that he really enjoyed showing off in Little Italy where people knew who he was. Of course, that has a negative side as well, especially if you're a marked man. I mean, if there really was a contract out on this guy, any goombah in that restaurant could have gone out to make a phone call to some other goombah, and eventually the wrong goombahs would get the word, and for the price of a twenty-five-cent call, Frank the Bishop Bellarosa's whereabouts would be fixed. But I don't think that's what actually happened on the night of September seventeenth. I'm pretty sure it was Lenny who fingered his boss, as they say.

But, anyway, I acquiesced to this dinner because, quite frankly, to say no to it would have been un-Machiavellian; i.e., I was still royally pissed off at old Frank and Mrs Sutter no matter how much I tried to cool down, but to show it would put them on their guard. What? Revenge? Vendetta? Had I lied to Frank and to myself? Was I still looking to get even? You bet. Though I had no idea what, if anything, I was going to do to or about these two, I wanted to keep their guards down and my options open.

So we sipped coffee and ate pastry. The normal security was in effect with Vinnie and Lenny at their favourite table near the door, while we were at Frank's favourite table in the rear corner. Frank sat in his very favourite chair, facing the front with his back to the wall.

Susan at one point in the evening had said to Frank, 'That's very good of you to buy your employees dinner. Most men just send their car and driver away until they're ready to leave.'

This was either the most facetious or the most naive statement I'd heard all year, and I wasn't sure which. Susan sometimes plays the *naif* as I mentioned, but the act was wearing a little thin.

I regarded Anna Bellarosa a moment. I hadn't spoken to her since that morning she tackled me at Alhambra. She was undoubtedly grateful to me for getting her husband sprung, but I was fairly certain that a traditional Italian woman did not telephone, write, or call on a man unless he was her father or brother. How suppressed these women were, I thought, how utterly dependent they were on their husbands for everything including their opinions and maybe even their feelings. I mean, the woman didn't even have a driver's licence. I wondered if Anna had an unmarried sister for me. Or maybe I'd ask the don for Filomena's hand.

Anyway, though we seemed to be having a good time during dinner, we weren't. For one thing, Frank was going out of his way to be cool to Susan, and going out of his way to praise me as the greatest lawyer in New York. Obviously the man was trying to demonstrate that there was absolutely nothing going on between him and my wife, and at the same time trying to jolly us back together. Bellarosa was a smart guy in a lot of ways, but this wasn't one of them.

Susan seemed uncomfortable with Bellarosa's obvious bad acting. She also seemed generally nervous, as you might expect.

There were times when the conversation was strained, as I suggested, and Frank just wasn't his scintillating self as he realized that the evening wasn't going as he'd planned. Anna, I think, noticed this, too, but I wondered if she was smart enough to know why. I had half a mind to announce to her, 'Your husband is fucking my wife.' But if she didn't believe that her husband was a Mafia boss, why would she believe that he was an adulterer? And if she did, what was she going to do about it?

Anyway, Frank paid the check with cash, and Vinnie and Lenny were already out the door. Frank said, 'You all stay here and finish your coffee. I'm gonna go see about the car.'

Anna stared down at the table and nodded. She knew the drill. Susan looked antsy to get moving, but like Anna she listened to Big Frank. I, on the other hand, didn't feel like sitting with the women while Mr Macho went out and secured the beachhead. So stupid John stood and said, 'I'll go with you.'

And I did. Bellarosa and I went to the door, and I saw Vinnie standing on the sidewalk, checking out the block. Our car pulled up, a black stretch Cadillac that Frank had ordered from his limousine company for the occasion. Lenny was at the wheel. Vinnie signalled to us, and we went through the door onto the sidewalk.

It was a very pleasant evening with a touch of autumn in the air. There were people strolling on the street as there always are in Little Italy, but none of them looked suspicious. And as always, no one knew where Bellarosa would be that night except Frank himself and his wife. Not even Susan or

I knew, though I had guessed, of course, that we were going to Giulio's. Vinnie and Lenny may have guessed also, though really, we could have been going to dinner at any one of about three thousand restaurants in New York, New Jersey, Connecticut, or Long Island. It was only after we had gotten to Giulio's that Lenny and Vinnie knew for sure, and Vinnie was never out of our sight. Only Lenny was when he parked the car in a garage down the street. As I said, anyone inside of Giulio's could have made the phone call, but I'm pretty sure it was Lenny the Cretin who did.

There were two of them, both wearing black trench coats and gloves. Where they came from exactly, I'm not sure, but they were standing on the other side of the limousine, and I had the impression they had been crouched behind it on the driver's side and had stood as Vinnie pulled on the rear passenger-side door handle, which caused the interior lights of the limo to go on. This may have been the signal, inadvertently given by Vinnie, for the two men to stand, because I seem to recall a connection between the two. Vinnie was still tugging on the door handle, which was apparently locked, and he banged on the window with his palm. 'Hey, Lenny! Unlock the fucking door. Whaddaya, stupid?' It was at that moment that Vinnie looked up and saw the two men across the roof of the car, and I heard him say, 'Oh, Mother of God . . .'

I should tell you that at one point in the evening, when the two women went off to powder their noses (as Anna referred to urinating), I had said to Bellarosa, 'Frank, this is not a good place to be at night.'

'You don't like the music?'

'Knock it off. You know what I mean.'

His reply had been, 'Fuck it.'

Well, I tried. I really did, because I couldn't stand by and say nothing. But Bellarosa's ego wouldn't allow him to make many changes in his lifestyle, and there was also the matter of Mr Peacock wanting to impress Mrs Sutter. Get it?

Well, back to the really bad stuff. I stared at these two guys and found myself looking down the muzzles of two double-barrelled shotguns not ten feet away. Both men steadied their aim on the roof of the limo, though with shotguns at ten feet you don't have to do a lot of aiming. This all happened very quickly, of course, though neither man seemed rushed or nervous, just sort of matter-of-fact.

I said, 'Frank . . .' and poked him.

Vinnie, of course, had gone for his gun, but the first blast caught him full in the face from about two feet away and literally blew his head off, sending pieces of it at me and Bellarosa.

Frank had turned toward the two assassins just as the first blast decapitated Vinnie. Bellarosa stepped back and held his hands out in a protective gesture, and he yelled out, 'Hey, hey!'

The second man fired both barrels at once, and Frank, who had been a foot or two away from my left shoulder, caught both barrels in his chest and was actually picked up off his feet and thrown backward, crashing through the front window of Giulio's.

The man who had fired the single barrel into Vinnie's face looked at me, and I looked at the shotgun pointing at me. But I'm a civilian, and I had nothing to worry about. Right? Right? Then why was the gun pointing at *me*? I sort of knew that I'd see the flash of the barrel but would probably never hear the explosion. People who have had similar experiences have described it as 'like waiting for an eternity'. That's exactly correct. And I even saw my life flash before my eyes.

Well, maybe the reason I'm able to tell you about this is that the guy smirked at me, and I wanted the last word so I flashed him the Italian salute. He smiled, swung the barrel of the shotgun away from me, and fired. I actually heard the buckshot fly past to my left, like buzzing bees, and I heard Bellarosa groan a few feet behind me. I looked and saw him sprawled on his back, half his body inside the restaurant and his legs dangling outside. His trousers were shredded, and I realized the last shot had peppered his legs. In fact, I saw blood running now, over his ankles and socks – he had lost his shoes at some point – and the blood was puddling on the sidewalk.

I heard a noise like another shot from the street and turned back to see that the two gunmen had gotten into the limo and the sound I'd heard was the door slamming shut. The long black car pulled away at normal speed. I noticed now that the two shotguns were lying in the street. My eyes moved downward, and I looked at Vinnie's body on the sidewalk, blood running out of his headless neck a few feet from my shoes. I stepped back.

No one on the street or sidewalk around me was screaming or running; they were all just standing very still. Of course, this sort of thing doesn't happen every night on Mott Street, but this was a savvy bunch, and no one around me was going to say later that they thought a car backfired or kids were shooting fireworks. No, everyone knew exactly what had happened, though no one saw a thing, naturally.

Inside the restaurant, however, there *was* a lot of screaming going on, and I could picture the scene in there with glass all over the place and Bellarosa's body sprawled across the window table, blood running onto the white tile floor.

Well, there was nothing to be done out on the street, so I turned and went inside the restaurant. I should point out that from the moment I saw the two gunmen to the time I walked back into the restaurant was probably less than two minutes. Susan and Anna were still at the corner table, though like everyone else, they were standing, and Anna looked at me with wide, terrified eyes. Susan looked at me, too, then her eyes sort of focused over my shoulder as if she were looking for Bellarosa. I realized that neither of them had understood that it was Frank Bellarosa who had reentered the restaurant through the window. I turned toward the window and saw why; there was a small crowd around, of course, but also, when he'd sailed through the window, he had taken the curtain rod and the red café curtain with him, and the curtain was lying partially over his face and body. His arms were outstretched and his head tilted back over the edge of the table on which he was half lying. Shards of plate glass lay everywhere, on the table, on the floor, and on Frank Bellarosa.

The pandemonium in the restaurant was dying down except that I could now hear Anna's voice shrieking, 'No! No! Frank! It's Frank! My God, my God!' and so forth.

As I moved toward Bellarosa's body, I glanced to my left and saw Susan standing a few feet away now, looking at Bellarosa's upside-down face. Her face was pale, but she seemed composed. Susan turned away from him, looked at me, and our eyes met. I knew I had blood or gore or some wet stuff on my clothes and even on my face, and I was pretty sure it wasn't *my* blood, but the remains of Vinnie's head. Susan, however, couldn't know that, yet she made no move toward me to see if I was all right.

Anna, on the other hand, broke away from some waiters and rushed toward her husband. She dropped to her knees on the glass and the blood-covered floor and took her husband's head in her hands, shrieking at the top of her lungs, then sobbing as she caressed his bloody face.

I was sort of out of it at this point, and I don't pretend that I noticed everything I'm describing at the exact time it happened, or that my impressions are as precise as they should have been. To give Susan the benefit of the doubt, for instance, she was probably in shock and that would explain her catatonic state.

Anyway, I got a grip on myself and knelt down in a tremendous pool of blood beside Anna, and I was about to comfort her and get her out of there. But then I noticed that the café curtain had slipped from Frank's face and that his eyes were open; not open dead, but open open. In fact, his eyes were watering and squinting in pain. I saw, too, that his chest was starting to heave. I ripped the red café curtain away from him and saw that though his tie, jacket, and shirt were full of holes, there was no big, gaping wound where the double-barrelled shotgun blast should have punched out his heart and lungs. I ripped his shirt open and saw, of course, a bulletproof vest with dozens of copper shots lying on the silvery-grey fabric.

I looked at Bellarosa's face and saw that his lips were moving, but more important, I saw the source of all that blood on the floor: a pellet or glass had penetrated the side of his throat, and blood was gushing from the wound under the collar and running onto the floor. The man was bleeding to death.

Well, that was too bad, wasn't it? Talk about a quick and simple solution to a complex problem. On the other hand, I hadn't been paid anything he owed me yet, but I could write that off as a life experience. Frank would have wanted it that way.

Meanwhile, all these customers and waiters were standing around, and I guess there wasn't a doctor in the house, and no one understood that Bellarosa needed first aid. Anna was still weeping, still clutching her husband's head.

Frank opened his eyes, and we looked at each other, and I think he smiled, but maybe not. I was certain his ribs were broken from the impact of the blasts, and I knew that if anyone moved him, his ribs would puncture his lungs. But so far, no blood was coming out of his mouth and his breathing was steady, though shallow. So what to do? *You a Boy Scout or something?* Well, as a matter or fact, yes. Eagle Scout, actually.

So I opened his collar and saw that the wound was probably in a carotid artery by the way it was gushing, and I felt around for the pulse below the wound and found it. I pressed my fingers on the pulse and the bleeding subsided. I then cradled the back of his neck in the crook of my arm to raise his head level with his heart so his brain could get blood, and I took a table napkin and pressed that against the wound itself. I didn't know if that was going to do the trick, but Mr Jenkins, my Troop Leader, would have been proud of my effort.

I looked around and said to the crowd in general, 'Please move back. Someone take his wife away. Thank you.'

So there I knelt, covered with Vinnie's brains and skull as I saw now in the better light of the restaurant, and smeared with Frank Bellarosa's blood, and my fingers on the don's neck where I'd wanted them for some time, though for different reasons. All things considered, I wasn't having one of my better evenings out.

I managed to get a look at my watch and saw it was a few minutes before midnight. I looked at Bellarosa's face and noticed that his skin was very white, which made his stubble look dark. But his breathing was still regular, and I could feel a good pulse. I also felt the *puttanesca* sauce rising in my stomach and up my oesophagus, but I got it down again.

I glanced back at his face and he was looking at me, although his eyes were unfocused. I said, 'Hang in there, Frank. You're doing fine. You'll be okay. Just relax,' and so forth. That's what you're supposed to do so they don't go into shock. Meanwhile, no one was giving *me* much encouragement, and my mouth was dry and my stomach was turning and my head felt light. *Hang in there, Sutter.*

I heard a police siren and I looked out through the broken window and saw that a crowd had gathered, and apparently seeing Vinnie's headless corpse on the sidewalk, they had formed a wide semicircle around the restaurant. The siren was right outside now, and I also heard an ambulance horn.

I looked back into the restaurant and discovered Susan a few tables away, sitting in a chair and watching me, her legs crossed and her arms folded across her chest as though she was angry with me for something.

There were police outside now, and when I glanced up, I saw one of them on the sidewalk and heard him say, 'Jesus Christ! Where's his head?'

On my tie.

Two cops burst through the door, guns drawn. They took stock of the situation and holstered their pistols. I said to one of them, 'This man has a severed artery, so don't tell me to move back. Get the EMS guys in here quick.'

And they did.

The two EMS guys listened to me for a few seconds, then took charge, getting Bellarosa into a wheeled stretcher without puncturing his lungs with his ribs, while a cop kept the pressure on his neck.

I stepped aside and let the pros handle it. Somewhere along the line, the boys in blue discovered the identity of the injured citizen – probably from one of the waiters, not from me – so it was up to them to decide whether or not they wanted to keep don Bellarosa from bleeding to death on the way to St Vincent's. Not my problem anymore.

Well, I was ready to go home now, having had enough excitement for one night, but my car was gone and my driver, Lenny the Rat, was probably on a flight to Naples by now.

Also, the detectives had arrived and they had this idea that I should go down to the station house and tell them all about it. 'Tomorrow,' I said. 'I'm in shock.' But they were positively insistent, so I worked out a deal whereby they would drive Susan back to Long Island and Anna to St Vincent's Hospital, in exchange for my going with them. You don't give nothing for nothing in this city, especially with the cops. Right, Frank?

While all this was going on, Lucio, the owner of the ill-fated establishment, had brought me a nice hot towel, and I got Vinnie off my hands and face, and Frank too. I said to Lucio, 'Sorry about this,' though it wasn't my fault, of course. But no one else was around to apologize for the window and the mess, and the free dinners. And I liked Lucio and his wife. But he'd make up the lost revenue now that Giulio's had joined other select dining and shooting establishments, with a Four Bullet rating.

And that reminded me of the press. They were undoubtedly on the way, and I didn't want to meet the press and be asked a lot of silly questions like, 'Did you see the faces of the men who shot Frank Bellarosa?' and so forth. I *might* have hung around if I thought Jenny Alvarez was on the way, but it was past midnight on a Friday, and she was probably home with a good book by now. Anyway, I said to a detective type, 'Get me out of here.'

'Okay. Let's go.'

'One minute.' Still holding my towel, I went to Anna, who was standing, but was being supported by three cops. I said to her, 'He's going to be all right. I promise.'

She looked at me as though she didn't recognize me, and in fact, her eyes were swollen nearly shut and blinded by tears. But then she put her hand out and touched my cheek. Her voice was very small. 'John . . . oh, John . . .'

'I'll try to see you later at the hospital.'

I moved away from Anna and walked over to where Susan was still sitting in the same chair. I said to her, 'The police will take you home. I have to go with them to the station.'

She nodded.

I said, 'He may make it.'

Again she nodded.

'Are you all right?'

'Yes.'

I had the impression again that she was annoyed at something. I mean, this *was* terribly inconvenient and all. I said, 'Okay. I'll see you later.'

'John?'

'Yes?'

'Did you save his life? Is that what you were doing there?'

'I suppose that's what I was trying to do. Yes.'

'Why?'

'He owes me money.'

She said, 'Well, I wouldn't have done it if I were you.'

Interesting. I said, 'I'll see you at home.' I turned and walked toward the detective who was waiting for me. I heard Susan call out, 'John.'

I turned and she smiled at me, then puckered those pouty lips in a kiss. *Madonn'*, she was nuts. But how sane was I to still love her?

I followed the detective out onto the sidewalk where dozens

of cops had cleared and barricaded a block of Mott Street. Police cars with revolving lights cast red and blue beams on the buildings, and it was a different block than it had been only a short time ago. The detective said to me, 'That your wife?'

'Yes.'

'Nice-looking lady.'

'Thank you.'

We walked toward an unmarked car and he asked me, 'Aren't you the lawyer? Sutter? Bellarosa's lawyer?'

'Right.'

'Maybe that's why they didn't take you out, too. They don't do lawyers.'

'Lucky me.'

He opened the passenger-side door for me and said, 'You ruined your suit, Mr Sutter.'

'It's an old one.' Though the tie was new.

So I spent the next few hours at Midtown south with two detectives, describing the events that had taken about ten minutes to happen. I really was being co-operative, though as an attorney, and especially as the victim's attorney, I could have blown them off and left anytime. In fact, when they started asking questions about who I thought had done the deed, I told them to stick to factual questions. One of the detectives, however, kept asking me about Sally Da-da, and I told him to go ask Sally Da-da about Sally Da-da. But Mr Da-da was in Florida as it turned out. How convenient.

So we went round and round, and this one detective, the bad-cop half of the team, asked me, 'Why'd you save his life?'

'He owes me money.'

The good cop said, 'He owes you his life. Collect on that.'

'How's he doing?'

Good cop replied, 'Still alive.'

I told them the joke about the Mafia guy who tried to blow up a police car, but they seemed sort of weary and barely chuckled. I was getting very yawny myself, but they kept pressing coffee on me.

Midtown South is not an ordinary station house, but is sort of like headquarters for that part of Manhattan, and the joint was bustling with detectives on the second floor where I was. There was also a big room on the second floor where they kept mug-shot books, and I sat in there for about an hour with a detective who was passing me these books labelled 'Wiseguys', which I thought was funny.

Well, I looked at more Italian faces in that hour than I see in Lattingtown in ten years, but I didn't recognize any of the photos as either of the two sportsmen with the shotguns. I remembered a phrase I heard in an old gangster movie once, and I said, 'Maybe they used outside talent. You know, a few boys blew in from Chicago. Check the train stations.'

'Train stations?'

'Well, maybe the airports.'

Anyway, we went from mug shots to a slide show of a few dozen *paesanos* caught by the candid camera in their natural habitats. The detective explained, 'These men have never been arrested, so we don't have mug shots, but they're all wiseguys.'

So I looked at the slide screen until my eyes were about gone and I was yawning and my head ached. A detective said, 'We really appreciate your co-operation.'

'No problem.' But was I really going to finger the two gunmen if I saw their faces? Did I want to be a witness in a mob murder trial? No, I didn't, but I would. Beyond all the bullshit of the last several months, I was still a good citizen, and had I seen the faces of either of those two men, I would have said, 'Stop! That's one of them.' But so far, no one looked familiar.

But then I started to see familiar faces and I blinked. The slides I was looking at now were unmistakably those shot from the DePauw residence with Alhambra in the background. It was, in fact, the Easter Sunday rotogravure, and the enlarged, grainy slides showed a lot of people in their Easter finery getting out of big black cars. I said, 'Hey, I remember that day.' And there was Sally Da-da with a woman who could well have been Anna's sister, and there was Fat Paulie with a woman who could have been his brother, and there were faces I recognized from Giulio's and from the Plaza Hotel, but none of those faces were the ones I had seen aiming down the barrels of those big cannons.

Then the screen flashed to a night view of Alhambra, and there was wiseass John Sutter waving to the camera with pretty Susan in her red dress beside me, giving me a look of puzzled impatience. I said, 'That's the guy! I'll never forget that face.'

The two detectives chuckled. One of them said, 'Looks like a killer.'

'Beady eyes,' agreed the other.

Well, the slide show ended, and to be honest, I couldn't identify the two men, but I said, 'Look, I'm willing to do this all over again, but not tonight.'

'It's best to do it while it's still fresh in your mind, sir.'

'It's too fresh. All I can see now is four black muzzles.'

'We understand.'

'Good. Well, good night.'

But not quite. I spent another few hours with a police sketch artist, a pretty woman, which made the thing sort of tolerable. I was very tempted to describe to her the features of Alphonse Ferragamo, but cops take this sort of thing seriously, and I guess I do, too. So I tried to re-create in words what two goombahs looked like on a dimly lit street, crouched behind a car with shotguns partially blocking their faces. Linda – that was the artist's name – gave me a book of sketches of eyes and mouths and all that, and it was sort of fun, like a mix-and-match game, and we sat shoulder to shoulder hunched over the sketch pad. She wore a nice perfume, which she said was Obsession. As for me, my deodorant had quit, and the little splatters of mortality on my clothes were getting ripe.

Anyway, she produced two sketches that, with some alterations, looked like the boys with the guns. But by this time,

I was so punchy I literally couldn't see straight. Linda said, 'You were very observant considering the circumstances. Most people blank, you know, sort of like a hysterical blindness, and they can't even tell you if the guy was black or white.'

'Thank you. Did I mention that the guy on the right had a tiny zit on his jaw?'

She smiled. 'Is that so?' She took a fresh pad and said, 'Sit still,' then did a quick charcoal sketch of me, which was a little embarrassing. She ripped off the sheet and slid it across the table. I picked it up and studied it for a moment. The woman had obviously been drawing felons too long, because the guy in the sketch looked like a bad dude. I said, 'I need some sleep.'

Well, it was approaching dawn, and again I figured I was through for the night, but who should show up at Midtown South but Mr Felix Mancuso of the Federal Bureau of Investigation. I asked him, 'Slumming?'

But he was in no mood for my wit. Neither was I, to tell you the truth.

I inquired, 'How is my client doing?'

'Alive, but not very well, I'm afraid. Lots of blood loss, and they're talking about possible brain impairment.'

I didn't reply.

Mr Mancuso and I spoke in private for ten or fifteen minutes, and I levelled with him, and he believed me that I knew absolutely nothing more than what I'd told the NYPD, and that I really hadn't been able to identify any of the mug shots or the faces on the slides. I did suggest, however, that Mr Lenny Patrelli was part of the conspiracy.

He replied, 'We know that. The limo was found parked out by Newark Airport and Patrelli's body was in the trunk.'

'How awful.'

Mr Mancuso looked at me. 'You could have been killed, you know.'

'I know.'

He said, 'They still may decide to kill you.'

'They may.'

'Do you think they're nice guys because they left you alive? Are you grateful?'

'I was. But it's wearing off.'

'Do you want federal protection?'

'No, I have enough problems. I really don't think I'm on the hit list.'

'You weren't, but you may be now. You saw their faces.'

'But that's not what we're telling the press, are we, Mr Mancuso?'

'No, but the guys who did the hit know you saw them up close, Mr Sutter. They probably didn't figure you would be that close to them or to Bellarosa, and they couldn't be sure who you were. Pros don't hit people they're not told to hit or paid to hit. You could have been a cop for all they knew, or a priest in civvies. So they let you stand rather than get in trouble with the guys who ordered the job. But now we have a different situation.' He looked at me closely.

I said, 'I'm really not too concerned. Those guys were pros as you said, and they're from someplace else, Mr Mancuso. They're long, long gone, and I wouldn't be too surprised if they turned up in a trunk, too.'

'You're a cool customer, Mr Sutter.'

'No, I'm a realistic man, Mr Mancuso. Please don't try to scare me. I'm scared enough.'

He nodded. 'Okay.' Then he made eye contact with me and said, 'But I told you, didn't I? I told you no good would come of this. I *told* you. Correct?'

'Correct. And I told *you*, Mr Mancuso, what Alphonse Ferragamo was up to. Didn't I? So if you want to find another accessory to this attempted murder, go talk to him.'

Poor Mr Mancuso, he looked sleepy and sad and really disgusted. He said, 'I hate this. This killing.'

I informed Saint Felix that I didn't care much for it either. And on the subject of mortality, I also informed him, 'I stink of blood. I'm leaving.'

'All right. I'll drive you. Where do you want to go?'

I thought a moment and replied, 'Plaza Hotel.'

'No, you want to go home.'

Maybe he was right. 'Okay. Do you mind?'

'No.'

So, after some NYPD formalities, including a promise by me not to leave town, we left Midtown South and got into Mr Mancuso's government-issued vehicle and went through the Midtown Tunnel, heading east on the expressway. The sun was coming up and it was a beautiful morning.

Mr Mancuso and I must have had a simultaneous thought because he asked me, 'Are you happy to be alive?'

'Absolutely.'

'I'm glad to hear that.'

So was I. I asked him, 'How is Mrs Bellarosa?'

'She looked all right when I saw her a few hours ago.' He asked me, 'And Mrs Sutter? Was she very upset?'

'She seemed composed when I last saw her.'

'These things sometimes have a delayed reaction. You should keep an eye on her.'

I should have kept an eye on her since April, and I think that's what he meant. 'She's a strong woman.'

'Good.'

We made small talk as we headed into the rising sun, and to his credit, he wasn't taking the opportunity to pump me about this or that, and so I didn't bug him about Ferragamo again.

Whatever we were talking about must have been boring because I fell asleep and awoke only when he poked me as we drove up Stanhope Hall's gates, which Susan had left open. Mancuso drove up to the guesthouse and I got out of the car and mumbled my thanks to him. He said, 'We'll keep an eye on the place. We're here anyway.'

'Right.'

'Do you want this sketch? Is this supposed to be you?'

'Keep it.' I stumbled out of the car, staggered to the door, and let myself in. On the way up the stairs, I peeled off my bloody clothes and left them strewn on the steps where Lady Stanhope could deal with the mess. I arrived at the guest bathroom stark naked (except for my Yale ring) and took a shower sitting down. *Madonn'*, what a lousy night.

I went into my little room and fell into bed. I lay there staring up at the ceiling as the morning sun came in the window. I heard Susan in the hallway, then heard her on the stairs. It sounded as if she was gathering up the clothes.

A few minutes later there was a knock on my door and I said, 'Come in.'

Susan entered, wearing a bathrobe and carrying a glass of orange juice. 'Drink this,' she said.

I took the orange juice and drank it, though I had a stomach full of coffee acid.

She said, 'The policeman who drove me home said you were a lucky man.'

'I'm definitely on a lucky streak. Tomorrow I'm going skydiving.'

'Well, you know what he meant.' She added, 'I'm lucky to have you home.'

I didn't reply, and she stood there awhile, then finally asked me, 'Is he dead?'

'No. But he's critical.'

She nodded.

'How do you feel about that?' I inquired.

She replied, 'I don't know.' She added, 'Maybe you did the right thing.'

'Time will tell.' I informed her, 'I'm tired.'

'I'll let you get some sleep. Is there anything else I can get for you?'

'No, thank you.'

'Sleep well.' She left and closed the door behind her.

As I lay there, I had this unsettling feeling that I *had* done the right thing, but for the wrong reason. I mean, my instinct as a human being was to save a life. But my intellect told me that the world would be well rid of Mr Frank Bellarosa. Especially this part of the world.

But I *had* saved his life, and I tried to convince myself that I did it because it was the right thing to do. But really, I had done it because I wanted him to suffer, to be humiliated knowing he was the target of his own people, and to face the judgement of society, not the judgement of the scum that had no legal or moral right to end anyone's life, including the life of one of their own.

Also, I wanted my piece of him.

But while I was telling myself the truth, I admitted that I still liked the guy. I mean, we had clicked right from the beginning. And if Frank Bellarosa had any conscious thoughts at that moment, he was thinking about what a good pal I was to stop him from bleeding to death. *Mamma mia,* we should have had pizza delivered.

Well, trying to clear your head and your conscience at the same time is pretty exhausting, so I tuned in to a fantasy about Linda the sketch artist and fell asleep.

CHAPTER 35

The tough son of a bitch survived, of course, thanks mostly to my Eagle Scout and army first-aid skills. The press had made a big deal about my saving Bellarosa's life, and one of those inane inquiring-photographer pieces in a tabloid asked: *Would you save the life of a dying Mafia boss?* All six respondents said yes, going on about humanity and Christianity and all that. Sally Da-da might have had a slightly different opinion if asked, and I sort of suspected he was pissed off at me.

Anyway, it was mid-October now, Columbus Day to be precise, and perhaps that had something to do with my deciding to pay a call on Mr Frank Bellarosa, who had been discharged from the hospital about two weeks before and was convalescing at Alhambra.

I hadn't seen or spoken to him since our unfortunate dinner at Giulio's, and in fact, I hadn't even sent a card or flowers. Actually, he owed *me* flowers. But I had followed the news accounts of his medical progress and so forth. Also, Jenny

Alvarez and I had been meeting in Manhattan for lunch now and then, and she gave me the latest mob gossip. The latest was this: Unlike with some failed Mafia hits where the intended victim survives and is granted a sort of stay of execution in return for acknowledging that he deserved what he almost got, the contract on Frank the Bishop Bellarosa was still in force.

Ms Alvarez and I, incidentally, had progressed in our relationship toward a more spiritual and intellectual plane, which means I wasn't screwing her. Just as well. That really complicates things.

So, on that sunny, mild Columbus Day morning, I walked across the back acreage to Alhambra, where I was stopped near the Virgin Mary by two men wearing blue windbreakers on which were stencilled the letters FBI. They both carried black M-16s. I introduced myself, and they asked for identification, though they seemed to know who I was. I produced my IDs and one of them used a hand-held radio to call someone. I could hear part of the conversation, and it sounded as if the guy on the other end had to go see if Mr Bellarosa was receiving, as they say. I guess he was, because one of the FBI guys said he had to frisk me and he did. He then escorted me toward the house.

I knew, of course, that the guard had changed at Alhambra. Well, two of them were dead for one thing. But Tony and the other characters I had seen floating around all summer had disappeared, either of their own volition or by government decree. Anyway, the Feds were in charge now, and Frank, though safer, was less free, like his birds in their gilded cages. He wasn't actually under arrest; he had apparently switched sides according to the press. Hey, would you blame him?

Anyway, the FBI guy with the M-16 said to me as we walked, 'You understand that he has dismissed you as his attorney, and anything he says to you is not privileged information.'

'I sort of figured that out.' Most FBI agents are lawyers, and maybe even this guy, with his government-issued L. L. Bean look-alikes and his rifle, was an attorney. I like to see attorneys do macho things. Good for the profession's image.

I asked, 'Is his wife home?'

'Not today. She stays with relatives on and off.'

'Is Mr Mancuso here?'

'I'm not sure.'

We crossed the patio, which was covered with autumn leaves, and passed by the pizza oven, whose door was rusty. We entered the great house through the rear doors where another agent, wearing a suit, took charge and escorted me into the palm court.

The palm court was filled with bouquets and baskets of get-well flowers and smelled like a funeral home. *Mamma mia*, these people were into cut flowers. I peeked at a few cards, and on the biggest flower arrangement was a card that said: *Frank, Welcome home. Feel better. Love, Sal and Marie.* No. Could that be Sally Da-da? What was Anna's sister's name? I think it *was* Marie. What incredible gall.

Anyway, there were a few other *federales* in the palm court, and one of them ran a metal detector over me while I admired the flowers.

The detector went off and the guy said, 'Please empty your pockets, sir.'

'It went off because I have brass balls,' I informed him, but I emptied my pockets just the same. I was wearing a tweed shooting jacket, perhaps not the best choice of attire for the occasion, and sure enough, in the side pocket was a clasp knife, which was missed by the frisk search, and which I use to extract jammed shotgun shells. But I didn't mention that because these guys looked tense enough.

'May I have that, sir?'

I gave him the knife and he ran the detector over me again. While this was going on, I spotted a female nurse walking across the palm court. She was an older woman, not a hanky-panky nurse, and she looked tough, the kind who gives ice-water enemas without lubrication.

So, the gent escorted me up the stairs, but I said, 'If he's in his den, I know the way.'

He replied, 'I have to take you all the way, sir.'

Good Lord, this place was getting grim.

We walked to the closed door of the den, and the agent knocked once and opened it. I walked in and the agent shut the door behind me.

Bellarosa was sitting in the easy chair where he'd sat that night we had grappa together. He was wearing a blue-striped bathrobe, and bedroom slippers, which somehow made him look older or perhaps just benign. I noticed he needed a shave.

Still sitting, he extended his hand toward me and said, 'I can't get up easy.'

I took his hand and we shook. I saw now that his usually tanned skin was sallow, and I noticed a few purplish scars on his face and neck where the buckshot had hit him. 'How are you, Frank?'

'Not bad.'

'You look like shit.'

He laughed. 'Yeah. I can't get around much. No exercise. They're still finding fucking pellets in my legs, and my chest feels like I got hit by a truck. I gotta use these canes now.' He grabbed a cane by the side of the chair. 'Like my grandmother.' He lifted the cane. 'I whack anybody who walks past.' He swung the cane and tapped me playfully on the hip and laughed. 'Like my old grandmother. Have a seat.'

I sat in the chair opposite him.

'You want some coffee? Filomena's still here. She's the only one left. The rest are fucking Feds. Even the nurses are fucking Feds. You want coffee?'

'Sure.'

He picked up a walkie-talkie and bellowed, 'Coffee!' He put the radio down and smiled. 'I keep them all busy.'

He really did look like shit, but I didn't sense any brain impairment. In fact, he seemed sharp as ever, just a bit subdued, though that might be a result of painkillers.

I asked, 'How's Anna?'

'She's okay. She's with her crazy sister in Brooklyn.'

'Marie? The one who's married to Sally Da-da?'

He looked at me and nodded.

I said, 'You know the Feds think it was your brother-in-law.'

He shrugged.

I went on, 'He's in charge now. Right?'

'In charge of what?'

'The empire.'

He laughed. 'Empire? I don't know about no empire.'

'You better know, Frank, or you'll wake up one morning and nobody's going to be outside with M-16s. It'll just be you and your canes and Sally Da-da paying a call. *Capisce?*'

He smiled. 'Listen to you. You sound like fucking Mancuso.'

'The papers said you were co-operating.'

He snorted. 'More bullshit. More Ferragamo bullshit, trying to make me look like a rat. The prick still wants me dead.'

In truth, I hadn't given much credence to the possibility that Frank Bellarosa was now working for Alphonse Ferragamo. I said, 'Look, Frank, I'm not your attorney anymore according to Jack Weinstein, but if I were, I'd advise you to co-operate with the government. I assume you're at least contemplating that, or you wouldn't be surrounded by FBI.'

He played with the crook of his cane for a while, and he looked like an old man, I thought. He said, 'I'm being protected because I'm a witness to a killing. Vinnie's killing. Just like you. You know? And I'm the target of organized crime.' He smiled.

I said, 'Frank, you don't owe any loyalty to people who tried to kill you. This is your last chance to stay out of jail, to stay alive, and to go someplace with Anna and start over.'

He looked at me for a full minute, then asked, 'What's it to you?'

Good question. I replied, 'Maybe I care about Anna. Maybe I care about justice.' I added, 'I'm a citizen.'

'Yeah? Well, let me tell you something, Mr Citizen. Frank Bellarosa doesn't talk to the Feds.'

'Your own people tried to kill you, Frank.'

'That was a misunderstanding. You know how that happened. Fucking Ferragamo set me up. But I got it all straightened out now with my people.'

'Do you? Then go take a ride in the country with Sally Da-da.'

'Hey, Counsellor, you don't know anything about this.'

'I know I saw the business end of two double-barrelled shotguns. I saw Vinnie's head splash open like a pumpkin, and I saw you do a backflip through the window.'

He smiled. 'You see why I pay my lawyers so much?'

Speaking of which, I hadn't seen a nickel from him so far, but I wasn't going to bring it up. I did say, however, 'I'd like you to explain to me why I was fired.'

He shrugged. 'I don't know. Lots of reasons. What did Jack tell you?'

'Not much. He just said I caught a break and I should be thrilled. This is true. He also said he would call me as your alibi witness if you wind up standing trial for murder. That is not so thrilling.'

'Yeah. Well, we'll see.' He added, 'The Feds don't like you. So I did them a little favour and let you go.'

'That's interesting. And what favour are they doing you in return?'

He didn't reply, but said, 'That don't mean we can't still be friends. In fact, we're better off as just friends and neighbours. Right?'

'I suppose. Am I still an honorary Italian?'

He laughed. 'Sure. Hey, better yet, I'm making you an honorary *Napoletano*. You know why? Because you stood there and flipped that guy the bird when he was thinking about putting you away.'

How in the name of God could he know that? But I knew better than to ask.

Bellarosa was getting himself into a lighter mood and

he said, 'Hey, you still fucking that Alvarez broad or what?'

'I'm a married man.'

He smiled.

I said, 'She did tell me that the word on the street is that your brother-in-law still has a contract out on you. And you let your wife sleep there?'

'One's got nothing to do with the other.'

I guess I still didn't understand Italian family relationships. I tried to imagine a situation where Susan went to stay with relatives who were trying to kill me. Actually, something like that happens every time she goes to Hilton Head. But William Peckerhead only *wants* me dead; he's too cheap to hire anyone to do the job. I said to Bellarosa, 'Sally sent you flowers. Does he come here and visit you?'

He didn't answer the question directly, but said, 'The guy's a Sicilian. The Sicilians have this expression: You hold your friends close, but your enemies closer. *Capisce?*'

'I do, but I think you're all nuts. *I* am not nuts, Frank. *You* are all nuts.'

He shrugged.

I asked him, 'Do they pay the two guys for a near miss?'

He smiled. 'They can keep the half they got up front. They don't get the other half.' He added, 'I woulda done it different.'

'How so?'

He replied as though he'd thought this out. 'Well, the shotguns were all right to knock people down and fuck up everybody's mind. You know? But you gotta finish the guy you're after with a bullet in the head, because lots of guys wear a vest now. Right?'

'Techniques vary, I'm sure. Hey, Frank, how come you were wearing a vest and not me?'

'I told you, you're a civilian. Don't worry about it. Hey, you want a vest? I'll give you one of mine.' He laughed.

There was a knock on the door, and an FBI guy came in followed by Filomena, who was carrying a tray. I stood to

601

help her, but she made it clear I was in her way, so I sat down. There aren't many women whose appearance would be improved by a beard, but Filomena was one of them.

She put a tray on the table and poured two cups of coffee. Frank said something to her in Italian, and she said something back to him, and they were at it again. While they argued about whatever, she fixed his coffee with cream and sugar and buttered a biscuit for him. I could tell, despite the arguing, that there was affection between the two. I said to Bellarosa, 'Tell her I like her.'

He smiled and spoke to Filomena in Italian.

She looked at me and made a sort of grunt, then snapped something at me.

Bellarosa translated, 'She said you have a beautiful wife and you should behave.' He added, 'Italian women think when you give them a compliment, you want to fuck them. They think all men are pigs.'

'They're right.'

Filomena gave me a glance and left.

I had some coffee, but I noticed that Bellarosa ignored his and ignored the biscuits. I said to him, 'Frank, I'm not here to do the government's work, but I have to tell you, you should put on your Machiavellian thinking cap and consider what's good for you and your wife and your sons.' I added, 'I tell you this because I like you.'

He seemed to be actually thinking about that, then replied, 'I'll tell you something, Counsellor, things are different now. Twenty years ago, nobody talked to the DA or the Feds. Now you got guys who want it both ways. They want to make the money, live the life, then they get into a little trouble with the law, and they don't want to do a little time. You know? So they sing. They don't understand that you got to be ready to do twenty years when you get into this business or you don't get into this business. But now they all have middle-class ambitions, these men. They want to sleep with their wives and girlfriends every night, see their kids off to school, play golf even. In my uncle's day, a man did his twenty years without a fucking peep, and he came out and his wife hugged him, his children kissed his hand, and his partners filled him in on the latest. Understand? But who's got that kind of balls today? So the fucking U.S. Attorney offers deals. But I don't make deals with Feds to save my own ass. My friends should've understood that. They should understand that Frank Bellarosa is not a fucking rat like half of them are. You know what I learned at La Salle? You lead by example. You don't compromise your honour. If this thing, this organization, it going to go on, then I got to show everybody how to make it go on. I got to set the example even if they tried to kill me, and even if I'm surrounded now by Feds. That's balls, Counsellor. Balls. *Capisce?*'

Indeed I did. Misplaced balls, but balls none the less. '*Capisco.*'

He smiled. 'Yeah. Hey, the organization may be a little fucked up these days, but you can't say they don't still have some class and style. They left you standing, didn't they?'

I replied, 'They understand bad press, too. Hitting you is one thing, hitting me is another.'

'Yeah. We still get good press. We want good press. We *need* good press. The *melanzane* and the Spanish shoot everybody, then they wonder why nobody likes them. Right?'

'Techniques vary, as I said.'

'Yeah, but those assholes don't have any technique.'

I really didn't want to debate the merits of competing criminal organizations. But Bellarosa had a point of sorts. To wit: Even if Sally Da-da wanted me dead because I annoyed him, he knew that killing me was not good press and not good business. So Gentleman John Sutter walked through blood and fire with nothing more than a ruined suit and tie, protected by an aura of perceived power and impeccable social credentials. No blue blood on the sidewalks of Little Italy. No wonder Frank didn't think I needed a bulletproof vest. Just the same, I would have preferred to be wearing one when the goombah pointed the gun at me.

I regarded Bellarosa a moment. Though his face looked

drawn and his frame looked somehow diminished to me, his paunch was trying to get out of his bathrobe. Truly, getting hit by three 8-gauge shotgun blasts, even when wearing a vest, was not good for one's health. Seeing him there, a physical wreck, I couldn't help but wonder if his mental state hadn't deteriorated as well. I mean, he seemed okay, but there was something different. Maybe it was the Feds in the house. That would depress anyone.

He asked me to get him a bottle of sambuca, which was hidden behind some books on a shelf, and I found it. I also saw a vase of freshly picked marigolds on the shelf, big yellow marigolds of the type George and I planted at Stanhope Hall. Interesting.

I gave him the bottle, and he poured a good shot of it into his coffee cup and drank it, then poured another. 'You want some?'

'It's a little early.'

'Yeah.' He said, 'That bitch of a nurse won't let me drink. Because of the antibiotics I'm taking. Shit, the fucking sambuca is an antibiotic. Right? Here, put this back.'

I put the bottle behind the books. My, how things had changed at Alhambra. Now *I* was depressed. I looked at my watch as if I had to leave. He saw me and said, 'Sit down a minute. I gotta tell you something.' He motioned me by his side and said, 'Sit here on this hassock.' He jerked his thumb at the ceiling, which I took to mean the place might be bugged.

I sat on the hassock close to him.

He leaned toward me and spoke softly, 'Let me give *you* some advice, Counsellor. I don't hear much from the outside these days, but I do hear that Ferragamo is after your ass. And he ain't doing that just to blow my alibi, he's doing it because you pissed him off in court, and because you saved my life and fucked up his whole thing. So now he's got vendetta on the brain. So watch yourself.'

'I know.' Irony of ironies; Frank Bellarosa was being offered a deal, and I was looking at ten years for perjury.

604

And the one man who could testify against me was Frank Bellarosa. Bellarosa understood this, of course, and I'm sure the irony wasn't lost on him. In fact, he smiled and said, 'Hey, Counsellor, I won't rat you out. Even if they get me by the balls and I got to give up some people, I won't rat you out to Ferragamo.'

I mean, this guy first got you into serious trouble, then got you out of it, then told you that you owed him a favour for his help, then you did him a favour that got you into more trouble, and round and round it went. Now I think he wanted me to say thank you. Speaking in the same low volume as he was, I said, 'Frank, please don't do me any more favours. I can't survive many more of your favours.'

He laughed, but his ribs must have been busted up pretty bad because he winced, and his face went even whiter. He swallowed the last of the sambuca, stayed motionless awhile until his breathing steadied, then sat up a bit and asked me, 'How's your wife?'

'Which one?'

He smiled. 'Susan. Your wife.'

'Why are you asking me? She comes here.'

'Yeah . . . but I haven't seen her in a while.'

'Neither have I. She just got home yesterday.'

'Yeah. She went to see the kids at school. Right?'

'That's right.' She had also taken another trip to Hilton Head before that, which included a journey to Key West to see her brother, Peter, who is apparently phototropic.

Susan and I never really did have a long talk, but we had a few sentences, and I suggested that she not come here anymore. She seemed to agree, but had probably come anyway; as recently as yesterday, in fact, if those flowers were from her. It must have slipped Frank's memory.

Of course, I should have moved out, but moving out is hard to do. For one thing, I knew I was partly responsible for everything that had happened to us since April. Also, Susan was gone more than she was home, so moving out wasn't a pressing issue. And Susan and I can go weeks and weeks without speaking, and my finances, to be honest, were shaky, and bottom line, I still loved her and she loved me and she had asked me to stay.

So there I was, a lonely house husband, living in my wife's residence, nearly broke, still on the hook as a witness for a Mafia don, the possible target of a rubout, a social pariah, a captain without a boat, and an embarrassment to my law firm. The firm, incidentally, had sent me a registered letter at the Locust Valley office, which I decided to open. The letter asked me to disassociate myself from Perkins, Perkins, Sutter and Reynolds, forthwith. The letter was signed by all the senior partners, active and retired, even the ones who couldn't remember their own names, let alone mine. One of the signatures was that of Joseph P. Sutter. Pop's a great kidder.

Well, screw Perkins, Perkins, Sutter and Reynolds. They all needed a few whacks with a lead pipe. Meantime, they could offer me some incentives to leave.

Bellarosa said, 'I'm glad she's not pissed at me.'

I looked at him. 'Who?'

'Your wife.'

'Why should she be?'

He replied, 'For almost getting her husband killed.'

'Don't be silly, Frank. Why, just the other day she was saying to me, "John, I can't wait for Frank to get better so we can all go to Giulio's again."'

He tried to keep from laughing, but he couldn't and his ribs hurt again. 'Hey . . . cut it out . . . you're killing me . . .'

I stood. 'Okay, Frank, here's something that's not so funny. You know fucking well that Susan and I are barely speaking and you know fucking well why. If she wants to come here, that's her business, but I don't want you talking to me about her as if you're making polite small talk. Okay?'

Bellarosa stared off into space, which I had learned was his way of showing that he wanted the subject changed. I said to him, 'I have to go.' I moved toward the door. 'Should I tell your nurse you need to use the potty?'

He ignored the taunt and said to me, 'Hey, did I ever thank you for saving my life?'

'Not that I recall.'

'Yeah. You know why? Because "thank you" don't mean shit in my business. "Thank you" is what you say to women and outsiders. What I say to you, Counsellor, is I owe you one.'

'Jesus Christ, Frank, I hope you don't mean a favour.'

'Yeah. A favour. You don't understand favours. Favours are like money in the bank with Italians. We collect favours, trade favours, count them like assets, hold them and collect on them. I owe you a big favour. For my life.'

'Keep it.'

'No. You gotta ask a favour.'

I looked at him. This was like having an Italian genie. But you can't trust genies. I said, 'If you went to trial for murder, and I asked you not to have Jack Weinstein call me as your witness, would you do that even if it meant your getting convicted for a murder you didn't commit?'

He didn't even hesitate. 'You ask, you get. I owe you my life.'

I nodded. 'Well, let me think about it. Maybe I can come up with a bigger and better favour.'

'Sure. Hey, stop by again.'

I opened the door, then turned back to him. 'Hey, these Indians are standing on the beach, you know, and Columbus comes ashore and says to them *"Buon giorno,"* and one of the Indians turns to his wife and says "Shit, there goes the neighbourhood."' As I closed the door behind me, I heard him laughing and coughing.

CHAPTER 36

I finally decided to go to my Wall Street office to tidy up my affairs there. I sat in my office, my father's old office, and wondered how I could have wasted so many years of my life in that place. But by an act of pure will, I got down to work and did for my firm and my clients basically what I'd done in the Locust Valley office; that is, I wrote memos on each client and each case, and I parcelled everything out to specific attorneys who I thought would be best suited to each case and each client. That was more than my father had done, and more than Frederic Perkins had done before he jumped from the window down the hall.

Anyway, despite my loyalty and conscientiousness, I was as welcome at 23 Wall Street as a four-hundred-point drop in the Dow. Nevertheless, I soldiered on for over a week, speaking to no one but my secretary, Louise, who seemed annoyed at me for having left her holding the bag for the last several months, trying to answer all sorts of questions from clients and partners regarding Mr Sutter's files and cases.

Anyway, in order to put in long days in the Wall Street office, and for other reasons, I was living at the Yale Club in Manhattan. This is a very large and very comfortable establishment on Vanderbilt Avenue, and the rooms are quite nice. Breakfast and dinner aren't bad either, and the bar is friendly. There's a stock market Teletype off the cocktail lounge so you can see if you can afford the place; there's a gym with a swimming pool and squash courts, and the clientele is Yale. What more can a man ask for? One could almost stay here for ever, and many members in my situation would do just that, but the club discourages overly long stays for wayward husbands, and in recent years, wayward wives. Regarding the latter, one could get into trouble at the club, but I had enough trouble, so after dinner I would just read the newspapers in the big lounge and have a cigar and port like the other old tweedbags, then go to bed.

I did bring Jenny Alvarez to dinner one night, and she said, apropos of the club, 'What a world you live in.'

'I guess I never gave it much thought.'

We chatted about the World Series, and she needled me about the Mets' pathetic four-in-a-row loss to the Yankees. Who would have believed it?

Anyway, we talked about everything except Bellarosa, television news, and sex, just to show each other, I guess, that we had a solid friendship based on many mutual interests. Actually as it turned out, other than baseball, we shared almost no interests. We wound up talking about kids, and she showed me a picture of her son. And though it was obvious that we were still hot for each other, I didn't ask her up to my room.

Well, I wound up spending nearly two weeks at the Yale Club, which was convenient in regard to not having to deal with friends and family on Long Island. On the weekend, I visited Carolyn and Edward at their schools.

By the middle of the following week, I had about run out of excuses for staying away from Lattingtown, so I checked out of the Yale Club and went back to Stanhope Hall to discover that Susan was about to leave for another visit to Hilton Head and Key West. You may envy people like us for the time and money we have to spend avoiding unpleasantness, and you may be right in being envious. But in my case, at least, the money was running out and so was the time, and the hurt was no less acute than if I'd been a contractor or a civil servant. Clearly, something had to be done. I said to Susan before she left, 'If we move away from here, permanently, I think I can come to terms with the past. I think we can start over.'

She replied, 'I love you, John, but I don't want to move. And I don't think it would do any good anyway. We'll solve our problems here, or we'll separate here.'

I asked her, 'Are you still visiting next door?'

She nodded.

'I'd like you not to.'

'I have to do this my way.'

'Do what?'

She didn't reply directly, but said to me, 'You visited next door. And you're not his attorney anymore. Why did you go?'

'Susan, it's not the same if I go there as when you go there. And don't piss me off by asking why it isn't.'

She replied, 'Well, but I will tell you that perhaps you shouldn't go there either.'

'Why not? Am I complicating things?'

'Maybe. It's complex enough.'

And on that note, she left for the airport.

Well, despite Susan's good advice, about a week later, on a raw, drizzly day in November, I decided to go collect the money that Bellarosa still owed me and, more important, to collect a favour. Because of the wet weather I went by way of the front gate. The three FBI men there were particularly officious, and I was briefly nostalgic for Anthony, Lenny, and Vinnie.

As I stood under the eave of the gatehouse, I could see this one FBI guy inside glancing at me through the window as he spoke to someone on the phone. Two other FBI guys stood near me with their rifles. I said to them, 'Is there something wrong with my passport? Is Il Duce not receiving? What's the problem here?'

One of the agents shrugged. After a while, the other guy came out of the gatehouse and informed me that Mr Bellarosa was not available. I said, 'My wife comes and goes here as she pleases. Now you get back on that fucking telephone and get me cleared pronto.'

And he did. Though he seemed upset with me for some reason.

So I was escorted up the cobble drive by one of the guys with the rifles, was turned over to another guy with a tie at the door, and got myself processed for dangerous metal objects. What they didn't understand was that if I wanted to kill Bellarosa, I would do it with my bare hands.

I noticed that the flowers were all gone now and the palm court looked somehow bigger and emptier. Then I realized that all the bird cages were gone. I asked one of the FBI men about that, and he replied, 'There's no one to take care of them. And they were getting on some of the guys' nerves.' He smiled and added, 'We only have one songbird left. He's upstairs.' So I was escorted up the stairs, but this time to Bellarosa's bedroom.

It was about five P.M., but he was in bed, sitting up though not looking well.

I had never been in the master bedroom of Alhambra, but I could see now that the room I was in was part of a large suite that included a sitting room off to my left and a dressing room to my front that probably included a master bath. The bedroom itself was not overly large, and the heavy, dark Mediterranean furniture and red velvets made it look smaller and somewhat depressing. There was only a single window against which the rain splattered. If I were sick, I'd rather be lying in the palm court.

Bellarosa motioned me to a chair beside the bed, the nurse's chair I suppose, but I said, 'I'll stand.'

'So, what can I do for you, Counsellor?'

'I'm here to collect.'

'Yeah? You need that favour? Tell me what you need.'

'First things first. I'm also here to collect my bill. I sent you a note and an invoice over two weeks ago.'

'Oh, yeah.' He took a glass of red wine from the night table and sipped on it. 'Yeah . . . well, I'm not a free man anymore.'

'Meaning what?'

'I sold myself like a whore. I do what they say now.'

'Did they tell you not to pay my bill?'

'Yeah. They tell me what bills to pay. Yours ain't one of them, Counsellor. That's your pal Ferragamo. But I'll talk to somebody higher up for you. Okay?'

'Don't bother. I'll write this one off to experience.'

'You let me know.' He asked, 'You want some wine?'

'No.' I walked around the room and noticed a book on his night table. It was not Machiavelli, but a picture book of Naples.

Bellarosa said to me, 'What really hurts me is that I can't take care of my people anymore. For an Italian, that's like cutting off his balls. *Capisce?*'

'No, and I never want to *capisce* a damned thing again.'

Bellarosa shrugged.

I said, 'So you work for Alphonse Ferragamo now.'

He didn't like that at all, but he said nothing.

I asked him, 'Can you tell me what those bulldozers are doing at Stanhope Hall?'

'Yeah. They're gonna dig foundations. Put in roads. The IRS made me sell the place to the developers.'

'Is that a fact? My whole world is fucked up, and now you tell me I'm about to be surrounded by tractor sheds.'

'Whaddaya mean tractor sheds? Nice houses. You'll have plenty of good neighbours.'

It wasn't my property that was being subdivided or surrounded anyway, so I didn't really care. But I asked him, 'What's happening to the Stanhope mansion?'

'I don't know. The developer has some Japs interested in it for a kind of rest house in the country. You know? Those people get all nervous, and they need a place to rest.'

This was really depressing news. A rest house for burnedout Japanese businessmen, surrounded by thirty or forty new houses on what was once a beautiful estate. I asked him, 'How did you get the zoning changed?'

'I got friends in high places now. Like the IRS. I told you, they want big bucks, so I get rid of everything with their help. And Ferragamo started a RICO thing against me so he's trying to get his before the fucking IRS gets theirs. They're like fucking wolves tearing me apart.'

'So you're telling me you're broke?'

He shrugged. 'Like I said once, Counsellor, give unto Caesar that which is Caesar's. Well, Caesar is in the next fucking room, and he wants his.'

I smiled. 'But never more than fifteen per cent, Frank.'

He forced a smile in return. 'Maybe this time he got more. But I can do all right on what's left.'

'That's good news.' I regarded him a moment, and indeed he looked like a beaten man. No doubt he was physically not well, but in a more profound way his spirit seemed crushed and his spark was gone. I guess this was what I'd hoped to see when I saved his life, but I wasn't enjoying it. In some perverse way we can all relate to the rebel, the pirate, the outlaw. His existence is proof that this life does not squash everyone and that today's superstate cannot get us all into lockstep. But life and the state had finally caught up with the nation's biggest outlaw and laid him low. It was inevitable, really, and he had known it even as he made plans for a future that would never come.

I said to him, 'And Alhambra?'

'Oh, yeah, I had to sell this place, too. The Feds want this house bulldozed. What bastards. Like they don't want people saying, "Frank Bellarosa lived there once." Fuck them. But I worked it out with them that Dominic gets to build the house for the guy who's going to buy the land. I'm going to make Dominic put up little Alhambras, nice little stucco villas with red tile roofs.' He smiled. 'Funny, huh?'

'I guess. And Fox Point?'

'The Arabs got it.'

'The Iranians?'

'Yeah. Fuck them. So all you bastards that didn't like me here on this street, you can all watch the sand niggers driving to their temple in their big cars, wailing all over the place.' He laughed weakly and coughed.

'Are you all right?'

'Yeah. Just a goddamned flu. That fucking nurse is a bitch. They fired Filomena one day without telling me and deported her or something, and they only let Anna come a few days at a time. She's in Brooklyn again. I got nobody to talk to here. Except the fucking Feds.'

I nodded. The Justice Department could indeed be nasty and petty when they chose to, and when you had the IRS on your case at the same time, you might as well put your head between your legs and kiss your ass good-bye. I said, 'And you let all this happen in exchange for what? For freedom?'

'Yeah. For freedom. I'm free. Everything's forgiven. But meantime I got to rat out everybody, and I got to let them play with me like I was a toy. Jesus Christ, these guys are worse than commies.' He looked at me. 'That was your advice, wasn't it, Counsellor? Sell out, Frank. Start a new life.'

I replied, 'Yes, that was my advice.'

'So, I took it.'

'No, you made your own decision, Frank.' I added, 'I think the operative part – the thing that is important – is that you start a new life. I assume you'll be leaving here under the new identity programme.'

'Yeah. I'm under the witness protection programme now. Next, I graduate to new identity if I'm good. In my new life I want to be a priest.' He forced a tired smile and sat up straight. 'Here, have some wine with me.' He took a clean water tumbler from his nightstand and poured me a full glass. I took it and sipped on it. Chianti *acido*, fermented in storage batteries. How could a sick man drink this stuff?

He said, 'I'm not supposed to tell nobody where I'm going, but I'm going back to Italy.' He tapped the book on his nightstand. 'Funny how we say "back", like we came from there. I'm third-generation here. Been to Italy maybe ten times in the last thirty years. But we still say "back". Do you say back to . . . where? England?'

'No, I don't say that. Maybe sometimes I think it. But I'm here for the duration, Frank. I'm an American. And so are you. In fact, you are so fucking American you wouldn't believe it. You understand?'

He smiled. 'Yeah. I know, I know. I'm not going to like living in Italy, am I? But it's safer there, and it's better than jail and better than dead, I guess.' He added, 'The Feds got it all worked out with the Italian government. Maybe someday you can come visit.'

I didn't reply. We were both silent awhile, and we drank our wine. Finally, Bellarosa spoke, but not really to me, I think, but to himself and maybe to his *paesanos*, whom he was selling out *en masse*. He said, 'The old code of silence is dead. There're no real men left anymore, no heroes, no stand-up guys, not on either side of the law. We're all middle-class paper guys, the cops and the crooks, and we make deals when we got to, to protect our asses, our money, and our lives. We rat out everybody, and we're happy we got the chance to do it.'

Again I didn't reply.

He said to me, 'I was in jail once, Counsellor, and it's not a place for people like us. It's for the new bad guys, the darker people, the tough guys. My people don't lay their balls on the table no more. We're like *you* people. We got too fucking soft.'

'Well, maybe you can work that farm outside of Sorrento.'

He laughed. 'Yeah. Farmer Frank. Fat fucking chance of that.' He looked me in the eye. 'Forget the word "Sorrento". *Capisce?*'

'I hear you.' I added in a soft voice, 'A word of advice, Frank. Don't trust the Feds to keep your forwarding address secret either. If they send you to Sorrento, don't stay too long.'

He winked at me. 'I was right to make you a *Napoletano*.'

'And I suppose Anna is going with you, so watch the postmarks on the letters she sends home. Especially to her sister.' I asked, 'She *is* going, right?'

He hesitated a moment, then replied, 'Yeah. Sure. She's my wife. What's she going to do? Go to college and work for IBM?'

'Is she as unhappy about the move as she was about moving here?'

'You got to ask? She never wanted to leave her mother's house, for Christ's sake. You know, you think about them immigrant women coming here from sunny Italy with nothing and making a life here in the tenements of New York. And now those women's daughters and granddaughters have a fit when the fucking dishwasher breaks. You know? But hey, we're no better. Right?'

'Right.' I said, 'Maybe she'll adjust better to Italy than to Lattingtown.'

'Nah. All Italian married women are unhappy. They are

happy girls and happy widows, but they are unhappy wives. I told you, you can't make them happy, so you ignore them.' He added, 'Anyway, my kids are still here. Anna is going nuts about that. Maybe they'll want to come over and live. Who knows? Maybe someday I can come back. Maybe someday you'll walk into a pizza joint in Brooklyn, and I'll be behind the counter. You want that pie cut in eight or twelve slices?'

'Twelve. I'm hungry.' Actually I couldn't picture me in a pizza joint in Brooklyn, nor could I picture Frank Bellarosa behind the counter, and neither could Frank Bellarosa. Some of this was just an act, maybe for me, maybe for the Feds if they were listening. A guy like Bellarosa may be down for a while, but never out. As soon as he got out from under the thumb of the Justice Department, he'd be back in some shady business. If he was ever in a pizza joint, it would be to shake down the owner.

He said, 'Well, you got me wondering about that favour I owe you.'

I put down my glass of wine and said, 'Okay, Frank, I'd like you to tell my wife it's over between you two and that you're not taking her with you to Italy, which is what I think she believes, and I want you to tell her that you only used her to get to me.'

We stared at each other, and he nodded. 'Done.'

I moved toward the door. 'We won't see each other again, but you'll forgive me if I don't shake your hand.'

'Sure.'

I opened the door.

He called out. 'John.'

I don't think he'd ever called me by my first name before, and it took me surprise. I looked back at him sitting in bed. 'What?'

'I'll tell her I used her if you want, but that wasn't it. You gotta know that.'

'I know that.'

'Okay.' He said to me, 'We're both on our own now,

Counsellor, and in years to come we'll think of this time as a good time, a time when we took and we gave and we got smarter by knowing each other. Okay?'

'Sure.'

'And watch your ass. You got some of my *paesanos* on your case now – Alphonse and the other guy. But you can handle it.'

'I sure can.'

'Yeah. Good luck.'

'You, too.' And I left.

CHAPTER 37

I had decided to visit Emily in Galveston, and I was packing enough clothes for an extended trip. Visiting relatives is sort of like walking out but under cover. Susan had her turn at it, and now that she was back, it was my turn.

I was going to take the Bronco rather than fly, because maybe the states west of New York were not just fly-over states, but places that should be seen, with people that should be met. It was a step in the right direction, anyway.

I was looking forward to my first stop at a McDonald's, to staying at motels made out of concrete blocks, and to buying an RC Cola at a 7-Eleven. The thought of self-service gasoline, however, was a bit anxiety-producing, because I wasn't sure how it was done. I suppose I could watch from the side of the road and see how everyone else did it. I think you pay first, then pump.

Anyway, I intended to leave in the morning at first light. It had only been a few days since my last call on Frank Bellarosa, and in that time, Susan had come home from her trip to Hilton Head and Florida looking very fit and tan. Her brother, she informed me, loved Key West and had decided to finally settle down and do something with his life.

'Like what?' I asked. 'Get a haircut?'

'Don't be cynical, John.'

She had greeted the news of my cross-country trip with mixed emotions. On the one hand, my absences removed a lot of strain from the situation, but she honestly seemed to miss me when we were separated. It's not easy to love two people at the same time.

Anyway, as I was packing that night, Susan came into the guest room where I was still in residence and said, 'I'm going for a ride.'

She was wearing riding breeches, boots, a turtleneck, and a tailored tweed jacket. She looked good, especially with her tan. I replied, 'The bulldozers have changed the terrain, Susan. Be careful.'

'I know. But it's bright as day tonight.'

Which was true. There was a huge, orange hunter's moon rising, and it was such a beautiful, haunting sort of night that I almost offered to join her. With the two estates about to become subdivisions, and Fox Point about to become Iranian territory, and with the remaining landed gentry not speaking to us, the days of horseback riding were drawing to a close, and even I was going to miss that. But that night, I decided not to ride. I think I had sensed she wanted to be alone.

She said, 'I may be late.'

'All right.'

'If I don't see you tonight, John, please wake me before you leave.'

'I will.'

'Good night.'

'Happy trails.'

And she left. In retrospect, she had seemed perfectly normal, but I told you she was nuts, and that full moon didn't help.

At about eleven P.M., I was contemplating retiring for the night as I wanted to be up before dawn and I had a long day on the road ahead of me. But Susan still wasn't home, and you know how husbands and wives are about falling asleep before the other is home. I suppose it's partly concern and partly jealousy, but whatever it is, the person at home wants to hear the car pull up in the driveway, even if they're not speaking to the other person.

In this case, I wasn't waiting for a car to pull up, of course, but for the sound of hoofbeats, which I can sometimes hear now that the stable is closer to the house. But it *was* a car that pulled up in front of the house, and I saw its headlights coming up the drive long before I heard the tyres on the gravel. I was in my second-floor bedroom at the time, still fully dressed, and as I came down the stairs, I heard the car door shut, then heard the doorbell ring.

A strange car in the driveway at eleven P.M. and a ringing doorbell is not usually good news. I opened the door to see Mr Mancuso standing there with an odd expression on his face. 'Good evening, Mr Sutter.'

'What's up?' was all I could think to say with my heart in my throat.

'Your wife – '

'Where is she? Is she all right?'

'Yes. I'm sorry, I didn't mean to . . . she's not hurt. But I think you should come with me.'

So, wearing corduroy jeans and a sweatshirt, I followed him out to his car, and we got in. We didn't speak as he made his way down the dark drive. As we went past the gatehouse, I saw Ethel Allard looking out the window, and we were close enough so that our eyes met, and I wondered if I looked as worried as she did.

We swung onto Grace Lane and turned left toward Alhambra. I said to Mr Mancuso, 'Is he dead?'

He glanced at me and nodded.

'I guess he wasn't wearing a bulletproof vest this time.'

'No, he wasn't.' He added, 'Do you have a good stomach?'

'I saw a man's head blown off on a full stomach.'

'That's right. Well, he's uncovered, and I guess you'll see him, because we held off on calling the police. I came and got you as a courtesy, Mr Sutter, a favour, so you can speak to your wife before the county detectives arrive.'

'Thank you.' I added, 'You didn't owe me any favours, so I guess I owe you one now.'

'All right. Here's the favour. Get what's left of your life together. I'd like that.'

'Done.'

Mancuso seemed in no hurry, as if he were unconsciously hesitating, and it took us a while to get up the long cobble drive. I noticed, irrelevantly, that every window in Alhambra was lit. Mancuso said to me, 'What a place. But like Christ said, "What is a man profited if he gain the whole world, and lose his own soul?"'

I didn't think St Felix understood the true nature of Frank Bellarosa. I replied, 'He didn't sell his soul, Mr Mancuso. He was more in the buying business.'

He glanced at me again. 'I think you're right.'

I said, 'Is Mrs Bellarosa here?'

'No. She's in Brooklyn.'

'Which was why my wife was here.'

He didn't reply.

I added, 'In fact, it was very convenient for Mr Bellarosa and Mrs Sutter having Mrs Bellarosa packed off to Brooklyn for extended visits.'

Again no reply.

I said, 'You not only allowed that, you aided and abetted it.'

He replied this time, 'That was not our business, Mr Sutter. It was your business. You knew.'

'I know you have to keep your witnesses happy, Mr Mancuso, but you don't have to pimp for them.'

'I understand your bitterness.'

'Understand, too, Mr Mancuso, that neither you nor I are as clean and pure as we were last Easter.'

'I know that.' He added, 'This was a very dirty case. And I can't even say that the ends justified the means. But I'll make my peace in my own way. I know you'll do the same.'

'I'll give it a shot.'

'Professionally, no one is very happy that Frank Bellarosa

620

died before he could tell us everything he knew. No one is very happy with what Mrs Sutter did. So maybe we got what we deserved for what we did, for bending the rules and letting her come here and never even running a metal detector over her. We have some answering to do for this. Maybe that makes you feel better.'

'Not a bit.'

The car stopped in front of Alhambra, and I got out quickly and went into the house. In the palm court were six FBI men, two in casual clothes with rifles slung across their backs and four in suits. They all turned and looked at me. I was approached by two of them and frisked, then got the metal detector routine that they should have given to my wife.

The first thing I noticed as I looked around was a large potted palm lying on its side near the archway that led to the dining room. The clay pot was cracked open, and soil and palm fronds were spread over the red tile floor. Partially hidden behind the big pot and the foliage was a man sprawled on the floor. I walked over to him.

Frank Bellarosa was lying on his back, his arms and legs outstretched and his striped robe thrown open, revealing his naked body. I could see the healed wounds and pockmarks where the shotgun blasts had hit his arms, neck, and legs some months before. There were three new wounds, one above his heart, one in his stomach, and one right in his groin. I wondered which shot she had fired first.

There was a lot of blood, of course, all over his body and his robe, all over the floor, and even on the plant. The three wounds had partly coagulated and looked like red custard. I noticed now that there was blood splattered some distance from his body, and I realized he had fallen from the railed mezzanine above. I looked up and saw that I was standing under where his bedroom door would be.

I looked back at Bellarosa's face. His eyes were wide open, but this time there was no life or pain in them, no tears, only eternity. I kneeled down and pressed his eyelids closed, and

I heard Mr Mancuso's voice behind me, 'Please don't touch anything, Mr Sutter.'

I stood and took a last look at Frank Bellarosa. It occurred to me that the Italians had always understood that at the core of life's problems are men with too much power, too much charisma, and too much ambition. The Italians made demigods of such men, but at the same time they hated them for these very same qualities. Thus, the killing of a Caesar, a don, a duce, was a psychologically complex undertaking, embodying both sin and salvation in the same act.

Perhaps Susan, not the sort of person to think of harming anyone for any reason, had absorbed some of her lover's psyche along with his semen, and had decided to use a Bellarosa solution to solve a Bellarosa problem. But how did I know that for sure? Maybe John is projecting.

Mancuso tapped my arm and drew my attention to the far side of the palm court.

Susan was sitting with her legs crossed in a wicker chair, between a pillar and a potted tree, out of the line of sight of the corpse. She was fully dressed in her riding outfit, though I did not know then nor would I ever know if she had been fully dressed earlier. Her long red hair, however, which had been tied up under her riding cap, was now loose and dishevelled. Otherwise she looked very composed. Very beautiful, actually. I walked toward her.

As I got within a few feet of her, she looked up at me but made no move to meet me. I saw now that an FBI man was standing near the pillar, watching her, guarding her actually. She glanced up at him, and he nodded, and she stood and came toward me. Odd, I thought, how even the highborn learn so quickly how to become prisoners. Depressing, actually.

We stood a few feet apart, and I saw that she had been crying, but she looked all right now. Composed, as I said. I suppose our audience was waiting for us to embrace or for someone to break down or maybe go for the other's throat. I was aware that six or seven men were ready to spring into action in the event of the latter. These guys were tense, of course, having already lost one person they were supposed to be safeguarding.

Finally I said to my wife, 'Are you all right?"

She nodded.

'Where did you get the gun?'

'He gave it to me.'

'When? Why?'

She seemed a little out of it, which was normal under the circumstances, but she thought a moment and replied, 'When he came home from the hospital. The FBI men were searching the house, and he had a gun hidden so he gave it to me to keep for him.'

'I see.' You blew it, Frank. But really, if it weren't a gun, it would have been a knife or a fireplace poker, or anything she could get her hands on. Hell hath no fury like a redheaded woman scorned. Believe it? I asked her, 'Did you make any statement to anyone here?'

'Statement . . .? No . . . I just said . . . I forgot . . .'

'Don't say anything to them or to the police when they arrive.'

'The police . . .?

'Yes, they're on the way.'

'Can't I go home?'

'I'm afraid not.'

'Am I going to jail?'

'Yes. I'll try to get you out tomorrow on bail.' Then again, maybe I won't.

She nodded and smiled for the first time, a forced smile, but genuine none the less. She said, 'You're a good lawyer.'

'Right.' I saw that she was pale and shaky, so I led her back to the chair. She glanced over at the mess at the far end of the palm court, then looked at me and said, 'I killed him.'

'Yes, I know.' I sat her down in the chair, knelt, and took her hand. 'Do you want something to drink?'

'No, thank you.' She added, 'I did this for you.'

I chose to ignore that.

The county police arrived, uniformed officers, plainclothes

623

detectives, the forensic unit, ambulance attendants, police photographers, and other assorted crime-scene types. The grandeur of Alhambra seemed more interesting to them than its dead owner, but eventually they got down to business.

Susan watched the activity as though it had nothing to do with her. Neither of us spoke, but I stayed with her, kneeling beside her chair and holding her hand.

I saw Mancuso speaking to a big beefy guy with a ruddy face, and they kept glancing over at Susan and me as they spoke. Finally, the big guy walked over to us and I stood. A uniformed female police officer joined him. The big guy said to me, 'You're her husband?'

'And her attorney. Who are you?'

He obviously didn't like my tone or my question, but you have to get off on the wrong foot with these guys, because that's where you're headed anyway. He said, 'I'm Lieutenant Dolan, County Homicide.' He turned to Susan and said, 'And you are Susan Sutter?'

She nodded.

'Okay, Mrs Sutter, I'm going to read you your rights in the presence of your husband, who I understand is your attorney.' Dolan had one of those little cheat cards like Mancuso had and began reading from it. Good Lord, you'd think they could remember a few simple lines after twenty years of saying them. I mean, I can still recite the entire prologue of the *Canterbury Tales* twenty-five years after I learned it, and that's in Middle English.

Dolan asked Susan, 'Do you understand your rights?'

Again she nodded.

He looked at me. 'She understands?'

'Not really,' I replied, 'but for the record, yes.'

He turned back to Susan. 'Do you want to make any statements at this time?'

'I –'

I interrupted. 'No. She is obviously not going to make any statements, Lieutenant.'

'Right.' Dolan signalled to the uniformed policewoman,

who approached, somewhat self-consciously I thought. Dolan turned back to Susan. 'Please stand, Mrs Sutter.'

Susan stood.

Dolan said to her, 'You are under arrest for murder. Please turn around.'

The policewoman actually turned Susan by the shoulder and was going to cuff her hands behind her back, but I grabbed the woman's wrist. 'No. In the front.' I looked at Dolan. 'She won't try to strangle you with the cuffs, Lieutenant.'

This didn't go over very well, but after a little glaring all around, Dolan said to the policewoman, 'In front.'

Before Susan was cuffed, I helped her off with her tweed jacket, and then the woman cuffed Susan's hands in front of her. This is more comfortable, less humiliating, and looks better because you can throw a coat over the cuffs, which I then did with Susan's jacket.

By this time, Dolan and I were getting to understand each other a little better, and we didn't like what we understood. Dolan said to the policewoman but also so I could hear, 'Mrs Sutter was searched by the federal types when they grabbed her, and they tell me she has no more weapons, but you have her searched again at the station house, and you look for poison and other means of suicide, and you keep a suicide watch on her all night. I don't want to lose this one.' He glanced at me, then said to the policewoman, 'Okay, take her away.'

'Hold on,' I said. 'I want to speak to my client.'

But Lieutenant Dolan was not going to be as co-operative as Mr Mancuso had been under similar circumstances in this very spot some months before. Lieutenant Dolan said, 'If you want to talk to her, come to the station house.'

'I intend to speak to her now, Lieutenant.' I had my hand on Susan's left arm, and the policewoman had her hand on Susan's right arm. Poor Susan. For the first time since I'd known her, she actually looked as if she wasn't in control of a situation.

Well, before the situation got out of everyone's control,

Mancuso ambled over and put his arm around Dolan, leading him away. They chatted a minute, then Dolan turned back toward us and motioned to the policewoman to back off.

I took Susan's cuffed hands in mine, and we looked at each other. She didn't say anything but squeezed my hands. Finally, I said, 'Susan . . . do you understand what's happening?'

She nodded. Actually she did seem more alert now, and she looked me in the eyes. 'John, I'm so sorry for the inconvenience. I should have waited until you left.'

That would have been a good idea, but Susan had no intention of letting me off that easy. I said, 'Maybe you shouldn't have killed him at all.'

Her mind was either elsewhere or she didn't want to hear that, because she said, 'Could you do me a favour? Zanzibar is tethered out back. Will you ride him home? He can't stay there all night.'

I replied, 'I'll certainly take care of Zanzibar.'

'Thank you. And you could see to Zanzibar and Yankee in the morning?'

'All right.'

'Will I be home by afternoon?'

'Perhaps. If I can make bail.'

'Well, my chequebook is in my desk.'

I replied, 'I don't think they take personal cheques, Susan. But I'll work something out.'

'Thank you, John.'

There really wasn't much else to say, I suppose, now that the horses were taken care of and I knew where her chequebook was. Well, maybe this wasn't the time for sarcasm, but if I told you I wasn't enjoying this at all, I'd be a liar. Still, I couldn't really enjoy it, nor for that matter could I weep over it unless I fully understood it. So, against my better judgement, I asked her, 'Why did you kill him?'

She looked at me as though that were a silly question. 'He destroyed us. You know that.'

Okay. So leave it at that. From that we had a chance to rebuild our lives together if we chose to. She did it for us.

End of story. But you can't build on lies, so I said, 'Susan, don't lie to me. Did he tell you he was leaving you? Did he tell you that he was not leaving Anna for you? That he was not taking you with him to Italy? Did he tell you that he only used you to get to me?'

She stared at me, through me actually, and I saw she was off again in Susan land. I supposed we could have this conversation some other time, though I was curious to discover if Bellarosa's telling Susan that he only used her to get to me was the proximate cause of his death. And you may wonder if he knew or suspected what would happen when I set that in motion. That is a complex question. I'd have to think about that.

I looked at Susan. 'If you did it for us, Susan, then thank you for trying to save our marriage and our life together. But you didn't have to *kill* him.'

'Yes, I *did*. He was evil, John. He seduced us both. Don't take his side. He was always taking *your* side about something or other and now you're taking his side. Now I'm angry with you both. Men are all alike, aren't they, always sticking up for one another, but he *was* different from other men, and I was obsessed with him, but I tried to control myself, I really did, but I couldn't keep away from him, even after you asked me to, and he took advantage of me, and he used me, and he promised me he was going to save Stanhope Hall, but he didn't, and he used you, too, John, and you knew what was happening, so don't look at me like that.'

Susan went on like this for a while, and I realized I could enter an insanity plea, but by morning she'd be herself again, which is not to say any less crazy, but at least she'd be quieter about it.

I took her head in my hands and played with her soft red hair. She stopped babbling and looked at me. Those catlike green eyes stared right into me, and with crystal-clear sanity now, she said to me, 'I did this because you couldn't, John. I did this to return your honour to you. *You* should have done it. You were right not to let him die, but you should have killed him.'

Well, if we had been living in another age or another country, she would be right. But not in this age, not in this country. Though perhaps like Frank Bellarosa, and like Susan, I *should* have acted on my more primitive instincts, on fifty thousand years of past human experience. Instead, I rationalized, philosophized, and intellectualized when I should have listened to my emotions, which had always said to me, 'He is a threat to your survival. Kill him.'

I looked at Susan and she said, 'Kiss me,' and pursed those magnificent pouty lips.

I kissed her.

She pressed her head into my chest and cried for a minute, then stepped back. 'Well,' she said in a crisp, cool voice, 'off to jail. I want to be out tomorrow, Counsellor.'

I smiled.

'Tell me you love me,' she demanded.

'I love you.'

'And I've always loved you, John. For ever.'

'I know.'

The policewoman approached and took Susan's arm gently, then led her toward the front door.

I watched until she was gone, but she never looked back at me. I was aware of a lot of quiet people around the palm court and thought it best if I left quickly so they could get back to their business.

I turned toward the rear of the house to go fetch Zanzibar as I had promised. As I walked across the court, I could hear my footsteps echoing on the tile floor, and I saw out of the corner of my eye Bellarosa's body still lying off to my left, uncovered. Frank Bellarosa was surrounded by people who found him interesting: the police photographer, two laboratory women, and the coroner.

As I walked past the body, I passed something off to my right. I stopped and turned back to look at it. It was a large brass display easel that held an oil painting framed in a soft green and white lacquered frame, quite a nice frame actually. The painting was of Alhambra's ruined palm court, of course, and I studied it. It was really quite good, perhaps one of the best that I've seen of Susan's works. But what do I know about art?

I stared at the painting of the ruined palm court, the streams of sunlight coming in from the broken glass dome, the decayed stucco walls, the vines twisting around the marble pillars, and the cracked floor sprouting scraggy plant life amid the rubble. And I saw this now not as a whimsical or romantic rendition of physical decay, but as a mirrored image of a ruined and crumbling mind; not a vanished world of past glory, but a vanished world of mental and spiritual health. But what do I know about psychology? I hauled off and put my fist through the canvas, sending it and the easel sprawling across the court.

No one seemed to mind.

CHAPTER 38

It was January, and the days were short and cold. It was about four P.M., and already the sunlight was fading, but I didn't need or want much light.

The wrought-iron gates of Alhambra had been sold by the developer and replaced with steel security gates that were fastened together with a chain but not tightly enough to prevent me from slipping through.

I walked past the gatehouse, which was now being used as the builder's sales office, but it was Sunday and the small house was dark. I walked up the long drive, bundled in my wool parka. The cobblestones, too, had been sold, and the drive was frozen mud, slippery in places, so I took my time. The flowers that bordered the drive were all gone, of course, but the poplars still stood, bare now, grey and spindly.

In the forecourt at the end of the drive, the ornamental fountain was still there, but someone had forgotten to drain it last autumn, and the marble was cracked and filled with dirty ice. And beyond the forecourt, where Alhambra had once stood, was a great heap of rubble: red roofing tile, white stucco, rafters, and beams. Indeed, they had bulldozed the entire mansion as Bellarosa had said they would. But I had no way of knowing if it was a spiteful act or if the developer simply wanted to be rid of the white elephant.

As it was Sunday, the earth-moving equipment was silent, and no one seemed to be around. It was very quiet, that sort of deep winter quiet where you can hear the ground crackle underfoot, and the trees creaking in the cold wind. I could tell you I heard ghostly hoofbeats on the solid earth, too, but I didn't, though I thought about Susan and me on one of our winter rides.

I thought, too, of last January, and of the black Cadillac that was here, or wasn't here, and the man whom I saw or didn't see. And it occurred to me that if he hadn't been lost that day and hadn't seen this place, then things would have been different today, most probably better since I couldn't imagine how they could be much worse.

Regarding Bellarosa's death, I still had mixed feelings about that. Initially, I had been relieved, nearly glad, to be honest. I mean, the man had caused me much unhappiness and had seduced my wife (or was it the other way around?), and his death solved a good many problems for me. Even seeing him lying there on the floor, half naked and covered with gore, had not affected me. But now, after some time, I realized that I actually missed him, and that he's gone for ever, and that I lost a friend. Well, but as I say, I still have mixed emotions.

Anyway, I noticed four long crates lying near the rubble and moved closer to them and saw that they held the four Carthaginian columns, all ready for shipping, though I didn't know where they were headed this time. Not back to Carthage, that was for certain, but maybe to a museum or to another rich man's house, or maybe the government had declared them a saleable asset and they'd sit forgotten in a warehouse for ever.

I continued my walk, veering around the heap of rubble toward the rear of the property. All around me were stacks of building materials and earth-moving equipment. I noticed engineer stakes stuck in the ground, connected by string with white strips of cloth hanging from the string, and there were surveyors' stakes as well, and masonry stakes and all sorts of other things stuck in the ground like dissecting pins on the carved-up earth.

As I walked, I could see that most of the fifty or so foundations had been dug and poured, and though many of the trees had been spared, the land was irrevocably altered, suffused with water and gas pipes and cesspools, and crisscrossed with power lines and paved with blacktop and concrete. Another few hundred acres had gone from rural to suburban, from pristine to scarred, and hundreds of people from someplace or another were on their way here, though they didn't know it yet, bringing with them their worries and their future divorces, and their propane barbecue grills and their mailboxes with numbers on them, and their hopes for a new life in a nicer place than the last. The American dream, you know, constantly needs new landscapes.

Stanhope Hall's acreage is gone, too, of course, and a few of the houses there are nearly complete, wood and Thermopane contemporaries with lots of skylights and oversize garages and central air-conditioning; not too bad, I admit, but not too good either.

The big house, the former Stanhope Hall, has indeed been sold intact to a Japanese firm of some sort, but I see no sign of twitchy Nipponese businessmen strolling around the paths or doing callisthenics on the great lawn. In fact, the place looks as deserted as it has been for nearly twenty years. Local rumour at McGlade's Pub, where I spend too much time, has it that the little people are going to dismantle the mansion stone by stone and send it to Japan, though nobody at McGlade's seems to know why.

The love temple, too, has survived, and the developer of the Stanhope acreage has used a picture of it in his ads, promising the splendour and the glory of Gold Coast living to the first hundred people who can come up with the down payments and mortgages on the half-million-dollar tractor sheds he's building.

The sacred grove is gone, however, as no one is interested in ten acres of dying plum trees in their backyards. But the gazebo and hedge maze are part of the great house, so they might survive, though I don't recommend the maze for strung-out Oriental businessmen.

So the Stanhope and Alhambra estates are divided like spoils in an ancient war, their walls and gates no longer useful for keeping people out, and their great structures destroyed or used for sport or for building material elsewhere. But that's not my problem anymore.

I kept walking over the hard ground until I came to where Alhambra's reflecting pool and fountain had been, or where I thought they had been, but there was an open foundation there, and an unpaved road passed through where the classical garden and imitation Roman ruins had once stood. Neptune and Mary were gone, probably having left in disgust.

I turned around and headed back toward the rubble heap, walking along the patch on which Anna had walked when she spotted me that Easter morning, and a smile came to my lips. I continued on and reached the back patio, which was still intact, though the post lights and pizza oven were gone.

I walked across the patio and looked at the demolished house. Half the rubble had been carted away, but I could still identify most of the rooms, especially the central palm court, and I could actually see where Frank Bellarosa had lain dead.

To my right was the kitchen and the breakfast room where the Bellarosas had entertained us in more ways than one, and to the left was the ballroom, sometimes known as the living room, where I had done a little soft-shoe for Susan. Behind this room was the conservatory, crushed now, a pile of broken glass, plant tables, and clay pots.

I turned away from the house and picked my way around

632

the construction debris in the failing light until I was back in front of the mansion, in the forecourt, near the broken fountain, where Susan's Jaguar had once sat and where she and I once stood, in a picture-perfect setting, like an ad for something good and expensive, and I fancied I saw Susan and me standing there waiting for someone to answer the door on that spring evening.

I walked back down the long drive hunched against the wind. Beyond the gates and across Grace Lane I saw the DePauw house, lights shining from its big colonial windows, a cheery sight unless you weren't in the mood for cheery sights.

As I walked, I thought of Susan the last time I'd seen her. It was in November, in Manhattan. A hearing had been convened at Federal Court in Foley Square, at which I was present, though not as Susan's attorney or husband, but as a witness to the events surrounding the death of a federal witness, Mr Frank Bellarosa. As it turned out, I was not even asked to give testimony, and the commission took only a few hours to recommend that the case not be presented to a grand jury, finding that Susan Sutter, while not justified in her actions, was not responsible for them. This seemed a little vague to me, but there was some talk of diminished capacity and a promise from the Stanhopes to seek professional help for their daughter. I hope William and Charlotte don't think that means art lessons or pistol practice. Anyway, the government took a dive on the case, of course, and Lady Justice didn't miscarry; she had an abortion. But I don't blame the government for aborting this tricky and sensitive case, and I'm happy they did, because my wife doesn't belong in jail.

I had made a point of running into Susan on the steps of the courthouse. She was surrounded by her parents, three of her parents' lawyers, and two family-retained psychiatrists. William didn't seem awfully thrilled to see me for some reason, and Charlotte stuck her nose in the air, I mean literally, like you see in old movies. You've got to be careful when you do that walking down steps.

Anyway, Susan broke away from the Stanhope guard and came over to me on the steps. She smiled. 'Hello, John.'

'Hello, Susan.' I had congratulated her on a successful court appearance, and she had been cheery and buoyant, which was to be expected after walking free on a murder that was witnessed by about six federal agents, who fortunately couldn't seem to recall the incident clearly.

We'd spoken briefly, mostly about our children and not about our divorce. I asked her at one point, 'Are you really crazy?'

She smiled. 'Just enough to get me out of that courthouse. Don't tell.'

I smiled in return. We agreed that we both felt bad for Anna, but that maybe she was better off, though that wasn't true, and Susan asked me if I had gone to Frank's funeral, which I had. Susan said, 'I should have gone, too, of course, but it might have been awkward.'

'It possibly could have been.' Since you killed him. I mean, really, Susan. But maybe she had already disassociated herself from that unpleasant incident.

She was looking very good, by the way, dressed in a tailored grey silk shirt and jacket, appropriate for courtroom appearances, and wearing high heels, which she probably couldn't wait to kick off.

I didn't know when or if I'd see her again, so I said to her, 'I still love you, you know.'

'You'd better. For ever.'

'Yes, for ever.'

'Me, too.'

Well, we parted there on the steps, she to go back to Hilton Head, and me to Long Island. I was sharing the Stanhope gatehouse with Ethel Allard, who had insisted on taking me in when Susan sold the guesthouse. Ethel and I are getting along a little better than we had in the past. I drive her to the stores and to church on Sunday, though I don't go to stores or churches much myself anymore. The arrangement seems to be working out, and I'm glad for the opportunity to help someone who needs help, and Ethel is glad she finally got a chance to take in a homeless person. Father Hunnings approves, too.

The guesthouse, incidentally, where Susan and I had spent our twenty-two years of married life, and where we had raised our two children, has been bought by an intense young couple who are here on a corporate transfer from Dubuque or Duluth or someplace out there, working their way up the corporate game of chutes and ladders. They both leave for Manhattan before dawn and return after dark. They're not quite sure where they are geographically or socially, but they seem anxious that the Stanhope subdivision be completed so they can have friends and start a bowling team or something.

Jenny Alvarez and I still see each other from time to time, but she's involved with a baseball star now, a Mets infielder of all things, but I don't rub that in when I see her.

I had actually gone to Bellarosa's funeral as I told Susan. The Mass was at Santa Lucia, of course, and Monsignor Chiaro gave a beautiful service and spoke well of the deceased, so I guess the cheque cleared.

The burial itself was at an old cemetery in Brooklyn, and it was a real mafioso affair with a hundred black limousines and so many flowers at graveside that they covered a dozen other graves in all directions. Sally Da-da was there, of course, and we nodded to each other, and Jack Weinstein was there, and we made indefinite plans to have lunch. Anthony was there, too, out on bail for some charge or other, and Fat Paulie was there, and a guy whose face was half eaten away who I guess was my godfather, Aniello, and there were whole faces, too, that I recognized from the Plaza soirée, and from Giulio's. Anna did not look particularly good in black, or particularly good at all for that matter. She had been surrounded by so many wailing women that she never saw me, which was just as well.

Also with Anna, of course, were her three sons, Frankie, Tommy, and Tony. I recognized Frankie as the oldest, a sort of big lummox who looked more benign than dangerous.

Tommy, the Cornell student, looked like an all-American kid, the sort who might wind up working for a Fortune 500 company. Tony, whom I had met, was in his La Salle uniform, looking very ramrod straight and clean-cut, but if you looked past the uniform and the short hair, you saw Frank Bellarosa. You saw eyes that appraised everyone and everything. In fact, he looked at me for a while as though he were sizing me up, and the resemblance to his father was so uncanny that I actually had to blink to make certain I wasn't seeing a ghost. At one point in the graveside service, I saw Tony staring at his Uncle Sal, aka Sally Da-da, and if I were Uncle Sal, I'd keep an eye on that kid.

Anyway, Mr Mancuso was present, but tactfully stood some distance away with four photographers recording the event for posterity or other reasons.

I recalled what old Monsignor Chiaro had said at graveside, quoting from Timothy: *We brought nothing into this world, and it is certain we can carry nothing out.* Which was the best news I'd heard since 'We pass this way but once.'

And so, I thought, as I walked between Alhambra's stately poplars that had so impressed Frank Bellarosa, there is an ebb and flow in all human events, there is a building up and a tearing down, there are brief enchanted moments in history and in the short lives of men and women, there is wonder and there is cynicism, there are dreams that can come true, and dreams that can't.

And there was a time, you know, not so long ago, as recently as my own childhood in fact, when everyone believed in the future and eagerly awaited it or rushed to meet it. But now nearly everyone I know or used to know is trying to slow the speed of the world as the future starts to look more and more like someplace you don't want to be. But maybe that is not a cultural or national phenomenon, only my own middle age, my present state of mind combined with this dark winter season.

But spring follows as surely as winter ends. Right? And I have my eye on a used Allied fifty-five footer that I can pick up for a song in the winter months if I can get my prestigious law firm to settle up with me. And Carolyn and Edward will crew for me over Easter week on a shakedown cruise, and by summer I'll be ready to set out again with my children if they want to come, or with anyone else who wants to crew aboard the *Paumanok II*. I'll stop in Galveston to see Emily, then if I can shanghai her and Gary or any two or three people who are game enough, we'll do a circumnavigation of the globe. Hey, why not? You only live once.

I slipped out through the gates of Alhambra and began the walk up Grace Lane toward the gatehouse and Ethel's Sunday roast.

And maybe, I thought, when I come back to America, I'll put in at Hilton Head and see if for ever is for ever.

PLUM ISLAND
Nelson DeMille

Wounded in the line of duty, NYPD detective
John Corey is convalescing on Long Island when
Tom and Judy Gordon are found murdered on
their patio. Corey knew the young, attractive
couple, and Sylvester Maxwell, the local police
chief, wants his big-city expertise. Maxwell,
however, gets more than he bargained for.

The early signs point to a burglary gone wrong,
but because the Gordons were biologists at Plum
Island, the off-shore animal disease research site
rumoured to be involved in germ warfare, it isn't
long before the media is suggesting that the dead
couple stole something very deadly.

John Corey's investigations lead him into the
lore, legends and ancient secrets of northern
Long Island. But they are secrets more dangerous
then he could ever have imagined – and he
becomes trapped in a crime with global
implications.

'An ingenious thriller. You'll be rewarded with a
climax as funny as it is tense' *Time Out*

'Chilling . . . that rare breed of suspense novel
that keeps you sitting on the edge of your beach
chair even while you're laughing out loud'
Newsday

WORD OF HONOUR
Nelson DeMille

Ben Tyson is a brilliant corporate executive. He's a family man, honest and handsome, admired by men and desired by women. Years ago Ben Tyson was a lieutenant in war-torn Vietnam. There, in 1968, the men under his command committed a murderous atrocity – and swore never to tell the world what they had done. But was their word their bond?

The press, army justice, and the events Ben Tyson tried to forget have caught up with him. And now his family, his career and his personal sense of honour hang precariously in the balance.

'An excellent piece of storytelling . . . compulsive reading' *Oxford Times*

'Nelson DeMille tackles a controversial subject with skill' *Evening Standard*

'The military scenes have the gunmetal ring of authenticity . . . a long, over-the-shoulder look at a time that grows larger as it recedes from sight' *Time Magazine*

Time Warner Paperback titles available by post:

☐	By the Rivers of Babylon	Nelson DeMille	£6.99
☐	Cathedral	Nelson DeMille	£6.99
☐	The Talbot Odyssey	Nelson DeMille	£6.99
☐	Word of Honour	Nelson DeMille	£6.99
☐	The Charm School	Nelson DeMille	£6.99
☐	The General's Daughter	Nelson DeMille	£6.99
☐	Spencerville	Nelson DeMille	£6.99
☐	Plum Island	Nelson DeMille	£6.99
☐	The Lion's Game	Nelson DeMille	£6.99

The prices shown above are correct at time of going to press. However, the publishers reserve the right to increase prices on covers from those previously advertised without prior notice.

timewarner
paperbacks

TIME WARNER PAPERBACKS
P.O. Box 121, Kettering, Northants NN14 4ZQ
Tel: 01832 737525, Fax: 01832 733076
Email: aspenhouse@FSBDial.co.uk

POST AND PACKING:
Payments can be made as follows: cheque, postal order (payable to Time Warner Books) or by credit cards. Do not send cash or currency.

All U.K. Orders	**FREE OF CHARGE**
E.E.C. & Overseas	25% of order value

Name (Block Letters) _____

Address _____

_____

Post/zip code: _____

☐ Please keep me in touch with future Time Warner publications

☐ I enclose my remittance £_____

☐ I wish to pay by Visa/Access/Mastercard/Eurocard

Card Expiry Date

_____